D1013279

THE BUTCHER'S THEATER

OTHER BOOKS BY JONATHAN KELLERMAN

FICTION

Over the Edge (1987)
Blood Test (1986)
When the Bough Breaks (1985)

NONFICTION

Helping the Fearful Child (1981)
Psychological Aspects of Childhood Cancer (1980)

THE BUTCHER'S THEATER

JONATHAN KELLERMAN

BANTAM BOOKS
TORONTO • NEW YORK • LONDON • SYDNEY • AUCKLAND

NOTE

This is a work of fiction. The characters in this novel are entirely the product of the author's imagination. Any similarity to actual events, locales, or persons, living or dead, is entirely coincidental.

THE BUTCHER'S THEATER
A Bantam Book / April 1988

Book design by Barbara N. Cohen.

Library of Congress Cataloging-in-Publication

Kellerman, Jonathan.
The butcher's theater.

I. Title.
PS3561.E3865B88 1988 813'.54 87-30660
ISBN 0-553-05251-9

Published simultaneously in the United States and Canada

Bantam Books are published by Bantam Books, a division of Bantam Doubleday Dell Publishing Group, Inc. Its trademark, consisting of the words "Bantam Books" and the portrayal of a rooster, is Registered in U.S. Patent and Trademark Office and in other countries. Marca Registrada. Bantam Books, 666 Fifth Avenue, New York, New York 10103.

PRINTED IN THE UNITED STATES OF AMERICA

BP 0 9 8 7 6 5 4 3

For Faye

Sincere and profound thanks to Eli Ben Aharon, Eli Bichler, Peter Guzzardi, Eran Israel, Barney Karpfinger, Baruch Ram, and Robert Rosenberg. And to Jesse, Rachel, and Ilana for being such exemplary travelers.

ISRAELI POLICE RANKS

Rav nitzav:	Commissioner
Nitzav:	Commander
Tat nitzav:	Deputy commander
Nitzav mishneh:	Assistant commander
Sgan nitzav:	Chief superintendent
Rav pakad:	Superintendent
Pakad:	Chief inspector
Mefakeah:	Inspector
Mefakeah mishneh:	Subinspector
Sgan mefakeah:	Deputy inspector
Rav samal rishon:	Staff sergeant major
Rav samal:	Sergeant major
Samal rishon:	Sergeant
Samal sheni:	Corporal
Rav shoter:	Lance corporal
Tura'i:	Rookie

BOOK ONE

1

Spring 1985

Yaakov Schlesinger could think only of food.

Idiot, he told himself. Immersed in such beauty and unable to take your mind off your belly.

Unclipping his flashlight from his belt, he beamed it briefly on the southern gate of the campus. Satisfied that the lock was in place, he hitched up his trousers and trudged forward in the darkness, determined to ignore the gnawing from within.

The Mount Scopus Road climbed suddenly, but it was a rise that he knew well—what was this, his two hundredth patrol?—and he remained sure-footed. Veering to the left, he walked toward the eastern ridge and looked out, with a pleasurable sense of vertigo, at nothingness: the unlit expanse of the Judean wilderness. In less than an hour dawn would break and sunlight would flood the desert like honeyed porridge dripping thickly into an earthenware bowl . . . *ach*, there it was again. Food.

Still, he rationalized, a bowl was exactly what it looked like to him. Or maybe a dinner plate. A broad, concave disk of desert, chalky-white, seamed with copper, dotted by mesquite and pocked with caves—a gigantic cracked dinner plate tipping into the Dead Sea. Any terrorist foolish enough to try to cross the wilderness would be as conspicuous as a fly on paper, certain to be spotted by the Border Patrol long before reaching the Ma'ale Adumim settlement. Which made *his* job, he supposed, little more than a formality. An old man's assignment.

He absently touched the butt of the M-1 carbine strapped over his shoulder and experienced a sudden rush of memories. A twinge of melancholy that he suppressed by telling himself he had nothing to complain about. That he should be thankful for the opportunity to volunteer. Grateful for the nightly exercise, the cool, fragrant air. Proud of the slap of the M-1 against his shoulder blades, the crisp Hagah uniform that made him feel like a soldier again.

A scurrying sound crackled somewhere beyond the ridge and caused his heart to jump. He pulled the carbine down, held it in both hands, and waited. Silence, then another scurry, this time easy to classify: the frantic dash of a rodent or shrew. Letting out his breath, he kept his right hand clamped around the M-1, took the flashlight in his left, and skimmed the beam over the brush. The light caught only rocks and shrubs. A clump of weeds. A filmy swirl of nightflying insects.

Stepping away from the ridge, he commenced walking south. The barrenness of the road was broken at the crest by a stolid, many-roofed mass huddled around a high, peaked tower: the Amelia Catherine Hospital, arrogantly colonial on this Levantine stretch of mountaintop. Because the hospital compound was U.N. property, it was excluded from his route, but sometimes he liked to stop and take a break just outside the grounds. Smoke a cigarette and watch as the odor of Turkish tobacco stirred the goats and donkeys penned behind the main building. Why, he wondered, were the Arabs allowed to keep animals there? What did that say for the hygiene of the place?

His stomach growled. *Absurd.* He'd eaten a hearty dinner at eight, spent the next four hours sitting on the balcony while slowly ingesting the food Eva set out for him before she went to bed: dried apricots and apples, a string of fat Calimyrna figs, tea wafers, lemon cookies, marzipan, tangerines and kumquats, toasted gar'inim, jagged chunks of bittersweet chocolate, jelly candies, halvah. Topped off by an entire liter bottle of grapefruit juice and a Sipholux full of soda—the last in hopes that gas bubbles might accomplish what solid matter had failed to do: fill him up. No such luck.

He'd lived with his hunger—and its accomplice, insomnia—for more than forty years. Long enough to think of them as a pair of living, breathing creatures. Abdominal homunculi implanted by the bastards at Dachau. Twin demons who scraped away at his peace of mind, evoking constant misery. True, it wasn't cancer, but neither was it trivial.

The pain fluctuated. At best, a dull, maddeningly abstract hollowness; at worst, real, grinding agony, as if an iron hand were clamped around his vitals.

No one took him seriously anymore. Eva said he was fortunate to be able to eat whatever he wanted and remain skinny.

This, as she pinched the soft ring around her own thickening waistline and examined the latest diet brochure handed out at the Kupat Holim clinic. And the doctors delighted in telling him there was nothing wrong with him. That the experiments had left no tangible scars. He was a superb specimen, they insisted, possessing the alimentary tract, and general constitution, of a man twenty years younger.

"You're seventy years old, Mr. Schlesinger," one of them had explained before settling back with a self-satisfied smirk on his face. As if that settled it. An active metabolism, another had pronounced. "Be thankful you're as active as you are, *adoni*." Still another had listened with apparent sympathy, raising his hopes, then dashing them by suggesting that he visit the Psychiatric Faculty at Hadassah. Which only illustrated that the man was just another civil-service idiot—the gnawing was in his belly, not his head. He vowed to cease all dealings with the clinic and find himself a private doctor, cost be damned. Someone who could understand what it was like to feel as if you were starving amid plenty, who could appreciate the bottomless ache that had plagued him since the Americans had discovered him, a barely breathing skeleton, lying limply atop a mound of stinking, broken corpses. . . .

Enough, fool. Ancient history. You're free, now. A soldier. The man in charge, armed and masterful. Privileged to patrol the most beautiful of cities at the most beautiful of hours. To watch her awaken, bathed in lavender and scarlet light, like a princess rising from a bed canopied with silk . . .

Schlesinger the poet.

He took a deep breath, filled his nostrils with the sharp perfume of Jerusalem pine, and turned away from the looming silhouette of the hospital. Exhaling slowly, he gazed out over the steeply sloping terraces of Wadi el Joz, toward the view from the southwest, the one he always saved for last:

The Old City, backlit in amber, turrets and battlements stitching a flame-colored hem across the pure black sky. Beyond the walls, faint shadowy contours of domes, spires, steeples, and minarets. At the southern end the vertical thrust of The Citadel. Dominating the north, the Haram esh-Sharif plateau, upon which sat the Great Mosque of the Rock, its golden dome burnished rosy in the half-light, nestled within the sleeping city like a brooch cradled in gray velvet.

Immersed in beauty like that, how could he think of his belly? And yet, the ache had intensified, quickened, taken on a pulse of its own.

Angry, he picked up his pace and crossed the road. Just off the asphalt was a shallow gully leading to the empty fields that anticipated the wadi. Casually, he ran the flashlight over familiar terrain. The same damned contours, the same damned shadows. This olive tree, that row of border stones. The rusty abandoned water heater that had been there for months, glints of broken glass, the sharp stink of sheep dung . . .

And something else.

An oblong shape, maybe a meter and a half long, tucked into a terraced pocket near the top of the north wall of the gully. Lying inert at the base of an olive sapling. Unmoving. A bomb? His instinctive answer was no—it looked too soft. But one couldn't be too careful.

As he considered his options, his arm began to move, seemingly of its own volition, sweeping the flashlight beam over the shape. Up and down, back and forth. This was definitely something new. Striped? No, two tones of fabric. Dark over light. A blanket over sheeting. A shroud. Glistening wet and dark around the edges.

The light continued to wash across the gully. Nothing. No one. He considered calling for help, decided it would be needlessly alarmist. Better to check first.

Carbine in hand, he inched to the rim of the gully, began climbing down, then stopped, legs suddenly leaden. Short of breath. Fatigued. Feeling his age. Deliberating some more, he berated himself: *Milksop*. A pile of blankets turns you to jelly? Probably nothing.

He resumed his descent, zigging and zagging toward the shape, extending his free arm horizontally in an attempt to maintain balance. Stopping every few seconds to aim the flashlight. Radar-eyed. Ears attuned to alien sounds. Prepared at any moment to drop the light and pull the M-1 into firing position. But nothing moved; the silence remained unblemished. Just him and the shape. The foreign shape.

As he lowered himself farther, the ground dipped abruptly. He stumbled, fought for equilibrium, dug his heels in, and remained upright. Good. Very good for an old man. Active metabolism . . .

He was almost there now, just a few feet away. *Stop*. Check the area for other foreign shapes. The hint of movement. Nothing. Wait. Go on. Take a good look. Avoid that mound of dung. Step around the panicky scatter of glossy black beetles. Tiny black legs scampering over clots of dung. Onto something pale. Something extending from the sheeting. Pale lozenges.

He was standing over the shape now. Kneeling. Chest tautened by breath withheld. Tilting his light downward, he saw them, soft and speckled like small white cucumbers: human fingers. The soft pad of palm. Speckled. Night-black. Edged with crimson. An outstretched hand. Beseeching.

Pinching a corner of the blanket between his fingers, he began peeling it back with the foreboding and compulsion of a child turning over a rock, knowing all the while that slimy things lived on the underside.

There. Done. He let go of the fabric and stared at what he'd exposed.

Lock-jawed, he moaned involuntarily. He was—had been—a soldier, had seen his share of abominations. But this was different. Clinical. So terribly reminiscent of something else . . .

Averting his eyes, he felt them swing back again and lock on to the contents of the blanket, imbibing the horror. Suddenly he was reeling, swaying, bobbing helplessly in a sea of images. Memories. Other hands, other nightmares. Hands. The same pose of supplication. Thousands of hands, a mountain of hands. Begging for mercy that never came.

Rising unsteadily, he took hold of an olive limb and exhaled in fierce, hot gusts. Sickened to the core, yet not unaware of the irony of the moment.

For what lay within the sheets had demolished the demons, freeing him for the first time in more than forty years.

He felt his viscera begin to churn. The iron hand letting go. A burning tide of bile rose uncontrollably in his gullet. Retching and heaving, he vomited repeatedly in the dirt, one part of him curiously detached, as if he were observing his own defilement. Careful to direct the spray away from the blankets. Not wishing to worsen what had already been done.

When he'd emptied himself he looked down again with a child's magical hope. Believing, for an instant, that his emesis had served as a ritual, a sacrificial atonement that had somehow caused the horror to vanish.

But the only thing that had vanished was his hunger.

2

The Ford Escort ran the red light at the intersection fronting the mouth of Liberty Bell Park. Turning left on King David, it hooked onto Shlomo Hamelekh as far as Zahal Square, then sped northeast on Sultan Suleiman Road, hugging the perimeter of the Old City.

The promise of daybreak had been newly fulfilled by a fiery desert sun that rose steadily over the Mount of Olives, warming the morning, tossing splashes of copper and gold across the ashen city walls with the abandon of a painter gone mad.

The Escort rushed through brightening cobbled streets, past sidewalks and alleys dotted with early risers: Bedouin shepherds nudging their flocks toward the northeast corner of the Old City walls in preparation for the Friday livestock market; veiled women from the nearby villages settling down with bright bolts of fabric and baskets of produce for the curbside bazaar at the entrance to the Damascus Gate; Hassidim in long black coats and white leggings walking in pairs and trios toward the Jaffa Gate, eyes affixed to the ground, hurrying to be in place at the Western Wall for the first *shaharit minyan* of the day; stooped, skullcapped porters bearing massive crates on narrow backs; bakers' boys carrying rings of sesame-studded *bagelah* suspended from stout iron bars.

Under other circumstances the driver of the Escort would have noticed all this, and more. His feelings for the city had never dimmed and no matter how many times he experienced her sights and sounds and smells, they never ceased to enchant him. But this morning his mind was on other things.

He turned the wheel and swung up Shmuel Ben Adayah. A quick left brought him onto the Mount of Olives Road toward the peak of Mount Scopus. The highest point in the city. The Eye of Jerusalem, where the outrage had taken place.

Flares and metal barriers had been laid across the road.

Behind the barriers stood a border policeman—a Druze the driver knew, by the name of Salman Afif. Afif maintained an impassive watch, legs spread and planted firmly, one hand resting on his holstered pistol, the other twirling the ends of enormous black mustaches. When the Escort approached he motioned for it to halt, came to the open window, and nodded in recognition. After a cursory exchange of greetings, the barriers were pulled aside.

As the Escort passed through, the driver surveyed the hilltop, examining the vehicles parked along the road: the mobile crime van; the transport van from the Abu Kabir pathology lab; a blue-and-white, its blue blinker still flashing; Afif's jeep; a white Volvo 240 with police plates. The technicians had already arrived, as had uniformed officers—but only two of them. Next to the Volvo stood Deputy Commander Laufer and his driver. But no police spokesman, no press, no sign of the pathologist. Wondering about it, the driver parked at some distance from the others, turned off the engine, and set the hand brake. There was a note pad on the passenger seat. He grasped it somewhat clumsily in his left hand and got out of the car.

He was a small, dark, neat-looking man, five foot seven, one hundred and forty pounds, thirty-seven years old but appearing ten years younger. He wore simple clothes—short-sleeved white cotton shirt, dark trousers, sandals without socks—and no jewelry except for an inexpensive wristwatch and an incongruously ornate wedding band of gold filigree.

His hair was thick, black, and tightly kinked, trimmed to medium length in the style the Americans called Afro, and topped with a small black *kipah srugah*—knitted yarmulke—bordered with red roses. The face below the Afro was lean and smooth, skin the color of coffee liberally laced with cream, stretched tightly over a clearly delineated substructure: high, sharp cheekbones, strong nose anchored by flared nostrils, wide lips, full and bowed. Only the upper surface of his left hand was a different color—grayish-white, puckered and shiny, crisscrossed with scars.

Arched eyebrows created the illusion of perpetual surprise. Deep sockets housed a pair of liquid, almond eyes, the irises a strange shade of golden-brown, the lashes so long they bordered on the womanish. In another context he could have been taken for someone of Latin or Caribbean descent, or perhaps Iberian melded with a robust infusion of Aztec. On at least one occasion he had been mistaken for a light-skinned black man.

His name was Daniel Shalom Sharavi and he was, in fact, a Jew of Yemenite origins. Time, circumstance, and *protekzia*—fortuitous connections—had made him a policeman. Intelligence and industriousness had raised him to the rank of *pakad*—chief inspector—in the National Police, Southern District. For most of his career, he'd been a detective. For the last two years he'd specialized in Major Crimes, which, in Jerusalem, rarely referred to the kind of thing that had brought him to Scopus this morning.

He walked toward the activity. The transport attendants sat in their van. The uniformed policemen were talking to an older man in a Civil Guard uniform. Daniel gave him a second look: late sixties to early seventies, thin but powerfully built, with close-cropped white hair and a bristly white mustache. He seemed to be lecturing the policemen, pointing toward a gully off the west side of the road, gesticulating with his hands, moving his lips rapidly.

Laufer stood several yards away, seemingly oblivious to the lecture, smoking and checking his watch. The deputy commander wore a black knit shirt and gray slacks, as if he'd lacked the time to don his uniform. In civilian clothes, bereft of ribbons, he looked pudgier, definitely less impressive. When he saw Daniel approaching, he dropped his cigarette and ground it out in the dirt, then said something to the driver, who walked away. Not waiting for Daniel to reach him, he moved forward, paunch first, in short, brisk steps.

They met midway and shared a minimal handshake.

"Horrible," said Laufer. "Butchery." When he spoke his jowls quivered like empty water bladders. His eyes, Daniel noticed, looked more tired than usual.

Laufer's hand fumbled in his shirt pocket and drew out a pack of cigarettes. English Ovals. Souvenirs from the latest London trip, no doubt. He lit a cigarette and blew the smoke out of his nose in twin drafts.

"Butchery," he said again.

Daniel cocked his head toward the Hagah man.

"He the one who found it?"

Laufer nodded. "Schlesinger, Yaakov."

"This part of his regular patrol?"

"Yes. From Old Hadassah, around the university, down past the Amelia Catherine, and back. Back and forth, five times a night, six nights a week."

"A lot of walking for someone his age."

"He's a tough one. Former palmahi. Claims he doesn't need much sleep."

"How many times had he been through when he discovered it?"

"Four. This was the last pass. Back up the road and then he picks up his car on Sderot Churchill and drives home. To French Hill."

"Does he log?"

"At the end, in the car. Unless he finds something out of the ordinary." Laufer smiled bitterly.

"So we may be able to pinpoint when it was dumped."

"Depending on how seriously you take him."

"Any reason not to?"

"At *his* age?" said Laufer. "He says he's certain it wasn't there before, but who knows? He may be trying to avoid looking sloppy."

Daniel looked at the old man. He'd stopped lecturing and stood ruler-straight between the policemen. Wearing the M-1 as if it were part of him. Uniform pressed and creased. The old-guard type. Nothing sloppy about him.

Turning back to Laufer, he lifted his note pad with his bad hand, flipped it open, and pulled out his pen.

"What time does he say he found it?" he asked.

"Five forty-five."

A full hour before he'd been called. He lowered the pen, looked at Laufer questioningly.

"I wanted things quiet," said the deputy commander matter-of-factly. Without apology. "At least until we can put this in context. No press, no statements, a minimum of personnel. And no needless chatter with any personnel not on the investigating team."

"I see," said Daniel. "Dr. Levi's been here?"

"Been and gone. He'll do the necropsy this afternoon and call you."

The deputy commander took a deep drag on his cigarette, got a shred of tobacco on his lip and spat it out.

"Do you think he's back?" he asked. "Our gray friend?"

It was a premature question, thought Daniel. Even for one who had made his mark in administration.

"Does the evidence fit?" he asked.

Laufer's expression made light of the question. "The site fits, doesn't it? Weren't the others found right around here?"

"One of them—Marcovici. Farther down. In the woodlands."

"And the others?"

"Two in Sheikh Jarrah, the fourth—"

"Exactly." Laufer cut him off. "All within a half-kilometer radius. Perhaps the bastard has a thing for this area. Something psychological."

"Perhaps," said Daniel. "What about the wounds?"

"Go down there and look for yourself," said the deputy commander.

He turned away, smoking and coughing. Daniel left him and climbed nimbly down into the gully. Two technicians, one male, one female, were working near the body, which was covered by a white sheet.

"Good morning, Pakad Sharavi," the man said with mock deference. He held a test tube up to the sunlight, shook it gently, and placed it in an open evidence case.

"Steinfeld," acknowledged Daniel. He ran his eyes over the site. Searching for revelations, seeing only the gray of stone, the dun of soil. Torsos of olive trees twisting through the dust, their tops shimmering silver-green. A kilometer of sloping rocky field; beyond it the deep, narrow valley of Wadi el Joz. Sheikh Jarrah, with its jumble of alleys and vanilla-colored houses. Flashes of turquoise: wrought-iron grills painted in the hue the Arabs believed would repel evil spirits. The towers and steeples of the American colony meshing with tangles of television antennas.

No blood spatter, no trail of crushed foliage, no bits of clothing adhering conveniently to jutting tree limbs. No geographical confession. Just a white form lying under a tree. Isolated, ovoid, out of place. Like an egg dropped out of the sky by some giant, careless bird.

"Did Dr. Levi have anything to say after his examination?" he asked.

"Clucked his tongue a lot." Steinfeld picked up another test tube, examined it, put it down.

Daniel noticed several plaster casts in the case and asked, "Any clear footprints?"

"Just those of the Hagah man," the technician said disgustedly. "If there were others, he obliterated them. He also threw up. Over there." He pointed to a dry, whitening patch a meter to the left of the sheet. "Missed the body. Good aim, eh?"

The woman was a new hire named Avital. She knelt in the dirt, taking samples of leaves, twigs, and dung, scooping them into plastic bags, working quickly and silently with an intent expression on her face. When she'd sealed the bags she looked up and grimaced. "You don't want to look at this one, *adoni.*"

"How true," said Daniel. He got down on his knees and lifted up the sheet.

The face had been left intact. It lay tilted in an unnatural position, staring up at him with half-closed, clouded eyes. Horribly pretty, like a doll's head fastened to the carnage below. A young face, dusky, roundish, lightly sprinkled with pimples on forehead and chin, wavy black hair, long and shining.

How old could she have been? he thought. Fifteen, maybe sixteen? A hot anger kindled in his abdomen. Avital was staring at him and he realized he was clenching his fists. Quickly he relaxed them, felt the fingertips tingle.

"Was the hair like this when you found it?" he asked.

"Like what?" asked Steinfeld.

"Clean. Combed."

The technicians looked at each other.

"Yes," said Avital.

Steinfeld nodded and paused expectantly, as if waiting for another question. When none came he shrugged and went back to work.

Daniel leaned in closer and sniffed. The stench of death had begun to issue from the corpse but through it he made out the clean, sweet scent of soap. Someone had washed her.

He raised his head and continued examining the face. The mouth hung slightly agape, revealing a hint of white but widely spaced teeth. The lower ones were crowded and chipped. An upper canine was missing. Not a rich girl. Pierced ears but no earrings. No tribal tattoos, scars, birthmarks, or blemishes.

"Any identification?"

"Life should be so easy," said Steinfeld.

Daniel stared a bit longer, then ceased his inspection of individual features. Shifting his perspective, he regarded the face as an entity and searched for ethnic characteristics. She appeared Oriental, but that meant little. It was a rare Jerusalem face that told a definite ethnic story—Arab, Ashkenazi, Druze,

Bukharan, Armenian. Each had its prototype, but the overlap was substantial. He'd seen too many blond, blue-eyed Arabs, too many swarthy Germans to be confident about racial guesses. Still, it would have been nice to find something, somewhere to start . . .

A shiny green fly settled on the lower lip and began exploring. He shooed it away. Forced his eyes downward.

The throat had been cut deeply from ear to ear, severing gullet and trachea, separating the ivory knobs of the spinal cord, millimeters from complete decapitation. Each small breast was circled by stab wounds. The abdomen had been sliced open under the ribs on the right side, swooping down to the pelvis and back up to the left. Glossy bits of tissue peeked out from under the flap of the wound. The pubic region was an unrecognizable mass of gore.

The fire in his belly intensified. He covered the body from the neck down.

"She wasn't killed here," he said.

Steinfeld shook his head in agreement. "Not enough blood for that. Almost no blood at all, in fact. Looks as if she's been drained."

"What do you mean?"

Steinfeld pointed to the wound flap. "No blood on the body. What's visible under the wound looks pale—like a lab specimen. Drained."

"What about semen?"

"Nothing conspicuous—we took scrapings. Levi's internal will tell you more."

Daniel thought of the destruction that had been visited upon the genitals. "Do you think Dr. Levi will be able to get anything from the vaginal vault?"

"You'll have to ask Dr. Levi." Steinfeld snapped the evidence case shut.

"Someone cleaned her up thoroughly," said Daniel, more to himself than to the techs.

"I suppose."

There was a camera next to the case.

"You've taken your pictures?"

"All the usual ones."

"Take some extra ones. Just in case."

"We've already shot three rolls," said Steinfeld.

"Shoot more," said Daniel. "Let's not have a repeat of the Aboutboul disaster."

"I had nothing to do with Aboutboul," said Steinfeld, defensively. But the look on his face bespoke more than defensiveness.

He's horrified, thought Daniel, and fighting to hide it. He softened his tone.

"I know that, Meir."

"Some defective from Northern District on loan to the National Staff," the technician continued to complain. "Takes the camera and opens it in a lighted room—bye-bye evidence."

Daniel's mind longed to be somewhere else, but he shook his head knowingly, forced himself to commiserate.

"*Protekzia*?"

"What else? Someone's nephew."

"Figures."

Steinfeld inspected the contents of his case, closed it, and wiped his hands on his pants. He glanced toward the camera, picked it up.

"How many extra rolls do you want?"

"Take two more, okay?"

"Okay."

Daniel wrote in his note pad, rose, brushed off his trousers, and looked again at the dead girl. The static beauty of the face, the defilement . . . Young one, what were your final thoughts, your agonies . . . ?

"Any sand on the body?" he asked.

"Nothing," said Avital, "not even between the toes."

"What about the hair?"

"No," she said. "I combed through it. Before that, it looked perfect—shampooed and set." Pause. "Why would that be?"

"A hair fetishist," said Steinfeld. "A freak. When you deal with freaks, anything's possible. Isn't that right, Pakad?"

"Absolutely." Daniel said good-bye and climbed back up. Laufer was back in his Volvo, talking on the radio. His driver stood behind the barrier, chatting with Afif. The old Hagah man was still sandwiched between the two officers. Daniel caught his eye and he nodded formally, as if in salute. Daniel began walking toward him but was stopped by the deputy commander's voice.

"Sharavi."

He turned around. Laufer had gotten out of the car and was waving him over.

"So?" the deputy commander demanded when they were face to face.

"As you said, butchery."

"Does it look like the bastard's work?"

"Not on the surface."

"Be specific," ordered Laufer.

"This one's a child. The Gray Man's victims were older—mid- to late thirties."

The deputy commander dismissed the point with a wave.

"Perhaps he's changed his taste," he said. "Acquired a lust for young whores."

"We don't know this one's a whore," said Daniel, surprised at the edge in his voice.

Laufer grunted, looked away.

"The wounds differ as well," said Daniel. "The Gray Man made his incision laterally, on the left side of the throat. He severed the major blood vessels but didn't cut nearly as deeply as this one—which makes sense, because the Gadish woman, the one who'd survived long enough to talk, described his knife as a small one. This poor girl was just about decapitated, which suggests a larger, heavier weapon."

"Which would be the case if he's gotten angrier and better-armed," said Laufer. "Progressively more violent. It's a pattern with sex fiends, isn't it?"

"Sometimes," said Daniel. "But the discrepancies go beyond intensity. The Gray Man concentrated on the upper trunk. Struck at the breasts, but never below the waist. And he killed his victims on the spot, after they began to fellate him. This one was murdered elsewhere. Someone washed her hair and combed it out. Scrubbed her clean."

Laufer perked up. "What does that mean?"

"I don't know."

The deputy commander grabbed another Oval, jammed it in his mouth, lit it, and puffed furiously.

"Another one," he said. "Another mad bastard prowling our streets."

"There are other possibilities," said Daniel.

"What, another Tutunji?"

"It needs to be considered."

"Shit."

Faiz Tutunji. Daniel uttered the name to himself and conjured the face that went with it: long, sunken-cheeked, snaggle-toothed, the same lazy eyes in every arrest photo. A petty thief from Hebron, with a talent for getting caught. Definitely small-time until a trip to Amman had turned him into a revolutionary. He'd come back spouting slogans, assembled six cohorts, and kidnapped a female soldier off a side street not far from the Haifa harbor. Gang-raped her in the Carmel mountains, then strangled her and cut her up to make it look like a sex murder. A Northern District patrol had caught up with them just outside of Acre, trying to force another *hayelet* into their van at gunpoint. The ensuing shootout had eliminated six out of seven gang members, including Tutunji, and the survivor had produced written orders from Fatah Central Command. Blessings from Chairman Arafat for an honorable new strategy against the Zionist interloper.

"Liberation through mutilation," spat Laufer. "Just what we need." He grimaced in contemplation, then said, "Okay. I'll make the appropriate inquiries, find out if any new rumblings have been picked up. If it turns into a security case you'll liaison with Latam, Shin Bet, and Mossad." He began walking up the road, toward the still-quiet southern border of the old Hebrew University campus. Daniel stayed by his side.

"What else?" said the deputy commander. "You said possibilities."

"Blood revenge. Love gone wrong."

Laufer digested that.

"A little brutal for that, don't you think?"

"When passion plays a role, things can get out of hand," said Daniel, "but yes, I think it's only a remote possibility."

"Blood revenge," Laufer reflected. "She look like an Arab to you?"

"No way to tell."

Laufer looked displeased, as if Daniel possessed some special insight into what Arabs looked like and had chosen to withhold it.

"Our first priority," said Daniel, "should be to identify her, then work backward from there. The sooner we assemble the team, the better."

"Fine, fine. Ben-Ari's available, as is Zussman. Which do you want?"

"Neither. I'll take Nahum Shmeltzer."

"I thought he retired."

"Not yet—next spring."

"None too soon. He's a dray horse, burned out. Lacks creativity."

"He's creative in his own way," said Daniel. "Bright and tenacious—well suited for records work. There'll be plenty of that on this case."

Laufer blew smoke at the sky, cleared his throat, said finally, "Very well, take him. In terms of your subinspector—"

"I want Yosef Lee."

"Free egg rolls, eh?"

"He's a good team worker. Knows the streets, indefatigable."

"How much homicide experience?"

"He put in time on the old woman from Musrara—the one asphyxiated by the burglar's gag. And he came onto Gray Man shortly before we . . . reduced our activity. Along with Daoud, whom I also want."

"The Arab from Bethlehem?"

"The same."

"That," said Laufer, "could prove awkward."

"I'm aware of that. But the benefits exceed the drawbacks."

"Name them."

Daniel did and the deputy commander listened with a bland expression on his face. After several moments of deliberation he said, "You want an Arab, okay, but you'll have to run a tight ship. If it turns into a security case he'll be transferred out immediately—for his own good, as well as ours. And it will go down on your record as an administrative blunder."

Daniel ignored the threat, put forth his next request. "Something this big, I could use more than one *samal.* There's a kid over at the Russian Compound named Ben Aharon—"

"Forget it on both counts," said Laufer. He turned on his heel, began walking back to the Volvo, forcing Daniel to follow in order to hear what he was saying. "Business as usual—one *samal*—and I've already chosen him. New hire named Avi Cohen, just transferred from Tel Aviv."

"What talent does he have to pull a transfer so soon?"

"Young, strong, eager, earned a ribbon in Lebanon." Laufer paused. "He's the third son of Pinni Cohen, the Labor MK from Petah Tikva."

"Didn't Cohen just die?"

"Two months ago. Heart attack, all the stress. In case you

don't read the papers, he was one of our friends in Knesset, a sweetheart during budget struggles. Kid's got a good record and we'd be doing the widow a favor."

"Why the transfer?"

"Personal reasons."

"How personal?"

"Nothing to do with his work. He had an affair with the wife of a superior. Asher Davidoff's blonde, a first-class *kurva*."

"It indicates," said Daniel, "a distinct lack of good judgment."

The deputy commander waved away his objection.

"It's an old story with her, Sharavi. She goes for the young ones, makes a blatant play for them. No reason for Cohen to eat it because he got caught. Give him a chance."

His tone indicated that further debate was unwelcome, and Daniel decided the issue wasn't worth pressing. He'd gotten nearly everything he wanted. There'd be plenty of quiet work for this Cohen. Enough to keep him busy and out of trouble.

"Fine," he said, suddenly impatient with talk. Looking over his shoulder at the Hagah man, he began mentally framing his interview questions, the best way to approach an old soldier.

". . . absolutely no contact with the press," Laufer was saying, "I'll let you know if and when a leak is called for. You'll report directly to me. Keep me one hundred percent informed."

"Certainly. Anything else?"

"Nothing else," said Laufer. "Just clear *this* one up."

3

After the deputy commander had been driven away, Daniel walked over to Schlesinger. He told the uniformed officers to wait by their car and extended his hand to the Hagah man. The one that gripped it in return was hard and dry.

"Adon Schlesinger, I'm Pakad Sharavi. I'd like to ask you a few questions."

"Sharavi?" The man's voice was deep, hoarse, his Hebrew

clipped short by the vestiges of a German accent. "You're a Yemenite?"

Daniel nodded.

"I knew a Sharavi once," said Schlesinger. "Skinny little fellow—Moshe the baker. Lived in the Old City before we lost it in '48, left to join the crew that built the cable trolley from the Ophthalmic Hospital to Mount Zion." He pointed south. "We put it up every night, dismantled it before sunrise. So the goddamned British wouldn't catch us sending food and medicine to our fighters."

"My uncle," said Daniel.

"*Ach*, small world. How's he doing?"

"He died five years ago."

"What from?"

"Stroke."

"How old was he, seventy?" Schlesinger's face had drawn tight with anxiety, the bushy white eyebrows drooping low over watery blue eyes.

"Seventy-nine."

"Seventy-nine," echoed Schlesinger. "Could be worse. He was a hell of a worker for a little guy, never griped. You come from good stock, Pakad Sharavi."

"Thank you." Daniel pulled out his note pad. Schlesinger's eyes followed him, stopped, focused on the back of his hand. Stared at the scar tissue. An observant one, thought Daniel.

"Tell me about your patrol," he said.

Schlesinger shrugged. "What's there to tell? I walk up and down the road five times a night, scaring away jackrabbits."

"How long have you been with Hagah?"

"Fourteen years, first spring out of the reserves. Patrolled Rehavya for thirteen of them, past the Prime Minister's house. A year ago I bought a flat in the towers on French Hill—near your headquarters—and the wife insisted I take something closer to home."

"What's your schedule?"

"Midnight to sunrise, Monday through Saturday. Five passes from Old Hadassah to the Ben Adayah intersection and back."

"Fifteen kilometers a night," said Daniel.

"Closer to twenty if you include curves in the road."

"A lot of walking, *adoni*."

"For an old fart?"

"For anyone."

Schlesinger laughed dryly.

"The brass at the Civil Guard thought so too. They worried I'd drop dead and they'd be sued. Tried to talk me into doing half a shift, but I convinced them to give me a tryout." He patted his midsection. "Three years later and still breathing. Legs like iron. Active metabolism."

Daniel nodded appreciatively. "How long does each pass take you?" he asked.

"Fifty minutes to an hour. Twice I stop to smoke, once a shift I take a leak."

"Any other interruptions?"

"None," said Schlesinger. "You can set your watch by me."

Perhaps, thought Daniel, someone had.

"What time did you find the girl?"

"Five forty-seven."

"That's very precise."

"I checked my watch," said Schlesinger, but he looked uneasy.

"Something the matter?"

The old man glanced around, as if searching for eavesdroppers. Touched the barrel of the M-1 and gnawed on his mustache.

"If you're not certain of the precise time, an estimate will do," said Daniel.

"No, no. Five forty-seven. Precisely."

Daniel wrote it down. The act seemed to increase Schlesinger's uneasiness.

"Actually," he said, lowering his voice, "that's the time I called in. Not when I found her."

Daniel looked up. "Was there much of a time lapse between the two?"

Schlesinger avoided Daniel's eyes.

"I . . . when I saw her I became sick. Tossed my dinner into the bushes."

"An understandable reaction, *adoni*."

The old man ignored the empathy.

"Point is, I was out of it for a while. Dizzy and faint. Can't be certain how much time went by before my head cleared."

"Did it seem more than a few minutes?"

"No, but I can't be certain."

"When did you last pass by the spot where you found her?"

"On the way up from the fourth trip. About an hour before."

"Four-thirty?"

"Approximately."

"And you saw nothing."

"There *was* nothing," said Schlesinger adamantly. "I make it a point to check the gully carefully. It's a good place for someone to hide."

"So," said Daniel, writing again, "as far as you could tell, she was brought there between four-thirty and five forty-seven."

"Absolutely."

"During that time, did you see or hear any cars?"

"No."

"Anyone on donkey or horseback?"

"No."

"What about from the campus?"

"The campus was locked—at that hour it's dead."

"Pedestrians?"

"Not a one. Before I found it . . . her, I heard something from over there, on the desert side." He swiveled and indicated the eastern ridge. "Scurrying, a rustle of leaves. Lizards, maybe. Or rodents. I ran my light over it. Several times. There was nothing."

"How long before you found her did this occur?"

"Just a few minutes. Then I crossed over. But there was no one there, I assure you."

Daniel lifted his hand to shield his eyes from the sun and looked out at the wilderness: jagged golden heights striped rust and green by ancient terraces, dropping without warning to the bone-white table of the Jordanian Rift; at vision's end, the shadow-like ellipse that was the Dead Sea. A leaden wedge of fog hovered over the water, dissolving the horizon.

He made a note to have some uniforms go over the slope on foot.

"Nothing there," repeated Schlesinger. "No doubt they came from the city side. Sheikh Jarrah or the wadi."

"They?"

"Arabs. This is obviously their dirty work."

"Why do you say that?"

"She was cut up, wasn't she? The Arab loves a blade."

"You said Arabs," said Daniel. "In the plural. Any reason for that?"

"Just being logical," said Schlesinger. "It's their style, the mob mentality. Gang up on someone defenseless, mutilate them.

It was a common thing, before your time—Hebron, Kfar Etzion, the Jaffa Gate riots. Women and children slaughtered like sheep. The goddamned British used to stand by and let it happen. I remember one time—end of '47—they arrested four of our boys and handed them over to a mob at the Damascus Gate. The Arabs ripped them apart. Like jackals. Nothing left to bury."

Schlesinger's face had grown hawklike, the eyes compressed to slashes, the mouth under the mustache thin-lipped and grim.

"You want to solve this, son? Knock on doors in East Jerusalem."

Daniel closed the pad. "One more thing, *adoni.*"

"Yes?"

"You said you live on French Hill."

"That's correct. Just up the road."

"That's within walking distance of your patrol route."

"Correct."

"And by your own account, you're a strong walker. Yet you drive your car and park it on Sderot Churchill."

Schlesinger gave him a stony look.

"Sometimes when I finish," he said, "I'm not ready to go home. I take a drive."

"Anywhere in particular?"

"Here and there. Anything wrong with that, Pakad?" The old man's gutturals were harsh with indignation.

"Nothing at all," said Daniel, but to himself he thought: *Ben adam afor,* Carmellah Gadish had gasped, when they'd found her. A gray man. Three barely audible words bubbling from between bloody lips. Then, the loss of consciousness, descent into coma. Death.

Ben adam afor. A feeble bit of information, perhaps nothing more than delirium. But it was the closest thing they had to evidence and, as such, had taken on an aura of significance. *Gray man*. They'd spent days on it. An alias or some kind of underworld code? The color of the slasher's clothing? A sickly complexion? Something characterological?

Or advanced age?

He looked at Schlesinger, smiled reassuringly. White hair and mustache. Sky-blue eyes, bordered by a ring of gray. White, light-blue. At night it could all look the same. *Gray.* It seemed crazy, almost heretical, to think of an old Palmahi doing something like that. And he himself had pointed out to Laufer the discrepancies between this death and the other five. But one never knew. Schlesinger had begun patrolling Scopus shortly after the last Gray Man murder. Thirteen years in one neighborhood, then a sudden move. Perhaps there was some connection, something oblique that he had yet to grasp. He resolved to look into the old man's background.

"I fought for this city," Schlesinger was saying, testily. "Broke my ass. You'd think I'd deserve better than being treated like a suspect."

Daniel wondered if his thoughts were that transparent, looked at Schlesinger and decided the old man was being touchy.

"No one suspects you of anything, *adoni,*" he soothed. "I was merely succumbing to curiosity—an occupational hazard."

Schlesinger scowled and asked if he could go.

"Certainly, and thank you for your time. I'll have the officers take you back to your car."

"I can walk just fine."

"I'm sure you can, but regulations dictate otherwise."

He called the uniforms over while the old man muttered about bureaucrats and red tape, had one of them walk him to the blue-and-white, and drew the other aside.

"Take a look at his car, Amnon. Nothing detailed, just a casual glance. Inform him that the carbine must be kept in the trunk and put it there yourself. When you do, check the trunk."

"Anything in particular to look for?"

"Anything out of the ordinary. Be sure to keep it casual—don't let on what you're doing."

The officer looked at Schlesinger's retreating form.

"Is he a suspect?"

"We're being thorough. He lives on French Hill. Escort him to the towers, and radio for two more men. Have them bring a metal detector and the four of you climb down there and do a grid search of the slope on the desert side. Concentrate on the immediate vicinity beyond the ridge—a two-kilometer radius should be sufficient. Look for footprints, blood, human waste, food wrappers."

"Anything out of the ordinary."

"Exactly. And no loose lips. The brass wants this kept quiet."

The officer nodded and left, talked to Schlesinger, and ushered him to the car. The blue-and-white drove off, followed shortly by the technical van. The transport drivers disappeared into the gully with a stretcher and a folded black plastic body bag and reappeared shortly with the bag filled. They slid it into the Abu Kabir van, climbed in, slammed the doors, and sped away. Daniel walked over to Afif and together they removed the barriers and loaded them into the jeep.

"Salman, what's the chance of someone sneaking in from the desert in the early morning hours?"

"Everything's been quiet," the Druze said stoically. "Well under control."

"What about from Isawiya?"

"Silent. We've got infrared scopes at our stations in the Rift. On the tenders and some of the jeeps as well. All we've been picking up are snakes and rabbits. Small band of Bedouins up north of the Ramot, they won't come down until summer."

"What about Ramallah?"

"Local unrest, but nothing beyond talk."

"The Bethlehem sector?"

"Patrol's been beefed up since the girl's funeral. No suspicious movement."

The girl. Najwa Sa'id Mussa. Fourteen years old and on her way to market when she'd been caught in the cross fire between a mob of stone-throwing Arabs and two nineteen-year-old soldiers who'd fired back in defense. A bullet to the head had turned her into a heroine, posters emblazoned with her picture slapped to the trunks of the fig trees that grew along the Hebron Road, the graffiti of vengeance marring walls and boulders. A near-riot of a funeral, and then things had gotten quiet again.

Or had they?

He thought about another dead girl and wondered.

By seven forty-five, students had begun drifting toward campus and the hum of traffic filtered down the road. Daniel crossed over and walked down toward the Amelia Catherine Hospital. He'd passed the place numerous times but had never been inside. During the Gray Man investigation, Gavrieli had taken the task of handling the U.N. people on his own. A good boss. Too bad he'd been careless.

As Daniel neared the compound he was struck by how out of place it seemed, perched atop Scopus, with its pink stone facade, obelisk bell tower, yawning gargoyles, and steeply pitched tile roofs. An overdressed Victorian dowager camped out in the desert.

An arched, ivied entry fronted the main building. Embedded in the limestone at the apex was a rectangle of gray granite, carved with a legend in English: AMELIA CATHERINE PILGRIMS' HOSPICE AND INFIRMARY, ERECTED BY HERMANN BRAUNER, AUGUST 15, 1898. An enameled plaque, white with blue letters, had been nailed just below: UNITED NATIONS RELIEF AND WORKS ASSOCIATION. CO-ADMINISTERED BY THE WORLD ASSEMBLY OF CHURCHES. English and Arabic, not a trace of Hebrew. Climbing white roses, their petals heat-browned, embraced the fluted columns that flanked the arch. The entry led to a large dusty courtyard, shaded at the hub by a spreading live oak as old as the edifice. Circling the trunk of the big tree were spokelike beds of flowers: tulips, poppies, irises, more roses. A high, carved fountain sat in one corner, dry and silent, its marble basin striated with dirt.

Just inside the entry sat a portly middle-aged Arab watchman on a flimsy plastic chair, sleepy-eyed and inert except for fingers that danced nimbly over a string of amber worry beads. The man wore gray work pants and a gray shirt. Under his armpits were black crescents of sweat. A glass of iced tamarindy rested on the ground, next to one leg of the chair, the ice cubes rounding to slush.

Daniel's footsteps raised the watchman's eyelids, and the Arab's face became a stew of emotions: curiosity, distrust, the muddled torpor of one whose dreams have been rudely curtailed.

Daniel greeted him in Arabic and showed him his badge. The watchman frowned, pulled his bulk upright, and reached into his pocket for identification.

"Not necessary," said Daniel. "Just your name, please."

"Hajab, Zia." The watchman avoided eye contact and looked out at a distant point over Daniel's left shoulder. Running a thick hand over crew-cut hair the color and texture of iron filings, he tapped his foot impatiently. His mustache was a charcoal patch of stubble, the lips below, thin and pale. Daniel noticed that his fingers were horned with callus, the fingernails broken and rimmed with grime.

"Are you from Jerusalem, Mr. Hajab?"

"Ramallah." The watchman drew himself up with regional pride. The hubris of a poor man from a rich city.

"I'd like to ask you some questions."

Hajab shrugged resignedly, continued to look away. "Ask, but I know nothing about it."

"About what?"

"Your police matters." Hajab sucked in his breath and began working on the beads with both hands.

"What time did you come on duty this morning, Mr. Hajab?"

"Six-thirty."

"Is that when you usually begin working?"

"Not usually. Always."

"And which road did you take from Ramallah?"

"None."

"Pardon?"

"No road. I live here."

"Here at the hospital?"

"Yes."

"Is that arrangement part of your job?"

"I maintain a beautiful home in Ramallah," said the watchman defensively. "A large garden, fig trees, and vines. But my skills must be easily available, so the hospital has provided me with a room. Lovely, clean, freshly painted, and well furnished."

"It's a lovely hospital," said Daniel. "Well built."

"Yes." Hajab was solemn.

"When is your custom to awaken?"

"Six."

"And your routine upon rising?"

"Ablutions, the morning prayers, a light breakfast, and straight to my post."

"How long have you lived here at the hospital, Mr. Hajab?"

"Thirteen months."

"And before that?"

"Before that, I lived in Ramallah. As I told you." Exasperated.

"Were you a sentry in Ramallah as well?"

"No." Hajab paused, massaged his beads. His brow had glossed with perspiration and he used one hand to wipe it.

"In Ramallah, I was an . . . automotive engineer."

Daniel wrote "mechanic" next to Hajab's name.

"What caused you to change occupations?"

Hajab's meaty face darkened with anger. "The station that employed me was sold. The new owner gave my job to his son-in-law." He looked at his beads, coughed, and cursed in Arabic under his breath: "*Zaiyel te'ban.*" Like a snake.

He coughed again, licked his lips and gazed longingly at the tamarindy.

"Please," said Daniel, indicating the drink, but the watchman shook his head.

"Go on with your questions," he said.

"Do you understand why I'm asking these questions?"

"An incident," said Hajab with forced disinterest.

Daniel waited for more and, when it didn't come, asked, "Do you have any knowledge of this incident?"

"As I told you, I know nothing of police matters."

"But you knew there had been an incident."

"I saw the barriers and the cars and assumed there was an incident." Hajab smiled mirthlessly. "I thought nothing of it. There are always incidents, always questions."

"Up here at the hospital?"

"Everywhere."

The watchman's tone was hostile and Daniel read the covert message: Life has been nothing but troubles since you Jews took over.

"Are you a sound sleeper, Mr. Hajab?"

"My dreams are peaceful. As sweet as roses."

"Did you dream sweetly last night?"

"And why not?"

"Did you hear or see anything out of the ordinary?"

"Nothing at all."

"No unusual movement? Voices?"

"No."

"How," asked Daniel, "did you come to work at the Amelia Catherine?"

"After I left my engineering position I experienced an illness and was treated at a clinic run by the hospital."

"What kind of illness?"

"Head pains."

"And where was the clinic?"

"In Bir Zeit."

"Go on, please."

"What's to go on about?"

"How you came to work here."

Hajab frowned. "The doctor at the clinic advised me to come here for tests. On the day I arrived I saw a notice on one of the walls, soliciting help. Sentry duty and repairs. I made inquiries and when my engineering talents were discovered by Mr. Baldwin, I was asked to join the staff."

"A bit of good fortune."

Hajab shrugged.

"*Al Maktoub,*" he said, casually. "It was written on my forehead."

"How is your head now?"

"Very well, bless the Prophet."

"Good. Tell me, Mr. Hajab, how many others live here at the hospital?"

"I've never taken count."

Before Daniel could pursue the point, a shiny black Lancia Beta drove up to the entrance. The sports car let out a belch, then shuddered as its engine died. The driver's door opened and out climbed a tall fair-haired man dressed in a khaki safari jacket over brown corduroy trousers. Under the jacket was a white shirt and green-and-red striped tie. The man was of indeterminate age—one of those smooth-faced types who could be anywhere from thirty to forty, wide-shouldered and narrow-hipped, with a heavy build and long arms that dangled loosely. His light hair was waxy and straight, thinning to outright baldness at the crown; his face, narrow and sunburned, topped by a high, freckled brow. His lips were chapped; his nose, uptilted, pink, and peeling. Mirrored sunglasses concealed his eyes. He faced Daniel, then Hajab. "Zia?" he said.

"Police, Mr. Baldwin," said Hajab, in English. "Questions."

The man turned back to Daniel, smiled faintly, then grew serious. "I'm Sorrel Baldwin, administrator of the hospital. What seems to be the trouble, Officer?"

His accent was American, tinctured by the kind of drawl Daniel had heard in cowboy movies. *Ah'm* for *I'm.*

"A routine investigation," said Daniel, offering his badge. Baldwin took it.

"An incident," said Hajab, growing bold.

"Uh hmm," said Baldwin, lifting his sunglasses and peering at the badge. His eyes were small, blue, shot through with red. Drinker's eyes? "And you're . . . an inspector."

"Chief inspector."

Baldwin handed back the badge.

"Any police dealings I've had have always been with Deputy Commander Gavrieli."

Buddies with the boss. Letting Daniel know that he was outclassed. But the fact that he thought Gavrieli's name still carried weight gave lie to his words. Daniel ignored the snub, got down to business.

"Mr. Baldwin, during the early hours of the morning a crime was committed—crucial evidence was found in that gully, just down the road. I'd like to talk to your staff, to find out if anyone saw something that could help us in our investigation."

Baldwin put his sunglasses back on.

"If anyone had noticed anything," he said, "they would have reported it, I assure you."

"I'm sure they would have. But sometimes people see things—small things—and are unaware of their significance."

"What kind of crime are we talking about?" asked Baldwin.

"A major one. I'm not at liberty to say more."

"Security censorship, eh?"

Daniel smiled. "May I talk to your staff?"

Baldwin kneaded his chin with one hand. "You realize, Officer . . ."

"Sharavi."

". . . Officer Sharavi, that we are an arm of the United Nations Relief and Works Agency and, as such, are entitled to diplomatic privilege with regard to police procedure."

"Of course, Mr. Baldwin."

"Understand also that involvement in local political matters is something we make a concerted effort to avoid."

"This is a criminal matter, sir. Not a political one."

"In this city," said Baldwin, "that's a fine distinction. One, I'm sorry to say, that the police don't often seem able to make." He paused, looked down at Daniel. "No, I'm sorry, Officer Sharavi, I just can't see clear to letting you disrupt our procedures."

As Daniel listened to the American, the image of the murdered girl intruded on his consciousness and he surrendered to a fantasy etched in anger: *He, the policeman, takes hold of the bureaucrat's arm and leads him to the gully, over the edge, right into the butchery. Presses his face close to the corpse, forces him to inhale the stench of evil. Breathe that, experience it. Viscerally. Is it criminal or political, pencil pusher?*

"I agree," he heard himself saying. "It is a very fine distinction. But one that we're getting better at recognizing. You remember, of course, the case of Corporal Takumbai?"

"Vaguely." Baldwin shifted his weight, looked uncomfortable. "Somewhere up north, wasn't it?"

"Yes it was. In Tiberias. Corporal Takumbai was part of a Fijian contingent assigned to the UNIFIL patrol in Southern Lebanon. He had a history of mental imbalance that no one thought was important. One night, during a holiday on the Sea of Galilee, he left his comrades, broke into an apartment, and raped two old women. Someone heard screams and called the police. When they tried to capture him, Takumbai wounded one officer and—"

"I really don't see what this has to do with—"

"—came close to killing another. Despite all that, *we let him go, Mr. Baldwin.* Back to Fiji, without prosecution. He was protected by his position with the United Nations and we respected that. We were able to separate the political from the criminal. There have been others, of course—a Frenchman, Grimaud, who was a compulsive shoplifter; a Finn named Kokkonen, who enjoyed getting drunk and beating up women. Even as we speak, the file of another Frenchman is being processed. This one was caught smuggling hashish resin out of the Beach Refugee Camp in Gaza. Like all the others, he'll be expelled without trial. Without public exposure. So you see, Mr. Baldwin, you have nothing to fear. We continue to protect the good name of the United Nations. We *are* able to make fine distinctions."

Baldwin glanced over his shoulder at Hajab, who'd listened to the exchange raptly, moving his head back and forth like a soccer fan. Reaching into his pocket, the American pulled out a set of car keys and tossed them to the watchman.

"Park the car, Zia."

Though clearly disappointed, the watchman complied. When the Lancia had driven off, Baldwin said to Daniel: "In any organization, there are going to be a few bad apples. That has nothing to do with the staff of this hospital. They're handpicked. Altruists. Good solid folk."

"I don't doubt that for a moment, Mr. Baldwin. As altruists they should be pleased to help."

The American peeled a papery shred of skin from his nose and looked toward the scene of the crime. A flock of crows rose from the gully. From somewhere behind the hospital came the bray of a donkey.

"I could," said Daniel, "go through channels. Which would mean a delay of the investigation—meetings, memoranda. We are a small country, Mr. Baldwin. News travels quickly. The longer something stretches out, the more difficult it is to keep it out of the public eye. People would want to know why so many criminals are avoiding punishment. One would hate to see the public image of the U.N. suffer needlessly."

When Baldwin didn't respond, Daniel added, "Perhaps I'm not speaking clearly. My English—"

"Your English is just fine," said Baldwin, smiling sourly.

Daniel returned the smile. "I had an excellent teacher," he said, then looked at his watch. Flipping over his note pad, he began to write. Several more moments passed. "All right," said Baldwin, "but let's try to keep it quick."

He turned on his heel, and Daniel followed him under the arch and across the silent courtyard. A lizard scampered up the trunk of the big oak and disappeared. Daniel breathed in deeply and the aroma of roses settled moistly in his nostrils. Like a cool spray of syrup, filtered through the hot, morning air.

4

The hospital had a history. Daniel had learned about it in '67, during training with the 66th, when rumors of war caused every paratroop officer to study his maps and his history books.

The Amelia Catherine had begun its life as a private residence —a great, lumbering manse at the crest of the watershed between the Jordan Valley and the Mediterranean.

Conceived by a wealthy German missionary as a wedding present for his young bride and named for her, the estate had been fashioned of native limestone and marble by the hands of local masons. But its plans had been drawn up in Munich by an Anglophile architect and the result was a self-conscious display of Victoriana transported to Palestine—oversized, decidedly snobbish, surrounded by formal gardens replete with boxwood hedges, beds of flowers, and velvet lawns that perished quickly in the Judean heat. The missionary was also a man of high taste, and he shipped over tinned meats and preserved delicacies, bottles of French wine stored in cavernous cellars beneath the mansion.

The object of all this architectural affection, a frail blond *fraulein* of twenty-one, contracted cholera two months after her arrival in Jerusalem and was dead three weeks later. After burying her near the Grove of Gethsemane, the grieving widower found himself shaken by a crisis of faith that sucked him back to Europe, never to return, abandoning his dream house to the ruling Ottomans.

The Turks had always entertained a disdain for Jerusalem and its structures and, during four centuries of reign, had transformed it from a teeming Crusader shrine into a dusty, disease-ridden, provincial village, home to beggars, lepers, and fanatic Jew-infidels. From the moment its foundation had been laid, the Amelia Catherine had been an affront to their world view—that a Christian-infidel should be allowed to build something so vulgar as a *house for a woman*, a house that looked down upon the mosques of Al Aqsa and the Rock, was a grievous insult to Allah.

Heavy taxes collected from the German fool had kept these religious reservations at bay. But once he was gone, the gardens were ordered fallow, the lawns burned, the great house transformed to a military warehouse. Soon, the stink of machine grease emanated from every marble corridor.

That state of affairs endured until 1917, when the British invaded Palestine. The debased mansion on Scopus was strategically located and its begrimed windows witnessed many a long bloody battle. When the gunfire died, on December 11, General Allenby was marching into Jerusalem and the Ottoman Empire was a thing of the past.

The British welcomed themselves with a ceremony of exceptional pomp—one that amused the poor Jews and Arabs whose families had inhabited the city for centuries—and like every conquering horde before them, the new rulers lost no time refurbishing the Holy City to their taste, starting with the Amelia Catherine.

Crews of workmen were ordered to scythe through ankle-ripping coils of weeds; limestone was abraded to its original blush; cisterns were emptied, cesspools drained and relined. Within weeks, suitably impressive headquarters for the British military governor had been created and the genteel mix of small talk and the clatter of teacups could be heard on the veranda.

In 1947 tensions between Palestinian Jews and Palestinian Arabs began boiling over. The British lost their taste for empire building and quickly pulled up stakes. Fighting broke out, followed by a cease-fire and a United Nations partition that created a jigsaw solution: The land was divided into six sections, with the southern and northern coastal regions and the heartland, including Jerusalem and most major cities, granted to the Arabs. The Jews received a strip of central coastline, an inland wedge of Galilee, and the barren Negev desert. Though they'd been deeded the lion's share of natural resources, the Arabs were dissatisfied with less than everything and, in 1948, attacked the Jews. Thousands of lives and one armistice later found the Jewish portion, now called Israel, enlarged to include the entire western section of Palestine but still smaller than the Arab portion, now called Jordan, which encompassed both sides of the Jordan River and spread to the east.

Faulty prophecy left Jerusalem bizarrely divided. The Holy City had been carved up hastily on November 30, 1948, during a temporary cease-fire. The process of division was an unceremonious exercise conducted in an abandoned building in the Musrara slum by the Jewish commander, a lieutenant colonel named Moshe Dayan, and the Arab commander, a lieutenant colonel named Abdullah Tal.

Neither Dayan nor Tal thought the truce would last and both considered their efforts temporary. The Jews hoped for a permanent peace treaty with their cousins, and Abdullah Tal still harbored fantasies of conquest, having boasted only days before of riding into Jewish Jerusalem on a white horse.

They went to work, using soft, waxy pencils—Dayan's red, Tal's green—on a 1:20,000 scale map of Jerusalem, drawing crude, arbitrary lines that corresponded to a land width of 50 meters. Lines that expanded as the wax melted, cutting through the centers of homes and backyards, shops and offices, splitting the city like Solomon's baby. Lines that didn't deserve serious attention because they were nothing more than transitory sketches.

But the commanders were sectioning a land that devours its prophets, where the only consistency is surprise. As the days stretched out, cease-fire matured to armistice, sketches became international borders, the space between the wax, a no-man's-land for nineteen years.

Due to its strategic value, Mount Scopus had been divided earlier, turned into a demilitarized zone administered by the United Nations. Israel retained the ruins of Hadassah Hospital and the Hebrew University; the eastern slope, housing the battered Amelia Catherine, was assigned to Jordan. All buildings on both sides of the mountain lay vacant and unused, though minimal patrols were permitted, the weeds were kept trimmed, and Arab farmers were allowed, illegally, to plough the fields surrounding the Amelia Catherine and grow truck crops.

In 1967 the Arabs attacked again and, once again, lost honor and land. Jerusalem fell under exclusive Jewish rule for the first time in more than three thousand years and Scopus was unified. The Amelia Catherine entered its fifth metamorphosis, as a hospital, operated jointly by the U.N. and a Swiss-based group of Protestant missionaries.

It was a hasty transformation, wholly lacking in sentiment: the compound enclosed by high chain-link fences, grand suites reduced to wards by particle-board partitions, the mansion's large paneled library painted a pale clinical green and apportioned into a warren of offices. Soon the high stone walls resonated with the moans and muffled sobs of human infirmity.

It was this diminished grandeur that Daniel saw as he followed Baldwin under a sweeping marble staircase and down a long, whitewashed corridor. The building seemed empty and, except for a sonata played haltingly on a typewriter, silent.

The administrator's office was midway down the hall, a small, light room with a high domed ceiling. Tacked to the back of the door was a schedule of mobile clinics.

The furnishings were cheap and efficient: an imitation Danish modern desk at the center, two matching straight-backed chairs, a striped cotton sofa along the left wall. Above the sofa hung a framed print of "The Last Supper" and two diplomas: a bachelor's degree in business from an agricultural college in San Antonio, Texas, and a master's in sociology from the American University in Beirut. Opposite the sofa was a wall of bracket shelves, half filled with textbooks and spiral-bound U.N. publications. A small electric fan blew air from one of the empty shelves. Next to it sat a cowboy hat with a leather band. Behind the desk, a pair of tall, arched windows exposed a panoramic view of the desert. Between the windows stood a glass display case filled with archaeological relics: coins, small clay urns, strips of parchment. Baldwin saw Daniel looking at them and smiled.

"All legal and proper, Officer Sharavi. Official property of the U.N."

Daniel returned the smile and the American moved behind the desk and reclined in his chair. Taking a seat across from him, Daniel held his note pad in his lap and searched for signs of personal attachment—family snapshots, the little curios that people bring to the workplace to remind them of home. Except for the hat, nothing.

"How many people are on your staff, Mr. Baldwin?"

"Full time only, or part time as well?"

"Everyone, please."

"In that case, I can't answer you other than to say that it's a long list."

"Does this list exist in written form?"

Baldwin shook his head. "It's not that simple, Officer. The Amelia Catherine concentrates on two spheres of activity: mobile outreach clinics to refugees and indigents, and weekly in-house clinics that we run right here—dermatology, eye care, neurology, women's problems, maternal and child health. Many of the local doctors and nurses volunteer their services; some are paid on a part-time basis; still others are full-time employees. What you'd call a dynamic situation."

"I'm interested," said Daniel, "in those who sleep in the building."

"That," drawled Baldwin, "narrows things down considerably." The American held up his hand, ticked off fingers as he spoke. "There are our nurses, Peggy Cassidy and Catherine Hauser—"

"What are their nationalities?"

"Peggy's an American—California, if that means anything to you. Catherine's Swiss."

"And both of them slept here last night?"

"Whoa," said Baldwin, holding out his hands, palms out. "You said 'sleep,' in general terms. As far as last night, specifically, I have no idea."

The man had a way of reacting to simple questions as if they were traps. The wariness, thought Daniel, of a criminal or a politician.

"Go on, please," he said, writing. "Who else?"

"Dr. Carter, Dr. Al Biyadi, possibly Dr. Darousha."

"Possibly?"

"Dr. Darousha lives in Ramallah. He's a very dedicated man, a fine physician. Comes here after seeing his private patients and sometimes works well into the night. We provide him with a room so that he doesn't have to drive home in a state of fatigue. I have no way of knowing if he used it last night."

"The doctors' first names, please."

"*Richard* Carter, *Hassan* Al Biyadi, *Walid* Darousha."

"Thank you. Any others?"

"Ma'ila Khoury, our secretary; Zia—whom you've met; and myself."

Daniel consulted his notes. "Dr. Carter is an American?"

"Canadian. Dr. Al Biyadi is a native of Jerusalem."

Daniel knew an Al Biyadi family. Greengrocers with a stall in the Old City, on the Street of Chains. He wondered about a connection.

"Ma'ila is Lebanese," Baldwin was saying, "Zia's a Palestinian, and I'm from the great Lone Star State of Texas. And that's it."

"What about patients?"

Baldwin cleared his throat.

"There are no clinics today, in honor of Muslim Sabbath."

"I mean hospitalized patients."

Baldwin frowned. "I explained before, we function primarily as an outpatient center and outreach facility. Our goal is to make contact with those who wouldn't ordinarily have access to health care. We identify problems and direct them to the appropriate source of treatment."

"A referral center."

"In a sense, but we do administer primary treatment at our clinics."

"So patients are never admitted here?"

"I wouldn't say never, but rarely."

Such a huge building, thought Daniel, housing only a handful of people. Vacant wards, empty beds. All that foreign money so that poor Arabs could see doctors who told them to go see other doctors. It seemed foolish, symbolism posing as function. Typical of the U.N. But that was neither here nor there.

"Mr. Hajab," he said. "What is his job?"

"Watchman, custodial work, general repairs."

"This is a large building to be maintained by one person."

"A cleaning crew—some women from East Jerusalem—do the daily mop-up. Zia helps with odds and ends."

"Both Mr. Hajab and Dr. Darousha are from Ramallah. Did they know each other before Mr. Hajab began working here?"

"Dr. Darousha recommended Zia for the job. More than that, I can't tell you."

"Mr. Hajab told me his first contact with the hospital was as a patient. Was Dr. Darousha his physician?"

"You'll have to talk to Dr. Darousha about that."

"Very well," said Daniel, rising. "I'd like to do just that."

Baldwin made a phone call and, when no one answered, took Daniel across the hall, to the source of the typing. Ma'ila Khoury was a lovely-looking woman of about twenty-five, with full pale lips, curly hennaed hair, and widely spaced khaki eyes. She wore smart Western clothes and her nails were long and polished. An emancipated woman of old Beirut. Daniel wondered why and how she'd come to Israel to work and received his answer a moment later when a quick look—something that implied more than boss and secretary—passed between her and Baldwin. The American spoke to her in poor Arabic and she answered in a cultured Lebanese accent.

"Did Dr. Darousha sleep here last night, Ma'ila?"

"I don't know, sir."

"Is he here in the hospital?"

"Yes, sir. In examining room four, with an emergency patient who just arrived."

"Come with me, Officer Sharavi."

The examining rooms were on the other side of the staircase, on the west wing of the building, five numbered doors that had once been servants' quarters. Baldwin knocked lightly on number four and opened it. The room within was peacock-blue paint over lumpy plaster, relieved by a single grilled window just below the arch of the ceiling. An olive-wood crucifix and a white metal first-aid box adhered to one wall. Filling most of the floor space was a chipped white examining table next to a chipped white cabinet. A hanging white lamp swung from the ceiling, emitting cold bluish light.

On the examining table lay a man—from the looks of his dusty clothing a farm laborer—stolid and unmoving, one arm by his side, the other resting limply in the grasp of a second man in a long white coat. The man holding the arm looked up at the intrusion.

"Good morning, Dr. Darousha," said Baldwin.

Darousha gave a wait-one-minute gesture and returned his

attention to the arm, which Daniel saw was as red and glossy as boiled sausage. The doctor was short, dark, fiftyish, froglike, with coarse, bushy hair and sad, drooping eyes behind black-rimmed glasses. His coat was starched and spotless, and he wore it buttoned, over a white shirt and dark tie and razor-pressed black slacks. A stethoscope hung scarflike around his neck. His feet were small and narrow in woven black loafers and, as he rocked from one to the other, seemed barely to touch the ground.

"How many wasps bit you?" he asked in a deep, authoritative voice.

"Hundreds. Maybe thousands."

Darousha scowled and laid the arm down gently. Inserting the prongs of the stethoscope in his ears, he placed the disc on the man's still-clothed chest, listened, and put the instrument away. Lifting the arm again, he said, "This is nasty. Very nasty." He stared down sternly at the farmer, who smiled weakly.

"Very well. I'm going to give you an injection of something that will fight the infection, as well as some pills. Take them twice a day for ten days and then come and see me again. If this isn't any better, I'll have to cut it open to drain it, which will hurt badly. Do you understand?"

"Yes, Doctor."

"Take every one of those pills, do you understand?"

"Yes, Doctor."

"How often must you take them?"

"Two times a day, Doctor."

"For how long?"

"Ten days."

"Roll over, facing the door."

Darousha pulled a hypodermic syringe out of the cabinet, went through the routine of filling, checking, and expelling air bubbles, and tugged down the waistband of the man's trousers, which were so loose they didn't need to be unfastened. Aiming the needle like a dart, he jabbed it into the farmer's buttocks. The man blinked at the pain, smiled at Daniel and Baldwin.

"Go on now. The nurse in number two will give you the pills."

"Thank you, Doctor."

When the farmer had gone, Darousha stepped out into the hallway and lit up a Rothmans. Daniel's presence didn't seem to bother him, and when Baldwin introduced him as a policeman, Darousha nodded, as if the visit had been expected.

"I've got a few things to look into," said Baldwin, taking a step. "Be back in a minute, okay?"

There was furtive tension in the American's eyes and Daniel wondered what he planned to do. Warn the others of impending interrogation? Sneak a drink? Flirt with Ma'ila?

"Okay," he said and watched Baldwin lope down the hallway, then turned back to Darousha, who was smoking the cigarette as if it were his last.

"What can I do for you?" asked the doctor. Daniel had expected to converse in Arabic but the man's Hebrew was perfect.

"A serious crime has been committed in the vicinity of the hospital, Doctor. I'm questioning the staff of the hospital about unusual occurrences."

Darousha remained placid. "What kind of unusual occurrences?"

"Sights, sounds, anything out of the ordinary."

"I saw and heard police cars. Otherwise, nothing."

"And you were here all night?"

"Yes."

"What time did you go to bed?"

"Shortly before midnight."

"When did you awaken?"

"Seven."

"How often do you sleep here, Doctor?"

"That depends upon my schedule. If it's late when I complete my obligations and I feel too tired to drive, I stay over."

"By 'obligations' you mean patients?"

"Or other matters. Yesterday, for example, I attended a daylong seminar at Hadassah. Emergency crises in children—anaphylaxis, choking. My afternoon patients were delayed until evening and I didn't finish until after eleven."

"Did the other doctors—Carter and Al Biyadi—attend the seminar as well?"

"Dr. Carter, yes. Dr. Al Biyadi, no."

"He remained here?"

"I have no idea." Darousha put the cigarette to his lips, inhaled, and added a millimeter of ash to the tip.

"You live in Ramallah."

"That's correct."

"Zia Hajab is also from there."

A nod. The ash tumbled.

"How well do you know him?"

"Our families are entwined. His grandfather worked for my grandfather, his father for my father."

"What kind of work did they do?"

"We owned orchards. They were field hands."

"Does that relationship persist?"

Darousha shook his head. "I'm my father's only son. After his death I decided to study medicine, and the orchards were leased to another family who had no need for Zia's services. I was gone at the time, studying medicine in Amman. Otherwise I would have intervened. As it turned out, he found part-time work at a petrol station."

"Until another family transaction edged him out."

"That's correct."

"Difficult for him and his family."

"For him, yes. There is no family. Both parents and a sister died of tuberculosis thirty years ago. His three brothers were inducted into the Arab Legion. All were killed in '67."

"Did he fight too?"

"Yes. He was taken captive."

"What about wife and children?"

"None."

Daniel found his interest in the watchman growing. For the picture Darousha was painting was one of chronic failure, habitual abuse by the fates. Why did Hajab have difficulty holding on to a job? And why, with bachelorhood virtually unknown among the Arabs, had he never purchased a woman, never spread his seed? It indicated social problems, the kind of downtrodden, isolated life that could lead to self-hatred. Or the resentment that sometimes blossomed into violence.

He needed to know more about the workings of the man's mind, but sensed that a direct question would put Darousha off. Taking an indirect path, he said, "Hajab told me he had headache problems. Did you treat him for his pain?"

"In a manner of speaking."

"Please explain."

Darousha's sad eyes drooped even further.

"His pain was a pain of the soul that chose to settle in his head. I offered reassurance and chalky syrup. My most effective medical intervention was helping him get a job."

"It was a psychosomatic disorder, then."

Darousha stiffened. "These are confidential matters. I cannot discuss them further."

"Doctor," said Daniel, "if there's something in Hajab's psychological makeup that would predispose him to antisocial behavior, it's essential that you tell me."

"He's a moody man," said Darousha. "Suffers from depression. But there's nothing criminal in him. Nothing that would interest you."

"How often does he get depressed?"

"Infrequently, perhaps once or twice a month."

"For prolonged periods of time?"

"Two or three days."

"And what are his symptoms?"

Darousha threw up his hands, impatiently.

"I shouldn't be discussing this, but if it will simplify matters, I'll tell you. He develops ambiguous pains—psychosomatic symptoms—the headaches, gets very weak and goes to sleep. There's no aggressiveness, no antisocial behavior. Now, if you'll excuse me, please, I really must be going."

The man's face was closed tight as a vault. Sensing that any further prodding would be useless, Daniel took down his home address and phone number, thanked him for his time, and ended the interview.

Alone in the hall, he thought for a while about Zia Hajab, was still thinking when Baldwin returned.

"All the others except Peggy are in the dining room," said the American. "They say they've seen or heard nothing."

"What did you tell them?" asked Daniel.

"Just what you told me. That there'd been a crime nearby. None of them knows anything that can help you."

"Nevertheless, I'll need to talk to them."

"Suit yourself."

The dining room was an airy blue rectangle furnished with half a dozen circular tables, five of them empty. The ceiling was white and edged with crown moldings. French doors led out to a patio that served as pecking grounds for dozens of pigeons. Their clucks and thrums could be heard through the glass. Each table was surrounded by folding chairs and covered with an aquamarine tablecloth. Arabic music played from a portable radio. A long table at the center of the room bore plates of pastry and fruit, glasses of orange juice. A brass samovar on a wheeled cart hissed coffee-flavored steam. Next to it stood Zia Hajab, solemn-faced, a white apron fastened over his work clothes, holding a cup under the spout.

Baldwin walked Daniel to a table by the window where the other two doctors and the Swiss nurse, Catherine Hauser, were seated together eating breakfast. After making the introductions, the administrator sat down with them. Before Baldwin's rump had settled on the chair, Hajab moved in quickly to serve him, filling his plate with dates and apples, pouring steaming coffee into his cup, punctuating the activity with obsequious bows.

No invitation to sit was offered Daniel and he remained standing. Three faces stared up at him. He needed to speak to each of them individually, and breaking up their klatch made him feel intrusive. He took Catherine Hauser first, drawing her to a table at the far end of the room, carrying her coffee cup for her and setting it down in front of her.

She thanked him and smiled, a plump, elderly woman dressed in a shapeless, colorless smock. Gray-haired and blue-eyed, with the same kind of parchment skin he'd seen on the older nuns at the Convent of Notre Dame de Sion. As he looked at her, coins of color rose on each cheek. She seemed friendly and cooperative but was sure she'd heard or seen nothing. What had happened? she wanted to know. A crime, he said, smiled, and ushered her back to her table.

The Canadian, Carter, he would have pegged for one of the Scandinavian backpackers who traipsed through the city each summer—big-framed and heavy-featured, with curly blond hair, narrow gray eyes, and a full ginger beard. He was in his early thirties and wore old-fashioned round gold-framed glasses. His hair was shaggy and longish and, like the rest of him, seemed carelessly assembled. His white coat was wrinkled and he wore it over a blue work shirt and faded jeans. Slow-talking and deliberate, he appeared to be lost in his own world, though he did express normal curiosity about the crime.

Daniel answered his questions with vague generalities and asked, "You attended the seminar with Dr. Darousha?"

"Sure did."

"Did you see patients afterward?"

"No," said Carter. "Wally went back by himself. I was off-shift, so I took a cab into East Jerusalem and had dinner. At the Dallas Restaurant." He chuckled and added: "Filet steak, chips, three bottles of Heineken." Another chuckle.

"Something amusing, Dr. Carter?"

Carter shook his head, ran his fingers through his beard, and smiled.

"Not really. Just that this sounds like one of those cop shows back home—where were you on the night and all that."

"I suppose it does," said Daniel, writing. "What time did you arrive back at the hospital?"

"Must have been close to ten-thirty."

"What did you do when you arrived?"

"Went to my room, read medical journals until they put me to sleep, and popped off."

"What time was that?"

"I really couldn't tell you. This was fairly boring stuff so it could have been as early as eleven. When was this crime committed?"

"That hasn't been established yet. Did you hear or see anything at all that was out of the ordinary?"

"Nothing. Sorry."

Daniel dismissed him and he shambled back to his table. A former hippie, Daniel guessed. The kind who might blunt life's edges with a hit of hashish now and then. A dreamer.

Dr. Hassan Al Biyadi, by contrast, was all points and angles, formal, dapper, and delicate—almost willowy—with skin as dark as Daniel's, short black hair, well-oiled, and a pencil-line mustache that had been trimmed to architectural precision. He looked too young to be a doctor, and his white coat and elegant clothes only served to enhance the image of a child playing dress-up.

"By any chance," Daniel asked him, "are you related to Mohammed Al Biyadi, the grocer?"

"He is my father," said Al Biyadi, suspiciously.

"Many years ago, when I was a uniformed officer, thieves broke into your father's warehouse and stole a new shipment of melons and squash. I was assigned to the case." One of his first triumphs, the criminals quickly apprehended, the merchandise returned. He'd swelled with pride for days.

As an attempt to gain rapport, it failed.

"I know nothing of melons," said the young physician coldly. "Ten years ago I lived in America."

"Where in America?"

"Detroit, Michigan."

"The automobile city."

Al Biyadi folded his arms across his chest. "What do you want of me?"

"Did you study medicine in Detroit, Michigan?"

"Yes."

"Where?"

"Wayne State University."

"When did you return to Israel?"

"I returned to *Palestine* two years ago."

"Have you worked at the Amelia Catherine all that time?"

"Yes."

"What is your specialty?"

"Family medicine."

"Did you attend the seminar at Hadassah?"

Al Biyadi's face contracted, almost shriveling with anger. "You know the answer to that, policeman. Why play games?"

Daniel looked at him calmly and said nothing.

"The same thing over and over," said Al Biyadi. "Something happens and you harass us."

"Have you been harassed by the police before, Dr. Al Biyadi?"

"You know what I mean," snapped the young Arab. He looked at his watch, drummed his fingers on the table. "I have things to do, patients to see."

"Speaking of seeing, did you see anything unusual last night?"

"No, nothing, and that's likely to be my answer to all of your questions."

"What about during the early morning hours?"

"No."

"No shouts or cries?"

"No."

"Do you own a car?" asked Daniel, knowing he was prolonging the interview in response to Al Biyadi's hostility. But it was more than a petty reaction: The young doctor's response was out of proportion. Was his anger politically rooted or something more—the edginess of the guilty? He wanted a bit more time to study Hassan Al Biyadi.

"Yes."

"What kind?"

"A Mercedes."

"What color?"

"Green."

"Diesel or petrol?"

"Diesel." From between clenched jaws.

"Where do you park it?"

"In the back. With everyone else's."

"Did you drive it last night?"

"I didn't go out last night."

"You were here all night."

"Correct."

"Doing what?"

"Studying, going about my business."

"Studying for what?"

Al Biyadi tossed him a patronizing look. "Unlike the less educated occupations, the field of medicine is complex, always changing. One needs constantly to study."

A woman in her late twenties came into the dining room. She saw Al Biyadi, walked over to him, and placed a hand on his shoulder.

"Good morning, Hassan," she said brightly, in heavily accented Arabic.

Al Biyadi mumbled a reply.

"Any more questions?" he asked Daniel.

The woman looked puzzled. She was plain, with a flat, pleasant face, snub-featured and freckled, devoid of makeup. She wore a sleeveless white stretch top over blue jeans, and low-heeled sandals. Her hair was thin, straight, medium-brown. It hung to her shoulders and was pulled back behind her ears with white barrettes. Her eyes were large and round and matched her hair in hue. They glided inquisitively over Daniel's face, then clouded in confusion at the sight of his *kipah*.

"Police," said Al Biyadi. "There's been some sort of crime and I'm being interrogated like a common criminal."

The woman absorbed his hostility, as if by osmosis. Imitated his crossed-arms posture and glared at Daniel as if to say *Now you've upset him. I hope you're happy*.

"Miss Cassidy?"

"That's right."

"I'm Chief Inspector Sharavi. Please sit down. You, Doctor, are free to go."

Being dismissed so quickly seemed to anger Al Biyadi as much as had being detained. He bounded out of his chair and stamped out of the room.

"You people," said Peggy Cassidy. "You think you can push everyone around."

"By *people*, you mean . . . ?"

The young woman smiled enigmatically.

"Please sit," Daniel repeated.

She stared at him, then lowered herself into the chair.

"Would you like some coffee, Miss Cassidy?"

"No, and can we get on with whatever it is you want?"

"What I want," said Daniel, "is to to know if you heard or saw anything unusual last night, or during the early hours of the morning."

"No. Should I have?"

"A crime was committed just up the road. I'm searching for witnesses."

"Or scapegoats."

"Oh?"

"We know how you feel about us, about those who want to help the Palestinian people."

"This isn't a political matter," said Daniel.

Peggy Cassidy laughed. "Everything's political."

Daniel took a few moments to write in his pad.

"Where in the States are you from, Miss Cassidy?"

"Huntington Beach, California."

"How long have you lived in Israel?"

"A year."

"And how long in Detroit?"

The question surprised her, but only for a moment. The look she gave Daniel bore the scorn reserved for a magician whose illusions have failed. "Three years. And yes, that's where I met Hassan."

"At Wayne State University?"

"At Harper Hospital, which is affiliated with Wayne State University. If you must know."

"When did the two of you meet?"

"Four years ago."

"Have you been . . . have you had a relationship since that time?"

"I don't see that that's any of your business."

"If I presumed too much, I apologize," said Daniel.

She studied him, searching for sarcasm.

"Hassan's a wonderful man," she said. "He didn't deserve what you did to him."

"And what was that?"

"Oh, come *on.*"

Daniel sighed, rested his chin on one hand, and looked at her.

"Miss Cassidy, as I told you, a crime was committed in the vicinity of this hospital. A serious crime. My interest in you or Dr. Al Biyadi is limited to what either of you can tell me about that crime."

"Fine," she said, rising. "Then you have no interest in us at all. Can I go now?"

He left the Amelia Catherine at nine. Several blue-and-whites were parked near the eastern slope—the grid search of the hillside had begun—and he drove the Escort near the cliff and asked one of the uniforms if anything had turned up in Schlesinger's trunk.

"Just a spare tire, Pakad."

"What about on the slope?"

"A Coke bottle with no fingerprints—nothing else yet."

Daniel spun the car around, descended Shmuel Ben Adayah and, when he reached the northeast tip of the Old City, turned left on Derekh Yericho, driving along the walls until he came to the parking lot just outside the Dung Gate. Swinging the Escort into a free space, he turned off the engine, got out, and opened the trunk. Inside were two black velvet bags that he removed and tucked under his left arm, next to his heart. The larger, about a foot square, was embroidered with gold and silver almond blossoms encircling a gold filigree Magen David. Half its size, the smaller bag was encrusted with a busy motif of gold curlicues and teardrops and studded with sequins.

Locking the trunk, he began walking toward the guard post just inside the Dung Gate, to his back the peaceful southern valley that had served as ancient Jerusalem's refuse dump. He passed the guards, walked under the graceful, scalloped arch, and stepped into the flow of people headed toward HaKotel Hama'aravi—the Western Wall.

The skies were a canopy of spring blue, cloudless and pure as only Jerusalem skies could be, so free from blemish that staring up at them could cause one to lose perspective. A cool, serene blue that belied the blanket of heat that had descended upon the city. By the time he reached the Wall, he was sticky with sweat.

The prayer plaza fronting the *Kotel* was uncrowded, the

women's section occupied only by a few hunched figures in dark clothing—righteous grandmothers praying on behalf of barren women, scrawling messages to the Almighty on scraps of paper and slipping them in the cracks between the stones. It was late, nearing the end of the *shaharit* period and the last of the Yemenite *minyanim* had ended, though he did see Mori Zadok reciting psalms as he stood face to the Wall, a tiny, white-bearded, ear-locked wisp, rocking back and forth in a slow cadence, one hand over his eyes, the other touching the golden stone. Other elders—Yemenite, Ashkenazi, Sephardi—had taken their customary places of meditation in the shadow of the Wall; their solitary devotions merged in a low moan of entreaty that reverberated through the plaza.

Daniel joined the only *minyan* still forming, a mixed quorum of Lubavitcher Hassidim and American Jewish tourists whom the Lubavitchers had corralled into praying. The tourists carried expensive cameras and wore brightly colored polo shirts, Bermuda shorts, and paper *kipot* that rested upon their heads with the awkwardness of foreign headdress. Affixed to some of their shirts were tour group identification labels (HI! I'M BARRY SIEGEL), and most seemed baffled as the Hassidim wound phylactery straps around their arms.

Daniel's own phylacteries lay in the smaller of the velvet bags, his *tallit* in the larger. On a typical morning he'd recite the benediction over the *tallit* and wrap himself in the woolen prayer shawl, then draw out the phylacteries and unwrap them. Following a second benediction, the black cube of the arm phylactery would be placed on his bicep, its straps wound seven times around his forearm, over the scar tissue that sheathed his left hand, and laced around his fingers. After uttering yet another *braha,* he would center the head phylactery over his brow, just above the hairline. The placement of the cubes symbolized commitment of both mind and body to God, and thus consecrated, he would be ready to worship.

But this morning was different. Laying the bags down on a chair, he pulled the drawstring of the larger and drew out not the *tallit* but a *siddur* bound in silver. Taking up the prayer book, he turned to the *Modeh Ani,* the Prayer of Thanks Upon Rising, which Laufer's call had prevented him from reciting at bedside. Facing the *Kotel,* he chanted:

Modeh ani lefaneha, melekh hai v'kayam,
"I offer thanks to Thee, O Everlasting King,"
Sheh hehezarta bi nishmati b'hemla.
"Who hast mercifully restored my soul within me."

To the Hassidim and tourists standing near him, the prayers of the small dark man seemed impassioned; his rhythmic cantillation, timeless and true. But he knew otherwise. For his devotion was encumbered by faulty concentration, his words baffled by an unwelcome hailstorm of memories. Of other souls. Those that hadn't been restored.

5

At ten he drove up El Muqaddas to French Hill, past the cluster of towers where Yaakov Schlesinger lived, and down to National Headquarters. The building was half a kilometer southeast of Ammunition Hill, a crisp, six-story cube of beige limestone, banded by windows and bisected by a flag tower. To the front sprawled an expansive apron of parking lot, half-filled; the entire property was hemmed by an iron fence. At the center of the fence was an electric gate controlled by a uniform inside a guard station. Daniel pulled up next to the observation window.

"Morning, Tzvika."

"Morning, Dani."

The gate opened like a yawn.

A steel revolving door provided access to the lobby. Inside, all was cool and quiet, the white marble floors spotless. A solitary woman in jeans and T-shirt sat on a bench kneading her fingers and waiting. Three uniforms stood behind the shiny black reception counter, joking and laughing, nodding at him without interrupting their conversation. He walked past them quickly, past the bomb display and the burglary prevention exhibit, ignored the elevators, swung open the door to the stairs, and bounded up to the third floor.

He stepped out into a long hallway and turned right, stopping at a plain wooden door. Only a strip of tape with his name on it distinguished it from the dozens of others that checkered the corridor. Ringing telephones and the white noise of conversation filtered through the hall in tidelike waves, but at a discreet level. Businesslike. He might have been in a law firm.

So different from the old Russian Compound, with its green copper domes and cold, dingy walls, the ancient plaster crackled like eggshell. The constant press of bodies, the eternal human parade. His cubicle had been noisy, cramped, bereft of privacy. Suspects rubbing elbows with policemen. Vine-laced leaded windows offering views of manacled suspects escorted across the courtyard, bound over for hearing at the Magistrates Hall, some shuffling, others fairly dancing to judgment. The bitter smell of sweat and fear, voices raised in the same old cantata of accusation and denial. The working space of a detective.

His Major Crimes assignment had meant a move to National Headquarters. But National Headquarters had been built with administrators in mind. Paper blizzards and the high technology of contemporary police work. Basement labs and banks of computers. Well-lit conference rooms and lecture halls. Clean, respectable. Sterile.

He turned the key. His office was spanking-white and tiny—ten by ten with a view of the parking lot. His desk, files, and shelves filled it, so that there was barely space for a single guest chair; more than one visitor meant a move to one of the interrogation rooms. On the wall was a framed batik Laura had done last summer. A pair of old Yemenite men, brown figures on a cream-colored background, dancing in ecstasy under a flaming orange swirl of sun. Next to it, a pictorial calendar from the Conservation League, this month's illustration a pair of young almond trees in full snowy blossom against a backdrop of gray rolling hills.

He squeezed behind the desk. The surface was clear except for a snapshot cube of Laura and the children and a stack of mail. At the top of the stack was a message to call Laufer if he had anything to report, some Research and Development questionnaires to be filled out as soon as possible, a memo explaining new regulations for submitting expense vouchers, and a final death report from Abu Kabir on the Dutch tourist who'd been found dead three days ago in the woodlands just below the

Dormition Abbey. He picked up the report and put the rest aside. Scanning the stiff, cruel poetry of the necropsy protocol ("This is the body of a well-developed, well-nourished white male . . ."), he dropped his eyes to the last paragraph: Extensive atherosclerotic disease including blockage of several main blood vessels, no sign of toxins or foul play. Conclusion: The man had been a heart attack waiting to happen. The steep climb to the abbey had done him in.

He put the report aside, picked up the phone, dialed the main switchboard, and got put on hold. After waiting for several moments, he hung up, dialed again, and was answered by an operator with a cheerful voice. Identifying himself, he gave her three names and left messages for them to contact him as soon as possible.

She read the names back to him and he said, "Perfect. There's one more, a Samal Avi Cohen. New hire. Try Personnel and if they don't know where he can be reached, Tat Nitzav Laufer's office will. Give him the same message."

"Okay. Shalom."

"Shalom."

The next number he tried was busy. Rather than wait, he left and climbed to the fourth floor.

The office he entered was one-third larger than his, but it housed two people. A pair of desks had been placed in an L. On the wall behind them, a single shelf held books, a collection of straw dolls, and a sachet that emitted a light aroma of patchouli.

Both youth officers were on the phone, talking to bureaucrats. Both wore pastel short-sleeved blouses over jeans. Otherwise, physically and stylistically, they were a study in contrasts.

Hanna Shalvi sat nearer to the door, diminutive, dark, bespectacled; baby-faced, so that she didn't look much older than the children she worked with. She asked a question about a family's fitness, nodded as she listened, said "yes" and "hmm" several times, repeated the question, waited, repeated.

A few feet away, Alice Yanushevsky hunched over her desk, jabbing her pencil in the air and smoking like a chimney. Tall and moon-faced, with straw-colored hair cut in a Dutch-boy, she demanded fast action from a recalcitrant pencil-pusher in a voice tight with impatience.

"This is a girl in jeopardy! We'll have no more delays! Am I understood?" Slam.

A sweet smile for Daniel. A drop in vocal pitch: "Good morning, Dani." She picked up a cardboard tube, opened it, and unfolded the contents. "Like my new poster?"

It was a blowup of the American rock band Fleetwood Mac.

"Very nice."

"Avner gave it to me because he says I look like one of them"—she swiveled and pointed—"the English girl, Christine. What do you think?"

"A little," he conceded. "You're younger."

Alice laughed heartily, smoked, laughed again.

"Sit down, Pakad Sharavi. Just what is it that you need?"

"Photographs of missing girls. Brunettes, probably fifteen or sixteen, but let's play it safe and go twelve to nineteen."

Alice's green eyes jumped with alarm.

"Something happened to one of them?"

"Possibly."

"What?" she demanded.

"Can't say anything right now. Laufer's put a gag on."

"Oh, come on."

"Sorry."

"All take, no give, eh? That should make your job easy." She shook her head scornfully. "*Laufer.* Who does he think he's kidding, trying to keep anything quiet around here?"

"True. But I need to humor him."

Alice stubbed out her cigarette. Another shake of the head.

"The girl in question has dark skin, dark hair," said Daniel. "Roundish face, pretty features, chipped teeth, one missing upper tooth. Anyone come to mind?"

"Pretty general except for the teeth," said Alice, "and that could have happened after the disappearance." She opened one of her desk drawers, pulled out a pile of about a dozen folders, and thumbed through them, selecting three, putting the rest away.

"All our open cases are being entered into the computer, but I have a few here that just came in recently. All runaways—these are the ones in your age range."

He examined the photographs, shook his head, gave them back.

"Let's see if she has any," said Alice. Rising, she stood over Hanna, who was still nodding and questioning. Tapping her on the shoulder, she said: "Come on, enough."

Hanna held up one hand, palm inward, thumb touching index finger. Signaling *savlanut.* Patience.

"If you haven't convinced them yet, you never will," said Alice. She ran her fingers through her hair, stretched. "Come on, enough."

Hanna conversed a bit more, said thank you, and got off the phone.

"Finally," said Alice. "Take out your recent files. Dani needs to look at them."

"Good morning, Dani," said Hanna. "What's up?"

"He can't tell you but you have to help him anyway. Laufer's orders."

Hanna looked at him, dark eyes magnified by the lenses of her glasses. He nodded in confirmation.

"What do you need?" she asked.

He repeated the description of the murdered girl and her eyes widened in recognition.

"What?"

"Sounds like a kid I processed two weeks ago. Only this one was only thirteen."

"Thirteen is possible," said Daniel. "What's her name?"

"Cohen. Yael Cohen. One second." She went into her files, talking as she sorted. "Musrara girl. Fooling around with a twenty-two-year-old *pooshtak.* Papa found out and beat her. Next day she didn't come home from school. Papa went looking for her, tried to beat up the boyfriend, too, got thrashed for his efforts. Ah, here it is."

Daniel took the file, homed in on the photograph, felt his spirits sink. Yael Cohen was curly-haired, bovine, and dull-looking. A missing tooth, but that was the extent of the resemblance.

"Not the one," he said, giving it back to Hanna. "The rest are in the computer?"

"In the process of being entered," said Alice.

"How many cases are we talking about?"

"Missing girls in that age range? About four hundred nationally, sixty or so from Jerusalem. But the files are classified alphabetically, not by age or sex, so you'd have to go through all of them—about sixteen hundred."

Tedious but workable.

"How can I get hold of them?"

"Go down to Data Processing and pull rank."

* * *

He spent the next two hours on the phone, phoning Dr. Levi at Abu Kabir and being told by an assistant that the pathologist was out of the office; requesting a copy of Schlesinger's service record from Civil Guard Headquarters; getting a records clerk to search for any sort of priors on the Amelia Catherine staff; attempting, without success, to find out if any of the three detectives had received his message. Letting Data Processing know that someone would be down to examine the missing-juvenile files. Filling out the mountain of requisition forms that legitimized each of the requests. Hampered at every step by his inability to satisfy the curiosity of the people whose cooperation he needed.

At twelve-fifteen, Levi called.

"Shalom, Pakad. I've finished the preliminary on the young one from this morning. I know it's priority so I'll read from my notes: Well-developed, well-nourished mid-adolescent female of Eastern descent. Multiple stab wounds, shock from voluminous loss of blood—she was drained."

"How?"

"Gravity, probably. Tipped over so that it flowed through the throat wound."

Like a butchered animal, thought Daniel. One hand tightened around the receiver. The other scrawled hastily as the pathologist continued to recite his findings:

"The ear pierces were old. Inside the hole was some blackening, which turned out to be steel oxide on the spectograph—non-gold wire, which means the earrings themselves probably weren't gold and they may have been removed recently."

"Could the wire have been gold-plated?"

"Possibly, or gold paint. Let me continue. There were no defense cuts or ligature marks, so she didn't resist and she wasn't tied up. Which would indicate lack of consciousness during the actual cutting, but there was no evidence of head trauma. However, I did find two fresh needle marks on the arms and the gas chromotography came up with opiates. Heroin. Not enough to kill her unless she had an idiopathic sensitivity, but enough to sedate her."

"Was she cut up before or after sedation?"

"From the lack of resistance, I'd say after. For her sake, I hope so."

"Anesthesia," said Daniel.

"Considerate of the bastard, eh?"

"Any sign that she was an addict?"

"On the contrary: The organs were clean, mucosa clear. No other marks besides the two fresh ones. All in all, a healthy young lady."

"What about sexual assault?"

"The whole damned thing was a sexual assault," said Levi. "You saw the genitalia. If you mean was there semen, no visible patches, but the region was too torn up for a complete analysis. The tests we ran were negative. Let's see what else . . . oh, yes, the wounds were caused by more than one instrument. At least two, maybe more."

"What kinds of instruments?"

"Knives. Very sharp. One with a curved blade, the other larger, straight-edged. The larger one was used on the throat. One strong slash from left to right, so we're probably dealing with a right-handed person, which doesn't help you much."

"Any similarity to the Gray Man homicides?"

"None whatsoever. Gray Man used a serrated blade, relatively dull—we hypothesized a kitchen knife, remember? Whoever did this used something finely honed."

"Like a razor?"

"Razor sharp but definitely larger than your standard safety blade."

"What about a straight razor?"

Levi's pause implied contemplation.

"From my inspection of the wound," he said, "I'd say the big one's larger than your average straight razor. There was little or no sawing—the initial cut went right through. Though I suppose it could be one of those old-fashioned heavy ones the barbers used to shave people with."

"What about the curved one?"

"Short-bladed. First thing I thought of was a curved scalpel, but I checked all of mine against the wounds and none of them fit. Which doesn't mean there isn't some kind of surgical knife that would. But it could just as easily be something else: woodcarver's tool, linoleum cutter, even a one-of-a-kind—anyone can buy a knife, shape it, and sharpen it. I took wound casts. If you bring me a weapon I can tell you if it fits."

"I'll keep that in mind. What about the sheet?"

"We're not finished with it but it looks like standard domestic issue so I doubt you'll get anywhere pursuing that line of inquiry. Same for the soap and shampoo she was washed with. Neka Sheva Green."

"What do you make of the fact that she was washed?"

"Someone was trying to get rid of physical evidence. And did a damned good job of it—so far we've come up with no fibers except for those from the sheet, no foreign secretions or residue other than a few grains of garden-variety silica sand. It took a lot of care to get her that clean."

"I was thinking more in terms of psychology," said Daniel. "A symbolic gesture. Washing away guilt."

"Lady Macbeth?" said Levi doubtfully. "I suppose anything's possible when you're dealing with twisted minds."

"You see this as the work of a madman?"

"Not a drooling, raving lunatic—too much planning and precision for that. But twisted, nonetheless. A sadistic psychopath."

"Any ideas about the ethnicity of the girl?"

"Eastern is as far as I'll go. I checked for clitorectomy but there was too much tissue damage to tell. Not that it's the marker it used to be—many of the Arabs have stopped circumcising their women. The only ones you can count on to do it routinely are the Bedouins, and this one's no Bedouin."

"Why do you say that?"

"No tattoos. The soles of her feet were too soft. And when they kill their own, they bury them in the desert. Besides, a Bedouin girl of this age would have been married already and not allowed far enough out of the tent to get into trouble." Levi paused. "Says something for primitive culture, eh?"

At one o'clock Daniel went down to the Forensics lab and received confirmation of Levi's assessment of the sand: nothing unique. Steinfeld had just begun developing photographs of the dead girl. One was a head shot, which revealed none of the wounds. Her face was placid and she could have been asleep. Daniel got the tech to print two dozen. Slipping the pictures in a large envelope, he left Headquarters and drove to the center of town.

Traffic was slow on Rehov King George, streets and sidewalks crammed with Sabbath shoppers, the babble of vendors and hawkers blending discordantly with diesel rumble, brake squeals, and the earsplitting blasts of auto horns. He got stuck at a red light behind an Egged bus and had to breathe in rancid exhaust mixed with wafts of hot grease from a nearby food stand. *Melekh HaFelafel.* "The Felafel King." Down the block was The Juice King, just around the corner The Emperor of Hamburgers. A nation of monarchs . . .

The bus moved and he sped forward, hooking a sharp left into the mouth of Rehov Ben Yehuda and parking illegally at the top of the street. Placing a police identification card on the dash of the Escort, he locked the car and left, hoping some underobservant rookie wouldn't clamp a Denver Boot on his tires.

The front door of The Star Restaurant was open, but he was early, so he walked past the restaurant and down the sloping street toward his father's shop.

Once just another auto-choked Jerusalem thoroughfare, Ben Yehuda had been closed to cars several years ago and transformed into a walking mall all the way to the big clock at Zion Square. He made his way through a wash of people—lovers holding hands as they window-shopped and traded dreams; children clinging to parental hands, their buttery faces smeared with pizza and ice cream; soldiers on leave; and artsy types from the Bezalel Institute, drinking iced coffee and eating paper-cradled napoleons at the parasoled tables of sidewalk cafés.

He walked past a shwarma stand, saw customers waiting eagerly as a counterman shaved juicy slices from a spinning, fat-topped cone of spiced lamb. Nearby, long-haired street musicians strummed American folk songs without passion, huddled like empty-eyed scarecrows over open instrument cases speckled with coins. One, a pale, skeletal, lank-haired woman, had brought a battered upright piano on wheels and was pounding out bad Chopin to a derisively grinning audience of taxi drivers. He recognized a Latam officer, Wiesel, at the rear of the group, avoided even momentary eye contact with the undercover man, and walked on.

The sign in his father's window said CLOSED, but he peered in through the front door and saw movement from the back room. A rap on the glass brought his father to the front, and when he saw Daniel, his face lit up and he unlocked it quickly.

"Shalom, Abba."

"Shalom, son! Come in, come in."

Standing on tiptoes, the older man embraced him, kissing

both his cheeks. In the process, his beret came loose and Daniel caught it for him. His father placed the hat atop his shiny dome and thanked him, laughing. Arm in arm, they entered the shop.

The odor of silver solder permeated the air. An elaborate filigree brooch lay on the workbench. Threadlike wire of silver looped around teardrop-shaped freshwater pearls, the outer perimeter of each loop a delicate braid of gold wire. Wire that seemed too thin to work with, but which his father's hands transformed to objects of strength and beauty. *Angel hair,* his Uncle Moshe had told him when he was a child. *Your abba spins the hair of angels into wondrous forms.*

Where does he get it, Dod Moshe?

From the heavens. Like manna. Special manna granted by Hakadosh Baruch Hu to those with magic hands.

Those same hands, nut-brown and hard as olive wood, cupped his chin now. More kisses, the momentary abrasion of the old man's beard. A flash of white-toothed smile through steel-wool whiskers. Black eyes flashing mischievously from a saddle-leather face.

"Something to drink, Daniel?"

"Just some water, please, Abba. I'll get it."

"Sit." Staying him with a finger, his father moved quickly to the back room and returned with a bottle of orange juice and two glasses. Taking a stool next to Daniel's, he filled both glasses, recited the *shehakol* blessing, and the two of them drank, his father sipping, Daniel emptying the glass in three swallows.

"How are Laura and the children?"

"Terrific, Abba. And you?"

"Couldn't be better. Just received a lovely commission from some tourists staying at the King David." He pointed at the brooch. Daniel picked it up gingerly, ran his index finger over the elaborate ridges and swirls. As fine and unique as fingerprints . . .

"It's beautiful, Abba."

His father shrugged off the compliment. "Wealthy couple from London. They saw something like it in the hotel gift shop, asked me what I would charge to make it up, and made their decision on the spot."

Daniel smiled, placed his hand on the old man's bony shoulder.

"I'm sure the decision was based on more than cost, Abba."

His father looked away, embarrassed. Busied himself with refilling Daniel's glass.

"Have you eaten? I have pita, hummus, and tomato salad in the refrigerator—"

"Thanks anyway, but I have a lunch appointment at The Star."

"Business?"

"What else. Tell me, Abba, has anyone tried to sell you a pair of cheap earrings recently?"

"No. The American longhairs try from time to time, but nothing recently. Why?"

"It's not important."

They drank in silence for several moments. His father was the first to speak.

"You're caught up in something ugly." A half-whisper. "Extreme violence."

Daniel stared at him, astonished.

"How did you know that?"

"It's not difficult. Your face has always been a mirror. When you came into the shop you looked burdened. Mournful. As if a cloud had settled over your brow. The way you looked when you came home from war."

Daniel had placed the brooch in his bad hand in order to drink; suddenly he felt his fingers close around it. The clumsy press of numbed flesh against frail filament. Stupidly destructive. Alarmed, he uncurled his fingers and placed the jewelry back upon the worktable. Looking at his watch, he stood.

"Have to be going."

His father climbed down from the stool, took his son's hands in his.

"I'm sorry if I've upset you, Daniel."

"No, no. I'm fine."

"Whatever it is, I'm sure you'll get to the bottom of it. You're the best."

"Thank you, Abba."

They walked to the door. Daniel pushed it open and let in the heat and noise of the plaza.

"Will you be praying with Mori Zadok tomorrow?" he asked.

"No," said his father sheepishly. "I have an . . . engagement."

"On Rehov Smolenskin?"

"Yes, yes."

Daniel couldn't suppress his grin. "Regards to Mrs. Moscowitz," he said.

The old man's eyebrows rose in exasperation.

"She's a nice woman, Abba."

"Very nice. The nicest. But not for me—that's no sin, is it?" A hand went up and adjusted the beret. "Now she's decided that the way to my heart is through my stomach—a Hadassah course in Yemenite cooking. Bean soup and kubaneh and kirshe every Shabbat. In addition to all her Ashkenazi food. I eat until I ache, for fear of hurting her feelings. Which is also why I haven't been able to tell her we're not a destined match." He smiled balefully at Daniel. "Can the police help in such matters?"

"Afraid not, Abba."

Shared laughter followed by an expectant silence.

"Shabbat shalom, Abba."

"Shabbat shalom. It was good to see you."

His father continued to hold his hands. Squeezing. Lingering. Suddenly, the old man brought the damaged hand to his lips, kissed the scar tissue, and let go.

"What you do is also an art," he said. "You must remember that."

6

On the way back up to The Star, he passed close to the shwarma stand, caught a glint of metal, and stopped: a long-bladed knife, flashing like a silver minnow in the hands of the counterman. Assaulting the meat as it turned slowly on the spit, the lamb splitting open and crackling with surrender as layer after layer fell from the cone. An everyday thing; he'd seen it thousands of times without noticing.

The counterman was a lanky Moroccan Jew, face wet with perspiration, apron dotted with gravy. He finished preparing a sandwich for a customer, saw Daniel staring, shouted out that the shwarma was fresh, and offered to cut the detective a juicy one. Shaking his head no, Daniel resumed his climb.

The door to The Star was wide open, leading to a small, dim entry hall backed by a curtain of painted wooden beads. Parting the beads, he walked in.

Luncheon business was brisk, the cedar-paneled front room fan-cooled and filled with a comfortable mix of tourists and regulars, the robust chorus of laughter and conversation competing with a background tape of French and Italian pop songs.

The walls of the restaurant were hung generously with pictures and figurines, all rendered in a stellar motif. Over the bar was an oil portrait of a younger David Kohavi, darkly fierce in his general's uniform. Just beneath the painting was a Star of David hewn from Jerusalem stone, at its center the word *HaKohav*—"the star"—and a dedication from the men of Kohavi's battalion in raised bronze letters. The fire-burnished bronze of melted bullet shells.

Emil the Waiter was washing glasses behind the bar, stooped and gnarled in a billowing starched shirt and black bow tie. When he saw Daniel he came forward and escorted the detective toward an unmarked door at the rear of the restaurant. Just as the waiter's hand settled on the doorknob, Kohavi himself emerged from the kitchen, dressed, despite the season, in dark suit and tie, a white-haired version of the man in the painting. Bellowing a greeting, he shook Daniel's hand and motioned Emil back to the bar.

"I've set up a table for you. Five, right?"

"If they all show up."

Kohavi pushed the door open. "One already has."

The rear banquet room was almost empty. Papered in a burgundy print and lit by crystal lamps in sconces, it sported a raised wooden stage at the far end and accommodated two dozen tables, all but one of them bare and unoccupied. A tablecloth of burgundy linen had been spread across a round table next to the stage. At it sat a nondescript man reading *Ha'aretz*. The sounds of footsteps caused him to glance up briefly from his paper before resuming his perusal.

"The fish is good today," said Kohavi, stopping midway. "So are the filet steak and the shishlik. I'll send the others back as they arrive."

"One of them's never been here," said Daniel. "Elias Daoud." He described Daoud physically.

"Daoud," said Kohavi. "The Arab involved in breaking up the Number Two Gang?"

"That's him."

"Nice piece of work. I'll see to it he doesn't get lost."

"Thanks."

The restaurateur left and Daniel walked to the newspaper reader and sat opposite him, propping the envelope of photos against one leg of his chair.

"Shalom, Nahum."

The paper lowered and the man gave a brief nod. "Dani."

He was in his mid-fifties, bald and thin, with features that had been cast with an eye toward anonymity: the nose slightly aquiline but unmemorable, the mouth a tentative hyphen of intermediate width, the eyes twin beads of neutral brown, their lack of luster suggesting sleepiness. A forgettable face that had settled into repose—the serenity of one who'd vanquished ambition by retreating from it. He wore reading glasses, a cheap digital watch on one hairless forearm, and a pale-blue sport shirt with a faint windowpane check, its pocket sagging with ballpoint pens. A navy-blue windbreaker had been folded neatly over the chair next to him. Over it was slung a shoulder holster bearing a 9 mm Beretta.

"Mice in the Golan are committing suicide," he said, tapping the newspaper and putting it down. "Jumping off cliffs, hundreds at a time. An instinctive reaction to overpopulation, according to the scientists."

"Noble," said Daniel.

"Not really," said the thin man. "Without a sufficient supply of mice, the owls who prey on them will die." He smiled. "If the owls complain to the U.N., we'll be brought up on cruelty-to-animal charges."

The door to the kitchen swung open and Emil the Waiter came to the table with a platter of salads—hummus, tehina, two kinds of eggplant, pickled cucumbers, bitter Greek olives—and a stack of pita for dipping. He set down a plate next to each of them and bowed formally.

"Something to drink, Pakad Sharavi?"

"Soda water, please."

"For you, Mefakeah Shmeltzer?"

"Another cola, no lime this time."

When he was gone, Daniel said, "Speaking of the U.N., I

was up at the Amelia Catherine this morning. It relates to our new one."

"So I've heard," said Shmeltzer, rolling an olive between his fingers. "Bloody cutting on Scopus."

"Are tongues flapping that energetically?" asked Daniel.

The edge in his voice made Shmeltzer look up.

"Just the usual grapevine stuff from the uniforms. You called for an extra car to search the hillside—people wanted to know why. What's the big deal?"

"No big deal. Laufer wants it kept quiet."

"I want world peace and harmony," said Shmeltzer. "Care to take bets on either?"

"What did you hear, exactly, Nahum?"

"Maniac homicide, maybe a whore, maybe another Gray Man. Does it match?"

Daniel shook his head. "Doubtful." He related what he'd learned about the case. The account seemed to subdue Shmeltzer.

"Insane," he said quietly. "We never used to see that kind of thing."

Emil returned with the drinks and, eyeing the untouched food, asked if everything was all right.

"Everything's fine," said Daniel. Rising, he went to a sink across the room and used a copper cup to wash both hands. Upon returning, he sat down, said the blessing over bread, broke off a piece of pita, salted it, and ate it. Dipping another piece into the hummus, he put it in his mouth, the pungency of cumin and garlic a pleasant shock upon his tongue. Emil nodded approvingly and turned on his heel.

"Get anything at the hospital?" asked Shmeltzer.

"Typical U.N. situation. Lip service and hostility."

"What do you expect? They live like little princes, the assholes—duty-free Mercedes, villas, diplomatic immunity. What do they pay their pencil pushers now—forty, fifty thousand a year?"

"Ninety."

"Shekels or American dollars?"

"Dollars," said Daniel. "Tax-free."

"Shit," said Shmeltzer. "Ten years' worth of wages for you and me. And for doing nothing." He dipped pita in eggplant salad, managed to frown while chewing. "I remember one guy I questioned in a burglary case. Nigerian, looked just like Idi

Amin. Safari suit, ivory-tipped walking stick, and an engraved calling card with a title you could eat for lunch: Executive Regional Director of the Sinai Border Commission, supposed to count how many Egyptians we kill and vice versa. No matter that we gave it all back at Camp David and there's no border anymore—this guy's job was to administer it because the hard-liners at the U.N. never recognized Camp David. Far as they're concerned it's still a war zone."

He sipped his cola, popped an olive in his mouth, removed the pit, and put it on his plate. Nibbling on another, he asked, "Anyone at the Amelia look like a suspect?"

"Nothing glaring," said Daniel. "Two of them were especially jumpy. Doctor named Al Biyadi and his girlfriend—an American nurse. She implied we've been persecuting him. Seemed to be a typical case of sheikh fever."

"Sure," said Shmeltzer. "Madly in love with Ahmed until he puts a bomb in her suitcase and sends her off on El Al. Where'd she meet him?"

"In America. Detroit, Michigan. Lots of Arabs there. Lots of PLO sympathy."

"What is it we're supposed to have done to Lover Boy?"

"Don't know yet," said Daniel. "Probably some kind of immigration problem. Records is running a check on both of them and on the other hospital people as well." He took a drink of soda, felt the bubbles dance against the back of his teeth. "Think this one could be political?"

Shmeltzer shrugged. "Why not? Our sweet cousins keep searching for new approaches."

"Levi said it's likely she was anesthetized," said Daniel. "Sedated with heroin."

"Kindly killer," said Shmeltzer.

"It made me think of a doctor, but then I thought a doctor would have access to all kinds of sedatives—no need to use something illegal."

"Unless the doctor was an addict himself. Maybe he and the girl had a heroin party. She overdosed. When he saw her he panicked, cut her up."

"I don't think so," said Daniel. "Levi says the dose wasn't fatal, and she was injected twice." He paused. "The way it was done, Nahum—the cutting was deliberate."

The door opened and Kohavi came in with another man.

Shmeltzer looked at the newcomer, then sharply back at Daniel.

"Speaking of sweet cousins," he said.

"He's first-rate," said Daniel. "If the girl's an Arab he'll be valuable."

Kohavi had slipped back to the front room and the new man walked toward them alone. Medium-sized, dark-complexioned, and in his twenties, he wore a tan suit, white shirt, and no tie. His face was long and big-boned, terminating in a heavy square chin. His hair was light reddish-brown and combed straight back, his mustache a faint ginger wisp over a wide, serious mouth. Narrow-set green eyes stared straight ahead, unwavering. When he reached the table he said, "Good afternoon, Pakad."

"Good afternoon, Elias. Please sit down. This is Mefakeah Nahum Shmeltzer of National Headquarters. Nahum, Samal Rishon Elias Daoud, of the Kishle Station."

"Elias." Shmeltzer nodded.

"The privilege is mine, sir." Daoud's voice was thin and boyish, his Hebrew fluent but accented—the rolling Arabic "r," the substitution of "b" for "p." He sat down and folded his hands in his lap, docile but inquisitive, like a schoolboy in a new class.

"Call me Nahum," said Shmeltzer. " 'Sirs' are fat guys who wear their medals to bed."

Daoud forced a smile.

"Have something to drink, Elias," said Daniel.

"Thank you. The proprietor is bringing me a coffee."

"Something to eat?"

"Thank you." Daoud took a pita and ate it plain, chewing slowly, looking down at the tablecloth, ill at ease. Daniel wondered how many Jewish restaurants he'd been to—how often, for that matter, did he come over to the western side of town?

"We're all impressed," he said, "with your work on the Number Two Gang case. All those creeps behind bars, the drugs kept off the street."

"I did my job," said Daoud. "God was with me."

Shmeltzer took a pickle and bit off the tip. "Here's hoping He stays with you. We've got a tough one. A maniac murderer."

Daoud's eyes widened with interest.

"Who was killed?"

"A young girl," said Daniel. "Mutilated and dumped on Scopus across from the Amelia Catherine. No ID. Here."

He picked up the envelope, drew out photos of the dead girl, and distributed copies to both detectives.

"Ring any bells?"

Shmeltzer shook his head. "Pretty," he said in a tight voice, then turned away.

Daoud continued to examine the picture, holding the edges with both hands, concentrating, grim.

"I can't place her," he said finally. "But there's something familiar about the face."

"What?" asked Daniel.

Daoud stared at the photo again. "I don't know why, but one of the villages keeps coming to mind. Silwan, perhaps. Or Abu Tor."

"Not Bethlehem?"

"No, sir," said Daoud. "If she were from Bethlehem, I'd know her."

"What about the other villages?" asked Shmeltzer. "Sur Bahir, Isawiya."

"Maybe," said Daoud. "For some reason Abu Tor and Silwan come to mind."

"Perhaps you've seen her in passing," said Daniel. "A brief glimpse through the car window."

Daoud thought for a while. "Perhaps."

He's worried, thought Daniel. About having spoken too soon with nothing to back it up.

"So you're saying she's an Arab," said Shmeltzer.

"That was my first impression," said Daoud. He tugged at his mustache.

"I've got a requisition in for all the missing-kid files," said Daniel. "Sixteen hundred of them. In the meantime, we'll be knocking on doors. The villages are as good a place to start as any. Take Silwan first, Elias. Show the picture around. If nothing clicks, go on to Abu Tor."

Daoud nodded and put the photo in his jacket pocket.

A shout came from across the room:

"All recruits at attention!"

A striking-looking man swaggered toward the table. Well over six feet, bulging and knotted with the heavy musculature of a weight lifter, he wore white shorts, rubber beach sandals, and a red sleeveless mesh shirt that exposed lots of hard saffron skin. His hair was blue-black, straight, parted in the middle and styled with a blow-dryer, his face wholly Asian, broad and flat like that of a Mongolian warrior. Eyes resting on high shelflike cheekbones were twin slits in rice paper. A blue shadow of beard darkened his chin. About thirty years old, with five years latitude on either side of the estimate.

"Shalom, Dani. Nahum." The man's voice was deep and harsh.

"Chinaman." Shmeltzer nodded. "Day off?"

"Till now," said the big man. He looked at Daoud appraisingly, then sat down next to him.

"Yossi Lee," he said, extending his hand. "You're Daoud, right? The ace of Kishle."

Daoud took the hand tentatively, as if assessing the greeting for sarcasm. Lee's shake was energetic, his smile an equine flash of long, curving white teeth. Releasing the Arab's hand, he yawned and stretched.

"What do they have to eat in this dump? I'm starved."

"Better this dump than somewhere else," said Shmeltzer.

"*Somewhere else* would be free," said Lee. "Free always tastes terrific."

"Next time, Chinaman," promised Daniel. He looked at his watch. Ten minutes late and the new man hadn't arrived.

Emil came in with menus.

"A beer," said the Chinaman.

"Goldstar or Maccabee?" asked Emil.

"Goldstar."

The waiter started to leave.

"Stick around," said Daniel. "We'll order now."

Shmeltzer and the Chinaman ordered stuffed marrow appetizers and a double mixed grill each. Daniel noticed Daoud examine the menu, shift his eyes to the price column, and hesitate. Wondering, no doubt, how far a brand-new sergeant's salary would carry him. Daniel had visited Daoud's home in Bethlehem shortly after the bust of the Number Two Gang, bringing news of the promotion and a gift of dried fruit. The poverty had surprised him, though it shouldn't have—most cops had serious money problems. The papers had just run a story about a bunch of new hires applying for welfare. And before joining the force Daoud had worked as a box boy in a souvenir shop, one of those cramped, musty places that sold olive-wood crucifixes and straw mockups of the Nativity to Christian tourists. Earning what—a thousand a year?

Now, watching the Arab scan the menu, the memory of that poverty returned: the Daoud household—three closet-sized rooms in an ancient building, mattresses on the floor, a charcoal stove for heat, prints of Jesus in agony on whitewashed walls. Children everywhere—at least half a dozen, toddling and tripping, in various stages of undress. A shy young wife gone to fat, a crippled mother-in-law knitting silently. Cooking smells and baby squalls.

Putting his own menu down, he said: "I'll have a mint salad."

"Mint salad," said Emil the Waiter, copying. "What else, Pakad?"

"That's it."

The waiter's eyebrows rose.

"Dieting?" said the Chinaman.

"Shabbat tonight," said Daniel. "Big meal."

Daoud handed his menu to Emil the Waiter.

"I'll have a mint salad too," he said.

"What else for you?"

"A coffee."

Emil grew wary, as if expecting to be the butt of a joke.

"Don't tell me," said the Chinaman. "You're eating at *his* house."

Daoud smiled.

"That'll be all," said Daniel to the waiter, who departed, muttering, "Salads, salads."

Daniel began laying out the case before the food came and continued after its delivery, ignoring his salad and talking while the others ate. Handing a photo of the dead girl to Lee, he placed another in front of the empty chair, and passed on what he'd learned so far. The detectives took notes, holding pens in one hand, forks in the other. Chewing, swallowing, but mechanically. A silent audience.

"Three possibilities come to mind immediately," he said. "One, a psychopathic murder. Two, a crime of passion—in that I include blood revenge. Three, terrorism. Any other suggestions?"

"Gang murder," said Shmeltzer. "She was someone's girl and got in the middle of something."

"The gangs use bullets and they don't kill women," said the

Chinaman. He slid cubes of shishlik off a skewer, stared at them, ate one.

"They never used to kill *anyone,*" said Shmeltzer. "There's always a first time."

"They hide their corpses, Nahum," said Lee. "The last thing they want is to make it public." To Daoud: "You guys never found any of the ones The Number Two boys hit, did you?"

Daoud shook his head.

"Any gang wars brewing that you know of?" Daniel asked Lee.

The Chinaman took a swallow of beer and shook his head. "The hashish gangs are stable—heavy supply down from Lebanon with enough to go around for everyone. Zik and the Chain Street Boys have a truce going on stolen goods. Zik's also cornered the opium market but for now it's too small for anyone to challenge him."

"What about the melon gangs?" asked Shmeltzer.

"The crop will be small this summer so we can expect some conflict, but that's a while off and we've never had a melon murder yet."

"All in due time," said the older detective. "We're growing civilized at an alarming rate."

"Look into the gangs, Chinaman," said Daniel. "And investigate the possibility of a pimp-whore thing—that she was a street girl who betrayed her *sarsur* and he wanted to make an example of her. Show her picture to the lowlifes and see if anyone knew her."

"Will do," said Lee.

"Any other hypotheses?" asked Daniel. When no one answered he said, "Let's go back to the first three, starting with terrorism. On the surface it doesn't look political—there was no message attached to the body and no one's claimed credit. But that may still be coming. We know they've been trying out street crime as a strategy—the one who stabbed Shlomo Mendelsohn shouted slogans, as did the punks who shot at the hikers near Solomon's Pools. Both of those cases were semi-impulsive—opportunistic—and this one looks more premeditated, but so was the job Tutunji's gang did on Talia Gidal, so let's keep our minds open. Nahum, I want you to liaison with Shin Bet and find out if they've picked up word of a sex murder strategy from overseas or any of the territories. Elias, have you heard anything along those lines?"

"There's always talk," said Daoud cautiously.

Shmeltzer's face tightened. "What kind of talk?" he asked.

"Slogans. Nothing specific."

"That so?" said the older detective, wiping his glasses. "I saw something specific the other day. Graffiti near the Hill of Golgotha. 'Lop off the head of the Zionist monster.' Could be someone followed instructions."

Daoud said nothing.

"When you get right down to it," Shmeltzer continued, "there's nothing new about Arabs mixing mutilation and politics." He jabbed his fork into a piece of grilled kidney, put it into his mouth, and chewed thoughtfully. "In the Hebron massacre they sliced the breasts off all the women. Castrated the men and stuffed their balls in their mouths. The Saudis still dismember thieves. It's part of the Arabic culture, right?"

Daoud stared straight ahead, tugging at his mustache until the skin around it reddened.

Daniel and the Chinaman looked at Shmeltzer, who shrugged and said, "This is Jerusalem, boys. A historical context is essential."

He returned his attention to his food, cutting into a baby lamb chop, masticating with exaggerated enthusiasm.

The silence that followed was ponderous and cold. Daoud broke it, speaking in a near murmur.

"For this murder to be political, the girl would have to be Jewish—"

"Or a member of an Arab family viewed as collaborationist," said Shmeltzer.

Daoud lowered his glance and pushed salad greens around his plate.

"All possibilities will be considered," said Daniel. "Let's move on to the second possibility. Crime of passion—unrequited love, an affair gone sour, soiled honor, blood revenge. Any of you know of family conflicts that could get nasty?"

"A couple of Moroccan families over in Katamon Tet have been punching each other out for the last few months," said the Chinaman. "Something about where the laundry should hang. Last I heard it'd cooled down. I'll check."

"Two betrothed families from Surif are feuding over a dowry," said Daoud. "It's been all words so far but the words are growing stronger and it may very well boil over into violence. But I know all the family members on both sides and she's not one of them. The only other thing I can think of is that Druze sheikh who was murdered last year."

"Hakim al Atrash," said Daniel.

"Yes. Common belief is that it was a land dispute and the Janbulat clan was behind it. It's an open situation—vengeance has yet to be accomplished. But when they kill someone it will be another man, not a young girl."

"Another remote possibility," said Daniel, "is Bedouins. They'd be quick to execute a lapsed virgin or an adulteress and a Bedouin girl this age could very well have been married or engaged. But the pathologist is certain that this one wore shoes and he made another good point: Bedouins bury their dead in the desert, away from prying eyes. There'd be no reason to bring her up into the city."

He took a drink of soda water, ate salad without tasting it, drank again, and said, "My intuition tells me this was no honor killing—all the ones I've seen or heard about have been done with a single throat-cut or a bullet to the head. Swift and clean. No body wounds or hacking of the genitals. No washing the corpse. I saw what had been done to her—the pictures don't capture it." He paused, chose his words. "It was butchery, ritualistic. Lots of rage, but calculated."

"A sex murder," said the Chinaman.

"It's our best working hypothesis."

"If it's a sex murder, we're out of our element," said Shmeltzer. "Working from textbooks again. Like goddamned rookies."

The remark angered Daniel, partly because it was true. A junior grade detective in any American city saw more in one year than he'd encounter in a lifetime. Serial killings, demonic rituals, child murders, back alley mutilations. A dark, ugly world that he'd read about but had never encountered. Until eight months ago, when Gray Man had come along. A welcome-back from vacation. Four slashings in two months. A one-man crime wave in a city that hosted nine or ten killings in a bad year, most of them the bloody offspring of family squabbles. Four dead women, victimized for selling phony love . . .

"Things are changing, boys." Shmeltzer was lecturing the Chinaman and Daoud. "And we're not equipped for it. Drug fiends, psychopaths—nut-case foreigners in rags. You never used to see them. Now they're all over the city. On the way here I saw one *meshuggener* lurching across Herzl, muttering to himself, frothing at the mouth, nearly got himself run over. Go into Independence Park and they're lying under the trees like mounds of dog shit."

"That's not the type we're looking for, Nahum," said Daniel. "Too disorganized, unable to plan. Dr. Ben David's profile of the Gray Man was a social misfit, withdrawn but outwardly normal."

"Terrific," said Shmeltzer. "Very scholarly guy, Dr. Ben David. Did us a hell of a lot of good."

What, Daniel wondered, was eating at him? Shmeltzer had always played the part of devil's advocate; Daniel didn't mind it—it kept him thinking. But today it seemed different, less constructive, as if the older man no longer had any interest in work. Perhaps Laufer had been right: The dray horse had outlived his usefulness. On a case like this he needed a rock-solid number two man—the type of detective Shmeltzer had always been before. Not the nay-saying cynic across the table. He looked at Shmeltzer drinking cola, face half-hidden by the glass; considered dealing with it right then and there, decided against it.

"Nahum," he said, "get the computer guys to update the list of sex offenders we pulled on Gray Man, subclassify again in terms of tendencies toward violence and use of a knife. Fondness for young girls and drug use are other variables to look for. Most of them are going to be guys we've already talked to, but they deserve going over again. A new *samal* named Avi Cohen will help you with the preliminary screening and I can get you a clerk for tabulation if you need one. Once we've established a good sublist, we'll start pulling them in for interviews. While you're waiting for the data, check the Scopus campus, see if anyone was working late, if any of the locks on the gates were tampered with.

"Our first priority," he said, picking up a photo, "will be identifying her. It's twenty-four-hour shift time. The earrings are a possible link—the killer may have taken them, but until we know what they look like, a jewelry store canvass isn't worthwhile. In addition, Dr. Levi said they weren't gold, so it's doubtful a professional jeweler would buy them. Still, if you come across someone who buys trinkets, ask them if anyone's tried to palm some earrings off on them."

He turned to Daoud. "Elias, take the villages—you can follow your hunch and start with Abu Tor and Silwan. If they don't pan out, do the others as well. Isawiya, in particular, is of interest, because you can walk across the desert and up to Scopus without traversing the rest of the city. The Border Patrol says everything's been quiet, but they're not infallible. If you learn nothing in any of the villages, start scouring the Old City up to the Damascus Gate, Sultan Suleiman, the area around the Arab bus station and the train station. Visit the orphanages. Talk to drivers, ticket clerks, porters, anyone who might have seen a young girl come in. I'll hit the main bus station this afternoon and do the same. Got it?"

"Yes, sir."

"Chinaman," Daniel continued, "cover the neighborhoods to the south of the crime scene—Sheikh Jarrah, the American Colony, Wadi el Joz, then Musrara and along the Green Line. I assume you'll be visiting the Watermelon Tents to do your gang check."

"Tonight, after midnight," said the Chinaman. "When the fun's in full bloom."

"If you don't get any leads there, go to the Green Line and talk to the whores. Find out if any strange customers have been hanging around. Don't hassle anyone but take note of weird ones. Warn the girls too, while you're at it—talk in general terms, no details."

"How general?" asked the Chinaman.

"Tell them they're in danger. Say nothing specific about the murder—that goes for all of us. Laufer wants this thing kept quiet—the tourist situation. So talk in terms of a missing girl, nothing more. The same thing applies to communications with other police personnel, which is why we're meeting away from Headquarters."

The Chinaman picked up an empty skewer, used it like a classroom pointer. "I'm supposed to tell the whores they're in danger. Then I show them the picture of the missing girl. You don't have to be the Chief Rabbi to put it together."

"There's no way to keep it under wraps for any significant length of time," agreed Daniel. "What the brass is hoping is that we jam up the grapevine for a while, get lucky, and wrap up the case quickly enough to feed the papers a three-line closed-file piece."

"Hope springs eternal," mumbled Shmeltzer.

"I'll be on beeper all through Shabbat," continued Daniel.

"If any of you get anything of substance, call me immediately. Tomorrow I'll be walking down to the lower Katamonim and knocking on doors—if she's poor and Jewish it seems the best place to start. I've got Records doing research into some people at the Amelia Catherine and the Civil Guardsman who discovered the body. Where I go from there depends on what they find. Anyone beep me if you get something good. If there's something worth sharing we'll call a meeting at my place, Sunday afternoon. Now, let's pay and get going."

After the bill had been settled, he instructed Daoud to remain at the table and walked Lee and Shmeltzer out of The Star. The Chinaman got onto a Vespa scooter he'd parked in front of the restaurant, thick thighs flaring, looking like a kid on a toy bicycle. He revved up, sputtered to King George, turned left, and sped away. Next to The Star was a three-story building whose ground floor housed an El Al agency and a children's clothing store. On the upper floors were lawyers' offices, all closed for the midday lunch break; to the right of the storefronts, a dark, tiled entrance leading to the stairs.

Daniel took Shmeltzer by the elbow, propelled him through the doorway, and said, "What's going on, Nahum?"

Shmeltzer's expression was innocent.

"Going on about what?"

"Your attitude. That little speech about Hebron, the side comments."

"Don't worry," said Shmeltzer, "I'll do my job."

"That's no answer," snapped Daniel. "If something's eating at you I want to know it."

Shmeltzer smiled placidly.

"What should be eating at me? I'm just a guy who likes to tell it straight."

"An irrelevant lecture on Arabic culture is telling it straight?"

A tremor of anger floated across the older man's face. He compressed his mouth and a ring of white encircled his lips.

"Look, Dani, you want to use him, that's your prerogative. You think he's hot, fine, maybe he is. But the hell if I'm going to change his diapers." Shmeltzer's glasses had slipped down a nose slippery with sweat, and he pushed them up. "That's the thing that pisses me off the most about them. They talk *around* things, using pretty words, *sir* this, *sir* that, welcome to my tent.

Turn your back and there's a fucking knife in it. I tell it straight, the rest of us tell it straight, and *he's* going to damn well have to live with that or go back to selling rosaries."

"I have no interest in protecting him," said Daniel. "He does his job or he's out. It's your frame of mind I want to be sure of. So we can get the job done."

"Have you ever known me to fuck up?"

"No. I brought you on because I thought you were the best."

For a moment Shmeltzer's face seemed to soften. Then his eyes grew strangely fierce before fading to neutrality.

"I'll give you no reason to change your mind."

"That's what I wanted to hear."

"You heard it," said Shmeltzer. "Now, if it's okay with you, I'd like to get to work." He put his hands in his pockets and slouched against the wall. A rubber ball bounced into the entry hall, followed by a child—a boy, six or seven—who scooped it up, stared at them, and ran back out to the mall.

"Go," said Daniel. "Shabbat shalom."

Shmeltzer straightened his windbreaker, adjusted his holster, and walked out of the entry. Daniel followed him and watched his thin form recede in the distance. Within moments he'd disappeared into the throng that streamed down Ben Yehuda.

When he got back to the banquet room, Emil the Waiter was clearing the table, working around Daoud, who sat staring at the picture of the girl, a demitasse of Turkish coffee in one hand. Daniel pulled out the chair next to him, sat, and waited until they were alone.

"I have one goal," he said. "Find the monster who killed her, prevent him from doing it again. I have no time for internal politics or bickering."

"I understand, Pakad."

"You took some garbage today. You'll probably take more in the future. You're a professional and I assume it won't disturb your sleep."

Daoud smiled faintly. "I'm a heavy sleeper."

"Good. If something gets in the way of your doing your job, tell me. Anything else, I don't want to hear about."

"Yes, sir."

They left the restaurant. Daoud walked to a tiny old gray Citroën that appeared to be held together with rope and baling wire. A blue Occupied Territories plate dangled crookedly from the battered front fender, embossed with the letter *bet* for Bethlehem, and an iron crucifix hung from the rearview mirror. Despite the police ID on top of the dash it looked like a perfect bomb crib, and Daniel wasn't surprised to see Wiesel, the undercover man, observing the car from a table at an adjacent café. When he saw Daniel he called for his check.

7

Friday, four P.M., Daniel exited the central bus station having learned nothing. No one had seen the girl. No one had looked at her photograph with even a hint of recognition.

A blind beggar was huddled on the sidewalk just outside the entrance to the depot, begrimed and toothless, his dry, sunken eyeholes raised to the sun. When Daniel passed, he held out a quaking clawlike hand and started to chant, a rhythmic keen not unlike prayer. *Kind sir, kind sir, the good deed of charity takes on special value as the Sabbath approaches, a good deed, kind sir, kind sir, amen, amen . . .*

Daniel reached into his pocket, drew out a handful of coins, and dropped them into the filthy palm without counting. The beggar began blessing him in a high-pitched wail. The bony hand continued to shake, sifting the money as if it were grain, probing, hefting, decoding its value. A mental total was reached; the beggar's mouth twisted into a gaping, black-gummed smile. The blessings increased in volume and vigor: *Daniel and his offspring for ten generations would be graced with good health and riches for time immemorial. . . .*

Suddenly a group of six other paupers appeared from nowhere. Hunched, lame, snaggletoothed, and twisted, they shuffled and limped toward the detective, proclaiming individual litanies of despair that merged to a toneless, mournful dirge. Before he could get to the Escort, they'd reached him. Forming a circle around him, they began chanting louder, beseeching the kind sir. Emptying his pockets, he gave something to each of them, compressing his nostrils to avoid their stench.

Finally he got away and into the Escort. The Middle Ages, he thought, driving off to the accompaniment of their phlegmy benedictions. For years the government had offered the beggars jobs, welfare, anything to rid the station of their presence. But they were the descendants of generations of beggars who regarded themselves as trained specialists, plying an honorable family trade. Many of them, it was said, made an excellent living—more than that of a policeman—so perhaps he was a fool to have donated. Still, one needed any blessings one could get.

A stop back at Headquarters produced meager rewards: the information on Schlesinger hadn't come in. The troubled watchman, Hajab, had no criminal record, nor had he been treated at any mental institution. Of the other Amelia Catherine people, only Dr. Al Biyadi was known to Records. That knowledge was summed up in four typewritten pages marked OFFICIAL ACCESS ONLY and placed on his desk in a sealed envelope. The data within were uninspiring.

It had been, as he'd suspected, a case of immigration complications. After seven years in Detroit, Al Biyadi had applied for and been granted American citizenship. After becoming an American, he'd attended two pro-PLO demonstrations at Wayne State and gotten his name in the FBI computer. The FBI had informed Mossad, and when Al Biyadi had applied for permission to reenter Israel and for a work permit to practice medicine, the computer had spat his name back out. Both requests had been refused pending a background investigation.

The usual paper storm had followed—an exchange of stiffly worded consular letters, U.N. protests, letters of support from Al Biyadi's congressman, and endorsements from medical school professors with Jewish surnames, all assuring the government that Dr. Hassan Al Biyadi was a man of sterling character. Some local newspaper coverage, as well, Daniel noted—personality pieces portraying the young physician as an idealist and a victim of discrimination.

In the end, the summary concluded, Al Biyadi had been determined to be "relatively apolitical," his involvement in PLO affairs confined to attendance at the rallies, his primary life interests listed as "expensive sports cars and haberdashery; expensive stereo equipment and electronic gadgetry; amorous relationships with a series of young American women, all of them nurses." Hardly a firebrand. Four months after applying, he'd been granted his papers.

Not bad, thought Daniel. Getting a phone installed in Jerusalem could take twice as long.

He put the envelope in the file he'd begun on the murder, left the office, and tried to put himself in a Sabbath frame of mind.

Five minutes after five and the shops were closing.

It was his custom every Friday to buy the wine, bread, and sweetmeats for Shabbat, and he hadn't called Laura to tell her this Friday would be any different. He sped down Rehov Sokolov toward Lieberman's grocery, got caught in traffic, and sat frustrated, hoping the store would still be open. The other drivers shared his frustration and reacted predictably: The air filled with a storm of curses and klaxon bursts before the jam cleared.

When he pulled to the curb, Lieberman was locking up, a shopping bag at his feet. The grocer saw him, pointed at his watch reproachfully, then smiled, brought the bag to the passenger side, and handed it to Daniel before the detective could get out of the car.

Daniel thanked him and put the groceries on the floor in front of the passenger seat. Lieberman rubbed his paunch and stuck his face into the car.

"I just called your wife and told her you hadn't come by. One of your kids is on the way over here to get it."

"Which one?"

"She didn't say." Laughing: "I could call and ask her."

"Not necessary, Mr. Lieberman. Thank you for saving it for us."

The grocer winked conspiratorially. "Caught up with work?"

"Yes."

"Hot case, eh?"

"The hottest." A longstanding routine. Daniel started the engine, looked down the street for sign of one of his children.

"Anything you want me to look out for, you tell me. Shady characters, saboteurs, anything."

"Thanks for the offer, Mr. Lieberman. If something comes up, I'll let you know."

"Always happy to help," said Lieberman, saluting. "I see a

lot sitting behind the counter. The human parade, if you know what I mean."

"I do, Mr. Lieberman. Shabbat shalom."

"Shabbat shalom."

Daniel guided the Escort back onto Sokolov and cruised slowly. A block later he spotted Shoshana, wearing a peach-colored Shabbat dress, half walking, half skipping. Singing to herself, as always.

He knew, without having to listen, what tunes danced across her lips: an odd mixture of pop songs and rope-jumping children's rhymes. An indication, according to Laura, of what it was like to be a twelve-year-old girl—the jumble of needs, the changing body. She'd been there herself, so he supposed she knew. His own memories of twelve were of simple times: lessons at the yeshiva. Playing ball in the alley behind the study hall. Hiding the soccer scores between pages of Talmud. Perhaps for boys it was different. . . .

He watched her for a few moments, smiling. Lost in her fantasies. Gazing dreamily at the sky, unaware of her surroundings. He coasted to a stop, gave a gentle honk that lowered her eyes. Initially confused, she looked around, saw him, and her face came alive with glee.

So beautiful, he thought, for the thousandth time. The oval face and brassy golden waves endowed by Laura. The dark skin, his. So, he'd been told, were her facial features, though it was hard for him to reconcile that kind of delicacy with anything that could have emanated from him. Her eyes were wide with delight—gray-green, enormous, filled with a light of their own. Totally original. In the delivery room, Laura had laughed over her tears: *We've created a mongrel, Daniel. A beautiful little mongrel.* Daniel had surprised himself by bursting into tears also.

"Abba! Abba!" She ran toward the car on stick-legs, opened the door, and flew in. Throwing her arms around him, she rubbed his chin and laughed. "You need a shave, Abba."

"How's my sweetie?" He nuzzled her, kissed her cheek.

"Terrific, Abba. I helped Eema cook, bathed Dayan, and took the boys to the park."

"Great. I'm proud of you."

"They were wild animals."

"Dayan and the boys?"

"Just the boys. Dayan was a gentleman." She gave a martyr's sigh and threw up her hands.

Like a beleaguered parent, thought Daniel; he suppressed a smile so she wouldn't think he was mocking her.

Not that her predicament was laughable. Five and a half years—three miscarriages—between her and Mikey; Benny's birth a year later adding to the insult. Five and a half years of only-childhood shattered by double windstorms. Too much age difference for friendship. She fancied herself a junior mother, demanded respect she never received.

"Wild animals," she repeated.

Daniel nodded and moved the bag of groceries to the rear of the car.

"Is that the stuff from Lieberman's?" she asked.

"Yes. I got there just in time. Thanks for going to pick them up."

"No problem, Abba." She got on her knees, stretched over the seat, and inspected the contents of the bag. "Yum. Chocolate."

She sat back down and fastened her seat belt, and Daniel began driving. When they'd traveled a block she asked, "Can we play poker tonight after dinner?"

"Gambling, Shoshi?" He mock-frowned. "On Shabbat?"

"Not for money. For raisins."

"And if you clean me out of raisins the way you cleaned me out of almonds last week, I'll have nothing to eat all Shabbat and I'll starve."

Shoshana giggled, then burst into laughter.

"Then I'll sell some back to you! At a discount!"

He clucked his tongue, gravely. "Aha! First gambling, now commerce on Shabbat. The sages were right: One sin leads to another."

"Oh, Abba!"

"Your Grandpa Al teaches you a few card games," he continued, "and next thing I know I've got a little gangster on my hands." Reaching across, he chucked her chin.

"Gangster," he repeated.

"Ten games, okay? After dinner."

"I'll have to check with Eema."

"Eema said it was okay. Ten games."

"Five."

"Twelve!"

"Ten. But go easy on me."

She sidled closer, wrapped one skinny arm around his bicep. "You're the nicest, Abba. A superstar."

He lived in the Talbieh district, southwest of the Old City, across the Valley of Hinnom. A quiet neighborhood of narrow, sloping, tree-lined streets and solid old two-story houses of golden *meleke* limestone, the stone veined with rust and rose and embraced by magenta tides of bougainvillea. Citrus, fig, and loquat trees sprouted from vest-pocket gardens; tendrils of honeysuckle clung to sculpted balconies. Most of the houses had been converted to apartments. A few of the grandest were leased to foreign governments as consulates and sat mutely behind high wrought-iron gates.

Home was a fourth-floor flat in a ten-year-old high-rise at the southern edge of the district. The building was a stylistic oddity—a sleek, bone-white projectile, devoid of architectural detail. Fifteen stories overlooking the flowered pergolas of Liberty Bell Park, with a long view of the Old City and the Mount of Olives beyond. Faced with limestone, in accordance with Jerusalem zoning laws, but a limestone so pale and unmarked by time that it stood out like a scar in the amber flesh of the hillside.

Between the building and the park was a large, sloping, vacant field. At the rear of the building was a gravel parking lot, three-quarters empty as usual. Modest but well-tended beds of grass and perennials ran along the border of the property, nourished by automatic sprinklers. Near the entrance to the high-rise was a stand of jacaranda trees, their lacy foliage shockingly purple. Pebbled-glass doors led to a marble entry hall. Inside, to the immediate right, was a small synagogue; to the left, three elevators that worked most of the time. The flats were large—six rooms and a generous terrace. To Daniel, luxury of the first degree, so different from how he'd been raised, from how his colleagues lived—though he'd been made to understand that in America it would be considered nothing out of the ordinary.

He'd come to live there through the good graces of others, and from time to time, especially when he remembered his origins, he felt like an interloper. A squatter in someone else's dream.

Today, though, it felt like home.

The radio was playing full blast and the boys were chasing

each other around the living room, naked, Dayan at their heels. When he saw Daniel, the little spaniel left the fray and leaped toward him, tail wagging, panting, yipping with joy. Daniel patted the dog's head, allowed himself to be licked, and called out a greeting to his sons. They looked up, shouted "Abba" in unison, and ploughed into him, their stocky little bodies as dense as sacks of flour. He kissed them, wrestled with them, threw them in the air, and let them wriggle free to resume their play.

"Monsters," said Shoshi, and went to her room. Dayan trotted after her.

Daniel walked through the dining area into the kitchen, where he placed the groceries on the counter. Pots simmered and hissed on the stove; a chicken baked in the oven. From the adjoining service porch came the whine and rumble of the washing machine. The room was hot, the air steamy and heavy with spices.

Laura stood at the sink with her back to him, the running water and kitchen noises obscuring the sound of his entry. She wore paint-stained jeans and a dark green T-shirt. Her soft blond hair had been pinned up but several wavy strands had come loose and created a lacy aura around her neck. He said *shalom* softly, so as not to frighten her, and when she turned around, took her in his arms.

"Hello, detective." She smiled. Drying her hands on her pants, she stood on tiptoes, held his face, and raised her own for a kiss. It began chastely enough, then deepened, and for a moment Daniel lost himself in it. Then she pulled away and said, "I sent Shoshi over to Lieberman's. Did you see her?"

"I got there first." He pointed to the bag. "Picked her up along the way. She's in her room, with the dog."

"Have you eaten at all today?" she asked.

"Business lunch."

"The same business that got you out of bed?"

"The same."

"Would you like a little something before dinner?"

"No, thanks. I'll wait for Kiddush."

"Drink something," she said, and went to the refrigerator.

He unbuttoned his shirt and sat down at the kitchen table. Laura fixed a glass of iced coffee and brought it to him. She filled a half a cup for herself and stood next to him sipping, with her hand on his shoulder. He swallowed a mouthful, closed his eyes, and exhaled. The coldness and sweetness of the coffee made his palate ache pleasurably.

Her hand took flight. He opened his eyes and saw her step away, adjust the dials on the stove, peer under the lid of a pot, swab her forehead with a paper towel. Without makeup she looked like a young girl, the fair skin heat-flushed and moist, the blue eyes open and curious. Returning to his side, she kissed the top of his head, took his bad hand, massaged the knuckles absently.

"When Lieberman called and said you hadn't made it over, I knew you'd had a wonderful day."

He nodded, finished the coffee, and asked, "How much time do I have until Shabbat?"

"Half an hour." She unbuttoned his cuffs, pulled his shirt off, and put it over a chair. "Go shower and shave. The boys were playing submarine in the bath but I've cleaned it up for you."

He stood, gave her hand a squeeze, left the kitchen, and walked back into the living room, stepping over an obstacle course of toys and books. As he passed the glass doors leading to the balcony he caught a glimpse of sunset: feathery streaks of coral and blue—the colors of a sailor's tattoo—sectioning the sky like layer cake. Detouring, he walked out on the balcony, placed his hands on the railing, and looked eastward.

An Arab boy herded a flock of goats through the open field that separated the building from Liberty Bell Park. Daniel watched the animals step nimbly through the weeds and rocks, then cast his gaze outward, past the artist apartments of Yemin Moshe and across Hinnom. Toward the Old City perched on its ridge—towers, ramparts, and parapets, like something out of a storybook.

His birthplace.

Behind him, the sun dropped and the ancient stone surfaces of the city within a city seemed to recede, dreamlike, into the Judean dusk. Then, all at once, electric lights came on, illuminating the crenellated walls. Spotlighting frieze and fissure, drawing forth the outlines of domes, turrets, and spires in brazen auric relief.

As if on cue, the surrounding villages began twinkling like nests of fireflies and he became conscious of encroaching darkness, aware that he was far from ready for Shabbat. He allowed himself a few more seconds of indulgence, closing his eyes and tuning in the smells and sounds of the city below. Petrol and chicken soup. Laughter and playground shouts rising from Liberty Bell Park. A hum of traffic from the King David intersection. The air, warm and sweet, bathed in a piney fragrance borne on puffs of desert breeze.

He breathed it all in, felt serene, then started thinking about the dead girl and was gripped with tension. When he opened his eyes, all was chaos. Lights and colors, shadows and secrets, the boundaries blurred, everything stirred up like some crazy broth.

Feeling overwhelmed and impotent, he quickly left the balcony, went to the bathroom, and stripped himself naked.

Standing under the needle spray of the shower, the water slapping him full-face, so hot he could barely stand it, he lathered himself and scrubbed his skin until it hurt.

Wondering who'd washed *her,* transformed her to a bloodless shell, like some horrible molt.

What kind of monster killed and then scrubbed up afterward, as if the victim were a dirty dish to be scoured and cast aside. As if the filth of the crime could ever be erased.

What kind of mind could celebrate such butchery?

He stepped out of the shower, clean but not cleansed.

8

He took all three children to the synagogue in the building, prayed with as much concentration as he could muster, and returned home to quiet order—Laura in a midnight-blue velvet gown, her hair covered by a white silk kerchief, curled on the couch with Dayan on her lap, turning the pages of an art book. The wine poured, the table set with white linen and Shabbat silver, the room dancing with the orange flicker of candlelight.

The five of them went to the table and sang "Shalom Aleichem," the poem that welcomed the Sabbath angels. Then he took Laura's hand and chanted "Woman of Valor" in an ancient Yemenite melody. After they'd embraced, he blessed the children, placing his hand on each of their heads, lingering on the words a little longer than usual.

* * *

In another part of the city, a ceremony of a different type unfolded. A consecration of the knives, as the grinning man liked to think of it. He'd played memory games and masturbated three times, which had relaxed him physiologically, though it hadn't slowed down the freight train that roared through the tunnels in his head.

How cozy, he thought, grinning, pushing past the roar. Domestic, yet self-sufficient. Soft music, a sandwich, a beer, his favorite reading material on the nightstand. The semen-soaked tissues, pleasantly ammoniac, crumpled in the wastebasket. And his little beauties, resting peacefully in their cozy velvet bed.

Carefully, tenderly, he unlatched the case, opened the lid. Stared at each of them. Lovingly.

Beauties.

Removing the smallest scalpel, he turned it in his fingers, thrilling at the buttery smoothness of the handle, the cold, sweet sting of the blade. Touching the cutting edge to one knuckle, barely grazing the skin, watching as a droplet of blood arose painlessly, then filled the knuckle-lines before flowing ticklishly down his finger. Lowering his tongue to the wound and drinking himself. Sperm out, blood in. Efficient. Self-sufficient.

He looked in the mirror above the bureau. Picked up the earrings and stared at them—cheap shit, but precious to him. He shuddered, put them down, took the scalpel and drew the blade across his throat, a millimeter short of contact. Pretending. A lovely pantomime. Feeling his erection return. Touching the handle of the scalpel to his cock, probing his balls, twiddling the short hairs around his anus.

"Little Dancer," he said, out loud, surprised at the hoarseness of his voice. Dry mouth. Another beer would taste good. In a minute.

He looked at the knife again, kissed the blunt edge. Laid it on his thigh and shivered.

Little Dancer. How it loved to waltz lightly on ballroom floors of flesh, tracing its progress in frothy scarlet. Dipping deeper and uncovering the mysteries within. Dance and skip, slice and delve.

Real science, the ultimate blend of real science and art.

Last night's dance party had gone well, so clean, so orderly. A lovely affair. Lovely.

9

Nahum Shmeltzer walked unnoticed through the lobby of the King Solomon Sheraton, made his way through a gaggle of tourists, and went down the stairs, past the Japanese restaurant and into the American one. Blond oak, dark-green upholstery and mirrored panels, plastic-coated menus, glass cases holding fake antiquities. Cute. The woman liked American food.

As usual, he was early and he expected to wait for her. But she'd arrived already and was sitting in a booth in a mirrored alcove, reading the menu—though she probably knew it by heart—a cup of coffee at her fingertips.

She saw him and waved. Smiling prettily.

Not bad for someone her age.

Though he knew the smile was contrived, he enjoyed looking at her. A lot more pleasant than the two hours of paperwork to get the sex offender programs run.

A hostess offered to seat him. He told her he was joining madame and walked to the booth. She greeted him with obvious warmth, held out a fine-boned hand, and said it had been a long time since they had seen each other.

"Too long," said Shmeltzer. "Must be three or four months." Three months since the last liaison. Ten months since that night in Eilat.

"Exactly. Please sit, dear."

A waiter came. Blond with a Yankee accent. Handed him a menu, took his order for hot tea with lemon, and left.

"You look well," Shmeltzer told her, meaning it, though it was part of the speech. She'd tinted her hair a dark chestnut-brown, but had allowed a few gray strands to remain. Her tailored suit was beige linen and the topaz brooch on her lapel set off the brown specks in her eyes. She'd applied her makeup effectively—softening the wrinkles instead of trying to mask them.

All in all, a classy production. Terrific bone structure. The kind who'd look right at home in the fancy places in any major city. He'd heard stories: that she'd been widowed in '56, worked the black-tie-and-Beretta circuit overseas, from London to Buenos Aires, then New York for a long time. That she'd made a fortune in the American stock market. That she'd been involved in the Eichmann capture. That she'd used her own kids as cover. No way to know how much was true, how much was bullshit. Now Shin Bet had her and she stayed close to home, though Shmeltzer still had no idea where her real home was. He'd looked through the files once, trying to find her, wanting a follow-up to Eilat. No address, no number. Nobody by that name, *adoni.*

She smiled, folded her hands in front of her, and Shmeltzer imagined the kind of assignments she was pulling now: society matron nibbling canapés at consulate parties. Doting grandma on a park bench, feeding sweets to her *aineklach,* diapers sharing space with the 9 mm in her purse. Rich tourist lady lounging in the hotel suite adjoining that of a certain visiting dignitary, stethoscope to the wall, fancy machines whirling and humming. No paperwork or garbage-bin stakeouts for her.

Too rich for his blood. Eilat had been a fluke, post-assignment tension release.

He looked around the restaurant. Across the room sat a group of American college kids. Three females, two males. Hebrew U., probably. Escaping dormitory cooking for a night out on the town. Nine-dollar hamburgers and Coca-Cola.

A young couple with two small children sat at the far end. The husband looked like a professor, bearded, with glasses; the wife, small, ginger-haired, a real looker. The kids were boys, one about six, the other younger. They drank milk, laughed, punched each other. He picked up scraps of conversation. American-accented English. All of them in brightly colored shorts and polo shirts. Probably exactly what they looked to be, though you could never be sure.

Otherwise, the place was dead—most of the tourists religious, taking their Shabbat meals at the King David or the Plaza, where the setup was more traditional.

"Not much business," he said.

"Past the dinner hour," said the woman.

The waiter brought his tea and asked if they were ready.

She ordered a minute steak and scrambled eggs with chips—calling them *french fries*—and more coffee. Still full from the mixed grill at Kohavi's, he settled for a basket of rolls, margarine, and jelly.

They made small talk as they ate and she had apple pie for dessert. After the waiter removed the dishes, she put her purse on the table, took out a compact, and opened it. Looking into the mirror, she smoothed back nonexistent strands of hair. As she freshened up, Shmeltzer noticed that she'd left the purse open so that he could see the tape recorder within—a miniaturized Japanese model, voice-activated, the size of a cigarette pack. High-tech. Her people loved it.

"I'm going shopping tomorrow, dear," she said, touching his hand. The touch brought back memories, soft white skin under black silk. "Is there anything you need?"

Enunciating clearly, he told her.

10

As the sun began to sink, Elias Daoud crossed himself and prayed for progress.

The village suburb of Silwan was a dense honeycomb of flat-roofed, porridge-colored dwellings notched into the hillside just southeast of the Old City, segregated from the city walls by the Valley of Kidron. Just north of the village, at the foot of the eastern wall, ran the Gihon Spring that fed the Pool of Siloam—the water supply for ancient Jerusalem. Women still went there to wash their laundry, and on his way up, Daoud saw a group of them—laughing and joking as they dipped sodden garments into the still, green water. Telling tales no man would ever hear.

And then he knew. That was where he'd seen her, during the course of his Number Two Gang investigation, when he'd assumed the identity of a dusty-faced punk with a hunger for dope.

He'd shuffled past the pools on his way to meet a dealer near the city walls, had seen her with a group of other, older women. Squatting, washing, laughing. The pretty face marred by the missing tooth.

Or had it been another? Was his mind playing tricks on him? His drive to succeed distorting his memory?

No, he was sure. The girl had been one of the washers. Her origins were here.

He trudged forward.

A spiraling, single-lane road provided access to the lowest level of the village. Narrow, jerry-built pathways and dirty alleys led to some of the upper houses; others could be reached only by donkey or on foot. He found it easiest to park the Citroën in an empty lot and walk most of the way.

It had been the same at Abu Tor, except that the Jews were starting to take over there, buying the biggest houses, renovating, settling in.

He'd concentrated on the poorer houses. Spent hours hiking and climbing, his thin-soled shoes steadily corroded by gravel and rock. The beige suit he'd worn to look good at the meeting, wilted and stained.

You couldn't talk to everyone, so his strategy had been to seek out the central meeting places, which, in a village, meant a cubbyhole café or soda stand on wheels. But Friday was Muslim Sabbath and everything was closed. The men were at the mosque or napping; in either event he couldn't interrupt and hope to get cooperation. And the women wouldn't speak to him without their husbands' permission. So he contented himself with stopping the occasional pedestrian, showing the girl's picture, asking his questions.

For the most part he encountered children or young men, walking in pairs and trios, aimless, with hungry eyes. The children giggled and scampered away. The young men responded to his greetings with curiosity and distrust, refused to believe he was a policeman until he showed his credentials; once they'd seen the badge, read his name, disbelief turned to instant hostility.

In and of itself, hostility was tolerable—he'd grown up in a

Muslim neighborhood and throughout his childhood had been labeled an infidel. Joining the police force had brought forth further accusations of infidelity from some of those he'd considered friends. Yet his faith in Christ the Savior and his ambition remained unshaken and he truly believed that he'd grown inured.

But hostility led to silence, and silence, to a detective, meant failure. Which was something he refused to tolerate. The case was important and he was determined to push himself. To prove himself to the Jews. Working under Sharavi was a stroke of good luck. The Yemenite had a reputation as a fair one, basing his decisions on merit, not religion. If a guy produced, it would be worth something. But there would be obstacles—the old guy, Shmeltzer, who'd be dogging him, waiting for a chance to show he was inferior. No way would Daoud give him anything to work with.

And the hostility of the Muslims.

Walking the tightrope, as usual.

As evening approached he was sour with impatience, bathed in his own sweat, marching forward on swollen feet, but remembering the girl's face as she washed clothes, then the death photo, knowing he had to continue.

An hour into Silwan he received his first smile of the day.

He'd just spent a fruitless five minutes with a gang of youths loitering near a disabled tractor and had climbed to the middle level of the village, walking along a dirt path barely wide enough for two people to pass. All the houses he passed were locked and quiet, the only sound the clucks of chickens and brays of goats. But at the end of the path he saw human movement on the steps of a tiny box of a building with turquoise shutters. A man sitting, swaying back and forth.

He walked toward the house and saw that it was cell-like, with a single window to the right of the door. The shutters were splintering and in need of paint, the steps framed by a rusty pipe arbor wrapped with the stiff brown tendrils of a dead grapevine. And the man was a boy. About seventeen, swaying as he peered closely at a book in his lap. Another surly one, no doubt.

But then he noticed that this boy looked different. Soft and slovenly. Hunched over, as if his spine were made of some pliable material. An undersized bullethead shaved to bristle length, sooty smears of peach fuzz on cheeks and chin. A weak chin. Moist, drooping, sheeplike eyes. The swaying, stiff and arrhythmic, punctuated by random finger flutters.

The boy continued reading, unresponsive to the presence of a stranger. Puzzled, Daoud stepped forward and cast a shadow over the book. The boy looked up and smiled. A smile of such innocence and warmth that the detective found himself smiling back.

"Good afternoon." Daoud's fingers drummed against the envelope that held the photo of the murdered girl.

More smiles, no answer. Thinking the boy hadn't heard, he repeated himself.

A blank stare. Another smile. Loose-lipped and gaptoothed.

Daoud looked at the book in the boy's spreading lap. The Arabic alphabet. A child's primer. Filthy, fluttering fingers held it awkwardly. A smell arose from the boy's homemade clothing. The stink of someone who didn't know how to wipe his ass properly.

An idiot. Figured.

"See you later," Daoud said, and the boy continued to stare, intensely, as if committing the detective's face to memory. But when Daoud stepped away the boy suddenly grew alarmed. Dropping the primer, he pulled himself clumsily to his feet and held on to the pipe arbor for support. Daoud saw that he was a tall one, with heavy, sloping shoulders, and wondered if he was dangerous. He tensed in anticipation of trouble, but the boy showed no signs of aggression, only frustration. Eyes rounding, he moved his lips furiously, churning soundlessly, until finally a croak emerged, followed by garbled noise that Daoud had to strain to understand:

"Hellosir. Nie-niceday!"

An idiot who could speak. A meager blessing, but maybe the poor guy had enough sense to be of some help.

"Good book?" he asked, looking at the fallen primer, shielding his nose with his hand to block out the stink. Trying to make conversation, establish rapport.

The boy was silent, staring at him, uncomprehending.

"Learning the alphabet, my friend?"

More blank stares.

"Want to look at something?" Daoud tapped the envelope. "A picture?"

The boy craned his neck, gawked at him. Rolled his eyes. Idiotically.

Enough of this, thought Daoud. He turned to leave.

The boy rocked on his feet and started gurgling and gesturing wildly. He pointed to his eyes, then to Daoud's lips, reached out suddenly to touch those lips with a grubby finger.

Daoud stepped nimbly away from the contact and the boy pitched forward, adding shouts to his gestures, slapping his own ears so hard it had to hurt.

Definitely trying to communicate, thought Daoud. He strained to understand.

"Seedwords! Seedwords! No ear, no ear!"

As the boy kept up his singsong, Daoud played it back in his head. *Seedwords?* Words? See dwords. See the words. No hear—

"You're deaf."

The boy's smile lit up his face. Clapping his hands, he jumped up and down.

Who was the real idiot? Daoud castigated himself. The poor kid could read lips but he—the brilliant detective—in his attempt to keep his nostrils unsullied had been hiding his nose and mouth when he talked.

"Seedwords, seedwords!"

"Okay." Daoud smiled. He came closer, made sure the boy had a clear view of his lips. Overenunciated: "What's your name, my friend?"

Straining neck cords, a moment's delay, then: "Ahmed." Muddily.

"Your family name, Ahmed."

"Nsif."

"Nasif?"

Smiles and nods.

"Hello, Mr. Ahmed Nasif."

"H'lo."

The effort of speaking made the boy's body go tense. Words were accompanied by the flapping of hands, the strange finger flutters.

This is more than just deaf, thought Daoud. Some sort of spastic condition. And mentally defective, just as he'd first thought. Speak to him as if to a child.

"I am Sergeant Daoud. I am a policeman."

More smiles. The crude pantomime of shooting a gun. "Boom boom." The boy laughed, and drool trickled down a corner of his mouth.

"That's right, Ahmed. Boom, boom. Would you like to look at a picture?"

"Boom, boom!"

Daoud pulled the photo out of the envelope, held it close enough for the sheep-eyes to see, not so close that the flapping hands could grab out and maul it.

"I'm looking for this girl, Ahmed. Do you know her?"

An emphatic nod. Eager to please.

"You do?"

"Dirl, dirl!"

"Yes, a girl. Does she live here in Silwan, Ahmed?"

The boy said "dirl" again, the word preceded by something Daoud couldn't make out.

"Say that again, Ahmed."

The boy pawed at the photo. Daoud pulled it back.

More pawing, as if he were trying to hit the picture.

"What's her name, Ahmed?"

"Badirl!"

"She's a bad girl?"

"Badirl!"

"Why is she a bad girl, Ahmed?"

"Badirl!"

"What has she done wrong?"

"Badirl!"

"Do you know her name, Ahmed?"

"Badirl!"

"All right, Ahmed. She's a bad girl. Now tell me her name, please."

"Badirl!"

"Where does she live, Ahmed?"

"Badirl!"

Sighing, Daoud put the picture away and started leaving. Ahmed gave a loud shriek and came after him, putting a padded hand on his shoulder.

Daoud reacted swiftly, turning and pushing the boy away. Ahmed stumbled and landed in the dirt. He looked up at

Daoud, pouted and burst into loud sobs. Daoud felt like a child abuser.

"Come on, Ahmed. Settle down."

The door to the house opened and a small woman stepped out, bosom drooping, round dark face emerging like a hickory nut from within the folds of her *melaya*.

"What is it?" she said in a high, sharp voice.

"Mama, Mama, Mama!" wailed the boy.

She looked at the fruit of her loins, then over at Daoud with a combination of sadness and muted anger. A look that said she'd been through this many times before.

The boy reached his hands out, cried "Mama." Daoud felt like apologizing but knew it was the wrong approach for someone like her. To the traditional ones, raised on beatings by fathers and husbands, kindness was interpreted as weakness.

"I'm Police Sergeant Daoud of the Kishle Substation," he said, stiffly. "I'm searching for someone who knows this girl." A wave of the photo. "Your son said he did and I was attempting to learn what he knew."

The woman snorted, came forward and glanced at the photo. Looking up without expression, she said, "He doesn't know her."

"Badirl!" said Ahmed, clucking his tongue.

"He said he did," said Daoud. "Seemed quite sure of it."

"Lessano taweel," snapped the woman. "He has a long tongue." She chattered rapidly: "His talk is like dung. Can't you see he's a fool?" Coming down the steps, she walked to the boy, slapped him sharply on the head, and took hold of his shirt collar.

"Up, you!"

"Mama, Mama!"

Slap, drag, slap. The boy got halfway to his feet and the woman, breathing hard, pulled him up the stairs toward the door.

"Badirl!" shouted the boy.

"One moment," said Daoud.

"A fool," said the woman, and she yanked the boy into the house and slammed the door.

Daoud stood alone on the steps and considered his options: He could knock, pursue the matter. But to what end? The picture had elicited no response from the woman, which meant the idiot son probably didn't know her either. A long-tongued idiot, as she'd said. Shooting off his mouth. A waste of time.

He took a deep breath and noticed that the skies had begun to darken. His job was far from done—covering the rest of the village would take hours. But the chance for human contact diminished with every degree the sun dropped. Better to wait until morning, a workday, with men on the streets. In the meantime he'd be better off asking his questions around more populated areas: the bus depot, the train station. Chasing shadows into the small hours.

It was decided, then. He'd leave Silwan, work Jerusalem until he couldn't keep his eyes open, come back tomorrow. First thing in the morning.

11

The collision of fist with face, firecracker-sharp.

The Chinaman sat in the tent, watching the movie. Waiting for Charlie Khazak to finish with the truck driver.

Bruce Lee on a big TV screen, surrounded by seven masked bad guys in black pajamas. Bare-chested and sweating, unarmed against the bad guys' knives and clubs. The bad guys moving in. A closeup of Bruce grimacing, screaming, a storm of lightning kicks and all the bad guys are down.

Not likely.

Applause and hoots came from some of the tables. Greasy-haired *pooshtakim* slouched with their arms around the bare shoulders of dumb, adoring girlfriends. Staring at the TV on the ladder as if it were some kind of god on a pedestal. Chain-smoking and drinking Turkish coffee, eating shishlik and watermelon, open-mouthed, spitting the seeds onto the dirt floor. Snotty little punks, laughing too loud. At this hour they should all be in bed. He picked out at least three or four he'd busted in the last year, probably others he couldn't remember. A couple of them met his eyes, tried to give him a little shit with defiant looks, but turned away when he held the stare.

A hot night, and he was overdressed for it—jeans, boots, a body shirt, a loose cotton sport coat to cover his shoulder holster. Tired and grumpy from walking all night through the Arab neighborhoods, showing the girl's picture and getting blank stares. Five hookers working the entire Green Line, all of them fat and ugly. Having to wait for one of them to finish blowing an Arab in the back of her car before he could question her; the other ones available but semiretarded. None of them knew the girl; none of them seemed to care, even after he'd warned them, even after Gray Man. Now, here he was, waiting again, for a shit like Charlie Khazak.

On the screen, Bruce had walked into a garden and encountered a fat bald guy with the body of a sumo wrestler. Was there a plot to this one? Bruce's footwork didn't seem to impress Fatso. Close-up of his ugly puss grinning. Bruce getting slammed around; then a neck chop and a two-hander to the back of the head turned the tables. More cheers and hoots. Someone had told him the guy had died from a brain tumor or something like that. Too many kicks to the head.

He took a cube of melon from his plate, let it melt in his mouth, looked around the tent, got restless, and walked outside. Charlie Khazak was still talking to the driver, standing next to the melon truck, playing dickering games.

The Chinaman kept his eye on the flow out of the Damascus Gate, watched a group of soldiers pass under the arch, patting one another on the back, looking like the teenagers they were. A couple of Arabs emerged, dressed in long white *jallabiyahs*. Another Arab, older, carrying a prayer rug. A solitary Hassid, tall, thin, wearing a wide mink hat. Like some black-garbed scarecrow, earlocks swinging as he walked. Where was a guy like that coming from at one in the morning on Shabbat—didn't they screw their wives on Friday night? What was his game—a late wrestle with the Talmud? Or some other kind of wrestle? During the stakeouts on Gray Man he'd learned about the righteous ones. . . .

Shouts of laughter poured out of Charlie's tent. No doubt Bruce had polished off someone else. As if in competition, the tent next door erupted in guffaws, backed by bass-heavy rock music.

Midnight party time at The Slave Market, every Friday, like clockwork. No party for Yossi Lee, walking through the tents, showing the picture to sleazy types and getting nothing.

By daybreak the tents would be down, the entire area just a dirt lot again, crowded with ten-dollar-a-day laborers waiting to be picked up by contractors. The only evidence of the party scene, the garbage: piles of broken bamboo shishlik skewers and melon rind, seeds dotting the dirt like dead bugs.

A Border Patrol jeep drove down Sultan Suleiman, stopped, and flashed blue lights over the walls, striping the Damascus Gate and driving on. Belly-dancing music came from one of the coffeehouses just inside the gate. A hangout for older Arabs—men only; the women were stuck at home. Card games and backgammon, the air a fog of tobacco smoke filtered through rosewater narghilas. Scratchy recordings of finger cymbals and whining violins, the same love song played for an hour—what use was all that romance, with no women around? Maybe they were all queer—the way they sucked on their narghilas, you could hear the gurgle.

Charlie Khazak paid the driver. Two boys materialized from behind the truck and started unloading the melons, carrying five, six at a time, back to the tent. Hot night like this, they'd sell faster than they came in.

The Chinaman stretched impatiently, walked over to Charlie, and said, "Come on."

"Patience." Charlie smiled and turned back to the Arab, who was counting his money with a tongue-moistened finger. Charlie smiled again, a vulture smile on a vulture face. Skinny, dark. Pocked, sunken cheeks, Iraqi beak nose, and one dark line of eyebrow. Bald on top with pointy sideburns and a long fringe of hair on the sides that ran over onto his collar. A purple and green paisley shirt with balloon sleeves, tight black pants, needle-toed patent-leather shoes. A *pooshtak* all grown up. The guy's father had been a rabbi in Baghdad; the wages of righteousness, a punk son.

"Patience, nothing," said the Chinaman and put his hand heavily on Charlie's shoulder. All bones. One good squeeze and the guy would be out of commission.

He exerted the tiniest bit of pressure and Charlie said good-bye to the Arab.

The two of them walked back to the tent, past the tables with *pooshtakim* greeting Charlie as if he were some sort of pop star, to the rear, where shishlik and skimpy hamburgers sizzled on charcoal grills and a sleepy-looking bartender filled orders behind a makeshift bar of melon cartons piled one on top of the other. Charlie grabbed a bottle of Coke from the ice bucket and offered it to the Chinaman, who took it and dropped it back in the bucket. Charlie shrugged, and the Chinaman motioned him into a dark corner next to a pyramid of melons, away from the eyes of the others.

"Look at this," he said, pulling out the picture. "Know her?"

Charlie took the photo, furrowed his forehead so that the single eyebrow dipped in the center.

"Cute. Is she sleeping or dead?"

"Ever sell her?"

"Me?" Charlie feigned hurt feelings. "I'm a restaurateur, not a flesh peddler."

A roar of approval rose from the crowd at the tables. Bruce Lee had just finished vanquishing a small army of bad guys.

"The mysteries of the Orient," said Charlie, watching the film. "Right up your alley."

"Cut the shit. I'm tired."

Something in the detective's voice wiped the smile off Charlie's face. Handing the photo back, he said: "Don't know her."

"Ever seen her around?"

The faintest hesitation, but the Chinaman picked up on it.

"No."

The Chinaman inched closer to Charlie, so that they could smell each other. "If you're holding out on me, I'll find out, shmuck. And I'll come back and jam one of those melons up your ass."

The bartender looked up. Smiling faintly, enjoying the sight of the boss being bossed.

Charlie put his hands on his hips. Raised his voice for the benefit of the bartender: "Get the hell out of here, Lee. I'm busy."

The Chinaman lifted a melon from the pyramid, knocked on it as if testing for freshness, then let it roll off his palm and fall to the ground. The melon landed with a dull thud and exploded, pink pulp and juice splattering in the dust. The barman looked up, remained in his place. No one else seemed to have noticed. All locked in on Bruce.

"Oops." The Chinaman smiled.

Charlie started to protest, but before he could say anything the Chinaman placed his right boot heel on the tent-keeper's right instep, leaned in, and put a little weight on it. Charlie's eyes opened wide with pain.

"What the—" he said, then forced himself to smile. The granddaddy *pooshtak,* toughing it out, not wanting to look like a pussy in front of his fans. Not that they had eyes for anyone but Bruce.

"Tell me what you know." The Chinaman smiled back.

"Off my foot, you baboon."

The Chinaman continued smiling. Pressed down harder and talked nonchalantly, as if the two of them were buddies. Having a chat about sports or something.

"Listen, Adon Khazak," he said, "I've no interest in finding out what naughtiness you've been up to. Tonight." More pressure. "Just tell me about this girl."

Charlie gasped and the bartender came closer, bottle of Goldstar in one hand. "Charlie—"

"Get the hell out of here, stupid! Do your job!"

The bartender cursed under his breath, went back to washing glasses.

"Like I told you," Charlie said between his teeth. Sweat ran down his nose, beading at the tip of the beak, rolling off into the dirt. "I don't know her. Now get the hell off my foot before you break something."

"You've seen her around."

"What of it? She's a face, a nothing."

"Where and when," said the Chinaman.

"Get off and I'll tell you."

The Chinaman gave a good-natured shrug and broke contact. Charlie spat into the ground, did a sneaky little dance. Concealed his pain by pulling out a pack of Marlboros and a box of matches, jamming a cigarette between his lips, and making a show of lighting a match against his thumbnail.

He sucked in smoke, blew it out through his nostrils. Re peated the gesture. Formed his features into a tough-guy grimace.

"Very impressive," said the Chinaman. "The girl."

"She's been around once or twice, okay? That's all."

"On a Friday?"

"That's the only time we're here, Lee." A kick at a stray chunk of pulp.

"Was she alone or with someone?"

"I saw her with a guy."

"What kind of guy?"

"An Arab."

"Name."

"How the hell should I know? They never came in. I just saw them hanging around. It was a long time ago."

"How long?"

"Month, maybe two."

"How do you know he was an Arab?"

"He looked like one. And he was talking Arabic." As if explaining to a moron.

"What did this Arab look like?"

"Skinny, lots of hair, mustache. Cheap clothes."

"How tall?"

"Medium."

"Be more specific."

"Not tall, not short. In the middle—maybe a meter eight."

"How old?"

"Eighteen or nineteen."

"What else about him do you remember?"

"Nothing. He looked like a million others."

"What'd you mean, lots of hair?"

"What does it mean to you?"

"Charlie," said the Chinaman, meaningfully.

"Thick, bushy, okay?"

"Straight or curly?"

"Straight, I think. Like yours." A smile. "Maybe he's your cousin, Lee."

"What style?"

"Who the hell remembers?"

"She an Arab too?"

"Who else would hang around with an Arab, Lee?"

"One of *your* cousins."

Charlie spat again. Inhaled his cigarette and ordered the bartender to clean up the mess.

"Street girl?" asked the Chinaman.

"How would I know that?"

The Chinaman cracked the knuckles of one hand.

"You're a cunt peddler is how, Charlie."

"I'm not into that shit anymore, Lee. I sell melons, that's all. Maybe this guy was pimping her, but all I saw was them hanging out. Once or twice."

"Ever see her with anyone else?"

"No. Just the two of them, hanging around—it was over a month ago."

"But you remember her."

Charlie grinned and patted his chest.

"I'm a connoisseur of beauty, you know? And she was good-looking. Big round ass, nice tits for someone that young. Even in those stupid clothes she was all right."

"She wore cheap clothes too?"

"Both of them. He was a nothing, a farmer. Give her a makeover, she'd be a fine piece."

"Tell me what else you know," said the Chinaman, restraining an urge to slap the little shit.

"That's it."

"Sure about that?"

Charlie shrugged, took a drag on his cigarette.

"Step on my foot again, Lee. From here on in, anything I tell you will be fairy tales."

"Ever see this Arab without her?"

"I don't look at boys. Do you?"

The Chinaman lifted his hand. Charlie recoiled, stumbling backward, and the Chinaman caught him before he fell. Lifted him by the scruff, like a rag doll.

"Tsk, tsk," he said, patting the tent-keeper's face gently. "Just a love pat."

"Go to hell, Lee."

"Shabbat shalom."

Back on his Vespa, he processed what he'd learned. Charlie's recognition had turned the girl from a picture into someone real. But when you got right down to it he didn't know much more than when he'd started.

She was loose, hung around with an Arab guy, which meant she was probably an Arab. Maybe a Christian—some of them were a little more modern. No way would a Muslim daddy allow his girl out at night, unchaperoned, least of all at The Slave Market.

Unless she was an orphan or a whore.

No one at the orphanages had known her.

A whore, probably. Or an unwanted daughter sold by her family—it was against the law, but some of the poorer families still did it. The girls, unwanted baggage, traded for cash to rich families in Amman or one of the oil states. The real slave market. Charlie had said her clothes were cheap. . . .

He kicked in the scooter's engine, flipped it around, drove south around the Old City. Past the Border Patrol jeep, which had stopped for a cigarette break near the Jaffa Gate. Swinging away from the walls, up to Keren Hayesod, zipping through the Rehavya district. Toward his flat on Herzl on the west side of town.

A lead, but pitiful. Good-looking, poor Arab girl with a poor Arab boyfriend. Big deal.

It was too late to knock on any more doors—not that that approach was worth much anyway. A day of it had brought him dumb stares, shakes of the head. Some of them pretending his Arabic was too poor to understand—pure crap; he was plenty fluent. Others simply shrugging. Know-nothing Ahmeds. For all he knew, he'd already talked to the right person and had been lied to.

If she had a family, they should have claimed her.

Probably a whore. But none of the pimps or the street girls knew her. Maybe a rookie. Short career.

Maybe the long-haired boy friend was the killer, or maybe he was just a guy who'd screwed her once or twice, then went on to something else. Thin, medium-sized, with a mustache. Like saying a guy with two arms, two legs. Nothing worth reporting to Dani.

Yossi Lee, ace investigator. He'd been on his feet for twelve hours, with little to show for it. Had gulped down greasy felafel that sat undigested in his stomach. Aliza had said she'd try to wait up for him, but he knew she'd be sleeping, little Rafi curled in the crib by the bed. Yesterday the kid had said "apple," which seemed pretty good for sixteen months. Muscles on him, too; ready for soccer before you knew it. Maybe he'd get a chance to bounce him around a little before hitting the street again. No walk in the park this Saturday, though. Shit.

The wind in his face felt good. He liked the city this way, sweet and empty. As if all of it belonged to him. King Yossi, the Jewish Genghis.

He'd drive around a little more. Give himself time to wind down.

12

Daniel awoke at three in the morning, troubled by vague remembrances of dark, bloody dreams. Metal through flesh, his hand severed, floating through space, out of reach. Crying like a child, mud-soaked and feeble . . .

He changed positions, hugged the pillow, wrapped himself in the top sheet and tried to relax. But instead, he grew edgier and rolled over again, facing Laura.

She was covered to her chin, breathing shallowly through barely parted lips. A wave of hair fell over one eye; a hint of tapered fingernail extended from beneath the sheet. He touched the nail, brushed away the hair. She stirred, made a throaty, contented sound, and stretched so that the sole of one foot rested on his ankle. He inched closer, kissed her cheeks, her eyes, dry lips tasting faintly of morning.

She smiled in her sleep and he moved up against her and kissed her chin. She opened her eyes, looked at him with confusion, and closed them again. Her body tensed, and she turned away from him. Then her eyes opened again. She mouthed the word *oh* and wrapped her arms around him.

They embraced, lying on their sides, face to face, kissing, nuzzling, rocking in a tangle of sheets. She raised one leg and rested it on his thigh, took him and guided him inside of her. They made love that way, slowly, sleepily, until climax brought them wide awake.

Afterward, they lay connected for a while. Then Laura said, "Daniel . . . I'm thirsty," with mischief in her voice.

"All right," he said, extricating himself.

He got out of bed, went into the kitchen, and filled a glass with cold mineral water. When he returned she was sitting up, bare above the waist, her hair pinned up. He handed her the glass and she emptied it in two long drafts.

"Want more?" he asked.

"No, this is fine." She moistened her finger on the rim of the glass, brushed it across her lips.

"Sure?" He smiled. "There's a half-gallon bottle in the refrigerator."

"Tease!" Fanning wet fingers, she splashed him lightly. "Can I help it if I get thirsty? That's the way my body works."

"Your body works just fine." He lay down beside her, put his arm around her shoulder. She set the glass on the nightstand, looked at the clock that rested there, and gave a low moan.

"Oh, no. Three-twenty."

"Sorry for waking you."

She reached beneath the covers, touched him lightly, and laughed. "All's well that ends well. Have you been up long?"

"A few minutes."

"Anything the matter?"

"Just restless," he said, feeling the tension return. "I'll get up and let you rest."

He began to move away but she touched his wrist and restrained him.

"No. Stay. We've hardly talked since you got that call."

She rested her head on his shoulder, made circles with her palm across his hairless chest. They sat without speaking, listening to night sounds—a faint whistle of wind, the hum of the clock, the synchrony of their heartbeats.

"Tell me about it," she said.

"About what?"

"What you avoided talking about by going to bed at nine."

"You don't want to hear about it."

"Yes, I do."

"It's horrible, believe me."

"Tell me, anyway."

He looked at her, saw the will in her eyes. Shrugged and began talking about the murder, reporting dispassionately, professionally. Leaving out as much as he could without patronizing her. She listened without comment, flinching only once, but when he finished her eyes were moist.

"My God," she said. "Fifteen."

He knew what she was thinking: not much older than Shoshi. He allowed himself to share the thought, and a stab of anxiety pierced him to the core. He defended against it the way he'd been taught to block out pain. Forcing pleasant images into his mind. Fields of wild poppies. The fragrance of orange blossoms.

"Heroin, sex murder, it doesn't . . . fit," Laura was saying. "We're not supposed to have that kind of thing here."

"Well, now we do," he said angrily. A second later: "Sorry. You're right. We're out of our element."

"That's not what I meant. I'm sure you'll solve it."

"Twenty-four-hour shifts until we do."

"It's just . . ." She groped for words. "When I was growing up, I heard about those kinds of things all the time. It wasn't that we accepted them, but . . . Oh, I don't know. Here, it just seems a heresy, Daniel. Demonic."

"I understand," said Daniel, but to himself he thought: That's exactly the kind of thing I have to avoid. Devils and demons, religious symbolism—the city makes you think that way. It's a *crime,* no more, no less. Perpetrated by a *human being.* Someone sick and fallible . . .

"What time will you be leaving?" Laura asked.

"Seven. I have to walk down to the Katamonim. If I'm not back by twelve-thirty, start lunch without me."

"The Katamonim? I thought you said she was an Arab."

"Daoud *thinks* she is. We won't know until we ID her."

She unpinned her hair, let it fall to her shoulders.

"The brass wants it kept quiet," he said. "Which means meetings away from Headquarters. If we get any leads, we'll be meeting here, Sunday evening. Don't prepare anything. If we're out of soda, I'll pick some up."

"What time in the evening?"

"Between five and six."

"Do you want me to pick up Luanne and Gene?"

Daniel slapped his forehead. "Oh, no, how could I forget. When are they coming in?"

"Seven P.M. if the flight's on schedule."

"Perfect timing. So much for grand hospitality."

"They'll be fine, Daniel. They'll probably be exhausted for the first day or so. I've arranged a walking tour of the Old City churches and Bethlehem on Tuesday, and I'll book them on an all-day trip to Galilee with an emphasis on Nazareth. That should keep them busy for a while."

"I wanted it to be personal, the way they treated us."

"There'll be plenty of time for that—they're here for four

weeks. Besides, if anyone should be able to understand, it's them. Gene probably sees this kind of thing all the time."

"Yes," said Daniel, "I'm sure he does."

At four Laura fell back asleep and Daniel drifted into a somnolent state, neither slumber nor arousal, in which dream-images flitted in and out of consciousness with a randomness that was unsettling. At six he got up, sponged off in the bathroom, dressed in a white shirt, khaki trousers, and rubber-soled walking shoes, and forced himself to swallow a glass of orange juice and a cup of instant coffee with milk and sugar. He took his *tallit* out on the balcony, faced the Old City, and prayed. By seven he was out the door, beeper on his belt, the envelope containing pictures of the dead girl in hand.

As on every other Shabbat, two of the elevators in the building were shut down, the third set automatically, stopping at every floor, so that religiously observant tenants could ride without having to push buttons—the completion of electric circuits was a violation of the Sabbath. But religious convenience also meant agonizingly slow progress, and when he saw that the car had just reached the ground floor, he took the stairs and bounded down four flights.

A man was in the lobby, leaning against the mailboxes, smoking. Young, twenty-two or -three, well built and tan, with dark wavy hair and a full clipped beard highlighted with ginger, wearing a white polo shirt with a Fila logo, American designer jeans, brand-new blue-and-white Nike running shoes. On his left wrist was an expensive-looking watch with a gold band; around his neck, a gold *Hai* charm. An American, thought Daniel. Some kind of playboy, maybe a rich student, but he doesn't belong here—everyone in the building was religious, no one smoked like that on Shabbat.

The young man saw him and ground out his cigarette on the marble floor. Inconsiderate, thought Daniel. He was about to ask him what his business was, in English, when the young man began walking toward him, hand extended, saying, in fluent, native Hebrew: "Pakad Sharavi? I'm Avi Cohen. I've been assigned to your team. I got the message late last night and thought I'd come over and check in personally."

Sophisticated rich kid, thought Daniel, irritated that his intuition had been wrong. North Tel-Avivnik. Politician's son with plenty of travel experience. Which explained the foreign threads. He took the hand and let go of it quickly, surprised at how much instant dislike he'd built up for the new hire.

"The briefing was yesterday," he said.

"Yes, I know," said Cohen, matter-of-factly, without apology. "I was moving into a new flat. No phone. Tat Nitzav Laufer sent a messenger over but he got lost."

A smile, full of boyish charm. No doubt it had worked wonders with Asher Davidoff's blonde. A *samal* connected to the deputy commander—what was a rich kid like this doing as a policeman?

Daniel walked toward the door.

"I'm ready, now," said Cohen, tagging along.

"Ready for what?"

"My assignment. Tat Nitzav Laufer told me it's a heavy case."

"Did he?"

"Sex cutting, no motive, no suspect—"

"Do you and Tat Nitzav Laufer confer regularly?"

"No," said Cohen, flustered. "He . . . my father—"

"Never mind," said Daniel, then remembered that the kid's father had died recently, and softened his tone.

"I was sorry to hear about your father."

"Did you know him?" asked Cohen, surprised.

"Just by reputation."

"He was a tough guy, a real ball-breaker." Cohen uttered it automatically, without emotion, as if it were a psalm that he'd recited hundreds of times before. Daniel felt his hostility toward the new hire rise again. Pushing the door open, he let it swing back for Cohen to catch and stepped out into the sunlight. There was an unfamiliar car in the parking lot. A red BMW 330i.

"My assignment, Pakad?"

"Your assignment is to be present for all meetings at precisely the time they're called."

"I told you, my flat—"

"I'm not interested in excuses, only results."

Cohen's eyebrows lowered. His icy blue eyes clouded with anger.

"Is that understood, Samal Cohen?"

"Yes, Pakad." The right thing to say, but with a hint of arrogance in the tone. Daniel let it pass.

"You'll be assigned to Mefakeah Nahum Shmeltzer. Call him

at eight tomorrow morning and do what he tells you to do. In the meantime, there are some files I want you to go through. At National Headquarters—the computer boys are getting them ready." He reached into the envelope, drew out a photo, and handed it to Cohen. "Go through each file and see if you can find a match with this one. Don't look only for exact matches—take into account that she may have changed her hair style or aged a bit since the file was opened. If there's any sort of resemblance, set it aside. Keep meticulous records, and when in doubt, ask questions. Got it?"

"Yes." Cohen looked at the picture and said, "Young."

"A very astute observation," said Daniel. Turning his back, he walked away.

He covered the three-kilometer walk quickly, with little regard for his surroundings, walking southwest, then west on Yehuda HaNasi, where he entered the Katamonim. The neighborhood started deteriorating when he came to Katamon Eight. Some evidence of renewal was visible: a newly painted building here, a freshly planted tree there. The government had been pushing it until the recession hit. But for the most part it was as he remembered it: curbless streets cracked and litter-strewn; what little grass there was, brown and dry. Laundry billowed from the rust-streaked balconies of decaying cinder-block buildings, the bunkerlike construction harking back to pre-'67 days, when south Jerusalem faced Jordanian guns, the sudden, murderous sniping attributed by the Arabs to a soldier "gone berserk."

Berserk marksmen. Lots of shootings. Bitter jokes had arisen: The psychiatric wards of Amman had been emptied in order to staff Hussein's army.

The change of borders in '67 had brought about a shift in character in other poor districts—Yemin Moshe with its cobbled alleys and artists' studios, so inflated now that only foreigners could afford it; even Musrara had begun looking a little better—but the lower Katamonim remained a living monument to urban blight.

During his rookie days, he'd driven patrol here, and though his own origins had been anything but affluent, the experience had depressed him. Prefab buildings knocked up hastily for tides of Jewish immigrants from North Africa, strung together like railroad cars and sectioned into dreary one-hundred-square-meter flats that seemed incurably plagued with mildew and rot. Tiny windows built for safety but now unnecessary and oppressive. Rutted streets, empty fields used for garbage dumps. The flats crammed with angry people, boiling in the summer, clammy and cold in the winter. Fathers unemployed and losing face, the wives easy targets for tirades and beatings, the kids running wild in the streets. A recipe for crime—just add opportunity.

The *pooshtakim* had hated him. To them, the Yemenites were an affront, poorer than anyone, different-looking, regarded as primitives and outsiders. *Smiling fools*—you could beat them and they'd smile. But those smiles reflected an unerring sense of faith and optimism that had enabled the Yemenites to climb up the economic ladder with relative haste. And the fact that their crime rate was low was a slap in the face to the poverty excuse.

Where else could that lead but to scapegoating? He'd been called Blackie more times than he could count, ridiculed and ignored and forced to come down hard on defiant punks. A hell of an initiation. He'd endured it, gradually ingratiated himself with some of them, and done his job. But though it had been his idea to work there in the first place, he'd welcomed the completion of his assignment.

Now he was back, on a Shabbat, no less, embarking on an outing that was a long shot at best.

On the surface, coming down here did have a certain logic to it. The girl was poor and Oriental, maybe a street girl. Though other neighborhoods bred that type, too, Eight and Nine were the right places to start.

But he admitted to himself that a good part of it was symbolic—setting a good example by showing the others that a pakad was still willing to work the streets. And laying to rest any suspicions that a religious pakad would use Shabbat as an excuse to loaf.

He despised the idea of disrupting the Sabbath, resented the break in routine that separated him from family and ritual. Few cases made that kind of demand on him, but this one was different. Although the dead girl was beyond help, if a madman was at work, he wouldn't stop at one. And the saving of a life overrode Shabbat.

Still, he did what he could to minimize the violation—wearing the beeper but carrying no money or weapon, walking instead of driving, using his memory rather than pen and paper to record his observations. Doing his best to think of spiritual things during the empty moments that constituted so much of a detective's working life.

An elderly Moroccan couple approached him, on their way to synagogue, the husband wearing an outsized embroidered *kipah,* mouthing psalms, walking several paces ahead of his wife. In Eight and Nine, only the old ones remained observant.

"Shabbat shalom," he greeted them and showed them the picture.

The man apologized for not having his glasses, said he couldn't see a thing. The woman looked at it, shook her head, and said, "No. What happened? Is she lost?"

"In a way," said Daniel, thanking them and moving on.

The scene repeated itself a score of times. On Rehov San Martin, at the southern tip of Nine, he encountered a group of muscular, swarthy young men playing soccer in a field. Waiting until a goal had been scored, he approached them. They passed the photo around, made lewd comments, and giving it back to him, resumed their game.

He continued on until eleven, eating a late breakfast of shrugs, ignorance, and bad jokes, feeling like a rookie again. Deciding that he'd been stupid to waste his time and abandon his family in the name of symbolism, he began the return trip in a foul mood.

On his way out of Eight, he passed a kiosk that had been closed when he'd entered the district, a makeshift stand where children stood in line for ice cream and candy bars. Approaching, he noticed that a particularly sickening-looking blue ice seemed to be the favorite.

The proprietor was a squat Turk in his fifties, with black-rimmed eyeglasses, bad teeth, and a three-day growth of beard. His shirt was sweat-soaked and he smelled of confection. When he saw Daniel's *kipah,* he frowned.

"No Shabbat credit. Cash only."

Daniel showed him his ID, removed the photo from the envelope.

"Aha, police. They force a religious one to work today?"

"Have you seen this girl?"

The man took a look, said casually, "Her? Sure. She's an Arab, used to work as a maid at the monks' place in the Old City."

"Which monks' place?"

"The one near the New Gate."

"Saint Saviour's?"

"Yeah." The Turk peered closely at the photo, turned serious. "What's the matter with her? Is she—"

"Do you know her name?"

"No idea. Only reason I remember her at all is that she was good-looking." Another downward glance: "Someone got her, right?"

Daniel took the picture away from him. "Your name, please, *adoni.*"

"Sabhan, Eli, but I don't want to get involved in this, okay?"

Two little girls in T-shirts and flowered pants came up to the counter and asked for blue ice bars. Daniel stepped aside and allowed Sabhan to complete the transaction. After the Turk had pocketed the money, he came forward again and asked, "What were you doing at the Saint Saviour's monastery, Adon Sabhan?"

The Turk waved his hand around the interior of the kiosk and gave a disgusted look.

"This is not my career. I used to have a real business until the fucking government taxed me out of it. Painting and plastering. I contracted to paint the monks' infirmary and finished two walls before some Arabs underbid me and the so-called holy men kicked me off the job. All those brown-robes—fucking anti-Semites."

"What do you know about the girl?"

"Nothing. I just saw her. Scrubbing the floor."

"How long ago was this?"

"Let's see—it was before I went bust, which would be about two weeks."

Two weeks, thought Daniel. Poor guy's just gone under. Which could explain all the anger.

"Did you ever see her with anyone else, Adon Sabhan?"

"Just her mop and pail." Sabhan wiped his face with his hand, leaned in, and said conspiratorially: "Ten to one, one of the brown-robes did her in. She was raped, wasn't she?"

"Why do you say that?"

"A guy has needs, you know? It's not normal, the way they live—no sex, the only women in sight a few dried-up nuns. That's got to do something to your mind, right? Young piece like that comes around, no bra, shaking like jelly, squatting down, someone gets heated up and boom, right?"

"Did you ever observe any conflict between her and the monks?"

Sabhan shook his head.

"What about between her and anyone else?"

"Nah, I was busy painting," said Sabhan, "my face to the wall. But take my word for it, that's what happened."

Daniel asked him a few more questions, got nothing more, and examined the Turk's business license. On it was listed a Katamon Two home address. He committed it to memory and left the kiosk, heart pounding. Quickening his pace to a jog, he retraced his path but turned east onto Ben Zakai, then northeast, making his way up toward the Old City.

He'd reached the David Remez intersection, just yards from the city walls, when his beeper went off.

13

"What's he like?" Avi Cohen asked Shmeltzer.

"Who?"

They were sitting in a gray, windowless room at Headquarters, surrounded by file folders and sheaves of computer printout. The room was freezing and Cohen's arms were studded with goose bumps. When he'd asked Shmeltzer about it, the old guy had shrugged and said, "The polygraph officer next door, he likes it that way." As if that explained it.

"Sharavi," said Cohen, opening a missing-kid file. He gazed at the picture and put it atop the growing mountain of rejects. Donkey work—a cleaning woman could do it.

"What do you mean, what's he like?"

Shmeltzer's tone was sharp and Cohen thought: Touchy bastards, all of them in this section.

"As a boss," he clarified.

"Why do you ask?"

"Just curious. Forget I asked."

"Curious, eh? You generally a curious fellow?"

"Sometimes." Cohen smiled. "It's supposed to be a good quality in a detective."

Shmeltzer shook his head, lowered his eyes, and ran his index finger down a column of names. Sex offenders, hundreds of them.

They'd been working together for two hours, collating, sorting, and for two hours the old guy had worked without complaining. Hunched over the list, making subfiles, cross-referencing, checking for aliases or duplicates. Not much of a challenge for a mefakeah, thought Cohen, but it didn't seem to bother him. Probably a burnout, liked playing it safe.

His own assignment was even more tedious: going through more than 2,000 missing-kid files and matching them up with the photo of the cutting victim. Only 1,633 were open cases, the computer officer had assured him. *Only.* But someone had mistakenly left more than 400 solved ones mixed in.

He'd made a remark about clerical incompetence to Shmeltzer, who replied, "Don't gripe. You never know where your next lead will come from. She could be one who'd been found, then ran away again—wouldn't hurt to look at all the closed ones." Great.

"He's a good boss," said Shmeltzer. "You hear any different?"

"No." Cohen came across a photo of a girl from Romema who resembled the dead girl. Not exactly, but close enough to put aside.

"Just curious, eh?"

"Right."

"Listen," said the old man, "you're going to hear stuff—that he made it because of *protekzia* or because he's a Yemenite. Forget all that crap. The *protekzia* may have gotten him started but"—he smiled meaningfully—"nothing wrong with connections, is there, son?"

Cohen blushed furiously.

"And as far as the Yemenite stuff goes, they may very well have been looking for a token blackie, but by itself that wouldn't have done the trick, understand?"

Cohen nodded, flipped the pages of a file.

"He got to where he is because he does his job and does it well. Which is something, Mr. Curious, that you might consider for yourself."

14

Daoud looked terrible. One glance told Daniel that he'd been up all night. His tan suit was limp and dirt-streaked, his white shirt grayed by sweat. Coppery stubble barbed his face and made his wispy mustache seem even more indistinct. His hair was greasy and disordered, furrowed with finger-tracks, his eyes swollen and bloodshot. Only the hint of a smile—the faintest upturning of lips—which he struggled manfully to conceal—suggested that the morning had been other than disastrous.

"Her name is Fatma Rashmawi," he said. "The family lives up there, in the house with the arched window. Father, two wives, three sons, four daughters, two daughters-in-law, assorted grandchildren. The men are all masons. Two of the sons left for work at seven. The father stays home—injured."

"The pools," said Daniel. "Your hunch was right."

"Yes," said Daoud.

They stood near the top of Silwan, concealed in a grove of olive trees. The residence Daoud indicated was of intermediate size, sitting at the edge of a dry white bluff, set apart from its neighbors. A plain house, ascetic even, the masonry arch above the front window the sole decorative detail.

"How did you find them?"

"An idiot helped me. Deaf kid name of Nasif, lives down there, with a widowed mother. I came across him yesterday and he seemed to recognize the picture, kept calling her a bad girl, but he was too stupid for me to believe it meant anything. Then the mother came out, showed no sign of recognition, and claimed the boy was talking nonsense. So I left and went to the Old City, did a little work in the Muslim Quarter. But it kept bothering me—I couldn't shake the feeling that I'd seen the girl at the pools. So I came back this morning and leaned on her for a while and finally she told me. After pleading with me not to let on that she'd talked—apparently the Rashmawis are a hotheaded bunch, old-fashioned. Father's the king; the kids stay under his thumb even after they marry. Fatma was the youngest and somewhat of a rebel—pop music, an eye for the boys. There were quarrels, the father and brothers beat her, and she ran away or was kicked out about two months ago—at least that's what Mrs. Nasif says. According to her, no one's seen Fatma since then and she claims no one has any idea where she went. But she may be lying, still holding back. She was frightened—the message between the lines was that the Rashmawis were capable of doing violence to the girl or anyone else who broke their rules."

Families, thought Daniel. The same old story? He found it hard to reconcile what had been done to Fatma Rashmawi with a family squabble. Still, the case was starting to take form. Names, places, the signposts of reality.

"I have an idea where she went," he said, and told Daoud the Turk's story about Saint Saviour's.

"Yes, that would make sense," said Daoud, green eyes sparkling from beneath thickened lids.

"You did excellent work," said Daniel. "Absolutely first-rate."

"Just following procedure," Daoud insisted, but he stood up straight, threw back his shoulders with pride.

A cock crowed and a warm breeze rustled the leaves of the olive trees. The ground was soft with fallen olives, the air marinated with the salt smell of rotting fruit.

Daniel looked up at the Rashmawi house.

"We'll go together and talk to them," he said. "But not right now. Drive over to Kishle and phone the others. Shmeltzer should be at French Hill, in Records. Tell him what we've learned and have him do background checks on the Rashmawis and any of their kin. Find out, also, if a file's ever been opened on Fatma. The Chinaman will probably be on beeper—have him come here and meet me. You go home, wash up, eat something, and come back at two. We'll proceed from there."

"Yes, sir," said Daoud, writing it all down.

The front door of the Rashmawi house opened and a young pregnant woman came out, carrying a rolled-up rug. A swarm of small children tumbled out behind her. The woman unfurled the rug, held it with one hand, and began beating it with a stick. The children danced around her as if she were a maypole, squealing with delight as they tried to grab hold of dissolving dust swirls.

"Anything else, Pakad?" asked Daoud.

"Nothing until two. Go home, spend some time with your family."

Daniel waited in the grove for the Chinaman to arrive, observing the comings and goings of the village, keeping one eye fixed upon the Rashmawi house. At twelve-thirty, a woman—not the rug beater—came out and purchased eggplant and tomatoes from a peddler who'd managed to wheel his cart to the upper level. By twelve thirty-nine she was back in the house. The kids ran in and out of the door, teasing and chasing each other. Other than that, no activity.

The case seemed to be drawing him back in time. This morning in the Katamonim, and now, Silwan.

He scanned the village, wondered which of the houses was the one where his great-grandfather—the man whose name he bore—had grown up. Strange, he'd heard so many stories about the old days but had never bothered to check.

Dinner table stories, recited like a liturgy. Of how hundreds of the Jews of San'a had fled the Yemenite capital, escaping from rising levels of Muslim persecution. Crossing the mountains and setting out in search of the Holy Land. Of how the first Daniel Sharavi had been one of them, arriving in Jerusalem in the summer of 1881, an undernourished ten-year-old in the company of his parents. Of how the Jews of San'a hadn't been welcomed with open arms.

The other residents of Jewish Jerusalem—the Sephardim and Ashkenazim—hadn't known what to make of these small, brown, kinky-haired people who stood at their doorsteps, near-naked and penniless but smiling. Speaking Hebrew with a strange accent and claiming to be Jews who had braved storm and pestilence, climbing mountains on foot, walking through the desert from Arabia, subsisting on seeds and honey.

Jerusalem, in those days, hadn't spread beyond the Old City walls—two square kilometers stuffed with ten thousand people, a third of them Jewish, almost all of them poor, living on donations from the Diaspora. Sanitation was primitive, raw sewage flowing through the streets, the cisterns polluted, epidemics of cholera and typhoid a way of life. The last thing the residents of the Jewish Quarter needed was a band of pretenders leeching off their beleaguered communities.

After much head scratching, a test of Jewishness had been

devised, the leaders of the Yemenites whisked into synagogue and tested on the finer points of Scripture by Sephardic and Ashkenazic rabbis.

Great-great-grandfather Sa'adia, so the story went, had been the first to be quizzed. A goldsmith and teacher, a learned man with a fine, pure nature. When called upon, he'd begun reciting rapidly from the Book of Genesis, letter-perfect, without pause. Questions regarding the most obscure tractates of Talmud elicited an identical response—text and commentaries recited fluently, the finer points of jurisprudence explained concisely and clearly.

The rabbis excused Sa'adia and called upon another man, who performed similarly. As did the next man, and the next. Yemenite after Yemenite knew the Torah by heart. When questioned about this, the little brown people explained that books were scarce in San'a, forcing everyone to use his head. In many cases a single volume was shared around the table, with one person learning to read conventionally, another upside down, still others from the left or right side. Happily, they demonstrated those talents, and the rabbis observed, astonished. The issue of Jewishness was laid to rest, the new arrivals allowed to share the poverty of their brethren.

In the beginning they settled just outside the walls, in the spot called Silwan, near the Siloam Pool, working as masons and laborers, living in tents while they built stone houses, moving, over the years, back into the Old City, into the Jewish Quarter the Arabs called *Al Sion,* in order to be nearer to the Wailing Place, a stone's throw from the Tomb of David.

It was there, within the walls, that Daniel's grandfather and father had been born, and from where he himself had been carried off as an infant in '48, rescued by strangers, squalling in terror under the thunder of gunfire.

My origins, he thought, gazing out at the village. But he felt no pangs of nostalgia, saw only the origins of a dead girl.

15

Warm beer, thought the Chinaman, quickening his pace. He'd been prepared to report his information on the girl, thought he'd done a pretty good job for one night out, until the Arab had called and told him of the ID. Sharp guy, Daoud. Still, the boyfriend angle was a contribution.

The village had come alive, shutters spreading, doors nudged open, a buzz of mutters and whispers trailing the detectives' footsteps. The corneal glint of the curious sparkled from grated windows, receding into the shadows at the hint of eye contact with the strangers.

"Probably looks like a raid to them," said the Chinaman.

Neither Daniel nor Daoud responded. Both were concentrating on walking quickly enough to keep up with the big man's stride.

They reached the Rashmawi house and climbed the front steps. The arched window was open but covered with a bright floral drape. From inside came a drone of Arabic music and the aroma of coffee laced with cardamom.

Daniel knocked on the door. There was no immediate answer and he knocked again, louder. At once the volume of the music lowered and was overriden by conversation. The sound of shuffling feet grew louder and the door opened. A young man stood in the doorway—eighteen or nineteen, slender, and round-faced with a prematurely receding hairline. A pair of heavy tortoise-shell eyeglasses dominated a mild face pitted with acne scars. He wore a cheap gray shirt, beltless gray trousers a size too large, and black bedroom slippers. Looking over his shoulder, he came out to the top step, closed the door behind him, and stared at each of them, dark eyes swimming behind thick lenses.

"Yes?" His voice was soft, tentative.

"Good afternoon," said Daniel, in Arabic. "I'm Chief Inspector Sharavi of the Police Department. This is Subinspector Lee and this is Sergeant Daoud. Your name, please?"

"Rashmawi, Anwar."

"What's your relationship to Muhamid Rashmawi?"

"He's my father. What's this about, sir?" There was a curious lack of surprise in the question. The flat, sad nuance of anticipated misfortune.

"We'd like to come in and talk with your father."

"He's not a well man, sir."

Daniel took out the photo of Fatma and showed it to him. The young man stared at it, lips trembling, eyes blinking rapidly. For a moment it seemed as if he would break into tears. Then he wiped his face clean of expression, held the door open for them, and said, "Come in, sirs."

They entered a long, narrow, low-ceilinged room, freshly whitewashed and surprisingly cool, its stone floor covered by frayed, overlapping Oriental rugs and mattresses draped with embroidered coverlets. A rug hung also from the rear wall, next to a row of coat hooks and a framed photograph of Gamal Abdel Nasser. All the other walls were bare.

Directly under Nasser's portrait was a portable television on an aluminum stand. The coffee aroma came from a small cooking area to the left: wood stove, hot plate, homemade shelves bearing pots and utensils. A battered iron saucepan sat on the stove, sizzling over a low fire. The stove's exhaust conduit rose and pierced the ceiling. Across the room, to the right, was a flimsy-looking wooden door and from behind it came female voices, the cries and laughter of children.

An old man sat on a mattress in the center of the room, thin, sun-baked, and wrinkled as an old shopping bag. His bare head was bald and conspicuously pale, his mustache a grizzled rectangle of white filling the space between nose and upper lip. He wore a pale-gray *jallabiyah* striped faintly with darker gray. An unfurled *kaffiyah* headdress and coil lay in his lap. To his right was a small carved table upon which sat an engraved brass pitcher and matching demitasse cup, a pack of Time cigarettes, and a string of worry beads. His left hand held a red plastic transistor radio. One of his feet was curled under him; the other extended straight out and was wrapped in bandages. Next to the ankle was an assortment of vials and ointments in squeeze-tubes. Just behind the medicines, another carved table held a well-foxed copy of the Quran within arm's reach.

He stared downward, as if studying the pattern of the rug, a cigarette dangling from his lips. The sound of the detectives' entry caused him to look up, squinting. Expressionless. It was then that Daniel noticed the resemblance to Fatma—the same synchrony of features, the handsome crispness lacking in the brother.

"Father," said Anwar, "these men are with the police."

Rashmawi gave his son a sharp look and the youth rushed over and raised him to tottering feet. Once upright, the old man gave a small head bow and said, in a low, rasping voice, *"Marhaba."* Welcome. *"Ahlan Wa Sahlan."* You've found in our home a wide valley.

The hospitality ritual. Daniel looked at the hard, weathered face, like a carved mask with its hollowed cheeks and deep eye sockets, unsure if the man behind it was victim or suspect.

"Ahlan Bek," he replied. The same welcome will be extended to you when you visit my home.

"Sit, please," said Rashmawi, and he allowed his son to lower him.

The detectives settled in a semicircle. The old man barked an order and Anwar crossed the room, opened the wooden door, and spoke into the opening. Two young women hurried out, dressed in dark robes, their hair covered, their feet bare. Averting their faces, they padded quickly to the cooking area and began a rapid ballet of pouring, scooping, and filling. Within moments the men were presented with demitasses of sweet, muddy coffee, platters laden with dishes of olives, almonds, sunflower seeds, and dried fruit.

Rashmawi waved his hand and the women danced away, disappearing into the room on the right. Another wave sent Anwar back with them. Almost immediately, an insectile buzz of conversation filtered through the thin wood of the door.

"Cigarette," said Rashmawi, holding out his pack. The Chinaman and Daoud accepted and lit up.

"You, sir?"

Daniel shook his head and said, "Thank you for your kind offer, but today is my Sabbath and I don't handle fire."

The old man looked at him, saw the *kipah* on his head, and nodded. He raised a dish of dried figs from the platter and waited until Daniel was chewing enthusiastically before settling back on the mattress.

"To what do I owe the honor of this visit?"

"We're here to talk about your daughter, sir," said Daniel.

"I have three daughters," said the old man casually. "Three sons as well, and many fat grandchildren."

One daughter less than Daoud had mentioned.

"Your daughter Fatma, sir."

Rashmawi's face went blank, the dry, well-formed features settling into paralytic stillness.

Daniel put down his demitasse, took out the picture, and showed it to Rashmawi, who ignored it.

"She was found yesterday," said Daniel, watching the old man's reaction.

Rashmawi made a tent of his fingers. Picked up his demitasse but put it down without drinking.

"I have three daughters," he said. "Sahar, Hadiya, and Salway. None are idle. Three sons as well."

The buzz behind the door had grown louder, solidifying into conversation—urgent, frightened female chatter. A tentative male response. Then a low moan rising steadily in pitch.

"How long has she been missing?" Daniel asked.

Rashmawi dragged deeply on his cigarette, drank coffee, and cracked an almond with long, knobby fingers. Removing the nut, he put it in his mouth and chewed slowly.

The moan behind the door escalated to a high-pitched wail.

"Silence!" thundered the old man and the wail dissipated into an artificial hush, broken once by a muffled sob.

Daniel showed him the photo again, caught his eye, and for a moment thought he saw something—pain, fear—pass across the weathered face. But whatever it was vanished instantaneously and Rashmawi folded his arms across his chest and stared past the detectives, as silent and unmoving as a stone idol.

"Sir," said Daniel, "it pains me to be the one to tell you this, but Fatma is dead."

Nothing.

Smoke from three untouched cigarettes ribboned lazily toward the ceiling.

"She was murdered, sir. Violently."

A long, maddening silence, every creak and exhalation, thunderous. Then:

"I have three daughters. Sahar, Hadiya, and Salway. None are idle. Three sons as well. Many grandchildren."

The Chinaman swore softly and cleared his throat. "It was a very brutal murder. Multiple stab wounds."

"We want to find the person who did it," said Daniel.

"To avenge her," added the Chinaman.

The wrong thing to say, thought Daniel. Revenge was the prerogative of the family. To suggest that an outsider could accomplish it was at best ignorant, at worst an insult. He looked at the Chinaman and gave his head a barely perceptible shake.

The big man shrugged and started gazing around the room, restless and eager for action.

Rashmawi was smiling strangely. He'd placed his hands on his knees and had started to sway, as if in a trance.

"Any information you can provide is essential, sir," said Daniel. "About anyone who could have done this to Fatma. Why anyone would have wanted to hurt her."

Anyone other than you or your sons . . .

"A bad influence, perhaps," said Daoud. "Someone who tried to corrupt her."

That, too, seemed the wrong thing to say, for the old man's face compressed with anger and his hands began to shake. He pushed down harder on his knees to avoid the appearance of feebleness. Clamped his eyes shut and continued swaying, further out of reach than ever.

"Mr. Rashmawi," said Daniel, more forcefully. "No young girl should have to come to such an end."

Rashmawi opened his eyes and Daniel examined them closely. Irises the color of the coffee in his demitasse, the whites soiled an unhealthy shade of gray. If eyes were the mirror of the soul, these mirrors reflected a weary soul beset by illness, fatigue, the pain of remembrance. Or was it guilt he was seeing, Daniel wondered—segregated from the heart by a fortress of silence?

Eloquent eyes. But you couldn't work a case based on unspoken eloquence.

"Tell us what you know, sir," said Daniel, fighting back impatience. "What she was wearing when she left, her jewelry."

Rashmawi's shoulders rounded and his head drooped, as if suddenly too heavy for his neck to support. He covered his face with his hands, swayed some more, then raised himself up, fueled by defiance.

"I have three daughters," he said. *"Three."*

"Hard-assed old bastard," said the Chinaman. "Didn't so much as look at the picture. Our best bet is to talk to the women."

They stood by the side of the dirt pathway, several yards from the house. The wailing had resumed and was audible at that distance.

"We could try," said Daniel, "but it would be a violation of their family structure."

"To hell with family structure. One of them may have sliced her, Dani."

"The point is, Yossi, that the family structure makes it impossible for us to get information. Without the father's permission, none of them is going to talk to us."

The big man spat in the dirt, pounded his fist into his hand.

"Then haul them in! A few hours in a cell and we'll see about their goddamned family structure."

"That's your plan, is it? Arrest the bereaved."

The Chinaman started to say something, then sighed and smiled sheepishly.

"Okay, okay, I'm talking shit. It's just that it's weird. The guy's daughter is butchered and he's as cold as ice, making like she never existed." He turned to Daoud: "That culturally normal?"

Daoud hesitated.

"Is it?" pressed the Chinaman.

"To some extent."

"Meaning?"

"To the Muslims, virginity is everything," said Daoud. "If the father thought Fatma lost hers—even if he just suspected it—he might very well expel her from the family. Excommunicate her. It would be as if she didn't exist."

"Killing her would accomplish the same thing," said the Chinaman.

"I don't see this as a family affair," said Daniel. "That old man was in pain. And after seeing the way they live, the factors I mentioned yesterday seem stronger—the Rashmawis are old-school, by the book. Had they chosen to execute a daughter, it would have taken place in the village—a swift killing by one of the brothers, semi-publicly in order to show that the family honor had been restored. Removing the body and dumping it for outsiders to find would be unthinkable. So would mutilating her."

"You're assuming," said the Chinaman, "that culture overrides craziness. If that was the case, they would have replaced us long ago with anthropologists."

The door to the Rashmawi house opened and Anwar came out, wiping his glasses. He put them back on, saw them, and went hastily inside.

"Now, that's a strange one," said the Chinaman. "Home when his brothers are working. Father banishes him to be with the women."

"I agree," said Daniel. "You'd expect him to be allowed to remain in the background—if for no other reason than to wait on the old man. Sending him in with the women—it's as if he's being punished for something. Any ideas about that, Elias?"

Daoud shook his head.

"A punitive family," Daniel reflected out loud.

"He wasn't surprised when you showed him the picture," said the Chinaman. "He knew something had happened to Fatma. Why don't we ask him about the earrings?"

"We will, but first let's watch him for a while. And keep our ears open. Both of you, circulate among the villagers and try to learn more about the family. See if you can find out whether Fatma ran away or was banished. And the specific nature of her rebellion. Find out what she was wearing, if anyone can describe the earrings. What about the Nasif woman, Elias? Do you think she's still holding back?"

"Maybe. But she's in a difficult position—a widow, socially vulnerable. Let me see what I can get from others before I lean on her again."

"All right, but keep her in mind. If we need to, we can arrange an interview away from prying eyes—a shopping trip, something like that."

A loud cry came from the Rashmawi house. Daniel looked at the unadorned building, noticed the empty land surrounding it.

"No neighbors," he said. "They keep to themselves. That kind of isolation breeds gossip. See if you can tap into any of it. Call

Shmeltzer and find out if any family member has popped up in a file. Keep an eye out, also, for the other two brothers. Far as we know they're on a job and should be getting back before sundown. Get to them before they reach home. If Anwar leaves the house, have a chat with him too. Be persistent but respectful—don't lean too heavily on anyone. Until we know any different, everyone's a potential source of help. Good luck, and if you need me, I'll be at Saint Saviour's."

16

Daniel walked west along the southern perimeter of the Old City, passing worshippers of three faiths, locals, tourists, hikers, and hangers-on, until he reached the northwest corner and entered the Christian Quarter through the New Gate.

The Saint Saviour's compound dominated the mouth of the quarter, with its high walls and green-tiled steeple. Double metal doors decorated with Christian symbols marked the service entry on Bab el Jadid Road; the arch above the door was filled by a blood-red crucifix; below the cross strong black letters proclaimed: TERRA SANCTA. Above the doors the steeple topped a four-sided pastry-white tower, exquisitely molded, ringed doubly with iron balconies and set with marble-faced clocks on all sides. As Daniel entered, the bells of the monastery rang out the quarter hour.

The courtyard within was modest and quiet. Inset into one of the inner walls was a nook housing a plaster figurine of a praying Madonna against a sky-blue background speckled with gold stars. Here and there were small plaques, repetitions of the *Terra Sancta* designation. Otherwise the place could have been a parking lot, the back door of any restaurant, with its trash bags and garages, functional metal stairs, pickup trucks, and jumble of overhead power lines. A far cry from the visitor's center on St. Francis Street, but Daniel knew that the plain-faced buildings housed a treasure trove: Travertine marble walls set off by contrasting columns of inlaid granite, statuary, murals, gold altars and candlesticks, a fortune in gold relics. The Christians made a grand show of worship.

A trio of young Franciscan monks exited the compound and crossed his path, brown-robed and white-belted, their lowered hoods exposing pale, introspective faces. He asked them, in Hebrew, where Father Bernardo could be found, and when they looked perplexed, thought: *new arrivals,* and repeated the question in English.

"Infirmary," said the tallest of the three, a blue-chinned youth with hot dark eyes and the cautious demeanor of a diplomat. From the sound of his accent, a Spaniard or Portuguese.

"Is he ill?" asked Daniel, aware now of his own accent. A Babel of a conversation . . .

"No," said the monk. "He is not. He is . . . caring for those who are the ill." He paused, spoke to his comrades in Spanish, then turned back to Daniel. "I take you to him."

The infirmary was a bright, clean room smelling of fresh paint and containing a dozen narrow iron beds, half of them occupied by inert old men. Large wood-framed windows afforded a view of Old City rooftops: clay domes, centuries old, crowned by TV antennas—the steeples of a new religion. The windows were cranked wide open and from the alleys below came a clucking of pigeons.

Daniel waited by the doorway and watched Father Bernardo tend to an ancient monk. Only the monk's head was visible above the covers, the skull hairless and veined with blue, the face sunken, near-translucent, the body so withered it was barely discernible beneath the sheets. On the nightstand next to the bed were a set of false teeth in a glass and a large, leather-bound Bible. On the wall above the headboard Jesus writhed on a polished metal crucifix.

Father Bernardo bent at the waist, wet a towel with water, and used it to moisten the monk's lips. Talking softly, he rearranged the pillows so that the monk could recline more comfortably. The monk's eyes closed, and Bernardo watched him sleep for several minutes before turning and noticing the detective. Smiling, he walked forward, bouncing silently on sandaled feet, the crucifix around his neck swinging in counterpoint.

"Pakad Sharavi," he said in Hebrew, and smiled. "It's been a long time."

Bernardo's waist had thickened since they'd last met. Otherwise he looked the same. The fleshy pink face of a prosperous Tuscan merchant, inquisitive gray eyes, large, rosy, shell-like ears. Snowy puffs of white hair covered a strong, broad head, the snowfall repeating itself below—in eyebrows, mustache, and Vandyke beard.

"Two years," said Daniel. "Two Easters."

"Two Passovers," Bernardo said with a smile, ushering him out of the infirmary into a dim, quiet corridor. "You're in Major Crimes now—I read about you. How have you been?"

"Very well. And you, Father?"

The priest patted his paunch and smiled. "A little too well, I'm afraid. What brings you here on a Shabbat?"

"This girl," said Daniel, showing him the photo. "I've been told she worked here."

Bernardo took the picture and examined it.

"This is little Fatma! What's happened to her!"

"I'm sorry, I can't discuss that, Father," said Daniel. But the priest heard the unspoken message and his thick fingers closed around the crucifix.

"Oh, no, Daniel."

"When's the last time you saw her, Father?" asked Daniel gently.

The fingers left the crucifix, floated upward, and began twisting white strands of beard.

"Not long ago, at all—last Wednesday afternoon. She didn't show up for breakfast Thursday morning and that's the last we saw of her."

A day and a half before the body had been found.

"When did you hire her?"

"We didn't, Daniel. One night, about three weeks ago, Brother Roselli found her crying, sitting in the gutter just inside the New Gate, on Bab el Jadid Road. It must have been in the early morning hours, actually, because he'd attended midnight mass at the Chapel of the Flagellation and was returning home. She was unwashed, hungry, generally knocked about, and sobbing. We took her in and fed her, let her sleep in an empty room at the hospice. The next morning she was up early, before sunrise, —scrubbing the floors, insisting that she wanted to earn her keep."

Bernardo paused, looking uncomfortable.

"It's not our practice to bring in children, Daniel, but she seemed like such a sad little thing that we allowed her to stay, temporarily, taking meals and doing little jobs so that she wouldn't feel like a beggar. We wanted to contact her family but any mention of it terrified her—she'd break out into heart-rending sobs and beg us not to. Perhaps some of it was adolescent drama, but I'm certain that a good deal of it was real. She looked like a wounded animal and we were afraid she'd run away and end up in some Godless place. But we knew she couldn't stay with us indefinitely and Brother Roselli and I had discussed transferring her to the Franciscan Sisters' Convent." The priest shook his head. "She left before we had a chance to bring it up."

"Did she tell you why she was afraid of her family?"

"She said nothing to me, but my feeling was that some kind of abuse had taken place. If she told anyone, it would have been Brother Roselli. However, he never mentioned anything to me."

"So she stayed with you a total of two and a half weeks."

"Yes."

"Did you ever see her with anyone else, Father?"

"No, but as I said, my contact with her was minimal, other than to say hello in the hallway, or suggest that she take a break—she was a hard worker, ready to scour and scrub all day."

"What was she wearing the day before she left, Father?"

Bernardo laced his fingers over his paunch and thought.

"Some sort of dress. I really don't know."

"Did she wear any jewelry?"

"Such a poor child? I wouldn't think so."

"Earrings, perhaps?"

"Perhaps—I'm not sure. Sorry, Daniel. I'm not good at noticing that kind of thing."

"Is there anything else you can tell me, Father? Anything that could help me understand what happened to her?"

"Nothing, Daniel. She passed through and was gone."

"Brother Roselli—have I met him?"

"No. He's new, been with us for six months."

"I'd like to speak to him. Do you know where he is?"

"Up on the roof, communicating with his cucumbers."

They climbed a stone stairway, Daniel sprinting, light-footed and energetic despite the fact that he hadn't had a real meal all day. When he noticed that Bernardo was huffing and pausing to catch his breath, he slowed his pace until it matched that of the priest.

A door at the top of the stairs opened to a flat area on the northeast quadrant of the monastery roof. Below was an Old City quilt of houses, churches, and vest-pocket courtyards. Just beyond the melange rose the plateau of Moriah, where Abraham had bound Isaac and where two Jewish temples had been built and destroyed, now called the Haram esh-Sharif and subjugated by the Mosque of the Rock.

Daniel looked out past the mosque's gold-leaf dome, toward the eastern city walls. From up here everything looked primitive, so vulnerable, and he was stabbed by a cruel, fleeting memory—of passing under those walls, through the Dung Gate. A walk of death, maddeningly endless—though the shock from his wounds provided a kind of sedation—as those in front of him and to his back fell under sniper fire, crumpling soundlessly, corsages of scarlet bursting through the olive-drab of battle-rancid uniforms. Now, tourists strolled along the ramparts, carefree, enjoying the view, the freedom. . . .

He and Bernardo walked toward the corner of the roof, where wine casks had been filled with planter's soil and set down in a long row within the inner angle of the rim. Some were empty; from others the first sprouts of summer vegetables nudged their way upward through the dirt: cucumbers, tomatoes, eggplant, beans, marrow. A monk held a large tin watering can and sprinkled one of the most productive casks, a large-leafed cucumber plant coiled around a stake, already abloom with yellow flowers and heavy with fuzzy fingers of infant vegetable.

Bernardo called out a greeting and the monk turned. He was in his forties, tan and freckled, with a tense, foxlike face, pale-brown eyes, thin pinkish hair, and a red beard cropped short and carelessly trimmed. When he saw Bernardo he put down the watering can and assumed a position of deference, head slightly lowered, hands clasped in front of him. Daniel's presence didn't seem to register.

Bernardo introduced them in English, and when Roselli said "Good afternoon, Chief Inspector," it was with an American accent. Unusual—most of the Franciscans came from Europe.

Roselli listened as Bernardo summarized his conversation with Daniel. The priest ended with: "The chief inspector isn't at liberty to say what's happened to her, but I'm afraid we can assume the worst, Joseph."

Roselli said nothing, but his head dipped a little lower and he turned away. Daniel heard a sharp intake of breath, then nothing.

"My son," said Bernardo, and placed a hand on Roselli's shoulder.

"Thank you, Father. I'm all right."

The Franciscans stood in silence for a moment and Daniel found himself reading the wooden tags: CORNICHON DE BOURBON, BIG GIRL HYBRID, AQUADULCE CLAUDIA (WHITE SEEDED), TRUE GHERKIN . . .

Bernardo whispered something to Roselli in what sounded like Latin, patted his shoulder again, and said to Daniel: "The two of you speak. I've chores to attend to. If there's anything else you need, Daniel, I'll be across the way, at the College."

Daniel thanked him and Bernardo shuffled off.

Alone with Roselli, Daniel smiled at the monk, who responded by looking down at his hands, then at the watering can.

"Feel free to continue watering," Daniel told him. "We can talk while you work."

"No, that's all right. What do you need to know?"

"Tell me about the first time you saw Fatma—the night you took her in."

"They're not the same, Inspector," said Roselli quietly, as if admitting a transgression. His eyes looked everywhere but at Daniel.

"Oh?"

"The first time I saw her was three or four days before we took her in. On the Via Dolorosa, near the Sixth Station of the Cross."

"Near the Greek Chapel?"

"Just past it."

"What was she doing there?"

"Nothing. Which was why I noticed her. The tourists were milling around, along with their guides, but she was off to the side, not trying to beg or sell anything—simply standing there. I thought it was unusual for an Arab girl of that age to be out by herself." Roselli hid the lower part of his face behind his hand. It seemed a defensive gesture, almost guilty.

"Was she soliciting for prostitution?"

Roselli looked pained. "I wouldn't know."

"Do you remember anything else about her?"

"No, it . . . I was on a . . . meditative walk, Inspector. Father Bernardo has instructed me to walk regularly, in order to cut myself off from external stimuli, to get closer to my . . . spiritual core. But my attention wandered and I saw her."

Another confession.

Roselli stopped talking, eyed the casks, and said, "Some of these are getting wilted. I think I *will* water." Lifting the watering can, he began walking along the row, probing, sprinkling.

The Catholics, thought Daniel, tagging along. Always baring their souls. The result, he supposed, of living totally in the head—faith is everything, thoughts equivalent to actions. Peek at a pretty girl and it's as bad as if you slept with her. Which could make for plenty of sleepless nights. He looked at Roselli's profile, as grim and humorless as that of a cave-dwelling prophet. A prophet of doom, perhaps? Tormented by his own fallibility?

Or did the torment result from something more serious than lust?

"Did the two of you talk, Brother Roselli?"

"No," came the too-quick answer. Roselli pinched off a brown tomato leaf, turned over several others, searching for parasites. "She seemed to be staring at me—I may have been staring myself. She looked disheveled and I wondered what had caused a young girl to end up like that. It's an occupational hazard, wondering about misfortune. I was once a social worker."

A zealous one, no doubt.

"Then what?"

Roselli looked puzzled.

"What did you do after you exchanged stares, Brother Roselli?"

"I returned to Saint Saviour's."

"And the next time you saw her was when?"

"As I said, three or four days later. I was returning from late Mass, heard sobs from the Bab el Jadid side, went to take a look, and saw her sitting in the gutter, crying. I asked her what the matter was—in English. I don't speak Arabic. But she just continued to sob. I didn't know if she understood me, so I tried in Hebrew—my Hebrew's broken but it's better than my Arabic. Still no answer. Then I noticed that she looked thinner than the first time I'd seen her—it was dark, but even in the moonlight the difference was pronounced. Which made me suspect she hadn't eaten for days. I asked her if she wanted food, pantomimed eating, and she stopped crying and nodded. So I gestured for her to wait, woke up Father Bernardo, and he told me to bring her in. The next morning she was up working, and Father

Bernardo agreed to let her stay on until we found her more suitable lodgings."

"What led her to drift through the Old City?"

"I don't know," said Roselli. He stopped watering, examining the dirt beneath his fingernails, then lowered the can again.

"Did you ask her about it?"

"No. The language barrier." Roselli flushed, shielded his face with his hand again, and looked at the vegetables.

More to it than that, thought Daniel. The girl had affected him, maybe sexually, and he wasn't equipped to deal with it.

Or perhaps he'd dealt with it in an unhealthy way.

Nodding reassuringly, Daniel said, "Father Bernardo said she was frightened about having her family contacted. Do you know why?"

"I assumed there'd been some sort of abuse."

"Why's that?"

"Sociologically it made sense—an Arab girl cut off from her family like that. And she reminded me of the kids I used to counsel—nervous, a little too eager to please. Afraid to be spontaneous or step out of bounds, as if doing or saying the wrong thing would get them punished. There's a look they all have—maybe you've seen it. Weary and bruised."

Daniel remembered the girl's body. Smooth and unblemished except for the butchery.

"Where was she bruised?" he asked.

"Not literal bruises," said Roselli. "I meant it in a psychological sense. She had frightened eyes, like a wounded animal."

The same phrase Bernardo had used—Fatma had been a subject of discussion between the two Franciscans.

"How long were you a social worker?" Daniel asked.

"Seventeen years."

"In America?"

The monk nodded. "Seattle, Washington."

"Puget Sound," said Daniel.

"You've been there?" Roselli was surprised.

Daniel smiled, shook his head.

"My wife's an artist. She did a painting last summer, using photographs from a calendar. Puget Sound—big boats, silver water. A beautiful place."

"Plenty of ugliness," said Roselli, "if you know where to look." He extended his arm over the rim of the roof, pointed down at the jumble of alleys and courtyards. "That," he said, "is beauty. Sacred beauty. The core of civilization."

"True," said Daniel, but he thought the comment naïve, the sweetened perception of the born-again. The core, as the monk called it, had been consecrated in blood for thirty centuries. Wave after wave of pillage and massacre, all in the name of something sacred.

Roselli looked upward and Daniel followed his gaze. The blue of the sky was beginning to deepen under a slowly descending sun. A passing cloud cast platinum shadows over the Dome of the Rock. The bells of Saint Saviour's rang out again, trailed by a muezzin's call from a nearby minaret.

Daniel pulled himself away, returned to his questions.

"Do you have any idea how Fatma ended up in the Old City?"

"No. At first I thought she may have gravitated toward The Little Sisters of Charles Foucauld—they wipe the faces of the poor, and their chapel is near where I saw her. But I went there and asked and they'd never seen her."

They'd come to the last of the casks. Roselli put down the watering can and faced Daniel.

"I've been blessed, Inspector," he said, urgently. Eager to convince. "Given the chance for a new life. I try to do as much thinking and as little talking as possible. There's really nothing more I can tell you."

But even as he said it, his face seemed to weaken, as if buckling under the weight of a burdensome thought. A troubled man. Daniel wasn't ready to let go of him just yet.

"Can you think of anything that would help me, Brother Roselli? Anything that Fatma said or did that would lead me to understand her?"

The monk rubbed his hands together. Freckled hands, the knuckles soil-browned, the fingernails yellowed and cracked. He looked at the vegetables, down at the ground, then back at the vegetables.

"I'm sorry, no."

"What kind of clothes did she wear?"

"She had only one garment. A simple shift."

"What color?"

"White, I believe, with some kind of stripe."

"What color stripe?"

"I don't remember, Inspector."

"Did she wear jewelry?"

"Not that I noticed."

"Earrings?"

"There may have been earrings."

"Can you describe them?"

"No," said the monk, emphatically. "I didn't look at her that closely. I'm not even sure if she wore any."

"There are many kinds of earrings," said Daniel. "Hoops, pendants, studs."

"They could have been hoops."

"How large?"

"Small, very simple."

"What color?"

"I have no idea."

Daniel took a step closer. The monk's robe smelled of topsoil and tomato leaves.

"Is there anything else you can tell me, Brother Roselli?"

"Nothing."

"Nothing at all?" pressed Daniel, certain there was more. "I *need* to understand her."

Roselli's eye twitched. He took a deep breath and let it out.

"I saw her with young men," he said, softly, as if betraying a confidence.

"How many?"

"At least two."

"At least?"

"She went out at night. I saw her with two men. There may have been others."

"Tell me about the two you saw."

"One used to meet her there." Roselli pointed east, toward the Greek Orthodox Patriarchate, with its grape arbors and fruit trees espaliered along the walls. "Thin, with long dark hair and a mustache."

"How old?"

"Older than Fatma—perhaps nineteen or twenty."

"An Arab?"

"I assume so. They talked to each other and all Fatma spoke was Arabic."

"Did they do anything other than talk?"

Roselli reddened.

"There was some . . . kissing. When it got dark, they'd go off together."

"Where to?"

"Toward the center of the Old City."

"Did you see where?"

The monk looked out at the city, extended his hands palms-up, in a gesture of helplessness.

"It's a labyrinth, Inspector. They stepped into the shadows and were gone."

"How many of these meetings did you witness?"

The word *witness* made the monk wince, as if it reminded him that he'd been spying.

"Three or four."

"During what time of day did the meetings occur?"

"I was up here, watering, so it had to be close to sunset."

"And when it got dark, they left together."

"Yes."

"Walking east."

"Yes. I really didn't watch them that closely."

"What else can you tell me about the man with the long hair?"

"Fatma seemed to like him."

"Like him?"

"She smiled when she was with him."

"What about his clothing?"

"He looked poor."

"Ragged?"

"No, just poor. I can't say exactly why I formed that impression."

"All right," said Daniel. "What about the other one?"

"Him I saw once, a few days before she left. This was at night, the same circumstances as the time we took her in. I was returning from late Mass, heard voices—crying—from the Bab el Jadid side of the monastery, took a look, and saw her sitting, talking to this fellow. He was standing over her and I could see he was short—maybe five foot five or six. With big glasses."

"How old?"

"It was hard to tell in the dark. I saw the light reflect off his head, so he must have been bald. But I don't think he was old."

"Why's that?"

"His voice—it sounded boyish. And the way he stood—his posture seemed like that of a young man." Roselli paused. "These are just impressions, Inspector. I couldn't swear to any of them."

Impressions that added up to a perfect description of Anwar Rashmawi.

"Were they doing anything other than talking?" Daniel asked.

"No. If any . . . romance had ever existed between them, it was long over. He was talking very quickly—sounded angry, as if he were scolding her."

"How did Fatma respond to the scolding?"

"She cried."

"Did she say anything at all?"

"Maybe a few words. He was doing most of the talking. He seemed to be in charge—but that's part of their culture, isn't it?"

"What happened after he was through scolding her?"

"He walked away in a huff and she sat there crying. I thought of approaching her, decided against it, and went into the monastery. She was up working the next morning, so she must have come in. A few days later she was gone."

"Following this meeting, what was her mood like?"

"I have no idea."

"Did she look frightened? Worried? Sad?"

Roselli blushed again, this time more deeply.

"I never looked that closely, Inspector."

"Your impression, then."

"I *have* no impression, Inspector. Her moods were none of my business."

"Have you ever been in her room?"

"No. Never."

"Did you see anything indicating she used drugs?"

"Of course not."

"You seem very sure of that."

"No, I'm . . . she was young. A very simple little girl."

Too pat a conclusion for a former social worker, thought Daniel. He asked the monk: "The day before she left she was wearing the striped white shift?"

"Yes," said Roselli, annoyed. "I told you she only had the one."

"And the earrings."

"If there were earrings."

"If," agreed Daniel. "Is there anything else you wish to tell me?"

"Nothing," said Roselli, folding his arms across his chest. He was sweating heavily, gripping one hand with the other.

"Thank you, then. You've been very helpful."

"Have I?" asked Roselli, looking perplexed. As if trying to decide whether he'd been virtuous or sinful.

An interesting man, thought Daniel, leaving the monastery. Jumpy and troubled and something else—immature.

When Father Bernardo had spoken about Fatma, there had been a clearly paternal flavor to his concerns. But Roselli's responses—his emotional level—had been different. As if he and the girl were on a peer level.

Daniel stopped on Bab el Jadid Road, near the spot where Roselli had twice seen Fatma. He tried to put his impressions of the monk into focus—something was cooking inside the man. Anger? Hurt? The pain of jealousy—that was it. Roselli had spoken of Fatma being wounded, but he seemed wounded himself. A spurned lover. Jealous of the young men she met at night.

He wanted to know more about the redheaded monk. About why Joseph Roselli, social worker from Seattle, Washington, had turned into a brown-robed roof-gardener unable to keep his mind on sacred meditation. And his thoughts off a fifteen-year-old girl.

He'd put one of the men—Daoud—on a loose surveillance of the monk, run a background check himself.

There were other matters to be dealt with as well. Who was Fatma's long-haired boyfriend and where did she go with him? And what of Anwar the Punished, who knew where his sister had found sanctuary. And had scolded her shortly before she disappeared.

17

Words, thought Avi Cohen. A flood of words, clogging him, choking him, making his head reel. Pure hell. And on Saturday night, no less. His heavy date: the goddamn files.

Looking at the missing-kid pictures had been tedious but tolerable—pictures were okay. Then Shmeltzer had gotten the phone call and announced that it had all been for nothing. That his job had changed; there was a new assignment: Go back over the same two thousand files and search for a name—a hell of a lot more complicated than it sounded, because the computer boys had scrambled the folders, and nothing was alphabetized. Pure hell. But the old guy hadn't seemed to notice his slowness—too caught up in his own work.

Finally he finished, having found no Rashmawis, and told Shmeltzer, who didn't even bother to look up as he gave him a new assignment: Go up to the Records Room and look for the same name in all the crime files. *All of them.* Rashmawi. Any Rashmawi.

The Records officer was a woman—nothing more than a clerk, but her three stripes outranked him. A hard-ass, too; she made him fill out a mountain of forms before giving him the computer lists, which meant writing as well as reading. More words—random assortments of lines and curves, a whirlpool of shapes that he could drown in unless he forced himself to concentrate, to use the little tricks he'd learned over the years in order to decipher what came so easily to others. Sitting at a school desk in a corner, like some overgrown retarded kid. Concentrating until his eyes blurred and his head hurt.

Exactly the kind of thing he'd joined the police to avoid.

He started with Offenses Against Human Life, the juiciest category and one of the smallest. At least this stuff was alphabetized. First step was locating the names in each subcategory that began with the letter *resh*—which could be confusing because *resh* and *dalet* looked so similar, and even though *dalet* was at the beginning of the alphabet and *resh* toward the end, his damned brain seemed to keep forgetting that. *Yud* could be a problem, too—same shape as *resh*—if you looked at it in isolation from the other letters around it and forgot that it was smaller. Several times he got flustered, lost his place, and had to start all over again, following his fingertip down columns of small print. But finally he managed to cover all of it: Murder, Attempted Murder, Manslaughter, Death by Negligence, Threats to Kill, and the Other Offenses listing that was always tagged on at the end. In 263 files, no Rashmawis.

Offenses Against the Human Body was absolute torture—10,000 Assault files, several hundred under *resh*—and his head hurt a lot more when he finished, hot pulses in his temples, a ring of pain around his eyes.

Offenses Against Property was even worse, a real nightmare; burglary seemed to be the national pastime, all those two-wage-earner homes easy pickings, over 100,000 files, only some of it computerized. Impossible. He put it aside for later. Shmeltzer had the Sex Offenses printout, which left Security, Public Order, Morals, Fraud, Economic, and Administrative crimes.

He began with Security crimes—the Rashmawis were Arabs. Of 932 cases, half had to do with violations of emergency laws, which meant the territories. No Rashmawis in the territories. No Rashmawis in the entire category. But wrestling with the words had caused the pain in his head to erupt into a giant, throbbing headache—the same hot, sickening pain he'd experienced all through school. *Brain strain* had been his secret name for it. His father had called it faking. Even after the doctors had explained it. *Bullshit. If he's strong enough to play soccer, he's strong enough to do his homework. . . .*

Bastard.

He got up, asked the Records officer if there was any coffee. She was sitting behind her desk reading what looked like the Annual Crime Report and didn't answer.

"Coffee," he repeated. "Do I have to fill out a form to get some?"

She looked up. Not a bad-looking girl, really. A petite brunette, with braided hair, a cute little pointed face. Moroccan or Iraqi, just the type he liked.

"What was that?"

He turned on the smile. "Do you have any coffee?"

She looked at her watch. "You're not finished yet?"

"No."

"I don't know what's taking you so long."

Cunt. He held on to his temper.

"Coffee. Do you have any?"

"No." She returned to the report. Started reading and shut him out. Really into the charts and statistics. As if it were some kind of romantic novel.

Cursing, he returned to his lists. Offenses Against Morals: 60 Pimping cases. Nothing. Soliciting: 130 cases. Nothing. Maintaining a Brothel, Seduction of Minors, Dissemination of Indecent Material, nothing, nothing, nothing.

The Loitering for the Purpose of Prostitution subcategory was tiny: 18 cases for the year. Two under *resh*:

Radnick, J. Northern District
Rashmawi, A. Southern District

He copied down the case number, laboring over each digit, double-checking to make sure he had it perfect. Getting up again, he walked to the counter and cleared his throat until the Records officer looked up from her goddamned report.

"What is it?"

"I need this one." He read off the numbers.

Frowning with annoyance, she came around from behind the desk, handed him a requisition form, and said, "Fill this out."

"Again?"

She said nothing, just gave him a snotty look.

Grabbing up the paper, he moved several feet down the counter, pulled out a pen, and sweated with it. Taking too long.

"Hey," said the girl, finally. "What's the problem?"

"Nothing," he snarled and shoved it at her.

She inspected the file, stared at him as if he were some kind of freak, goddamn her, then took the form, went into the Records Room, and returned several minutes later with the RASHMAWI, A. file.

He took it from her, went back to the school desk, sat down, and read the name on the tag: Anwar Rashmawi. Flipping it open, he sloughed through the arrest report: The perpetrator had been busted three years ago on the Green Line, near Sheikh Jarrah, after he and a whore had gotten into some kind of shoving match. A Latam detective had been on special assignment nearby—hidden in some bushes looking for terrorists—and had heard the noise. Tough luck for Anwar Rashmawi.

The second page was something from Social Services, then what looked like doctors' reports—he'd seen enough of those. Words, pages of them. He decided to scan the whole file, then go back over it, word by word, so that he'd be able to make a good presentation to Shmeltzer.

He turned another page. Ah, now here was something he could deal with. A photograph. Polaroid, full color. He smiled. But then he looked at the picture, saw what was in it, and the smile died.

Shit. Look at that. Poor devil.

18

Sunday, nine A.M., and the heat was punishing.

The Dheisheh camp stunk sulfurously of sewage. The houses—if you could call them that—were mud-brick hovels wounded by punch-through windows and roofed with tarpaper; the paths between the buildings, boggy trenches.

A shithole, thought Shmeltzer, as he followed the Chinaman and the new kid, Cohen, brushing away flies and gnats and walking toward the rear of the camp, where the little pisser was supposed to live.

Issa Abdelatif.

The way the Chinaman told it, the villagers of Silwan had been less than talkative. But Daoud had leaned on an old widow and finally gotten a name for Fatma's long-haired boyfriend. She'd overheard the Rashmawis talking about him. A lowlife type. She had no idea where he came from.

The name cropped up again, in the Offenses Against Property files, subcategory: Theft by Employee or Agent. He'd sent Cohen looking for it and the kid had stayed away so long Shmeltzer wondered if he'd drowned in the toilet or walked off the job. He'd gone looking for him, ran into him jogging up the stairs. Grinning ear to ear, with a look-at-me expression on his pretty-boy face. Dumb kid.

The file itself was petty stuff. Abdelatif had worked the previous autumn as a ditch digger at a construction site in Talpiyot, and whenever he was around, tools started disappearing. The contractor had called in the police, and a subsequent investigation revealed that the little punk had been stealing picks, trowels, and shovels and selling them to residents of the refugee camp where he lived with his brother-in-law and sister. Following his arrest, he led the police to a cache at the rear of the camp, a hole in the ground where many of the tools were still hidden. The contractor, happy at getting most of his goods back and wanting to avoid the nuisance of a trial, refused to press charges. Two days in the Russian Compound jail, and the punk was back on the streets.

A rat-faced little pisser, thought Shmeltzer, recalling the arrest photo. Long stringy hair, a weak chin, a pitiful mustache, rodent eyes. Nineteen years old and no doubt he'd been stealing all his life. Forty-eight hours behind bars wasn't what lowlifes like that needed. A little hard time—getting his ass battered at Ramle—and he would have thought twice about misbehaving. Then maybe they wouldn't be trudging through donkey shit looking for him. . . .

All three of them carried Uzis, in addition to the 9 mms. Armed invaders. An army truck was stationed outside the entrance to the camp. Establishing a strong presence, showing who was in charge. But still they had to look over their shoulders as they sloshed through the muck.

He hated going into these places. Not just the poverty and the hopelessness, but the fact that it made no damned sense at all.

All that crap about the Arabs and their strong sense of family, and look how they treated their own.

Fucking King Hussein. In the nineteen years he'd occupied Judea and Samaria, he hadn't done a goddamned thing in the way of social welfare. Too busy building himself that goddamned palace on the Hebron road and knocking up his goddamned American wife—no, back then it was still one of the Arab ones.

Once a year the refugees sent letters to the Welfare and Labor Ministry in Amman, and if they were lucky, each family received a few dinars or nine kilograms of flour three months later. Thank you, King Shit.

But the do-gooders—the private agencies—were all over the place, or at least their offices were. Air-conditioned places on the nicer streets of Bethlehem and East Jerusalem. The Saint Victor's Society, the American Friends Services Committee, the Lutherans, AMIDEAST, UNIPAL, ANERA, with all that American oil money behind it. And the U.N., with its big white sign plastered across the front of the barbed-wire fence that surrounded the camp. ADMINISTERED BY THE UNITED NATIONS RELIEF AND WORKS AGENCY. Administered. What the hell did that mean?

Not to mention the Saudis and the Kuwaitis. And the fucking PLO, big business with its banks and factories and farms and its airports in Africa—a report he'd just seen estimated the bastards' net worth at 10 billion. Abu Mussa got a hundred grand American each month just for entertainment expenses.

All that money, all the goddamned do-gooders, and the people in the camps still lived like wretches. Where the hell did all of it go? The U.N. guy's Mercedes parked right in front of the camp was a partial answer—they got them subsidized for $4,000 American—but Mercedes alone didn't start to explain it.

A big scam—the kind of theft he would have loved to investigate.

The U.N. guy was a sour-looking Norwegian with a *kaffiyah* hanging around his neck. Playing Great White Father, with his clipboard and pen on a chain, gazing down on the sixty or seventy people queuing up in front of him for some sort of privilege. When the three of them came in he'd looked down his nose at them, as if *they* were the bad guys. Gave them a hassle even though he had no legal jurisdiction over anything. But Dani had said not to make waves, so they put up with it for a while, watching the bastard fill out forms, screw around, and give them lemon-sucking looks before coming up with Abdelatif's address. Meanwhile the people in the queue had to wait for whatever morsel the Norwegian was doling out. Typical.

As if it were up to the Jews to solve the problem the Arabs had created—to eat the shit that nobody else had an appetite for. And the goddamned government fell into it, playing the liberal game—putting the refugees on the Israeli welfare rolls, giving them houses, schooling, free medical care. Since '67 their infant mortality had dropped way down. More little pissers to contend with.

Far as he was concerned, the people in the camp were cowards and the descendants of cowards. They'd run away from Jaffa and Lod and Haifa and Jerusalem because the Arab Legion had scared the shit out of them with those hysterical radio broadcasts back in '48. He'd been a wet-eared kid of eighteen, remembered it well. Harsh voices screaming that the Jews ate babies alive, would cut the tits off their women, grind their bones, fuck their eye sockets, and drink their blood.

Jihad had begun, the voices promised. A Holy War to end all wars. The infidels have been attacked and will soon be routed and driven into the Mediterranean. Leave at once and return soon with the victorious forces of the United Arab Armies. Not only will you reclaim your homes, noble brothers, but you will be privileged to confiscate everything the filthy Zionists have accumulated.

Thousands of them listened and believed, falling over one another to escape. Swarming up into Syria and Lebanon and Gaza, pouring into Jordan in such numbers that the Allenby Bridge sagged under their weight. And when they got there, what did their Arab brethren with the strong family ties do for them? Built camps and locked them up. Just temporary, Ahmed. Wait in your nice little tent. Paradise is coming soon—dead Jews and endless virgins to fuck.

Still waiting, he thought, eyeing a shriveled old woman sitting in the dirt and pounding chickpeas in a bowl. The door to her hovel was open; inside was an equally shriveled old man, lying on a mattress, smoking a narghila. Fucking political footballs.

The educated ones had found jobs, settled all over the world. But the poor ones, the defective and stupid ones, stayed in the camps. Living like barnyard animals—breeding like them too. There were 400,000 of them still penned up in Lebanon and Jordan and Syria, another 300,000 dumped in Israel's lap after '67, with 230,000 in Gaza alone. Far as he was concerned, you build a wall around the Strip, stash them all there, and call it Palestine.

Three hundred thousand wretches. The spoils of victory.

The location the Norwegian had given them was midway through the camp, a mud house that looked as if it were melting. Empty oil drums were stacked along one side. Lizards ran over them, chasing insects.

Maksoud, the brother-in-law, sat at a card table in front of the house in a greasy white shirt and snot-shiny black pants, playing *sheshbesh* with a kid of about twelve. The firstborn son. Privileged to sit with the old man and piss his life way.

Not that the old man was so old. A sleepy-looking guy, pasty-faced, maybe thirty, with a ratty-looking mustache no better than Abdelatif's, skinny arms, and a potbelly. A livid worm of scar tissue ran the length of his left forearm. Nasty-looking.

He shook the dice, looked at their Uzis, rolled, and said, "He's not here."

"Who's not here?" asked Shmeltzer.

"The pig, the leech."

"Does the pig have a name?"

"Abdelatif, Issa."

A thick-skinned lizard ran up the side of the building, stopped, bobbed its head, and climbed out of sight.

"What makes you think we're looking for him?" asked the Chinaman.

"Who else?" Maksoud moved two backgammon discs. The kid picked up the dice.

"We'd like to look inside your home," said Shmeltzer.

"I have no home."

Always polemics.

"This house," said Shmeltzer, letting him know by the tone of his voice that he was in no mood to take any shit.

Maksoud looked up at him. Shmeltzer looked right back, kicked the side of the house. Maksoud gave a phlegmy cough and yelled, "Aisha!"

A short, thin woman opened the door. In her hand was a grimy dish towel.

"These are police. They're looking for your pig brother."

"He's not here," said the woman, looking scared.

"They're coming in to see our *home.*"

The boy had rolled double sixes. He moved three discs into his home zone and removed one from the board.

"Ahh," said Maksoud, and he rose from the table. "Put it away, Tawfik. You learn too well."

There was an overtone of threat in his voice, and the boy complied, looking frightened, just like his mother.

"Get out of here," said Maksoud and the boy ran off. The brother-in-law pushed the wife out of the way and went inside. The detectives followed him.

Just what you'd expect, thought Shmeltzer. Two tiny rooms and a cooking area, hot, filthy, smelly. A baby on the floor wearing a skullcap of flies, a chamber pot that needed emptying. No running water, no electricity. Crawling bugs decorating the walls. *Administered.*

The wife busied herself with drying a dish. Maksoud sat down heavily on a torn cushion that looked as if it had once been part of a sofa. His paleness had taken on a yellowish cast. Shmeltzer wondered if it was the light or jaundice. The place felt dangerous, contagious.

"Have a smoke," he told the Chinaman, wanting something to burn away the smell. The big man pulled out his pack of

Marlboros, offered it to Maksoud, who hesitated, then took one and let the detective light it for him.

"When's the last time you saw him?" Shmeltzer asked when the two of them were puffing away.

Maksoud hesitated and the Chinaman didn't seem interested in waiting for an answer. He started walking through the room, looking, touching things, but lightly, without seeming intrusive. Shmeltzer noticed that Cohen seemed lost, not knowing what to do. One hand on the Uzi. Scared shitless, no doubt.

Shmeltzer repeated the question.

"Four or five days," said Maksoud. *"Insha'Allah,* it will stretch to eternity."

The woman gathered enough courage to look up.

"Where is he?" Shmeltzer asked her.

"She knows nothing," said Maksoud. A glance from him lowered her head just as surely as if he'd pushed it down with his hands.

"Is it his habit to leave?"

"Does a pig have habits?"

"What did he do to piss you off?"

Maksoud laughed coldly. *"Zaiyel mara,"* he spat. "He is like a woman." The ultimate Arabic insult, branding Abdelatif as deceitful and irresponsible. "For fifteen years I've been putting him up and all he creates is trouble."

"What kind of trouble?"

"From the time he was a baby—playing with matches, almost set the place on fire. Not that it would be a great loss, eh? Your government promised me a house. Five years ago and I'm still in this shithole."

"What else besides the matches?"

"I told him about the matches, tried to knock sense into him. Little pig kept doing it. One of my sons got burned on the face."

"What else?" Shmeltzer repeated.

"What else? When he was about ten he started to knife rats and cats and watch them die. Brought them inside and watched. *She* didn't do a thing to stop him. When I found out about it I beat him thoroughly and he threatened to use the knife on me."

"What did you do about that?"

"Took it away from him and beat him some more. He didn't learn. Stupid pig!"

The sister suppressed a sniffle. The Chinaman stopped walking. Shmeltzer and Cohen turned and saw the tears flowing down her cheeks.

Her husband stood up quickly and turned on her, screaming. "Stupid woman! Is this a lie? Is it a lie that he's a pig, descended from pigs? Had I known what lineage and dowry you brought I would have run from our wedding, all the way to Mecca."

The woman backed away and bowed her head again. Wiped a dish that had dried long ago. Maksoud swore and settled back down on the cushion.

"What kind of knife did he use on the animals?" asked the Chinaman.

"All kinds. Whatever he could find or steal—in addition to his other fine qualities, he's a thief." Maksoud's eyes scanned the putrid house. "You can see our wealth, how much money we have to spare. I tried to get hold of his U.N. allotment, to force him to pay his share, but he always managed to hide it—and steal mine as well. All for his stinking games."

"What kinds of games?" asked Shmeltzer.

"*Sheshbesh*, cards, dice."

"Where did he gamble?"

"Anywhere there was a game."

"Did he go into Jerusalem to play?"

"Jerusalem, Hebron. The lowest of the coffeehouses."

"Did he ever make any money?"

The question enraged Maksoud. He made a fist and shook one scrawny arm in the air.

"Always a loser! A parasite! When you find him, throw him in one of your prisons—everyone knows how Palestinians are treated there."

"Where can we find him?" asked Shmeltzer.

Maksoud shrugged expansively. "What do you want him for anyway?"

"What do you think?"

"Could be anything—he was born to steal."

"Did you ever see him with a girl?"

"Not girls, whores. Three times he brought home the body lice. All of us had to wash ourselves with something the doctor gave us."

Shmeltzer showed him the picture of Fatma Rashmawi.

"Ever seen her?"

No reaction. "Nah."

"Did he use drugs?"

"What would I know of such things?"

Ask a stupid question . . .

"Where do you think he's gone?"

Maksoud shrugged again. "Maybe to Lebanon, maybe to Amman, maybe to Damascus."

"Does he have family connections in any of those places?"

"No."

"Anywhere else?"

"No." Maksoud looked hatefully at his wife. "He's the last of a stinking line. The parents died in Amman, there was another brother left, lived up in Beirut, but you Jews finished him off last year."

The sister buried her face and tried to hide herself in a corner of the cooking area.

"Has Issa ever been up to Lebanon?" asked Shmeltzer—another stupid question, but they'd walked through shit to get here, why not ask? His Sheraton companion had turned up nothing political, but it had been short notice and she had other sources yet to check.

"What for? He's a thief, not a fighter."

Shmeltzer smiled, stepped closer, and looked down at Maksoud's left forearm.

"He steal that scar for you?"

The brother-in-law covered the forearm, hastily.

"A work injury," he said. But the belligerence in his voice failed to mask the fear in his eyes.

"A knife man," said the Chinaman, as they drove back to Jerusalem.

The unmarked's air conditioning had malfunctioned and all the windows were open. They passed an army halftrack and an Arab on a donkey. Black-robed women picked fruit from the huge, gnarled fig trees that lined the road. The earth was the color of freshly baked bread.

"Very convenient, eh?" said Shmeltzer.

"You don't like it?"

"If it's real, I'm in love with it. First let's find the bastard."

"Why," asked Cohen, "did the brother-in-law speak so freely to us?" He was behind the wheel, driving fast, the feel of the auto giving him confidence.

"Why not?" said Shmeltzer.

"We're the enemy."

"Think about it, *boychik*," said the older man. "What did he really tell us?"

Cohen sped up around a curve, felt the sweat trickle down his back as he strained to remember the exact wording of the interview.

"Not much," he said.

"Exactly," said Shmeltzer. "He brayed like a goat until it came down to substance—like where to find the pisser. Then he clammed up." The radio was belching static. He reached over and turned it off. "The end result being that the bastard got a bunch of shit off his chest and told us nothing. When we get back to Headquarters, I'm sending him a bill for psychotherapy."

The other detectives laughed, Cohen finally starting to feel like one of them. In the back the Chinaman stretched out his long legs and lit up a Marlboro. Taking a deep drag, he put his hand out the window and let the breeze blow off the ashes.

"What about the Rashmawi brothers?" asked Shmeltzer.

"The defective one never came out of the house all night," said the Chinaman. "The two older ones were hard-asses. Daoud and I questioned them before they got home and they didn't even blink. Tough guys, like the father. Knew nothing about anything —not an eye-blink when we told them Fatma was dead."

"Cold," said Avi Cohen.

"What's it like," asked Shmeltzer, "working with the Arab?"

The Chinaman smoked and thought.

"Daoud? Like working with anyone else, I guess. Why?"

"Just asking."

"You've got to be tolerant, Nahum," the Chinaman said, smiling. "Open yourself up to new experiences."

"New experiences, bullshit," said Shmeltzer. "The old ones are bad enough."

19

On Sunday at six P.M., Daniel came home to an empty apartment.

Twenty-four hours ago he'd left Saint Saviour's and gone walking through the Old City, down the Via Dolorosa and through the Christian Quarter with its mass of churches and rest spots commemorating the death walk of Jesus, then over through El Wad Road to the covered bazaar that filled David Street and the Street of the Chain. Talking to Arab souvenir vendors hawking made-in-Taiwan T-shirts aimed at American tourists (I LOVE ISRAEL with a small red heart substituted for the word *love*; KISS ME, I'M A JEWISH PRINCE above a caricature of a frog wearing a crown). He entered the stalls of spice traders presiding over bins of cumin, cardamom, nutmeg, and mint; talked to barbers deftly wielding straight razors; butchers slicing their way through the carcasses of sheep and goats, viscera hanging flaccidly from barbed metal hooks affixed to blood-pinkened tile walls. Showed Fatma's picture to metalsmiths, grocers, porters, and beggars; touched base with the Arab uniforms who patrolled the Muslim Quarter, and the Border Patrolmen keeping an eye on the Western Wall. Trying, without success, to find someone who'd seen the girl or her boyfriend.

After that, there had been a quick break for prayer at the *Kotel,* then the conference with the other detectives in a corner of the parking lot near the Jewish Quarter. What was supposed to have been a brief get-together had stretched out after Daoud had reported pulling Abdelatif's ID out of Mrs. Nasif, and Shmeltzer had arrived with the arrest information on both the boyfriend and Anwar Rashmawi. The five of them had traded guesses, discussed possibilities. The case seemed to be coming together, taking form, though he was far from sure what the final picture would look like.

By the time he'd gotten home last night, it had been close to midnight and everyone was asleep. His own slumber was fitful and he rose at five thirty, full of nervous energy. Abdelatif's family had been located in the Dheisheh camp, and he wanted to reconfirm the trip with the army, to make sure that everything went smoothly.

He'd traded sleepy good-byes with Laura and kissed the kids on their foreheads while buttoning his shirt. The boys had rolled away from him, but Shoshi had reached out in her sleep, wrapped her arms around him so tightly that he'd had to peel her fingers from his neck.

Leaving that way had made him feel wistful and guilty—since the case had begun he'd barely had time for any of them, and so soon after Gray Man. Foolish guilt, really. It had been only two days, but the nonstop pace made it seem longer, and the loss of Shabbat had disrupted his routine.

As he walked out the door, the image of his own father filled his childhood memories—always there for him, ready with a smile or words of comfort, knowing exactly the right thing to say. Would Shoshi and Benny and Mikey feel the same way about *him* in twenty years?

Those feelings resurfaced as he arrived home on Sunday evening, weary from empty hours of surveillance and hoping to catch Laura before she left to pick up Luanne and Gene. But all was quiet except for Dayan's welcoming yips.

He petted the dog and read the note on the dining room table: ("Off to Ben Gurion, love. Food's in the refrig., the kids are at friends.") If he'd known which friends, he could have dropped by, but they had so many, there was no way to guess.

He stayed just long enough to eat a quick dinner—pita and hummus, leftover Shabbat chicken that he'd never had a chance to eat hot, a handful of black wine grapes, two cups of instant coffee to wash it all down. Dayan kept him company, begging for scraps, the black patch surrounding the little spaniel's left eye quivering each time he cried.

"Okay, okay," said Daniel. "But just this little piece."

Finishing quickly, he wiped his face, said grace after meals, changed his shirt, and was out the door at six twenty-five, behind the wheel of the Escort and speeding back toward Silwan.

Sunday night. The end of Christian Sabbath and all the church bells were ringing. He parked on the outskirts of the village and covered the rest of the journey on foot. By seven he was back in the olive grove, with Daoud and the Chinaman. Watching.

"Why don't we just go in there and lay it on the line with them?" said the Chinaman. "Tell them we know about Abdelatif and ask them if they took care of him?" He picked up a fallen olive, rolled it between his fingers, and tossed it aside. Ten forty-three, nothing had happened, and he couldn't even smoke in case someone saw the glow. The kind of night that made him think about another line of work.

"They're hardly likely to tell us," said Daniel.

"So? We're not finding out anything this way. If we confront them, at least we've got the element of surprise working for us."

"We can always do that," said Daniel. "Let's wait a while longer."

"For what?"

"Maybe nothing."

"For all we know," persisted the Chinaman, "the guy's still alive, flown off to Amman or Damascus."

"Looking into that is someone else's job. This is ours."

At eleven-ten, a man came out of the Rashmawi house, looked both ways, and walked silently down the pathway. A small dark shadow, barely discernible against a coal-black sky. The detectives had to strain to keep him in their sights as he made his way east, to where the bluff dipped its lowest.

Climbing gingerly down the embankment, he began walking down the hill, in the center of their visual field. Merging in the darkness for stretches of time that seemed interminable, then surfacing briefly as a moonlit hint of movement. Like a swimmer bobbing up and down in a midnight lagoon, thought Daniel as he focused his binoculars.

The man came closer. The binoculars turned him into something larger, but still unidentifiable. A dark, fuzzy shape, sidling out of view.

It reminded Daniel of '67. Lying on his belly on Ammunition Hill, holding his breath, feeling weightless with terror, burning with pain, his body reduced to something hollow and flimsy.

The Butcher's Theater, they called the hills of Jerusalem. Terrain full of nasty surprises. It carved up soldiers and turned them into vulture fodder.

He lowered the binoculars to follow the shape, which had grown suddenly enormous, heard the Chinaman's harsh whisper and abandoned his reminiscence:

"Shit! He's headed straight here!"

It was true: The shape was making a beeline for the grove.

All three detectives shot to their feet and retreated quickly to the rear of the thicket, hiding behind the knotted trunks of thousand-year-old trees.

Moments later the shape entered the grove and became a man again. Pushing his way through branches, he stepped into a clearing created by a tree that had fallen and begun to rot. Cold, pale light filtered through the treetops and turned the clearing into a stage.

Breathing hard, his face a mask of pain and confusion, the man sat down on the felled trunk, put his face in his hands, and began to sob.

Between the sobs came gulping breaths; at the tail end of the breaths, words. Uttered in a strangulated voice that was half whisper, half scream.

"Oh, sister sister sister . . . I've done my duty . . . but it can't bring you back . . . oh sister sister . . . we of the less favored wife . . . sister sister."

The man sat for a long time, crying and talking that way. Then he stood, let out a curse, and drew something from his pocket. A knife, long-bladed and heavy-looking, with a crude wooden handle.

Kneeling on the ground, he raised the weapon over his head and held it that way, frozen in ceremony. Then, crying out wordlessly, he plunged the blade into the earth, over and over again. Unleashing the tears again, snuffling wetly, sobbing *sister sister sister*.

Finally he finished. Pulling out the knife, he held it in his palms and stared at it, tearfully, before wiping it on his trouser leg and placing it on the ground. Then he lay down beside it, curled fetally, whimpering.

It was then that the detectives came toward him, guns drawn, stepping out of the shadows.

20

Daniel kept the interrogation simple. Just him and the suspect, sitting opposite one another in a bare, fluorescent-bright room in the basement of Headquarters. A room wholly lacking in character; its normal function, data storage. The tape recorder whirred; the clock on the wall ticked.

The suspect cried convulsively. Daniel took a tissue out of a box, waited until the man's chest had stopped heaving, and said, "Here, Anwar."

The brother wiped his face, put his glasses back on, stared at the floor.

"You were talking about how Fatma met Issa Abdelatif," said Daniel. "Please go on."

"I . . ." Anwar made a gagging sound, placed a hand on his throat.

Daniel waited some more.

"Are you all right?"

Anwar swallowed, then nodded.

"Would you like some water?"

A shake of the head.

"Then please go on."

Anwar wiped his mouth, avoided Daniel's eyes.

"Go on, Anwar. It's important that you tell me."

"It was at a construction site," said the brother, barely audible. Daniel adjusted the volume control on the recorder. "Nabil and Qasem were working there. She was sent to bring food to them. *He* was working there also and he snared her."

"How did he do that?"

Anwar's face constricted with anger, the pockmarks on his pale cheeks compressing to vertical slits.

"Pretty words, snake smiles! She was a simple girl, trusting—when we were children I could always fool her into thinking anything."

More tears.

"It's all right, Anwar. You're doing the right thing by talking about it. What was the location of this site?"

"Romema."

"Where in Romema?"

"Behind the zoo . . . I think. I was never there."

"How, then, do you know about Fatma meeting Abdelatif?"

"Nabil and Qasem saw him talking to her, warned him off, and told father about it."

"What did your father do?"

Anwar hugged himself and rocked in the chair.

"What did he do, Anwar?"

"He beat her but it didn't stop her!"

"How do you know that?"

Anwar bit his lip and chewed on it. So hard that he broke skin.

"Here," said Daniel, handing him another tissue.

Anwar kept chewing, dabbed at the lip, looked at the crimson spots on the tissue, and smiled strangely.

"How do you know Fatma kept seeing Issa Abdelatif?"

"I saw them."

"Where did you see them?"

"Fatma stayed away too long on errands. Father grew suspicious and sent me to . . . watch them. I saw them."

"Where?"

"Different places. Around the walls of Al Quds." Using the Arabic name for the Old City. "In the wadis, near the trees of Gethsemane, anywhere they could hide." Anwar's voice rose in pitch: "He took her to hidden places and defiled her!"

"Did you report this to your father?"

"I had to! It was my duty. But . . ."

"But what?"

Silence.

"Tell me, Anwar."

Silence.

"But what, Anwar?"

"Nothing."

"What did you think your father would do to her once he knew?"

The brother moaned, leaned forward, hands outstretched, eyes bulging, fishlike, behind the thick lenses. He smelled feral, looked frantic, trapped. Daniel resisted the impulse to move away from him and, instead, inched closer.

"What would he do, Anwar?"

"He would kill her! I knew he would kill her, so before I told him I warned her!"

"And she ran away."

"Yes."

"You were trying to save her, Anwar."

"Yes!"

"Where did she go?"

"To a Christian place in Al Quds. The brown-robes took her in."

"Saint Saviour's Monastery?"

"Yes."

"How do you know she went there?"

"Two weeks after she ran away, I took a walk. Up to the olive grove where you found me. We used to play there, Fatma and I, throwing olives at each other, hiding and looking for each other. I still like to go there. To think. She knew that and she was waiting for me—she'd come to see me."

"Why?"

"She was lonely, crying about how much she missed the family. She wanted me to talk with Father, to persuade him to take her back. I asked her where I could reach her and she told me the brown-robes had taken her in. I told her they were infidels and would try to convert her, but she said they were kind and she had nowhere else to go."

"What was she wearing, Anwar?"

"Wearing?"

"Her clothing."

"A dress . . . I don't know."

"What color?"

"White, I think."

"Plain white?"

"I think. What does it matter?"

"And which earrings was she wearing?"

"The only ones she had."

"Which are those?"

"Little gold rings—they put them on her at birth."

Anwar began to cry.

"Solid gold?" asked Daniel.

"Yes . . . no . . . I don't know. They looked gold. What does it matter!"

"I'm sorry," said Daniel. "These are questions I have to ask."

Anwar slumped in his chair, limp and defeated.

"Did you talk to your father about taking her back?" asked Daniel.

A violent shake of the head, trembling lips. Even at this point, the fear of the father remained.

"No, no! I couldn't! It was too soon, I knew what he would say! A few days later I went to the monastery to talk to her, to tell her to wait. I asked her if she was still seeing the lying dog and she said she was, that they *loved* each other! I ordered her to stop seeing him but she refused, said I was cruel, that all men were cruel. All men except for *him*. We . . . argued and I left. It was the last time I saw her."

Anwar buried his face.

"The very last?"

"No." Muffled. "One more time."

"Did you see Abdelatif again, as well?"

The brother looked up and smiled. A wholehearted grin that made his ravaged face glow. Throwing back his shoulders and sitting up straighter, he recited in a clear, loud voice: "He who does not take revenge from the transgressor would better be dead than to walk without pride!"

Reciting the proverb seemed to have infused new life into him. He balled one hand into a fist and recited several other Arabic sayings, all pertaining to the honor of vengeance. Took off his glasses and stared myopically into space. Smiling.

"The obligation . . . the honor was mine," he said. "We were of the same mother."

Such a sad case, thought Daniel, watching him posture. He'd read the arrest report, seen the reports from the doctors at Hadassah who'd examined Anwar after the assault arrest, the psychiatric recommendations. The Polaroid pictures, like something out of a medical book. A fancy diagnosis—*congenital micropenis with accompanying epispaedia*—that did nothing but give a name to the poor guy's misery. Born with a tiny, deformed stump of a male organ, the urethra nothing more than a flat strip of mucous membrane on the upper surface of what should have been a shaft but was only a useless nub. Bladder abnormalities that made it hard for the guy to hold his water—when they'd stripped him before booking him he'd been wearing layers of cloth fashioned into a crude homemade diaper.

One of God's cruel little jokes? Daniel had wondered, then stopped wondering, knowing it was useless.

Plastic surgery could have helped a little, according to the Hadassah doctors. There were specialists in Europe and the United States who did that kind of thing: multiple reconstructive surgeries over a period of several years in order to create something a bit more normal-looking. But the end result would still be far from manly. This was one of the severest cases any of them had ever seen.

The whore had thought so too.

After years of conflict and deliberation, propelled by cloudy motivations that he ill understood, Anwar had walked, late one night, toward the Green Line. To a place near Sheikh Jarrah where his brothers said the whores hung out. He'd found one leaning against a battered Fiat, old and shopworn and coarse, with vulgar yellow hair. But warm-voiced and welcoming and eager.

They'd come quickly to terms, Anwar unaware that he was being blatantly overcharged, and he'd climbed into the backseat of her Fiat. Recognizing the terror of inexperience, the whore had cooed at him, smiled at him, and lied about how cute he was, stroking him and wiping the sweat from his brow. But when she'd unbuttoned his fly and reached for him, the smiling and cooing had stopped. And when she'd pulled him out, her shock and revulsion had caused her to laugh.

Anwar had gone crazy with rage and humiliation. Lunging for the whore's throat, trying to strangle the laughter out of her. She'd fought back, bigger and stronger than he, pummeling and gouging and calling him freak. Screaming for help at the top of her lungs.

An undercover cop had heard it all and busted poor Anwar. The whore had given her statement, then left town. The police had been unable to locate her. Not that they'd tried too hard. Prostitution was a low-priority affair, the act itself legal, solicitation the offense. If the whores and their customers kept quiet, it was live and let live. Even in Tel Aviv, where three or four dozen girls worked the beaches at night, making plenty of noise, busts were rare unless things got nasty.

No complainant, first offense, no trial. Anwar had walked

free with a recommendation that his family obtain further medical consultation and psychiatric treatment. Which the family was about as likely to accept as conversion to Judaism.

Pathetic, thought Daniel, looking at him. Denied the things other men took for granted because of missing centimeters of tissue. Treated as something less than a man by family and culture—any culture.

Sent in with the women.

"Would you like something to eat or drink now?" he asked. "Coffee or juice? A pastry?"

"No, nothing," said Anwar, with bravado. "I feel perfect."

"Tell me, then, how you avenged Fatma's honor."

"After one of their . . . meetings, I followed him. To the bus station."

"The East Jerusalem station?"

"Yes." There was puzzlement in the answer. As if there was any other station but the one in East Jerusalem. To him the big central depot on the west side of town—the Jewish station—didn't exist. In Jerusalem, a kilometer could stretch a universe.

"What day was this?"

"Thursday."

"What time of day?"

"In the morning, early."

"You were watching them?"

"Protecting her."

"Where was their meeting?"

"Somewhere behind the walls. They came out of the New Gate."

"Where did she go?"

"I don't know. That *was* the last time."

Anwar saw Daniel's skeptical look and threw up his hands.

"It was him I was interested in! Without him she'd come back, be obedient!"

"So you followed him to the station."

"Yes. He bought a ticket for the Hebron bus. There was some time before it left. I walked up to him, said I was Fatma's brother, that I had money and was willing to pay him to stop seeing her. He asked how much money and I told him a hundred dollars American. He demanded two hundred. We haggled and settled on a hundred and sixty. We agreed to meet the next day, in the olive grove, before the sun rose."

"Wasn't he suspicious?"

"Very. His first reaction was that it was some kind of trick." Anwar's face shone with pride. His glasses slid down his nose and he righted them. "But I played him for a fool. When he said it was a trick, I said okay, shrugged, and started to walk away. He came running after me. He was a greedy dog—his greed got the better of him. We had our meeting."

"When?"

"Friday morning, at six-thirty."

Just shortly after Fatma's body had been discovered.

"What happened at the meeting?"

"He came ready to rob me, with the knife."

"The knife we found you with tonight?"

"Yes. I arrived first and was waiting for him. He pulled it out the minute he saw me."

"Did you see from which direction he'd come?"

"No."

"What did he look like?"

"A thief."

"His clothes were clean?"

"As clean as they'd ever be."

"Go on."

"He had the knife, ready to do me harm, but I'd come armed too. With a hammer. I kept it hidden behind the trunk of the tree that had fallen. I pulled out ten dollars. He grabbed it out of my hands and demanded the rest. I said the rest would come in installments. Five dollars a week for every week he stayed away from her. He started adding it up in his head. He was slow-witted—it took him a while. 'That's thirty weeks,' he said. 'Exactly,' I answered. 'There's no other way to deal with a thief.' That made him crazy. He started to walk toward me with the knife, saying I was dead, just like Fatma. That she was nothing to him, garbage to be dumped. That all the Rashmawis were garbage."

"Those were his words? That she was dead? Garbage to be dumped?"

"Yes." Anwar started crying again.

"Did he say anything else?"

"No. From the way he said it I knew he'd . . . hurt her. I'd come up there with intentions of killing him and knew now that the time had come. He was coming closer, holding the knife in his palm, his eyes on me, beady, like those of a weasel. I started laughing, playing the fool, saying I was only joking and that the rest of the money was right there, behind the tree stump.

" '*Get it,*' he ordered, as if talking to a slave. I told him it was buried under the stump, that it was a job for two men to roll it away."

"You took a chance," said Daniel. "He could have killed you and come back later for the money."

"Yes, it was risky," said Anwar, clearly pleased. "But he was greedy. He wanted everything right then and there. 'Push,' he ordered me. Then he knelt down beside me, holding the knife in one hand, using the other to try to roll the stump. I pretended to roll, too, reached out and pulled hard at his ankles. He fell, and before he could get up I grabbed the hammer and hit him with it. Many times."

A dreamy look surfaced behind the eyeglasses.

"His skull broke easily. It sounded like a melon breaking on a rock. I took his knife and cut him. Kept it for a memorial."

"Where did you cut him?" asked Daniel, wanting a wound match on tape, all the details taken care of. The body had been dug up and sent to Abu Kabir. Levi would be calling within a day or so.

"The throat."

"Anywhere else?"

"The . . . the male organs."

Two out of the three sites where Fatma had been butchered.

"What about his abdomen?"

"No." Incredulity, as if the question were absurd.

"Why the throat and genitals?"

"To silence him, of course. And prevent further sin."

"I see. What happened after that?"

"I left him there, went to my house, and returned with a spade. I buried him, then used the spade to roll the log over his grave. Right where I showed you."

Abdelatif's remains had been lifted from a deep grave. It must have taken Anwar hours to dig it. The trunk hiding the excavation. Which made Daniel feel a little less foolish about sitting for hours, just a couple of meters away. Watching the house, keeping a dead man company.

"The only money you paid him was ten dollars," said Daniel.

"Yes, and I took it back."

"From out of his pocket?"

"No. He had it clenched in his greedy hand."

"What denomination?" asked Daniel.

"A single American ten-dollar bill. I buried it with him."

Exactly what had been found on the corpse.

"Is that all?" asked Anwar.

"One more thing. Was Abdelatif a drug user?"

"It wouldn't surprise me. He was scum."

"But you don't know it for a fact."

"I didn't know him," said Anwar. "I merely killed him."

He wiped the tears from his face and smiled.

"What is it?" asked Daniel.

"I'm happy," said Anwar. "I'm very happy."

21

Like a suite at the King David, thought Daniel, walking into Laufer's office. Wood-paneled and gold-carpeted, with soft lighting and a fine desert view. When it had been Gavrieli's, the decor had been warmer—shelves overflowing with books, photos of Gorgeous Gideon's equally gorgeous wife.

In one corner stood a case full of artifacts. Coins and urns and talismans, just like the collection he'd seen in Baldwin's office at the Amelia Catherine. Bureaucrats seemed to go in for that kind of thing. Were they trying to dress up their uselessness with imagined links to the heroes of the past? Over the case hung a framed map of Palestine which appeared to have been taken from an old book. Signed, inscribed photographs of all the Prime Ministers, from Ben Gurion on down, graced the walls—the pointed suggestion of friends in high places. But the inscriptions on the photos were noncommital, none of them mentioned Laufer by name, and Daniel wondered if the pictures belonged to the deputy commander or had been pulled out of some archive.

The deputy commander was in full uniform today, sitting behind a big Danish teakwood desk and drinking soda water. An olive-wood tray holding a Sipholux bottle and two empty glasses sat near his right arm.

"Sit down," he said, and when Daniel had done so, pushed a piece of paper across the desk. "We'll be releasing this to the press in a couple of hours."

The statement was two paragraphs long, stamped with today's date, and entitled POLICE SOLVE SCOPUS MURDER AND RELATED REVENGE KILLING.

POLICE DEPUTY COMMANDER AVIGDOR LAUFER ANNOUNCED TODAY THAT THE MAJOR CRIMES DIVISION, SOUTHERN DISTRICT, HAS SOLVED THE CASE OF A YOUNG GIRL FOUND STABBED TO DEATH FOUR DAYS AGO ON MOUNT SCOPUS. THE INVESTIGATION HAS REVEALED THAT FATMA RASHMAWI, 15, A RESIDENT OF SILWAN, WAS KILLED BY ISSA QADER ABDELATIF AL AZZEH, 19, RESIDENT OF THE DHEISHEH REFUGEE CAMP WHO WAS KNOWN TO THE POLICE BECAUSE OF A HISTORY OF THIEVERY AND ANTISOCIAL BEHAVIOR. ABDELATIF'S BODY WAS FOUND IN A GROVE NEAR SILWAN WHERE IT HAD BEEN BURIED BY ONE OF THE VICTIM'S BROTHERS, ANWAR RASHMAWI, 20. RASMAWI, WHO ALSO HAS A POLICE RECORD, CONFESSED TO MURDERING ABDELATIF IN ORDER TO AVENGE THE HONOR OF HIS SISTER. HE IS CURRENTLY IN POLICE CUSTODY.

THE INVESTIGATION WAS CARRIED OUT BY A TEAM OF DETECTIVES FROM MAJOR CRIMES, HEADED BY CHIEF INSPECTOR DANIEL SHARAVI AND SUPERVISED BY DEPUTY COMMANDER LAUFER.

Public relations, thought Daniel. Names on paper. Worlds removed from the streets and the stakeouts. From the Butcher's Theater. He put the statement on the desk.

"So?" demanded Laufer.

"It's factual."

Laufer drank some soda, looked at the bottle as if debating offering some to Daniel, then thought better of it, and said, "Factual."

He sat back in his chair and stared at Daniel, waiting for more.

"It's a good statement. Should make the press happy."

"Does it make *you* happy, Sharavi?"

"I still have reservations about the case."

"The knife?"

"For one." Abdelatif's weapon was thick-bladed and dull.

Not even remotely similar to the wound molds taken from Fatma's body.

"He was a knife man," said Laufer. "Carried more than one weapon."

"The pathologist said at least two had been used on Fatma, which means he would have had to carry three. No others have turned up, but it's a discrepancy I can live with—he hid the murder weapons or sold them to someone. What really bothers me is the foundation of the case: We're depending exclusively on the brother's story. Apart from what he's told us, there's no real evidence. Nothing placing Abdelatif near or around Scopus, no explanation for how he got up there—for why he dumped her there. At least twenty hours passed between Fatma's leaving the monastery and the discovery of the body. We have no idea what they did during that time."

"He cut her up is what they did."

"But where? The brother said he bought a ticket for the Hebron bus. The girl went somewhere on her own. Where? On top of that, we've got no motive for why he killed her in the first place. Anwar said they parted after a tryst, with no signs of hostility. And there's the physical context of the murder to consider—the washing of the body, the way it was prepared, the hair combed out, the sedation with heroin. We didn't find a single fiber, footprint, or fingerprint. It indicates calculation, intelligence—a cold type of intelligence—and nothing we've learned about Abdelatif makes him sound that bright."

The deputy commander leaned back in his chair. Laced his hands behind his head and spoke with deliberate casualness.

"Lots of words, Sharavi, but what it boils down to is that you're searching for answers to every little detail. It's not a realistic attitude."

Laufer waited. Daniel said nothing.

"You're overreacting," said the deputy commander. "Most of your objections can be easily understood given the fact that Abdelatif was a thief and a lowlife psychopath—he tortured animals, burned his cousin, and cut up his uncle. Is murder that far removed from that kind of crap? Who knows why he killed or why he chose to dump her in a certain way? The head doctors don't understand those types and neither do you or I. For all we know he *was* intelligent—a damned genius when it came to murder. Maybe he's cut up and washed other girls and never been caught—the people in the camps never call us in. Maybe he carried *ten* knives, was a damned knife *fanatic*. He stole tools—why not blades? As far as where he did it, it could be anywhere. Maybe she met him at the station, he took her home, carved her up in the camp."

"The driver of the Hebron bus is reasonably certain Abdelatif was on it and Fatma wasn't."

Laufer shook his head scornfully. "The number of people they stuff in, all those chickens, how the hell could he notice anything? In any event, Rashmawi did the world a favor by polishing him off. One less psycho to worry about."

"Rashmawi could just as easily be our culprit," said Daniel. "We know he's psychologically disturbed. What if he killed both of them—out of jealousy or to impress his father—then concocted the story about Abdelatif in order to make it sound honorable?"

"*What if*. Do you have any *evidence* of that?"

"I'm only raising it as an example—"

"During the time his sister was murdered, Rashmawi was home. His family vouches for him."

"That's to be expected," said Daniel. Anwar's confession had turned him from freak to family hero, the entire Rashmawi clan marching to the front gate of the Russian Compound, making a great show of solidarity at the prison door. The father beating his breast and offering to trade his own life for that of his "brave, blessed son."

"What's expected can also be true, Sharavi. And even if the alibi were false, you'd never get them to change it, would you? So what would be the point? Leaning on a bunch of Arabs and getting the press on our asses? Besides, it's not as if Rashmawi will be walking the streets. He'll be locked up at Ramle, out of circulation." Laufer rubbed his hands together. "Two birds."

"Not for long," said Daniel. "The charge is likely to be reduced to self-defense. With psychiatric and cultural mitigating factors. Which means he could be walking the streets in a couple of years."

"*Could be*'s and *maybe*'s," said Laufer. "That's the prosecutor's problem. In the meantime we'll proceed based on the facts at hand."

He made a show of shuffling papers, squirted soda from the injection bottle into a glass, and offered a drink to Daniel.

"No, thanks."

Laufer reacted to the refusal as if it were a slap in the face.

"Sharavi," he said tightly. "A major homicide has been solved in a matter of days and there you sit, looking as if someone had died."

Daniel stared back at him, searching for intentional irony in his choice of words, the knowledge that he'd uttered a tasteless joke. Finding only peevishness. The resentment of a drill major for one who'd broken step.

"Stop searching for problems that don't exist."

"As you wish, Tat Nitzav."

Laufer sucked in his cheeks, the flab billowing as he exhaled.

"I know," he said, "about your people walking across the desert from Arabia. But today we have airplanes. No reason to do things the hard way. To wipe your ass with your foot when a hand is available."

He picked up the press release, initialed it, and told Daniel he was free to leave. Allowed him to reach the doorknob before speaking again: "One more thing. I read Rashmawi's arrest report—the first one, for throttling the whore. The incident took place some time before Gray Man, didn't it?"

Daniel knew what was coming.

"Over two years before."

"In terms of a Major Crimes investigation, that's not long at all. Was Rashmawi ever questioned in regard to the Gray Man murders?"

"I questioned him about it yesterday. He denied having anything to do with it, said except for the incident with the prostitute, he never went out of the house at night. His family will vouch for him—an unassailable alibi, as you've noted."

"But he wasn't questioned originally? During the active investigation?"

"No."

"May I ask why not?"

The same question he'd asked himself.

"We were looking at convicted sex offenders. His case was dismissed before coming to trial."

"Makes one wonder," said Laufer, "how many others slipped by."

Daniel said nothing, knowing any reply would sound mealy-mouthed and defensive.

"Now that the Scopus thing has been cleared up," continued the deputy commander, "there'll be time to backtrack—go over the files and see what else may have been missed."

"I've started doing that, Tat Nitzav."

"Good day, Sharavi. And congratulations on solving the case."

22

On Wednesday night, hours after the Scopus case closed, the Chinaman celebrated by taking his wife and son out for a free dinner. He and Aliza smiled at each other over plates heaped high with food—stir-fried beef and broccoli, sweet and sour veal, lemon chicken, crackling duck—holding hands and sipping lime Cokes and enjoying the rare chance to be alone.

"It's good that it's over," she said, squeezing his thigh. "You'll be home more. Able to do your share of the housework."

"I think I hear the office calling."

"Never mind. Pass the rice."

Across the room, little Rafi sucked contentedly on a bottle of apple juice, cradled in his grandmother's arms, receiving a first-class guided tour of the Shang Hai as she took him from table to table, introducing him to customers, announcing that he was her *tzankhan katan*—"little paratrooper." At the rear of the restaurant, near the kitchen door, sat her husband, black silk yarmulke perched atop his hairless ivory head, playing silent chess with the *mashgiah*—the rabbi sent by the Chief Rabbinate to ensure that everything was kosher.

This *mashgiah* was a new one, a youngster named Stolinsky with a patchy dark beard and a relaxed attitude toward life. During the three weeks since he'd been assigned to the Shang Hai, he'd gained five pounds feasting on spiced ground veal pancakes with hoisin sauce and had been unable to capture Huang Haim Lee's king.

The restaurant was lit by paper lanterns and smelled of garlic and ginger. Chinese watercolors and calendars hung on red-lacquered walls. A rotund, popeyed goldfish swam clumsily in a bowl next to the cashier's booth. The register, normally Mrs. Lee's bailiwick, was operated tonight by a moonlighting American student named Cynthia.

The waiter was a tiny, hyperactive Vietnamese, one of the boat people the Israelis had taken in several years ago. He rushed in and out of the kitchen, bouncing from table to table carrying huge trays of food, speaking rapidly in pidgin Hebrew and laughing at jokes that only he seemed to understand. The large center table was occupied by a party of Dutch nuns, cheerful, doughy-faced women who chewed energetically and laughed along with Nguyen as they fumbled with their chopsticks. The rest of the customers were Israelis, serious about eating, cleaning their plates and calling for more.

Aliza took in the activity, the polyglot madness, smiled and stroked her husband's forearm. He reached out and took her fingers in his, exhibiting just a hint of the strength stored within the oversized digits.

It had taken her some time to get used to it. She'd grown up a farm girl, on Kibbutz Yavneh, a bosomy, big-boned redhead. Her first beaus, robust, tractor-driving youths—male versions of herself. She'd always had a thing for big men, the muscular, bulky types who made you feel protected, but never had she imagined herself married to someone who looked like an oversized Mongol warrior. And the family: her mother-in-law your basic *yiddishe mama*, her hair in a babushka, still speaking Hebrew with a Russian accent; Abba Haim an old Buddha, as yellow as parchment; Yossi's older brother, David, suave, always wearing a suit, always making deals, always away on business.

She'd met Yossi in the army. She'd worked in requisitions and had been attached to his paratrooper unit. He'd stormed into her office like a real *bulvan,* angry and looking ludicrous because the uniform that had been issued to him was three sizes too small. He started mouthing off at her; she mouthed back and that was it. Chemistry. And now little Rafi, straw-haired, with almond eyes and the shoulders of a working man. Who'd have predicted it?

As she'd gotten to know Yossi, she'd realized that they came from similar stock. Survivors. Fighters.

Her parents had been teenaged lovers who escaped from Munich in '41 and hid for months in the Bavarian forest, subsisting on leaves and berries. Her father stole a rifle and shot a German guard dead in order to get them across the border. Together they traveled on foot, making their way through Hungary and Yugoslavia and down to Greece. Catching a midnight boat ride to Cyprus and paying the last of their savings to a Cypriot smuggler, only to be forced off the boat at gunpoint, five miles from the coast of Palestine. Swimming the rest of the way on empty stomachs, crawling half-dead onto the shores of Jaffa. Avoiding the scrutiny of Arab cutthroats long enough to reach their comrades at Yavneh.

Yossi's mother had also escaped the Nazis by walking. In 1940. All the way from Russia to the visa-free port of Shanghai, where she lived in relative peace, along with thousands of other Jews. Then war broke out in the Pacific and the Japanese interned all of them in the squalid camps of Hongkew.

A tall, husky theology student named Huang Lee had been held captive there, too, suspected of collaborating with the Allies, because he was an intellectual. Dragged out periodically to endure public floggings.

Two weeks before Hiroshima, the Japanese sentenced Huang Lee to death. The Jews took him in and he evaded execution by hiding in their midst, being passed from family to family under the cover of darkness. The last family he stayed with had also taken in an orphan from Odessa, a black-haired girl named Sonia. Chemistry.

In 1947, Sonia and Huang came to Palestine. He converted to Judaism, took the name Haim—"life"—for he considered himself reborn, and they married. In '48 both of them fought with the Palmah in Galilee. In '49 they settled in North Jerusalem so that Huang Haim could study in Rabbi Kook's Central Yeshiva. When the children came—David in 1951, Yosef four years later—Huang went to work as a post-office clerk.

For twelve years he stamped packages, noticing all the while the enthusiasm with which his co-workers devoured the dishes he brought for lunch—food from his childhood that he'd taught Sonia to cook. After saving up enough cash, the Lees opened the Shang Hai Palace, on Herzl Boulevard, in back of a Sonol petrol station. It was 1967, when spirits were high, everyone eager to forget death and find new pleasures, and business was brisk.

It had remained brisk, and now Huang Haim Lee was able to hire others to wait on tables, free to spend his day studying

Talmud and playing chess. A contented man, his sole regret that he hadn't been able to transmit his love for religion to his sons. Both were good boys: David, analytic, a planner—the perfect banker. Yossi, wholly physical, but brave and warmhearted. But neither wore a *kipah*, neither kept Shabbat nor was attracted to the rabbinic tractates that he found irresistible—the subtleties of inference and exegesis that captivated his mind.

Still, he knew he had little to complain about. His life had been a tapestry of good fortune. So many brushes with eternity, so many reprieves. Just last week he'd shoveled dirt over the bare roots of his new pomegranate tree, the last addition to his biblical garden. Experienced the privilege of planting fruit trees in Jerusalem.

Aliza saw him smile, a beautiful Chinese smile, so calm and self-satisfied. She turned to her husband and kissed his hand. Yossi looked at her, surprised by the sudden show of affection, smiled himself, looking just like the old man.

Across the room, Huang Haim moved his bishop. "Checkmate," he told Rabbi Stolinsky, and got up to take the baby.

Elias Daoud's wife had grown fatter each year, so that now it was like sharing a bed with a mountain of pillows. He liked it, found it comforting to reach out in the middle of the night and touch all that softness. To part thighs as yielding as custard, submerge himself in sweetness. Not that he would have ever expressed such sentiments to Mona. Women did best when they were keyed up, just a little worried. So he teased her about her eating, told her sternly that she was consuming his salary faster than he could earn it. Then silenced her tearful excuses with a wink and a piece of sesame candy he'd picked up on the way home.

Nice to be off-duty, nice to be in bed. He'd acquitted himself well, done an excellent job for the Jews.

Mona sighed in her sleep and covered her face with a sausage of an arm. He raised himself up on his elbows. Looked at her, the dimpled elbow rising with each breath. Smiling, he began tickling her feet. Their little game. Waking her gently, before climbing the mountain.

She was exactly the kind of girl his father would have hated, Avi knew. Which made her all the more attractive to him.

Moroccan, to begin with, purely South Side. One of those working-class types who lived to dance. And young—not more than seventeen.

He'd spotted her right away, talking with two other chickies who were total losers. But no loser, this one—really cute, in an obvious look-at-me kind of way. Far too much makeup. Long hair dyed an improbable black and styled in a fancy, feathery cut—which made sense because she'd told him she cut hair for a living; it was only logical that she'd want to show it off. The face under the feathery bangs was sweet enough: glossy cherry lips, huge black eyes, at the bottom a little pointy chin. And she had a great body, slender, no hair on her arms—which was hard to find in a dark girl. Tiny wrists, tiny ankles, one with a chain around it. And best of all, big soft breasts. Too big for the rest of her, really, which played off against the slenderness. All of it packed into a skintight black jumpsuit of some kind of wet-looking vinyl material.

The fabric had given him his opening line.

"Spill your drink?" Giving her the Belmondo smile, curling it around the cigarette, putting his hands on his hips and showing off his tight physique under the red Fila shirt.

A giggle, the bat of an eyelash, and he knew she'd agree to dance with him.

He could feel the big breasts, now, as they did the slow dance to an Enrico Macias ballad, the discotheque finally quiet after hours of rock. Nice soft mounds flattening against his chest. Twin pressure points, the hardness in his groin exerting a pressure of its own. She knew it was there and though she didn't press back, she didn't back away from it either, which was a good sign.

She ran her hand over his shoulder and he let his fingers explore lower, caressing her tailbone in time with the music. One fingertip dared going lower, probing the beginnings of her gluteal cleft.

"Naughty, naughty," she said, but made no attempt to stop him.

His hand dipped lower again, moving automatically. Cupping one buttock, nice and rubbery, all of it fitting into his palm. He pinched lightly, went back to massaging her lower back in time with the music, humming in her ear and kissing her neck.

She raised her face, mouth half-open, kind of smiling. He

brushed her lips with his, then moved in. There was a tangy taste to the kiss, as if she'd eaten spicy food and the heat had remained imbedded in her tongue. His breath, he knew, was bitter with alcohol. Three gin and tonics, more than he usually allowed himself. But working the murder case had made him nervous—all that reading, not knowing what he was doing, petrified of looking stupid—and now that it was over he needed the release. His first night back in Tel Aviv since the hassle with Asher Davidoff's blonde. It wouldn't be his last.

In the end it hadn't turned out bad. Sharavi had asked him to write up the final draft of the report, wanting him to be some damned secretary. The thought of all those words had made his knees go weak and he'd surprised himself by opening his mouth.

"I can't do it, Pakad."

"Can't do what?"

"Anything. I'm going to quit the police force." Blurted it out, just like that, though he hadn't come to a decision about it yet.

The little Yemenite had nodded as if he'd expected it. Stared at him with those gold-colored eyes and said, "Because of the dyslexia?"

It had been his turn to stare then, nodding dumbly, in shock, as Sharavi kept talking.

"Mefakeah Shmeltzer told me you take an extraordinary amount of time to read things. Lose your place a lot and have to start over again. I called your high school and they told me about it."

"I'm sorry," Avi had said, feeling stupid the moment the words left his lips. He'd trained himself long ago not to apologize.

"Why?" asked Sharavi. "Because you have an imperfection?"

"I'm just not suited for police work."

Sharavi held up his left hand, showed him the scars, a real mess.

"I can't box with bad guys, Cohen, so I concentrate on using my brains."

"That's different."

Sharavi shrugged. "I'm not going to try to talk you into it. It's your life. But you might think of giving yourself some more time. Now that I know about you, I could keep you away from paperwork. Concentrate on your strengths." Smiling: "If you have any."

The Yemenite had taken him for a cup of coffee, asked him

about his problem, gotten him to talk about it more than anyone ever had. A master interrogator, he realized later. Made you feel good about opening up.

"I know a little bit about dyslexia," he had said, looking down at his bad hand. "After '67, I spent two months in a rehabilitation center—Beit Levinstein, near Ra'nana—working on getting some function back in the hand. There were kids there with learning problems, a few adults too. I watched them struggle, learning special ways to read. It seemed like a very difficult process."

"It's not that bad," Avi replied, rejecting the pity. "A lot of things are worse."

"True," said Sharavi. "Stick around Major Crimes and you'll see plenty of them."

The girl and he had been dancing and kissing for what seemed like hours but had to be only minutes because the Macias song had just ended.

"Anat," he said, escorting her off the dance floor, away from the crowd, away from her loser buddies, to a dark corner of the discotheque.

"Yes?"

"How about going for a drive?" Taking her hand.

"I don't know," she said, but coyly, clearly not meaning it. "I have to work tomorrow."

"Where do you live?"

"Bat Yam."

Deep south. Figured.

"I'll drive you home then." Her back was to the wall and Avi put his arm around her waist, leaned in and gave her another kiss, a short one. He felt her body go loose in his arms.

"Umm," she said.

"Would you like another drink?" Smile, smile, smile.

"I'm not really thirsty."

"A drive, then?"

"Uh . . . okay. Let me tell my friends."

Later, when she saw the red BMW, she got *really* excited, couldn't wait to get in.

He switched off the alarm, held the door open for her, said, "Seat belt," and helped her fasten the harness, touching her breasts in the process, really feeling them, the nipples hard as pencil erasers. Giving her another kiss and then ending it abruptly.

Walking around to the driver's side, he got in, started up the engine, gave it gas so that it roared, slipped an Elvis Costello tape in the deck and drove away from Dizengoff Circle. He took Frischmann west to Hayarkon Street, then headed north on Hayarkon, parallel with the beach. Ibn Gvirol would have been a more direct route to the destination he had in mind, but the water—hearing the waves, smelling the salt—was more romantic.

Years ago Hayarkon had been Tel Aviv's red light district, actual scarlet bulbs glowing atop the entrances to sleazy sailor bars. Fat Romanian and Moroccan girls in hot pants and net stockings slouching in the doorways, the color of the light making them look like sunburnt circus clowns. Crooking their fingers and warbling *bohena yeled!* "Come here, little boy!" When he was in high school he'd gone there plenty, with his North Side friends, getting laid, smoking a little hash. Now Hayarkon was fast becoming respectable, the big hotels with their cocktail lounges and nightclubs, the cafés and bars that picked up the overflow crowd, and the hookers had moved on, farther north, to the dunes of Tel Baruch.

Avi shifted into fourth and drove quickly toward those dunes, Anat grooving to Costello, snapping her fingers and singing along with "Girl Talk," her hand resting casually on his knee, not even bothering to point out that Bat Yam was in the opposite direction.

He drove past the bathing beach, came to the entrance to the port, where Hayarkon ended. Speeding over the Ta'Arukha Bridge, he crossed the Yarkon River and kept going until he reached a construction site just south of the dunes, but with a view of the cars parked in the sand.

Coming to a stop in the shadow of a crane, he turned off the engine and switched off the lights. From the dunes came the sound of music—drumbeats and guitars, the whores partying, sashaying in the sand, trying to create a mood for prospective customers. He visualized what was going on there, the action in each of the cars parked in the sand, and it turned him on.

He looked at Anat, took her hand in his, used the other to pull down the zipper of her jumpsuit, slide inside, and feel those amazing tits.

"What?" she asked. Which sounded silly, but he knew all about saying the wrong thing at the wrong time.

"Please," she said. Not making it clear if it was *please go on* or *please stop.*

It was all on the line now, time to go for it.

"I want you," he said, kissing each of her fingers. "I've got to have you." With just a touch of begging, the eagerness that he knew they all loved.

"Ohh," she sighed, as he began nuzzling her palm, licking, doing what he did best. What really made him feel important. Then sudden tension in that wonderful little body: "I don't know . . ."

"Anat, Anat." Slipping the jumpsuit off her shoulders, the vulnerability of sudden nakedness causing her to cling to him. "So beautiful," he said, taking a good look at the unfettered breasts, milky white in the night light. Not having to fake it.

He played with her, kissing each of the tiny, pebbly nipples, sucking on her tongue, and stroking her labia through the shiny black fabric. Taking her hand and guiding it to his erection.

When she didn't pull away he started to relax. When she began to wiggle and squirm, he smiled to himself. Mission accomplished.

Nahum Shmeltzer listened to scratchy Mozart and ate chickpeas from a can. On the arm of his easy chair was a plate containing slices of yellow cheese that had begun to stiffen around the edges and a pool of unflavored yogurt. He'd mixed the instant coffee too weak, but it didn't matter. It was the heat he wanted—to hell with the taste.

His home was a single room on the street level of a building in Romema. A sorry structure that had been built during the Mandate and remained unmodified since that time. The landlords were rich Americans who lived in Chicago and hadn't been to Jerusalem in ten years. He mailed his rent check to an agency on Ben Yehuda each month and expected nothing in return but basics.

Once upon a time, he'd owned a farm. Five *dunams* in a quiet *moshav* not far from Lod. Peaches and apricots and grapes and a plot for vegetables. A tired old plow horse for Arik to ride, a flower greenhouse for Leah. A chicken coop that yielded enough eggs for the entire *moshav*. Fresh omelettes and dewy cucumbers and tomatoes each morning. Back when taste had been important.

The road to Jerusalem had been lousy back then, nothing like the highway you had today. But he hadn't minded the daily drive to the Russian Compound. Nor the double load—working the streets all day, coming home to break his ass farming. The work was its own reward, the good feeling that came when you sank into bed each night, aching and ready to drop, knowing you'd given it your best. That you were making a difference.

ARBEIT MACHT FREI the Nazis had put on the signs they hung in the death camps. Work creates freedom. Those fucking assholes had meant something different, but there was truth in it. Or so he'd believed then.

Now everything was all fucked up, the boundaries gone—the borders between sane and insane, worthwhile and worthless . . . He caught himself, stopped. Philosophizing again. Must mean he was constipated.

The record stopped.

He got up out of the chair, turned off the phonograph, then walked two steps to the kitchen area and dumped the uneaten food into a cracked plastic wastebasket. Lifting a bottle of hundred-proof slivovitz from the counter, he carried it back with him.

Sipping slowly from the bottle, he let the liquor run down his gullet, feeling it burn a pathway straight to his stomach. Internal erosion. He imagined the damage to his tissue, enjoyed the pain.

As he grew progressively intoxicated, he began thinking of the butchered girl, her crazy eunuch of a brother. The punk they'd dug up in the olive grove, the maggots already holding a convention on his face. The case stunk. He knew it and he could tell that Dani knew it. Too clean, too cute.

That crazy, dickless eunuch. Pathetic. But who gave a shit—fucking Arabs slicing each other up over crazy pseudocultural nonsense. *Lumpen proletariat*. How many countries did they have—twenty? Twenty-five?—and they whined like shit-assed babies because they couldn't have the few square kilometers that belonged to the Jews. All that *Palestinian* bullshit. Back when he was a kid, the Jews had been Palestinians too. *He'd* been a goddamned Palestinian. Now it was a fucking catch phrase.

If the government was smart it would use *agents provocateurs* to fuck all the Arab virgins, convince the families that Ahmed next door had done it, supply them all with big knives, and set off a wave of revenge killings. Let them wipe themselves out—how long would it take? A month? Then we *Zhids* could finally have peace.

A laugh. With the Arabs gone, how long would it take for the Jews to chew each other up? What was the joke—a Jew had to have two synagogues. One that he went to, one that he rejected.

We're the princes of self-hatred, the standard-bearers of self-destruction; all you had to do was read the Torah—brothers fucking over brothers, raping their sisters, castrating their fathers. And murder, plenty of it, nasty stuff. Cain and Abel, Esau going after Jacob, Joseph's brothers, Absalom. Sex crimes, too—Amnon raping Tamar, the Concubine of Gilead gang-banged to death by the boys from Ephraim, then cut into twelve pieces by her master and mailed to all the other tribes, the rest of them taking revenge on Ephraim, wiping out all the men, capturing the women for you-know-what, enslaving the kids.

Religion.

When you got down to it, that was human history. Murder, mayhem, bloodlust, one guy fucking over another, like monkeys in a cramped cage. Generation after generation of monkeys dressed in people-suits. Screeching and cackling and scratching their balls. Pausing just long enough to cut one another's throats.

Which made him, he supposed, a fucking historian.

He raised the bottle to his lips and took a deep, incendiary swallow.

How he loathed humanity, the inevitable movement toward entropy. If there *was* a God, he was a fucking comedian. Sitting up there laughing as the monkey-men yammered and bit each other in the ass and jumped around in the shitpile.

Life was shit; misery the order of the day.

That's the way it was. That's definitely the way it was.

He gave a boozy belch and felt a wave of acid pain rise in his esophagus.

Another belch, another wave. Suddenly he felt nauseated and weak. More pain—good, he deserved it for being such a weak, naïve shmuck.

For understanding the way it was but being unable to accept it. Unable to throw out the pictures. Goddamned fucking framed snapshots on the table next to his cot. He woke up each morning and saw them first thing.

Starting the day off right.

Pictures. Arik in uniform, leaning on his rifle. *To Abba and Eema, With Love*. The kid had never been original. Just good.

Leah at the Dead Sea, in a flowered bathing suit and matching cap, covered to her knees with black mud. Rounded belly, lumpy hips—looking at the picture he could feel them under his fingertips.

Tomorrow morning he'd throw out the pictures. Right now he was too tired to move.

Bullshit. He was a coward. Trying to hold on to something that didn't exist anymore.

One year they were there; the next, gone, as if they'd never been real, only figments of his imagination.

A good year for death, 1974.

Eleven fucking years and he still couldn't deal with it.

Not only that, but it was getting to him more, working on Gray Man, now this one, the cruelty. The fucking stupidity.

Monkeys.

Tough guy.

Shmuck.

He drank some more, disregarding the pain. Pushing himself toward the blackness that always came.

The kid had been bivouacked in the Sinai, reading a book in his tent—Hegel, no less, according to the military messenger. As if that made a fucking bit of difference. Picked off by some faceless Egyptian sniper. Next year, on the same spot, a bunch of assholes from Canada built a luxury hotel. A few years later, all of it was back in Egypt. Traded for Sadat's signature. The word of a fucking Nazi collaborator.

Thank you very much.

Leah never recovered. It ate her like a cancer. She wanted to talk about it all the time, always asking why us, what did we do to deserve it, Nahum? As if he had an answer. As if an answer existed.

He had no patience for that kind of thing. Got to where he couldn't stand the sight of her, the crying and the whining. He avoided her by burying himself in the double load, catching assholes, growing peaches. He came home one day, ready to avoid her again, and found her laid out on the kitchen floor. Cold as slate, waxy gray. He didn't need a fucking doctor to tell him what the story was.

Cerebral aneurysm. She'd probably been born with it. No way to know, tsk, tsk, sorry.

Thank you very much.

Fuck you very much.

23

Gene and Luanne wanted something authentic, so Daniel and Laura took them to The Magic Carpet, a Yemenite restaurant on Rehov Hillel, owned by the Caspi family. The dining room was long and low, bathed in dim, bluish light, the walls alternating panels of white plaster decorated with Yemenite baskets, and blown-up photographs of the '48 airlift after which the restaurant had been named. Swarms of robed and turbaned Yemenite Jews alighting from gravid prop planes. The Second Wave of emigration from San'a. The one everyone knew about. If you were Yemenite they assumed you'd come over on the Carpet, were genuinely shocked when they found out Daniel's family had lived in Jerusalem for over a century. Which in most cases meant longer than theirs.

"You were right," said Luanne. "This is very hot, almost like Mongolian food. I like it. Isn't it good, honey?"

Gene nodded and continued spooning the soup into his mouth, hunched over the table, big black fingers holding the utensil tightly, as if it threatened to float away.

The four of them sat at a corner table shadowed by hanging plants as they feasted upon steaming bowls of *marak basar* and *marak sha'uit*—chili-rich meat soup and bean soup.

"It took me a while to get used to it," said Laura. "We'd go over to Daniel's father's house and he'd make all these wonderful-looking dishes. Then I'd try them and my mouth would catch fire."

"I've toughened her up," said Daniel. "Now she takes more spice than I do."

"My taste buds are shot, sweetheart. Beyond all pain." She put her arm around him, touched his smooth brown neck. He looked at her—blond hair down and combed out, wearing a little makeup, a clinging gray knit dress, and filigree earrings—and let his hand drop to her knee. Felt his feelings surface, the same feelings as when they'd first met. The *mutual zap,* she'd called it. Something to do with American comic books and magic powers . . .

The waitress, one of the six Caspi daughters—Daniel could never remember who was who—brought a bottle of Yarden Sauvignon and poured the wine into long-stemmed glasses.

"In your honor," said Daniel, toasting. "May this be only the first of many visits."

"Amen," said Luanne.

They drank in silence.

"So you enjoyed the Galilee," said Laura.

"Nothing's like Jerusalem," said Luanne. "The vitality—you can just feel the spirituality, from every stone. But Galilee was fantastic, just the same."

She was a handsome woman, tall—almost as tall as Gene—with square, broad shoulders, graying hair marcelled into precise waves, and strong African features. She wore a simple boat-necked dress of off-white silk striped diagonally in navy-blue, a strand of pearls, and pearl earrings. The dress and the jewelry set off her skin, which was the same color as Daniel's.

"To be able to actually see everything you've read about in the Scriptures," she said. "The Church of the Annunciation, realizing that you're putting your feet down in the same spot where He walked—it's unbelievable."

"Did the guide take you to see the Church of Saint Joseph also?" asked Laura.

"Oh, yes. And the cave underneath—I could just visualize Joseph's workshop, him working there on his carpentry, Mary upstairs, maybe cooking or thinking about when the baby was going to come. When I come back and tell my class about it, it will inject a real sense of life into our lessons." She turned to Gene: "Isn't it just amazing, honey, seeing it like that?"

"Amazing," said Gene, the word coming out slurred because he was chewing, the heavy jaws working, the big gray mustache revolving as if gear-driven. He broke off a piece of pita and put it in his mouth. Emptied his wineglass and mouthed *thank you* when Daniel refilled it for him.

"I'm keeping a log," said Luanne. "Of all the holy spots we visit. For a project that I promised the children—a Holy Land sojourn map to hang up in the classroom." She reached into her purse and took out a small note pad. Daniel recognized it as the type that Gene used, marked LAPD.

"So far," she said, "I've got eighteen churches listed—some of them we haven't actually gone into but we've passed them close by, so I consider it legal to include them. Then there are the natural landmarks: This morning we saw a stream in Tiberias that fed Mary's well, and yesterday we visited the Gethsemane garden and the hill of Golgotha—it really does look like a skull, doesn't it?—though Gene couldn't see it." To her husband: "I certainly saw it, Gene."

"Eye of the beholder," said Gene. "Are you eating all of your soup?"

"Take it, honey. All the walking we did, you need your nutrition."

"Thanks."

The waitress brought a plate of appetizers: stuffed peppers and marrows, chopped oxtail, kirshe, pickled vegetables, slices of grilled kidney, coin-sized barbecued chicken hearts.

"What's this?" asked Gene, tasting some of the kirshe.

"It's a traditional Yemenite dish called kirshe," said Laura. "The meat is chopped pieces of cow's intestine, boiled, then fried with onion, tomatoes, garlic, and spices."

"Chitlins," said Gene. Turning to his wife: "Excuse me, chitterlings." He took some more, nodded approvingly. Picking up the menu, he put on a pair of half-glasses and scanned it.

"Got a lot of organ meats here," he said. "Poor folks' food."

"Gene," said Luanne.

"What's the matter?" asked her husband innocently. "It's true. Poor folks eat organs 'cause it's an efficient way of getting protein and rich folks throw it away. Rich folk eat sirloin steaks and get all the cholesterol and clogged arteries. Now you tell *me* who's smarter?"

"Liver is an organ meat and liver is *loaded* with cholesterol," said Luanne. "Which is why the doctor took *you* off it."

"Liver doesn't count. I'm talking hearts, lungs, glands—"

"All right, dear."

"Those people," said Gene, pointing to pictures on the walls. "Every one of them is skinny. They all look in great shape, even the old ones. From eating organs." He speared several chicken hearts with his fork and swallowed them.

"It's true," said Laura. "When the Yemenites first arrived,

they had less heart disease than anyone. Then they started assimilating and eating like the Europeans and developed the same health problems as everyone else."

"There you go," said Gene, looking at the menu again. "What's this expensive stuff—'geed'?"

Daniel and Laura looked at each other. Laura burst out laughing.

"*Geed* means penis," explained Daniel, struggling to remain straight-faced. "It's prepared like kirshe—sliced and fried with vegetables and onions."

"Ouch," said Gene.

"Some of the old people order it," said Laura, "but it's pretty obsolete. They put it on the menu but I doubt they have it."

"Penis shortage, huh?" said Gene.

"Honey!"

The black man grinned.

"Get the recipe, Lu. We get back home you can cook it for Reverend Chambers."

"Oh, Gene," said Luanne, but she was stifling a giggle herself.

"Can't you just see it, Lu? We're sitting around at the church supper, with all your tight-girdled bridge buddies jabbering on and tearing people down, and I turn to them and say, 'Now, girls, stop gossiping and eat your penis!' What kind of animal they use?"

"Ram, or bull," said Daniel.

"For the church supper, we'd definitely need bull."

"I think," said Luanne, "that I'd like to go powder my nose."

"I'll join you," said Laura.

"Ever notice that?" said Gene, after the women had left. "Put two females together and they have this instinctive urge to go to the bathroom at the same time. Just let two fellows do that and people start to figure there's something funny about them."

Daniel laughed. "Maybe it's hormones," he said.

"Gotta be, Danny Boy."

"How are you enjoying your visit?"

Gene rolled his eyes and picked a crumb out of his mustache. He leaned closer, pressing his palms together prayerfully.

"Rescue me, Danny Boy. I love that woman to death, but she's got this religious thing—always has. At home I don't mind it because she raises Gloria and Andrea straight and narrow—

she certainly gets the credit for what they are. But what I'm fast finding out is that Israel's one big religious candy store—everywhere you go there's some sort of church or shrine or Jesus Slept Here whoozis. And Lu can't bear to miss one of them. I'm a profane person, start seeing double after a while."

"There's a lot more to Israel than shrines," said Daniel. "We've got the same problems as anyone else."

"Tell me quick. I need a shot of reality."

"What do you want to hear about?"

"The *job,* guy, what do you think? What kind of stuff you've been working on."

"We just finished a homicide—"

"This one?" asked Gene, reaching into his pocket and drawing out a newspaper clipping. He handed it to Daniel.

Yesterday's *Jerusalem Post.* Laufer's press release had been used verbatim—just like in the Hebrew papers—with the conspicuous addition of a tag line:

. . . LED BY CHIEF INSPECTOR DANIEL SHARAVI. SHARAVI ALSO HEADED THE TEAM THAT INVESTIGATED THE ASSASSINATION OF RAMLE PRISON WARDEN ELAZAR LIPPMANN LAST AUTUMN, AN INQUIRY THAT LED TO THE RESIGNATION AND PROSECUTION OF SEVERAL SENIOR PRISON OFFICIALS ON CHARGES OF CORRUPTION AND . . ."

He put the clipping down.

"You're a star, Danny Boy," said Gene. "Only time I ever received that kind of coverage was when I got shot."

"If I could wrap up the publicity and give it to you, I would, Gene. Tied with a ribbon."

"What's the problem, threatening the brass?"

"How'd you know?"

Gene's smile was as clean as a paper cut. Pure white against umber, like a slice out of a coconut.

"Ace detective, remember?" He picked up the clipping, put his half-glasses on again. "All that good stuff about you and then they just throw in the other guy—Laufer—at the end. No matter that the other guy is probably a Mickey Mouse pencil-pusher who didn't do a thing to deserve having his name in there in the first place. Executive types don't like being preempted. How'm I doing?"

"A-plus," said Daniel and thought of telling Gene about his *protekzia* with Gavrieli, how he'd lost it and now had to deal with

Laufer, then reconsidered and talked about the Rashmawi case instead. All the loose ends, the things he didn't like about it.

Gene listened and nodded. Starting, finally, to enjoy the vacation.

They broke off the discussion when the women returned. The conversation shifted to children, schools. Then the entrees came—a heaping mixed grill—and all conversation died.

Daniel watched, with awe, as Gene consumed lamb chops, sausage, shishlik, kebab, grilled chicken, serving after serving of saffron rice and bulghur salad. Washing it down with beer and water. Not wolfing—on the contrary, eating slowly, with an almost dainty finesse. But steadily and efficiently, avoiding distraction, concentrating on the food.

The first time he'd seen Gene eat had been in a Mexican restaurant near Parker Center. Nothing kosher there—*he'd* nursed a soft drink and eaten a salad, watching the black detective attack an assortment of tasty-looking dishes. He'd learned the names since Tio Tuvia had come to Jerusalem: burritos and tostadas, enchiladas and chile rellenos. Beans, pancakes, spicy meat—except for the cheese, not all that different from Yemenite food.

His first thought had been that if the man ate like that all the time, he would weigh two hundred kilos. Learning, over the course of the summer, that Gene did eat like that all the time, had no use for exercise, and managed to stay normal-looking. About a meter nine tall, maybe ninety kilos, a bit of a belly but not bad for a guy in his late forties.

They'd met at Parker Center—a bigger, shinier version of French Hill Headquarters. In orientation, listening to an FBI agent talk about terrorism and counterterrorism, the logistics of keeping things safe with that many people around.

The Olympics job had been a real plum, the last one Gavrieli had handed him before the Lippmann case. The opportunity to go to Los Angeles, all expenses paid, gave Laura a chance to see her parents and visit old friends. The kids had been talking about Disneyland since Grandpa Al and Grandma Estelle had told them about it.

The assignment had turned out to be a quiet one—he and eleven other officers tagging along with the Israeli athletes. Nine in Los Angeles, two with the rowing team in Santa Barbara, ten-hour shifts, rotating schedules. There had been a couple of weak rumors that had to be taken seriously anyway. Some hate mail signed by the Palestine Solidarity Army and traced, the day before the Games, to an inmate of the state mental hospital in Camarillo.

But mostly it was watching, hours of inactivity, eyes always on the lookout for anything that didn't fit: heavy coats in hot weather, strange contours under garments, furtive movements, the look of hatred on a jumpy, terrified face—probably young, probably dark, but you never could be sure. The look imprinted on Daniel's brain: an aura, a storm warning, before the seizure of stunning, stomach-churning violence.

A quiet assignment, no Munich in L.A. He'd ended each shift with a tension headache.

He'd sat in the front of the room during the orientation lecture and grown aware, before long, that someone was looking at him. A few backward glances located the source of scrutiny: a very dark black man in a light-blue summer suit, a SUPERVISOR identification badge clipped to his lapel. Local police.

The man was heavily built, older—late forties to early fifties, Daniel figured. Bald on top with gray hair at the sides, the hairless crown resembling gift candy—a mound of bittersweet chocolate nestled in silver foil. A thick gray mustache flared out from under a broad, flat nose.

He wondered why the man was looking at him, tried smiling and received a curt nod in response. Later, after the lecture, the man remained behind after the others had left, chewed on his pen for a few seconds, then pocketed it and walked toward him. When he got close enough, Daniel read the badge: LT. EUGENE BROOKER, LAPD.

Putting on a pair of half-glasses, Brooker looked down at Daniel's badge.

"Israel, huh. I've been trying to figure out what you are."

"Pardon me?"

"We've got all types in town. It's a job to sort out who's who. When I first saw you I figured you for some sort of West Indian. Then I saw the skullcap and wondered if it was a yarmulke or some type of costume."

"It's a yarmulke."

"Yeah, I can see that. Where are you from?"

"Israel." Was the man stupid?

"*Before* Israel."

"I was born in Israel. My ancestors came from Yemen. It's in Arabia."

"You related to the Ethiopians?"

"Not to my knowledge."

"My wife's always been interested in Jews and Israel," said Brooker. "Thinks you guys are the chosen people and reads a lot of books on you. She told me there are some black Jews in Ethiopia. Starving along with the rest of them."

"There are twenty thousand Ethiopian Jews," said Daniel. "A few have immigrated to Israel. We'd like to get the others out. They're darker than me—more like you."

Brooker smiled. "You're no Swede, yourself," he said. "You've also got some Black Hebrews over in Israel. Came over from America."

A delicate topic. Daniel decided to be direct.

"The Black Hebrews are a criminal cult," he said. "They steal credit cards and abuse their children."

Brooker nodded. "I know it. Busted a bunch of them a couple of years ago. Con artists and worse—what we American law-enforcement personnel call *sleazeballs*. It's a technical term."

"I like that," said Daniel. "I'll remember it."

"Do that," said Brooker. "Sure to come in handy." Pause. "Anyway, now I know all about you."

He stopped talking and seemed embarrassed, as if not knowing where to go with the conversation. Or how to end it. "How'd you like the lecture?"

"Good," said Daniel, wanting to be tactful. The lecture had seemed elementary to him. As if the agent were talking down to the policemen.

"I thought it was Mickey Mouse," said Brooker.

Daniel was confused.

"The Mickey Mouse of Disneyland?"

"Yeah," said Brooker. "It's an expression for something that's too easy, a waste of time." Suddenly he looked puzzled himself. "I don't know how it came to mean that, but it does."

"A mouse is a small animal," suggested Daniel. "Insignificant."

"Could be."

"I thought the lecture was Mickey Mouse, too, Lieutenant Brooker. Very elementary."

"Gene."

"Daniel."

They shook hands. Gene's was large and padded, with a solid

core of muscle underneath. He smoothed his mustache and said, "Anyway, welcome to L.A., and it's a pleasure to meet you."

"Pleasure to meet you too, Gene."

"Let me ask you one more thing," said the black man. "Those Ethiopians, what's going to happen to them?"

"If they stay in Ethiopia, they'll starve with everyone else. If they're allowed out, Israel will take them in."

"Just like that?"

"Of course. They're our brothers."

Gene thought about that. Fingered his mustache and looked at his watch.

"This is interesting," he said. "We've got some time—how about lunch?"

They drove to the Mexican place in Gene's unmarked Plymouth, talked about work, the similarities and differences between street scenes half a world apart. Daniel had always conceived of America as an efficient place, where initiative and will could break through the bureaucracy. But listening to Gene complain—about paperwork, useless regulations handed down by the brass, the procedural calisthenics American cops had to perform in order to satisfy the courts—changed his mind, and he was struck by the universality of it all. The policeman's burden.

He nodded in empathy, then said, "In Israel there's another problem. We are a nation of immigrants—people who grew up persecuted by police states. Because of that, Israelis resent authority. There's a joke we tell: Half the country doesn't believe there's such a thing as a Jewish criminal; the other half doesn't believe there's such a thing as a Jewish policeman. We're caught in the middle."

"Know the feeling," said Gene. He wiped his mouth, took a drink of beer. "You ever been to America before?"

"Never."

"Your English is darned good."

"We learn English in school and my wife is American—she grew up here in Los Angeles."

"That right? Whereabouts?"

"Beverlywood."

"Nice neighborhood."

"Her parents still live there. We're staying with them."

"Having a good time?"

Interrogating him, like a true detective.

"They're very nice people," said Daniel.

"So are *my* in-laws." Gene smiled. "Long as they stay in Georgia. How long have you been married?"

"Sixteen years."

Gene was surprised. "You look too young. What was it, a high school romance?"

"I was twenty; my wife was nineteen."

Gene calculated mentally. "You look younger than that. I did the same kind of thing—got out of the army at twenty-one and married the first woman who came along. It lasted seven months—burned me good and made me careful. For the next couple of years I took my time, played the field. Even after I met Luanne, we had a long engagement, working all the bugs out. Must have been the right thing to do, 'cause we've been together for twenty-five years."

Up until then, the black detective had come across as tough and dour, full of the cynical humor and world-weariness that Daniel had seen in so many older policemen. But when he talked about his wife, his face creased in a wide smile and Daniel thought to himself: He loves her intensely. He found that depth of feeling something he could relate to, causing him to like the man more than he had in the beginning.

The smile remained as Gene pulled out a bruised-looking wallet, stuffed with credit card slips and fuzzy-edged scraps of paper. He unfolded it, pulled out snapshots of his daughters and showed them to Daniel. "That's Gloria—she's a teacher, like her mother. Andrea's in college, studying to be an accountant. I told her to go all the way, become a lawyer and make a lot more money, but she's got her own mind."

"That's good," said Daniel, producing snapshots of his own. "Having your own mind."

"Yeah, I suppose so, long as the mind's in the right place." Gene looked at the pictures of the Sharavi children. "Very cute—husky little guys. Aha, now *she's* a beauty—looks like you, except for the hair."

"My wife is blond."

Gene gave the pictures back. "Very nice. You got a nice family." The smile continued to linger, then faded. "Raising kids is no picnic, Daniel. The whole time my girls were growing up I was watching for danger signs, probably drove them a little crazy. Too many temptations, they see stuff on TV and want it without having to wait for it. Instant highs, which is why they get onto dope—you've got that, too, don't you, being close to the poppy fields?"

"Not like in America, but more than we ever had before. It's a problem."

"There are two ways to solve it," said Gene. "One, make all of it legal so there's no incentive to deal, and forget all about morality. Or two, execute all the dealers and the users." He made a gun with his fingers. "Bang, you're dead, every one of them. Anything short of that doesn't stand a chance."

Daniel smiled noncommittally, not knowing what to say.

"Think I'm joking?" asked Gene, calling for the check. "I'm not. Twenty-four years on the force and I've seen too many kacked-out junkies and dope-related crimes to think there's any other way."

"We don't have capital punishment in Israel."

"You hung that German—Eichmann."

"We make an exception for Nazis."

"Then start thinking of dope scum as Nazis—they'll kill you the same way." Gene lowered his voice. "Don't let what's happened here happen over there—my wife would be very disillusioned. She's a serious Baptist, teaches in a Baptist school, been talking about seeing the Holy Land for years. Like it's some kind of Garden of Eden. Be terrible for her to learn any different."

Luanne was back on the subject of churches. The Holy Sepulchre, in particular. Daniel knew the history of the place, the infighting for control that went on constantly between the different Christian groups—the Greeks battling the Armenians, who battled the Roman Catholics, who battled the Syrians. The Copts and the Ethiopians banished to tiny chapels on the roof.

And the orgies that had taken place during the Ottoman era—Christian pilgrims fornicating in the main chapel because they believed a child conceived near Christ's burial place would be destined for greatness.

It didn't shock him. All it proved was that Christians were humans, too, but he knew Luanne would be appalled.

She was an impressive woman, so wholehearted in her faith. One of those people who seem to know where they're going, make those around them feel secure. He and Laura listened attentively as she talked about the feelings that came from standing in the presence of the Holy Spirit. How much she'd grown after three days in the Holy Land. He didn't share her beliefs, but he related to her fervor.

He promised himself to give her a special tour, Jewish and Christian places, as many as time would allow. An insider's visit to Bethlehem, to the Greek Patriarchate and the Ethiopian chapel. A look at the Saint Saviour's library—he'd call Father Bernardo in the morning.

The waitress—this one was Galia, he was almost certain—served Turkish coffee, melon, and a plate of pastries: Bavarian creams, napoleons, rum-soaked *Savarinas*. They all sipped coffee and Gene went to work on a napoleon.

Afterward, logy from food and wine, they walked down Keren Hayesod, hand in hand like double-daters, enjoying the freshness of the night, the silence of the boulevard.

"Umm," said Luanne, "smells like out in the country."

"Jerusalem pines," said Laura. "They set their roots in three feet of soil. Beneath that, everything is solid rock."

"A strong foundation," said Luanne. "Has to be."

The next day was Friday and Daniel stayed home. He allowed the children to skip school and spent the morning with them, in Liberty Bell Park. Kicking a soccer ball around with the boys, watching Shoshi skate around the roller rink, buying them blue ices and eating a chocolate casatta himself.

Just after noon an Arab on a camel came riding through the parking lot adjacent to the park. Pulling the animal to a halt just outside the south gate of the park, he dismounted and rang a brass bell hanging around its neck. Children queued up for rides and Daniel allowed the boys to have two turns each.

"How about you?" he asked Shoshi as she untied her skates.

She stood, put her hands on her hips, and let him know the question was ridiculous.

"I'm no baby, Abba! And besides, it smells."

"Rather drive a car, eh?"

"Rather ride while my husband drives."

"Husband? Do you have someone in mind?"

"Not yet," she said, leaning against him and putting her arm around him. "But I'll know him when I meet him."

After the rides were over, the Arab helped Benny off the

camel and handed him to Daniel, kicking and giggling. Daniel said, "Sack of potatoes," and slung the little boy over his shoulder.

"Me too! Me too!" demanded Mikey, pulling at Daniel's trousers until he relented and hoisted him up on the other shoulder. Carrying both of them, his back aching, he began the walk home, past the Train Theater, through the field that separated the park from their apartment building.

A man was walking toward them, and when he got close enough Daniel saw that it was Nahum Shmeltzer. He shouted a greeting and Shmeltzer gave a small wave. As he approached, Daniel saw the look on his face. He put the boys down, told the three of them to run up ahead.

"Time us, Abba!"

"Okay." He looked at his watch. "On your mark, get set, go."

When the children were gone he said, "What is it, Nahum?"

Shmeltzer righted his eyeglasses. "We've got another body, in the forest near Ein Qerem. A repeat of the Rashmawi girl, so close it could be a photocopy."

Book Two

24

As a small child, the Grinning Man had been a poor sleeper. Fidgety during the day and afraid of the dark, he went as rigid as hardwood during slumber, easily startled by the faintest night sound. The type of youngster who could have benefited from warm milk and bedtime stories, consistency and calm. Instead, he was yanked awake regularly by a raging of voices: the bad-machine sound of his parents tearing each other apart.

It was always the same, always terrible. He'd find himself sitting upright in bed, cold and wet from pee, toes curled so tightly that his feet hurt, waiting with a burnt-rubber taste in his mouth until the ugliness came into focus.

Once in a while, in the beginning, they did it upstairs—either of their bedrooms could serve as a killing ground—and when this happened, he'd climb out of bed and tiptoe from the Child's Wing across the landing, make a stumble-sneak to the Steinway grand, then slide under the giant instrument and settle there. Sucking his thumb, letting his fingertips brush against the cold metal of the foot pedals, the undercarriage of the piano looming above like some dark, voluptuous canopy.

Listening.

Usually, though, they fought downstairs, in the walnut-paneled library that looked out to the garden. *Doctor's room.* By the time he was five, they did it there all the time.

Everyone except *her* called his father Doctor, and for the first years of his life, he thought that was his father's name. So he called him Doctor, too, and when everyone laughed, he thought he'd done something terrific and did it again. By the time he learned that it was a stupid affectation and that other boys called their fathers Dad—even boys whose fathers were also doctors—it was too late to change.

Lots of times Doctor was cutting all day and into the night and slept at the hospital instead of coming home. When he did come home, it was always really late, way after the boy had been put to bed. And since he left for rounds an hour before the boy woke up, father and son rarely saw each other. One result of this, the Grinning Man believed, was that as an adult he had to struggle to retrieve a visual image of Doctor's face, and the picture he did produce was fragmented and distorted—a cracked death mask. He was also convinced that this problem had spread like a cancer, to the point where anyone's face eluded him—even when he managed to dredge up a mental picture of another human being, it vanished immediately.

It was as if his mind was a sieve—damaged—and it made him feel weak, lonely, and helpless. Really worthless when he let himself think about it. Out of control.

Only one type of picture stuck well—*real science* brought power—and only if he worked at it.

At first he thought Doctor was gone a lot because of work. Later he came to understand that he was avoiding what waited for him when he crossed the threshold of the big pink house. The insight was useless.

On Home Nights, Doctor usually put his black bag down in the entry hall and headed straight to the kitchen, where he fixed himself a sloppy sandwich and a glass of milk, then took the food into the dark-paneled library. If he wasn't hungry, he headed for the library anyway, sank into his big leather chair, loosened his tie, and sipped brandy while reading surgical journals by the light of a glass-shaded lamp with a weird-looking dragonfly on the shade. Unwinding before plodding heavily up the stairs for a few hours of sleep.

Doctor was a fitful sleeper, too, though he didn't know it. The boy knew because the door to Doctor's bedroom was always left open and his thrashing and moans were scary, echoing harshly across the landing. So scary it made the boy feel as if his insides were rattling and turning to dust.

Her bedroom—*le boudoir,* she called it—was never open. She locked herself in there all day. Only the smell of battle brought her out sniffing, like some night-prowling she-spider.

Though he could count on the fingers of one hand the number of times he'd been allowed in there, his memories of the place were vivid: cold space. *An ice palace*—that was the image that had stayed with him after all these years.

As white and bleak as a glacier. Treacherous marble floors,

white porcelain trays crammed with diamond-faceted crystal bottles, the facets sharp enough to wound, beveled mirrors that spat back skewed reflections, filmy hangings of white lace, dead and sickeningly ephemeral, like the molt of some soft-boned albino reptile.

And satin. Shimmering acres of it, shiny, cold, snotlike to the touch.

At the center of the glacier was an immense white fourposter bed on a platform with a tufted satin headboard, smothered by gelatinous layers of satin—sheets and comforters and draperies and pendulous window valances; even the closet doors were padded with panels of the slimy stuff. His mother was always naked, lying exposed from the waist up under a frothy satin tide, propped up by a satin bed-husband, cocktail glass in hand, taking small sips of an oily-looking colorless liquid.

Her hair was long and loose, Harlow-blond, her face ghostly and beautiful, like that of an embalmed princess. Shoulders white as soap, with little bumps where the collarbones arched upward. Rouged nipples like jelly candy.

And always the cat, the hateful Persian, fat and spineless as a cotton ball, snuggled against her breast, piggy, water-colored eyes shining with defiance at the boy, hissing ownership of all that female flesh, branding him an intruder.

Come-a-here, Snowball. Come to Mama, sweet thing.

The stink, also. More intense as he got closer to the bed. Shit-breath. The oily liqueur, redolent of juniper. French perfume, *Bal à Versailles,* so cloying even the recollection made him gag.

She slept all day and left the glacier at night to do battle with Doctor. Throwing open the door to her room and surging down the stairs in a swirl of satin.

They'd start. He'd wake up, jolted by the bad-machine sound—a cruel roar that wouldn't stop, as if he'd been locked in a shower, the water turned on full force. He'd get up, still groggy, trace a hypnotic path from his room to the top of the stairs, then down each step, feeling the heat of *her* bare feet radiating from the carpet. *Thirteen stairs.* He always counted in his head, always stopped at number six before sitting down to listen. Not daring to move as the machine sounds began to separate in his mind, his brain breaking the roar down into lip-smacking growls and bone-crunching syllables.

Words.

The same words, always. Hammer blows that made him cringe.

Good evening, Christina.

Don't good evening *me.* Where have you been!

Don't start, Christina. I'm tired.

You're tired? *I'm* tired. Of how you treat me. Where were you until ten after one!

Good night, Christina.

Answer me, you bastard! Where the *hell* have you been?

I don't have to answer your questions.

You goddamn *do* have to answer my questions!

You're entitled to your opinion, Christina.

Don't you dare smirk at me like that! WHERE HAVE YOU BEEN!

Lower your voice, Christina.

Answer me, damn you!

What do you *care?*

I care because this is my house, not some goddamned motel that you check in and out of!

Your *house? Amusing. What mortgage checks have you written lately?*

I pay the *real* bills, you bastard, from my soul—I gave up everything to be your whore!

Oh, really?

Yes, really, damn you.

And what is it exactly that you're supposed to have given up?

My career. My goddamned soul.

Your soul. I see.

Don't you dare smirk at me, you bastard!

All right, all right, no one's smirking. Just get out of here and no one will smirk at anyone.

I paid for *everything,* damn you—with blood and sweat and tears.

Enough, Christina. I'm tired.

You're tired? From what? Running around with your candy-striper whores—

I'm tired because I've been cracking chests all day.

Cracking chests. Big shot. Lousy bastard. Whore-fucker.

You're *the whore, remember? By your own admission.*

Shut up!

Fine. Now crawl back upstairs and leave me alone.

Don't you tell me what to do, you bastard! You're not my boss. I'm my own boss!

You're drunk, *is what you are.*

You drive me to drink.

Right, your weaknesses are my *responsibility.*

Don't laugh at me, I'm warning you—

You drink, *Christina, because you're weak. Because you can't face life. You're a coward.*

Bastard goddamned bastard! What's that *you're* guzzling, Coca-Cola?

I can handle my liquor.

I can *handle* my liquor.

Don't imitate me, Christina.

Don't *imitate* me, Christina.

Fine. Now get the hell out of here. Drink yourself cirrhotic and leave me alone.

Drink yourself *cirrhotic*. You and your fucking jargon, think you're a hotshot. Everyone thinks you're a pompous asshole—when I worked Four West, everyone said so.

Didn't stop you from licking my balls, did it?

It made me want to throw up. I did it for your money.

Fine. You've got my money. Now get the hell out of here.

I'll stay wherever the hell I want to.

You're out of control, Christina. Rambling. Make an appointment with Emil Diefenbach tomorrow and have him check you out for organic brain disease.

And you're a limpdick asshole.

Pathetic.

Stop smirking, limpdick!

Pathetic.

Maybe I am pathetic, maybe I am! At least I'm human, unlike you the fucking *machine* who can handle *everything. You're* perfect—Mister Per . . . *Doctor* Perfect! Handles anything except getting a hard-on! Doctor Limpdick Perfect!

Pathetic lush.

What is that, Coca-fucking-*Cola*!

Get away, Christina, I'm—

Sure doesn't taste like Coca-fucking—

Get away—

-Cola!

—Oh, shit, you spilled it all over me.

Poor baby, poor limpdick! Serves you right! Slob! Whore-fucker!

Get out of the way, you goddamned bitch! Get out of the way, *damn you! I need to clean this off!*

Just throw it out, Doctor Limpdick. Fucking Italian suit makes you look like a greaseball, anyway.

Move, Christina!

Whore-fucker.

MOVE!

Fuck you!

I'm warning *you!*

I'm *warning* you— Ow! You—oh, you pushed me you hurt me, you lousy stinking bastard! Oh! Ow, my foot—

Look at you. Dribbling. Pathetic.

You *pushed* me, you goddamned *cock*sucker!

Drunken cow!

Piece of shit!

Fucking lush!

STINKING FUCKING KIKE BASTARD!

Ah! There it is!

You're goddamned fucking *right* there it is, you filthy hook-nosed kike *limpdick*!

Go ahead, let it all out. Show your true colors, bitch!

JEW BASTARD!

White trash cunt!

KIKEKIKEKIKE! CRUCIFYING BASTARD!

25

The second victim was identified quickly.

After he'd picked up the sheet and looked at her, Daniel's first thought was: Fatma's older sister. The resemblance was that strong, down to the missing earrings.

They'd started working on the missing-kid files again, getting nowhere. But the interdepartmental gag was off, the story had hit the papers immediately, and passing her picture around brought results on Sunday, forty-eight hours after the body had been found: A detective from the Russian Compound, a recent transfer from Haifa, remembered her as someone he'd busted a few months ago, for soliciting down by the harbor. A phone call to Northern District brought her file down by police courier, but she'd been let go with a warning and there wasn't much to learn from it.

Juliet Haddad ("They call me *Petite* Julie"), born in Tripoli, a professional whore. Twenty-seven years old, dark and pretty, with a baby face that made her appear ten years younger.

The illusion of youth ended below the slashed neck—what remained of her body was flabby, mottled, the thighs lumpy and scarred with old cigarette burns. The uterus was gone, severed and lifted out like some bloody treasure, according to Dr. Levi's report, but tissue analyses of the other organs revealed evidence of gonorrhea and primary syphilis, successfully treated. Like Fatma, she'd been sedated with heroin, but for her it was no maiden voyage: scores of sooty, fibrosed needle marks surrounded the pair of fresh ones. Additional marks in the bend of her knees.

"She was washed as clean as the other," Dr. Levi told Daniel. "But physiologically speaking, she was far from spotless—a damaged young woman, probably abused for years. There were hairline fractures all over the skull—like spider-webbing. Some evidence of minor damage to the dura of the occipital and frontal lobes of the brain."

"Would that have affected her intelligence?"

"Hard to say. The cerebral cortex is too complex to assess retroactively. Loss of function in one area can be compensated for by another."

"How about an educated guess?"

"Not if you'll hold me to it."

"Off the record."

"Off the record, she may have had visual problems—distortions, blurring—and a dulling of emotional responses, like the patients the Russians do psychosurgery on. On the other hand, she may have functioned perfectly—there's no way to tell. I've examined brains that have necrosed to nothing—you'd bet the owner was a vegetable. Then you talk to the family and find out the guy played chess and solved complex math problems up until the day he died. And others that look picture-perfect and the owners were morons. You want to know how smart she was, find someone who knew her when she was alive."

"Any theories about the uterus?"

"What did the psychiatrists say?"

"I haven't spoken to any of them yet."

"Well," said Levi, "I suppose I can guess as well as they can. Hatred of women, destruction of femininity—removal of the root of femininity."

"Why take this one and not Fatma's?"

"Maniacs change, Dani, just like anyone else. Besides, Fatma's uterus was virtually obliterated, so in some sense he was destroying her womanhood, too. Maybe he removed this one in order to take his time with it, do God-knows-what. Maybe he's decided to start a collection—didn't Jack the Ripper start off by carving, then progress to removing organs? One of the kidneys, if I remember correctly, wasn't it? Sent a chunk to the police, claimed to have eaten the rest of it."

"Yes," said Daniel, thinking: butchery, cannibalism. Until Gray Man, such horrors had been pure theory, cases in the homicide textbook. The kind of thing he never thought he'd need to know about.

Levi must have read his mind.

"No sense escaping it, Dani," said the pathologist. "That's what you've got here—another Jack. Better bone up on maniacs. He who forgets history is condemned and all that."

According to Northern District, Juliet had claimed to be a Christian, a political refugee from East Beirut, wounded in the invasion and fleeing the Shiites and the PLO. Asked how she'd gotten into the country, she'd told a story of hitching a ride with an Israeli tank unit, which seemed far-fetched. But she'd showed the interrogators a recent head wound and a Kupat Holim registration card from Rambam Hospital to back the story up, along with a Haifa address and temporary-resident ID, and the police, busy with more serious matters than another small-change streetwalker, had accepted her story and let her go with a warning.

Which was unfortunate, because just a cursory investigation revealed that the story was a sham. Immigration had no record of her, the Haifa address was an abandoned building, and a visit by Shmeltzer and Avi Cohen to Rambam Hospital revealed that she'd been treated in the emergency room—for epilepsy, not a wound.

The doctor who'd seen her was gone, on a fellowship in the States. But his handwriting was clear and Shmeltzer read aloud from his discharge notes:

> Treated successfully with phenobarbitol and Dilantin, full abatement of overt seizure activity. The patient claims these seizures were her first, and stuck to this, despite my explicit skepticism. I wrote a prescription for a month's worth of medication which was provided to her by the hospital pharmacy, gave her Arabic-language brochures on epilepsy and admitted her for observation, including comprehensive neurologic and radiographic studies. The following morning, her bed was empty and she was nowhere to be found. She has not recontacted this institution. Diagnosis: Grand mal epilepsy. Status: Self-Discharged, Against Medical Advice.

"Translation," said Shmeltzer, "she was a little liar, conned them into free medication."

Avi Cohen nodded and watched the older man flip through the pages of the medical chart.

"Well, well, take a look at this, *boychik*. Under *Nearest Relative or Admitting Party,* there's a little army stamp."

Cohen leaned over, pretending he could make sense of it.

"Yalom, Zvi," read Shmeltzer. "*Captain* Zvi Yalom, Tank Corps—goddamned army captain checked her in. She was leveling about the tank unit." He shook his head. "The little slut had an official military escort."

To listen to Yalom, he'd acted solely out of compassion.

"Listen, you were there—you know how it was: the Good Border and all that. We fed hundreds of them, gave them free medical care."

"Those were political refugees," said Avi Cohen. "Christians. And all of them went back."

"She was Christian too."

"Got to know her pretty well, didn't you?"

Yalom shrugged and took a drink of orange soda. He was a handsome, somewhat coarse-looking man in his late twenties, blond, ruddy, and broad-shouldered, with immaculately manicured hands. In civilian life, a diamond cutter at the Tel Aviv Exchange. His home address in Netanya had been traced quickly through army records, and Avi had invited him for lunch at a sidewalk café near the beach.

A beautiful Monday morning. The sky was as blue as the sapphire in Yalom's ring; the sand, granulated sugar. But Netanya had changed, Avi decided. A lot different from the days when his family used to summer there—a suite at the Four Seasons, calls to room service for hamburgers and Cokes with maraschino cherries, all of them staying too long in the sun, getting burned pepper-red. After-dinner strolls, his father pointing out the gangsters sitting at café tables. Exchanging greetings with some of them.

Now, the buildings seemed shabbier, the streets more crowded, thick with traffic and exhaust fumes, like a miniature Tel Aviv. Just a block away he could see black people sitting on the front stoop of a decrepit-looking apartment building. Ethiopians—the government had settled hundreds of them here. The men wore *kipot*; the women covered their hair, too. Religious types, but in blackface. Strange.

"You going to get me into trouble?" asked Yalom.

Avi smiled noncommittally. He liked this, enjoyed the feeling of authority. Sharavi had made good on his word, kept him away from reading, given him a real assignment.

He's a Lebanon vet. You should be able to relate to him.

Thank you, Pakad.

Doing your job well will be sufficient thanks.

"It could really fuck me up, Avi," said Yalom.

Overly familiar, thought Avi, using my first name like that. But some military officers had an attitude problem, thought of the police as second-class soldiers.

"Speaking of fucking," he said, "is that how you met her?"

Yalom squinted with anger. He kept a smile on his lips and drummed his perfect fingertips on the table. "You a virgin, kid?"

"How about," said Avi, starting to stand, "we continue this conversation at National Headquarters."

"Wait," said Yalom. "Sorry. It's just that I'm nervous. The tape recorder bothers me."

Avi sat down again. Moved the recorder closer to Yalom.

"You've got good reason to be nervous."

Yalom nodded, reached into his shirt pocket, and offered a pack of Rothmans to Avi.

"No, thanks, but suit yourself."

The diamond cutter lit up, turning his head so that the smoke blew in the direction of the beach, the sea breeze catching it, thinning it to wispy ribbons. Avi looked over his shoulder, saw girls in bikinis carrying towels and beach baskets. Watched the little dimples in their backs, just above the ass-slit, and longed, for a moment, to be with them.

"She was scared," said Yalom. "The place she worked was on the Christian side of Beirut, private club, members only. She was afraid the Shiites would come and get her after we left."

"What kinds of members?" asked Avi, remembering what Sharavi had told him about the skull fractures, the cigarette burns.

"Foreigners. Diplomats, businessmen, professors from the American University. The place was too expensive for the locals, which was one of the reasons she wanted to get out—some fundamentalists had threatened to bomb the building, slapped up a poster calling it a receptacle for the semen of infidels, or something like that."

"You see that poster yourself?"

"No," said Yalom quickly. "I was never there. This was all from her."

"Where'd you meet her, then?"

"We were pulling out of the city. She was standing in the middle of the road, near the barriers between East and West. Waving her hands and crying. She refused to move and I couldn't just squash her, so I got out, checked for snipers, talked to her, felt sorry for her, and gave her a lift. She was supposed to go as far as Bin Jbeil, but then she started having seizures and I decided to take her all the way."

"Considerate of you."

Yalom grimaced. "All right, looking back it was stupid. But I felt sorry for her—it was no felony."

Avi sipped his beer.

"How many of you banged her?" he asked.

Yalom was silent. The hand holding his cigarette began to shake. Bad trait for someone in his line of work, thought Avi. He sipped and waited.

Yalom looked around at the adjoining tables, moved closer and lowered his voice.

"How the hell was I supposed to know she was going to get carved up?" he said. Avi saw that there were tears in his eyes, the tough-guy posture all gone. "I just got married a couple of months ago, Samal Cohen. It's my wife I'm more worried about than the army."

"Then why don't you just tell me the truth and I'll do my best to keep your name out of the papers."

"All right, all right. What I told you about picking her up out of sympathy is right—I was trying to be human. Look where it got me—when we let the Arabs massacre each other we're fucked and when we try to be human, the same damned thing. No way to win."

"You picked her up out of sympathy," said Avi, prompting. "But . . ."

"But a bunch of us had her, okay? She offered it for free, she was cute-looking, and we'd just been through two months of hell—the snipers, two of my best drivers were blown up by mines . . . For God's sake, you know what it was like."

Avi thought of his own tour in Lebanon. Hand-to-hand fighting in the streets of Beirut, routing the PLO, putting his own ass on the line in order not to shoot the women and children—the human shields those bastards used habitually. Then, a month of guard duty at Ansar Prison, feeling out of control as he stood watch over sulking hordes of PLO captives wearing the blue jogging suits the army issued them. Unable to stop the tough guys from bullying the weaker ones, unable to prevent them from building homemade spears and daggers. Hugging his Uzi like a lover as he watched the tough ones circle the flock, picking off the effeminate ones. Choosing the softest boys to be brides at mock weddings. Dressing them up like girls, painting their faces and plucking their eyebrows and beating them when they cried.

Gang-fucks when the lights went out. Avi and the other soldiers trying to shut out the screams that rose, like bloody clouds, above the grunts and heavy breathing. The "brides" who survived were treated the next morning for shock and torn anuses.

"I know," said Avi, meaning it. "I know."

"Three fucking years," said Yalom, "and for what? We've replaced the PLO with Shiites and now *they're* shooting Katyushas at us. You going to blame us for having a free taste? We didn't know if we were going to get out of there alive, so we had her, had a few giggles—it was temporary relief. I'd do it all over again—" He stopped himself. "Maybe I wouldn't. I don't know."

"What else did she say about her clients?" asked Avi, following the outline the Yemenite had suggested to him.

"They went in for rough stuff," said Yalom. "The brothel was designed to accommodate that type. Professors, educated types, you'd be surprised at the things that turned them on. I asked her how she could stand it. She said it was okay, pain was okay."

"As if she liked it?"

Yalom shook his head. "As if she didn't care. I know it sounds strange, but she *was* strange—kind of dull, half asleep."

"Like a defective?"

"Just dull, as if she'd been knocked around so much nothing mattered to her anymore."

"When she begged you to take her with you it mattered."

Yalom's face registered self-disgust. "She conned me. I'm a fool, okay?"

"You saw the needle marks on her arms, right?"

Yalom sighed. "Yes."

"She mention any friends or suppliers?"

"No."

"Anything about her past that could connect her to anyone? Maybe one of the educated ones?"

"No. We were in back of the halftrack, riding south in the dark. There wasn't much conversation."

"Nothing about the seizures?"

"No, that took me by surprise. All of a sudden she's all rigid, moving back and forth, teeth chattering, frothing at the mouth—I thought she was dying. You ever see that kind of thing?"

Avi remembered the epileptic kids in the Special Class. Retards and spastics, shaking and drooling. He'd felt like a freak being with them, cried hysterically until his mother had pulled him out.

"Never," he said. "What was she doing when it started to happen?"

"Sleeping."

"Lucky, huh?"

Yalom looked at the detective, puzzled.

"Lucky," said Avi, smiling, "that she wasn't going down on you when she started to shake. Hell of a way to pick up a war wound."

26

There was no record of Juliet's whereabouts during the four months following her release by Northern District. No pimp or whore or drug dealer admitted to knowing her; no substation had booked her. She hadn't applied for welfare or any other kind of public assistance, nor had she worked in a legitimate job and gotten on the tax rolls.

It was as if she'd gone underground, thought Daniel, like some kind of burrowing animal, surfacing only to be torn apart by a waiting predator.

She could have plied her profession independently, he knew, pulling tricks on side streets in out-of-the-way neighborhoods. Or taken an unregistered side job—as a charwoman or fruit picker. In neither case were they likely to find out about it. An employer would be less than enthusiastic about admitting he'd hired her illegally, and those who'd purchased her favors were sure to keep silent.

The strongest thing they had going for them was the epilepsy angle and the best way to work that was footwork: a canvass of doctors, hospitals, Kupat Holim clinics, and pharmacists. The medication she'd received at Rambam had run out some time ago, which meant she'd have gotten a refill somewhere.

They started, all of them, checking out neurologists and neurological clinics; when none of that bore fruit, moved on to general practitioners and emergency rooms. Showing Juliet's picture to busy people in white uniforms, searching for her name in patient rosters and charts. Eye-straining work, reeking of tedium. Avi Cohen was less than useless for most of it, so Daniel had him handle the telephones, cataloging crank calls and following the false leads and compulsive confessions that the newspaper articles had started to bring in.

By the end of the week they'd learned nothing and Daniel knew that the whole endeavor was questionable. If Juliet had been streetwise enough to get her hands on fake ID within days of coming across the border, she probably had multiples, with false names and birth dates. Her baby face would have allowed her to claim anything from seventeen to thirty. How could you trace someone like that?

Even if they managed to connect her to some doctor or druggist, what good would it do? This was no crime of passion, the victim's destiny interlaced with that of the killer. She'd been slain because of a chance meeting with a monster. Persuasive words, the exchange of money, perhaps. Then a rendezvous in some secret, dark place, the expectation of hurried sex, a recreational shot of dope. Blackness. Surgery.

He hoped neither she nor Fatma had ever known what was happening to them.

Surgery. He'd started thinking of it in medical terms, because of the anesthesia, the washing, the removal of the uterus, though Levi assured him that no special medical knowledge had been necessary to perform the extraction.

Simple stuff, Dani. A butcher or shohet *or nurse or medical corpsman could have done it without special training. If I gave you an anatomy book you could do it yourself. Anyone could. Whenever something like this happens people always start looking for a doctor. It's nonsense.*

The pathologist had sounded defensive, protective of his profession, but Daniel had no reason to doubt what he was saying.

Anyone.

But here they were, talking to doctors.

Hospitals.

Right after Fatma's murder, he'd thought about the Amelia Catherine, the proximity of the hospital to the dumping ground, how easy it would have been to hide the body in a big, empty building like that, sneak out at the right time during Schlesinger's shift in order to dump it. But apart from a rumor that Dr. Walid Darousha was homosexual, the Amelia Catherine people had turned up clean on every record check. And the trail he'd followed up through Silwan had made him forget about the U.N. hospital.

Did U.N. clinics, he wondered, see epilepsy patients? He was almost certain they had to—the disorder was common. Those files would be off-limits to his men. Unless he wanted to make a stink about it, get embroiled with Sorrel Baldwin and others like him. All that U.N. bureaucracy.

Baldwin—now there was something interesting. Before coming to Jerusalem, the American had lived in Beirut, Juliet's former home base. He'd earned a degree from the American University—sociology; Daniel remembered the diploma. According to the tank captain Cohen had interviewed, Juliet's brothel had catered to foreigners. American University personnel—Yalom had mentioned that specifically. A coincidence? Probably. The university was a breeding ground for Arabists; lots of them ended up working for the U.N. Still, it would have been interesting to talk to Baldwin in depth. Impossible without going through the brass.

Evidence, Laufer would bark at him. What evidence do you have for me to get my hands dirty, Sharavi? Challenging their diplomatic immunity? Stick with the case and don't run off on another tangent, Sharavi.

Since the discovery of Juliet's body, the deputy commander was in foul spirits. Pickled by his own press release, fermenting in ruined optimism. Firing off memos that inquired shrilly about progress. Or the lack of it.

Evidence. Daniel knew he had none. There was nothing to tie Juliet in with Baldwin or anyone else at the Amelia Catherine. Her body had been dumped clear across town, in the pine forest near Ein Qerem, on the southwest side of town. About as far from Scopus as you could get.

A Jewish National Fund forest, financed by the penny-in-a-blue-box donations of schoolchildren. The corpse wrapped in white sheeting, just like Fatma's. Discovered by a pair of early morning hikers, teenage boys, who'd run from the sight, goggle-eyed with fear. The Russian nuns who lived nearby at the Ein Qerem Convent had seen and heard nothing.

Then there was the matter of Brother Joseph Roselli. Daniel had dropped by Saint Saviour's hours after the discovery of the second body, found the monk on his rooftop, and showed him Juliet's death picture. Roselli had exclaimed: "She could be Fatma's sister!" Then his face had seemed to collapse, features falling, restructuring suddenly in a tight-lipped mask. His demeanor from that point had been hard and cold, taut with outrage. A completely different side of the man. Daniel supposed he couldn't be faulted for his indignation: Men of God weren't accustomed to being considered murder suspects. But the shift was sudden. Strange.

He couldn't shake the feeling that Roselli was harboring some secret, *struggling* with something . . . but the resumption of Daoud's nighttime surveillance had turned up nothing so far.

No evidence and two dead girls.

He thought about Fatma and Juliet for a while, tried to establish some kind of connection between the runaway from Silwan and the whore from Beirut, then scolded himself for going off on tangents. Obsessing about the victims instead of trying to understand the killer, because the victims had names, identities, and the killer was an enigma.

Seven days had separated the two murders. Now, a week had passed since Juliet had been found.

Was something happening right now? Another helpless woman seduced into endless sleep?

And if so, what was there to do?

He kept thinking about it—cursing his helplessness—until his belly filled with fire and his head felt ready to burst.

After a Shabbat supper during which he nodded and smiled at Laura and the children, hearing them but not listening, he went into the laundry room that Laura had converted to a studio, carrying an armful of books and monographs checked out of the library at National Headquarters. The room was bright—he'd left the light on before Sabbath, stacked Laura's stretched canvases neatly on the floor. Sitting among rolls of fabrics and tins of wax, jars filled with brushes and paint-encrusted palettes, he began to read.

Case histories of serial killers: Landru; Herman Mudgett; Albert Fish, who murdered and ate little children; Peter Kurten, a nauseating excuse for a human being who had well earned the nickname Dusseldorf Monster. According to one expert, the Germans produced a disproportionate number of sex murders—something to do with an impoverished collective unconscious.

And, of course, Jack the Ripper. Rereading a book on the Ripper case gave him pause, because some experts were convinced the scourge of Whitechapel had been a Jew—a *shohet* whose experience as a ritual slaughterer made him an expert in anatomy. He remembered what Dr. Levi had said, and he thought of the *shohtim* he knew: Mori Gerafi, a tiny, kind Yemenite who seemed too gentle for the job. Rabbi Landau, who worked out of the Mehane Yehuda market. Learned men, pious and scholarly. The thought of them carving up women was absurd.

He put the Ripper book aside and forged onward.

Krafft-Ebing's *Psychopathia Sexualis*—people chasing pleasure in hideous ways. Interpol and FBI reports—the German theory notwithstanding, America seemed to have more serial killers than any other country. One estimate said there were thirty or forty of them doing their dirty work at any given time, more than five hundred unsolved serial murders. The FBI had begun to program a computer in order to catalog all of it.

Thirty roving monsters. Such cruelty, such evil.

Street-corner Mengeles. Why had God created them?

He finished at two in the morning, dry-mouthed and heavy-lidded, Laura's drawing lamp the sole illumination in the silent, dark apartment.

Was it happening right now? The ritual, the outrage—an inert body laid out for dissection?

Knowing his dreams would be polluted, he went to sleep.

He awoke at dawn, expecting bad news. None came and he faked his way through Shabbat.

At nine on Sunday morning he filled an attaché case with papers and went to see Dr. Ben David. The psychologist's main office was at Hebrew University but he kept a suite for private consultations in the front rooms of his flat on Rehov Ramban.

Daniel arrived early and shared the claustrophobic waiting room with a tired-looking woman who hid from eye contact behind the international edition of *Time* magazine. Ten minutes before the hour, Ben David came out of the treatment room with a skinny, large-eyed boy of about five. The boy looked at Daniel and smiled shyly. The detective smiled back and wondered what could trouble such a young child so deeply that he needed a psychologist.

The woman put the *Time* into her purse and stood.

"All right," said Ben David heartily, in English. "I'll see Ronny the same time next week."

"Thank you, Doctor." She took her son by the hand and the two of them left quickly.

"Daniel," said Ben David, taking the detective's hand in both of his and shaking it energetically. He was a young man, in his early thirties, medium-sized and heavyset, with bushy black hair, a full dark beard, light-blue eyes that never rested, and a fitful nature that had taken Daniel by surprise the first time they'd met. He'd always thought of psychotherapists as passive, quiet. Listening and nodding, waiting for you to talk so they could pounce with interpretations. The one he'd seen at the rehab center had certainly fit the stereotype.

"Hello, Eli. Thank you for seeing me."

"Come in."

Ben David ushered him into the treatment room, a smallish, untidy office lined with bookshelves and furnished with a small desk, three sturdy chairs, and a low circular table upon which sat a dollhouse in the shape of a Swiss chalet, doll furniture, and half a dozen miniature human figurines. Behind the desk was a credenza piled high with papers and toys. Next to the papers were an aluminum coffeepot, cups, and a sugar bowl. No couch, no inkblots. A single Renoir print on the wall. The room smelled pleasantly of modeling clay.

Daniel sat on one of the chairs. The psychologist went to the credenza.

"Coffee?"

"Please."

Ben David prepared two cups, gave Daniel his, and sat down opposite him, sipping. He was wearing a faded burgundy polo shirt that exposed a hard, protuberant belly, baggy dark-green corduroy trousers, and scuffed loafers without socks. His hair looked disheveled; his beard needed trimming. Casual, careless even, like a graduate student on holiday. Not like a doctor at all, but such were the perquisites of status. Ben David had been an academic prodigy, chief of the army's psychological service at twenty-seven, a full professor two years later. Daniel supposed he could dress any way he pleased.

"So, my friend." The psychologist smiled cursorily, then shifted in the chair, moving his shoulders with almost tic-like abruptness. "I don't know what I can tell you that we haven't covered on Gray Man."

"I'm not sure, myself." Daniel pulled the forensic reports

and crime summaries out of his case and handed them over. He drank coffee and waited as the psychologist read.

"Okay," said Ben David, scanning quickly and looking up after a few moments. "What do you want to know, specifically?"

"What do you think about the washing of the bodies? What's the meaning of it?"

Ben David sat back in his chair, flipped one leg over the other, and ran his fingers through his hair.

"Let me start with the same warning I gave you before. Everything I tell you is pure speculation. It could be wrong. Okay?"

"Okay."

"Given that, my best guess is that the pathologist may very well be right—the killer was attempting to avoid leaving physical evidence. Something else to consider—and the two notions aren't mutually exclusive—would be a power play, playing God by preparing and manipulating the body. Were the corpses positioned in any way? *Posed*?"

Daniel thought about that.

"They looked as if they were set down neatly," he said. "With care."

"When you saw the first body what was your initial impression?"

"A doll. A damaged doll."

Ben David nodded enthusiastically. "Yes, I like that. The victims may very well have been *used* as dolls."

He turned and pointed to the miniature chalet. "Children engage in doll-play in order to achieve a sense of mastery over their conflicts and fantasies. Artists and writers and composers are driven to produce out of similar motivations. The creative urge—everyone wants to be godlike. Sex killers do it by destroying life. Gray Man tossed his victims aside. This one's more creative."

It sounded blasphemous to Daniel. He said nothing.

"Collecting accurate data on sex killers is difficult, because we have access only to the ones who get caught—which may be a biased sample. And all of them are liars, so their interview data are suspect. Nevertheless, the Americans have done some good research, and a few patterns seem to hold—the things I told you about Gray Man. Your man's an exceptionally immature psychopath. He's grown up with a chronic and overwhelming sense of powerlessness and helplessness—a creative blockage, if you will. He's been constructing power fantasies since early childhood and building his life around them. His family was intact. His family life was a mess but may have appeared outwardly normal to the casual observer. Normal sex doesn't work for him. He needs violence and domination—helplessness of the victim—to get aroused. In the beginning, violent fantasies were enough to satisfy him. Then, while still a child, he moved on to torturing and possibly having sex with animals. As an adolescent, he may have progressed to human rape. When that no longer fulfilled his power needs, he began killing. Murder serves as a substitute for intercourse: beginning with some sort of subjugation and following it with stabbing and hacking—the exaggerated sexual metaphor, the *literal* piercing and entry of the body. He chooses women as victims but may be latently homosexual."

Thinking of the rumor about Dr. Darousha, Daniel asked, "What about an active homosexual?"

"No," said Ben David. "The key word is *latent*. He's fighting to suppress those impulses, may even be hypermasculine—a real law-and-order type. There are homosexual sex killers, of course, but they usually murder men." Ben David thought for a moment. "There are records of a few pansexual murderers—Kurten, the Dusseldorf Monster, did away with men, women, children. But unless you start turning up male victims, I'd concentrate on latent homosexuals."

"How can a latent homosexual be spotted?"

"He can't."

Daniel waited for more. When it didn't come, he asked, "What about the earrings? Gray Man didn't take anything."

"Gray Man was crude, scared—slash and run. The earrings are *trophies,* as was the uterus taken from your second victim. Other killers take underwear, clothing. Your corpses were found naked, so your killer may have taken clothing as well. The trophies are a temporary substitute for killing again. *Mementoes,* similar to the heads collected by hunters. They're used for masturbation, to retrigger the power fantasies."

Ben David glanced at the reports again. "The ultimate power play is necrophilia. No mention is made of rape. Did your killer have post-mortem intercourse with the victims?"

"The pathologist found no semen," said Daniel. "It may have been washed away."

"Possible impotence," said the psychologist, "or he could have masturbated away from the body. It would make serum typing impossible—more avoidance of physical evidence. Not a stupid murderer, Dani. Definitely smarter than Gray Man."

Daniel thought: Stupid, "crude" Gray Man had eluded capture.

Ben David raised his cup and emptied it, then dried his beard with the back of one hand. "In order to dominate, you need subjugation. Some killers tie up their victims. Yours used heroin to subjugate, but it amounts to the same thing. Total control."

"Do you attach any significance to the use of drugs?"

The psychologist got up, walked to the credenza, and poured a second cup of coffee. "I don't know," he said, upon return. "Perhaps he'd experienced some sort of peak sexual experience related to drug use. A lot of what turns people on is the result of chance associations—the coupling of some random but significant event with sexual arousal."

It took a moment for Daniel to assimilate that. "An accident?"

"A *Pavlovian* accident—in this case, repetitive pairings of sex and violence. It may very well be the root of sexual deviance—generations of English sadomasochists were created by the practice of caning public school students. Beat a horny adolescent frequently enough and you're going to establish a mental connection between pain and arousal. The same may be true of sexual psychopaths—most of them claim to have been abused as children, but then again, they'd say anything that was self-serving."

"Could the use of sedation indicate someone with medical experience?" asked Daniel. "Along with the fact that he took care to avoid physical evidence?"

"Do you have a physician suspect?"

"No."

"Did the pathologist feel the mutilation indicated exceptional surgical skill?"

"No."

"Then I wouldn't place much stock in that hypothesis. Why would a doctor use something crude like heroin, when he could get his hands on more precise anesthetics? What it *does* indicate is someone with drug experience, which, unfortunately, is no longer a small club in this country. Anything else?"

"When we talked about Gray Man, you said he would probably be withdrawn, an antisocial loner. Do you feel the same about this one?"

"At the core, all psychopaths are antisocial. They're incapable of achieving intimacy, view people as objects, have no sense of empathy or compassion. Gray Man was impulsive and meek, which led me to *guess* that he was socially inadequate. But this one isn't so clear-cut. He's cold, calculating, takes great care to wash the body, prepare it, clean it—he's a stage director. Arrogant and intelligent, and those types often come across as sociable, even charming. Some even have apparent romances with women, though when you examine the relationship closely it turns out to be warped or platonic. The more sophisticated sex killer doesn't necessarily shun the public eye. In fact, he may even jump right into it. He may be attracted to politics because it's also a power game: There was an Englishman—one of the homosexual killers—named Dennis Nilsen. Labor union activist, well liked by everyone, terrific social consciousness when he wasn't strangling boys. The American, Ted Bundy, was a law student, also politically active, good-looking, suave. Another American, Gacy, entertained children with a clown act, raised funds for the Democratic party and had his picture taken with President Carter's wife. Semipublic figures, every one of them."

Ben David leaned forward.

"Internally, your man's a cesspool, Dani. Get to know him on an *intimate* level and the psychopathy starts popping out—lies, false claims, inconsistencies in personal history, poor impulse control, situational conscience. He believes in rules but *doesn't* believe they apply to *him*. But outwardly, he may very well look normal. Better than normal—a persuasive manipulator."

Daniel thought of Fatma's naïveté, Juliet's possible brain damage. Easy pickings for someone like that.

"What about religious fanatacism?" he asked.

Ben David smiled. "The avenging murderer cleansing the world of whores? Movie nonsense. Some of these guys claim they've got some greater moral purpose, but it's more self-serving garbage and if no one buys it, they quickly drop it. Basically, they kill to achieve orgasm." He looked at the reports again.

"Both your victims were Arabs," he said. "One thing you should consider strongly is the political component."

"Neither Mossad nor Shin Bet has come up with any terrorist connections—"

"That's not what I meant," the psychologist cut in, impatiently. "Don't limit your thinking to some organized political cell. As I said, psychopaths are attracted to political issues because politics is power. I'm suggesting to you a solitary psychopathic killer whose violent fantasy life is interwoven with political elements."

Ben David shot out of his chair, went to the bookshelves, ran his fingers along the spines of the volumes, and pulled out several.

"Here," he said, placing the books in Daniel's lap.

The first three were American paperbacks. Cheap, cracked editions with brittle, yellowed paper. Daniel studied the cover illustrations: lurid, cartoonish paintings of impossibly voluptuous women, naked, bound and gagged, and tormented by hypermuscular, whip-wielding men in leather costumes so glossy they looked wet. Costumes emblazoned with swastikas and iron crosses and the SS death's-head logo. In one illustration, ribbons of blood ran down the woman's meaty thighs. In another a slavering, razor-toothed Doberman pinscher aimed its snout in the vicinity of the victim's crotch.

The women strained against their bonds and their eyes were wide with terror. Their tormentors grinned and fondled groins bulging grotesquely.

The titles: *Eat This, Jewbitch. Nazi Lovemasters. Gestapo Rape.*

Daniel opened one of them, read several lines of explicit, sadomasochistic pornography, and put the books down angrily.

"Disgusting."

"I got them when I was at Harvard," said Ben David, "in a used-book store near the campus. There's a small but steady market for this type of thing."

Daniel opened the fourth book. A hard-cover volume entitled *This Must Not Happen Again: The Black Book of Fascist Horror.* He turned pages, saw grainy photographs. Mountains of human skeletons. A row of empty-eyed corpses, partially corroded by lime, lying three-deep in a muddy ditch. Severed arms and legs, waxily artificial. The leer of a German soldier as he shot a naked woman in the back.

"Read the chapter on 'Murder for Profit,' " said the psychologist. "The surgical experiments."

Daniel found the section, skimmed it, then closed the book, his anger growing. "What's the point?"

"The *point* is that racist politics and psychopathy can be comfortable bedfellows. Mengele, all the other camp doctors, were psychopaths. Hannah Arendt claimed they were normal, banal men, but their psychological evaluations indicate otherwise. They were attracted to the Nazi philosophy because it fit with their psychopathic natures. Hitler reinforced and legitimized them with power and status and technology—serial killers in the employ of the State. The point is, Dani, that if Arab girls keep turning up slaughtered, you'd do well to consider that your psychopath has a thing against Arabs."

"A Jewish race murderer?" Daniel thought of the Ripper book. The *shohet* theory.

"It could be a self-hating Arab," said Ben David. "Serial killers often turn against their own kind. But don't exclude the possibility that a member of our tribe is running around butchering Arabs just because it's an unappetizing contingency. We're not all lambs. There's a reason for the sixth commandment."

Daniel was silent. Ben David misread the look on his face as resistance and threw up his hands.

"I don't like it either, my friend. You wanted my speculations, you got them."

"I was reading about psychopathic killers last night," Daniel reflected, "and found myself thinking about them in Nazi terms. A phrase came to mind: street-corner Mengeles."

"You see"—the psychologist smiled—"you don't need me. Your unconscious is guiding you in the right direction."

He handed the reports back to Daniel, who put them into his case and removed a folder. The summary on Schlesinger, it had finally arrived yesterday from Civil Guard Headquarters. He gave it to Ben David, saying, "What do you think of this one?"

More rapid scanning. "This tells me nothing," said the psychologist. "An old man with stomach pains—Kupat Holim claims it's in his head. The classic psychosomatic dodge."

"He was the Hagah man patrolling Scopus the night the first one turned up," said Daniel, "giving him excellent opportunity. An old palmahi, hates Arabs—which could give him a motive. He likes to drive around the city at night and he has psychological problems."

Ben David shook his head, held up the summary.

"There's nothing in here about psychological problems. He has stomach pains and persistent hunger pangs that the doctors can't identify. So they cover for their feelings of inadequacy by using psychology to blame the victim." He gave the folder to Daniel. "I'm not saying this Schlesinger isn't your man. If you have evidence, go for him. But there's nothing in here that's relevant." Ben David looked at his watch. "Anything else?"

"Not for now," said Daniel. "Thanks."

The two of them stood and Ben David walked him back into the waiting room. A young couple sat at opposite ends of the sofa, arms folded, eyes cast downward. When the door opened, both of them looked up briefly, then returned to staring at the rug. Daniel saw their fear and shame, wondered why Ben David didn't have a separate exit for his patients.

"One moment," the psychologist told the couple. He accompanied Daniel out the front door and to the curb. The morning had filled with traffic and sunshine, the hum of human discourse filtering from Keren Hayesod to the quiet, tree-shaded street. Ben David took a deep breath and stretched.

"Psychopaths can be arrogant to the point of self-destructiveness," he said. "He may get careless, make a mistake, and tell you who he is."

"Gray Man never did."

Ben David tugged at his beard. "Maybe your luck will change."

"And if it doesn't?"

Ben David placed a hand on his shoulder. His eyes softened as he searched for a response. For the first time, Daniel saw him in a different light—paternal, a therapist.

Then, all at once, he drew away and said,

"If it doesn't, more blood."

27

He interviewed sex offenders and false confessors all day—wretched men, for the most part, who seemed too downtrodden to plan anything more complicated than putting one foot in front of the other. He'd talked to many of them before. Still, he considered each of them a pathological liar, put them through the entire grilling, reducing some to tears, others to a near-catatonic fatigue.

At seven he returned home to find Gene and Luanne there, the table set for guests. He didn't recall Laura mentioning a visit, but lately he'd been far from attentive, so she might very well have spelled it out for him without its sinking in.

The boys attacked him, along with Dayan, and he wrestled with them, absently, noticing that Shoshi hadn't come forward to greet him.

The reason was soon obvious. She and Gene were playing draw poker in a corner of the living room, using raisins for chips. From the size of the piles it was clear who was winning.

"Flush," she said, clapping her hands.

"Oh, well," said Gene, throwing his cards down.

"Hello, everyone," said Daniel.

"Hello, Abba." Preoccupied.

" 'Lo, Danny. Your turn to deal, sugar."

The boys had run to the back of the apartment, taking the dog with them. Daniel stood alone for a moment, put his attaché case down, and went into the kitchen.

He found Laura and Luanne at the table, both in light cotton dresses, examining a large white scrapbook—his and Laura's wedding album.

"You were both so *young,*" said Luanne. "Oh, hello, Daniel."

"Hello, Luanne." A smile for Laura.

She smiled back but got up slowly, almost reluctantly, and he felt more like a stranger than ever.

"I just called your office," she said, pecking his cheek. "Dinner's getting cold."

"Sorry."

"No problem." She gave his hand a quick squeeze, released it, and went to examine the roast in the oven.

"You were some couple," said Luanne. "My, my, look at all those coins. That is simply gorgeous."

Daniel looked down at the picture that had captured her attention. The formal wedding portrait: he and Laura, holding hands, next to a ridiculously large wedding cake—his mother-in-law's idea.

He wore a white tuxedo with a silly-looking ruffled shirt, plum-colored cummerbund and bow tie—the rental store had insisted it was all the rage. Smiling but looking baffled, like a child dressed up for a dance party.

Laura looked majestic, nothing silly about her. Swallowed

up by the Yemenite wedding gown and headdress that had been in the Zadok family for generations but belonged, really, to the Yemenite community of Jerusalem. A treasure, centuries old, lent to any bride who requested it. A tradition that stretched back to San'a, celebrating social equality: The daughters of rich men and beggars came to the *huppah* dressed in identical splendor, each bride a queen on her special day.

The gown and headdress and accompanying jewelry were as heavy as chain mail: tunic and pantaloons of crisp gold brocade; three rings on every finger, a trio of bracelets around each wrist; scores of necklaces—strings of silver and gold coins, filigree balls glowing like silver gumdrops, amber beads, pearls and gemstones. The headdress high and conical, layered with alternating rows of black and white pearls and topped by a garland of white and scarlet carnations, the pearl chin-piece hanging down to the clavicle like a glittering, shimmering beard; a fringe of tiny turquoise pendants concealing the top half of the brow, so that only the center of Laura's face was visible. The young, beautiful features and enormous pale eyes framed and emphasized.

The night before, she'd had her palms and soles smeared red in the henna ceremony, and now this. She'd barely been able to walk; the merest flick of a wrist elicited a flash of gemfire, the jangle of metal against metal. The old women tended to her, jabbering incomprehensibly, holding her upright. Others scraped out complex rhythms on finger cymbals, coaxed near-melodies from antique goatskin drums. Whooping and chanting and singing women's songs, the Arabic lyrics subtly erotic. Estelle had gotten right in with them, a small woman, like her daughter. Light-footed, laughing, whooping along.

The men sat in a separate room, eating, drinking Chivas Regal and arak and raisin brandy and Turkish coffee augmented with arak, linking arms and dancing in pairs, listening to Mori Zadok sing men's songs in Hebrew and Aramaic. Stories of the Great Ones. The Rambam. Sa'adia Gaon. Mori Salim Shabazi. The other elders followed him, taking turns delivering blessings and *divrei Torah* that praised the joys of marriage.

Daniel sat at the center of the table, drinking the liquor that was placed in front of him, remaining clear-headed in the manner of the Yemenites. He was flanked by his father, who sang along in a high, clear tenor, and his new father-in-law, who remained silent.

Al Birnbaum was fading away. The liquor was turning him pinker by degrees. He clapped his hands, wanting to be one of them, but succeeded only in looking baffled, like an explorer cast among primitives. Daniel felt sorry for him, didn't know what to say.

Later, after the *yihud* ceremony, Al had cornered him, hugging him, slipping money into his pocket and planting a wet kiss on his cheek.

"This is wonderful, son, wonderful," he blurted out. His breath was hot, heavy with arak. The band had started playing "Qetsad Merakdim"; celebrants were juggling and dancing before the bride. Al started to sway and Daniel placed a hand on his shoulder.

"Thank you very much, Mr. Birnbaum."

"You'll take care of her—I know you will. You're a good boy. Anything you need, ask."

"Thank you very much. I appreciate that."

"You're welcome, son. The two of you will make a beautiful life together. Beautiful." A trickle of tears hurriedly wiped and camouflaged by a fit of coughing.

Later, of course, the phone calls had come. Static-laden long-distance calls buzzing across two continents. Poorly concealed cries of parental loneliness that always seemed to interrupt love-making. Not-so-subtle hints about how wonderful things were in California, how was the two-room flat working out, was the heating fixed yet, did it still smell of insecticide? Al had a friend, a lawyer, he might be able to use someone with investigative skills; another friend owned an insurance agency, could steer him into something lucrative. And if he got tired of police work, there was always room in the printing business. . . .

Eventually, the Birnbaums had accepted the fact that their only child wasn't coming home. They purchased the Talbieh apartment, all those bedrooms, the kitchen full of appliances, supposedly for themselves. ("For summer visits, darling—would you kids be good enough to house-sit?")

The visits took place every year, like clockwork, the first two weeks in August. The Birnbaums arriving with half a dozen suitcases, half of them full of gifts for the kids, refusing the master bedroom and sleeping in the boys' bunk. Mikey and Benny moving in with Shoshi.

Thirteen summers, sixteen visits—one extra for the birth of each child.

The rest of the time, the Sharavis house-sat. More luxury than a policeman could expect . . .

"You looked like a princess, Laura," said Luanne, turning a page and studying pictures of dancing Yemenites.

"I lost two pounds perspiring," laughed Laura. She poked at the roast with a fork. Then her face grew serious and Daniel thought he saw her fight back a tear.

"It was a beautiful gown," she said. "A beautiful day."

Daniel walked over to her, put his arm around her waist, enjoying the feel of her, the sharp taper inward, the sudden flare of hip under his palm. She raised the fork and he felt a current of energy dance along the surface of her skin, involuntary and tremulous like the quivering flanks of a horse after exercise.

He kissed her cheek.

She winked at him, put the roast on a platter, and handed it to him.

"Help me serve, Pakad."

During dinner, Luanne and Gene talked about their trip to Eilat. Snorkeling in the crystalline waters of the Red Sea, the coral forests below, schools of rainbow-colored fish that swam placidly up to the shoreline. The long gray shapes Gene was certain had been sharks.

"One thing I noticed," said Luanne, "was the shrimp. Everyone was selling it or cooking it or eating it. I didn't feel I was in a Jewish country."

"First-rate shrimp," said Gene. "Good-sized, deep-fried."

After dessert, everyone pitched in clearing the dishes, Mikey and Benny laughing uproariously as they balanced stacks of plates, Shoshi admonishing them to be careful.

Then the children retreated to Shoshi's room to watch a videotape of *Star Wars*—the TV, VCR, and tape, donations from Los Angeles—and the women went back to the wedding album. Gene and Daniel stepped out on the balcony and Gene pulled out a cigar and rolled it between his fingers.

"I didn't know you smoked," said Daniel.

"Once in a great while I sneak one in after a really good meal. These are Cubans—picked them up in the duty-free at Zurich." Gene reached into his pocket and pulled out another. "Want one?"

Daniel hesitated. "Okay. Thank you."

They sat, put their feet over the railing, and lit up. At first the bitter smoke made Daniel wince. Then he found himself loosening up, feeling the heat swirl around inside his mouth, enjoying it.

"Speaking of sharks," said Gene, "how's your case?"

"Not good." Daniel told him about Juliet, the endless interviews of doctors and nurses, the pressure exerted on hordes of sex offenders, all useless so far.

"Boy, do I know the name of that tune," said Gene, but there was a lilt in his voice, the mellow satisfaction of homecoming. "Sounds like you've got a real winner on your hands."

"I spoke to a psychologist this morning, trying to get a profile."

"What'd he tell you?" asked Gene. He lay back and put his hands behind his head, looked up at the black Jerusalem sky, and blew smoke rings at the moon.

Daniel gave him a summary of the consultation with Ben David.

"He's right about one thing," said Gene. "The psych stuff's darned close to worthless. I've worked Lord knows how many homicides, gotten bushel-basketfuls of psych profiles, never solved a case with one of them yet. And that includes the nut-case serials."

"How *do* you solve them?" On the surface a foolish question, far too artless. But he felt comfortable with Gene, able to speak openly. More open than he could be with his own family. It bothered him.

Gene sat up, edged his chair closer to Daniel's.

"From where I sit, sounds like you're doing everything right. Truth is, lots of times we don't solve them. They stop killing or die and that's that. When we do catch them, nine times out of ten it's because of something stupid—they park their car near the murder scenes, get a couple of parking tickets which show up on the computer. A records check, just like you're doing. Some angry girlfriend or wife turns them in. Or the killer starts playing games, letting us know who he is, which means he's basically catching himself. We've done nothing but cut along the dotted line."

The black man sucked on his cigar and blew out a jetstream of smoke. "These cases are hell on the ego, Danny Boy. The public gets hold of them and wants instant cure."

Keep pounding the pavement and wait for the killer to give himself away. The same thing Ben David had told him.

He could have done without hearing it twice in one day.

He got into bed, hugged and kissed Laura.

"Ooh, your breath—have you been smoking?"

"One cigar. I brushed my teeth. Want me to brush again?"

"No, that's all right. I just won't kiss you."

But moments later, her legs wrapped around him, the fingers of one hand languidly caressing his scrotum, the other entangled in his hair, she opened her mouth and relented.

He woke up in the middle of the night, his mind still going like a dieseling engine. Thinking of death camps and hypodermics and long-bladed knives that could sever a neck without sawing. Blood flowing in gutters, disappearing down sewer drains. A city drenched in blood, the golden stone turned to crimson. Headless dolls crying out for salvation. Himself suspended in mid-air, like one of Chagall's birds. Frozen in space, unable to swoop. Helpless.

28

The first time the war between the grown-ups ended differently, he'd been caught by surprise.

Usually they'd shout themselves into exhaustion, the viciousness defused by alcohol and fatigue, trailing off in a mumble of last words.

Usually *she* would outlast Doctor, spitting out the final curse, then lurching upstairs, woozily, the boy anticipating her retreat and running ahead of her, safe in bed, hidden under the covers, as her footsteps grew faint, her dirty talk faded to silence.

Doctor usually stayed in the library for a while, walking back and forth, drinking and reading. Sometimes he fell asleep on the tufted leather sofa, still in his clothes. When he came upstairs, he, too, trudged heavily. Leaving the door open in a final act of generosity, so that the boy could share his nightmares.

The time it was different, he'd been six years old.

He knew this with certainty because his sixth birthday had been three days before, a non-event marked by gaily wrapped gifts from the most expensive toy store in town, a cutting-of-the-cake ceremony grudgingly attended by both parents. Then a double-bill monster movie accompanied by one of the maids, the one with the horse face, who had no use for children and hated him in particular.

During intermission he went to the theater bathroom and peed all over the wall, then bought so much popcorn and candy that twenty minutes later he was back in the bathroom, throwing up into his pee puddles.

So he was sure he was six.

On the night it ended differently, he wore pale-blue pajamas with a monkey and parrot pattern, sat curled on the sixth stair, massaging a polished wood baluster. Hearing the usual bad-machine sounds, happy because it was something he was used to.

Then a surprise: no dirty talk. Silence.

The tearing and ripping ended so suddenly that for a moment the boy thought they'd actually destroyed each other. Blam.

Then he heard the sound of heavy breathing, a moan—was someone being hurt?

Another moan, more breathing. Fear wrapped itself around him, cold, icy fingers squeezing his chest.

Could this be it? Was this the end?

Cautiously, like one of the robot monsters he'd seen in the movie, he made his way down the remaining seven stairs. The heavy double doors to the library were partially open. Through the opening came a narrow triangle of yellow light. Ugly yellow, like the pee puddles.

He heard more moans, tasted something sweet and bitter, and was seized with an urge to throw up. He held his breath, put his hand on his tummy, and pressed in hard to make the feeling go away. Telling himself: Go away.

"Oh!"

His mother's voice, but she sounded different. Scared. The breathing continued without her, huffing, not stopping, like a toy train: Doctor.

"Oh!"

What was happening?

"Oh, Charles!"

He gathered up his courage, tiptoed to the door. Peeked through the yellow space and saw them.

Doctor was sitting on the couch, still wearing his white shirt and tie, but with his pants and underpants down around his ankles. His legs looked gross, all hairy and thick, like a gorilla's.

She was naked, white as her nightgown, her back to the door, her white-yellow hair loose and shiny.

Her head was on Doctor's shoulder, her chin kind of squeezing into his neck. Like she was trying to vampire-bite him.

She was sitting on Doctor. Her hands were in his hair. She was rubbing his hair, trying to pull it out.

Oh, no, look at her butt!

It was hanging down like two giant eggs and there was something between it. Something going *into* it. A pole with black hair-fuzz around it, like a pink grapefruit popsicle. No, a pole, a wet, pink pole—his father's *thing*!

Oh, no. He wanted to throw up again, gagged, swallowed the bad taste, and felt it burn him down to his tummy.

The thing was a *weapon*. An egg masher.

You could use it as a *weapon*!

He stared, unable to breathe, chewing on his fingers.

It was *in* her. In and *out*. Oh, no, it was *stabbing* her, hurting her—that's what was making her cry and moan. She was being stabbed by Doctor's thing!

He could see Doctor's face rolling back and forth over her shoulder, like someone had cut it off but it was still alive, all sweaty. A sweaty zombie head, with a mean smile. All scrunched up and pink and wet, just like his *thing*.

Doctor was forcing her—both of his big hairy hands were on her butt, squeezing, the fingers disappearing into soft white skin. Squeezing her until she cried, and the neck-biting and hair-pulling couldn't stop him—he was a monster who didn't feel pain and he was forcing her, forcing his thing into her, and it was hurting her and she was crying!

"Oh . . . oh, Charles . . ."

Pink and white, pink *into* white. He thought of a glass of milk with blood dripping into it; when the blood hit the surface of the milk it swirled and turned all pink.

"Oh, God!" she called out. Now she was praying—it was

really hurting her bad. She started moving faster, bouncing, trying to bounce off of him, to get away from *him* and his egg stabber, but he held on to her—he was forcing her!

"Oh, God!"

She was praying for help. Should he help her? His feet felt glued to the floor. His chest was all tight and it hurt. What could he do . . . ?

"Yes," said Doctor, grinning and clenching his teeth and grinning again, a wet monster grin. "Oh, yes. *Yes."*

"Oh, God! Harder, you bastard! *Harder!"*

What was this?

"*Give* it to me, you bastard!"

Bounce, bounce.

Bounce, bounce, moan.

She was *smiling,* kind of.

"Harder, damn you!"

She was *telling* Doctor to stab her. She was *telling* him to hurt her!

She liked being hurt!

Doctor was monster-growling and monster-grinning, pushing the words out in between breaths that sounded like a steam engine puffing: *"Here, look at it, take it."*

"Oh, I hate . . . you."

"You love it."

"I hate you."

"Want me to stop, bitch?"

"No, oh, no."

"Say it!" Growling.

"No—don't stop, damn—"

"Say it!" Grinning.

"I love it."

"That's better. Again."

"I love it Iloveit!"

"Here, look, I'm fucking you. Feelit."

"Oh. Oh, oh. Jew . . . bastard . . . oh, oh."

"Take it."

". . . goddamned kike . . . cock. OH!"

All of a sudden Doctor was thrusting himself up, raising his hairy butt off the couch, lifting her with him. Stabbing fast and hard and yelling "Damn!"

She flopped like a rag doll. She yelled, "I hate you!" Made a noise that sounded like she was choking. Then her fingers came loose from Doctor's hair and started to wiggle around like white worms, the kind the boy sometimes found under wet rocks in the garden.

"Oh."

"*Bitch.*"

Then, all of a sudden, she stopped moving and Doctor was slapping her butt and laughing and grinning and the boy was running upstairs gasping and tripping, his heart fighting to burst out of his chest.

He threw up on the floor, got into the bed and wet it.

He spent an eternity under the covers, shaking and biting his lips, scratching his arms and his face until he bled. Tasting his blood. Squeezing his thing. Hard.

Hurting himself, to see if you could like it.

You could, kind of.

It wasn't until later, when he heard her come up the stairs, sobbing, that he realized she was still alive.

29

When the woman opened the door, Shmeltzer was surprised. He'd expected someone older, the same age as the Hagah man, maybe just a little younger. But this one was *much* younger, in her early fifties, younger than *him.* A round, girlish face, plump and pretty, though the gray eyes seemed grim. A little makeup applied well, thick dark hair pulled back in a bun, just beginning to streak with gray. A heavy, sagging bosom that took up most of the space between neck and waistline. The waistline well-padded, as were the hips. Small ankles for a heavy woman. Just like Leah. No doubt she fretted over her weight.

"Yes?" she said, sounding wary and unfriendly.

Then he realized he was being stupid, a fine detective. The fact that she'd opened the door didn't make her the wife. A niece, maybe, or a guest.

But when he introduced himself, showed his badge and asked for Schlesinger, she said, "He's not here now. I'm Eva—Mrs. Schlesinger. What do you want?"

"When do you expect him back?"

The woman stared at him and bit her lip. Her hands were small and soft; they started kneading one another.

"Never," she said.

"What's that?"

She started to say something, clamped her lips shut, and turned her back on him, retreating into the apartment. But she'd left the door open and Shmeltzer followed her inside.

The place was simple, bright, immaculately maintained. Lean Danish furniture that had probably been purchased as an ensemble from Hamashbir. Bowls of nuts and candies and dried fruits on the coffee table. Crystal animals and porcelain miniatures, all female stuff—the Hagah man probably didn't give a hoot about decorating. A teak bookcase filled with volumes on history and philosophy. Landscape prints on the walls, but no photos of children or grandchildren.

A second marriage, he told himself: the old guy hot for a young one, maybe divorcing the first one, maybe waiting for widowhood. Then he remembered that Schlesinger had been in Dachau and the age difference took on a different context: Wife number one murdered by the Germans, perhaps a couple of kids gone too. Come to Palestine, fight for your life, and start anew—a familiar story; plenty of his *moshav* neighbors had gone through the same thing.

Were the two of them childless? Maybe that was why she looked so unhappy.

She'd gone into the kitchen and was drying dishes. He followed her in.

"What did you mean by 'never'?"

She turned around and faced him. She inhaled and her bosom heaved impressively. She noticed Shmeltzer looking at her and covered her chest with her dish towel.

What an interview, thought Shmeltzer. Very professional.

"My husband is in the hospital. I just got back from there. He's got cancer all over him—in the stomach and the liver and pancreas. The doctors say he's going to die soon. Weeks, not months."

"I'm sorry." What an inane thing to say. He'd hated it when others had said it to him. "How long has he been ill?"

"For a week," she snapped. "Does that give him a good enough alibi?"

"Gveret Schlesinger—"

"He told me the police suspected him—some Yemenite accused him of being a murderer. A few days later he had cancer!"

"No one accused him of anything, *gveret*. He's a material witness, that's all."

Eva Schlesinger looked at him and threw her dish down on the floor. She watched it shatter, then burst into tears, knelt, and started to pick up the pieces.

"Careful," said Shmeltzer, getting down beside her. "That's sharp—you'll cut your hands."

"I hope so!" she said and began grabbing at the shards quickly, automatically, like someone batch-sorting vegetables. Shmeltzer saw pinpoints of blood freckle her fingers, pulled her hands away, and brought her to her feet. He steered her to the sink, turned on the tap, and put the wounded fingers under the water. After a few seconds most of the bleeding stopped; only a few red bubbles persisted. Small cuts, nothing serious.

"Here," he said, tearing a piece of paper towel from a wall-mounted roll. "Squeeze this."

She nodded, complied, started crying again. He guided her into the living room, sat her down on the couch.

"Something to drink?" he said.

"No, thank you, I'm fine," she whispered between sobs, then realized what she'd said and started laughing. An unhealthy laugh. Hysterical.

Shmeltzer didn't know what to do, so he let her go on for a while, watching her alternate between tears and laughter, then finally growing silent and covering her face with her hands. She started to mutter, "Yaakov, Yaakov."

He waited, looked at the blood-speckled paper towel wrapped around her fingers, the view of the desert from the living room window. A good view, rocky crags and pinhole caves, but architecturally the French Hill complex made no sense—towers on top of a mountain. Some developer bastard fucking up the skyline . . .

"He had pain for years," said Eva Schlesinger. To Shmeltzer it sounded as if she were accusing him, blaming him for the pain.

"He was always hungry—he ate like a wild animal, a human garbage disposal, but he was never satisfied. Can you imagine what that felt like? *They* told him it was in his head."

"Doctors," commiserated Shmeltzer. "Most of them are jerks. How's your hand?"

She ignored the question, leaned her uninjured hand on the coffee table, and tossed out words like machine-gun bullets: "He tried to tell them, the fools, but they wouldn't listen. Instead they told him he was nuts, said he should see a psychiatrist—head doctors, they're the biggest nuts of all, right? What did he need them for? His *stomach* hurt, not his head. It's not normal to have pain like that. It doesn't make sense, does it?"

"Not at all—"

"All they want is to keep you waiting for hours, then pat you on the head and tell you it's your fault—as if he wanted the pain!" She stopped, pointed a finger at Shmeltzer. "He was no murderer!"

Shmeltzer saw the fire in her eyes. The bosom, moving as if imbued with a life of its own.

"Of course he wasn't—"

"Don't give me your double talk, Inspector! The police thought he was a murderer—they blamed him for that Arab girl. *They* killed him, put the cancer in him. Right after the Yemenite accused him, the pain started to get worse! What do you think of that? Nothing helped it—even food made it worse! He refused to go back and see more doctors. He was gritting his teeth and suffering in silence—the man's a rock, a *shtarker*. What he's been through in his life, I won't tell you—he could take the pain of ten men. But this was worse. At night he'd crawl out of bed—he had an iron constitution, could take anything, and this pain made him crawl! He'd crawl out and walk around the apartment groaning. It would wake me up and I'd go out and find him, crawling. Like an insect. If I went to him he screamed at me, told me to leave him alone—what could I do?"

She pounded her fist on the table, put her hands on her temples, and rocked.

Shmeltzer considered what to say and decided to say nothing.

"Such pain, it's not right, after what he'd been through. Then I saw the blood, from all ends—he was urinating it and coughing it up and spitting it. The life was flowing out of him." She unwrapped the paper towel, looked at it, and put it on the coffee table. "That's what happens to people—that's what happens to Jews. You live a good life, work hard; then you fall apart—everything comes out of you. We had no kids. I'm glad they're not here to see it."

"You're right," said Shmeltzer. "You're one hundred percent right."

She stared at him, saw that he was serious, and started to cry again, pulling at her hair. Then she looked at him again, shook a fist.

"What the hell do you know! What am I doing talking to you!"

"Gveret—"

She shook her head no, got up from the couch, stood and took a step forward, catching her foot on a leg of the coffee table and reeling.

Shmeltzer moved quickly, catching her before she fell. He put his arms under her armpits and kept her upright. She reacted to the support by punching at him and cursing him, spraying him with saliva, then going all loose and limp, letting her arms fall to her sides. He felt her pressed against him, her soft bulk astonishingly light, like meringue. She buried her face in his shirtfront and cursed God.

They stood that way for a while, the woman sobbing in anticipation of widowhood. Shmeltzer holding her. Confused.

30

The gag cards on the wall of Fink's Bar were tacky, decided Wilbur. The kind of thing you'd see in a hick-town tavern, back in the States. Combine that with enough Wild Turkey and you could forget where you were. For a moment.

He picked up *The Jerusalem Post,* read the piece again, and took a sip of bourbon. Another scoop heard from.

He'd been on his vacation—ten days of R and R in Athens—when the murders story broke. The international *Trib* hadn't carried it—the first he'd heard of it was a page-two item in the *Post* he'd picked up on the plane back to Ben Gurion.

Like most foreign correspondents, he spoke no Hebrew or Arabic and depended upon native journalists for his information—the *Post* for the Jewish angle, the English edition of *Al Fajr* for the Arab side. Both were highly partisan, but that was okay; it spiced up his pieces. Anyway, it was either that or bird-dog the government spokesmen, and Israeli mouthpieces were cagey, paranoiac, always grooming themselves for victim status. Always worried someone was out to get them, invoking military censorship when they didn't want to deal with something.

The vacation had been a good one. He'd met up with an Italian photojournalist named Gina, a skinny, bleached-blond free-lance with an appetite for sautéed calamari and cocaine; they'd met on the beach, traded meaningful looks, puffed-up bios, and shared a line from a vial that she carried in her beach bag. She had a room in his hotel, checked out of it, and moved in with him, living off his expense account for a week and a half of fun and games, then woke him up early one morning with a blowjob and breakfast, left him eating dry toast as she tossed him a *ciao* and was out the door, back to Rome. Wild girl, not pretty, but adventurous. He hoped she hadn't given him a dose of anything.

He took another swallow of Turkey, motioned for a refill. Two murders—potential start of a serial. It just might play back home, the kind of thing the wire services sometimes went for. No doubt the *Times* men—New York and L.A.—had gotten hold of it, but they usually stayed away from crime stories, milked the political stuff, which was always in heavy supply. So maybe there was still something to work with.

Being out of the country when it broke bothered the Jimmy Olsen part of him, but after six months in Israel he'd needed the time off. The country was hyperkinetic; the pace could drive you crazy.

Stuff never stopped coming at you, but most of it was noise. Grabowsky had loved it—he was a certified information junkie, firing off pieces right and left, breaking productivity records before he'd ventured too far into the Bekaa and gotten his arm blown off. The day after he'd been certified a cripple, the wire service had called Wilbur in from Rio. Farewell to a beautiful assignment. A little boring—how much could you write about *favelitos*, generals, and sambas, and Mardi Gras was a once-a-year thing—but my, my, what a culture, white sand, all those women sashaying topless along Ipanema, caramel asses hanging out of G-string bikini bottoms.

After three fat years under the Brazilian sun, Manhattan seemed poisonous, unhealthily clamorous, a headache machine. Welcome home, Mark. *Home.* Backslapping and speeches from the boys in the New York office, kudos to old Grabowsky, drink to the one-armed Hemingway (could he, Wilbur wondered, learn to type with that prosthesis?), and keep the fire burning in the Holy Land, Mark. Rah, rah.

Not his style. He'd laid his *Front Page* fantasies to rest a long time ago, wanted to take things easy, enjoy life. The wrong man for the Israel bureau.

The pace.

A story that was milkable for a week anywhere else faded in a day here, crowded out by something new before the ink was dry. Crazy coalition government, had to be at least twenty political parties—he was a long way from knowing all of them—constantly taking shots at one another, clawing for little smidgens of power. Knesset meetings turned invariably to shouting matches; last week there had been a fist fight. They couldn't talk softly; a real Brooklyn deli scene—the constant charges and countercharges of corruption, virtually all of it noise. The Arabs were no better, always whining, buttonholing him, wanting to see their names in print. Cries of oppression from guys driving Mercedes and living off the U.N. dole.

Everyone had an axe to grind; in the six months he'd been there, a week hadn't gone by without some kind of major political demonstration. Usually there were two or three. And the strikes—the doctors, the nurses, the postal workers. Last month the taxi drivers had decided they wanted more money from the Transportation Ministry, blocked the main thoroughfares of Jerusalem and Tel Aviv with their cabs, burned an old jalopy in the middle of King George Street, the tires stinking to high heaven. Wilbur had been forced to leave his car at home and walk everywhere, which inflamed his corns and heightened his antipathy toward the country, the obstreperousness—the *Jewishness* of it.

He finished his drink, put the glass down on the bar, and looked around. Six tables, five empty. Two guys in a corner:

Margalit from *Davar,* Aronoff from *Yediot Aharonot*—he hadn't gotten close to either of them. If they'd noticed him come in, they didn't show it, eating peanuts, drinking ginger ale, and talking in low voices.

Ginger ale. Another problem. Newshounds who didn't take their drinking seriously. No one did. The country had no drinking age—a ten-year-old could waltz into a grocery and buy hundred-proof—and yet, no one went for it. A kind of snobbery, as far as he was concerned. As if they considered sobriety some sort of religious virtue, regarded booze as a goy weakness.

He called for another Turkey. The bartender was the owner's nephew, quiet kid, not a bad sort. In between orders, he studied from a math book. He nodded in response to Wilbur's call and brought the bottle over, poured a full measure without comment, asked Wilbur if he wanted something to eat.

"What do you have?"

"Shrimp, lobster cocktail."

Wilbur felt himself grow irritated. Patronized.

"What about soup?" He smiled. "Chicken soup. With matzo balls."

The kid was impassive. "We've got that too, Mr. Wilbur."

"Bring me a shrimp cocktail."

Wilbur looked across the bar as the kid disappeared into the kitchen, read the gag cards again. An eye chart that spelled out TOO MUCH SEX MAKES YOU GO BLIND if you read it the right way; a placard announcing ONCE A KING, ALWAYS A KING, BUT ... ONCE A KNIGHT IS ENOUGH!

The door to the street swung open, letting in heat, and Rappaport from the *Post* walked in. Perfect. It was Rappaport's byline on the murder story, and he was an American, Princeton grad, a former hippie type who'd interned at the Baltimore *Sun.* Young, Jewish, and fast-talking, but he didn't mind a tipple once in a while.

Wilbur motioned toward the empty stool on his left and Rappaport sat down. "Steve, old boy."

"Hello, Mark."

The *Post* man was wearing a short-sleeved safari shirt with oversized pockets, denim walking shorts, and sandals without socks.

"Very casual," said Wilbur appraisingly.

"Got to beat the heat, Mark." Rappaport took a bulldog

pipe, tobacco pouch, and matches out of one of the big pockets and placed them on the bar.

Wilbur noticed that the other two Israeli journalists were also informally attired. Long pants, but lightweight sport shirts. Suddenly his seersucker suit, button-down shirt, and rep tie, which had looked natty when he'd dressed this morning, seemed out of place, superfluous.

"Righto." He loosened his tie and pointed to the rolled-up *Post*. "Just finished reading your piece. Nice chunk of work, Steve."

"Routine," said Rappaport. "Straight from the source. The police covered up the first one, fed us a false quick-solve, and we swallowed it, but there were rumors that it was too easy, too cute, so we had our feelers out and were ready for them the second time around."

Wilbur chuckled. "Same old bullshit." He picked up the newspaper, used it for a fan. "Nasty stuff, from the sound of it."

"Very. Butchery."

Wilbur liked the sound of that. He filed it away for future use.

"Any leads?"

"Nothing," said Rappaport. He had long hair and a thick handlebar mustache that he brushed away from his lips. "The police here aren't used to that kind of thing—they're not equipped to handle it."

"Amateur hour, huh?"

The bartender brought Wilbur's shrimp.

"I'll have some of that too," said Rappaport. "And a beer."

"On me," Wilbur told the bartender.

"Thank you much, Mark," said Rappaport.

Wilbur shrugged it off. "Gotta keep the expense account going or the main office gets worried."

"I won't tell you about my expense account." Rappaport frowned. "Or lack thereof."

"Police beating their meat?" asked Wilbur, trying to get the conversation back on track. It was a little too obvious and Rappaport seemed to have caught it. He picked up the pipe, rolled it in his palm, then filled it, lit it, and regarded Wilbur over a rising plume of smoke.

"Same thing back home," said Wilbur, backtracking casually. "Stepping over each other's feet and snowing the press."

"No," said Rappaport. "That's not the situation here. Major Crimes is a fairly competent unit when it comes to their specialty—security crimes, bombs left in trash bins, et cetera. The problem with this kind of thing is lack of experience. Sex murders are virtually unknown in Israel—I went into the archives and found only a handful in thirty years. And only one was a serial—a guy last year, cutting up hookers. They never caught him." He shook his head, smoked. "Six months in Baltimore, I saw more than that."

"Last year," said Wilbur. "Could it be the same guy?"

"Doubtful. Different M.O.'s."

M.O.'s. The kid had been reading too many detective novels.

"Two in a row," said Wilbur. "Maybe things are changing."

"Maybe they are," said Rappaport. He looked concerned. The sincere worry of a good citizen. Unprofessional, thought Wilbur. If you wanted to be effective you couldn't be part of it.

"What else you been up to, Steve?" he asked, not wanting to sound too eager.

"Sunday puff piece on the new Ramat Gan mall—nothing much else."

"Till the next pseudo-scandal, eh?"

Before Rappaport could reply, his shrimp and beer came. Wilbur slapped down his American Express card and called for another Turkey.

"Thanks again," said Rappaport, tamping his pipe out and laying it in an ashtray. "I don't know, maybe we *are* changing. Maybe it's a sign of maturity. One of the founders of the state, Jabotinsky, said we wouldn't be a real country until we had Israeli criminals and Israeli whores."

We. The guy was overinvolved, thought Wilbur. And typically arrogant. The Chosen People, thinking they invented everything, turning everything into a virtue. He'd spent four years on a midtown Manhattan beat for the *New York Post*, could tell the kid plenty about Israeli criminals.

He smiled and said, "Welcome to the real world, Steve."

"Yup."

They drank and ate shrimp, talked about women and bosses and salaries, finally got around to the murders again. Wilbur kept a running tab going, cajoled Rappaport into having another shrimp cocktail. Three more beers and the *Post* man started reminiscing about his student days in Jerusalem, how safe it had been, everyone keeping their doors unlocked. Paradise, to listen to him, but Wilbur knew it was self-delusion—nostalgia always was. He played fascinated listener and, by the time Rappaport left, had filed away all his information and was ready to start writing.

31

Ten days since the discovery of Juliet's body, and nothing new, either good or bad.

They'd narrowed the sex offender list down to sixteen men. Ten Jews, four Arabs, one Druze, one Armenian, all busted since Gray Man. None had alibis; all had histories of violence or, according to the prison psychiatrists, the potential for it. Seven had attempted rape, three had pulled it off, four had severely beaten women after being refused sex, and two were chronic peepers with multiple burglary convictions and a penchant for carrying knives—a combination the doctors considered potentially explosive.

Five of the sixteen lived in Jerusalem; another six resided in communities within an hour's drive of the capital. The Druze's home was farther north, in the village of Daliyat el Carmel, a remote aerie atop the verdant, poppy-speckled hills that looked down upon Haifa. But he was unemployed, had access to a car, and was prone to taking solitary drives. The same was true of two of the Arabs and one of the Jews. The remaining pair of Jews, Gribetz and Brickner, were friends who'd gang-raped a fifteen-year-old girl—Gribetz's cousin—and also lived far north, in Nahariya. Before going to prison they'd shared a business, a trucking service specializing in picking up parcels from the Customs House at Ashdod and delivering them to owners' homes. Since their release they'd resumed working together, tooling along the highways in an old Peugeot pickup. Looking, Daniel wondered, for more than profit?

He interviewed them and the Druze, trying to make some

connection between Juliet Haddad's Haifa entry and home bases near the northern border.

Gribetz and Brickner were surly, semiliterate types in their mid-twenties, heavily muscled louts who smelled unwashed and gave off a foul heat. They didn't take the interrogation seriously, nudged each other playfully and laughed at unspoken jokes, and despite the tough-guy posturing, Daniel started perceiving them as lovers—latent homosexuals perhaps? They seemed bored by discussion of their crime, shrugged it off as a miscarriage of justice.

"She was always loose," said Gribetz. "Everyone in the family knew it."

"What do you mean by 'always'?" asked Daniel.

Gribetz's eyes dulled with confusion.

"*Always*—what do you think?" interceded Brickner.

Daniel kept his eyes on Gribetz. "She was fifteen when you raped her. How long had she been . . . loose?"

"Always," said Gribetz. "For years. Everyone in the family knew it. She was born that way."

"They'd have family parties," said Brickner. "Afterward everyone would take a drive with Batya and all the guys would have a go at her."

"You were there too?"

"No, no, but everyone knew—it was the kind of thing everyone knew."

"What we did was the same as always," said Gribetz. "We went for a spin in the truck and had her good, but this time she wanted money and we said fuck you. She got mad and called the cops, ruined our lives."

"She really fucked us up," confirmed Brickner. "We lost all our accounts, had to start from scratch."

"Speaking of your accounts," Daniel asked him, "do you keep a log of your deliveries?"

"For each day. Then we throw it out."

"Why's that?"

"Why not? It's our personal shit. What's the matter, the government doesn't give us enough paperwork to store?"

Daniel looked at the arrest report Northern Division had written up on the two. The girl had suffered a broken jaw, loss of twelve teeth, a cracked eye socket, ruptured spleen, and vaginal lacerations that had needed suturing.

"You could have killed her," he said.

"She was trying to take our money," protested Brickner. "She was nothing more than a whore."

"So you're saying that it's okay to beat up whores."

"Well, ah, no—you know what I mean."

"I don't. Explain it to me."

Brickner scratched his head and inhaled. "How about a cigarette?"

"Later. First explain me your philosophy about whores."

"We don't need whores, Hillel and me," said Gribetz. "We get plenty of pussy, any time we want."

"Whores," said Brickner. "Who the hell needs them."

"Which is why you raped her?"

"That was different," said Brickner. "His whole family knew about her."

An hour later, they'd given him nothing that cleared them, but neither had they implicated themselves. During the nights of the murders they claimed to have been sleeping in bed, but both lived alone and lacked verification. Their memories failed to stretch back to the period preceding Fatma's murder, but they recalled delivering parcels to Bet Shemesh the day before Juliet's body had been found. A painstaking check of Ashdod Customs records revealed an early morning pickup; Shmeltzer was still trying to get hold of the bills of lading from the week of Fatma's death.

The timing vis-à-vis Juliet was feasible, Daniel knew. Bet Shemesh was just outside Jerusalem, which would have given them ample opportunity to drop off the packages, then go prowling around. But where would they have killed her and cut her up? Neither had residence nor connections in Jerusalem and the lab boys had found no blood in the truck. They denied ever laying eyes on Juliet or going into the city, and no witness placed them there. As for what they'd done with the afternoon, they claimed to have driven back north, spent the afternoon at a deserted stretch of beach just above Haifa.

"Anyone see you there?" asked Daniel.

"No one goes there," said Brickner. "The ships leak shit in the water—it smells. There's tar all over the beach that can gook you up if you're not careful."

"But you guys go there."

Brickner grinned. "We like it. It's empty—you can piss in the sand, do whatever you like."

Gribetz laughed.

"I'd like for both of you to take a polygraph test."

"Does it hurt?" asked Brickner in a crude imitation of a child's voice.

"You've had one before. It's in your file."

"Oh, yeah, the wires. It fucked us over. No way."

"No way for me either," said Gribetz. "No way."

"It incriminated you because you were guilty. If you're innocent, you can use it to clear yourselves of suspicion. Otherwise you'll be considered suspects."

"Consider away," said Brickner, spreading his arms.

"Consider away," said Gribetz, aping him.

Daniel called for a uniform, had them taken back.

A repulsive pair but he tended to believe them. They were low-impulse morons, explosive and psychopathic, playing on each other's pathology. Certainly capable of damaging another woman if the right situation came up, but he didn't see them for the murders. The cold calculation that had echoed from the crime scenes wasn't their style. Still, smarter men than he had been fooled by psychopaths, and there was still the earlier Ashdod material to be looked at. Perhaps something would be found that refreshed their memories about Fatma. Before he ordered them released, he slowed down the paperwork so that they'd be cooling their heels for as long as possible, assigned Avi Cohen to drive up to Nahariya and find out more about them, keep a tight surveillance on them when they got home.

The Druze, Assad Mallah, was also no genius. One of the peepers, he was a withdrawn, stammering type, just turned thirty, with jailhouse pallor, watery blue eyes, and a history of neurological abnormalities that had exempted him from army service. As a teenager he'd burgled Haifa apartments, gorged himself on food from the victims' refrigerators, and left a thank-you card before departing: a mound of excrement on the kitchen floor.

Because of his age he'd been given youth counseling, which never took place because at that time there'd been no Druze counselors; no one from Social Welfare had bothered to drive up to Daliyat el Carmel to bring him in. But he had received treatment of sorts—severe and regular beatings at the hand of his father—which seemed to have done the trick, because his record stayed clean. Until one night, ten years later, he was caught ejaculating noisily against the wall of an apartment building near the Technion, one hand gripping the casement of a nearby bedroom window, the other flogging away as he cried out in ecstasy.

The tenants were a married couple, a pair of graduate physics students who'd forgotten to draw their drapes. Hearing the commotion, the husband rushed out, discovered Mallah, beat him senseless, and called the police. During his questioning by Northern District, the Druze immediately confessed to scores of peeping incidents and dozens of burglaries, which went a long way in clearing the local crime records.

He was a blade man too. At the time of his arrest, there had been a penknife in his pocket—he claimed to use it to whittle and slice fruit. No forensic evidence had been found to contradict him at the time and Northern District had confiscated the weapon, which had since disappeared. At his trial he had the misfortune of drawing the only Druze judge at Haifa Magistrates Hall and received the maximum sentence. In Ramle he behaved well, got good recommendations from the psychiatrists and the administrators, and was released early. One month before Fatma's murder.

Another penknife had been found on him the day he'd been picked up for questioning. Small-bladed, dull, it bore no similarity to Levi's wound molds. He was also, Daniel noticed, left-handed, which, according to the pathologist, made him an unlikely candidate. Daniel spent two sluggish hours with him, scheduled a polygraph, and made a phone request to Northern District for a loose surveillance: no intrusion into the village; keep track of his license plate; report his whereabouts if he went into town.

At the same time, the Chinaman and Daoud were interrogating other suspects, working with dogged rhythm, going down the list. They agreed to do a good-guy, bad-guy routine, switching off so that the Chinaman would lean hard on the Jews, Daoud zero in on the Arabs. It threw the suspects off guard, kept them guessing about who was who, what was what. And reduced the possibility of racism/brutality charges, though that would happen no matter what you did. A national pastime.

Two days later, ten of the sixteen had been judged improbable. All agreed to be hooked up to the polygraph; all passed. Of the six possibles, three also passed, leaving three refusers—the

Nahariya buddies and an Arab from Gaza. Daoud was assigned to watch the Arab.

Late in the afternoon, Shmeltzer came into Daniel's office with photocopies of the customs material from Ashdod. During the days preceding Fatma's murder, Brickner and Gribetz had picked up an unusually full load of cargo—part of an overflow shipment held up at the docks for three weeks due to a stevedore strike. The parcels were destined for the north-central region—Afula, Hadera, and villages in the Bet She'an valley, a good seventy kilometers above Jerusalem. Which was still driveable if they'd gotten off early.

Daniel, Shmeltzer, and the Chinaman got on the phone, calling each name on the bills of lading, received confirmation that the buddies had been busy for two days straight, so busy that they'd spent the night in Hadera, parking their truck in a date grove belonging to one of the package owners, still asleep when the guy went to check his trees. He remembered them well, he told Daniel, because they'd awoken filthy-mouthed, stood on the truck bed and urinated onto the ground, then demanded breakfast.

"Were there packages in the truck bed?"

"Oh, yeah. Dozens. They stood right on top of them—didn't give a damn."

Idiots, thought Daniel, they could have supplied themselves with alibis all along, had been too stupid or too contrary to do so. Maybe being thought of as potential murderers fed their egos.

Dangerous, they bore watching, but were no longer his present concern.

The Arab from Gaza, Aljuni, was their last chance—not that probable, really, except that he was a killer who liked blades and hated women. He'd carved up one wife in a fit of rage over improperly cooked soup, maimed another, and, three months out of prison, was engaged to a third, sixteen years old. Why did women hook up with that type? Latent death wish? Was being alone worse than death?

Irrelevant questions. Daoud had nothing to report on Aljuni: The guy kept regular habits, never went out at night. No doubt he'd come to naught as a prospect. The winnowing of the sex files had been futile.

He looked at his watch. Eight P.M. and he hadn't called

home. He did so, got no answer, and puzzled, phoned the message operator and asked if Gveret Sharavi had tried to get in touch with him.

"Let me see—yes. Here's one from her that came in at four forty-three, Pakad. She wants to know if you'll be joining her, the children, and . . . it looks like the Boonkers—"

"Brookers."

"Whatever. She wanted to know if you'll be joining them for dinner at seven-thirty."

"Did she say where?"

"No," said the operator reproachfully. "She probably expected you to call sooner."

He hung up, took a swallow of cold coffee from the cup on his desk, and put his head down. A knock on the door raised him up and he saw Shmeltzer enter, looking angry, a sheaf of papers clutched in his hand.

"Look at this, Dani. I was driving home, noticed a guy plastering this to walls, thought you might want to see it."

The papers were handbills. At the center was a head-shot photo of a Hassid, fortyish, full-bearded, with extravagant side curls. The man looked fat, with flat features and narrow eyes behind black-framed eyeglasses. He wore a dark jacket and a white shirt buttoned to the neck. Atop his head was a large, square *kipah*. Hanging around his neck was a sign with the letters NYPD, followed by several numbers.

A mug shot.

BEWARE OF THIS MAN! was emblazoned under the photo, in Hebrew, English, and Yiddish. SENDER MALKOVSKY IS A CRIMINAL AND A CHILD RAPER!!!!!! HIDE YOUR YOUNG ONES!!!!!! Below the warnings were clippings from New York newspapers, reduced to the point where the print was barely legible. Daniel squinted, read with tired eyes.

Malkovsky was from the Williamsburg section of Brooklyn, a father of six, a teacher of religious studies, and a tutor. A student had accused him of forced molestation and the charge had brought forth similar stories from dozens of other children. Malkovsky had been arrested by the New York Police, arraigned, released on bail, and failed to appear at his trial. One of the articles, from the *New York Post,* speculated that he'd run off to Israel, citing connections to "prominent Hassidic rabbis."

Daniel put the handbill down.

"He's living here, the bastard," said Shmeltzer. "In a fancy flat up in Qiryat Wolfson. The guy I found pasting these up is also a longbeard, named Rabinovitch—also from Brooklyn, knew Malkovsky's case well, thought Malkovsky was in jail. He moves to Israel, buys a flat in the Wolfson complex, and one day he spots Malkovsky coming out of an apartment a hundred meters away. It drove him crazy—he has seven kids of his own. He marches straight to Malkovsky's *rebbe* and tells him about the shmuck's history, *Rebbe* nods and says Malkovsky had done repentance, deserves a second chance. Rabinovitch goes crazy and runs to the printer."

"A tutor," said Daniel. "Skips bail and moves into one of the fanciest developments in town. Where does he get that kind of money?"

"That's what Rabinovitch wanted to know. He figured Malkovsky's fellow Hassidim donated it on the *rebbe*'s orders. That may be rivalry talking—Rabinovitch is from a different sect; you know how they like to go at each other—but it makes sense."

"Why didn't Rabinovitch notify us?"

"I asked him that. He looked at me as if I were crazy. Far as he's concerned the police are in on it—how else could Malkovsky get into the country, be running around free?"

"How else, indeed?"

"It stinks, Dani. I don't remember any Interpol notices or extradition orders, do you?"

"No." Daniel opened a desk drawer, took out the Interpol bulletins and FBI bulletins and flipped through them. "No Malkovsky."

"No immigration warnings, either," said Shmeltzer. "Nothing from the brass or Customs. This *rebbe* must have massive *protekzia*."

"Which *rebbe* is it?"

"The Prostnitzer."

"He's new, " said Daniel. "From Brooklyn. Has a small group that broke off from the Satmars—couple of planeloads of them came over last year."

"To Wolfson, eh? No Mea She'arim for these saints?"

"Most of them live out in the Ramot. The Wolfson thing is probably special for Malkovsky—to keep him under wraps. How long's he been in the country?"

"Three months—enough to do damage. He's a kiddy-diddler, but who knows what a pervert will do? Maybe he's shifted his preferences. In any event, someone's making us look like idiots, Dani."

Daniel slammed his fist down on the desk. Shmeltzer, surprised at the uncharacteristic display of emotion, took a step backward, then smiled inwardly. At least the guy was human.

32

Qiryat Wolfson was luxury American-style; a penthouse in the complex had recently sold for over a million dollars. Crisp limestone towers and low-profile town houses, a maze of landscaped walkways and subterranean parking garages, carpeted lobbies and high-speed elevators, all of it perched at the edge of a craggy bluff near the geographical center of the municipality, due west of the Old City. The view from up there was commanding—the Knesset, the Israel Museum, the generous belts of greenery that surrounded the government buildings. To the southwest, an even wider swatch of green—the Ein Qerem forest, where Juliet had been found.

In the darkness the complex jutted skyward like a clutch of stalagmites; from below came the roar of traffic on Rehov Herzl. Daniel drove the Escort into one of the underground lots and parked near the entrance. Some of the spaces were occupied by American cars: huge Buicks, Chevrolets, Chryslers, an old white Cadillac Coupe de Ville sagging on underinflated tires. Dinosaurs, too wide for Jerusalem streets and alleys. Why had the owners bothered to bring them over?

It took him a while to find his way around, and it was just past nine by the time he reached Malkovsky's flat—a first-floor town-house unit on the west side of the complex, built around a small paved courtyard. The door was unmarked, armored with three locks. Daniel knocked, heard heavy footsteps, the sliding of bolts, and found himself face to face with the man in the handbill.

"Yes?" said Malkovsky. He was huge, bearishly obese, the beard fanning over his chest like some hirsute bib, reaching almost to his waist. A thick reddish-brown pelt that masked his cheekbones and tapered raggedly just beneath the lower rims of his eyeglasses. His complexion was florid, lumpy, dominated by a nose squashed pita-flat and dotted with open pores. His forehead was skimpy, the hair above it dense and curly. He wore the same square skullcap as in the picture, but had pushed it back to the crown.

Swallowed up by hair, thought Daniel. Like Esau. So big, he blocked most of the doorway. Daniel looked past him, peering through slivers of space: a living room still redolent of a boiled chicken supper, the floor littered with toys, newspapers, an empty baby bottle. He saw a blur of motion—children chasing each other, laughing and screaming in Yiddish. A baby wailed, unseen. A kerchiefed woman passed quickly through the sliver and disappeared. Moments later the crying stopped.

"Police," said Daniel, in English. He took out his identification and held it up to Malkovsky's glasses.

Malkovsky ignored it, unimpressed. A wave of annoyance rumpled the knobby blanket of his face. He cleared his throat and drew himself up to his full height.

"A *frummer*?" he said, focusing on Daniel's *kipah*.

"May I come in?"

Malkovsky wiped his brow. He was sweating—from exertion, not anxiety—eyeglasses fogged, perspiration stains browning the armpits of a tentlike V-neck undershirt. Over the undershirt he wore a black-striped woolen *tallit katan*, the ritual fringed garment prescribed for daily use, a rectangle of cloth with a hole cut out for the head, the fringes looped through perforations on each corner. His pants were black and baggy. On his feet were black bubble-toed oxfords.

"What do you want?" he demanded, in Hebrew.

"To talk to you."

"Who is it, Sender?" a female voice called out.

"Gornisht." Malkovsky stepped out into the hallway and closed the door behind him. When he moved he shook. Like the cubes of jellied calf's leg in the display case at Pfefferberg's.

"Everything's been arranged," he said. "I don't need you."

"Everything?"

"Everything. Just perfect. Tell your boss I'm perfect."

When Daniel gave no evidence of moving, Malkovsky nibbled his mustache and asked, "*Nu*, what's the problem? More papers?"

"I have no papers for you."

"What is it, then?"

"I'm conducting a criminal investigation. Your criminal history came to my attention and I thought it best that we talk."

Malkovsky flushed, sucked in his breath, and his eyes kindled with anger. He started to say something, stopped himself, and wiped his brow again. Turning his hands into fists the size of Shabbat roasts, he began bouncing them against the convex surface of his thighs.

"Go away, policeman," he said. "My papers are in order! Everything's been arranged!"

"To what arrangement are you referring, Mr. . . . or is it *Rabbi* Malkovsky?"

Malkovsky folded his arms across his chest. The flush beneath the beard was tinged with purple and his breathing sounded labored.

"I don't have to talk to you."

"That's your privilege," said Daniel, "but I'll be back in an hour with papers of my own, along with a *minyan* of police officers to help me deliver them. Your neighbors are sure to be intrigued."

Malkovsky stared down at him, clenching and unclenching those massive fists.

"Why are you harassing me!" he demanded, but his resistance had started to fizzle, indignation giving way to naked fear.

"As I told you, Rabbi—"

"I'm not a rabbi!"

"—your history makes it necessary for me to speak with you concerning some crimes that have taken place since you've immigrated to Israel."

"This is stupid talk. There is no history. I don't know what you're talking about." Malkovsky opened his hands, turned them palms-down, and passed one over the other in a gesture of closure. "*G'nuk*. Enough."

"No, not *g'nuk*, not until we talk."

"There's nothing to talk about. I'm a permanent resident. My papers are in order."

"Speaking of papers," said Daniel. He removed a handbill from his pocket, unfolded it, and gave it to Malkovsky.

The immense man stared at it, lips formed into a silent O. With one hand he crumpled the paper; with the other he covered his face. "Lies."

The hand opened and the paper ball dropped to the floor.

"There are others, Mr. Malkovsky, hundreds of others, plastered to walls, kiosks, all over town. It's just a matter of time."

"Lies," said Malkovsky. "Sinful gossip." He turned, half-faced the wall, pulling at his beard, ripping loose long, wiry strands of hair.

Daniel took Malkovsky's arm, feeling his fingers sink into softness. A clay man, he thought. A *golem*.

"We need to talk," he said.

Malkovsky said nothing, continued to shred his beard. But his posture had slackened and he allowed Daniel to lead him outside, to a quiet corner of the courtyard shaded by pepper trees in terra-cotta planters. The outdoor lighting was dim, weak orange spotlights casting electric blemishes upon the giant's knurled countenance.

"Tell me everything," said Daniel.

Malkovsky stared at him.

Daniel repeated: "Tell me."

"I was a sick man," said Malkovsky, as if by rote. "I had a sickness, a burden the *yetzer horah* cast upon my shoulders."

Self-pitying hypocrite, thought Daniel. Speaking of the Evil Impulse as if it were divorced from his free will. The sight of the man, with his beard and *peyot* and religious garments, dredged up feelings of revulsion that were almost overwhelming.

"You've transferred that burden to the shoulders of others," he said coldly. "Very small shoulders."

Malkovsky trembled, then removed his glasses, as if clarity of perception were painful. Unshielded, his eyes were small, down-slanted, restlessly evasive.

"I've worked hard to repent," he said. "True *tshuva*—last Yom Kippur, my *rebbe* praised my efforts. You're a *frummer mensh*, you understand about *tshuva*."

"A necessary part of *tshuva* is *vidduy*," said Daniel. "Full confession. All I've heard from you is self-pity."

Malkovsky was indignant. "I've done a proper *vidduy*. My *rebbe* says I'm making good progress. Now you forget about me—leave me alone!"

"Even if *I* would, others won't." Daniel pulled out another handbill, set it down on Malkovsky's broad lap.

Malkovsky pounded his chest and began uttering the Yom Kippur confession in a high, constricted whisper. Stood there torturing his beard, spitting out a litany of transgressions.

"We have trespassed, we have dealt treacherously, we have stolen, we have spoken slander, we have committed iniquity . . ."

When he reached the last offense, he put a finger in his mouth and bit down upon it, eyes closed, *kipah* askew. Breathing rapidly and noisily.

"Did you ever," asked Daniel, "do it with any of your own children, or did you limit yourself to the children of others?"

Malkovsky ignored the question, kept praying. Daniel waited, repeated his question. Let the big bastard know he wouldn't be getting off with lip service.

A while later, Malkovsky answered.

33

The library was the best room in the house.

The living room was boring—all those couches and paintings and furniture, and stuff under glass bells that you weren't allowed to touch. When he'd been real little the maids wouldn't let him go in there at all, and now that he was nine he didn't even want to.

The kitchen was okay if you wanted food or something, but otherwise it was boring. The extra bedrooms in the Children's Wing were always locked, and his bedroom smelled of pee and throw-up. The maids said it was his imagination, it smelled fine. They refused to scrub it anymore.

He'd been in Doctor's room a couple of times, going through the drawers, squeezing the soft, striped underwear and the blue pajamas with white trim around the edges and Doctor's initials on the front pocket. The rest of the stuff was socks, sweaters; suits and pants in the closet—all boring. The only interesting thing he'd ever come across was a thick black fountain pen with a gold tip, kind of stuck between two sweaters, hiding from him.

He stole it, took it into his room, and tried to write with it, and when it didn't work he smashed it with a hammer until it turned into black dust. He tasted it. It was bad and he spit it out, wiping his tongue to get the grit off, trails of grayish drool trickling down his chin.

The ice palace was always locked. Of course. She only let him in there when she was really drunk and needed him to get her an aspirin from the bathroom. Or when Sarah came to visit, which was only two or three times a year but always got her upset.

On Sarah days, she was always calling for him in a high, wiggly voice that was kind of scary—*"Darling! Come he-ere! Daarling!"*—telling him to get into bed, drawing him in under the slimy-satin covers and putting a soft, bare arm around his shoulder. He could feel her hand squeezing him, soft and wet and sticky, her mouth breathing all that gin-breath on him, hot and sweet, but a disgusting sweet, like she'd been throwing up candy.

On Sarah days, she'd get really disgusting, lean over him so that her titties were pushing into his chest, the tops all white and shaky. Sometimes she'd lean real low so that he could look down and see the nipples, like big pink gumdrops. Slurping his cheek and saying, "Come on, baby, tell Mama. Is that nasty little bitch high-hatting you? Is she lording it over you, is she?" While she'd be slobbering all over him, the cat would stare at him, all jealous, sneak a scratch in, then pull back so you couldn't accuse it of anything.

He didn't understand what she was talking about—high-hatting, lording—so he just shrugged and looked away from her, which got her going again, waving her empty glass and talking all wiggly.

"Little *snot,* thinks she's so much *better* than you and me, thinks she's so goddamned *smart—they* always *do.* Too smart for their own damned good, the chosen people, yeah. Chosen to ruin the world, right? Right? Answer me!"

Shrug.

"Cat got your tongue, eh? Or maybe she spooked you—the chosen people hex. Ha. *Chosen* for big *noses,* if you ask me. Don't you think her nose is big? She's horrid and ugly, don't you think? *Don't* you?"

He actually thought Sarah was okay. She was seven years older, which made her sixteen, almost a grown-up, and kind of pretty, with thick dark hair, soft brown eyes, and a wide, pretty mouth. Her nose looked okay to him, too, but he didn't say so, just shrugged.

"Horrid little *bitch*."

Even though she stayed in the room next to his, they didn't see each other much. Sarah was either swimming or reading or calling her mother at her hotel, or going out at night with Doctor. But when they passed each other in the hall she always smiled at him, said hi. One time she brought a tin of sugared fruits all the way from the city where she lived and shared it with him, didn't even mind when he ate all the cherries.

"Don't you think she's *terrible*—a horrid little hook-nosed *nothing*? Answer me, damn you!"

He felt his arm being pinched hard, twisted between cold, wet fingers. Bit his lip to keep from crying out.

"*Isn't* she!"

"Sure, Mom."

"She really *is* a little bitch, you know. If you were older you'd understand. Ten years it's been and she still won't give me the time of day, the conceited little kike—*kikette*! Isn't that a *fun* way to say it, darling?"

"Sure, Mom."

A hot, ginny sigh and a wet-hand hug, the fingers digging in as if for another pinch, then opening and rubbing him. Down his arm to his wrist, dropping onto his leg. Rubbing.

"We're all we've got, darling. I'm so glad we can confide in each other this way."

Sarah's mother always brought her. A taxi would drop them off in front of the house; Sarah would get out first, then her mother. Her mother would kiss her good-bye, walk her to the door, but never come inside. She was a short, dark woman named Lillian, kind of pretty—Sarah looked a lot like her. She wore fancy clothes—shiny dresses, shoes with really high heels, long coats with fur collars, sometimes a hat with a veil—and she smiled a lot. One time she caught him looking at her through the living room window, smiled and waved before she got in the taxi and rode off. He thought it was a pretty nice smile.

If Doctor was home, he'd go outside and talk to Lillian, shake her hand, and pick up Sarah's suitcases. They seemed to like each other, talking all friendly, as if they had lots to talk about, and he couldn't figure out why, if they got along so good, they'd gotten divorced. He wondered if *his* mother and Doctor had ever been friendly like that. As long as he could remember, it had always been fighting, the night-wars.

Twice during each visit Doctor and Sarah went out together. Once for dinner, once for ice cream. He knew about it because he heard them talking, planning what they were going to eat. Rack of lamb. Prime rib. Baked Alaska. Rice pudding. His mother heard it, too, called him in and whispered in his ear: "They're a pair of little *piggies,* absolutely disgusting. They go to nice places and eat like pigs and people stare at them. I refuse to go along anymore—it's disgusting. You should see his shirts when he's through. *She* eats chocolate ice cream and gets it all over herself. Her dresses look like used toilet paper!"

He thought of that, chocolate ice cream stains looking like shit stains, and wondered what people shit tasted like. One time he'd taken a tiny piece of the cat's shit out of the litter box and put it on his tongue and then spit it out real fast because it was so terrible. Tasting it had made his stomach hurt and he wanted to throw up for three days. All over his mother's bed—that would be good, big globs of barf all over the white satin. On Doctor and Sarah and the maids too. Running all over the house—no, *flying*! *Dive bombing everyone* with shit bombs and throw-up bombs. Pow!

Power!

One time he saw Sarah in the cabana next to the pool. There was an open window and he looked through it. She was peeling off her bathing suit and looking at herself in the mirror before putting on her clothes.

She had small titties with chocolate centers.

Her body was tan except for a white tit belt and a white butt belt and her puss was covered with black hair.

She touched her puss and smiled at herself in the mirror. Then shook her head no and lifted her leg in order to put on her panties.

He saw a pink, squiggly line peeking out from under the middle of the hair, like one of the wounds in Doctor's books.

Her butt was like two eggs, small, the brown kind. He thought of cracking them open, yellow stuff coming out.

Her head hair was dark, but not as dark as her puss hair. She stood there in her panties and brushed it, making it shine.

Raising her arms so that her titties went flat and disappeared and only the chocolate tips were sticking out. Humming to herself.

He wanted to take bites out of her, wondered what she tasted like.

Thinking about it made his pecker get all stiff and hurt so bad he was afraid it would crack and fall off and all the blood would come pouring out of the hole and he would die.

It took a long time for the pain to go away.

He hated Sarah a little after that, but he still thought she was okay. He wanted to sneak into her room, go through her drawers, but she always kept the door locked. After she went back home and before the maids had a chance to lock it, he went in and opened all the drawers. All that was left was a nylon stocking box and a perfumey smell.

It made him real angry.

He kind of missed her.

He thought of cutting her up and eating her, imagined that she tasted like sugared fruit.

The house was so big it always felt empty. Which was okay—the only ones around were the maids and they were stupid, talked with an accent and hummed weird songs. They hated him—he could tell from the way they looked at him and whispered to each other when he walked by. He wondered what their pusses looked like. *Their* titties. Thought they probably tasted sour, like vegetables. Wondering about it made him stare at them. When they noticed it they got angry, muttered under their breaths, and walked away from him, talking foreign.

The neat thing about the library was that the double doors were always closed; once the maids were through cleaning, you could go in, turn the key in the lock, and nobody would know you were in there.

He liked the big, soft leather chairs. And the books. Doctor's books, full of terrific, scary pictures. He had favorites, would always turn to them first. The nigger guy with elephantiasis (a big word; it took him a long time to figure it out), his balls were big—*huge!*—each one as big as a watermelon. He couldn't believe it the first time he saw it. The picture showed the guy sitting on a chair with his hands in his lap, the balls hanging down to the floor! He looked pretty worried. Why didn't someone just come along and chop them off so he could walk again? Clean him up and stop his worries?

Other ones he liked were the retarded people with no foreheads, and tongues as big as salamis that just hung out of their mouths. A weird-looking naked retarded lady with a real flat face standing next to a ruler; she was only thirty-seven inches tall and had no hair on her puss, even though she was old. Naked midgets and giants, also next to rulers. People missing fingers and arms and legs. One guy without arms *or* legs—that looked really stupid and made him laugh.

Lots of other naked people, with sores and spots and bent bones and weird bumps. Buttholes and lips with splits down the middle. And naked fat people. *Really* fat people, so fat that they looked like they were wearing squishy clothes all full of wrinkles and folds. One woman had a belly that hung down past her knees, covering her whole puss. Her elbows were covered by hang-downs of fat. Someone, a surgeon like Doctor, should come along and cut off all that fat, maybe use it for candles or something or to give to skinny people to keep them warm. The fat people could be peeled and cleaned up to make them look nice. The ones in the books probably didn't do it because it was too expensive. They'd have to walk around like that, all covered with fat-clothes, for the rest of their lives.

One time, after looking at the fat people, he left the library, went up to his room, and made squishy, fat people out of modeling clay. Then he took a pencil and a nail file and made holes and slit-cuts all over them, chopped off their heads and arms and legs and peeled them until they were nothing more than little chunks and pieces. Then he grabbed up the chunks and squeezed real hard, let the clay squish through his fingers. Flushed them down the toilet and imagined they were drowning. Screaming: *Oh, no! Oh, God!* Watching them go around and around and finally disappear made him feel like the boss, made his pecker hard and sore.

On the top shelf of the carved bookcase was this big green book, really heavy; he had to stand on a chair to get it, be really careful not to drop it on Doctor's leather-topped desk, break the skull that Doctor used for a paperweight. A monkey skull, too small to have come from a person, but he liked to pretend it was from a person. One of the midgets in the pictures. Maybe he'd tried to attack the boy's family and the boy had killed him and saved everyone, like a big hero, then peeled off the skin to get the skull.

The green book was old—the date on it was 1908—and it had a long title: *The Atlas of Clinical Surgery* by Professor Bockenheimer or some weird name like that, from a place called Berlin; he looked it up in his junior encyclopedia and found out it was in Germany.

Someone had written something inside the cover of the book, in this weird, thin handwriting that looked like dead bugs and spider legs, it took him a long time to figure it out.

To Charles, my learned colleague, with deepest gratitude for your kind hospitality and stimulating conversation.

Best wishes,
Dieter Schwann

What was neat about the green book was that the pictures looked really real, as if you could put your hand out and touch them, just like looking through a 3-D stereoscope. The book said they were pictures of models. Models made by some guy named F. Kalbow from the—this was a really hard one—Pathoplastic Institute of Berlin.

One model was a guy's face with a hole in it called a sarcoma. The hole covered the guy's nose and mouth. All you could see was eyes and then the hole—inside it was all pink and yellow. Another one was a pecker all squashed up, with some grayish, wrinkly thing around it and a big sore on the tip. Kind of like an earthworm with a red head. One he really liked to look at was this big picture of a butthole with pink flowerlike things all over it. A butthole flower garden.

It was dirty stuff. He wanted to take a knife and cut it all away and peel it, make everything clean and nice.

To be the boss, and save everyone.

The other things he *really* liked were the knives and tools in the big black leather case that sat next to the monkey skull.

The inside of the case was red velvet. Gold letters were stamped into it: *Jetter und Scheerer: Tuttlingen und Berlin*. There it was again, that same place, Berlin. It was a doctor city, probably. Full of doctor stuff.

The knives and tools were held in place by leather straps. There were a lot of them; when you picked up the case it kind of clinked. The blades were silvery metal, the handles some smooth, white, shiny stuff that looked like the inside of a seashell.

He liked to unfasten the straps and take the knives out, one by one, then arrange them like ice-cream sticks, making letters and designs with them on the desk top. His initials, in knife-letters.

They were *really* sharp. He found out by accident when he touched the tip of one of them to his finger and all of a sudden his skin had opened, as if by magic. It was a deep cut and it scared him but he felt good, seeing the different layers of skin, what was inside of him. It didn't even hurt, at first; then it started to bleed—a lot—and he felt a sharp, pumping pain. He grabbed a tissue, wrapped it around his finger, and squeezed, watching the tissue turn from white to red, sitting there a long time until the blood finally stopped coming out. He unwrapped the finger, touched the tissue to his tongue, tasted salt and paper, crumpled it, and stuffed it into his pocket.

After that he cut himself from time to time. On purpose—he was the boss over the knives. Little tiny cuts that didn't bleed for long, notches nicked into the tops of his fingernails. There was a squeezing tool in the case, off to one side, and he used it to squeeze his finger until it turned purple and hot and throbbing and he couldn't stand it any longer. He used tissues to soak up the blood, collected the bloody pieces of paper, and hid them in a toy box in his closet.

After playing with the knives, he sometimes went up to his room, locked the door, and took out nail files, scissors, safety pins, and pencils. Laying them out on his own desk, slapping together clay people and doing operations on them, using red clay for blood, making sarcoma holes and butthole flowers, cutting off their arms and legs.

Sometimes he imagined the clay people screaming. Loud, wiggly screams of *Oh, no!* and *Oh, my god!* Chopping off their heads stopped that.

That'll show you to scream!

He played with the knives for weeks before finding the knife book.

The knife book had no people in it, just drawings of knives and tools. A catalog. He turned pages until he found drawings that matched the knives in the black leather case. Spent a long time finding matches, learning the names and memorizing them.

The seven ones with the short blades were called *scalpels.*

The folding one on top with the little pointed blade was a *lancet.*

The ones with the long blades were called *bistouries.*

The skinny, round things were *surgical needles.*

The sharp spoon was a *probe and scoop.*

The one that kind of looked like a fork with two points was a *probe-detector.*

The hollow tube was a *cannula;* the pointy thing that fit into it was a *trocar.*

The fat one with the thick, flat blade was a *raspatory.*

The squeezing one off on the side, by itself, was a *harelip clamp.*

At the bottom of the case was his favorite one. It really made him feel like the boss, even though he was still scared to pick it up, it was so big and felt so dangerous.

The amputating knife. He needed two hands to hold it steady. Swing it in an arc, a soft, white neck its target.

Cut, slice.

Oh, god!

That'll show you.

There was other neat stuff in the library too. A big brass microscope and a wooden box of prepared slides—flies' legs that looked like hairy trees, red blood cells, flat and round like flying saucers. Human hair, bacteria. And a box of hypodermic needles in one of the desk drawers. He took one out, unwrapped it, and stuck it in the back of one of the leather chairs, on the bottom, next to the wall, where no one would notice it. Pretending the chair was an animal, he gave it shots, jabbing the needle in again and again, hearing the animal screaming until it turned into a person—a naked, ugly person, a girl—and started screaming in words.

Oh, no! Oh, god!

"There!" Jab. "That'll show you!" Twist.

He stole that needle, took it up to his room, and put it in with the bloody tissues.

A neat room. Lots of neat stuff.

But he liked the knives the best.

34

More interviews, more dead ends; five detectives working like mules.

Lacking any new leads, Daniel decided to retrace old ones. He drove to the Russian Compound jail and interviewed Anwar Rashmawi, concentrating on the brother's final conversation with Issa Abdelatif, trying to discern if the boyfriend had said anything about where he and Fatma had stayed between the time she'd left Saint Saviour's and the day of her murder. If Abdelatif's comment about Fatma's being dead had been more specific than Anwar had let on.

The guard brought Anwar in, wearing prison pajamas three sizes too big for him. Daniel could tell right away the brother was different, hostile, no longer the outcast. He entered the interrogation room swaggering and scowling, ignored Daniel's greeting and the guard's order to sit. Finally the guard pushed him down into the chair, said, "Stay there, you," and asked Daniel if there was anything more he needed.

"Nothing more. You may go."

When they were alone, Anwar crossed his legs, sat back in his chair, and stared at the ceiling, either ignoring Daniel's questions or turning them into feeble jokes.

Quite a change from the puff pastry who'd confessed to him two weeks ago. Bolstered, no doubt, by what he imagined to be hero status. According to the guards, his father had been visiting him regularly, the two of them playing *sheshbesh,* listening to music on Radio Amman, sharing cigarettes like best pals. The old man smiling with pride as he left the cell.

Twenty fruitless minutes passed. The room was hot and humid. Daniel felt his clothes sticking to him, a tightness in his chest.

"Let's go over it again," he said. "The exact words."

"Whose exact words?"

"Abdelatif's."

"Snakes don't talk."

Like a broken record.

Daniel opened his note pad.

"When you confessed, you said he had plenty to say. I have it here in my notes: '. . . he started to walk toward me with the knife, saying I was dead, just like Fatma. That she was nothing to him, garbage to be dumped.' You remember that, don't you?"

"I remember nothing."

"What else did he say about Fatma's death?"

"I want my lawyer."

"You don't need one. We're not discussing your crime, only Fatma's murder."

Anwar smiled. "Tricks. Deceit."

Daniel got to his feet, walked over to the brother, and stared down at him.

"You loved her. You killed for her. It would seem to me you'd want to find out who murdered her."

"The one who murdered her is dead."

Daniel bent his knees and put his face closer to Anwar's. "Not so. The one who murdered her has murdered again—he's still out there, laughing at all of us."

Anwar closed his eyes and shook his head. "Lies."

"It's the truth, Anwar." Daniel picked up the copy of *Al Fajr,* waved it in front of Anwar's face until his eyes opened, and said, "Read for yourself."

Anwar averted his gaze.

"Read it, Anwar."

"Lies. Government lies."

"*Al Fajr* is a PLO mouthpiece—everyone knows that, Anwar. Why would the PLO print government lies?"

"Government lies."

"Abdelatif didn't murder her, Anwar—at least not by himself. There's another one out there. Laughing and plotting."

"I know what you're doing," said Anwar smugly. "You're trying to trick me."

"I'm trying to find out who murdered Fatma."

"The one who murdered her is dead."

Daniel straightened, took a step backward, and regarded the brother. The stubbornness, the narrowness of vision, tightened his chest further. He stared at Anwar, who spat on the floor, played with the saliva with the frayed toe of his shoe.

Daniel waited. The tightness in Daniel's chest turned hot, a fiery band that seemed to press against his lungs, branding them, causing real, searing pain.

"Idiot," he heard himself saying, words springing to his lips, tumbling out unfettered: "I'm trying to find the one who butchered her like a goat. The one who sliced her open and scooped out her insides for a trophy. Like a goat hanging in the *souq*, Anwar."

Anwar covered his ears and screamed. "Lies!"

"He's done it again, Anwar," Daniel said, louder. "He'll keep doing it. Butchering."

"Lies!" shouted Anwar. "Filthy deceit!"

"*Butchering,* do you hear me!"

"Jew liar!"

"Your revenge is incomplete!" Daniel was shouting too. "A dishonor upon your family!"

"Lies! Jew trickery!"

"Incomplete, do you hear me, Anwar? A sham!"

"Filthy Jew liar!" Anwar's teeth were chattering, his hands corpse-white, clutching his ears.

"Worthless. A dishonor. A joke for all to know." Daniel's mouth kept expectorating words. "Worthless," he repeated, looking into Anwar's eyes, making sure the brother could see him, read his lips. "Just like your manhood."

Anwar emitted a wounded, rattling cry from deep in his belly, jumped out of the chair, and went for Daniel's throat. Daniel drew back his good hand, hit him hard against the face with the back of it, his wedding ring making contact with the eyeglasses, knocking them off. A follow-up slap, even harder, rasping the bare cheekbone, feeling the shock of pain as metal collided with bone, the frailty of the other man's body as it tumbled backward.

Anwar lay sprawled on the stone floor, holding his chest and gulping in air. A thick red welt was rising among the crevices and pits of one cheek. An angry diagonal, as if he'd been whipped.

The door was flung open and the guard came in, baton in hand.

"Everything okay?" he asked, looking first at Anwar hyperventilating on the floor, then at Daniel standing over him, rubbing his knuckles.

"Just fine," said Daniel, breathing hard himself. "Everything's fine."

"Lying Jew dog! Fascist Nazi!"

"Get up, you," said the guard. "Stand with your hands against the wall. Move it."

Anwar didn't budge, and the guard yanked him to his feet and cuffed his hands behind his back.

"He tried to attack me," said Daniel. "The truth upset him."

"Lying Zionist pig." An obscene gesture. *"Qus Amak!"* Up your mother's cunt.

"Shut up, you," said the guard. "I don't want to hear from you again. Are you all right, Pakad?"

"I'm perfectly fine." Daniel began gathering up his notes.

"Finished with him?" The guard tugged on Anwar's shirt collar.

"Yes. Completely finished."

He spent the first few minutes of the ride back to Headquarters wondering what was happening to him, the loss of control; suffered through a bit of introspection before putting it aside, filling his head instead with the job at hand. Thoughts of the two dead girls.

Neither body had borne ligature marks—the heroin anesthesia had been sufficient to subdue them. The lack of struggle, the absence of defense wounds suggested they'd allowed themselves to be injected. In Juliet's case he could understand it: She had a history of drug use, was accustomed to combining narcotics with commercial sex. But Fatma's body was clean; everything about her suggested innocence, lack of experience. Perhaps Abdelatif had initiated her into the smoking of hashish resin or an occasional sniff of cocaine, but intravenous injection—that was something else.

It implied great trust of the injector, a total submission. Despite Anwar's craziness, Daniel believed he'd been telling the truth during his confession. That Abdelatif had indeed said something about Fatma being dead. If he'd meant it literally, he'd been only a co-participant in the cutting. Or perhaps his meaning had been symbolic—he'd pimped his ewe to a stranger. In the eyes of the Muslims, a promiscuous girl was as good as dead.

In either event, Fatma had gone along with the transaction, a big jump even for a runaway. Had the submission been a final cultural irony—ingrained feelings of female inferiority making her beholden to a piece of scum like Abdelatif, obeying him simply because he was a man? Or had she responded to some characteristic of the murderer himself? Was he an authority figure, one who inspired confidence?

Something to consider.

But then there was Juliet, a professional. Cultural factors couldn't explain her submission.

During his uniformed days in the Katamonim, Daniel had gotten to know plenty of prostitutes, and his instinctual feelings toward them had been sympathetic. They impressed him, to a one, as passive types, poorly educated women who thought ill of themselves and devalued their own humanity. But they disguised it with hard, cynical talk, came on tough, pretended the customers were the prey, they the predators. For someone like that, surrender was a commodity to be bartered. Submission, unthinkable in the absence of payment.

Juliet would have submitted for money, and probably not much money. She was used to being played with by perverts; shooting heroin was no novelty—she would have welcomed it.

An authority figure with some money: not much.

He put his head down on the desk, closed his eyes, and tried to visualize scenarios, transform his thoughts into images.

A trustworthy male. Money and drugs.

Seduction, rather than rape. Sweet talk and persuasion—the charm Ben David had spoken of—gentle negotiation, then the bite of the needle, torpor, and sleep.

Which, despite what the psychologist had said, made this killer as much a coward as Gray Man. Maybe more so, because he was afraid to face his victims and reveal his intentions. Hiding his true nature until the women lost consciousness. Then beginning his attack in a state of rigid self-control: precise, orderly, *surgical.* Getting aroused by the blood, working himself up gradually, cutting deeper, hacking, finally losing himself completely. Daniel remembered the savage destruction of Fatma's genitals—that had to be the orgasmic part, the explosion. After that, the cool-off period, the return of calm. Trophy-taking, washing, shampooing. Working like an undertaker. Detached.

A coward. Definitely a coward.

Putting himself in the killer's shoes made him feel slimy. Psychological speculation, it told him nothing.

Who, if you were Fatma, would you trust to give you an injection?

A doctor.

Where would you go if you were Juliet and needed epilepsy medicine?

A doctor.

The country was full of doctors. "We've got one of the world's highest physician-to-citizen ratios," Shmeltzer had reminded him. "Over ten thousand of them, every goddamned one of them an arrogant son of a bitch."

All those doctors, despite the fact that most physicians were government employees and poorly paid—an experienced Egged bus driver could earn more money.

All those Jewish and Arab mothers pushing their sons.

The doctors they'd spoken to had denied knowing either girl. What could he do, haul in every M.D. for interrogation?

On the basis of what, Sharavi? A hunch?

What was his intuition worth, anyway? He hadn't been himself lately—his instincts were hardly to be trusted.

He'd been waking at dawn, sneaking out the door each morning like a burglar. Feasting on failure all day, then coming home after dark, not wanting to talk about any of it, escaping to the studio with graphs and charts and crime statistics that had nothing to teach him. No daytime calls to Laura. Eating on the run, his grace after meals a hasty insult to God.

He hadn't spoken to his father since being called to view Fatma's body—nineteen days. Had been an absymal host to Gene and Luanne.

The case—the failure and frustration so soon after Gray Man—was changing him. He could feel his own humanity slipping away, hostile impulses simmering within him. Lashing out at Anwar had seemed so natural.

Not since the weeks following his injury—the surgeries on his hand, the empty hours spent in the rehab ward—had he felt this way.

He stopped himself, cursed the self-pity.

How self-indulgent to coddle himself because of a few weeks of job frustration. To waste time when two women had been butchered, God only knew how many more would succumb.

He wasn't the job; the job wasn't him. The rehab shrink, Lipschitz, had told him that, trying to break through the depression, the repetitive nightmares of comrades exploding into pink mist. The urge, weeks later, to hack off the pain-wracked, useless hunk of meat dangling from his left wrist. To punish himself for surviving.

He'd avoided talking to Lipschitz, then spilled it all out one session, expecting sympathy and prepared to reject it. But Lipschitz had only nodded in that irritating way of his. Nodded and smiled.

You're a perfectionist, Captain Sharavi. Now you'll need to learn to live with imperfection. Why are you frowning? What's on your mind?

My hand.

What about it?

It's useless.

According to your therapists, more compliance with the exercise regimen would make it a good deal more useful.

I've exercised plenty and it's still useless.

Which means you're a failure.

Yes, aren't I?

Your hand's only part of you.

It's me.

You're equating your left hand with you as a person.

(Silence.)

Hmm.

Isn't that the way it is in the army? Our bodies are our tools. Without them we're useless.

I'm a doctor, not a general.

You're a major.

Touché, Captain. Yes, I am a major. But a doctor first. If it's confidentiality you're worried about—

That doesn't concern me.

I see. . . . Why do you keep frowning? *What are you feeling at this moment?*

Nothing.

Tell me. Let it out, for your own good. . . . Come on, Captain.

You're not . . .

I'm not what?

You're not helping me.

And why is that?

I need advice, not smiles and nods.

Orders from your superiors?

Now you're mocking me.

Not at all, Captain. Not at all. Normally, my job isn't to give advice, but perhaps in this case I can make an exception.

(The shuffling of papers.)

You're an excellent soldier, an excellent officer for one so young. Your psychological profile reveals high intelligence, idealism, courage, but a strong need for structure—an externally imposed structure. So my guess is that you'll stay in the military, or engage in some military-like occupation.

I've always wanted to be a lawyer.

Hmm.

You don't think I'll make it?

What you do is up to you, Captain. I'm no soothsayer.

The advice, Doctor. I'm waiting for it.

Oh, yes. The advice. Nothing profound, Captain Sharavi, just this: No matter what field you enter, failures are inevitable. The higher you rise, the more severe the failure. Try to remember that you and the assignment are not the same thing. You're a person doing a job, no more, no less.

That's it?

That's it. According to my schedule, this will be our last session. Unless, of course, you have further need to talk to me.

I'm fine, Doctor. Good-bye.

He'd hated that psychologist; years later, found him prophetic.

The job wasn't him. He wasn't the job.

Easy to say, hard to live.

He resolved to retrieve his humanity, be better to his loved ones, and still get the job done.

The job. The simple ones solved themselves. The others you attacked with guesswork masquerading as professionalism.

Doctors. His mind kept returning to them, but there were authority figures besides doctors, others who inspired obedience, submission.

Professors, scientists. Teachers, like Sender Malkovsky—the man looked just like a rabbi. A man of God.

Men of God. Thousands of them. Rabbis and sheikhs, imams, mullahs, monsignors and monks—the city abounded in those who claimed privileged knowledge of sacred truths.

Spires and steeples. Fatma had sought refuge among their shadows.

She'd been a good Muslim girl, knew the kind of sympathy she could expect from a mullah, and had run straight to the Christians, straight to Joseph Roselli. Was it far-fetched to imagine Christian Juliet doing the same?

But Daoud's surveillance had revealed no new facts about the American monk. Roselli took walks at night; he turned back after a few minutes, returned to Saint Saviour's. Strange, but not murderous. And phone calls to Seattle had turned up nothing more ominous than a couple of arrests for civil disobedience—demonstrations against the Vietnam War during Roselli's social-worker days.

Ben David had raised the issue of politics and murder, but if there was some connection there, Daniel couldn't see it.

During the daylight hours Roselli stayed within the confines of the monastery, and Daniel alternated with the Chinaman and a couple of patrol officers in looking out for him. It freed the Arab detective for other assignments, the latest of which had nearly ended in disaster.

Daoud had been circulating in the Gaza marketplace, asking questions about Aljuni, the wife-stabber, when a friend of the suspect had recognized him, pointing a finger and shouting "Police! Traitor!" for all to hear. Despite the unshaven face, the *kaffiyah* and grimy robe, the crook remembered him as "that green-eyed devil" who had busted him the year before on a drug charge. Gaza was rife with assassins; Daniel feared for his man's life. Aljuni had never been a strong possibility anyway, and according to Daoud, he stayed at home, screaming at his wife, never venturing out for night games. Daniel arranged for the army to keep a loose watch on Aljuni, requested notification if he traveled. Daoud said nothing about being pulled off the assignment, but his face told it all. Daniel assured him that he hadn't screwed up, that it happened to everyone; told him to reinterview local villagers regarding both victims, and save his energies for Roselli.

If it bothered Daoud's Christian conscience to be tailing a man of the cloth, his face didn't show it.

Malkovsky, the other paragon of religious virtue, was under the surveillance of Avi Cohen. Cohen was perfect for the assignment: His BMW, fancy clothes, and North Tel Aviv face blended in well at the Wolfson complex; he could wear tennis clothes, carry a racquet, and no one would give it a second thought.

He was turning out to be an okay kid, had done a good job

on Yalom and on Brickner and Gribetz—avoiding discovery by the slimy pair, making detailed tapes and doing the same for Malkovsky.

But despite the details, the tapes made for boring listening. The day after Daniel confronted him, the child raper spent hours traipsing around the neighborhood with four of his kids, tearing handbills off walls, throwing the scraps in paper bags, careful not even to litter.

According to Cohen, he was rough on the kids, yelling at them, ordering them around like a slavemaster, but not mistreating them sexually.

Once the handbills were taken care of, his days became predictable: Early each morning he went to *shaharit minyan* at the Prosnitzer *rebbe*'s yeshiva just outside Mea She'arim, driving a little Subaru that he could barely fit into, staying within the walls of the yeshiva building until lunchtime. A couple of times Avi had seen him walking with the *rebbe,* looking ill at ease as the old man wagged his finger at him and berated him for some lapse of attention or observance. At noon he came home for lunch, emerged with food stains on his shirt, pacing the halls and wringing his hands.

"Nervous, antsy," Avi said into the recorder. "Like he's fighting with his impulses."

A couple more minutes of pacing, then back into the Subaru; the rest of the day spent hunched over a lectern. Returning home after dark, right after the *ma'ariv minyan,* no stop-offs for mischief.

Burying himself in study, or faking it, thought Daniel.

He'd asked the juvenile officers to look into possible child abuse at home. Tried to find out who was protecting Malkovsky and had met with official silence.

Time to call Laufer for the tenth time.

Men of God.

He arrived home at six-thirty, ready for a family dinner, but found that they'd all eaten—felafel and American-style hamburgers picked up at a food stand on King George.

Dayan barked a greeting and the boys jumped on him. He kissed their soft cheeks, promised to be with them in a minute. Instead of persisting, they ran off cuffing each other. Shoshi was doing her homework at the dining room table. She smiled at him, hugged and kissed him, then returned to her assignment, a page of algebra equations—she'd completed half.

"How's it going?" Daniel asked. Math was her worst subject. Usually he had to help her.

"Fine, Abba." She bit her pencil and screwed up her face. Thought a while and put down an answer. The correct one.

"Excellent, Shosh. Where's Eema?"

"Painting." Absently.

"Have fun."

"Uh huh."

The door to the studio was closed. From under it seeped the smell of turpentine. He knocked, entered, saw Laura in a blue smock, working on a new canvas under a bright artist's lamp. A cityscape of Bethlehem in umbers, ochers, and beige, softly lit by a low winter sun, a lavender wash of hillside in the background.

"Beautiful."

"Oh, hi, Daniel." She remained on her stool, leaned over for a kiss. Half a dozen snapshots of Bethlehem were tacked to the easel. Pictures he'd taken during last year's Nature Conservancy hayride.

"You ate already," he said.

"Yes." She picked up the brush, laid in a line of shadow along the steeple of the Antonio Belloni church. "I didn't know if you were coming home."

He looked at his watch. "Six thirty-six. I thought it would be early enough."

She put the brush down, wiped her hands on a rag, and turned to him. "I had no way of knowing, Daniel," she said in a level tone of voice. "I'm sorry. There's an extra hamburger in the fridge. Do you want me to heat it up for you?"

"It's all right. I'll heat it up myself."

"Thanks. I'm right in the middle of this—want to finish a few more buildings before quitting."

"Beautiful," he repeated.

"It's for Gene and Luanne. A going-away present."

"How are they doing?"

"Fine." Dab, blend, wipe. "They're up in Haifa, touring the northern coast. Nahariya, Acre, Rosh Hanikra."

"When are they coming back down?"

"Few days—I'm really not sure."

"Are they having a good time?"

"Seem to be." She got off the stool. For a moment Daniel thought she was going to embrace him. But instead she stepped back from the canvas, measured perspective, returned to her seat, and began blocking in ocher rectangles.

He waited a few seconds, then left to make himself dinner. By the time he'd eaten and cleaned up, the boys had busied themselves again with the *Star Wars* videotape. Eyes filled with wonderment, they declined his offer to wrestle.

35

Stacks of newspaper clippings covered Laufer's desk. The deputy commander began fanning them out like oversized playing cards.

"Garbage-sifting time," he said. "Read."

Daniel picked up a clipping, put it down immediately after realizing it was one he'd already seen. *Ha'aretz* was his paper; he liked the independence, the sober tone—and the reporting on the murders was typical: factual, concise, no thrills for ghouls.

The party-affiliated papers were another story. The government organ gave the crimes short shrift on a back page, an almost casual downplay, as if hiding the story would make it go away.

The opposition paper played a shrill counterpoint, using Daniel's name to segue into the Lippmann case, offering a blow-by-blow rehash of the scandal, making much of the fact that prior to his assassination the late, discredited warden had been a darling of the ruling party. Implying, not so subtly, that any rise in violent crime was the government's fault: Failure to raise police salaries had led to continued corruption and ineptitude; a poorly administered Health Ministry had failed to handle the issue of dangerous mental patients; the psychological frustration caused by the ruling party's economic and social policies engendered "deep-rooted alienation and concomitant hostile impulses in the general populace. Impulses that are at risk for spilling over into bloodshed."

The usual partisan nonsense. Daniel wondered if anyone took it seriously.

Haolam Hazeh and the other tabloids had done their heavy-breathing bit: lurid headlines and hints of perverted sex in high places. Gory-detail crime stories fighting for space with photos of naked women. Daniel put them down on the desk.

"Why the rehash? It's been two weeks since Juliet."

"Go on, go on, you're not through," Laufer said, drumming his fingers on the desk. He picked up a thick batch of clippings and shoved it at Daniel.

These excerpts were all in Arabic: *Al Fajr, Al Sha'ab,* other locals at the top of the pile, foreign stuff on the bottom.

Arabic, thought Daniel, was an expansive, poetic language, lending itself to hyperbole, and this morning the Arab journalists had been in fine hyperbolic form: Fatma and Juliet restored to virginity and transformed to political martyrs victimized by a racist conspiracy—abducted, defiled, and executed by some night-stalking Zionist cabal.

The local publications called for "hardening of resolve" and "continuation of the struggle, so that our sisters have not perished in vain," stopping just short of a call for revenge—saying it outright could have brought down the heavy hand of security censorship.

But the foreign Arab press screamed it out: officially sanctioned editorials from Amman, Damascus, Riyadh, the Gulf states, brimming with hate and lusting for vengeance, accompanied by crude cartoons featuring the usual anti-Jewish archetypes—stars of David dripping blood; hook-nosed, slavering men wearing *kipot* and side curls, pressing long-bladed knives to the throats of veiled, doe-eyed beauties wrapped in the PLO flag. The *kipot* emblazoned with swastikas—the Arabs loved to co-opt the Nazi stuff, spit it back at their cousins. The Syrians went so far as to link the murders to some occult Jewish ritual of human sacrifice—a harvest ceremony that the writer had invented.

Vile stuff, thought Daniel, reminiscent of the *Der Stürmer* exhibit he'd seen at the Holocaust Memorial, the *Black Book* that Ben David had shown him. But not unusual.

"The typical madness," he told Laufer.

"Pure shit. This is what stirred it up."

He gave Daniel an article in English, a cutting from this morning's international *Herald Tribune.*

It was a two-column wire service piece bearing no byline and entitled "Is a New Jack the Ripper Stalking the Streets of Jerusalem?" Subtitle: "Brutal Slayings Stymie Israeli Police. Political Motives Suggested."

The anonymous journalist had given the killer a name—the Butcher—an American practice that Daniel had heard Gene decry ("Gives the bad guy the attention he craves, Danny Boy, and makes him larger than life, which scares the heck out of the civilians. Every day that goes by without a bust makes us look more and more like clods"). The actual information about the killings was sparse but suggestively spooky and followed by a review of the Gray Man case, using copious quotes from "sources who spoke on condition they would not be identified" to suggest that both serial killers were likely to remain at large because Israeli police officers were inept homicide investigators, poorly paid, and occupying "lowly status in a society where intellectual and military accomplishments are valued but domestic service is demeaned." Illustrating that with a rehash of the six-month-old story about new recruits having to apply for welfare, the wives' picket of the Knesset.

The *Herald Tribune* article went on to wallow in armchair sociology, pondering whether the murders were symptomatic of "a deeper malaise within Israeli society, a collective loss of innocence that marks the end of the old idealistic Zionist order." Quotes from political extremists were given equal weight with those from reasoned scholars, the end result a weird stew of statistics, speculation, and the regurgitated accusations of the Arab press. All of it delivered in a morose, contemplative tone that made it sound reasonable.

The final paragraph was saturated with pessimism that seemed almost gleeful: "Tourism has always constituted a vital part of the fragile Israeli economy and in light of current economic difficulties, Israeli officials have put forth especially strong efforts to negate their country's image as a dangerous place to live and visit. But given the recent handiwork of the Gray Man and the Butcher, experts' predictions of increasing violence against both Arabs and Jews, and the subsequent inability of the Israeli police to cope with that violence, those efforts may be doomed to failure."

Daniel put the clipping down and said, "Who wrote this?"

"Wire service *putz* by the name of Wilbur. Replaced Grabowski—the one who ignored cordons up in Bekaa and got his arm blown off. This one came over six months ago, spends most of his time at Fink's, drinking himself numb."

Daniel recalled a press conference he'd attended a few months ago. One of the faces had been new.

"Dark, puffy-looking, gray hair, bloodshot eyes?"

"That's him, a goddamned *shikur*—just what we need." Laufer shoved aside papers and created a clearing in the middle of the desk top. "His last big story was a feature on the fig harvest—glorious Arab workers, bonded to the soil."

"Is he pro-PLO?"

"From what we can tell he has no political leanings one way or the other. Anti-*work* is what he is—gets his stuff secondhand and plays around with it in order to make it sound profound. All that shit about 'unnamed sources.' " The deputy commander sat down and glared at Daniel.

"This time he stirred up the shitpile but good—puffs up a two-week-old story and gets every other hack hot to outdo him. Nothing would give me greater pleasure than feeling his ass under my boot, but we're stuck with him—free press and all that. We're the ultimate democracy, right? Out to prove to the goyim how righteous we are."

Laufer picked up the *Herald Tribune* piece, looked at it, and ripped it in half, then in half again. "Now that he's seen how successful he's been, he'll be exploiting this *Butcher* shit as long as it remains unsolved. And you can bet the others keep falling over one another to outdo him. Bastards." A sickly smile spread across the pouchy face: "The Butcher. Now your killer has a name."

Your killer. Like one parent blaming another for the behavior of a delinquent child.

"I don't see how we can concern ourselves with the press," said Daniel.

"The point is," continued Laufer, "that your team has accomplished nothing tangible. You're giving them all a giant tit to suck."

Daniel said nothing.

Laufer raised his voice: "I've sent you four memos of inquiry in the last six days. None have been answered."

"There was nothing to report."

"I don't give a goddamn what there was to report! When I send a memo, I expect a response."

"I'll be more conscientious," said Daniel, "about responding to your inquiries."

The deputy commander stood, placed his knuckles on the top of the desk, and leaned on them, thick torso swaying, looking like a gorilla.

"Cut the crap," he said. "Get the patronizing tone out of your voice." A thick hand slapped the desk. "Now catch me up—what do you have?"

"As I said, nothing new."

"What route did you take to reach that glorious destination?"

Daniel gave him a review of procedures, the interrogation of the sex offenders, the surveillances and record checks, the matching wound molds that confirmed both women had been cut with the same knives. Knowing any mention of similarities between Fatma and Juliet would be a slap across the deputy commander's flabby face, a reminder that his quick-solve press release was now a departmental joke.

But Laufer seemed almost to revel in the misery, making Daniel repeat himself, go over picayune forensic details that had no bearing upon the cases. When he finally seemed sated, Daniel took a copy of the handbill out of his attaché case and handed it to Laufer.

The deputy commander glanced at the paper, crumpled it, tossed it into the wastebasket.

"What of it?"

"I wasn't notified of his presence."

"That's correct."

"We're investigating two sex murders, and a sex offender moves into the community—"

"He's a child molester, Sharavi, not a murderer."

"Sometimes," said Daniel, "they go hand in hand."

Laufer raised one eyebrow. "Upon what do you base that statement?"

Ignorant pencil-pusher, thought Daniel. And the man had attained his post all because of him. He fought to hold on to his temper.

"Upon American crime data, FBI reports . . . Several serial murderers have been found also to be child molesters. Sometimes they alternate between killing and molesting phases; sometimes the crimes occur in tandem. If you'd like, I can show you the sources."

Laufer chewed his lip, tormenting the rubbery flesh. Cleared his throat and tried to regain face.

"You're telling me that *most* serial murderers are molesters?"

"Some."

"What percentage?"

"The sources didn't say."

"If you quote statistics, be prepared to back them up with numbers."

Daniel was silent. Laufer smiled. Now it was his turn to patronize.

"*Some* murderers, Sharavi, are also thieves. *Some* are reckless drivers. The pedophile thing may be nothing more than a random correlation—nothing to make Malkovsky a suspect."

"What," Daniel asked, "does this guy have going for him in order to earn this kind of *protekzia*?"

"*Protekzia* has nothing to do with it," snapped Laufer. "He's never been convicted of anything."

"He escaped before trial."

"He's a Jew, Sharavi. You saw that beard—as long as Moses'. Entitled to entry under the Law of Return."

"So was Meyer Lansky, but we sent him back to America."

"Malkovsky's no Lansky, believe me. Besides, we've received no extradition request from the Americans."

"Yet," said Daniel. "What happens when we do?"

Laufer ignored him. "In the meantime, he's well supervised. His *rebbe* vouches for him."

"I didn't know," said Daniel, "that we employed *rebbes* as probation officers."

"That's enough! A decision was made, in a specific context. A decision that you needn't concern yourself with."

"The man," said Daniel, "is seriously disturbed. He admitted to me having erotic feelings for his own daughters, denied molesting them, but I think he's lying."

"*You* think? You've harassed him, have you?"

"I've spoken to him."

"When and where?"

"Yesterday, at his apartment."

"What else have you done?"

"He's under surveillance."

"By whom?"

"Cohen."

"The new hire—how's he doing?"

"Fine."

"Told you he was a good kid. Anyway, call him off and reassign him."

"Tat Nitzav—"

"Call him off, Sharavi. Malkovsky is being handled. Stick to your own case and it might even get solved."

Daniel's abdomen was hot as a fry pan, his jaw so tight he had to consciously relax it in order to speak.

"If you don't approve of how I've done my job, feel free to remove me from the case."

Laufer looked at him hard, then applauded.

"Very theatrical, Sharavi. I'm impressed."

He pulled an English Oval out of his shirt pocket. Lit it, smoked, and let the ashes fall on the clippings. A stray ember rolled from the papers onto the desk top and he stubbed it out with a fingertip. Examining the gray-smudged finger, he said, "If and when you're removed, the decision won't be yours. In the meantime, stay out of administrative matters and concentrate upon the job at hand. Tell me, how many staff meetings have you had?"

"Staff meetings?"

"Getting the team together, sharing information."

"I'm in daily contact with each of them."

"How many times have all of you gotten together?"

"Twice."

"Not nearly enough. In cases such as these, communication is paramount. Collating, correlating, the tying up of loose ends. You may have missed something—another Anwar Rashmawi."

Laufer played with the cigarette ashes, allowed his words to sink in.

"Communicate," he said. "Vertically and horizontally. And expand your thinking. Open up new avenues of investigation."

Daniel took a deep breath, let it out silently. "Such as?"

"Such as Arab girls are being cut up like kebab meat. Such as maybe the Arab papers aren't all wrong. Have you thought of talking to Moshe Kagan and his gang?"

"Am I to consider Rabbi Kagan a suspect?"

"*Rabbi* Kagan thinks he's another Kahane. Arabs are subhuman—unclean animals. He goes to their villages and calls them dogs to their faces. He and his *Gvura* hooligans are a giant pain in the ass—bunch of misfits and nut cases. All they want is an excuse to go around breaking heads. Is it illogical to suppose that one of them has convinced himself it's a *mitzva* to slaughter unclean animals?"

"No," said Daniel, "not illogical at all. But we ran a check on them last year, after Kagan was elected. Found no evidence of violence beyond tough talk and a couple of light skirmishes with the communists."

But even as he spoke, he recalled what Ben David had told him: *Racist politics and psychopathy can be comfortable bedfellows. . . . We're not all lambs. There's a reason for the sixth commandment. . . .*

"Times change," Laufer was saying. "Crazies get crazier."

"The other thing to consider is that he's a Member of the Knesset—"

"One lousy seat," said Laufer. "An aberration—next election he'll be out on his ass. Couple of years from now he'll be back battling blacks in Brooklyn."

Brooklyn, thought Daniel. In a couple of years, where would Malkovsky be? He said nothing, but his thoughts were transparent and Laufer read them.

"Obviously, you like talking to rabbis, so talk to this one. Your *kipah* should help forge a bond between the two of you. I also heard that he likes Yemenites, tries to recruit them to prove he's not a racist. Go, drop in on him, send him regards from the whole damned department—two hundred thousand dollars American his last demonstration cost us in extra man-hours, barricades, new windshields. Send him regards and ask him if his hooligans have turned into slaughterers."

Laufer looked down and began shuffling papers. Smoking and rubber-stamping and signing his name. Daniel stood there for several moments, knowing if he left without being formally dismissed, the DC would dump on him.

"Anything else, Tat Nitzav?"

Laufer glanced up, feigning surprise at his presence. "Nothing. Get going. Go about your business."

He went back to his office, radioed Avi Cohen at Wolfson, had him come back to Headquarters and, when he arrived twenty minutes later, told him of Laufer's decision.

"Pencil-pushing prick," exploded the young samal. "Just when I'm getting a feel for the pervert—he's getting more and more nervous, always looking over his shoulder. Scratching his head and his crotch, pacing the courtyard. This morning he drove by a school, stopped for a few moments, and looked through the gate. I know he's up to something, Pakad."

"Which school?"

"The religious public school—Dugma, on Rehov Ben Zvi."

Mikey and Benny's school. Daniel visualized Malkovsky's enormous body silhouetted against the fence, pressing against the chain link.

"His own kids don't go there?"

"No, they're at the Prostnitzer Heder, near Mea She'arim. He'd already dropped them off and was on the way home when he stopped at Dugma."

"Did he do anything besides look?"

Avi shook his head. "Look was all, but I tell you he's getting more and more jumpy—yelling at his wife, showing up later and later at the yeshiva. And he's always alone. I haven't seen him with the *rebbe.* Yesterday he left early, went home, and stayed inside all day—no evening *minyan,* nothing. Maybe he had a cold or something, but I wouldn't count on it. For all we know he could be abusing his own daughters." Avi shook his head in disgust. "He's going to pop. I can feel it. This is the worst time to back off."

His handsome face shone with excitement. The thrill of the hunt, a detective's joy. The kid would work out fine, Daniel decided.

"Dammit," said Avi, "isn't there some way to get around it?"

"No. The order was clear."

"What kind of *protekzia* does he have?"

"I don't know." In Daniel's mind the bearish silhouette had pushed its way through the chain link, metal buckling and splitting open under the massive weight. Tiny bodies in the background, playing and whooping, unaware of the approaching monster. When the bodies took on faces, round and chubby-cheeked, with black curly hair, dusky skin, and Laura's features, he put the image out of his head, found that he'd been clenching his fist so hard it ached.

"Your new assignment," he told Avi, "is to hook up with the Chinaman, do what he tells you." The big detective was circulating around the Old City, combing the *souqs* and stalls and coffeehouses, walking every cobbled step of the dark, arched streets.

Seeking out pimps and lowlifes, anyone who would talk, still looking for someone who'd seen Fatma or Juliet.

"What does he need me for?"

"He'll inform you of that when you get there," said Daniel. A bureaucrat's answer—both he and Cohen knew it.

Avi pouted, then just as quickly shrugged and smiled broadly, flashing even white teeth, blue eyes bouncing with mischief.

"Sounds like an easy job, Pakad."

"Don't count on it. Yossi's got plenty of energy."

"Oh, yeah, I know, a real *gever.* But I'm no girl. I can keep up."

"Good for you," said Daniel, wondering about the sudden change of mood, the return of the rich-kid arrogance. Cohen might have instincts, but he still needed taming. "Have fun."

Instead of leaving, Avi came closer.

"What I'm saying is that it won't keep me too busy."

"Are you complaining about the assignment?"

"No, Dani," grinned Avi, sounding inappropriately familiar. It was the first time he'd addressed Daniel by anything other than *Pakad.* "Terrific assignment, a real plum. What I'm saying, Dani, is that I'll have plenty of energy left over. For extra work." He held out his hands, waited expectantly.

"No," said Daniel. "Forget it. The orders came down from the top."

"Thing is"—Avi's grin was wide—"there's more than just work involved. I met this girl at Wolfson, rich, kind of pretty, parents live in South Africa. She goes to Hebrew U., lives in this terrific apartment all by herself. Great chemistry. Who knows, it could be true love."

"Mazal tov," said Daniel. "Invite me to the wedding."

"True love," repeated Avi. "No crime in visiting my little sweetie, is there? Playing tennis and swimming in the pool? No crime in the pursuit of love, is there?"

"No," smiled Daniel. "That's no crime at all."

Cohen looked at his watch. "In fact, with the Pakad's permission, I've got to run right now. Got a lunch date with her in a few minutes. Blintzes and iced tea, on her balcony." More teeth. "Great view from that balcony."

"I'll bet."

"No crime in lunch, is there?"

"Get out of here," said Daniel. "Call Yossi after you've eaten your blintzes."

Avi rubbed his hands together, saluted, and was off.

As soon as the door closed, Daniel radioed the Chinaman. The connection was bad and they shouted at each other through a rain of static before Daniel told him to get to a phone. A few minutes later, the big man called; there was Arabic music in the background, the rattling of trays, a hum of voices.

"Where are you, Yossi?"

"Thousand Nights Café, just up from the Damascus Gate. Lots of eyes glued to my back. What's up?"

"How's it going?"

"Shitty—no one's talking; everyone looks pissed off. They're believing what they're reading, Dani—all that Zionist conspiracy garbage. I've even heard rumors about a general strike to protest the killings. Man, you should see how they're looking at me right now. It's the owner's phone—I sent him to serve coffee. Anyway, I spoke to the Border Patrol—they're keeping a watch out. You might tell Latam to send out more undercover guys, just for good measure."

"Good idea. I called to tell you Cohen will be contacting you in a couple of hours. He's assigned to you now. Keep him busy."

"What happened with the kid-raper?"

"We're off him, Laufer's orders."

"Why the hell?"

"*Protekzia*. Don't say it. I know. Cohen thinks he's ripe to do something sick—saw him looking at school kids."

"Wonderful," said the Chinaman.

"My kids' school, in fact. I'll be keeping an eye out, maybe dropping in to talk with the teacher, bring them lunch. Haven't been involved enough lately anyway."

"Absolutely. Got to be a good daddy. When my little ox starts school, I'll be involved too. Meanwhile, what do you want me to do with Cohen?"

"He's turning out to be a decent interviewer. Show him the ropes. If you think he's up to it, give him a go at some of your lowlifes." Daniel paused. "Of course, if you need to send him on errands, that's okay too."

There was a longer pause; then the Chinaman laughed. "Long errands? Clear across town?"

"Long errands are fine. He's confident of his energy."

More laughter.

"But if his energy runs out," said the Chinaman, "you wouldn't want me breaking his ass, nice kid like that. Forcing him to work a full shift if his frail little body just can't keep up."

"Never," said Daniel. "The current memo from Manpower says we must respect our officers. Treat them as if they were human beings."

"As if," laughed the Chinaman. "Which means if he sneezes or blows his nose I should be careful not to overwork him, maybe even send him home for beddy-bye. We wouldn't want little Avi to catch a fever."

"God forbid."

"God forbid," laughed the Chinaman. "God forbid."

36

The cat had been a big step forward, *real* science.

He was twelve when it happened, well into sex thoughts, two years into heavy-duty jacking-off, the hair starting to grow out of his face, but no pimples like some of the other kids—he had good skin, clean.

Twelve brought the noise in his head: sometimes just a hum, other times a race-car roar. All that bad machinery—he wondered how it got in there.

When he jacked off it went away, especially when the sex thoughts got all combined with good pictures: blood; his bug experiments; her on Doctor's lap, them screaming at each other, killing each other, but *doing* it.

He imagined doing it to a girl on his lap—squeezing her eggs, hurting her, finishing her off, making everything clean. No girl in particular, lots of them. He invented them from different pieces of different girls—pictures in his head collected from magazines and movies and real girls that he saw on the street. All kinds, but the best ones were dark and short, like Sarah. Big tits and pretty mouths that screamed really good.

Sarah had big tits now.

She was in college, had come visiting last semester break,

but with a boyfriend, some lame-o named Robert who was studying to be a lawyer and liked to hear himself talk. They slept in separate rooms. He knew why, had heard his mother screaming at Doctor that she wasn't going to have any hook-nosed little slut fornicating in *her* house. But sometimes at night or early in the morning, Sarah got up and went to Robert's room.

Now there was something else to listen to.

When Sarah visited, Doctor took her out every night. The fights in the library were postponed. When she left, they continued even worse—but only once in a while. Doctor wasn't home much. Which made them kind of special.

At twelve he'd gotten smarter, even though his grades were still the same. He understood more about life, could figure out some of the things that had mixed him up when he was a kid. Like what his mother and Doctor were doing when she climbed into his lap after they fought, stabbing herself and bouncing around, screaming and calling him a fucking kike bastard.

What.

But not why.

The library fights gave him a giant hard-on. He carried tissues in the pocket of his robe.

They were both lame fucks. He hated them, wished they'd die while they were doing it and leave him the house and all the money. He'd buy lots of good stuff, fire the maids and hire pretty girls with dark hair to be his slaves.

She was always drunk now, every minute of the day. Tripping over her own feet when she got out of bed. The whole room stank of gin and bad breath. And she'd gotten all puffy and fat and dark around the eyes; her hair looked like dry straw. She was really had-out.

Doctor didn't give a shit about anything. He'd stopped pretending. Once in a while they ran into each other in the morning—he'd be waiting near the curb for the school bus and Doctor would drive up in his big soft car, coming home to pick up a change of clothes or something. He'd get out of the car, looking all embarrassed, say hello, stare at a bush or a tree or something, then walk on, not even bothering anymore with his bullshit questions about how school had been, was he making friends.

Hello, son.

Hello.

Lame fuck.

Both of them.

She was a total zero, when she called for him now, he didn't answer, just let her keep calling until she gave up. He was twelve, with hair, didn't have to take any of her shit, her ass-breath and tits hanging out. She was too had-out to come after him, could barely keep her eyes open. He did what he wanted, probably had more freedom than any kid in the world. More than *anyone*.

Except the cat.

Usually it stayed up in the ice palace, eating human food and getting stroked and running its little pink tongue around the inside of the gin glass. Getting drunk and falling asleep on the big satin bed.

Snowball. C'mere, sweetie.

The only thing she bothered to take care of, washing and shampooing and combing out fleas with this little metal comb, then pinching them between her fingers and dropping them into a glass of liquid bleach. Once she asked him to empty the glass. He spilled it on the bathroom floor, let the fleas stay there on the tiles, little black freckles—he would have liked to see them on her face.

After grooming sessions, the cat got special treats: these crackers that came from an expensive store and were made by a cat chef. The fish ones looked like fish, the beef ones like little cows; the chicken ones were the head of a chicken. She broke off little pieces, teased the cat with them while she blow-dried its fur and rubbed oil into it, put little pink ribbons on its stupid head.

A boy cat, but they'd cut its balls off. Now it wore pink ribbons.

A real faggy cat, fat and nasty. It lay on the bed all day, too drunk to walk, peed wherever it wanted to.

But one night it walked.

A special night: They were going at it in the library.

He was listening on the stairs, not sure if they were going to *do* it afterward, not sure if he was going to jack off to reality or to thoughts, but prepared, wearing his bathrobe, with tissues in the pockets.

They were really going at it.

You cocksucking kike.

Shut up, you dumb cunt.

Borrring.

They yelled some more, then he heard something break.

Goddamn you, Christina, that ashtray was from Dunhills!

Fuck you, Charles.

Doctor said something, but mumbled it. He had to lean in closer to hear it.

She yelled back.

Borrring.

More yelling, for a long time. Then it stopped. Maybe? Silence.

Heavy breathing. All right!

First time in a long time. He felt himself get a hard-on, tiptoed down the stairs, wanting to be as close as possible. Stepped on something soft and slippery, heard a sound that made his heart jump so hard it hurt his chest—like someone being strangled, but it wasn't coming from the library. It was right here, right near him!

He stood up. The soft thing was still squirmy under his foot, knocking around on the carpet. Felt a sharp pain in his ankle—something had scratched him!

He backed away from it and looked down, feeling scared enough to pee his pajamas.

The cat hissed at him and bared its claws. Its eyes were shining in the dark. He tried to kick it. It screamed again, jiggled up the stairs making little crying noises.

What the hell was that!

Nothing, Christina, forget it.

That's—it sounded like Snowball—ohmigod!

It was nothing. Where do you think you're *going!*

He's hurt! Snowball, honey!

Oh, no, you don't. You—

Let go of me!

—can't start something and just—

Let go of me, you bastard. I have to find him!

I don't believe this. Once a year you— Ow, dammit!

(A grunt. Padded footsteps.)

Fine, just stay the hell out, you dumb cunt!

The footsteps got louder.

Snowball!

She was coming. He had to escape but his body was frozen. Oh, shit, he was caught. It was over. He was dead!

Snowball! C'mere, sweetie!

Move, feet, get unfrozen. Ohgod, finally they're warm again . . . running . . . can't breathe . . .

Where are you, sweetheart?

She was out of the library, moving drunkenly up the stairs. Calling for the cat, so maybe she wouldn't hear him ten feet ahead of her, running, not breathing, pleasegod don't let her hear . . .

Here, darling, here, puss. Come-a-here! Come-a-here to Mama.

He made it to his room just as she came to the top of the stairs, threw himself in bed, and pulled the covers over himself.

Oh, Snowball-sweet, where are you? Don't hide, sugar-puss. Mama's got a treat *for you!*

She was in her room, coming out of it now, half-calling, half-singing: *Pu-uss!*

He was all wrapped up like the Mummy, grabbing the mattress to keep from shaking.

Puss? Sweetie?

He'd forgotten to close his door! She was coming near his room!

Snowball!

She was standing in the doorway. He could smell her, *Bal à Versailles* and gin. All of a sudden he had to hiccup. Holding it in was making his heart go crazy. He heard it swooshing in his ears, was sure she could hear it too.

Now where's my bad little boy?

Hiding, sorry, never do it again, promise promise.

C'mere, you bad boy.

No anger in her voice. Oh, no! Oh, God!

Bad little lover bo-oy!

Saved. She wasn't talking to him!

Pu-uss!

Swoosh, swoosh, like it was going to slide all the way up into his brain and start shooting blood all over the inside of his skull and he'd choke on it and die.

She kept standing in the doorway, calling in that drunken, shaky, opera-singer voice. . . .

Kissy, kissy, Snowball. If you're hurt, Mama will make it all better!

The roar in his head was louder than ever. He was biting down on his lip to keep the sound from coming out.

Come-a-here! Mama's got a treat for you—your favey-fave, tuna!

The voice was far away, getting farther and farther. The

danger had passed. A moment later she was saying *Snowball! Sweetheart!*, making disgusting, sloppy noises that let him know she'd found the fucking animal, was kissing it.

Close call.

It wouldn't happen again.

He waited eighteen days. By that time everything was planned, everything really good.

Eighteen days because that's how long it took for her to forget to lock her door.

It was in the afternoon, he'd come home from school, eaten a snack, and gone up to his room. The maids were downstairs, blabbing and telling their foreign jokes and faking as if they were working.

He was faking, too, sitting at his desk, pretending to be doing his homework. The door wide open, so he could hear the signal sounds: throwing up, the toilet flushing—a sign that she was getting rid of her afternoon pastries.

She was doing that more and more, the barfing. It didn't help—she was still getting fat and puffy. Afterward, she always drank more gin and fell deep asleep. Nothing could wake her.

He waited, really patient. Enjoying the wait, actually, because it stretched things out, gave him more time to think about what was going to happen. He had it all planned, *knew* he'd be in charge.

When he was certain she was asleep, he tiptoed to the door, looked up and down the hallway, then down over the balcony. The maids were still accounted for—he could hear the vacuum cleaner, them blabbing to each other.

Safe.

He opened the door.

She was lying on the fourposter, all lamed-out, her mouth wide open. A weird whistling sound was coming from it. The cat was curled next to her pillow—both of them fucking lame-os. It opened its eyes when he came in, gave him a dirty look as if it owned the place and he was some robber.

He cleared his throat, as a test. If she woke up he'd ask how she was feeling, if she needed anything. The same test he used before sneaking into the library and locking himself in so that he could play with the knives, read Schwann's big green book and the others, look through the stuff in the closet.

Nothing. She was out.

Another throat-clear.

Out cold.

He reached into his pocket, pulled out the Tuna Treet, and showed it to the cat.

The blue eyes narrowed, then widened.

Interested, you little fucker?

The cat moved forward, then sank back on the satin bed.

Lazy and fat, like her. It got everything it needed, wouldn't surprise him if she jacked it off—no, she couldn't, no balls. It probably couldn't get a hard-on.

He waved the Tuna Treet.

The cat stared at it, then him, then back at the fish-shaped cracker, water-eyes all greedy. It licked its lips and got all tight, like it was ready to spring.

C'mere, sweetie. *TOOONA!*

It didn't. It knew something was up.

He touched the Treet to his lips, smiled at the cat.

Lick lick, look what I've got that you don't.

The cat moved forward again, froze.

He put the Tuna Treet back in his pocket. The cat's ears perked.

Come-a-here, come-a-here. Pu-uss . . .

The cat was still frozen, smelling the cracker but not knowing what to do, dumb dickhead.

He took a step backward, as if he didn't give a flying fuck. The cat watched him.

Out came the Treet again. Another lick, a big smile. Like it was the best thing he'd ever eaten in his life.

The cat took a couple of cautious steps, rocking the bed.

Lick.

Yum yum.

He waved the Tuna Treet, put it between his teeth, and started to leave the room.

The cat jumped off the bed and landed silently on the white carpet, stepping on *her* to do it, using her grossed-out belly as a diving board. She was so out of it she didn't even feel it.

He kept walking toward the door, real casual.

C'mere, sweetie.

A piece of the Treet broke off in his mouth—actually it didn't taste that bad.

Maybe I'll eat it *myself,* you furry little piece of shit.

The cat was following him from a distance as he backed out of the room, smiling and licking the Tuna Treet.

They were out on the landing now. He closed the door to the ice palace.

The cat meowed, making like it was his friend.

Beg, dickhead.

He kept walking backward, nibbling on the Tuna Treet. Not bad, actually. Kind of like fried fish.

The cat followed him.

Here, kitty, stupid, fucking kitty.

Walk, follow, walk, follow.

A look-down to see what the maids were doing.

Still blabbing and vacuuming. The coast was clear.

Into his room, licking, waving.

In came the cat.

Close the door, lock it, grab the furry fucker by the neck and throw it *hard* against the wall.

Thud. It cried out and slid down the wall and landed on his bed, alive but something was broken. It just lay there looking funny.

He unlocked the bottom drawer of his desk, pulled out the hypodermic needle that he'd prepared. Lidocaine from one of the little rubber-topped bottles Doctor kept in the library closet, along with boxes of disposable needles, packages of gloves, bandages, and the empty doctor's bag—a Gladstone bag, it was called—which made this fantastic *thunk* when you opened and closed it. A couple of times he'd taken stuff, put it in the bag, and brought it up to his room.

Big smile: *Hi, I'm Dr. Terrific. What seems to be the problem?*

He'd used lidocaine on bugs and worms and the mouse that he'd found half-dead in the trap in the cellar. Mostly it killed them right away, so he figured it was too strong. But bugs were no fun anyway—so small, just sticking them with the needle fucked them totally up. And the mouse had been all crushed, almost dead when he found it.

A cat, now that was a different story—a step forward, real science.

In school, he was flunking science because it wasn't real science—the teacher was a lame-o, all words, no reality.

The cat tried to crawl off the bed, stopped, just lay there.

This was real. He'd been *real* scientific, taken the time to plan everything. There was a pediatrics book in the library—he read it for hours before finding a drug dosage chart for newborn infants, then used it to dilute the lidocaine, then added even more water, mixing all of it together in a juice glass, hoping he hadn't ruined the lidocaine.

Only one way to find out.

The cat was trying to get off the bed, again. Its eyes were all cloudy and its back legs were dragging.

Fuck you, dickhead, messing things up like that!

He picked it up by the scruff, stuck the needle in its chest, and shot in the lidocaine. Did it a bunch more times, the way it said in the book, trying to get *pinpoint anesthesia.*

The cat made squeaky sounds, struggled for a while, then shuddered and then went all stiff.

He placed it on his desk, belly-up, on top of the layers of newspaper he'd spread all over.

It wasn't moving—shit! No fair!

No, wait . . . Yeah, there it was, the chest going up and down. Fucker was still breathing, weak, you could barely see it, but still breathing!

All *right*!

He opened the bottom drawer again, took out the two knives that he'd chosen from the box in the library: the biggest scalpel and a curved bistoury. He held them in his hands, watching the cat breathe, knowing this was real science, not any bugs or half-dead mouses.

Hi, I'm Dr. Terrific.

What seems to be the problem, Mr. Cat, Mr. Snowball? Mr. Little Dickhead who almost ruined my life?

The cat just lay there.

Big problems for you.

Things got all red in front of his eyes.

The roar in his head got louder.

He took a deep breath. A bunch of them, until things got clear again.

Hello, Mr. Cat.

Time for surgery.

37

Friday. Daoud's nights keeping Roselli under surveillance had been as productive as tilling concrete.

For the past week, the monk had remained within the walls of Saint Saviour's, taking only one brief walk Wednesday night, shortly after midnight. Not even a walk, really. Fifty steps before turning on his heel—abruptly, as if he'd experienced anxiety, a sudden change of heart about venturing out—and heading back quickly for the refuge of the monastery. Daoud had just begun to trail him, walking maybe ten meters behind, disguised as a Franciscan, the hood pulled down. After Roselli changed direction, Daoud kept on going and, as they passed each other, retracted his head into the brown folds of his robe and stared downward, as if lost in contemplation.

When Roselli had gone twenty more steps, nearing the curve at Casa Nova Road, Daoud permitted himself a half-turn and a look back. He watched the monk round the bend and disappear; then Daoud headed swiftly toward the monastery on silent, crepe-soled feet, getting to the curve just in time to see his quarry vanish behind the large doors. He stopped, listened, heard retreating footsteps, and waited in the darkness for an hour before satisfying himself that Roselli was in for the night.

He kept the surveillance going until daybreak, shuffling back and forth on St. Francis Road, down Aqabat el Khanqa to the Via Dolorosa, reading the Arabic Bible that he'd brought for a prop, always keeping one eye on the tower of the monastery. He stuck it out until the city awoke under a golden banner of sunlight, watched early risers emerging from the shadows, and, tucking the Bible under his arm, started walking away in an old man's halting pace, blending in with the burgeoning stream of workers and worshippers, allowing himself to be carried along in the human flow that exited the Old City at the New Gate.

Engine roars and bleats and guttural commands filled his

ears. Fruit and vegetable vendors were unloading their cargo; flocks of sheep were being herded toward the city walls for market. He inhaled the rotten sweetness of wet produce, made his way through dancing spirals of dung-laden dust, and walked the two kilometers to his car, still dressed as a monk.

The night-watch assignment was a little boring, but he enjoyed the solitude, the coolness of dark, empty streets. Took strange pleasure in the coarse, heavy feel of the robe, the large, leather-bound Bible he'd brought from home. As he drove home to Bethlehem, he wondered what it would have been like had he devoted his life to Christ.

Shmeltzer continued the week's routine of double-checking doctors, finding them arrogant, stingy with their time, a real bunch of little princes. Friday morning he had breakfast with his Shin Bet friend at the Sheraton, watched her eat buckwheat pancakes with powdered sugar and maple syrup, and asked the tape recorder in her purse to contact Mossad and check out Juliet Haddad's Beirut brothel. Afternoon was more record-searching and collating, the detailed, patience-straining work that he found enjoyable.

Friday evening he spent, as he had the past five evenings, with Eva Schlesinger, waiting in the corridor at the Hadassah Oncology Ward, then taking her arm as she walked shakily out of the room where her husband lay unconscious, hooked up to monitors and nourished by tubes.

Shmeltzer leaned against a gurney and watched people hurrying up and down the hospital halls, oblivious to his presence. Nurses, technicians. More doctors—he couldn't get away from them. Not that they were worth a damn. He remembered their reactions to Leah's aneurysm, the damned shrugs and false sympathy.

One time he'd peeked into Schlesinger's room, amazed at how far the old man had faded in so short a time. The tubes and needles were all over him, like the tentacles of some kind of sea monster—a giant jellyfish—wrapping themselves around what remained of his body. Meters and machines beeping away as if it meant something. All that technology was supposed to be *life supporting*—that was the story the white-coats told—but to Shmeltzer it seemed to be sucking the life out of the old palmahi.

A couple of times the hospital visits had been followed by tea at a café, an hour or so of winding down from the damned hospital ambience, small talk to hide from the big issue. But tonight Eva told him to take her straight home. During the drive back to French Hill, she was silent, sitting up against the passenger door, as far from him as possible. When they got to her door, she turned the key in the lock, gave him a look full of anger—no, more than that: hatred.

Wrong time, wrong place, he thought, and braced himself for something unpleasant, feeling like an idiot for getting involved in a no-win situation, for getting involved at all. But instead of spitting out her pain, Eva bored her eyes into his, breathed in deeply, took his hand, and pulled him into the apartment. Moments later they were lying next to each other in her bed— Tell it straight, shmuck: *their* bed, hers and the old man's. Schlesinger wouldn't be sleeping in it again but Shmeltzer still felt like an adulterer.

They remained that way for a while, naked and sweating atop the covers, holding hands, staring at the ceiling. Both of them mute, the words knocked out of them, a mismatched pair of *alter kockers,* if he'd ever seen one. He, a scrawny bird; she, all pillows, wonderfully upholstered, her breasts heavy and flattened, thighs as soft and white as hallah dough.

She began crying. Shmeltzer felt the words of comfort lump up in his gullet, congealed by inhibition. He lifted her hand, touched dimpled knuckles to his mouth. Then, suddenly, they were rolling toward each other, slapping against each other like magnets of opposite polarity. Cleaving and clawing, Shmeltzer cradling her, listening to her sobs, wiping wet cheeks, feeling—and this was really crazy—young and strong. As if time were a pie and a large slice had been restored by some compassionate god.

The Chinaman spent another Friday night in and around the Damascus Gate, alternating between joking around with the low-lifes and pressuring them. Receiving promises from all of them, Arabs and Jews, that the moment they saw or heard anything, blah blah blah.

At one in the morning a series of behind-the-hand whispers steered him to a petty sleaze named Gadallah Ibn Hamdeh, and known as Little Hook, a diminutive, crook-backed thief and swindler who sidelined by running girls out on the Jericho Road. The

Chinaman knew him by sight but had never dealt with him personally and wasn't familiar with his haunts. It took an hour to find him, halfway across the Old City, in Omar Ibn el Khatab Square, inside the Jaffa Gate. Talking to a pair of backpackers at the top of the steps that led down to David Street, just past the facade of the Petra Hotel.

The Chinaman stood back for a moment and watched them conferring in the dark, wondering if it was a drug deal. Ibn Hamdeh was bowing and scraping, gesticulating wildly with his arms as if painting a picture in the air, reaching back every so often to touch his hump. The backpackers followed every movement and smiled like trusting idiots. Except for a solitary street sweeper who soon turned down the Armenian Patriarchate Road, the three of them were alone in the square; the Aftimos Market and all the other shops on David Street, dark and shuttered.

Too conspicuous for dope, decided the Chinaman. Had to be some kind of swindle.

The backpackers looked to be around nineteen or twenty, a boy and a girl, tall and heavily built, wearing shorts and tank tops and hiking boots, and carrying nylon knapsacks supported by aluminum frames. Scandinavian, he guessed, from the goyische features and blond, stringy hair. They towered over the little hunchback as he kept jabbering on in a steady stream of broken English. Laying on the shit in a high, choppy voice.

When the boy pulled out money, the Chinaman approached, nodding at the backpackers and asking Little Hook, in Arabic, what the hell he was up to. The hunchback seemed to shrivel. He backed away from the money and the detective. The Chinaman whipped out his arm and grabbed him by the elbow. A look of protective aggression came into the male backpacker's eyes. He had peach fuzz on his chin, a narrow mouth set in a perpetual pucker.

"He's my friend, man."

"He's a crook," said the Chinaman in English, and when the boy continued to look hostile, showed him his police badge. The backpackers stared at it, then at each other.

"Tell them," the Chinaman commanded Little Hook, who was grimacing as if in agony, doing a little dance, calling the Scandinavians "my friends, my friends," playing the part of victim, outrageously overacting.

"Hey, man," said the backpacker. "We were seeking a place for the night. This fellow was helping us."

"This fellow is a crook. Tell them, Hook."

Ibn Hamdeh hesitated. The Chinaman squeezed his arm and the little thief started crowing: "I'm crook. Yes." He laughed, displaying toothless upper gums, lower incisors jacketed with steel. "I'm nice guy, but crook, ha ha."

"What did he tell you?" the Chinaman asked the backpackers. "That his sister has a nice place, warm bed, running water, and free breakfast—you give him a finder's fee and he'd take you there?"

The girl nodded.

"He has no sister. If he did, she'd be a pickpocket. How much did he ask for?"

The Scandinavians looked away in embarrassment.

"Five American dollars," said the girl.

"Together, or each?"

"Each."

The Chinaman shook his head and kicked Ibn Hamdeh in the seat of the pants. "How much money can you spend on a room?" he asked the backpackers.

"Not much," said the boy, looking at the bills in his hands and putting them back in his pocket.

"Try the YMCAs. There's one in East Jerusalem and one in West Jerusalem."

"Which one's cheaper?" asked the girl.

"I think they're the same. The east one's smaller, but closer." He gave them directions, the boy said, "Thanks, man," and they loped off. Stupid babies.

"Now," he said, dragging Ibn Hamdeh up David Street and pushing him against the grate of a souvenir shop. He flipped the little rascal around, frisked him for weapons, and came up with a cheap knife with a fake pearl handle that he pulverized under his heel. Spinning Ibn Hamdeh around so that they were face to face, he looked down on him, down on greasy hair, fishy features, the hump covered by a flowered shirt that reeked of stale sweat.

"Now, Gadallah, do you know who I am?"

"Yes, sir. The . . . police."

"Go on, say what you were going to say." The Chinaman smiled.

Little Hook trembled.

"Slant Eye, right?" said the Chinaman. He took hold of Ibn Hamdeh's belt, lifted him several inches in the air—the shmuck weighed less than his concrete-can barbell. "Everything you've heard about me is true."

"Most certainly, sir."

The Chinaman held him that way for a while, then lowered him and told him what he'd heard on the street, got ready for resistance, the need to exert a little pressure. But rather than harden the hunchback's defenses, the inquiry seemed to cheer him. He opened up immediately. Laying on the sirs and talking fast in that same choppy voice about a man who had scared one of his girls the previous Thursday night, on the Jericho Road just before it hooked east, just above Silwan. An American with crazy eyes who'd seemed to materialize out of nowhere, on foot—the girl had seen no car, figured he'd been hiding somewhere off the road.

Eight days ago, thought the Chinaman. Exactly a week after Juliet's murder.

"Why'd you take so long to report it, asshole?"

Little Hook began an obsequious dance of shuffles and shrugs. "Sir, sir, I didn't realize—"

"Never mind. Tell me what happened exactly?"

"The American asked her for sex, showed her a roll of American dollars. But his eyes scared her and she refused."

"Is she in the habit of being picky?"

"Everyone's scared now, sir. The Butcher walks the streets." Ibn Hamdeh looked grave, putting on what the Chinaman thought was a reproachful look, as if to say: You've not done your job well, policeman. The Chinaman stared him down until the shmuck resumed looking servile.

"How'd she know he was an American?"

"I don't know," said Little Hook. "That's what she told me."

The Chinaman gripped his arm. "Come on. You can do better than that."

"By the prophet! She said he was American." Little Hook winked and smiled. "Maybe he carried an American flag—"

"Shut your mouth. What kind of sex did he ask for?"

"Just sex, is all she told me."

"Is she in the habit of doing kinky stuff?"

"No, no, she's a good girl."

"A real virgin. What did he do then? After she refused?"

"Nothing, sir."

"He didn't try to force her?"

"No."

"Didn't try to persuade her?"

"He just walked away, smiling."

"Which way did he walk?"

"She didn't say."

"She didn't look?"

"She may have—she didn't tell me."

"You're sure of that?"

"Yes, sir. If I knew, I would certainly tell you."

"What was wrong with his eyes?"

Little Hook painted in the air, again, caressed his hump. "She said they were flat eyes, very flat. Mad. And a strange smile, very wide, a grin. But the grin of a killer."

"What made it a killer's grin?"

The hunchback's head pushed forward and bobbed, like that of a turkey pecking at corn. "Not a happy grin, very crazy."

"She told you that."

"Yes."

"But she didn't tell you which way he walked?"

"No, sir, I—"

"That's enough whining." The Chinaman pressed him for more: physical description, nationality, clothing, asking again what had been crazy about the eyes, wrong with the grin. He got nothing, which was no surprise. The pimp hadn't seen the man, had heard everything secondhand from his girl.

"If I could tell you more, I certainly would, sir."

"You're a fine upstanding citizen."

"Very surely, sir. I want dearly to cooperate. I sent out the word so you would find me. Truly."

The Chinaman looked down at him, thought: The little bastard looks pretty crazy himself, waving his arms, rubbing that hump like he's masturbating.

"I'm going to talk to the girl myself, Gadallah. Where is she?"

Ibn Hamdeh shrugged expansively. "Ran away, sir. Maybe to Amman."

"What's her name?"

"Red Amira."

"Full name."

"Amira Nasser, of the red lips and the red hair."

Not physically similar to the first two victims. The Chinaman felt his enthusiasm waning. "When did you see her last?"

"The night she saw Flat Eyes. She packed her bag and was gone."

"Wednesday night."

"Yes, sir."

"And you just let her go?"

"I am a friend, not a slavemaster."

"A real pal."

"Yes, sir."

"Where does her family live?"

"I don't know, sir."

"You said Amman. Why there?"

"Amman is a beautiful city."

The Chinaman frowned skeptically, raised a fist. Ibn Hamdeh flashed stainless steel.

"Allah's truth, sir! She worked for me for two months, was productive, quiet. That's all I know."

Two months—a short shift. It jibed with what he'd been told about Ibn Hamdeh. The hunchback was small-time all the way, not even close to a professional flesh peddler. He promised novice whores protection and lodgings in return for a percentage of their earnings but couldn't hold on to them for very long. When they found out how little he delivered, they abandoned him for sturdier roosters. The Chinaman pressed him a while longer, showed him pictures of both victims and got negative replies, wrote down a general physical description of Amira Nasser, and wondered if he'd see her soon, cut open and shampooed and wrapped in white sheeting.

"May I go now, sir?"

"No. What's your address?" Ibn Hamdeh told him the number of a hole in an alley off Aqabat el Mawlawiyeh, and the Chinaman wrote it down and radioed Headquarters for verification, requesting simultaneous record checks on both the hunchback and Amira. Ibn Hamdeh waited nervously for the data to come in, tapping his feet and caressing his deformity. When the radio spat back an answer, the address was correct. Ibn Hamdeh had been busted a year ago for pickpocketing, let off with probation, nothing violent in his file. Nothing at all on any Amira Nasser.

The Chinaman gave Ibn Hamdeh a business card, told him to call him if he heard anything more about the flat-eyed man, pointed him toward the Jaffa Gate, and ordered him to get lost.

"Thank you, sir. We must rid the city of the abomination. Life is not good, this way." The hunchback stopped before the gate, made a sharp turn on Christian Quarter Street, and disappeared into the darkness.

Flat eyes, thought the Chinaman, continuing east on David Street, then hooking north and taking the Souq Khan e-Zeit toward the Damascus Gate. A crazy grin. A redheaded whore. Probably another dead end.

The *souq* had been watered before closing, the cobblestones still wet and glowing in the bands of moonlight that seeped between the arches. The market street was deserted, save for Border Patrolmen and soldiers, giving way to noise and lights as he approached the Damascus Gate. He walked past the coffeehouses, ignoring the revelry and fanning away cigarette smoke, exited gratefully into the cool night air.

The sky was a starlit dome, as black as mourning cloth. He flexed his muscles, cracked his knuckles, and began circulating among the tents of the Slave Market, buying a soda at one and standing at the back drinking it, watching a European-looking girl do a clumsy belly dance. Flat eyes, a crazy grin. The hunchback was probably a habitual liar, so maybe it was just another con—false cooperation aimed at weaseling out of a larceny bust. Or maybe not. Maybe he *had* put out the word because he wanted to talk.

Still, the time frame made sense: a week between murders, the killing on Thursday night, the dumping Friday morning. If Red Amira had been tagged as number three, her escape helped explain why the time lapse since Juliet. Maybe this guy had some sort of schedule that allowed him out only on Thursday and Friday.

On the other hand, the red hair didn't match. Maybe the whole story was bullshit.

He took a big gulp of soda, planned his next moves: Check out this Red Amira—too late for that right now. Examine the spot where the American had propositioned her, see if there was a place for someone to hide, if there was room to conceal a car. Also a daylight job.

If he found anything interesting, he'd call Dani tomorrow

night. He had nothing yet that justified disturbing the guy's Shabbat.

The bellydancer shook her cymbals and ground her abdomen; *pooshtakim* hooted and cheered. *Bland*, appraised the Chinaman, definitely European, a college girl picking up extra shekels. No zest, too skinny to make it work—you could see her ribs when she undulated. He left the tent, saw Charlie Khazak standing outside his pleasure palace, sucking on a cigarette and wearing a snot-green shirt that seemed to glow in the dark. The shithead hadn't forgotten their little heel-on-instep dance. When he saw who was looking at him, he threw away the smoke and backed into the tent, was gone when the Chinaman got there. Forty minutes later, he showed up, only to find the Chinaman stepping out of the shadows, using a shishlik skewer for a toothpick, yawning like some giant yellow cat.

"Shabbat shalom, Charlie."

"Shabbat shalom. I've been asking around for you, trying to help out."

"Gee," said the Chinaman, "I'm really touched."

"I'm serious, Lee. This murder shit is bad for all of us. Bad atmosphere, people staying home."

"How sad." The Chinaman broke the skewer with his teeth, began chewing the wood, swallowing it.

Charlie stared at him. "Want some dinner? On me."

"Nah, already had some. On you." The Chinaman smiled, pulled eight more skewers out of his pocket, and let them drop to the dirt. He stretched and yawned again, cracked giant knuckles. More than a cat, Charlie decided. Fucking slant-eyed tiger, he should be caged.

"So," said the detective, "business stinks. What a pity. Who knows, you might have to turn to honest labor." He'd been hearing the same tales of woe from other pimps and dealers. Since the papers had started pumping the Butcher story, there'd been a fifty percent slowdown on the Green Line, worse in the small pockets of iniquity that peppered the Muslim Quarter—sinholes deep within the core of the Old City surrounded by a maze of narrow, dead-black streets, nameless alleys that went nowhere. You had to want something very badly to go there. The hint of a scare and the places shut down completely. All the whores were kicking about working with strangers, girls on the border staying off the streets, opting, temporarily, for the comforts of hearth and home. The pimps expending more effort to keep them in line, receiving less reward for their efforts.

"Everything stinks," said Charlie, lighting a cigarette. "I should move to America—got a cousin in New York, drives a Rolls-Royce."

"Do it. I'll pay for your ticket."

The big screen TV was turned up loud; from behind the flaps came the sound of squealing tires.

"What's on tonight?"

"French Connection."

"Old," said the Chinaman. "Got to be . . . what? Fifteen, twenty years old?"

"A classic, Lee. They love the car chases."

"Then how come so few of *them* are *watching*? Your man behind the bar told me you had a newer one scheduled. *Friday the Thirteenth,* lots of knives and blood."

"Wrong time, wrong place," said Charlie, looking miserable.

"A temporary attack of good taste?" The Chinaman smiled. "Cheer up. It'll pass. Tell me, Rabbi Khazak, what do you know about a whore named Amira Nasser?"

"She the latest?"

"Just answer."

"Brunette, cute, big tits."

"I thought she was a redhead."

Charlie thought for a moment. "Maybe. Yeah, I've seen her with red hair—but that's a wig. Her natural color is dark."

"Does she usually go dark or red?"

"She takes turns. I've seen her as a blonde too."

"When did you last see her?"

"Maybe three weeks ago."

"Who runs her?"

"Whoever wants to—she's an idiot."

The Chinaman sensed that he meant it literally. "Retarded?"

"Or close to it. It's not obvious—she looks fine, very adorable. But talk to her and you can see there's nothing upstairs."

"Does she make up stories?"

"I don't know her that well, Lee. She connected to the Butcher?"

The Butcher. Fucking press.

"Little Hook says he's been running her."

"Little Hook says all sorts of shit."

"Could he be?"

"Sure. I told you she's an idiot."

"Where does she come from?"

"Hell if I know."

The Chinaman placed a hand on Charlie's shoulder.

"Where's she from, Charlie?"

"Go ahead, beat me, Lee," said Charlie wearily. "Why the hell would I hold back? I want this thing cleared up more than you do."

The Chinaman took hold of Charlie's shirt, rubbed the synthetic fabric between his thumb and forefinger, half expecting it to throw off sparks. When he spoke, his voice was knotted with tension.

"I doubt that, asshole."

"I didn't mean—" Charlie sputtered, but the big man released him and walked away, heading back toward the Damascus Gate in a long, loose, predator's stride.

"What's so interesting down there?" the girl called from bed.

"The view," said Avi. "There's a beautiful moon out tonight." But he didn't invite her to share it.

He wore skintight red briefs and nothing else, stood on the balcony and stretched, knowing he looked great.

"Come on in, Avraham," said the girl, in her best sultry voice. She sat up, let the covers fall to her waist. Put a hand under each healthy breast and said, "The babies are waiting."

Avi ignored her, took another look across the courtyard at the ground-floor apartment. Malkovsky had gone in three hours ago. It was doubtful he'd be out again. But something kept drawing him back to the balcony, making him think magically, the way he had as a child: An explosion would occur the moment he withdrew his attention.

"*Av*-ra-ham!"

Spoiled kid. Why was she rushing? He'd already satisfied her twice.

The door to the apartment remained closed. The Malkovskys had finished their meal by eight, singing Shabbat songs in an off-key chorus. Fat Sender had come waddling out once at eight-thirty, loosening his belt. For a moment Avi thought he was going to see something, but the big pig had simply eaten too much, needed air, a few extra centimeters around the waist. Now it was eleven—he was probably in bed, maybe mauling his wife, maybe worse. But in for the night.

Still, it was nice out on the balcony.

"Avi, if you don't come here real soon, I'm going to sleep!"

He waited a few moments, just to make sure she knew she couldn't push him around. Gave one last look at the apartment and walked inside.

"Okay, honey," he said, standing at the side of the bed. He put his hands on his hips and showed off his body. "Ready."

She pouted, folded her arms across her chest, the breast tops swelling with sweet promise. "Well, I don't know if *I* am."

Avi peeled off his briefs, showed himself to her, and touched her under the covers. "I think you are, my darling."

"Oh, yes, Avi."

38

Friday, at ten-thirty in the morning, Daniel called Beit Gvura. Though the settlement was near—midway between Jerusalem and Hebron—phone connections were poor. A chronic thing—Kagan had protested it on the Knesset floor, claimed it was all part of a government conspiracy. Daniel had to dial nine times before getting through.

One of Moshe Kagan's minions answered, announcing "Gvura. Weakness is death" in American-accented Hebrew.

Daniel introduced himself and the man said, "What do you want?"

"I need to talk with Rabbi Kagan."

"He's not here."

"Where is he?"

"Out. I'm Bob Arnon—I'm his deputy. What do you want?"

"To talk with Rabbi Kagan. Where is he, Adon Arnon?"

"In Hadera. Visiting the Mendelsohns—maybe you heard of them."

The sarcasm was heavy. Shlomo Mendelsohn, cut down at

nineteen. By all accounts a kind, sensitive boy who'd combined army service with three years of study at the Hebron yeshiva. One afternoon—a Friday, Daniel remembered; yeshiva boys got off early on Erev Shabbat—he'd been selecting tomatoes from an outdoor stall at the Hebron *souq* when an Arab emerged from the throng of shoppers, shouted a slogan, and stabbed him three times in the back. The boy had fallen into the bin of vegetables, washing them crimson as he bled to death, unaided by scores of Arab onlookers.

The army and the police had moved in quickly, dozens of suspects rounded up for questioning and released, the murderer still at large. A splinter group in Beirut claimed credit for the kill, but Headquarters suspected a gang of punks operating out of the Surif area. The best information was that they'd escaped across the border to Jordan.

Moshe Kagan had been campaigning for Knesset at the time; the case was custom-made for him. He jumped in, comforted the family and got close to them. Shlomo's father made public statements calling Kagan Israel's true redeemer. After the thirty days of mourning were up, Kagan led a parade of enraged supporters through the Arab section of Hebron, arm in arm with Mr. Mendelsohn. Displaying the dead boy's angelic face on slogan-laden placards, trumpeting the need for an iron-fist policy when it came to "mad dogs and Arabs." Windows were broken, knuckles bloodied; the army was called in to keep the peace. The papers ran pictures of Jewish soldiers busting Jewish protesters and when the election was over, Kagan had garnered enough votes to earn a single Knesset seat. His detractors said Shlomo had been his meal ticket.

"When do you expect him back?" asked Daniel.

"Don't know."

"Before Shabbat?"

"What do you think? He's *shomer shabbat,*" said Arnon with contempt.

"Connect me to his house. I'll talk to his wife."

"Don't know."

"Don't know what?"

"If I should let you bother her. She's cooking, preparing."

"Mr. Arnon, I'm going to speak with her one way or another, even if it means coming out there in person. And I'm *shomer shabbat* myself—the trip will disrupt *my* Shabbat preparation."

Silence on the line. Arnon snorted, then said, "Hold on. I'll connect you. If *your* government hasn't screwed up the lines completely."

Daniel waited several minutes, began to wonder if he'd been cut off, before Kagan's wife came on. He'd seen her at rallies—a tall, handsome woman, taller than her husband, with wide black eyes and pale skin free of makeup—but had never spoken to her and was surprised at the quality of her voice, which was soft and girlish, untainted by hostility.

"I'm sorry, Inspector," she told him, "my husband's out of town and I don't expect him back until shortly before Shabbat."

"I'd like to speak with him as soon after Shabbat as possible."

"We're having a *melaveh malkah* Saturday night, honoring a new bride and groom. Would Sunday morning be all right?"

"Sunday would be fine. Let's say nine o'clock. In your home."

"Thank you, Inspector. I'll write it down."

"Thank you, Rebbetzin Kagan. Shabbat shalom."

"Shabbat shalom."

He hung up thinking *What a gracious woman,* filed his papers, and looked at his watch. Ten-thirty A.M. He'd been at the office since five forty-five, reading and reviewing, recycling useless data—succumbing to Laufer's suggestion that he'd missed something. Waiting for the discovery of another body.

But there had been no call, just a troubling inertia.

Two full weeks—two Friday mornings—since Juliet, and nothing. No rhythm, not even the certainty of bloodshed.

He was disappointed, he realized. Another murder might have yielded clues, some bit of carelessness that would finally establish a firm lead to the killer.

Praying for murder, Sharavi?

Disgusted with himself, he checked out and left for the day, determined to forget the job until the end of Shabbat. To get his soul back in alignment, be able to pray with a clear head.

He visited his father at the shop, stayed longer than usual, eating pita and drinking orange juice, admiring several new pieces of jewelry. When he invited his father to come for Saturday lunch, he received the usual answer.

"I'd love to, son, but I'm already obligated."

A shrug and a grimace—his father was still embarrassed after all this time. Daniel smiled inwardly, thinking of plump, cheerful Mrs. Moscowitz pursuing Yehesqel Sharavi, with soup and cholent and golden roast chicken. They'd been carrying on this way for over a year, his father complaining but making no attempt to escape. The man had been a widower for so long, perhaps he felt powerless in the presence of a strong woman. Or maybe, thought Daniel, *he* was underestimating this relationship.

A stepchild at thirty-seven. Now that would be something.

"After lunch, then, Abba. We have guests from America, interesting people. Laura and the children would love to see you."

"And I, them. What do you think of the pin I gave Shoshana?"

"I'm sorry, Abba. I haven't seen it."

His father showed no surprise.

"A butterfly," he said. "Silver, with malachite eyes. I conceived it in a dream I had two nights ago—springtime in the Galilee, flocks of silver butterflies covering the sky, alighting on a stand of cypress. Such a powerful image, I began work yesterday at sunrise and finished by the afternoon, just before Laura came by with the children."

"They were here yesterday?"

"Yes, after school. Laura said they were shopping at Hamashbir and decided to drop in. It must have been destiny"—the old man smiled—"because I'd just gone out to shop myself and had a brand-new chocolate bar in my pocket, Swiss, with raspberry jelly in the middle. Michael and Benjamin pounced on it like little lions. I offered some to Shoshana, too, but she said candy was for babies, she was too old for it. So I gave her the butterfly. The green of the malachite went perfectly with those wonderful eyes. Such a beautiful little girl."

"I got home after she was asleep," said Daniel, thinking *How cut off have I been?* "I'm sure she'll show it to me tonight."

His father sensed his shame, came over, stroked his cheek, and kissed it. The tickle of whisker evoked a flood of memories in Daniel, made him feel like a small boy—weak, but safe.

"I've been consumed with work," he said.

His father's hand rested on his shoulder, butterfly-light. Yehesqel Sharavi said nothing.

"I feel," said Daniel, "as if I'm being drawn into something . . . unclean. Something beyond my control."

"You're the best there is, Daniel. No man could do more."

"I don't know, Abba. I really don't know."

They sat together in silence.

"All one can do is work and pray," said his father, finally. "The rest is up to God."

Spoken by anyone else, it would have sounded pat—a cliché

employed to kill discussion. But Daniel understood his father, knew he really meant it. He envied the old man's faith and wondered if he'd ever reach that level, where reliance upon the Almighty could dissolve all doubt. Could he hope to attain the kind of religious serenity that obliterated nightmares, steadied a heart beating out of control?

Never, he decided. Serenity was out of reach. He'd seen too much.

He nodded in agreement, said "Amen, God be blessed," playing the dutiful son, the unquestioning believer. His father must have known it was an act; he looked at Daniel quizzically and stood, began circulating among the jewelry, tidying, fussing with velvet, and adjusting displays. Daniel thought he looked sad.

"You've been helpful, Abba. As always."

His father shook his head. "I bend wire, Daniel. I don't know about much anything else."

"That's not true, Abba—"

"Son," said his father, firmly. He swiveled and stared, and Daniel felt the little boy take over again. "Go home. Shabbat is approaching. Time to rest and renew. Everyone rests, even God."

"Yes, Abba," said Daniel, but he thought: Does Evil have respect for God's calendar? Does Evil ever rest?

He got home at eleven-thirty, saw the look on Laura's face, and knew they'd either work things out or have a terrible fight. He stayed with her in the kitchen, plying her with smiles and unswerving attention, ignoring the lack of response, the seemingly frantic preoccupation with simmering pots and meat thermometers. Finally she softened, allowed him to rub her neck, and laughed when he got underfoot, the two of them knocking shins in the small, hot room.

She wiped her hands with a towel, poured iced coffee for both of them, and gave him a heartfelt kiss with cold lips and tongue. But when he tried for a repeat, she backed away and asked him to sit down.

"Listen," she said, settling opposite him, "I understand what you're trying to do. I appreciate it. But we have to talk."

"I thought we were."

"You know what I mean, Daniel."

"I've been overinvolved. It won't happen again."

"It's more than that. For the last few weeks you've been in

another world, I feel as if you've locked me—all of us—out of your life."

"I'm sorry."

Laura shook her head. "I'm not trying to wring an apology out of you. What we need to do is *talk*. Sit right here and tell each other what's on our minds. What we're feeling." She placed her hand on his, white linen over mahogany. "I can only imagine what you've been going through. I want to *know*."

"It's very ugly, nothing you'd want to hear."

"But I do! That's the point! How can we be intimate if we skate on the surface?"

"Share with me what *you've* been doing," said Daniel. "How's the Bethlehem painting going?"

"Dammit, Daniel!" She pulled her hand away. "Why are you being so withholding!"

"Sharing is mutual," he said quietly. "You have things of beauty to share—your art, the home, the children. I have nothing to offer in return."

"Your work—"

"My work is cruelty and blood."

"I fell in love with a policeman. I *married* a policeman. Did it ever occur to you that I think what you do is beautiful? You're a guardian, a protector of the Jewish state, of all the artists and the mothers and the children. There's nothing ugly about that."

"Some protector." He looked away from her and took a sip of coffee.

"Come on, Daniel. Stop punishing yourself for the horrors of the world."

He wanted to satisfy her, thought of how to begin, the right way to phrase things. But the words spun around in his head like clothes in a dryer, random sounds, nothing seemed to make sense.

He must have sat that way for a long time, because Laura was patient by nature, and finally she got up, looking defeated. The same look he'd just seen on his father's face.

You're a real harbinger of cheer, Pakad Sharavi.

"If you can't deal with it right now, fine. I can accept that, Daniel. But eventually you're going to have to."

"I can," said Daniel, taking hold of her wrist. "I want to."

"Then do it. There's no other way."

He took a deep breath and forced himself to begin.

* * *

At twelve-fifteen, feeling freer than he had in a long time, he drove to Lieberman's and picked up the groceries, dancing a verbal ballet with the garrulous shopkeeper in order to avoid discussing the case. His next stop was a florist on Rehov Gershon Agron, where he bought a bouquet of daisies and had them arranged against a bed of leather fern along with a card on which he wrote *I Love You.*

Battling the traffic, he managed to get to the Dugma school by twelve twenty-eight, just in time to pick up the boys. He idled the car by the curb, searched for Sender Malkovsky's bulk among the group of parents waiting for their children.

The child molester was nowhere to be seen, which was hardly surprising—no way would he be that obvious. Looking for him had been an irrational bit of desperation, but compulsive, like checking under the bed for ghosts.

Two minutes passed slowly and Daniel filled them with speculation, wondering what Malkovsky was up to. If Avi was on him, right now, or back in the Old City, pounding the pavement with the Chinaman. Then he realized he was back on work-thoughts and forced them out of his mind. Replaced them with butterflies.

Mikey and Benny came out of the gate, saw him, and whooped. They tumbled into the car like dervishes, keeping up a steady stream of insults and kid jokes as he headed for Shoshi's school. When he got there, she was just leaving, walking with a group of other girls, all of them swinging the oversized plastic purses that had come into fashion, skipping and laughing, chirping like birds.

She was definitely the prettiest, he decided. None of the others came close.

She passed right by him, engrossed in conversation. He honked and she looked up—disappointed. Usually she walked home; he'd picked her up as a nice surprise, but could see that she was embarrassed at being treated like a little kid. She said something to the other girls and ran to the car. The butterfly brooch was pinned to her blouse.

"Hello, Abba. What's the occasion?"

"Does there have to be an occasion?"

"You always say walking is good for me."

"I got home early, thought we'd all do something together."

"What are we doing?" asked Mikey.

"The zoo," said Benny. "Let's go to the zoo."

"Are we going to the zoo, Abba?" asked Mikey. "Okay, okay!"

Shoshi glared at them. "Will you both please shut up? The zoo is dumb, and besides, it closes early on Erev Shabbat."

"The zoo is smart," said Mikey. "*You're* dumb."

"Quiet, all of you," said Daniel. "Eema will need us to help out in about an hour. In the meantime, we could go down to the park, throw the ball around or something."

Shoshi's friends began walking. She noticed the movement, turned and shouted, "One second!" but they kept on going. Facing Daniel, she said, "Abba, I'm in the middle of something. Can I go?"

"Sure. Have fun."

"You're not mad?"

"Not one bit. Be home by two."

"Thanks." She blew him a kiss and ran to catch up, the purse knocking against one narrow hip.

"Now can we go to the zoo?" asked Benny as Daniel put the car into gear.

"What do I need a zoo for? I've got wild animals right here."

"Rahhr," said Mikey, screwing up his little face and attempting to snarl. "Rahhr."

"Rahhr, me too," said Benny. He curled his hands into claws and raked the air.

Daniel looked at them in the rearview mirror. Little lions, his father had called them. More like kittens.

"Rahhrr!"

"Very fierce, boys. Let's hear it again."

39

Shabbat felt like Shabbat. A rosy, springtime glow seemed to settle around Daniel from the moment he woke up on Saturday.

He was in synagogue for the beginning of the *shaharit* services, stayed after services, wrapped in his *tallit,* listening to a visiting rabbi expound on the weekly Torah portion. He came home at noon, meeting Gene and Luanne as they got off the elevator. They'd brought flowers, a dozen red roses from the shop at the Laromme Hotel. Laura put them in water, next to the daisies. Daniel made Kiddush over a bottle of Hagefen Riesling and everyone helped bring out the food.

They ate themselves drowsy for an hour, cleared the dishes, then returned to the table for dessert and conversation, coffee and arak. Shoshi pulled Gene away for raisin poker, winning four games out of seven before the black man dozed off on the couch.

"Oh, Gene," said Luanne, and continued talking about their tour of the Negev.

At two-thirty Daniel's father came over, wearing his heavy black Sabbath suit, a snowy-white shirt, and a large black *kipah* embroidered with gold. The children jumped on him shouting "Saba! Saba!," covered his beard with kisses, and the old man pressed pieces of hard candy into their palms. The boys ran off, unwrapping their treasures. Shoshi pocketed hers.

"Abba Yehesqel," said Laura, hugging her father-in-law.

"Leora, beautiful as always!" he said, using her Hebrew name.

Daniel introduced his father to Luanne, cleared a place for him at the head of the table, and brought him the bottle and a glass. When he sat down, Shoshi climbed onto his lap.

"Nice to meet you, Mr. Sharavi," said Luanne. "That butterfly is lovely."

"Saba made Eema's earrings too," said Shoshi, pointing. Laura pushed her hair aside and revealed a lacy silver pendant shaped like a spice box. From the bottom of the earring hung tiny gold flags.

"Lovely."

"My Saba is the best."

Yehesqel smiled, shrugged, and drank arak. Laura left and came back with a box full of jewelry, spread the pieces out on the tablecloth.

"These are all my father-in-law's creations."

"Such delicacy," said Luanne, examining the pieces. She picked up a filigree bracelet set with turquoise and held it up to the light.

"I learned to bend wire as a child," said the old man in heavily accented English. "What a man learns as a child, he remembers."

"My father is being modest," said Daniel. "He's a master of his art."

"Bezalel was an artist," said his father. "He carved the Temple vessels with God's hand guiding his. I am a craftsman. I learn by making mistakes." He turned to Luanne. "We Jews became craftsmen because we were forced to. In Yemen we lived under the Muslims, and the Muslims hated the crafts and gave them over to the Jews."

"How strange," said Luanne.

"It was their belief. They called us *usta*—masters—but put us under them, on the bottom. Seventy crafts we did: weaving, leather, pottery, baskets, making swords. A craftsman is a good job for a Jew, because it doesn't stop the learning of the Torah. A man makes a pot—when it cooks in the oven, he opens a book and studies. The Muslim understands that—he loves his Quran."

"I've been told," said Luanne, "that the Jews living in Arab lands were treated with respect."

Yehesqel smiled. When he spoke again, his speech took on a singsong rhythm.

"In the beginning, Muhammid thought the Jews would all become Muslim. So he said nice things about us, made Moses a big prophet in Islam. He even put parts of the Torah into the Quran—the *Israilyat.* It's still there. But when we said no, we want to stay Jews, Muhammid got very angry, told everyone that the Jews were *cofrim* . . . what's the word in English, Daniel?"

"Infidels."

"*Infidels.* The Christians, too, were infidels. Sometimes infidels were killed; sometimes they were kicked outside. In Yemen we were kept and protected—like children. We lived in small villages in the mountains. Even San'a, the capital, was just a big village. We lived very poorly. Many of the Arabs were poor also, but we were the poorest because we couldn't own land, couldn't be merchants. They kept us as craftsmen, because they wanted the Jewish crafts. Each village had a *tekes* . . ."

"Ceremony," said Daniel.

"The strongest imam in the village would kill a goat and make a Muslim prayer, tell Allah the Jews belonged to him. We paid a big tax to the imam—the *geziyah*—did the craft he needed. If our imam lost a war to another, we belonged to the winner."

Yehesqel mouthed a blessing, chewed on a piece of honey cake, and washed it down with arak.

"Not respect, Mrs. Brooker, but better than dying. We lived that way for hundreds of years, under the Sunni. Then the Zaydi Shiia conquered the Sunni and wanted to make a very strong Islam. All the Jewish boy babies were taken away and given to Muslim families. A very bad time, like the slavery of Egypt. We tried to hide our sons—those who got caught were killed. In 1646 the Judge Muhammid al Sahuli made the *gezerah ha Meqamsim*—the scraping rule. The honor of scraping all the *batei shimush*—the toilets—in Yemen was given to the Jews. In 1679, al-Mahdi, the imam of Yemen, kicked us out of San'a. We had to walk across the desert to a place called Mauza, a very sick place, a *bitza* . . ."

"Swamp."

"A *swamp* full of sickness. Many of us died on the way, many more when we reached Mauza."

"You say *us* and *we*," said Luanne. "As if you were there. It's a part of you."

Yehesqel smiled. "I *was* there, Mrs. Brooker. The rabbis tell us that every soul was created at one time. The soul lives forever—there is no yesterday or today. That means my soul was in Egypt, at Mount Sinai, in San'a, at Auschwitz. Now it has come to rest in *Eretz Yisrael*, free to live as a Jew. If God is kind, it will stay free until Messiah." He broke off another piece of cake and began raising it to his lips.

"Saba," said Shoshi, "tell about Mori Yikhya."

The cake stopped mid-air. "Ah, Mori Yikhya."

"Let Saba eat," said Laura.

"It's okay," said the old man. He put the cake down, chucked Shoshi under the chin. "Who was Mori Yikhya, *motek*?"

"A great *khakham* of San'a."

"And?"

"A great *tzadik*."

"Excellent."

"*Khakham* means wise man," explained Daniel. "*Tzadik* means righteous man."

"What was Mori Yikhya's full name, Shoshana?"

"Mori Yikhya Al Abyad. Please, Saba, tell about the disappearing Torahs and the magic spring. Please."

Yehesqel nodded, resuming the singsong. "Mori Yikhya Al Abyad, the great *tzadik*, was one of those who died during the march to Mauza. He lived in San'a and worked as a *sofer*—he wrote *mezuzot* and *tefillin* and *sifrei Torah*. The *Halakhah*—the Jewish law—tells us that when a *sofer* writes a Torah, he must have a clean mind, no sin inside. This is most important when the *sofer* writes God's name. Many *sofrim* go to the *mikvah*—the special bath—before they write God's name. Mori Yikhya did it another way. What was that way, Shoshana?"

"He jumped into an oven!"

"Yes! Before he wrote God's name, he threw himself into a big oven fire and was cleaned. His *tzidkut*—his righteous—protected him, and his Torahs became special. How were they special, Shoshana?"

"If a bad man reads them, the words disappear."

"Excellent. If a man with sin in his heart reads one of them, Mori Yikhya's Torah turns yellow and the letters fade."

"There are scrolls, here in Jerusalem," Daniel told Luanne, "that people attribute to Mori Yikhya. No one dares to use them." He smiled. "They wouldn't last long."

"The magic spring, Saba," said Shoshi. She wrapped the coils of her grandfather's beard around her slender fingers. "Ple-ease."

Yehesqel tickled her chin, took another swallow of arak, and said, "When Mori Yikhya died, it was a terrible thing. He lay down in the sand and stopped breathing in the middle of the desert, a place without water—we were all dying. The *Halakhah* says that a body must be washed before it is buried. But there was no water. The Jews were sad—we didn't know what to do. We prayed and said *tehillim* but knew we couldn't wait a long time—the *Halakhah* also says a body must be buried quickly. All of a sudden something happened, something special."

He held out his hand to Shoshi.

"The magic spring came up!"

"Yes. A spring of water came up from the middle of the sand, a great miracle in honor of Mori Yikhya Al Abyad. We washed him, gave him honor, and buried him. Then we filled our water bottles and drank. Many lives were saved because of Mori Yikhya. As his soul entered heaven, the spring dried up."

"A wonderful story," said Luanne.

"The Yemenites are fabulous storytellers," said Laura. She added, laughing, "It's why I married Daniel."

"What stories did Abba tell you, Eema?" asked Shoshi.

"That I was a millionaire," said Daniel. "My name was

Rockefeller, I owned a hundred white horses, and could turn cabbage to gold."

"Oh, Abba!"

"There are books of beautiful poems called *diwans,*" said Laura. "They're meant to be sung—my father-in-law knows them all by heart. Would you sing for us, Abba Yehesqel?"

The old man tapped his Adam's apple. "Dry as the desert."

"Here's your magic spring," said Daniel, filling his glass with arak. His father emptied it, had another half glass, and was finally cajoled into performing. He stood, righted his beret, and cleared his throat.

"I will sing," he said, "from the *diwan* of Mori Salim Shabazi, the greatest Yemenite *tzadik* of all. First, I will sing his *peullot.*"

Accompanying himself with hand and body movements, he began to chant, first softly, then louder, in a clear, reedy tenor, reciting in Hebrew as Daniel whispered translation in Luanne's ear. Using original melodies more than four hundred years old to sing the *peullot*—the miraculous deeds—of the Great Teacher Shabazi, who put an end to the exile to Mauza by bringing down an affliction upon the imam of San'a. Mori Shabazi, whose grave at Ta'izz became a sacred shrine, even to the Muslims. Who was so humble and God-fearing that each time worshippers tried to grace the grave with flowers, the whitewash flaked off the headstone, the monument finally disintegrating into thin air.

Gene opened his eyes and sat up, listening. Even the boys stopped their play and paid attention.

The old man sang for a full half-hour, of the yearning for Zion, the Jew's eternal quest for spiritual and physical redemption. Then he took a break, wet his gullet with more arak, and looked at Daniel.

"Come, son. We will sing of our ancestor Mori Shalom Sharavi, the weaver. You know that *diwan* well."

The detective got up and took his father's hand.

At four the old man left for his afternoon Torah class and Laura pulled a book out of the case.

"This is a recent translation of Yemenite women's songs, put out by the Women's Center in Tel Aviv. My father-in-law would never sing them—he's probably never even seen them. In Yemen the sexes were segregated. The women never learned to read or write, were taught no Hebrew or Aramaic—the educated languages. They got back at the men by making up songs in Arabic—closet feminism, really—about love, sex, and how foolish men are, ruled by lust and aggression."

"Amen," said Luanne.

"This is getting dangerous," Gene said to Daniel. He rose from the couch, hitched up his trousers.

"My favorite one," said Laura, flipping pages, "is 'The Manly Maiden.' It's about a girl who dresses up as a man and becomes a powerful sultan. There's this great scene where she gives a sleeping powder to forty-one robbers, takes off their clothes, and inserts a radish in each one of their—"

"That," said Gene, "is my exit line."

"Mine too," said Daniel.

They left the women laughing, took the children and Dayan down to Liberty Bell Park.

As Daniel came out of the apartment, his eyes were assaulted by the sunlight. He could feel his pupils expanding, the heat massaging his face. As he walked, he noticed that everything looked and felt unnaturally vivid—the grass and flowers so bright they seemed freshly painted, the air as sweet as sun-dried laundry. He looked at Gene. The black man's face remained impassive, so Daniel knew it was his own perceptions that were heightened. He was experiencing the hypersensitivity of a blind man whose sight has miraculously been restored.

"Some guy, your dad," said Gene, as they made their way through the field that bordered the northern edge of the park. "How old is he?"

"Seventy-one."

"He moves like a kid. Amazing."

"He is amazing. He has a beautiful heart. My mother died in childbirth—he was mother and father to me."

"No brothers or sisters?"

"No. The same with Laura. Our children have no aunts or uncles."

Gene eyed the boys and Shoshana, running ahead through the tall grass.

"Looks like you've got plenty of family, though."

"Yes." Daniel hesitated. "Gene, I want to apologize for being such a poor host."

Gene dismissed him with a wave. "Nothing to apologize for. Tables were turned, I'd be doing the same."

They entered the park, which was crowded with Shabbat strollers, walked under arched pergolas roofed with pink and white oleanders, past sand-play areas, rose beds, the replica of the Liberty Bell donated by the Jews of Philadelphia. Two men out on a stroll, two out of many.

"What is this, Father's Day?" said Gene. "Never seen so many guys with kids."

The question surprised Daniel. He'd always taken Shabbat at the park for granted. One afternoon a week for mothers to rest, fathers to go on shift.

"It's not like that in America?"

"We take our kids out, but nothing like this."

"In Israel, we have a six-day workweek. Saturday's the time to be with our children." They continued walking. Daniel looked around, tried to see things through Gene's perspective.

It was true. There were teenagers, couples, entire clans. The Arabs came over from East Jerusalem, three generations all banded together, picnicking on the grass.

But mostly it was Daddies On Parade. Big brawny guys, pale, studious-looking fellows. Graybeards and some who looked too young to sire. Fathers in black suits and hats, *peyot* and beards; others who'd never worn a *kipah*. Truck drivers and lawyers and shopkeepers and soldiers, eating peanuts and smoking, saying "Yes, yes, *motek*," to toddlers tugging at their fingers.

One guy had staked out a spot underneath an oak tree. He slept on his back as his children—four girls—constructed houses out of ice-cream sticks. A two-year-old ran bumpily across Daniel and Gene's path, sobbing and grubby-faced, arms extended to a blond man in shorts and T-shirt, crying "Abba! Abba!" until the man scooped the child up in his arms, assuaged her misery with kisses and tongue-clucks.

The two detectives stopped and sat on a park bench. Daniel looped Dayan's leash around a back slat, said, "Sit," and when the spaniel ignored him, dropped the subject. He looked around for Mikey and Benny, spotted them clear across the park, climbing a metal structure shaped like a spaceship. Shoshi had met up with a girlfriend, was walking with her near the guardrail of the roller skating rink. Both girls had their heads lowered, lost in a conversation that looked serious.

The boys reached the top of the spaceship, clambered down, and ran toward the Train Theater, disappearing behind the boxcars.

"You let them get out of your sight like that?" said Gene.

"Sure. Why not?"

"In L.A. you can't do that—too many weirdos hanging out at the parks."

"Our parks are safe," said Daniel, chasing away the leering image of Sender Malkovsky.

Gene looked as if he were going to say something. Something related to the case, Daniel was certain. But the American stopped himself, bit his lip, said, "Uh huh, that's good," and stretched his legs out.

They sat there, surrounded by shouts and laughter, but lulled into inactivity by empty minds and full bellies.

Gene's arms dropped to his sides. "Very nice," he said, and closed his eyes. Soon his chest was heaving, and his mouth opened slightly, emitting a soft, rhythmic whistle. Poor guy, thought Daniel. Luanne had dragged him all over the country. ("Sixty-three churches, Danny Boy—she's been keeping score.")

He sat there next to the sleeping man, felt himself sinking into the bench and didn't fight it. Time to let his guard down. Rest and renew, as his father had said. Time to remove his policeman's eyes—suspicious eyes trained to home in on discrepancy, the odd, disturbing flaw that an ordinary person wouldn't notice.

No protector, no detective. Just one of the fathers. A guy out with his kids in Liberty Bell Park.

His eyelids were heavy, he yielded to their weight. Shabbat shalom. True Sabbath Peace.

So complete was his surrender that he had no idea he was being watched. Had been observed, in fact, since his entry to the park.

A big nigger and a little nigger-kike. And a little worm of a dog that would be good for a few minutes of fun.

Beautiful, just beautiful.

Amos and Andy. King Kong and Ikey-Kikey in blackface.

Nigger-kike—the very idea was a joke. De-evolution at its nadir, selective breeding for stupidity and weakness.

The little asshole *was* stupid, which was why he listed his name in the phone book. Everyone in this fucking country did—you could look up the mayor, go to his house, and blow his face off when he came out the front door.

Come and get me. Instant victim: Just add Jew genes.

Reminded him of that invention he'd thought of as a kid. Insta-Auschwitz, little green box on wheels. Quick disposal of unwanted pets. And other *untermensch* nuisances. Clean it all up. Cut it away.

Look at that. Rufus and Ikey-Kikey Blackface limped out on the bench like a couple of grokked-out winos.

What did you get when you crossed a nigger with a kike—a janitor who owned the building? A shylock who ripped himself off?

One big hook-nose squashed flat.

One hell of a circumcision—have to use a chain saw.

The man felt the laughter climbing up through his esophagus, forced himself to keep it bottled up. He feigned relaxation, seated on the grass among all the other people, half-hidden behind a newspaper, wearing a wig and mustache that made him someone else. Scanning the park with cold eyes concealed behind sunglasses. One hand on the paper, the other in his pocket, fondling himself.

All those kids and families, kikes and sand-niggers. He would have loved to come rolling in with a giant chain saw of his own. Or maybe a lawn mower or a combine, something relentless and gas-powered . . . No, nuclear-powered, with gigantic blades, as sharp as his little beauties but *big.* As big as helicopter rotors.

And loud, making a sound like an air-raid siren. Panic-feeding, ear-bleeding loud. Blood-freezing loud.

Come rolling in with the nuke-mower, just pushing it through the human lawn, listening to the screams, churning everything up.

Back to the primordial soup.

Some terrific game, a real pleasure diddle. Maybe one day.

Not yet. He had other things to do. *Hors d'oeuvres.*

Project Untermensch.

The one who'd refused him had set things back, fucked up the weekly rhythm, really gotten him upset.

Stupid sand-nigger bitch, his money hadn't been good enough.

He'd watched her for a couple of days, gotten interested because of her face, the perfect fit for his mind-pictures. Even when she put on the tacky red wig, it was all right. He'd take it off. Along with everything else.

Everything came off.

Then she goes and fuck-you's him.

Unreal.

But that's what he got for improvising, deviating from the plan.

Trying to be casual—that never worked.

The important thing was structure. Following the rules. Keeping everything clean.

He'd gone home that night and punished himself for stepping out of bounds.

Using one of the little dancing beauties—the smallest bistoury—he'd incised a series of curved discipline cuts in the firm white skin of his inner thighs. Close to the scrotum—don't slip, ha, ha, or there'll be a major endocrine adjustment.

Cut, cut, dance, dance, crosses with bent ends. Rotated. One on each thigh. The crosses had seeped blood; he'd tasted it, bitter and metallic, poisoned by failure.

There, that'll show you, filthy boy.

Stupid sand-nigger whore.

A delay, but no big deal. The schedule could be fouled if the goal was kept sacred.

Project Untermensch. He heard children laughing. All these inferior slimefucks—it made his head hurt, filled his skull with a terrible roar. He hid his face behind the paper, concentrated on making the noise go away by thinking of his little beauties asleep in their velvet bed, so shiny and clean, extensions of his will, techno-perfection.

Structure was the answer. Keeping in step.

Goose step.

Dance, dance.

40

Moshe Kagan seemed amused rather than offended. He sat with Daniel in the living room of his home, a cheaply built four-room cube on a raised foundation, no different from any of the others in the Gvura settlement.

One corner of the room was filled with boxes of clothes. On the wall behind Kagan was a framed poster featuring miniature oval portraits of great sages. Next to it hung a watercolor of the Western Wall as it had been before '67—no sunlit expanse of plaza; the prayer space narrowed by a rear wall and shadowed by jerry-built Arab houses. Daniel remembered coming upon it like that, after making his way through dead bodies and hailstorms of sniper fire. How demeaned the last remnant of the Temple had looked, rubble and rotting garbage piled up behind the wall, the Jordanians trying to bury the last reminder of three thousand years of Jewish presence in Jerusalem.

Underneath the watercolor was a hand-printed banner featuring the blue clenched-fist logo of the Gvura party and the legend: TO FORGET IS TO DIE. To the left of the banner was a glass-doored bookcase containing the twenty volumes of the Talmud, a *Mikra'ot Gedolot* Pentateuch with full rabbinic commentary, *megillot,* kabbalistic treatises, the Code of Jewish Law. Leaning against the case were an Uzi and an assault rifle.

An angry red sun had set itself resolutely in the sky and the drive down the Hebron Road had been hot and lonely. The unpaved turnoff to Beit Gvura anticipated Hebron by seven kilometers, a twisting and dusty climb, hell on the Escort's tires. Upon arrival, Daniel had passed through a guarded checkpoint, endured the hostile stares of a gauntlet of husky Gvura men before being escorted to Kagan's front door.

Lots of muscle, plenty of firearms on display, but the leader himself was something else: mid-fifties, small, fragile-looking, and cheerful, with a grizzled beard the color of scotch whisky and drooping blue eyes. His cheeks were hollow, his hair thinning, and he wore a large black velvet *kipah* that covered most of his head. His clothes were simple and spotless—white shirt, black trousers, black oxfords—and bagged on him, as if he'd just lost weight. But Daniel had never seen him any heavier, either in photos or onstage at rallies.

Kagan took a green apple out of the bowl on the coffee table that separated him from Daniel and rubbed it between his palms. He offered the bowl to the detective and, when Daniel declined, made the blessing over fruit and bit in. As he chewed, knotty lumps rose and fell in his jaw. His sleeves were rolled up to his elbows, revealing thin forearms, sunburnt on top, fish-belly white on the inner side. Still banded, Daniel noticed, with the strap marks of the morning phylacteries.

"A terrible thing," he said, in perfect Hebrew. "Arab girls getting cut up."

"I appreciate your taking the time to talk to me about it, Rabbi."

Kagan's amusement spread into a smile. He ate half the apple before speaking.

"Terrible," he repeated. "The loss of any human life is tragic. We are all created in God's image."

Daniel felt he was being mocked. "I've heard you refer to Arabs as subhuman."

Kagan dismissed the comment with a wave of his hand. "Rhetoric. Hitting the ass across the face in order to get its attention—that's an old American joke."

"I see."

"Of course if they choose to reduce themselves to animals by acting in a subhuman manner, I have no compunction about pointing it out."

Kagan chewed the apple down to the core, bit into the core, and finished it too. When only the stem was left, he pulled it out of his mouth and twirled it between his fingertips.

"Sharavi," he said. "Old Yemenite name. Are you descended from Mori Shalom Sharavi?"

"Yes."

"No hesitation, eh? I believe you. The Yemenites have the best *yikhus,* the finest lineage of any of us. Your *nusakh* of prayer is closest to the original, the way Jews *daven*ed before the Babylonian exile. What *minyan* do you attend?"

"Sometimes I pray at the *Kotel.* Other times I go to a *minyan* in my building."

"Your building—ah, yes, the toothpick in Talbieh. Don't look so surprised, Inspector. When you told Bob Arnon you were religious I had you checked out, wanted to make sure it wasn't just government subterfuge. As far as my contacts can tell, you are what you say you are—that *kipah* isn't for show."

"Thank you for your endorsement," said Daniel.

"No need to get upset," said Kagan genially. "Blame the government. Four months ago they tried to slip in an undercover agent—I don't suppose you'd know anything about that, would you? Yemenite fellow, as a matter of fact—isn't that a coincidence? He, too, wore a *kipah,* knew the right things to say, bless this, bless that—blessings with false intention, taking God's name in vain. That's a major transgression, not that the government cares about transgressions."

Kagan took another apple out of the bowl, tossed it in the air and caught it. "No matter. We found him out, sent him home to his masters a little the worse for wear." He shook his head. "Tsk, tsk. Jews spying on Jews—that's what thousands died for, eh? If the spineless old ladies of the ruling party spent as much time tracking down terrorists as they did harassing good Jews, we'd have an *Eretz Yisrael* as the Almighty planned it for us—the one place in the world where a Jew could walk down the street like a prince. Without fear of pogroms or being stabbed in the back."

Kagan paused for breath. Daniel heard him wheezing—the man was an asthmatic of some kind. "Anyway, Inspector Sharavi, the *minyan* in your building is Ashkenazi, not for you. You should be maintaining your noble Yemenite heritage, not trying to blend in with the Europeans."

Daniel pulled out his note pad. "I'll need a list of all your members—"

"I'm sure you've already got that. In quadruplicate, maybe more."

"An updated list, along with each member's outside job and responsibilities here at the settlement. For the ones who travel, their travel logs."

"Travel logs." Kagan laughed. "You can't be serious."

"This is a very serious matter, Rabbi. I'll begin interviewing them today. Other officers will be arriving this afternoon. We'll stay until we've talked with everyone."

"The children too?" said Kagan sarcastically.

"Adults."

"Why exclude the little ones, Inspector? We train them to butcher Arabs as soon as they're off the breast." Kagan spread his arms, closed them, and touched a hand to each cheek. "Wonderful. Secular Zionism at its moment of glory." He put the apple down, stared into Daniel's eyes. "What wars have you fought in? You look too young for '67. Was it Yom Kippur or Lebanon?"

"Your contacts didn't tell you that?"

"It wasn't relevant. It won't be hard to find out."

"The '67 war. The Jerusalem theater."

"You were one of the privileged ones."

"Where were you in '67, Rabbi?"

"Patrolling the streets of Crown Heights, Brooklyn. Taking on *shvartzes* in order to prevent them from mugging old Jewish ladies and stealing their social security checks. Not as glorious as liberating Jerusalem, but philosophically consistent with it. Or at least it was until the Jews of Israel got as soft and stupid as the Jews of America."

Daniel shifted his gaze down to his note pad. "Some of your members have police records. Have any new people with criminal backgrounds joined the settlement?"

Kagan smiled. "I have a police record."

"For disturbing the peace and illegal assembly. I'm more interested in those with a violent background."

That seemed to insult Kagan. He frowned, retrieved the second apple, and bit into it hard, so that the juice trickled over his beard. Wiping himself with a paper napkin, he held out the bowl again.

"Sure you wouldn't like some fruit, Inspector?"

"No, thank you."

"A polite Israeli? Now I'm really suspicious."

"Please answer my question, Rabbi. Have any new people joined who have violent histories?"

"Tell me, Inspector, did you risk your life in '67 so that the Jew could reach a new level of self-denigration?"

"Rabbi," said Daniel, "the investigation is going to proceed one way or the other. If you cooperate, everything will go faster."

"Cooperate," enunciated Kagan, as if learning a new word. "How long have you been involved in this *investigation*?"

"From the beginning."

"From the beginning," echoed Kagan. "So, no doubt you've visited an Arab home or two in the course of your *investigation.* And no doubt you were offered food in those homes—the vaunted culture of Arab hospitality, correct?"

"Rabbi Kagan—"

"One moment. Bear with me, Inspector." Kagan spoke softly but with intensity. "You were offered food by the Arabs—quaint little dishes of nuts and fruits and seeds. Maybe they rubbed it in donkey meat before bringing it out. Maybe they spit in it. But you smiled and said thank you, sahib, and ate it all up, didn't you? Your training taught you to respect their culture—God forbid one of *them* should be offended, right? But here you are, in *my* home, *I* offer you fruit, and you turn *me* down. *Me* you're not worried about offending. Who gives a *damn* if the Jew is insulted?"

Kagan stared at Daniel, waiting for an answer. When he'd had his fill of silence, he said, "A lovely little secular Zionist democracy we've got here, isn't it, Daniel Sharavi, descendant of Mori Shalom Sharavi? We bend over backward to pay homage to those who despise us, but *kvell* in the abuse of our brethren. Is that why you fought in '67, Inspector? Were you shooting and stabbing Arabs in order to liberate them—so that you'd have the privilege of providing them with free health care, welfare checks, turn them into your little burnoosed buddies? So that they could propagate like rats, push us into the Mediterranean by out*breeding* us? Or was it materialism that kept your gunsights in place? Maybe you wanted video-recorders for your kids. *Playboy* magazine, hashish, abortion, all the wonderful gifts the goyim are more than happy to give us?"

"Rabbi," said Daniel. "This is about murder, not politics."

"Ah," said Kagan, disgustedly, "you don't see the point. They've indoctrinated you, ripped your fine Yemenite spine right out of your body."

He stood up, put his hands behind his back, and paced the room.

"I'm a member of Knesset. I don't have to put up with this nonsense."

"No one's immune from justice," said Daniel. "If my investigation led me to the Prime Minister, I'd be sitting in his house, asking him questions. Demanding his travel log."

Kagan stopped pacing, turned to Daniel and looked down at him.

"Normally I'd dismiss that little speech as garbage, but you're the one who dug up the Lippmann mess, aren't you?"

"Yes."

"How did your investigation *bring* you to me?"

"I won't tell you that. But I'm sure you can see the logic."

"The only thing I *see* is political scapegoating. A couple of Arabs get killed—blame it on Jews with guts."

Daniel opened his attaché case, knowing there was truth to what Kagan was saying and feeling like a hypocrite. He pulled out crime-scene photos of Fatma and Juliet, got up and gave them to Kagan. The Gvura leader took them and, after looking at them unflinchingly, handed them back.

"So?" he said casually, but his voice was dry.

"That's what I'm up against, Rabbi."

"That's the work of an Arab—Hebron, 1929. No member of Gvura would do anything like that."

"Let me establish that and I'll be out of your way."

Kagan rocked on his heels and tugged at his beard. Going over to the walnut case, he pulled out a volume of Talmud.

"Fine, fine," he said. "Why not? This whole thing is going to backfire on the government. The people aren't stupid—you'll turn me into a persecuted hero." He opened the book, moistened his finger, and began turning pages. "Now be off, Inspector. I have to learn Torah, have no more time to waste on your *naarishkeit*." Another look of amusement. "And who knows, maybe after you've spent some time with us, something will rub off on you. You'll see the error of your ways, start *daven*ing with the proper *minyan*."

The Gvura members were a motley bunch. He interviewed them in their dining hall, a makeshift concrete-floored space roofed with tent canvas and set up with aluminum tables and folding chairs. Clatter and the smell of hot oil came from the kitchen.

About half were Israelis—mostly younger Moroccans and Iraqis, a few Yemenites. Former street kids, all of them hard-eyed and stingy with words. The Americans were either religious types with untrimmed beards and oversized *kipot* or tough-talking secular ones who were hard to categorize.

Bob Arnon was one of the latter, a middle-aged man with curly gray hair, long, bushy sideburns, and a heavy-jawed face assembled around a large broken nose. He'd been living in Israel for two years, had acquired three disorderly-conduct arrests and a conviction for assault.

He wore faded jeans and crossed gun belts over a NEW YORK YANKEES T-shirt. The shirt was tight and showed off thick, hairy arms and a substantial belly. Poking up into the belly was the polished wooden grip of a nickel-plated .45-caliber revolver—an American-made Colt. The gun rested in a hand-tooled leather holster and made Daniel think of a little boy playing American cowboy.

In addition to the Colt, Kagan's deputy wore a hunting knife ensconced in a camouflage-cloth case, and carried a black baseball bat, the handle wrapped in adhesive tape that had long ago turned filthy gray. He was a combat veteran, he informed Daniel, and more than happy to talk about himself, starting in American-accented Hebrew but shifting to English after Daniel responded to him in that language.

"Saw hard action in Korea. Those were tough little suckers we were fighting—no Arabs, that's for certain. When I got back to the States I knocked around."

"What do you mean by 'knocked around'?"

Arnon winked. "Little of this, little of that—doing my thing, doing favors for people. Good deeds, you understand? My last hitch was a bar in New York—up in Harlem, gorgeous place, you ever heard of it? Five years I worked the place, never had a single problem with the shvoogies." This last comment was punctuated by a toothy grin and a slap of the bat.

"May I see your knife, please?"

"This? Sure. Genuine buck, great all-purpose weapon, had it for fifteen years." Arnon took it out of its case and gave it to Daniel, who turned it over in his palm, inspecting the wide, heavy blade, the serrated edge honed to razor-sharpness. A nasty piece of work, but from what Levi had told him, not the one he was looking for. Gray Man, on the other hand, had used a serrated blade. But duller, smaller . . .

He gave the knife back to Arnon.

"Do you own any other knives, Mr. Arnon?"

"Others? Oh, yeah. Got a tackle box that I brought over from the States—haven't had a chance to use it yet. They say there's great fishing in the Sea of Galilee. That true?"

"Yes. Your other knives, Mr. Arnon."

"A gutter and a scaler in the box, along with a Swiss Army—least, I think it's still there. Maybe a spare scaler too. Then there's another buck for under the pillow and an antique Japanese samurai sword that I picked up in Manila. Want to know about the guns, too?"

"Not right now. Some other detectives will be here soon. They'll want to see your weapons."

"Sure." Arnon smiled. "But if I was the one cut up those Arab whores I wouldn't be advertising it, now would I? Leaving the knife around to show you."

"What *would* you be doing, Mr. Arnon?"

"Wiping it clean, oiling it, and hiding it somewhere. That's *if,* mind you. Hypothetical."

"Is there anything else you want to tell me—hypothetical?"

"Just that you're barking up the wrong tree. Gvura doesn't concern itself with an Arab here, an Arab there. It's a sociological problem—they've all gotta go."

The women were an odd mix of toughness and subservience, filing in after the men had been questioned. Stoic and unsmiling, they brought their children with them, resisted Daniel's suggestion that the youngsters leave.

"The questions I'll be asking aren't fitting for a child's ears," he told one of the first. She came in with three small ones, the oldest a girl of no more than four, the youngest an infant who squirmed in her grasp.

"No. I want them to see," she said. "I insist upon it." She was young, pallid, and thin-lipped, and wore a long-sleeved striped shift that reached below her knees. Her hair was covered completely with a white kerchief, and an Uzi was strapped over her shoulder. The baby's tiny fingers reached out and touched the barrel of the submachine gun.

"Why?" asked Daniel.

"To show them what it's like."

She sounded like a kid herself. A teenager asserting herself with her parents. So young, he thought, to have three of them. Her eyes were bright, vigilant, her breasts still heavy with milk.

"What *what*'s like, Gveret Edelstein?"

"*The world.* Go on, ask your questions." A glance downward, the ruffling of hair. "Listen carefully, children. This is called harassment. It's part of being Jewish."

* * *

By noon he'd talked to a third of them, found no one who interested him, other than Arnon, with his knives and assault conviction. And even *he* seemed more bluster than substance, an aging tough guy living out his mid-life fantasies. His assault conviction itself wasn't much—the result of a confrontation at a rally. Arnon's left hook had landed on the nose of a PEACE NOW placard-bearer; when the police came to break it up, Arnon resisted. First offense, no jail time. Not exactly your psychopathic killer, but you could never tell. He'd have the others follow up on Cowboy Bob.

At twelve-thirty the lunch bell rang and settlement members swarmed into the dining room for salad and fried fish. They took their places automatically and Daniel realized seats were preassigned. He vacated his chair and left the hall, meeting Kagan and his wife as they came in.

"Any luck, Inspector?" asked the leader loudly. "Find any crazed killers among us?"

Mrs. Kagan winced, as if her husband had told an off-color joke.

Daniel smiled noncommittally and walked down the path toward the guard post. As he left he could hear Kagan talking to his wife. Something about melting pots, a fine old culture, what a shame.

At twelve forty-six, Shmeltzer and Avi Cohen drove up to the guard post in Cohen's BMW. Laufer had wanted four detectives questioning the Gvura people. Daniel had given in partially by pulling Avi out of the Old City for the afternoon, but this was no job for Daoud and he had no intention of removing the Chinaman from his current assignment.

He was interested in the big man's story about the flat-eyed American with the strange grin, despite Little Hook's credibility problem, because it was *something*—a solitary buoy bobbing in a great sea of nothingness. He double-teamed the Chinaman and Daoud again—the Arab helping out until sundown, before he began the Roselli surveillance. Those two and Cohen were to put all their energies into finding some backup for Little Hook's story, someone else who might have encountered Flat Eyes. And in locating Red Amira Nasser. The dark hair and the fact that she was dull-witted put her in league with Fatma and Juliet. So far the only thing they'd come up with was a rumor that she had family in Jordan, had escaped there. And a medical chart at Hadassah Hospital—treatment six months ago for syphilis. No welfare payments, no other government records; a true professional, she lived off her earnings.

Avi parked the BMW next to Daniel's Escort. He and Shmeltzer got out and trudged up the sloping pathway, kicking up dust. Daniel greeted them, summed up his procedures, gave them the list of Gvura members, and told them to do a weapons check on all of them, paying special attention to Bob Arnon. Any blade that remotely fit Levi's descriptions was to be taken and tagged.

"Anything about this Arnon that makes him interesting?" asked Shmeltzer.

"He's an American, he likes to play with guns and knives, he beat up on a leftist last June, and he hates Arabs."

"Are his eyes flat?" Shmeltzer smiled sourly. He knew Little Hook from his days on the pickpocket detail, was far from being convinced of the hunchback's story.

"Bloodshot," said Daniel. "Otherwise unremarkable."

"Fucking political games, coming down here. A total waste of our time."

Avi nodded along like a dutiful son.

"Okay, let's get it over with," said Daniel. "Send a report to Laufer and move on."

"Laufer knew my father," said Cohen. "He thinks I'm his boy. I think he's a shithead."

"What's with Malkovsky?" Daniel asked him.

"Nothing. Still edgy. I wish I were there instead of playing the shithead's game."

"The shithead cornered me in the hall this morning," said Shmeltzer. "Wanted to know what we've gotten out of these sweet souls—just itching for another press release. I told him we just started, it was too early to tell, but from the way it looked, they were all blameless as newborn lambs—did the esteemed Tat Nitzav wish us to continue in the same vein? 'What do you mean?' he says. I say, 'Should we start checkin' out the other MK's and their people too?' "

Daniel laughed. "What did he say to that?"

"Made like an old car—sputters and snorts, metal against metal—then headed straight for the bathroom. Primed, no doubt, for a little vertical communication."

* * *

Daniel got back to Jerusalem at two-thirteen, bought a felafel from a street vendor near the train station, and finished it while driving to Headquarters. Back in his office he began transcribing the interview with Kagan onto official forms, wanting to be rid of it as quickly as possible, then called the operator and asked for radio contact with the Chinaman. Before she completed the transmission, she interrupted, saying: "There's one for you coming in right now. Do you want it?"

"Sure." He endured a minute of static, was connected to Salman Afif, the mustachioed Druze, phoning from his Border Patrol jeep.

"I'm out here with some Bedouins—the ones we spoke about that first morning. They've migrated south, found something I think you'll want to see."

He told Daniel what it was and reported his location, using military coordinates. Daniel pulled out a map and pinpointed the spot, three and a half kilometers due north from the Scopus ridge. Fifteen hundred meters past the perimeter of the grid search he'd ordered after viewing Fatma's body.

So close.

"What's the best way to get there?"

"I can drive up into the city," said Afif, "and take you back, retracing on the donkey paths, but it would be quicker for you to climb down the first kilometer or so on foot—to where the slope eases. From there it's a straight ride. How are your shoes?"

"They'll survive. I'm leaving now—meet you there. Thanks for keeping your eyes open."

"Nothing to it," said the Druze. "A blind man couldn't have missed it."

Daniel hung up, put his papers away, and called Forensics.

41

He parked the Escort across the road from the Amelia Catherine, put on a narrow-brimmed straw hat to block out the relentless Judean sun, tightened the buckles on his sandals, and got out. The watchman, Zia Hajab, was sitting at the entry to the hospital. Slumped in the same plastic chair, apparently sleeping.

Taking a quick backward look at the gully where Fatma had been found, Daniel sprinted toward the ridge, climbed over, and began his descent.

Walking sideways on bent legs, he made rapid progress, feeling nimble and fit, aware of, but unperturbed by, dry fingers of heat radiating upward from the broiling desert floor.

Summer was approaching—twenty-three days since the dumping of Fatma, and the case was snaking its way toward the new season. The rainy season had been brief this year, attenuated by hot easterly winds, but clumps of vegetation still clung to the terraced hillsides, denying the inevitability of summer. Digging his heels in and using his arms for balance, he half-walked, half-jumped through soft expanses of rusty terra rossa. Then the red earth began yielding to pale strips of rendzina—the chalky limestone that looked as dead as plastic but could still be friable if you knew how to work it—until soon all was pale and hard and unyielding—a crumbling, rocky course the color of dried bones. Land that would rather dissolve than accommodate, the emptiness relieved only by the last starved weeds of spring.

Afif's jeep was visible as a khaki spot on the chalk, its diameter expanding as Daniel drew near. Daniel removed his hat and waved it in the air, saw the blue Border Patrol light flash on and off. When he was forty meters away, the jeep's engine started up. He trotted toward it, unmindful of the grit that had lodged between his toes, then remembering that no sand had been found on either body.

Afif gave the jeep gas and it rocked on its bearings. Daniel climbed in and held on as the Druze made a sharp U-turn and sped off.

The ride was spine-jarring and loud, the jeep's engine howling in protest as Afif tortured its transmission, maneuvering between low outcroppings of limestone, grinding single-mindedly through dry stream beds. The Druze's pale eyes were hidden by mirrored sunglasses. A red bandanna was tied loosely around his neck, and the ends of his enormous mustache were blond with dust.

"Which Bedouin clan is this?" Daniel shouted.

"Locals, like I told you. Unrelated to any of the big clans. They run goats and sheep from here up toward Ramallah, come in for the summer, camping north of the city."

Daniel remembered a small northern campsite, nine or ten low black tents of woven goat-hair, baking in the heat.

"Just past the Ramot, you said?"

"That's them," said Afif. He downshifted into a climb, twisted the wheel, and accelerated.

"How long have they been herding here?"

"Eight days."

"And before that?"

"Up north, for a month or so."

Bedouins, thought Daniel, holding on to his seat. Real ones, not the smiling, bejeweled businessmen who gave tent tours and camel rides to tourists in Beersheva. The most unlikely of informants.

The Bedouin saw themselves as free spirits, had contempt for city dwellers, whom they regarded as serfs and menial laborers. But they chose to live at bare subsistence level in terrain that had the utmost contempt for them and, like all desert creatures, had turned adaptation into a fine art.

Chameleons, thought Daniel. They told you what you wanted to hear, worked both sides of every fence. Glubb Pasha had built the Arab Legion on Bedouin talent; without them the Jordanian Army wouldn't have lasted twenty-four hours. Yet, after '67, they'd turned right around and volunteered for the Israeli Army, serving as trackers, doing it better than anyone. Now there were rumors that some of them were working for the PLO as couriers—grenades in saddlebags, plastique drop-offs in Gaza. Chameleons.

"Why'd they come forward?" Daniel asked.

"They didn't," said Afif. "We were on patrol, circling southeast from Al Jib—someone had reported suspicious movement along the Ramot road. It turned out to be a construction crew, working late. I was using the binoculars, saw them, decided to go in for a close look."

"Ever had any trouble with them?"

"No, and we check on them regularly. They're paupers, have enough trouble keeping their goats alive long enough to get them to market without getting into mischief. What caught my eye was that they were all gathered in one place. It looked like a conference, even though their camp was a good kilometer north. So I drove over and found them huddled around the mouth of the cave. They started to move out when they heard us coming, but I kept them there while I checked it out. When I saw what was inside, I had them pull up camp and regroup by the cave while I called you."

"You don't think they had anything to do with it?"

The Druze twirled one end of his mustache. "How can you be sure with the Bedouin? But, no, I think they're being truthful. There weren't any signs of recent activity in the cave. Old dried dung—looked like jackal or dog."

"How many of them actually went into the cave?"

"The kid who found it, his father, a couple of others. We got there fairly soon after they did, kept the rest out."

"I'll need fingerprints and foot casts from them for comparison. Forensics should be here within the hour. It'll be a long day."

"I'll handle it, no problem."

"Good. How many men do you have with you?"

"Ten."

"Have them do a search within a one-and-a-half-kilometer radius from the cave. Look for anything unusual—other caves, clothing, personal articles, human waste—you know the routine."

"Do you want a grid search?"

"You'll need reinforcements for that. Is it worth it?"

"It's been weeks," said Afif. "There was that strong khamsin eleven days ago."

He stopped talking, waited for Daniel to draw the conclusion: The chance of a footprint or clue withstanding the harsh easterly heat-storm was minimal.

"Do a grid within half a kilometer from the cave. If they find another cave, tell them to call in and wait for further instructions. Otherwise, just a careful search of the rest of it will be enough."

The Druze nodded. They dipped, traversing a network of shallow wadis strewn with rocks and dead branches, the jeep's underbelly reverberating hollowly in response to an assault of dancing gravel. Afif pushed his foot to the accelerator, churning up a dust storm. Daniel pulled down the brim of his hat, slapped one hand over his nose and mouth, and held his breath. The jeep climbed; he felt himself rise out of his seat and come down hard. When the particles had settled, the Bedouin camp came into focus along the horizon: dark, oblong smudges of tent, so low they could have been shadows. As they got closer, he could see the rest of the Border Patrol unit—two more jeeps and a canvas-top truck, all of them sporting revolving blue lights.

The truck was pulled up next to a ragged mound of limestone and surrounded by a mottled brown cloud that undulated in the heat: goatherds shifting restlessly. A single shepherd stood motionless at the periphery, staff in hand.

"The cave's over there," said Afif, pointing to the mound. "The opening's on the other side."

He aimed the jeep at the flock, came to a halt several meters from the goats, and turned off the engine.

Two Bedouins, a boy and a man, stood next to the canvas-topped truck, flanked by Border Patrolmen. The rest of the nomads had returned to their tents. Only the males were visible, men and boys sitting cross-legged on piles of brightly colored blankets, silent and still, as if tranquilized by inertia. But Daniel knew the women were there, too, veiled and tattooed. Peeking from behind goatskin partitions, in the rear section of the tent, called *haramluk,* where they huddled among the wood stoves and the cooking implements until beckoned for service.

A single vulture circled overhead and flew north. The goats gave a collective shudder, then quieted in response to a bark from the shepherd.

Daniel followed Afif as the Druze pushed his way through the herd, the animals yielding passively to the intruders, then closing ranks behind them, settling into a mewling, snorting pudding of hair and horns.

"The family is Jussef Ibn Umar," said Afif as they approached the pair. "The father is Khalid; the boy, Hussein."

He handed their identification cards to Daniel, walked up

to the Bedouins, and performed the introductions, calling Daniel the Chief Officer and making it clear he was someone to be respected. Khalid Jussef Ibn Umar responded with an appropriate bow, cuffed his son until the boy bowed too. Daniel greeted them formally and nodded at Afif. The Druze left and began instructing his men.

Daniel inspected the ID cards, made notes, and looked at the Bedouins. The boy was ten, small for his age, with a round, serious face, curious eyes, and hair cropped close to the skull. His father's head was wrapped with wide strips of white cloth held in place by a goat-hair cord. Both wore loose, heavy robes of coarse dark wool. Their feet were blackened and dusty in open sandals, the nails cracked and yellow. The smallest toe on the boy's left foot was missing. Up close, both of them gave off the ripe odor of curdled milk and goat flesh.

"Thank you for your help," he told Ibn Umar the elder. The man bowed again. He was thin, stooped, sparsely bearded, and undersized, with dry, tough skin and one eye filmed by a slimy gray cataract. His face had the collapsed look of toothlessness and his hands were twisted and crisscrossed with keloid scars. According to the card he was thirty-nine, but he looked sixty. Stunted and damaged, like so many of them, by malnutrition, disease, inbreeding, the ravages of desert living.

At forty, it was said, a Bedouin was old, approaching uselessness. Not exactly T. E. Lawrence's noble desert conqueror, thought Daniel, looking at Khalid, but then again, most of what the Englishman had written was nonsense—in high school he and his friends had laughed at the Hebrew translation of *The Seven Pillars of Wisdom* until their sides ached.

The boy stared at the ground, then looked up, catching Daniel's eye. Daniel smiled at him and his head snapped back down.

Clear eyes, clear complexion, a bright-looking kid. The short stature within the range of normalcy. Compared to his father, the picture of health. The result, no doubt, of ten summer weeks camped outside the Ramot. Forays by social workers, tutors, mobile health units, immunizations, nutritional supplements. The despised ways of the city dweller . . .

"Show me the cave," he said.

Khalid Jussef Ibn Umar led him to the other side of the ragged limestone mound. Hussein followed at his heels. When they reached the mouth of the cave, Daniel told them to wait.

He stepped back, took a look at the mound. A nondescript eruption, fringed with scrub. The limestone was striated horizontally and pitted, a decaying layer cake. Ancient waters had run down the north wall for centuries and sculpted it into a snail-shell spiral. The mouth of the shell was slitlike, shaped like a bow hole. Daniel's first impression was that it was too narrow for a man to enter. But as he came closer, he could see it was an optical illusion: The outer lip extended far enough to conceal a hollow in the stone, a dishlike depression that afforded more than enough space for passage. He slipped through easily, motioned the Bedouins in after him.

The interior of the cave was cool, the air stagnant and heavy with some musky, feral perfume.

He'd expected dimness, was greeted by mellow light. Looking upward he found the source: At the apex of the spiral was an open twist. Through it shot an oblique ray of sunshine, softened by refraction and dancing with dust specks.

The light was focused, as surely as if it had been a hand-held torch, spotlighting the center of a low, flat loaf of rock about two meters long, half as wide, then tapering to blackness in all directions.

On the rock was a rusty stain—a stone guitar. A woman-shaped stain. The outer contours of a female body, vacant at the center and delineated by reddish-greenish borders that ended in starburst fringes in some places, spreading in others to the edge of the rock and over. Fanning and flowing in lazy dribbles.

A silhouette of human sacrifice, stretched out on some altar. Etched in relief, as if by some lost-wax process.

He wanted to go closer, take a better look, but knew he had to wait for Forensics and contented himself with observing from a distance.

The legs of the outline were slightly apart, the arms positioned close to the trunk.

Etched. The lost-blood process.

Blood deteriorated fast. Exposure to the elements could turn it gray, green, blue, a variety of nonsanguinary colors. But Daniel had seen enough of it to know what this was. He glanced at the Bedouins, knew they would have recognized it too. They slaughtered their own animals, got blood on their clothes all the time; when water was lacking they went weeks without washing. Even the boy would have known.

Khalid shifted his weight. His eyes were restless with uncertainty.

Daniel turned his attention back to the rock.

The outline was headless, ending at the neck. He visualized a body splayed out helplessly, the head tilted back, the neck slashed open. Draining.

He thought he saw something—a patch of white—stuck to the upper edge of the rock, but the light evaded that part of the altar and it was too dark to be sure.

He scanned the rest of the cave. The ceiling was low and curved, arched as if by design. On the side of one wall he saw some spots that could also have been blood. There were footprints near the rock/altar. In one corner he made out a jumble of detritus: balls of dried dung, broken twigs, crushed rock.

"How did you find this?" he asked Khalid.

"My son found it."

He asked Hussein: "How did you find this cave?"

The boy was silent. His father squinted down at the top of his head, poked the back of his neck, and told him to speak.

Hussein mumbled something.

"Speak up!" ordered the father.

"I was . . . herding the animals."

"I see," said Daniel. "And then what happened?"

"One of the young ones ran loose, into the cave."

"One of the goats?"

"A baby. A ewe." Hussein looked up at his father: "The white one with the brown spot on the head. She likes to run."

"What did you do then?" asked Daniel.

"I followed it." The boy's lower lip trembled. He looked terrified.

Just a kid, Daniel reminded himself. He smiled and squatted so that he and Hussein were at eye level.

"You're doing very well. It's brave of you to tell me these things."

The boy hung his head. His father took hold of his jaw and whispered fiercely in his ear.

"I went inside," said Hussein. "I saw the table."

"The table?"

"The rock," said Khalid Jussef Ibn Umar. "He calls it a table."

"That makes sense," Daniel told the boy. "It looks like a table. Did you touch anything in the cave?"

"Yes."

"What did you touch?"

"That piece of cloth." Pointing to the shred of white.

A forensics nightmare, thought Daniel, wondering what else had been disturbed.

"Do you remember what the cloth looked like?"

The boy took a step forward. "Over there, you can pull it off."

Daniel restrained him with a forearm. "No, Hussein, I don't want to move anything until some other policemen get here."

The terror returned to the boy's face.

"I . . . I didn't know—"

"That's all right," said Daniel. "What did the cloth look like?"

"White with blue stripes. And dirty."

"Dirty with what?"

The boy hesitated.

"Tell me, Hussein."

"Blood."

Daniel looked at the cloth again. He could see now that it was larger than he'd thought. Only a small portion was white. The rest had blended in with the bloodstained rock. Enough, he hoped, for a decent analysis.

Hussein was mumbling again.

"What's that, son?" asked Daniel.

"I thought . . . I thought it was the home of a wild animal!"

"Yes, that would make sense. What kinds of animals do you see out here?"

"Jackals, rabbits, dogs. Lions."

"You've seen lions? Really?" Daniel suppressed a smile; the lions of Judea had been extinct for centuries.

Hussein nodded and turned his head away.

"Tell the truth, boy," commanded his father.

"I've heard lions," said the boy, with unexpected assertiveness. "Heard them roaring."

"Dreams," said Khalid, cuffing him lightly. "Foolishness."

"What," Daniel asked the boy, "did you do after you touched the cloth?"

"I took the ewe and went out."

"And then?"

"I told my father about the table."

"Very good," said Daniel, straightening himself. To the father: "We're going to have to take your son's fingerprints."

Hussein gasped and started crying.

"Quiet!" commanded Khalid.

"It won't hurt, Hussein," said Daniel, squatting again. "I promise you that. A police officer will roll your fingers on a pad of ink, roll them again on a piece of paper, making a picture of the lines on your fingertips. Then he'll wash them off. That's it. He may also take a picture of your feet, using white clay and water. Nothing will hurt."

Hussein remained unconvinced. He wiped his nose, hid his eyes with his arm, and continued to sniffle.

"Hush. Don't be a woman," admonished the father, pulling the arm away. He dried the boy's tears with the back of his sleeve.

"You've done a very good job," Daniel told Hussein. "Thank you." He offered a smile that went unreciprocated, turned to Khalid, and asked, "Did anyone else touch anything in the cave?"

"No," said Khalid. "No one went near. It was an abomination."

"How long have you been grazing near this cave?"

"Eight days."

"And where were you before that?"

"Up." The Bedouin pointed to the ceiling.

"North?"

"Yes."

"How long were you grazing up north?"

"Since the end of Ramadan."

One lunar month, which jibed precisely with what Afif had told him.

"In all that time have you seen anyone else out here? Especially at night?"

"Only the jeeps with the blue lights. They come all the time. Sometimes an army truck too."

"No one else?"

"No."

"What about sounds? Have you heard anything unusual?"

"Nothing at all. Just the sounds of the desert."

"Which sounds are those?"

Jussef Ibn Umar scratched his chin. "Rodents, a leaf bending in the breeze. A beetle gnawing at a piece of dung."

His words—the precision of his perceptions—brought back memories. Of bowel-tightening night watches, learning that there was no such thing as silence.

"Night music," said Daniel.

Khalid looked at him appraisingly, trying to figure out if this urban fool was ridiculing him. When he decided the comment had been tendered in earnest, he nodded and said, "Yes, sir. And no false notes have been heard."

Steinfeld stepped out of the cave, frowning. He removed his gloves, brushed off his trousers, and walked toward Daniel. Several other techs were fingerprinting the Bedouins, taking foot casts and fiber samples from their robes. Afif's men were walking slowly across the immediate vicinity, carrying collecting sacks, eyes locked to the ground.

"Party time," said Steinfeld, eyeing the nomads. "The goats smell better than they do."

"What can you tell me?"

"Not much yet. I've taken distilled water samples, run the *ortho-tolidine* test, and it's blood all right. The luminol spray's the best for the rest of the cave but I need darkness to see the glow spots clearly. You'll have to cover that sky hole."

Daniel called over a Border Patrolman, instructed him to throw a tarp over the hole.

"Tight," Steinfeld called out as the officer departed. "I did an ABO right there," he told Daniel. "All of it's O, same as both of your victims and forty-three percent of the population, so no big deal there. In terms of the other groupings, I think there was some difference between the two of them on a couple—maybe the haptoglobin, but don't hold me to it. I could be wrong. Anyway, don't get your hopes up. Blood decomposes fast, especially out here in the open. You're unlikely to get anything you can use in court."

"Forget court," said Daniel. "I'd be happy with an identification."

"Don't even hope for that. The best thing I can do is take the samples back to the lab. Maybe something'll still be reactive. I've got a guy in there chipping off pieces of rock, another one scooping up everything, including the shit, which is weeks old and definitely canine—if it barked you couldn't be surer. If we find something interesting, you'll be the first to know."

"What about the cloth?"

"Looks like cotton," said Steinfeld. "It might match your number one, but it's very common stuff. In answer to your next question, the footprints are fresh—from the sandals of our nomadic friends. A few fingerprints have turned up, probably also theirs." He looked at his watch. "Anything else? That blood isn't getting any fresher."

"No. Thanks for coming so quickly. When can you give me your results?"

Steinfeld snorted. "Yesterday. That's when you need it, right?"

42

She went crazy about the cat, screaming and crying and just generally being lame, staggering all over the house, throwing open closets and drawers and tossing stuff onto the floor for the maids to clean up. Going into the kitchen, the cellar, *his* room—places she hadn't been for years. Sing-crying in that weird shaky opera voice.

"Snow-ball, come-a-here, come-a-here!"

He got a little nervous when she invaded his room and started going through it, even though he knew he'd been careful.

Have you seen my baby? Tell me, damn you!

No, Mom.

Oh, God! Sob, cry, tear hair.

He'd cleaned up really good—not a speck of blood remained. Used the surgical scissors from the case and cut up what was left of the body into little pieces, wrapped them up in newspaper, and dropped different parts in different sewer drains all over the neighborhood. Doing it at night when it was fresh and cool, the summer flowers blooming and giving out this really sweet smell that lasted forever.

An adventure.

She went out, too—the first time he'd ever seen her out of the house. Put on this satin robe that looked ridiculous on the street and actually made it halfway down the block singing, "Snow-ball, come-a-here, bad boy, naughty lover!" before having to rush back all scared and pale and locking herself in her room and throwing up so loud you could hear her heaving through the door.

When she finally realized the little fucker was gone for good, she started to get paranoid, certain that someone had killed it, convincing herself it had been Doctor, catching him in the library and accusing him of it.

Doctor ignored her, and she kept screaming that he was a murderer, had murdered Snowball for some kike blood ritual, using the blood for his fucking matzo.

Finally Doctor got mad and said, "Maybe it ran away because it was sick of you, Christina. Couldn't stand watching you drink and puke yourself to death."

After that it became just another fight, and he climbed down the stairs and took his regular seat on number six. Listening and stroking himself and filing sex-pictures for future jack-off sessions.

The next morning she called the Humane Society, told them her husband was an animal murderer, had killed her prize Persian and taken it to the hospital for experiments. Then she phoned the hospital and the Medical Board and reported Doctor for cruelty to animals.

The minute she opened her mouth everyone could tell she was crazy. No one paid any attention to her.

During surgery, the roaring had stopped. He'd felt about eight feel tall; everything had gone great.

A success, real science. Cutting carefully and peeling back all the layers, seeing all the colors: yellow fat, meat-red muscle, purple liver, tannish-pinkish intestines, all those bluish membranes covered with a network of blood vessels that looked like roads on a map.

The little heart pumping, kind of leaking around the edges.

It made him like the cat, feel that it was *his* pet.

The insides of animals were beautiful, just like the charts he'd seen in one of Doctor's books. The *Atlas of Human Anatomy*—plastic sheets, layers of them, with different stuff painted on each one. They lay in a pile, one on top of the other. You peeled them off one by one, starting with a whole person—naked—and then peeling and getting the muscles, kind of a striped, red muscle man. Then off came the muscles and you got the organs, then a fringey-looking man made only of nerves and a brain, then a skeleton.

Two of them, actually. A plastic man and a plastic woman.

He liked the woman better, liked learning that inside, tits were mostly fat.

Funny.

Insides were beautiful, all the colors, really complicated.

School was fruit flies and words, not reality, nothing like this.

Not science.

When he was finished with the cat, he cut its diaphragm and it stopped breathing.

Then he cleaned up, took his time doing it, being supercareful.

That was the key, to clean up really good. You'd never get caught.

Without the cat *she* got worse, crazier. Spent a lot of time in her room talking to herself and barfing her meals—she was definitely losing it. The maids called her *Senora Loca,* didn't even bother to hide the fact that they thought she was nuts.

He wondered why she and Doctor stayed together, why Doctor didn't just kick her ass out. Then he heard them fighting once, she accusing Doctor of fucking candy-stripers at the hospital, saying that he better not pull the shit he'd pulled on Lillian—*she'd* take him to the cleaners if he ever tried that shit on her. He'd be taking the bus to work, eating beans for dinner before she was finished with him.

Doctor didn't answer, so he figured there was something to the threat.

Not that the fights happened too often anymore, 'cause they didn't. Because Doctor was almost never home. But when he was, the shit *really* hit the fan.

He missed going down and listening. Even though his mind was working good, he had plenty of mental pictures and kill-sex memories to work with, there was nothing like actually hearing it, actually peeking through the door and seeing it.

They had a real good one when he was fifteen. A week after his fifteenth birthday, which no one had celebrated. He hadn't expected anything—she was too drunk and Doctor had ignored his birthdays since he'd refused to have a Bar Mitzvah.

Fuckbrain never did anything religious—why the fuck should *he* learn all that Jewish shit?

He'd waited for it to feel like a birthday. When it didn't, said fuckit, fuck them, and went out for a night walk. He found the dog a couple of blocks away—a ragged-looking terrier with no collar—choked it out, then brought it home hidden under his coat. Up in his room he anesthetized it and set up a terrific anatomy session, using the big Liston amputating knife and really enjoying the weight of it. The power.

Later that night he had terrific dreams, bunches of animals and girls all dancing and screaming and begging him to do it to them; he was sitting on this throne-type chair looking down on this pit that was half fire, half blood. An outrageous scene that he cleaned up perfectly and felt good about.

They woke him with their fight.

All *right*! Happy *birthday*!

He was down there again on step six, feeling rich with memories, really comfortable.

He'd missed part of it but could tell it had to do with Sarah—the best ones always did.

She'd graduated college with honors, had been accepted to the first medical school of her choice, and Doctor was flying up to see her, rewarding her with money, a new wardrobe, and a trip abroad, all expenses paid—first-class airfare, the best hotels, a couple of charge cards.

When the hell did you ever give me anything like that?

When the hell did you ever deserve it?

Screw you, you cheap bastard. I gave you my life, that's all. Ruined myself for you!

Here we go again.

Don't sigh at me, you bastard. You're damned *right* here we go again. Don't think for a minute I don't know what you're doing.

And what's that?

Giving her all your money so there won't be any left in the community property.

Thinking about inheritance, are you?

Damned right. What else is there to live for?

Way you're going with the booze and the purging, Christina, I wouldn't count on being around to inherit anything.

Just you wait, you bastard. I'll be standing there when they put you under, laughing, dancing on your grave.

Don't count on it.

I'm counting.

Ten to one your electrolytes are out of whack, God knows how much liver you've got left—you even smell like a drunk. Jesus.

Don't Jesus me. Jesus *loves* me and he hates *you,* 'cause *you're* a Jesus killer. Don't you *dare* roll your eyes at me, you fucking kike Christ-killer.

All of a sudden you're religious.

I've *always* been religious. Jesus loves me and I love him.

You and Jesus have a regular thing going, do you?

Laugh all you want, you bastard. I'll be saved and you'll burn—along with that little hook-nosed bitch and her hook-nosed mother. I'd take you to the cleaners right now, show the world what a thief you are if it didn't mean *they'd* stick their grubby hands in the pot, get their kike shyster lawyers to take it all away from me.

I thought I was giving it to them, anyway.

Don't try to shit me, Charles. I know what you're up to.

Fine, fine, whatever you say.

I say your hook-nosed bitches are going to burn along with you. I say I'll be damned if they clean me out before they do it.

Sarah's a terrific kid. She's earned it. I'll give her what I want.

I'll bet.

What's that supposed to mean?

No smile anymore? You know exactly what I mean.

You're disgusting. Get the hell out of my sight.

And your little hook-nose bitch, she's pure class, with her hairy legs and nose like a—

Lillian's a thousand times the woman you'll ever be.

—parrot beak. Real classy, that nose, huh?

Shut up, Christina.

Shut up, Christina—trying to throw me out with the trash, are you? Well, I wasn't so disgusting when you wanted shiksa pussy, was I? Ignoring me, hotshot? You didn't ignore me when you wanted shiksa pussy, when shiksa pussy was *all* you wanted. You kicked your hook-nose bitch out so you could have some of this, c'mere, look—all blonde and sweet and ready to—

You're repulsive. Cover yourself.

Hook-nosed bitches don't have this, do they? Hook-nosed bitches are all hairy and smelly and dirty, just like the animals they are. Hook-nose Lillian, hook-nose Sarah—

Shut your mouth!

Ah, that wipes the smile off your face, the thought of your little angel having a dirty—

Shut up before I—

Before you what? Beat me up? Kill me? Go ahead. I'll come back to haunt you, dance on your grave.

Enough.

Not enough, Charles. It's never enough, because you're a thieving, lying bastard who wants to give away what's mine to some little slut because she's convinced him she's the fucking Virgin Mary or something. What do you think, you stupid bastard, she doesn't have one too? How do you think she got into med school? Got on her knees for some admissions officer and—

Shut your goddamned filthy mouth.

The truth hurts, doesn't it?

Listen, you stupid, drunken moron! She got into med school because she was a straight-A student, summa cum laude, Phi Beta Kappa, and has more brains in her little finger than you have in your entire alcohol-besotted brain.

A straight-A slurper.

All right, Christina, I'm not going to let you get to me. You're jealous of Sarah because she's a fabulous specimen and she threatens you.

She's a little hook-nose bitch, just like her mother.

Her mother's a first-class lady. I should have stayed with her.

Then why didn't you?

God only knows.

God knows, all right. Jesus knows. That you're a hypocrite and a fucking liar. She was frigid and boring and hairy. You wanted smooth white legs, some nice shiksa pussy, come in the Virgin Mary's mouth—wanted it so bad that you took me right in the examining room, all those patients still in the waiting room, and raped me, you bastard!

If any raping went on, it was you that did it—

Raped me and used me. Now you want to give what I earned—my blood money—to your hook-nosed bitch.

Enough, I'm tired. I have to operate early.

You're tired? I'm tired too. Of your bullshit. Giving her all those clothes and that trip—she's already spoiled rotten.

She's a great kid and she deserves it. Discussion ended.

She slurps, just like her mother.

Her mother gave me a first-class kid.

And me? What did I give you? Tore myself up—I've never been the same!

Tore *yourself? That's a laugh. You had a pelvis someone could drive a truck through.*

It *tore* me, you fucking bastard. What did *I* give you, you fucking bastard?

A weirdo.

Fuck you!

He's a weird kid, Christina. No two ways about it.

Listen to me, you fucking kike. He's beautiful—that hair, like a Greek god! Those dreamy eyes. A *small, straight nose.* And tall—he's already your size, going to be taller than you, going to be able to beat the shit out of you when I tell him to, to protect his mama.

He's weird, Christina—got all of your weird genes. Ever try to talk to him? Course not—how could you? Too damn pickled—

Fuck you, he's beaut—

Try it some time, you drunken moron. Say hello and catch the weird smile he gives you. He's like you—bizarre, stays in his room all day, all night. God knows what he does in there.

He's studying. He's an intellectual—it's in his eyes.

Studying what? He's flunking out of school, hasn't gotten better than a D in three years. But you wouldn't know about that, would you? The headmaster doesn't call you*—nobody calls you because everyone knows you're too drunk to talk. They call* me. *Teachers, counselors, every one of them thinks he's weird. The headmaster called me last week. In fact, I had to bribe him with a new science lab to keep your beautiful kid from getting booted out.*

Did you tell the headmaster he had a crazy, cruel father who never paid any attention to him or to his mother, whom he raped? That his father killed Jesus and wanted to kill his wife, too, so he could fuck candy-stripers? Did you tell him—

*No friends, no attention span, sits in class all day staring off into space—*your *genes, all the way, Christina. God only knows if he can overcome it. The headmaster suggested that he get psychiatric help. I talked to Emil Diefenbach—he works with a few teenagers, said he'd be happy to meet him.*

You're not taking him to any kike head-shrinker.

I'll take him anywhere I damn well please.

Not my son.

He's a goddamned weirdo, Christina—that's what you gave me, a freak. Maybe he can be helped, I don't know. I'm going to give it a shot.

Over my dead body, you filthy, scheming bastard. All you want is to destroy him—poison his brain the way you poisoned mine, take away his share so you can give all of it to your hook-nosed—

Pathetic.

—bitch. I won't let you!

And how do you propose to stop me?

I'll get a lawyer. A mother has rights.

You're no mother. You're nothing, Christina. You haven't been a mother—or anything else—for a long time.

I'm his parent. Jesus put me here to protect him.

I'm his parent too. The only sane one he's got.

Don't you dare mess with his head, you bastard!

Good night, Christina.

He's not yours to mess with, you bastard! There's not an ounce of you in him!

Discussion closed, Christina. Get out of my way.

Take a good look at him, you bastard! His hair, his nose—there's no kike in him. He's not yours.

If only it were true. Let go of my arm.

It's *true,* you stupid kike bastard. He's not yours—he's Schwann's!

(Silence.)

He's Schwann's, you asshole. Don't you see the resemblance?

What the hell *are you talking about?*

Ah, now he's upset, now he wants to kill me. Get away from me—I'll scream.

I said, *what are you talking about, Christina?*

The summer Schwann stayed with us, he had me every day is what I'm talking about. We did it in the house, on the beach, in the pool!

(Silence.)

Take a good look at him. Remember Schwann's face. Strong resemblance, isn't it, Charles?

Absurd.

You were absurd, Charles. Playing hotshot doctor, giving

Schwann your pompous speeches about surgery and its place in society, thinking he was looking up to you and thought you were so hot, calling you *Herr Doktor* Professor, and all the time it was *me* he was after. *I* was the reason he kept kissing up to you, telling you how goddamned wonderful you were. The moment you walked out the door and left him here with your books, I was Johnny-on-the-spot and we were climbing all over each other and loving it and he gave me a beautiful baby with no filthy kike blood in it, SO STAY AWAY FROM HIM, YOU BASTARD, DON'T YOU DARE TOUCH HIM, HE'S NOT YOURS!

(Silence. Heavy footsteps.)

Ah! Now he's quiet, walking off with his tail tucked between his legs. *Now* he's got nothing snotty to say!

43

"The shithead will be proud of you," said Shmeltzer as he entered the conference room. "Is this communication going to be horizontal or vertical?"

"Diagonal," said Daniel. He was tacking a map of Jerusalem and its exurbs onto the wall next to the blackboard. The spots where both victims had been dumped were circled in red crayon, as was the cave.

Shmeltzer took his place at the table. He nodded at the Chinaman and Daoud while reaching for the coffeepot. It was eight in the morning, twenty hours after the discovery of the bloody rock. The room was on the ground floor of Headquarters, white-walled and refrigerated by an overexuberant air conditioner.

Daniel finished hanging the map and picked up a pointer. Shmeltzer passed him the coffeepot and he filled his cup. The Chinaman and Daoud lit up. The cold air filled quickly with smoke and tension.

"Where's Cohen?" Daniel asked the Chinaman.

"Don't know. He was supposed to meet me at seven, do a walk-through of the Armenian Quarter. I haven't seen him or heard from him."

"Ah, the vagaries of youth," said Shmeltzer. He filled his cup, took a long swallow.

"We can't afford vagaries," said Daniel. He picked up the phone, left a message with the switchboard for Samal Cohen to call in immediately, then hung up, irritated. Just when he'd thought the kid was shaping up. So much for flexibility.

"Let's begin," he said, tapping the pointer to the map. Last night he'd called each of them, informed them about the cave. Now he went over the basics, gave them time to take notes before returning to his seat and picking up the Forensics report.

"We owe Meir Steinfeld a dinner at Cow on the Roof. He worked all night and came up with more than we could have hoped for. There were two classes of animal blood in the cave—rodent and canine—and one human sample, type O, Rh positive. Both Fatma and Juliet were O-positive, but they differed on the haptoglobin test. Juliet was type two, the commonest, but Fatma was type one, which shows up in only about fifteen percent of the population. All Steinfeld found was type one, so it looks as if Juliet wasn't killed in the cave."

"That's no proof Fatma *was*," said Shmeltzer. "Fifteen percent isn't that rare."

"No proof," said Daniel, "but strong indications. Steinfeld estimates the volume of blood loss as monumental. Dr. Levi confirms it would have had to be fatal. The anthropometric analysis of the outline on the rock indicates a slender female of Fatma's height. A copious amount of dried blood was found in the dirt at the head of the rock, suggesting a deep, draining head or neck wound. The blood flow over the sides indicates smaller, multiple wounds on the trunk. Know of any other victims who fit that description?"

"For the sake of argument," said Shmeltzer, "here's another scenario: The Bedouins cut up one of their own women on that rock. Executed her for fucking the wrong guy or talking out of turn, then buried her somewhere in the desert."

"The time frame doesn't work," said Daniel. "Steinfeld estimates the age of the blood at three to six weeks—nothing he'll swear to, but it's definitely older than eight days, which is how long the Bedouin have been grazing in that part of the desert. Border Patrol's had a good fix on them for some time—since the end of the rainy season they've been up north, nowhere near the cave. And the shred of cloth fits the description of the shift

Fatma was last seen wearing." He paused. "It's not ironclad, but it's well worth pursuing."

Shmeltzer nodded and drank more coffee. "All right," he said, "two killing grounds. Why?"

"I don't know," said Daniel. "And neither body was washed in that cave—there's been no water down there for four months and both bodies were washed thoroughly."

"You could bring water into the desert in bottles," said the Chinaman. "Last summer we spent a couple of weeks at my wife's kibbutz. They put me to work at the carp ponds, schlepping bottles of distilled back and forth in order to backflush the filters. Big plastic ones—they hold eight liters each, weigh about thirty kilos. Two would be enough to wash a body, don't you think?"

Shmeltzer got up and took a close look at the map. "We're talking a four-kilometer climb, Yossi. Down a mountainside in the dark. Know anyone who could pull that off while hauling sixty kilos of water, maybe a forty-kilo corpse as well?"

The Chinaman grinned and flexed a huge bicep.

"Is that a confession, Goliath?" Shmeltzer shook his head and returned to his seat.

"The water could have been carried down on donkeyback," said Daniel, "but no one's spotted any donkeys down there, and it would be tremendously inefficient. The more logical assumption is that Fatma was murdered in the cave and most of her blood was allowed to drain out there. The body was then moved to the second place, where the final cleanup took place. Maybe the same place Juliet was killed."

"He kills her, then moves her to wash her," said the Chinaman. "Very weird. What's the point?"

"Like a sacrifice on an altar," said Shmeltzer. "A *korban*, straight out of the Bible." He smiled sourly. "Maybe we should have grilled Kagan's people more thoroughly."

Korbanot, the ancient Judaic sacrifices that antedated prayer. Daniel had thought of it himself—the implications disturbed him. Looking across the table, he sought out the single non-Jewish face. Daoud's expression was noncommittal.

"Yes," he said. "More of that same ceremonial quality." He found a piece of chalk and wrote on the blackboard:

FATMA: Killed in cave, washed ?
JULIET: Killed ? , washed ?

"There are caves near Ein Qerem," said Daoud. "Not far from where Juliet was found. And some of the streams there are still running."

Daniel nodded. "The Border Patrol began searching them at sunrise. Afif called in an hour ago—they've found nothing so far."

"Maybe we've got more than one kill spot," said Shmeltzer, "because we've got more than one killer. Why not a whole group of murderous bastards, some crazy cult? Way things are going, it wouldn't surprise me. They could bring water down to the cave in small containers. If they used their homes, there'd be God knows how many kill spots to choose from."

"A caravan of people would be conspicuous in the desert," said Daniel. "Afif's men would have been likely to spot them with the infrared."

"Those boys are eagle-eyes but they're not infallible," said Shmeltzer. "They missed a murderer hiking four kilometers with a body over his back and gear—the knives, the sheet, some kind of portable light. Assuming he cut her at night."

"All right," said Daniel, "we won't rule it out." He wrote: MULTIPLE KILLERS? on the board. Pausing to take a sip of coffee, he found it had turned tepid and replaced the cup on the table.

"Something else," he said. "From the outside, the cave looks impenetrable. Someone would have had to inspect it to know about it. It's not exactly a garden spot—the guides don't take tourists down there."

"Which is why I thought of the Bedouins," said Shmeltzer. "They know every crack in the sand. Or maybe we've got murderous archaeologists on our hands."

"Contact the university, Nahum, and the Nature Conservancy. Find out if any digs have been planned in the area, any groups taken on hikes down there within the last year or so."

Shmeltzer nodded and made a note.

"Next order of business," said Daniel. "I got a call from the army about Aljuni—the wife murderer from Gaza. He got tired of being watched, finally agreed to a polygraph. Tel Aviv will do it and send us the report. Any other updates? Then on to Little Hook's story about the flat-eyed American."

"Little Hook's a treacherous piece of dirt," said Shmeltzer. "He'd just as soon lie as breathe."

"Any reason for him to make up a story like this one?" asked Daniel.

Shmeltzer held out one hand and ticked off fingers. "Avoiding a larceny bust, trying to curry favor with us, attention seeking."

"I don't think so, Nahum," said the Chinaman. "The lowlife have come around to our side on this one. This Butcher shit is wiping them out financially. Red Amira may have spun a yarn for Little Hook, but my bet is that he's repeating it faithfully."

"Putting aside Little Hook's credibility," said Daniel, "there are problems fitting the story to our case. From the way it sounds, Flat Eyes was looking for a curbside pickup. Nothing about our killer indicates that type of impulsive selection. And neither of our victims was working the streets: Fatma was no whore; Juliet had just gotten into town—she had no time to set up her brothel contacts and had no street experience here in Israel."

"She streetwalked in Haifa," said the Chinaman.

"For one day before she got caught. And she was clumsy—the Northern District detective who picked her up told me he was surprised she was a professional. She had no idea sex for hire was legal as long as she kept her mouth shut. He caught her breaking the soliciting law aggressively, throwing herself at sailors. No doubt she would have gotten smarter had she stayed alive and eventually found employment, but the whores and pimps you've spoken to never spotted her or Fatma working Jerusalem, did they, Yossi?"

"No," admitted the big man. "Neither of them have been seen at the pickup places. But Juliet could have done some back-alley stuff. And it's possible Fatma wasn't that innocent. Her boyfriend was slime—maybe he sold her to others."

"Maybe," said Daniel. "According to the brother, Abdelatif said she was dead, which could have meant she'd turned promiscuous, but no one spotted her hooking and the regular girls always notice newcomers." He shook his head. "No, I don't see either of them meeting the killer at curbside. This wasn't just quick sex—they were shot up with heroin, injected without resistance. To me that says some kind of seduction was used to snare them. Juliet was a drug user, so for her the heroin may have actually been the lure. But what convinced a traditional girl like Fatma to lie there and get stuck?"

"First thrills," said the Chinaman. "When they fall, they fall fast."

"We have evidence she hadn't fallen that far. A few days

before she left the monastery, she waited in the olive grove for Anwar, begged him to help her reconcile with the family. So her corruption was far from complete. Taking that needle was a big step—someone very credible had to convince her to do it, or trick her. Someone exploiting a position of trust. Which is why we spent so much time on the doctors, why I put Elias on the monk." To Daoud: "How's that going?"

"The same. He starts walking, then all of a sudden he stops and heads back for the monastery. The farthest he's ever gotten is to the end of the Via Dolorosa. Usually he returns after just a few steps. As if something's bothering him."

"Stick with it. Maybe you'll find out what it is."

Daoud nodded, then said, "One question, Pakad."

"What is it?"

"The issue of the casual pickup. We're dealing with a psychologically disturbed person, a deviate. Perhaps he deviated from his own rules and yielded to impulse."

"Perhaps he did, Elias. But why would he go for Amira Nasser? Fatma and Juliet looked remarkably alike, which implies he's after a certain type—small, pretty brunettes wearing earrings. And he probably likes them young—Juliet's baby face fooled him. Without her wig, Amira is a petite brunette, but someone watching her work wouldn't know that. He'd see a redhead, hot pants and fishnets, all plastered with makeup."

"Maybe he goes for different types for different things," said the Chinaman. "Redheads for sex, brunettes for killing."

"Wait a minute," said Shmeltzer. "Before we go any further with this, let's bear in mind that this American guy didn't do a damned thing that was incriminating. He offered cash, the whore turned him down, he walked away, end of story. *Supposedly* he scared her because she didn't like his smile. *Supposedly* he had flat eyes—whatever that means. Very weak, boys. And the fact that it comes via the hunchback makes it weaker than weak."

"I agree with you," said Daniel, "but weak is better than nothing. And having stated all the problems with the story, it still holds my interest. The fact that Amira was scared by this guy can't be brushed off—prostitutes get good at assessing their customers because their safety depends on it. If Amira thought there was something weird about him, there probably was. And the time frame is appealing: Thursday night—a murder a week. Now, exactly how did she describe him, Yossi?"

The Chinaman flipped through his note pad.

"According to Little Hook he was 'an American with crazy eyes . . . he came out of nowhere . . . she figured he'd been hiding somewhere off the road.' I took a look at the area—there's a small field someone could hide in. Forensics found some tire marks, lots of footprints, but all of it was too indistinct to identify."

"Go on," said Daniel.

" 'He offered sex for money, but his eyes scared her and she refused.' I asked Little Hook what was wrong with the eyes and he said Amira had told him they were 'flat. Mad . . . A strange smile, very wide, a grin. But the grin of a killer.' As to what made it a killer's grin, he said, 'Not a happy grin, very crazy.' "

The big man closed the pad. "I tried to get more—squeezed him hard enough to get juice, but that's all there is. If you want, I can pick him up again."

"Just see that he stays in town." Daniel got up, wrote AMERICAN? on the board.

"To Amira," he said, "*American* could have meant any number of things—a genuine American, someone who spoke English or wore American clothes. Or someone who *looked* American, which could translate to fair-skinned, big-boned, a T-shirt with the American flag—who knows? But at the very least we're talking about some kind of foreigner—a man with a non-Levantine appearance. Which gives us a possible line of inquiry."

"Comparisons with foreign homicides," said Shmeltzer. "America and Europe."

"Exactly. Our new Interpol liaison in Bonn is a fellow named Friedman. I've been trying to reach him since Yossi told me Little Hook's story. He's out of town—no one in his office will say where. When he calls in I'm going to have him contact all the Interpol chiefs in Europe, see if they can find records of similar crimes within the past ten years. It shouldn't be difficult, with the exception of the Germans, their homicide rates are generally as low as ours. A vicious one will stand out. The American situation's more complicated: They record tremendous numbers of sex murders each year and there's no central reporting—each city has its own police jurisdiction. They seldom communicate with one another. Lately, though, the FBI's gotten involved—they've been collating homicides and finding serial murderers who travel across the country, killing people. They're in the process of setting up a computer bank, and I think I have a way of hooking into it without going through all the red tape. In the meantime, though, it would be nice to talk to Amira. Any information on her whereabouts, Yossi?"

"All three of us picked up rumors that she's back in Jordan," said the Chinaman, "living in one of the towns outside Amman. Elias and I heard she's in Suweilih. Cohen was told Hisban. When we tried to trace the origin of the rumors, all we got is something that somebody told somebody after he heard it from somebody."

"Weaker than weak," said Shmeltzer. "Speaking of rumors, Shin Bet's confirmed Darousha's definitely homosexual. Had an affair last year with a Jewish doctor. Hajab the watchman spends his off-hours at Darousha's place in Ramallah, doing odd jobs. Maybe they're into funny business. Want Shin Bet to stay on it?"

"It's low priority," said Daniel, remembering what Ben David had said about latent homosexuals. "More important, have them contact the Mossad operative in Amman and run a trace on Amira."

"They weren't overjoyed about the Beirut brothel, won't like this any better, Dani. The whore's no security risk. The case isn't political. Having an operative leave Amman to comb the smaller towns is damned conspicuous."

"This whole mess has turned political," said Daniel. "Laufer made a point of informing me that the Syrians are preparing a U.N. resolution 'condemning the Zionist occupation for the wanton slaughter of innocent Arab women.' After the automatic majority pushes it through, the heat's going to be turned way up, so you may get more cooperation than you expected. Besides, we don't need anything flashy from the operative, just a location."

"If they locate her, then what? Abduction?"

"First let's see if they can trace her. We'll take it from there."

"Okay," said Shmeltzer, thinking of another breakfast with his Sheraton friend. It would be all business from now on—no more fantasies of pillow play. Since he'd met Eva, other women seemed fashioned of cardboard.

"Any other questions?" said Daniel.

The Chinaman raised a finger. "What happens if we do get something interesting from Interpol or the Americans?"

"Then we check out airline arrivals from the country where the matching crime occurred. Pare down our lists and start interviewing foreigners."

The big man groaned.

"Yes, I know," said Daniel. "Fun for all of us."

The phone rang. Daniel picked it up, heard Avi Cohen say "Dani?" in an infuriatingly cheerful tone of voice.

"Yes, Cohen. You'd better have a good reason for missing the meeting."

"Real good, Dani." The kid was gushing. "The best."

44

It was kind of funny the way it happened, thought Avi. Ironic, even. But he'd pulled it off.

He left the Russian Compound and walked to the cobbled parking lot, exhilarated, holding on to his good mood even after four hours of paperwork. He'd sweated through every word of it, had called no one for assistance. Wanting to prove to Sharavi that he could handle anything when he put his mind to it.

The BMW was parked between two unmarkeds. He unlocked it, got in, popped the clutch, and spun out of the compound on squealing tires, past the disapproving eyes of two uniforms. Turning onto Rehov Yafo, he sped west for twenty meters before screeching to a halt behind a cement truck with an engine as loud as a fighter jet.

A traffic jam. The glut of cars on Yafo was thick as pitch, motorists leaning on their horns, pedestrians taking advantage of the situation and jaywalking between the inert automobiles. He watched as a uniform on horseback blew his whistle and tried, without success, to get things moving.

Classy, he thought, watching the mounted officer prance in and out of the jam. The horse was a fine-looking Arabian, its rider an older guy, looked Moroccan. Still a *samal,* Avi noticed. No career advancement, but the guy sat tall in the saddle. Keeping his dignity amidst all the fumes and clamor.

The first time he'd seen a mounted policeman had been right after the '67 liberation, on a trip to Jerusalem with his father, some sort of official business. They'd been stuck in a traffic jam just like this one, Avi a timid kid of five, eating sunflower seeds and spitting them out the car window, his father punching the horn and cursing, griping that an administrative assistant to an MK deserved better.

That's what I want to be, Abba.

What, an administrative assistant?

A horse policeman.

Don't be silly, boy. They're showpieces, useless. A bit of candy for the Eastern types.

They eat candy, Abba?

His father rolled his eyes, lit one of those smelly Panamanian cigars, gave Avi an absent pat on the knee, and said:

Back in Iraq and Morocco the Jews weren't allowed to ride horses—the Arabs wouldn't let them. So when they came to Israel, the first thing they wanted to do was jump on a horse. We bought a few for them, told them they could ride if they became policemen. It made them happy, Avi.

That one doesn't look happy, Abba. He looks tough.

He's happy, believe me. We made all of them happy, that's what politics is all about.

Avi looked in the rearview mirror, saw a light turn green, and watched a herd of westbound cars rushing to join the tail end of the jam. He put on the emergency brake, got out of the BMW, and walked to the center of the road in order to see what the problem was.

"Get back in, you idiot!" someone shouted. "Don't be standing there when it's time to move!"

Avi ignored the chorus of horns that rose behind him. Little chance of anything moving, he thought. Traffic was at a standstill clear up to the King George intersection.

"Idiot! Subversive!"

He could see what was causing it now: An eastbound cab had stalled. For some reason the driver had attempted to push his vehicle across the road into westbound traffic and had ended up straddling both sides, trapped by gridlock. Now all lanes in both directions were blocked and tempers were heating.

Avi looked for escape—he'd jump the sidewalk if he had to. But both sides of Yafo were bordered by shops, not even a break for a wrong-way alley.

Wonderful—he'd be late for his appointment with Sharavi. The Yemenite had sounded none too pleased about his missing the staff meeting.

No problem there. He'd be pleased when he found out how well things had gone. All the paperwork wrapped up neatly.

He heard a whistle, looked up, and saw the mounted policeman shouting at him and waving him back inside. He pulled out his police ID but the uniform had already turned his back and didn't see it.

"Showpiece," said Avi, and got back in the car. Rolling up the windows and turning on the air conditioner, he lit up a cigarette, turned off the engine, put the key in auxiliary, and slipped a Culture Club cassette into the tape deck. "Karma Chameleon" came on. That crazy George guy was as queer as a five-legged sheep but he could really sing.

Avi turned up the volume, hummed along to lyrics he didn't fully understand, and blessed his good fortune.

To hell with horses and meetings and superior officers. Nothing was going to spoil his good mood.

He reclined the seat, sat low, and reminisced about last night.

Ironic, really funny, how he'd almost missed it. Because the balcony had become almost a hobby, he'd been spending so much time out there the South African girl was starting to nag. ("Are you some kind of *voyeur,* Avraham? Shall I buy you a *telescope?*")

Generally he could keep her annoyance at bay with affection and time-outs for first-rate sex—the little extra moves that let a girl know you had her pleasure in mind. He made sure always to give her a good workout, varying the positions, stretching it out until she was right on the brink, then backing off, then moving in again, so when she came she was really tired and fell right asleep. Unaware, moments later, when he left the bed.

Then back to the balcony.

Last night, though, he'd been exhausted himself. The girl had prepared two giant steaks for dinner—her monthly allowance was unbelievable; the only time he'd seen filet mignon like that was when his family traveled to Europe.

Steak and fried potatoes and chopped salad. Along with a bottle of Bordeaux and half a chocolate cake. After all that, Avi had felt fuzzy around the edges but still able to oblige, thank you, madame.

She'd taken hold of him, pulled him to the bed, giggling. Then forty-four minutes (he'd timed it) of straightaway pumping with the girl holding on to him as if he were a life preserver, Avi feeling himself sweat, the wine popping out of him in fermented droplets.

After that one, he'd been tired too. Listening to the rhythm of the girl's breathing, then sinking into deep, dreamless sleep.

No balcony, for the first time since he'd been on the Wolfson surveillance.

Then screams—he didn't know how many of them he'd missed. But loud enough to yank him awake, shuddering. The girl awoke, too, sat up holding the sheet to her body, just like in the movies—what the hell was she hiding?

Another scream. Avi swung his legs out of bed, shook his head to make sure it was really happening.

"Avraham," the girl croaked. "What's going on?"

Avi was up now. The girl reached out for him.

"Avraham!"

The grogginess had made her look ugly, thought Avi. Damaged. And he knew that it was the way she'd look in five years. All the time. While running to the balcony he decided he'd break it off with her, soon.

"What is it, Avraham?"

"Shh."

Malkovsky was in the courtyard, barefoot and wearing a white robe that made him look like a polar bear. Lumbering in circles, chasing a child—a girl of about twelve.

One of the daughters, second to the oldest. Avi remembered her because she always looked so serious, walked separately from the others.

Sheindel—that was her name.

Sheindel was in pajamas. Her blond hair, usually braided, fanned around her shoulders as she ran from the polar bear.

Screaming: *"No, no, no! No more!"*

"Come here, Sheindeleh! Come here. I'm sorry!"

"No! Get away! I hate you!"

"Shah shtill! Quiet!" Malkovsky reached out to grab her, moving sluggishly because of his weight.

Avi ran back into the bedroom. Throwing on trousers and a shirt that he didn't bother to button, he kept his ears attuned to the cries from below.

"No! Get away from me! I hate you! Aahh!"

"Stop running, I order you!"

"I hate you! I hate you! Aaahhh!"

Avi put the light on. The South African honey yelped and threw herself under the covers. He fumbled as his eyes adjusted to the sudden brightness. Where were his handcuffs, dammit! Always prepared and now look at him . . . the wine . . . Ah, there on the nightstand. He pocketed them. Now the gun . . .

"Help!" Sheindel was screaming.

"Shut your mouth, stupid girl!"

"No, no, get away! Help!"

Avi's eyes were clear now. He found the 9 mm hanging in its holster over the chair, pulled the gun out, stuck it under his waistband, and ran for the door.

"Is it terrorists?" asked the girl, still under the covers.

"No. Back to sleep." Avi flung open the door, thinking: There are different types of terrorism.

He sprinted for the stairwell, leaped down the stairs four at a time, pumped up and strangely elated. When he got to the courtyard, lights were switching on throughout the nearby apartments, checkering the complex.

Malkovsky's back was to him. Sheindel was nowhere in sight. Then Avi heard sucking sobs and hyperventilation and realized that she was hidden behind her father, concealed by his mass. She'd backed herself into a corner. Malkovsky was advancing toward her, huffing, arms spread wide.

"Sheindel," he cajoled. "I'm your *tateh.*"

"No!" Sob, breath. "You're a"—sob, breath—*"rasha!"* Evil man.

"Don't touch her," said Avi.

Malkovsky jerked around, saw the Beretta pointed at him. His eyes were agitated, his face moonlight-pale and greasy with perspiration.

"What?" he said.

"I'm a police detective. Get away from her, Malkovsky. Lie on the ground."

Malkovsky hesitated. Avi walked up to him, keeping the gun aimed. Malkovsky stepped backward. Avi grabbed the lapel of the white robe with one hand, put one foot around Malkovsky's ankle, and tripped him with a judo move he'd learned in basic training.

The bigger they were, the easier they fell, he thought, watching Malkovsky collapse facedown. Something to do with leverage, according to the self-defense instructor, but until now Avi had never really believed it.

Working swiftly, enjoying his competence, he yanked Malkovsky's arms behind his back. The man's corpulence made it hard to stretch the limbs far enough to cuff them, but he tugged hard and finally clamped the cuffs over soft, hairy wrists.

"Oy, you're hurting me," said Malkovsky. His breathing was labored and rapid. He turned his head to the side and Avi saw blood seeping into his mustache and beard; the fall had bruised him.

"Tsk, tsk," said Avi, making sure the cuffs were secure.

Malkovsky moaned.

Wouldn't it be funny if the fat bastard gave out right here—heart attack or something? True justice, but the paperwork would be a nightmare.

"Oy."

"Shut up."

Malkovsky safely trussed, Avi turned to the child. She was sitting on the ground, knees drawn up, head buried in her arms.

"It's okay," he said. "You're all right."

Her small body convulsed. Avi wanted to comfort her, didn't know if touching her was the right thing to do.

Footsteps sounded in the courtyard. An older couple—neighbors coming to gawk. Avi showed them his police identification and told them to go back inside. They stared at Malkovsky's prostrate bulk. Avi repeated his order and they complied. More tenants came filing into the courtyard. Avi shooed them away, forcefully, until finally he was alone again with Malkovsky and the girl. But the others were still there, watching. He could hear windows sliding open, whispers and mutters. Saw their silhouettes, outlined muddily in the half-light.

Real voyeurs. A damned exhibition.

Where the hell was the mother?

Malkovsky started praying, something familiar—Avi had heard it before but couldn't place it.

The girl sobbed. He put his hand on her shoulder and she jerked away.

He told Malkovsky to stay put, kept his eye on Sheindel, and went to the door of the Malkovsky apartment. The wife opened the door before he'd finished the first knock; she'd been waiting behind it all the time.

She just stood there, staring at him. Her hair was long and blond—first time he'd ever seen it uncovered.

"Come outside," Avi told her.

She walked out slowly, as if sleepwalking. Looked at her husband and began cursing him in Yiddish.

Well, listen to that, thought Avi—*piece of shit, whoremaster*—he wouldn't have thought a religious one knew words like that.

"Bayla, please," said Malkovsky. "Help me."

His wife walked over to him, smiled at Avi, then began kicking the fat man violently in the ribs.

Malkovsky bellowed with pain, squirmed helplessly, like a steer trussed for slaughter.

Sheindel was biting her knuckles to keep from hyperventilating.

Avi pulled the wife away, told her: "Cut it out, take care of your daughter."

Mrs. Malkovsky curled her hands into claws, looked down at her husband, and spat on him.

"Momzer! Meeskeit! Shoyn opgetrent?"

Sheindel let go of her knuckles and started to wail.

"Oy," moaned Malkovsky, praying as his wife cursed him. Avi recognized the prayer, now. The *El Molei Rakhamim*, the prayer for the dead.

"Shtik dreck! Yentzer!" screamed Bayla Malkovsky. *"Shoyn opgetrent? Shoyn opgetrent—gai in drerd arein!"* She lunged at Malkovsky. Avi restrained her and she twisted in his grasp, spitting and cursing, then began clawing at *him*, going for *his* eyes.

Avi slapped her across the face. She stared at him, stupidly. A pretty woman, actually, when you looked past the grimness and the hysteria and the baggy dress. She started crying, clenched her jaws shut to stem the tears. Meanwhile the kid was sobbing her heart out.

"Cut it out," he told the mother. "Do your job, for God's sake."

Mrs. Malkovsky went limp and started to weep, joining her daughter in a sobbing duet.

Great. Yom Kippur.

"Oy," she said, tearing at her hair. *"Riboynoy shel oylam!"*

"Oy, nothing," said Avi. "God helps those who help themselves. If you'd done your job in the first place, this wouldn't have happened."

The woman stopped mid-sob, frozen with shame. She yanked out a healthy clump of hair and nodded her head violently. Up and down, up and down, bobbing like some kind of robot whose controls had short-circuited.

"Take care of your daughter," said Avi, losing patience. "Go inside."

Still bobbing, the woman capitulated, walking over to Sheindel and touching her lightly on the shoulder. The girl looked up, wet-faced. Her mother stretched out arms that had been forced into steadiness, uttered vague maternal comfort.

Avi watched the kid's reaction, the gun still trained on Malkovsky's broad back.

"Sheindeleh," said Mrs. Malkovsky. "Bubbeleh." She knelt, put her arm around the girl. Sheindel allowed herself to be embraced but made no move to reciprocate.

Well, thought Avi, at least she hadn't pushed her away, so maybe there was something still there. Still, to let it go this far . . .

Mrs. Malkovsky stood and raised Sheindel to her feet.

"Get inside," said Avi, surprised by how gruff he sounded.

The two of them walked into the apartment.

"Now, as for you," Avi told Malkovsky.

The fat man groaned.

"What's the matter?" said a new voice. "What's going on?"

A little bald man with a gray bandage of a mustache had come out into the courtyard. He was wearing a sport coat over pajamas, looked ridiculous. Greenberg, the building manager. Avi had seen him nosing around.

"You," said Greenberg, staring at the Beretta. "The one who uses the tennis court and swimming pool all the time."

"I'm Detective Cohen, on special assignment from police headquarters and I need you to make a call for me."

"What has *he* done?"

"Broken the laws of God and man. Go back to your flat,

phone 100, and tell the operator that Detective Avraham Cohen needs a police wagon dispatched to this address."

Malkovsky started praying again. A symphony of window-squeaks and whispers played in counterpoint to his entreaties.

"This is a nice place, very tidy," said Greenberg, still trying to absorb the reality of the moment.

"Then let's keep it that way. Make that call before everyone finds out you rent to dangerous criminals."

"Criminals? Never—"

"Call 100," said Avi. "*Run.* Or I'll shoot him right here, leave the mess for you to clean up."

Malkovsky moaned.

Greenberg ran.

45

Laufer's secretary liked Pakad Sharavi, had always thought of him as kind of cute, one of the nicer ones. So when he entered the waiting room she smiled at him, ready for small talk. But the smile he offered in return was brittle, a poor excuse for cordiality, and when he brushed past her instead of sitting down, she was caught off guard.

"Pakad—you can't do that! He's in a conference!"

He ignored her, opened the door.

The deputy commander was conferring with his soda water bottle, polishing the metal, peering up the spout. When he saw Daniel he put it down quickly and said, "What is this, Sharavi!"

"I need to know where he is."

"I have no time for your nonsense, Sharavi. Leave at once."

"Not until you tell me where he is, Tat Nitzav."

The deputy commander bounded out of his chair, came speeding around the desk, and marched up to Daniel, stopping just short of collision.

"Get the hell out."

"I want to know where Malkovsky is."

"He's not your concern."

"He's my suspect. I want to question him."

"Out."

Daniel ignored the digression. "Malkovsky's a suspect in my murder case. I needed to talk to him."

"That's crap," said Laufer. "He's not the Butcher—I ascertained that myself."

"What evidence did he present to convince you of his innocence?"

"Don't try to interrogate me, Sharavi. Suffice it to say he's out of your bailiwick."

Daniel struggled with his anger. "The man's dangerous. If Cohen hadn't caught him, he'd still be raping children under official protection."

"Ah, Cohen," said the deputy commander. "Another bit of insubordination that you—and he—will be answering to. Of course, the charges against *him* will be mitigated by inexperience. Improper influence by a commanding officer."

"Cohen was—"

"Yes, I know, Sharavi. The girlfriend at Wolfson, one of life's little coincidences." Laufer extended a finger, poked at the air. "Don't insult me with your little games, you bastard. You want to play games? Fine. Here's a new one called suspension: You're off the Butcher case—off *any* case, without pay, pending a disciplinary hearing. When I'm finished with you, you'll be directing traffic in Katamon Tet and feeling grateful about it."

"No," said Daniel. "The case is mine. I'm staying with it."

Laufer stared at him. "Have you lost your mind?"

When Daniel didn't answer, the deputy commander went behind his desk, sat, took out a leather-bound calendar, and began making notes.

"Traffic detail, Sharavi. Try calling the pretty boy in Australia if you think it'll help you. Your *protekzia*'s long gone—dead and buried." The deputy commander laughed out loud. "Funny thing is, it's your own doing—you fucked yourself, just like now. Nosing into things that don't concern you." Laufer lifted a pack of English Ovals off the desk, found it empty and tossed it aside. "Like a little brown rat, rooting in garbage."

"If I hadn't rooted," said Daniel, "you'd still be pushing paper in Beersheva."

Laufer made a strangling noise and slammed his hand on

the desk. His eyes bulged and his complexion turned the color of ripe plums. Daniel watched him inhale deeply, then expel breath through stiffened lips, saw the rise and fall of his barrel chest, the stubby fingers splayed on the desk top, twitching and drumming as if yearning to do violence.

Then suddenly he was smiling—a cold, collaborative smirk.

"Aha. Now I understand. This, beating Rashmawi, it's all something psychiatric, eh, Sharavi? You're trying for a stress pension."

"I'm fine," said Daniel. "I want to work on my case. To catch criminals rather than protect them."

"You *have* no case. You're on suspension as of this moment." Laufer held out a fleshy palm. "Hand over your badge."

"You don't really want it."

"What!"

"If I walk out of here under suspension, the first place I'm going is the press."

"All contact between you and the press is forbidden. Violate that order and you're finished for good."

"That's okay," said Daniel. "I'm allergic to traffic."

Laufer leaned back in his chair, stared at the ceiling for several moments, then lowered his gaze and directed it back at Daniel.

"Sharavi, Sharavi, do you actually think you're intimidating me with your threats? What if you do talk? What will it amount to? A nosy little detective, unable to solve the case he's charged with, tries to distract attention away from his incompetence by whining about administrative manners. Small stuff, even by local standards."

The deputy commander folded his hands over his paunch. His face was calm, almost beatific, but the fingers kept drumming.

A poor bluffer, thought Daniel. Shoshi would wipe him out in poker.

"I'm not talking local," said Daniel. "I'm talking international. The foreign press is sure to love this one—child rapist shielded by the police as he stalks the streets of Jerusalem, secret deals cut with Hassidic *rebbe.* 'The suspect was apprehended assaulting his own daughter while under privileged protection of Deputy Commander Avigdor Laufer. The officer who apprehended him has been disciplined—' "

"It goes higher than Avigdor Laufer, you fool! You don't know what you're dealing with!"

"The higher the better. They'll eat it with a spoon."

Laufer was on his feet again. Glowering, pointing. "Do it and you'll be finished, permanently—a blighted record, loss of security rating, no pension, no future. Any decent job will be closed to you. You'll be lucky to find work shoveling shit with the Arabs."

"Tat Nitzav," said Daniel, "we don't know each other well. Let me acquaint you with my situation. Since the first day of my marriage, my in-laws have been trying to get me to move to America. They're fine Jews, believe deeply in the state of Israel, but they want their only daughter near them. I've a standing offer of a new house, new car, tuition for my kids, and a job with my father-in-law's corporation. A *very* decent job—executive responsibility, regular hours, and more money than I'll ever earn here, more than *you* ever will. The only hold the job has over me is the job itself—doing it properly."

The deputy commander was silent. Daniel took his badge out of his wallet.

"Still want it?"

"Damn you," said Laufer. "Damn you to hell."

Lucky, thought Daniel, that he was a pencil pusher, no detective. Al Birnbaum had never owned a corporation, had spent his working years selling paper goods to printing companies. And even that was old news—he'd been retired for a decade.

46

He left Laufer's office and went to his own, having gotten what he'd wanted but feeling no flush of victory.

He'd missed the chance to interview Malkovsky because Cohen had run the whole arrest as a one-man show, booking the suspect without calling in. And if the child raper was a killer, they'd never know—another unsolved, like Gray Man.

He thought of calling Cohen in, dressing him down, and kicking him off the team. But the kid had saved Malkovsky's daughter, his performance on the stakeout had been impeccable, and his intentions on the bust had been good. There'd been no way for him to suspect what was going on while he sweated over the paperwork.

Some paperwork too. All the details of the arrest precisely documented on the correct forms, perfect penmanship, not a single spelling error. It must have taken him most of the night. In the meantime, bye-bye, Malkovsky, trundled out the back door under police escort, handcuffed to a Shin Bet operative dressed as a Hassid. A quick ride to Ben Gurion, bypass of Passport Control and Security, and first-class seating for both of them on the next El Al jet to Kennedy.

Good scandal potential, but short-lived—people forgot quickly; bigger and better things were sure to come along—so he'd decided to use it while it was still worth something. To keep Cohen—and himself—safe, keep Anwar Rashmawi's lawyer at bay, put an end to any nonsense about disciplinary hearings. And to get Laufer to describe his interrogation of Malkovsky, if you could call it that—three or four hasty questions in a back room at the airport, then good-bye, good riddance. Under duress, the deputy commander also agreed to have Mossad make contact with the New York investigators and attempt to question Malkovsky about the murders of Fatma and Juliet.

A symbolic triumph, really, because Daniel no longer considered Malkovsky a serious suspect—not in light of the bloody rock discovery. The man was grossly overweight and out of shape; at the jail he'd complained of shortness of breath. An examining doctor had said his blood pressure was dangerously high. It was unlikely he'd have hiked through the desert carrying a body, though Daniel supposed he could have been part of one of Shmeltzer's murder cults.

Killer Hassidim—too crazy to consider.

But that wasn't the point. The brass hadn't known about the rock when they'd shipped him back to New York. They'd intruded on his case, sullied it with politics.

He'd lived through that before, refused to endure it again.

Rooting in the garbage.

Try calling Australia.

He wondered about Gavrieli, wondered if he liked Melbourne,

how he was taking to the duties of an embassy attaché. Gorgeous Gideon wore a tuxedo well, knew how to make conversation at parties, the right wine to drink; still, Daniel was certain he was far from fulfilled.

Rooting and nosing. Biting the hand that had fed him—and fed him well, not scraps.

Laufer was a fool, but his words had opened up old wounds. The guilt.

Not that there had been any choice.

He still wondered why Lippmann had been assigned to him. Gavrieli had never answered that one, had avoided Daniel since the day the report was filed.

Surely he must have known it would all come out.

Or had he expected a cover-up—or failure, a premature wrap-up? All the talk about Daniel's talents just more toothy subterfuge used to capture another pawn, place him into position?

Gavrieli had always had a way with words.

They'd met in '67, in early May, just after Passover, in the army training camp near Ashdod. A beautiful spring, balmy and dry, but rumors had settled over the base like storm clouds: Nasser was planning to move troops into the Sinai. No one was sure what would happen.

Daniel had been a nineteen-year-old inductee, a year out of the yeshiva, an honors graduate of paratroop training still basking in the memory of his jumps—the deathly thrill of human flight. Newly assigned to the 66th Battalion, he'd reported to base in sergeant's chevrons, a red beret, and trooper's boots, all of it so new it felt like a Purim costume.

At the 66th, he was put through a battery of physical and psychological tests, then assigned to a night-attack unit. Gideon Gavrieli was the commander. From his reputation, Daniel had expected a leather-face, but encountered instead a young man, tall, black-haired and blue-eyed, endowed with movie-actor looks and a double portion of arrogance.

Gorgeous Gideon. Only six years older than Daniel, but decades more seasoned. Both parents lawyers and big in the ruling party, the father a retired general on top of that. A nice childhood in a Zahala villa, riding lessons at the Caesarea Country Club, season tickets to the Philharmonic and Habimah, summers abroad. Then three top-rated years in the army, decorations in marksmanship and hand-to-hand, a captain at twenty, onward to Hebrew U. and election as student body president. One month short of his own law degree when the southern border had started to simmer and he'd been summoned back to command. Soon, they said, he'd be a major, one of the youngest, with no intention of stopping there.

He'd singled Daniel out right away, called him to the command post and offered him water wafers and instant coffee.

You're Yemenite.

Yes.

They say Yemenites are intelligent. Does that apply to you?

I don't think that's for me to say.

This is no time for modesty. No matter what you've heard, the Egyptians are going to attack us. Soon you'll be shooting at more than paper targets. Are you intelligent or not?

I am.

Good. I'm glad you realize it. Now I'll tell you, your tests confirm it. I want you to take some additional exams next week. They'll help you qualify for lieutenant and I expect you to receive an excellent score, is that clear?

Yes.

Tell me, what does your father do for a living?

He's a jeweler.

In the event you survive, what do you plan to do with your life?

I don't know.

Do you make jewelry too?

Some.

But you're not as good as your father.

No.

And never will be.

Never.

A common problem. What are your other career options?

I've thought of law.

Forget it. Yemenites are too straightforward to be good lawyers. What else?

I don't know.

Why not?

I haven't thought about it in detail.

A mistake. Start thinking about it now, Sharavi. There's no use merely floating when you can learn how to swim.

Four weeks later they were belly-down on a muddy slope northwest of Scopus, crawling in the darkness through the crosshatch of fortified trenches that surrounded Ammunition Hill. Two survivors of a five-man machine-gun detail sent to flush out Arab Legion snipers.

No-man's-land. For nineteen years the Jordanians had fortified their side of the hill, laying in their positions in anticipation of *Jihad*: trenches—forty concrete-lined wounds slashed into the hillside, some so well camouflaged they were invisible even in daylight.

No daylight now. Three A.M., an hour since the assault had begun. First, the ground had been softened by artillery bombardment; then tanks had been used to set off enemy mines. In their wake, sappers had arrived with their noisy toys, blowing up the fences—Israeli and Jordanian—that had bifurcated the hillside since the cease-fire of '49.

In the other theaters, the Israeli Air Force had been employed to fine effect—Nasser's jets destroyed before they got off the ground, the Syrians swallowing a bitter pill in the Golan. But Jerusalem was too precious, too many sacred places to risk large-scale air attack.

Which meant hand-to-hand, soldier against soldier.

Now the only ones left were desperate men on both sides. Hussein's Arab Legion troops ensconced in two long bunkers atop the hill and hunkered down in the network of trenches below. The men of the 66th, squirming upward through the dirt like human worms. Measuring their progress in meters while racing the rising sun—the cruel light of morning that would highlight them like bugs on a bed sheet.

The last thirty minutes had been a nightmare of artillery barrage and screams, the splintering of olive trees that whispered eerily as they fell, calls for stretchers and medics, the moans of the dead and dying echoing longer than could be explained by any law of physics. Three hundred meters to the southwest, the Old British Police School was ablaze, the UNRWA stores used as sniping posts by the Jordanians crackling like a campfire. Curved trajectory shells arced from Legion positions, followed by grenades and automatic-weapons fire that tilled the soil in murderous puffs, sowing hot metal seeds that would never bear fruit.

The first two men in the company had fallen simultaneously, just seconds after setting out for a shallow trench that fronted the U.N. water tank, a sniper hideout that the infrared scopes had been unable to pinpoint. The third to die was an apple-cheeked kibbutznik named Kobi Altman. The fall of his comrades had inspired him to improvise—leaping up and exposing himself on all sides as he stormed the trench, spraying it with his Uzi. Killing ten Jordanians before being cut down by the eleventh. As he buckled, Gavrieli and Daniel rushed forward, firing blindly into the trench, finishing off the last Legionnaire.

Gavrieli knelt by the rim of the trench, inspecting it, his Uzi poised for fire. Daniel slung Kobi's body over his shoulder and waited.

No sounds, no movement. Gavrieli nodded. The two of them hunched low and crept forward slowly, Gavrieli taking hold of Kobi's feet in order to share the burden. They searched for a safe spot to leave the body, a vantage point from which a grenade could be lobbed at the spindly legs of the water tower. Their plan was clear: Shielded by the aftermath of explosion, they'd run toward the big bunker on the northwest of the hill where scores of Legionnaires had settled in, firing without challenge. Lobbing in more grenades, hoping the concrete would yield to their charges. If they lived, they'd come back for Kobi.

Gavrieli scanned the slope for shelter, pointed finally to a stunted olive sapling. They slithered two meters before the thunder of recoilless guns slapped them back toward the trench.

The big guns fired again. The earth shuddered under Daniel; he felt himself lifted like a feather and slammed back down. Clawing at the soil, he dug his nails in so as not to fall backward into the mass of corpses that filled the trench. Waiting.

The recoilless attack ended.

Gavrieli pointed again. A tracer bullet shot out from the big bunker and died in a mid-air starburst, casting scarlet stripes over the commander's face. No arrogance now—he looked old, dirt-streaked and damaged, acid-etched by grief and fatigue.

The two of them began crawling toward the sapling, toward where they'd left Kobi's body, turned at the same time at the sound from the trench.

A man had crawled out, one of the corpses come to life—a ghost that stood, swaying in the darkness, clutching a rifle and searching for a target.

Gavrieli charged the apparition and took a bullet in the chest.

He crumpled. Daniel feinted to the right and retreated into

the darkness, dropping silently to the ground, his Uzi pinned beneath him. He needed to get at the weapon but feared that any movement would betray his location.

The Jordanian advanced, stalking, firing where Daniel had been, missing but getting warmer.

Daniel tried to roll over. The underbrush crackled faintly. His heart was pounding—he was certain the Legionnaire could hear it.

The Jordanian stopped. Daniel held his breath.

The Jordanian fired; Daniel rolled away.

Moments of silence, stretched cruelly long; his lungs threatened to burst.

Gavrieli groaned. The Jordanian turned, aimed, prepared to finish him off.

Daniel rose to his knees, grabbing the Uzi at the same time. The Legionnaire heard it, realized what was happening, made a split-second decision—the right one—firing at the unwounded enemy.

Daniel had no chance to return fire. He dropped, felt the bullet shave his temple.

The Jordanian kept firing. Daniel molded himself into the earth, wanting to merge with it, to seek the safety of burial.

The fall had knocked the Uzi loose. It clattered against a rock. The Jordanian swiveled and shot at it.

Daniel propelled himself forward, grabbed for the Legionnaire's ankles. The two of them went down, tumbling backward into the ditch.

They snarled and sobbed, tore and bit, rolling through muck and gore. Siamese twins, the rifle sandwiched between them like some deadly umbilical cord. Pressing against each other in a deadly death-hug. Beneath them was a cushion of dead flesh, still warm and yielding, stinking of blood and cordite, the rancid issue of loosened bowels.

Daniel's face was pushed into the cushion; he felt a lifeless hand graze his mouth, the fingers still warm. A syrupy stickiness ran over his face. He twisted around and got his hands around the rifle. The Jordanian managed to regain superiority, freed the weapon.

The Legionnaire was hatless. Daniel took hold of his hair and yanked the man toward him, could see he was young—smooth-faced and thin-lipped with a feathery mustache.

He tried to bite the Jordanian's chin.

The Jordanian writhed out of his grasp. They tugged and flailed, fighting for the rifle, avoiding the bayonet that capped the barrel.

All at once the Jordanian let go of the rifle. Daniel felt sweaty hands clamp around his neck. An internal darkness began to meld with the one that time had wrought. He pried the fingers loose, kicked violently at the Jordanian's groin.

The Jordanian cried out in pain. They rolled and thrashed through a sea of dead flesh. Daniel felt the bayonet nick his cheek. He clawed purposefully, went for the Jordanian's eyes, got a thumb over the lower ridge of the socket, kept clawing upward and popped the eyeball loose.

The Legionnaire stopped for a split second; then agony and shock seemed to double his strength. He struck out wildly, sunk his teeth in Daniel's shoulder and held on until Daniel broke three of his fingers, hearing them crack like twigs.

Incredibly, the Jordanian kept going. Gnashing and grunting, more machine than man, he pulled away from the murderous embrace, lifted the rifle, and brought the butt down on Daniel's solar plexus. The flesh-cushion lightened the impact of the blow but Daniel felt the air go out of him. He was swimming in pain and momentarily helpless as the Jordanian raised the rifle again—not attempting to fire, trying to take this Jew's life in a more intimate manner: stabbing down with the bayonet, his eyeless socket a deep black hole, his mouth contorted in a silent howl.

I'm going to be killed by a ghost, thought Daniel, still sucking for air as the bayonet came down. He forced himself to roll; the blade made a dull sound as it sank into a corpse. As the Legionnaire yanked it loose, Daniel reached out to grab the weapon.

Not quick enough—the Jordanian had it again. But he was screaming now, begging Allah for mercy, clawing at his face. His eyeball was hanging from its cord, bobbing against his cheek, artificial-looking like some macabre theater prop. The reality of his injury had hit him.

Daniel tried to push himself upward, found himself swallowed by torsos and flaccid limbs.

The Jordanian was trying to push the eye back in with his broken fingers. Fumbling pitifully as his other hand stabbed wildly with the bayonet.

Daniel grabbed for the moving weapon, touched metal, not wood. Felt the tip of the bayonet enter his left hand through the palm, a biting, searing pain that coursed down his arm and into the base of his spine. His eyes closed reflexively, his ears rang, he tried to break free, but his hand remained impaled by the bayonet as the Jordanian pushed him down, twisting, *destroying* him.

It was that image of destruction, the thought of himself as just more human garbage added to the heap in the trench, that fueled him.

He raised both feet and kicked, arched his body upward like a rocket. The wounded hand remained pinioned, sinking into the corpse-cushion.

He was throwing the rest of himself at the Jordanian now, not caring about the fiery mass that had once been his left hand, just wanting something to remain intact.

Wrenching upward with abandon, he felt the blade churning, turning, severing nerves, ligaments, and tendons. Gritting his teeth, he traveled somewhere beyond pain as his boot made contact with the Jordanian's jaw and he was finally free.

The rifle fell to one side, tearing more of the hand. He pulled loose, liberated the ravaged tissue.

The Jordanian had recovered from the kick, was trying to bite him again. Daniel slammed the heel of his good hand under the bridge of the man's nose, went after him as he fell, ripping at his face like a jackal gone mad—tearing an ear off, gouging out the other eye, turning the *enemy* to garbage that whimpered helplessly as Daniel formed a talon with his undamaged hand and used it to crush the Jordanian's larynx.

He kept both hands around the Legionnaire's neck. The injured one was a useless, leaking pad, but what else was there to do with it? Squeezing and clawing and forcing out the life spirit.

When the young Jordanian had stopped twitching, Daniel turned his head and vomited.

He collapsed, lay there for a second, atop the pile of bodies. Then gunfire and Gavrieli's whimpers brought him to his elbows. He foraged in the trench, managed to pull a bloody shirt off a corpse and used a clean corner of the garment to bind his hand, which now felt as if it had been fried in hot grease.

Then he crawled out of the trench and went to Gavrieli.

The commander was alive, his eyes open, but his breathing sounded bad—feeble and echoed by a dry rattle. Gavrieli struggled, tossing and shaking as Daniel labored to unbutton his shirt. Finally he got it open, inspected the wound, and found it a neat, smallish hole. He knew the exit side could be worse, but couldn't move Gavrieli to check. The bullet had entered the right side of the chest, missing the heart but probably puncturing a lung. Daniel put his face close to the ground, touched blood, but not enough to make him give up hope.

"You're all right," he said.

Gavrieli lifted one eyebrow and coughed. His eyes fluttered with pain and he started to shiver.

Daniel held him for a while, then climbed back into the trench. Fighting back his own pain, he yanked combat jackets off of two dead Jordanians. Clambering back up, he used one for a blanket, rolled the other into a pillow and placed it under Gavrieli's feet.

He found Gavrieli's radio and whispered a medic call, identifying his location and the status of the rest of the company, informing the communications officer that the trench had been neutralized, then wriggled over to Kobi's body. The kibbutznik's mouth was open; other than that, he looked strangely dignified. Daniel closed the mouth and went searching for both the Uzis.

After several moments of groping in the dark, he found Kobi's, then his, handle dented but still functional. He brought the weapons back to where Gavrieli lay and huddled beside the wounded man. Then he waited.

The battle continued to rage, but it seemed distant, someone else's problem. He heard machine-gun fire from the north, a recoilless response that shook the hills.

Once, Gavrieli gasped and Daniel thought he'd stopped breathing. But after a moment his respiration returned, weak but steady. Daniel stayed close by, checking him, keeping him warm. Cradling the Uzis, his arm enveloped by pain that seemed oddly reassuring.

Suffering meant life.

It took an hour for the rescuers to arrive. When they put him on the stretcher, he started to cry.

Three months later Gavrieli came to visit him at the rehab center. It was a hot day, choked by humidity, and Daniel was sitting on a covered patio, hating life.

Gavrieli had a beach tan. He wore a white knit shirt and

white shorts—*après* tennis, very dashing. The lung was healed, he announced, as if the state of his health had been Daniel's primary worry. The cracked ribs had mended. There was some residual pain and he'd lost weight, but overall he felt terrific.

Daniel, on the other hand, had started seeing himself as a cripple and a savage. His depression was deep and dark, surrendering only to bouts of itchy irritability. Days went by in a numbing, gray haze. Nights were worse—he fell into smothering, terrifying dreams and awoke to hopeless mornings.

"You look good too," Gavrieli lied. He poured a glass of fruit punch and, when Daniel refused it, drank it himself. The discrepancy between their conditions embarrassed Gavrieli; he coughed, winced, as if to show Daniel that he, too, was damaged. Daniel wanted to tell him to leave, remained silent, bound by manners and rank.

They made small talk for a turgid half hour, reminisced mechanically about the liberation of the Old City: Daniel had fought with the medics to be released for the march through the Dung Gate, ready to die under sniper fire. Listening to Rabbi Goren blow the shofar had made him sob with joy and relief, his pain spirited away for a golden moment in which everything seemed worthwhile. Now, even that memory was tarnished.

Gavrieli went on about the new, enlarged state of Israel, described his visit to Hebron, the Tomb of the Ancestors. Daniel nodded and blocked out his words, desiring only solitude, the selfish pleasures of victimization. Finally, Gavrieli sensed what was happening and got to his feet, looking peeved.

"By the way," he said, "you're a captain now. The papers should be coming any day now. Congratulations. See you soon."

"And you? What's your rank?"

But Gavrieli had started to walk away and didn't hear the question. Or pretended not to.

He had, in fact, been promoted to lieutenant colonel. Daniel saw him a year later at Hebrew U. wearing a lieutenant colonel's summer uniform bedecked with ribbons, strolling through campus among a small throng of admiring undergraduates.

Daniel had attended his last class of the day, was on the way home, as usual. He'd completed a year of law studies with good grades but no sense of accomplishment. The lectures seemed remote and pedantic, the textbooks a jumble of small-print irrelevancies designed to distract from the truth. He processed all of it without tasting, spat it out dutifully on exams, thinking of his courses as tubes of processed food ration, the kind he'd carried in his survival kit—barely enough to sustain him, a long way from satisfaction.

Gavrieli saw him, called out. Daniel kept walking—his turn to feign deafness.

He was in no mood to talk to Gorgeous Gideon. No mood to talk to anyone. Since leaving the rehab center he'd avoided old friends, made no new ones. His routine was the same each day: morning prayers, a bus ride to the university, then a return, immediately after classes, to the apartment over the jewelry store, where he cleaned up and prepared dinner for his father and himself. The remainder of the evening was spent studying. His father worried but said nothing. Not even when he collected the jewelry he'd made as a teenager—mediocre stuff, but he'd saved it for years—and melted it down to a lump of silver that he left on a workbench in the shop's back room.

"Dani, hey. Dani Sharavi!"

Gavrieli was shouting. Daniel had no choice but to stop and acknowledge him. He turned, saw a dozen faces—the undergraduates following their hero's glance, staring at the short, brown student with the *kipah* pinned to his African hair, the scarred hand like something the butcher had thrown away.

"Hello, Gideon."

Gavrieli said a few words to his fans; they dispersed grudgingly, and he walked over to Daniel. He peered at the titles of the books in Daniel's arms, seemed amused.

"Law."

"Yes."

"Hate it, don't you? Don't tell me stories—I can see by the look on your face. Told you it wouldn't suit you."

"It suits me just fine."

"Sure, sure. Listen, I just finished a guest lecture—war stories and similar nonsense—and I have a few minutes. How about a cup of coffee?"

"I don't—"

"Come on. I've been planning to call you anyway. There's something I want to talk to you about."

They went to the student cafeteria. Everyone seemed to know Gavrieli; the woman serving the pastries took extra time to pick out an especially large chocolate roll for him. Daniel, basking in the light reflected by the halo, got the second-biggest one.

"So, how've you been?"

"Fine."

"Last time I saw you, you were pretty damned low. Depressed. The doctors said you'd been that way for a while."

Damn liar Lipschitz. "The doctors should have kept their mouths shut."

Gavrieli smiled. "No choice. Commanding officer has a right to know. Listen, I understand your hating law—I hate it, too, never practiced a day, never intend to. I'm leaving the army, too—they want to turn me into a paper shuffler."

The last statement was uttered with dramatic flourish. Daniel knew he was supposed to react with surprise. He drank his coffee, took a bite of chocolate roll. Gavrieli looked at him and went on, undaunted.

"A new age, my friend. For both of us. Time to explore new territories—literally and metaphorically, time to loosen up. Listen, I understand your depression. I was there myself. You know the first few weeks after I got out of the hospital, all I wanted to do was play games—kid's games, the stuff I never had time for because I was too busy studying and serving. Checkers, chess, *sheshbesh*, one from America called Monopoly—you become a capitalist, amass land, and wipe the other guy out. I played with my sister's kids, game after game. Everyone thought I was crazy, but I was just starved for novelty, even stupid novelty. After that I ate nothing but hamburgers and champagne for three weeks. You understand."

"Sure," said Daniel, but he didn't. New experiences were the last thing he wanted. The things he'd seen and done made him want to pass through life with a minimum of disruption.

"When I finished with the games," Gavrieli was saying, "I knew I had to do something, but not law, not the army. A new challenge. So I'm joining the police."

Unable to conceal his surprise, Daniel said, "I wouldn't have thought it."

"Yes, I know. But I'm talking about a new police force, highly professional—the best technology, a boost in pay, parity with the army. Out with morons, in with intelligent, educated officers: university types, high school diplomas at minimum. I'm being put in as a pakad, which is still a significant drop from my army rank, but with major supervisory duties and plenty of action. They want me to reorganize the Criminal Investigation Division, draw up a security plan for the new territories, report directly to the district commander, no underlings, no red tape. In six months he's promised me rav pakad. After that it's straight up, in time for his retirement." Gavrieli paused. "Want to join me?"

Daniel laughed. "I don't think so."

"What's to laugh at? Are you happy doing what you're doing?"

"I'm fine."

"Sure you are. I know your personality—law won't work for you. You'll sit on your ass wondering why the world's so corrupt, why the good guys don't win. On top of that the payoff is always muddled, nothing's ever solved. And there's already a glut—the big firms aren't hiring. Without family connections it'll be years before you make a living. You'll have to handle tenant-landlord disputes and other nonsense just to scratch by. Sign up with me, Dani, and I'll see to it that you zip through the rookie course, skip through all the dirty work."

Gavrieli made a square frame with his fingers, put Daniel's face at the center. "I picture you as a detective. The hand won't make a difference because you'll be using your brains, not your fists. But it's still action, street work, not talk. You'll get priority for every advanced course, be assigned to CID and leap-frogged to rav samal. Which means the best cases—you'll build up a record quickly, be a mefakeah in no time. As I move higher, I'll take you with me."

"I don't think so," Daniel repeated.

"That's because you haven't thought at all. You're still floating. Next time you're studying, take a good look at those law books, all that English common-law crap, another gift from the Brits—their judges wear wigs and fart into their robes. Stop and consider if that's really what you want to do with the rest of your life."

Daniel wiped his lips and stood. "I've got to be going."

"Need a ride somewhere?"

"No, thanks."

"All right, then. Here's my card, call me when you change your mind."

Two weeks into the new academic year, he called. Ninety days later he was in uniform, patrolling the Katamonim. Gavrieli had offered to skip him through it, but he declined the favor, wanting to walk the streets, get a feel for the job that Gideon would never have—for all his intelligence and savvy, there was a certain naïveté about him, a delusion of invincibility that surviving Ammunition Hill had only served to strengthen.

A psychic partition, thought Daniel, that separated him from the darker side of life.

It had caused him be in the wrong place at the wrong time, swept along, inevitably, with the sewage from Lippmann.

Gideon had played from his own script. There was no reason to feel guilty about what had happened. No reason for Daniel to apologize for doing his job.

He looked at his watch. What time was it in Melbourne? Eight hours later, well into the evening.

An embassy party, perhaps? Gorgeous Gideon sticking close to the ambassador, manicured fingers curled around a cocktail glass as he charmed the ladies with flattery and clever anecdotes. His evening jacket tailored to conceal the 9 mm.

Executive attaché. When all was said and done, he was just a bodyguard, a suit and a gun. He had to be miserable.

As opposed to me, thought Daniel. I have plenty to be happy about. A killer on the loose, bloody rocks, and heroin. Mad Hassidim and *korbanot* and strange monks and missing whores frightened by flat-eyed strangers.

Sitting in this white cell, trying to put it all together. Half a kilometer southeast of Ammunition Hill.

47

A sticky summer. He was seventeen, three months away from eighteen, when he walked into the library and asked Doctor for a car. Had to ask twice before the fucker looked up from his surgical journal and paid attention.

"What's that?"

"A car."

"Why do you want one?"

"All the kids have their own."

"But what do *you* need one for?"

"Go places, get to school."

"School's that important to you, huh?" Smile.

Shrug.

"I mean, you're flunking most of your subjects. I didn't think school meant that much to you."

Shrug.

"No, I don't see why I should get you a car just like that."

Smiling in that fucking superior way. The asshole had two cars of his own, a big soft one and a low-slung sports job that looked like a hard-on, neither of which he let anyone else drive. *Her* car was a big soft one, too, big bucks, but it hadn't been out of the garage for a long time; Doctor had had the crankcase drained, put it up on blocks.

The fucker was loaded, all that money, all those cars, and *he'd* had to learn how to drive on a jalopy that belonged to one of the maids, a rusty clunker with no power steering, a real bitch to park—he'd failed the test twice because of it.

"Loan me the money. I'll pay you back."

"Oh, really?" Amused.

"Yeah."

"And how do you propose to do that?"

"I'll get a job."

"A job."

"Yes."

"And what kind of work do you deem yourself qualified to perform?"

"I could work at the hospital."

"At the hospital."

"Yes."

"Doing what?"

"Anything."

"Anything?"

"Anything."

Doctor talked to the head janitor—a nigger retard—and got him a job in maintenance. The nigger hadn't liked the idea; he and Doctor had discussed it while *he* waited a few feet away. The two of them talking about him as if he were invisible.

"I dunno, Doc, it's a dirty job."

"That's fine, Jewel. Just fine."

The nigger put him to work, mopping up vomit and piss off sickroom floors, emptying catheter bags and taking out garbage—not much to find there.

After two weeks of it he smelled bad, carried the smell with him all the time. When he went near Doctor, the fucker winced.

Then the director of personnel found out about it and transferred him out of there, not wanting the son of the head honcho heart surgeon doing shitwork like that.

He got sent to the mail room, which was *excellent*. He didn't even have to stand around and sort—just serve as a courier, taking stuff from place to place.

He did it all summer, got a real good feel for the hospital—every office, every lab.

It was amazing how careless people were, leaving stuff unlocked—petty cash drawers, their purses out on the desk when they went to the john.

He pilfered small amounts of cash that added up to big bucks.

He stole prescription blanks and drugs, always in small amounts. Demerol and Percodan and Ritalin and Seconal and stuff like that, sold it to the junkies who roamed Nasty Boulevard, just a few blocks away.

Sometimes he opened envelopes that had checks in them and sold them at five percent of face value to the junkies. Once in a while someone was stupid enough to send a cash donation to the hospital charity fund. That belonged to him immediately.

He opened book cartons and took the interesting ones home—fancy medical texts about sex and cutting. Once he found a stack of porno books in one of the lockers in the interns' lounge—white men fucking nigger women and vice versa—took it home and cut up the women until he could work up some good scream-pictures, stared at it until it turned him on and he could really get off.

Slowly but surely, he turned the minimum-wage situation into something excellent.

The key was to be careful. To make a plan and stick with it and clean up well afterward.

He smiled at everyone, was prompt, courteous, always willing to do favors for people. Very popular. A couple of the nurses seemed to be ogling his dick; also one of the orderlies, who he was sure was a fag. But none of them interested him, unless they could scream it was borrrring.

A great summer, very educational. He delivered mail to the pathology department—those were cool fuckers, eating their lunch with stiffs all around. The head honcho pathologist was this tall guy with a British accent and a clipped white beard. He chain-smoked menthol cigarettes and coughed a lot.

One time he delivered a package of gloves to Pathology. No one was in the office. He started opening the drawers of the secretary's desk, looking for stuff, when suddenly he heard this buzzing from down the hall—one of the labs that adjoined the offices.

He went over and took a look. The door was open; the room was cold. Whitebeard was standing over this stiff. The stiff lay on a stainless-steel table—a man; it had a dick. Its skin was a dull green-gray.

Whitebeard was using an electric saw with a little round wheel—it looked like a pizza cutter—to lop off the top of the stiff's skull. There was this weird burning smell. He stood there smelling it. It sickened him but really turned him on.

"Yes?" said Whitebeard. "What have you there?"

"Box of gloves."

"Put it over there."

Whitebeard started sawing again, looked up, saw him staring. All the knives and tools. The Y-shaped cut in the stiff's chest, pinned back, the body cavity hollow, all the good stuff scooped out—you could see the spine. An older guy, the dick all shriveled; he needed a shave. On the steel tables were organ samples in trays—he recognized them all, felt good about that. A bucket of blood, vials of fluid, not that different from his experiments, but a nice big room, all out in the open.

Real science.

Whitebeard smiled. "Interested?"

Nod.

Whitebeard continued to saw, pulled off the top of the scalp like a kike's beanie cap. Funny if the stiff had *been* a kike—the dick was too shriveled to tell.

"The cerebral cortex," said Whitebeard, pointing. "The cosmic jelly that creates delusions of immortality."

What shit.

He wanted to say: I know what it is, asshole. I've seen plenty of them, scooped them out just as cool as you're doing.

Instead he just nodded. Play dumb. Play it safe.

Whitebeard lifted the brain, weighed it in a scale that looked like the one they used for vegetables in the supermarket.

"Heavy," he said. A smile. "Must have been an intellectual."

He didn't know what to say, just nodded and stared, until Whitebeard got this uptight look on his face and said, "Don't you have something to do?"

His drug sales alone were quadruple his shitty salary. It turned out to be a very profitable summer. In more ways than one.

For the first time in his life he got to watch Doctor in his natural habitat. The fucker was an even bigger asshole than he'd imagined—ordering people around, never passing a mirror without looking at himself, though why the hell would he want to look at that hook nose and that potbelly, the skin getting all red and blotchy? Red skin meant he was sick—fucker was probably going to drop dead of a heart attack one day, not be able to cut himself open and cure himself, that was for sure.

Drop dead and probably leave all the money to Sarah. Dr. Sarah, soon. But she wanted to be a psychiatrist, no cutting. *Unfuckingbelievable.*

He checked Doctor out real good, got to know him for the first time. Fucker never knew he was being studied. They could have been standing next to each other and he wouldn't have noticed.

To Doctor he was a freak. Weird. Some piece of shit that didn't exist.

It made him invisible, which was excellent.

Doctor liked the young ones. He found out there was truth to all *her* screaming about him fucking candy-stripers.

Fucker flirted with all of them, got serious with one in particular. Audrey, this little brunette, seventeen years old, fucking *high school student* just like Mr. Invisible. But she knew her way around.

Short but curvy—big ass, big tits, wore her hair in this ponytail and wiggled a lot when she walked.

Doctor could have been her father.

Yet they were doing it, he was sure of it. He watched her go into Doctor's office after the secretary had gone home. At first she knocked and Doctor answered; later she started to use her own key. After a half hour, she'd peek her head out to see if the coast was clear, giggle, then wiggle out the door. Wiggle down the hall, swinging her purse, with this bouncy little *high school* walk that said *I'm a winner.*

Thinking no one saw.

Someone saw.

The invisible man, carrying a big carton that blocked his face. Even if he'd been visible he was safe. Pow.

He would have loved to cut her up, clean her up.

Mind picture.

Scream-picture.

Once Doctor and Audrey had a close call: One of the janitors got to work early, opened Doctor's office, and was immediately escorted out by Doctor, looking pissed. No white coat for the fucker now. Just pants and a shirt, the tie loose, the buttons not done right.

After that they started leaving the hospital. Going out, once or twice a week, to a motel just off Nasty Boulevard. Dirty-looking place, three dozen rooms around a sunken motor court, hand-painted signs on the roof advertising water beds and electric massage.

Really filthy. It offended him that people could stoop so low.

He followed them, walking because he still had no car, but it was close to the hospital, five blocks. He had long legs—no problem.

He set up his position behind a tall bush, squatted, and watched.

Doctor always drove. But he parked his car half a block away, on a dark side street, and the two of them walked to the motel, Doctor's big arm over her shoulder, Audrey wiggling and giggling. They were predictable: always went into the same room, number twenty-eight, way at the end. Borrring.

The clerk was this skinny slant, all yellow and sunken-cheeked, like he spent his off hours in an opium den. He had a small bladder, went to the bathroom every half hour or so. Or maybe he was shooting up—the guy wore long sleeves.

The room keys hung in duplicate from hooks on a particle-board rack just behind the reception desk.

He laid out his plan, ran it through his head for three weeks in a row. Just watching, trying to ignore the roaring in his head that got louder when he thought of what they were doing in there.

The key was to plan.

Week number four was action time. He'd brought his equipment, dressed in black like some *ninja,* feeling all tight and good and knowing he was fighting for a good cause.

The first day it didn't work. When the clerk went to pee/shoot up, there was another slant in the office, also looked like a junkie. Slant Two just stood around. When the clerk came out they talked to each other for a while.

The second day, it happened. Slant One split. The minute the office was empty, he ran in, vaulted the counter, grabbed the duplicate to twenty-eight, and vaulted back. By the time One was back, he was outside the door to twenty-eight, all ready with his equipment.

It was dark. There were a few cars; some of the other rooms were occupied, but all the drapes were drawn. No one was around—it was the kind of place you didn't want to be seen in.

He waited, with a giant hard-on, so hard he felt he could break down the door with it.

Put his ear to the door and heard mumbling, what sounded like sex-noise.

Waited some more until they *had* to be doing it, then slipped the key in, pushed, and ran in, turning on the lights and dancing around the room laughing and snapping pictures.

He caught them in a good pose. Audrey was sitting on Doctor, playing the egg game, just like *she* used to. Her eggs were smaller and firmer and kind of tan, but it was the same game, in and out.

Snap.

Screams.

What the hell— You!

Snap.

Audrey got hysterical, started crying, struggled to get off. Doctor holding on to her out of fear, shouting at *him,* but it ended up in *her* ear.

Comedy.

It looked like they hated each other, but they were still connected, couldn't get free of each other!

Excellent. Snap, snap! The mind pictures would be even

better than the real ones, watching them struggle and scream, he was close to coming in his pants.

Snap.

They tried to disconnect. Fear made them clumsy, and they fell sideways.

Snap, another pose.

Snap snap.

Finally Audrey was loose, running naked and sobbing to the bathroom. He kept snapping Doctor, heard her throwing up—probably a habit with women.

Doctor's face was deep purple, his hard-on fading. He grabbed at sheets, tried to cover himself.

Snap.

"You little—" Doctor sprang up and came at him.

The guy was flabby, unhealthy. He pushed him on the chest and Doctor tumbled backward on the bed, ass to the camera.

Snap.

Doctor stood up again.

He put the camera away, smiled, and sauntered to the door.

"See you later. Dad."

The next day there was a note on his bed.

What kind of car do you want?

He got two. A Jaguar XKE Roadster for fun, a Plymouth sedan for when he didn't want to be noticed.

He drove them for a couple of weeks, let Doctor think that was it. Then walked, one afternoon, past the secretary, without even asking permission, opened the door marked PRIVATE, went in and shut it behind him.

The fucker was at his desk, writing in a medical chart. He looked up, tried to look stern, put on the head-honcho look, but couldn't pull it off. Obviously scared shitless.

"What is it?"

"We have to talk. Dad."

"Sure. Sit down."

There was a cedar humidor full of cigars on Doctor's desk. Stupid for a heart surgeon, but the guy had never practiced what he preached anyway.

He stared at Doctor, took a cigar out, licked it, and lit it.

Doctor started to say something. Something parental. Then stopped himself.

"What do you want?"

Straight out with it, no "son," no pretending it was anything other than business.

He didn't answer, let an ash grow on the cigar, flicked it on the carpet.

Doctor clenched his jaw to keep from talking.

He blew smoke rings.

"Well, Dad," he said finally, "the pictures are in a safe place with instructions to open them if anything happens to me, so if you've been thinking that fucking me over will help you, forget it."

"Don't be ridiculous. Harming you is the furthest thing from my—"

"Right."

"Believe me, all I've ever wanted for you—"

"Cut the shit." He leaned forward, dropped a gray worm of ash on the desk. On Doctor's charts. Picked up a chart.

"You can't look—"

"Why's that?"

"It's confidential patient information."

"Tough shit."

Doctor sighed, put on a nicey-nicey tone: "Listen, I know our relationship hasn't been—"

"Cut the shit, I said!" He said it loud. Doctor looked nervously at the door.

He leafed through the chart. No good pictures. Borrring. Put it down.

"The photos are in packets. Dad. One addressed to Mom, one to Dr. Schoenfeld, one to Audrey's parents. I can do anything I want to."

Doctor stared at him. His eyes got narrow.

Neither of them said anything for a while.

"What do you want?" Doctor finally said.

"Favors."

"What kinds of favors?"

"Whatever I want."

Doctor kept staring at him.

The cigar was starting to taste like shit. He ground it out on the shiny wooden surface of Doctor's desk, left the butt lying there like an old turd.

"Not a lot of favors. Dad. Just a few important ones."

"Such as?" Trying to tough it out, but *totally* scared shitless.

Now it was *his* turn to smile. "I'll let you know."

He got up, walked around to where Doctor was sitting. Slapped him on the shoulder and smiled again.

"We'll be in touch, stud."

48

At one-fifteen Daniel received news from Tel Aviv that Aljuni, the Gaza wife-stabber, had passed his polygraph. At one-thirty P.M. he made radio contact with the Chinaman. Nothing new from the Old City.

"What's with Cohen?" he asked.

"Still feels like a dumb shit about Malkovsky, but he seems to be doing his job."

"How's Daoud doing with Roselli?"

The big man laughed.

"Share the joke," said Daniel.

"Daoud spent the morning dressed as a beggar with palsy, whining for alms near the Fourth Station of the Cross. Did such a good job that an Arab policeman smacked the soles of his feet with his baton, screamed at him to stop defiling the holy places."

"How is he?"

"Proud as hell, and sore. You should see him, Dani—all shaking and filthy. If anyone can pick up idle chatter, he can."

"Drop a shekel in his can for me," said Daniel.

"I already did. Talk to you later."

At two o'clock, Shmeltzer called in.

"The Hebrew U. archaeology department and the nature people promise to get me their hike lists as soon as possible. I had breakfast with the lady. Our request to look for the Nasser whore is being taken under consideration."

"That the best they could do?"

"There was cooperation floating between the lines—I got a breakfast date immediately, so they're taking it seriously. My feeling is they'll look for her if they can do it safely. Problem is the Amman operatives took a long time to plant—they're not going to shut down the entire operation because of something like this."

"Stay in touch with it," said Daniel. "If we need to push a little, let me know."

"I don't think pushing will help," said Shmeltzer. "Something else came up. I'm in Tel Aviv, at Beilison Hospital—the reason I didn't call sooner. I got a call from one of the doctors I talked to a couple of weeks ago—eye surgeon named Krieger, had something to say about one of his colleagues, anesthesiologist named Drori. Remember the flap last year about the doc who refused to give gas to an Arab kid? A cross-eyed baby—they were wheeling him into the operating room and the mother started praising Allah for straightening her little lion's eyes so he'd be able to throw stones at the Zionists. The doctor got pissed off, told her to screw herself, he hoped the kid went blind, then walked off the case. That was Drori."

"I remember. One of the leftist MKs wanted him brought up on charges."

"Right—Sardoffsky and his usual Marxist crap. Anyway, it blew over in two days—that was that. But according to this Krieger, Drori has a real thing for Arabs. Since the incident with the baby, he's gotten even more militant, interrogates Arab patients before he agrees to work on them, has them recite this pledge that they support the state and think Yasser Arafat's a perfidious dog. If anyone on the staff tries to talk to him about separating politics and medicine, he gets irrational—that's Krieger's term. It's come close to blows. On top of that, he's a loner, unmarried, antisocial. Krieger says several times when he's been on night shift, he's seen Drori leave the hospital, get into his car, and come back early in the morning wearing the same clothes, unshaven. Says it's obvious the guy hasn't slept, has been doing something else all night."

"Something like stalking and killing."

"That's what Krieger thinks. At first he didn't want to believe it, but the more he thought about it, the better Drori looked as our guy. He wasn't too happy about telling me all this, of course. Felt like an informer. But civic duty and all that."

"Think this could be some issue between them?"

"It's possible, but Drori sounds strange enough to look into."

"What else do you know about him?"

"His employment records show he immigrated two years ago from England—Scotland, actually. Original name was Denzer—Selwyn Denzer. Divorced his wife and left her and some kids there. Personnel notes say he's got a very good reputation medically, but hard to live with."

"Has the lack of sleep affected his performance?"

"Not yet, but they're watching him for slip-ups. They'd love an excuse to get rid of him."

"Where does he live?"

"In Petah Tikva."

"Not exactly local."

"No, but with the new highway he could be driving back and forth in ample time. Who knows, maybe our second kill spot's out of town. A guy this fanatical could be into rituals, making some sort of symbolic statement."

"Any connection between him and Kagan?"

"According to Krieger, Drori thinks Gvura's too moderate."

"Okay," said Daniel. "Find out what he was doing the nights of both murders."

"Will do."

After Shmeltzer hung up, Daniel phoned Bonn for the tenth time and asked for the Interpol man. A secretary assured him that Mr. Friedman had indeed received the Pakad's messages, would be returning them shortly. All attempts to push the issue were met with cool secretarial indifference.

He collected his maps and his files, left the office, and drove to the Laromme Hotel. The lobby was thick with people, tourists queued up at the desk, checking in and settling their accounts, an army of clerks attending to their needs.

The courtesy phones were all in use. Daniel searched for the manager, spotted him standing near one of the mobile luggage racks berating a bellman. When the bellman had departed, Daniel walked over and said, "Please ring Mr. and Mrs. Brooker, Yigal. I'm not sure of the room number."

The manager's eyebrows rose. "Is there something I should know about them?"

"They're friends of mine."

"Oh. In that case, no need to call. She went out this morning at ten, met a blond woman—good looker—near the taxi stand. He's out by the pool."

"Impressive, Yigal. Want to join my staff?"

The manager shrugged. "They're easy to spot."

Daniel walked to the pool area—lots of bikinis and laughter, the clink of glasses. The water in the pool was turquoise dappled with navy. The only ones swimming were children and one old man doing a slow breast stroke.

Gene was asleep on a chaise longue, next to an umbrellaed table, one arm thrown over his eyes, the other resting at his side. On the decking near his fingertips were a bottle of Heineken and a half-full glass of beer. He wore green-and-white striped trunks. His legs were speckled with gray fuzz; his belly asserted itself above the waistline in a sleek, ebony billow.

Like a seal, thought Daniel. A bull seal, basking on a rock.

He settled in a deck chair. A waitress approached and took his order for a Coke with lime. When she returned with the drink, he sipped slowly, watching Gene sleep, and was halfway through the ice when the black man began to stir.

The arm lifted, peeling away audibly from the tar-colored face. Gene's eyes closed tighter, then opened and focused on Daniel.

"Hey," he said, sitting up and extending his hand.

Daniel shook it. "You look at peace with the world, Lieutenant Brooker."

Gene smiled, stretched, and pulled a towel down from the table. "Working on my tan." He wiped his brow, ran the towel over his face. "Lu's at the museum, some lecture on biblical archaeology—matter of fact, I think Laura's with her. What's up?"

"I need to talk to the FBI, Gene. I'd like your help."

That brought the black man to his feet.

"My, my," he said. "I thought you'd never ask."

They drove the two blocks to Daniel's apartment. Laura had left a note saying Shoshi was staying late at school to work on a science project; the boys were at friends'; she and Luanne would be back by five, five-thirty the latest.

Gene sat down at the dining room table and stroked Dayan as Daniel brought out files, maps, pencils, and a stack of paper. He uncoiled the phone wire, put the phone down next to Gene, and sat down. Taking a sheet from the stack, he began writing, jotting a column of numbers parallel with the left-hand margin, placing notations next to each number. When he was through, he handed the list to Gene, who put on a pair of half-glasses and read.

"The program's fairly new—called VICAP," Gene said. "Stands for Violent Criminal Apprehension Program—the Feds love acronyms."

"They also love paperwork, which is why I'm bothering you. They usually delay us for weeks."

"If that's an apology, I'm ignoring it." Gene read for a while longer. "Not much to work with, Danny. Your basic generic sex killer mutilation—neck, breasts, privates. I've seen plenty of it over the years."

"There was a difference between the victims," said Daniel. "The genitals were cut up on One, removed from Number Two."

"Yeah, I see—that could work for us or against us, depending on how they've programmed the computer. If all they've got in there is wound pattern, we'll lose, because we're giving them two sets of data, reducing the chances of finding something in common with ours. On the other hand, if they've put in sequences—and I don't know that they have—and come up with another chop-the-first, steal-the-second pattern, we'll get a tighter match, something a little thought-provoking."

Gene read further. "Maybe the washing will pan out, but even that's not that weird—good way to get rid of evidence. Most of these turkeys like to fool with the body, manipulate it, have sex with it. We had a case back in L.A. in '49, the Black Dahlia, pretty famous. She was scrubbed and drained just like your two. They never found the guy who did it. How far back do you want them to go?"

"As far as they can."

"If I remember correctly, the file bottoms out at ten-year-old unsolveds. Most of the stuff is pretty recent. There seems to be more and more of it each year—world's getting sweeter."

He scanned the list again, put it down. "All right, let's get to it. Let's see, the time difference from here to L.A. is ten hours, which would make it seven hours from here to Virginia—just after eight A.M. Okay, McGuire should be there by now. Set me up."

Daniel dialed the international code, got a recorded message that all overseas cables were in use. He phoned the local operator, after several minutes of debate, obtained an international line. Gene took the receiver, dialed Virginia, and waited.

"No ring yet."

"Sometimes it takes a while."

The black man nodded, tapped the phone with his finger. "McGuire's a very nice guy—cooperative for a Fed. He's in Disputed Documents at the FBI Academy in Quantico, used to be in the L.A. office. We worked together on a forgery case that turned into— All right, it's ringing."

A moment later he was talking to his contact, speaking in a low, level voice:

"Hello, Sam? This is Gene Brooker. I'm calling from the Middle East . . . Yup, you heard right. Doing some international consulting . . . Yeah, I'll tell you about it when I get back. Anyway, I need access to VICAP—Serial Killer Data Bank in particular. Got some homicides with a possible international connection, want to run the wound patterns and *modus,* see if anything you guys have matches up. . . . No, nothing iffy politically . . . not at all—you've got my word on it, Scout's honor. Just trying to catch a bad guy with a possible wide radius of operations . . . Yes, I know it's still in development. Any profiles worked out?. . . Okay, I'll take what I can get. So who do I speak to? . . . You will? Terrific. I owe you. Got a pen? These are the parameters. . . ."

When he was through discussing the list with McGuire, he gave his room number at the Laromme for callback, covered the mouthpiece, and said, "Want to use your office for a backup number?"

"Yes," said Daniel, "and here." He wrote down both numbers and Gene gave them to the FBI man.

Thanking McGuire again, Gene hung up and said, "All set. Couple of days, maybe longer. They're not set up for profiling yet. Just basic statistics and collation."

"Thank you, Gene."

"Don't mention it."

They went over the case again, Gene offering empathy and suggestions, but nothing Daniel hadn't thought of. One part of Daniel regretted the lack of new ideas. The other felt good that an outsider had little to offer.

At three-thirty his stomach rumbled and he realized he'd skipped breakfast and lunch. "Hungry?" he asked Gene.

"I could eat."

He got up to fix cheese sandwiches and brew coffee when the phone rang: an operator from Headquarters informing him that a Mr. Friedman from Bonn was on the phone and threatening to hang up if they didn't find Pakad Sharavi within thirty seconds.

"Put me through," he said.

"You should tell us when you leave the office," said the operator, and connected him to Bonn.

"Sharavi."

"Sharavi, this is Friedman. I hear you've got problems." The Interpol man's voice was hoarse. He talked loud and fast, like someone shouting farewells from a moving train.

"We could use some help."

"That's for sure. Had a hell of a time reaching you—no one over there seems to know what they're doing."

Two months in Germany and the man considered himself an *ubermensch.* Daniel let the slur pass, told him what he wanted, ending with detailed descriptions of the wounds.

"Ugly," said Friedman. "Do you want Greece too?"

"Yes."

"It's going to take some time."

"Do the best you can."

"Bear in mind that there's a time lag with the computer—some of our so-called current data's over a year old. Anything really recent's going to require personal calls."

"I'm aware of that. Four weeks is our cutoff. I'd appreciate the calls."

"What's your lead to Europe?"

"Possible ID of a foreign suspect."

"What do you mean by 'possible'?"

"The source said American but that could mean European."

"The source stupid or just being cagey?"

"Unavailable, whereabouts unknown. The ID's secondhand."

"Sounds weak to me," said Friedman.

"If I had the case solved, I wouldn't be calling you."

"No need to get sensitive. I'll get you what you want. All I'm telling you is that it sounds weak. Anything else I should know about?"

"Nothing."

"Because if there is, I need to have it up front. They're not pleased with us—think all their terrorist problems are our fault. Being able to give them something would help grease the skillet."

"Whenever we get something, you're always the first to know," said Daniel. He gave the Interpol man his home number and hung up. As he put the phone in its cradle, he saw Gene smile knowingly from across the table.

"Friendly chat," said the black man.

"New man," said Daniel. "We don't owe each other anything, yet."

He went into the kitchen, finished setting up the coffeepot, and started laying slices of yellow cheese on rye bread.

Gene followed him in, said, "Changing of the guard's always wonderful. I spent six years building up a relationship with one captain, got a new one and had to start proving myself from scratch."

"I know all about that," said Daniel, opening the refrigerator. "Do you like mustard?"

49

No one was talking to Wilbur, but he could live with that. No problem.

A Butcher story a week had kept New York happy. The pieces had a terrific pickup rate, both in the States and worldwide. So terrific, he'd managed to cadge a byline on the last three.

The key was to be creative, work with what you had. On something like this, facts were less important than flavor.

And no shortage of flavor on this one: ancient city, Thousand Nights' ambience, ethnic tensions, a fiend with a knife.

Terrific visuals—he'd started thinking about a screenplay.

There was always the political angle too. Arabs getting killed—the implications were obvious.

He approached it from the human-interest perspective first, went to Silwan, and knocked on the door of the first one's family, hoping for a victim piece.

When they wouldn't let him in, he got hold of a sociology professor from Bir Zeit University: Columbia-educated little snot named El Said, in love with himself and a real publicity hound, which made him more than eager to offer quotable quotes about the political roots of violent crime in a racist society.

When that had been milked, it was time to backtrack, round out the historical perspective. He spent hours at the *Jerusalem Post* archives—unimpressive place on the north side of town, near a sooty industrial stretch. You entered through the back of the building, had to walk between the newspaper delivery trucks, through some kind of loading dock. Nearby was a slaughterhouse or chicken processing plant; as he entered the archive, he heard the birds squawking, smelled the stench of burnt feathers.

Inside wasn't any better: rows of sagging floor-to-ceiling bookcases, scarred tables, cracked linoleum floors, not a computer in sight. And the librarian was a stooped, shuffling old character with wet eyes and an unhealthy complexion.

Central-casting Dickens, decided Wilbur, half-expecting the geezer to creak when he walked.

But the geezer was *competent,* knew where everything was. He took Wilbur's money and was back with the file before the correspondent finished counting the change.

Deciding to give the political thing a rest, he did a sex-murder search, hoping to shatter some myths. The local press kept repeating what Steve Rappaport had told him that first afternoon at Fink's: Psycho homicides were virtually unknown in Israel. But that could have been just another bit of self-congratulation on the part of the Chosen People. He wasn't ready to accept it at face value.

He scoured clippings and reports, pulled Rappaport's file and those of a couple of other reporters who'd covered the crime beat, went back to '48 and found that it checked out: The violent crime rate was low and had remained relatively constant over the thirty-seven-year life of the state. The homicides they did have were mostly family blowups, manslaughters, and second degrees; serials and bizarre snuffs were virtually unheard-of. And from what he could tell, it didn't seem due to cover-ups or underreporting. Since '48, the press had been free.

So no scoop, but the fact that two serials had arisen in rapid succession gave him a new slant: Thoughtful theoretical pieces about societal changes responsible for the sudden increase in brutality. No need for new sources; El Said and other academic types were more than happy to pontificate upon command.

With that kind of spice, the pickup rate soared, especially in

Europe. New York asked for more. The other foreign correspondents caught flak for not being there first—now none of them wanted anything to do with him. Ditto for Rappaport—kid was green-faced with envy, convinced he'd been robbed.

Another source dried up. And the police weren't saying a damn thing.

But no problem. He had other things on his mind: The more he thought about it, the more attractive a screenplay started to look.

He began an outline, realized he needed more to flesh it out.

He researched the first series of killings, attributed to some ghoul they'd tagged the Gray Man, got one long retro piece out of that, and learned that the head detective on the first serial was the same one working the Butcher—Major Crimes detective named Sharavi. There were no quotes from him, no pictures. Probably a strong, silent type, or maybe he just didn't want to field questions about his solve rate.

Wilbur called the guy's office at French Hill, got no answer, which was hardly surprising. He had the geezer dig up whatever he could on the detective, found a series of clippings from the previous autumn that opened his eyes nice and wide:

Elazar Lippmann, former Member of Knesset. Ruling party loyalist with a progressive voting record and a special interest in criminology and prison reform. He'd been appointed warden of Ramle Prison, talked a lot about humane changes, education and rehabilitation. Real golden boy, little Omar Sharif mustache, good teeth—everyone seemed to like him. Good old Stevie Rappaport had even done a Friday Supplement interview with him—amateur stuff that reeked of hero worship.

So it surprised everyone when, six months later, Lippmann was ambushed and assassinated on the way to work—machine-gunned to death along with his driver.

Daniel Sharavi had headed the investigation, appointed directly by the deputy commander, which, considering Gray Man hadn't been solved, meant he was either hot or well-connected.

Efficient fellow, and thorough, Wilbur decided, making his way through the Lippmann clippings and getting a feel for the rapid pace of the inquiry: the prison turned upside down, everyone interviewed, guards as well as inmates; gang leaders and their buddies on the outside hauled in for interrogation, Palestinian activists questioned by the busload, even talks with clients

Lippmann had represented as an attorney a decade ago, before going into politics.

Plenty of intrigue, but in the end it had turned out to be just another tacky corruption case. Far from a hero, Lippmann had been a first-class sleaze. Four weeks after his death, the press murdered him again.

Sharavi had solved this one—and quickly. Dug up the dirt on Lippmann and found the prick had been venal from day one, hit his stride when he got the warden job: two fat Swiss accounts, one in the Bahamas, a small fortune amassed selling favors—extra visitations, early release dates, exemptions from work details, even illegal weekend passes for dangerous felons. Those who reneged on payment made it up in pain—Jews locked in Arab cell blocks and vice versa, handpicked guards looking the other way when the blood started to flow.

Given that setup, the assassins were easy to find—three brothers of an eighteen-year-old convicted burglar who'd welshed and had his nose flattened and his anus enlarged.

Fun guy, Warden Lippmann—in more ways than one.

One of Sharavi's men caught a deputy warden rifling through the boss's desk, shredded photos in his pocket. The pictures were put together like a jigsaw, found to be snapshots of call girls carousing with politicos—nothing kinky, just wine, hors d'oeuvres, low-cut gowns, jolly party scene. The politicos got canned. One of them turned out to be the deputy commander, another golden boy named Gideon Gavrieli. *His* picture they ran—Warren Beatty look-alike with a high-school quarterback smile.

Except for attending one party, Gavrieli claimed to be clean. Someone believed him, shipped him out to Australia.

Sharavi was promoted to chief inspector.

Intriguing fellow, thought Wilbur. Two unsolved serials, a fuck-the-boss exposé sandwiched in between. Man in that situation couldn't be too popular with the higher-ups. Be interesting to see what happened to him.

Wilbur was sitting at his desk at Beit Agron when the mail came, staring at the fly fan and sipping Wild Turkey from a paper cup.

There was a knock on the door. Wilbur emptied the cup, tossed it in the trash basket. "Enter."

A skinny blond kid ambled in. "The mail, Mr. Worberg."

Mutti, the high school sophomore who functioned as a part-time office boy. Which meant Sonia, the poor excuse for a secretary, had taken lunch again without asking permission.

"Toss it on the desk."

"Yes, Mr. Worberg."

Half a dozen envelopes and the current issues of *Time, Newsweek,* and the *Herald Tribune* landed next to his typewriter. In the machine was a piece of Plover bond headed THE BUTCHER: A SCREENPLAY by Mark A. Wilbur. Below the heading, blank space.

Wilbur pulled the sheet out, crumpled it, tossed it on the floor. He picked up the *Herald* and looked for his most recent Butcher piece. Nothing. That made three days running. He wondered if he was starting to wear out the welcome mat, felt a stab of anxiety, and reached for the drawer with the Turkey. As he put his hand on the bottle, he realized Mutti was still standing around smiling and gawking, and withdrew it.

Dumb kid—father was one of the janitors at the press building. Mutti wanted to be the Semitic Jimmy Olson. Grabowsky, being a soft touch, had taken him on as a gofer; Wilbur had inherited him. Obedient sort, but definitely no rocket scientist. Wilbur had long ago given up trying to teach him his name.

"What is it?"

"Do you needing anything else, Mr. Worberg?"

"Yeah, now that you mention it. Go down to Wimpy's and get me a hamburger—onions, mayonnaise, relish. Got that?"

Mutti nodded energetically. "And for drink?"

"A beer."

"Okay, Mr. Worberg." The boy ran off slamming the door behind him.

Alone once again, Wilbur turned to the mail. A confirmation, finally, of his expense vouchers from the Greek vacation. Invitation to a Press Club party in Tel Aviv, regrets only; overseas express letter from a Nashville attorney dunning him for back alimony from Number Two. That one made him smile—it had been routed through Rio and New York, taking six weeks to arrive. Two weeks past the deadline the legal eagle had set before threatening to move on to "vigorous prosecution." Wilbur dropped it in the circular file and examined the rest of the mail. Bills, the Rockefeller Museum newsletter, an invite to a buffet/press conference thrown by the WIZO women to announce the groundbreaking of a new orphanage. Toss. Then something, midway through the stack, that caught his eye.

A plain white envelope, no postage, just his name in block letters written with such force that the W in Wilbur had torn through the paper.

Inside was a sheet of paper—white, cheap, no watermark.

Glued to the paper were two paragraphs in Hebrew, both printed on glossy white paper that appeared to have been cut out of a book.

He stared at it, had no idea what any of it meant, but the presentation—the hand delivery, the force of the writing, the cutouts—smacked of weirdness.

He kept staring. The letters stared back at him, random angles and curves.

Incomprehensible.

But definitely weird. It gave him a little twist in the gut.

He knew what he needed.

When Mutti got back with the food, he greeted him like a long-lost son.

50

A sweltering Thursday. By the time Daniel arrived at the scene, the air was acrid with scorched rubber and cordite, the pastoral silence broken by gunfire and poisoned by hatred.

Roadblocks had been thrown up across the Hebron Road just south of the entrance to Beit Gvura—steel riot grills, manned by soldiers and flanked by army trucks. Daniel parked the Escort by the side of the road and continued on foot, his pakad's uniform earning free passage.

A cordon of troops, four rows deep, stood ten meters beyond the barriers. Gvura people were massed behind the soldiers, eye to eye with MPs who walked back and forth, suppressing spurts of forward movement, shepherding the settlers back toward the mouth of the settlement. The Gvura people brandished fists and shouted obscenities but made no attempt to storm the MPs. Daniel remembered their faces from the interview, faces now twisted with rage. He searched for Kagan or Bob Arnon, saw neither of them.

On the other side of the cordon was a seething mob of Arab youths who had marched from Hebron bearing placards and PLO flags. Some of the placards lay tattered in the dust. A grainy mist shimmered in the heat and seemed to hover over the Arabs—some of them had rolled old auto tires from town and set them afire. The flames had been extinguished, the tires scattered by the side of the road, steaming like giant overcooked doughnuts.

The command post was an army truck equipped with full radio capability, stationed by the side of the road in a dusty clearing ringed by a dozen ancient fig trees. Surrounding the truck were several canvas-covered MP jeeps, all unmanned.

Just beyond the trees was another clearing, then a small vineyard, emerald leaves shading clusters of fruit that glistened like amethysts in the afternoon sun. Four military ambulances and half a dozen transport vans filled the clearing. Some of the vans were bolted shut and under the guard of soldiers. Next to them was a civilian vehicle—a small mud-colored Fiat with Hebron plates, sagging on flattened tires, its hood pocked with bullet holes, its windshield shattered.

A pair of vans and one of the ambulances pulled out, driving in the dirt by the side of the road until past the barriers, then turning onto the asphalt, sirens blaring, speeding north, back to Jerusalem. Daniel saw activity near another of the ambulances: white blurs, crimson blood bags, the clink and glow of intravenous bottles. He spotted Colonel Marciano's distinctive figure at the front bumper of the truck and walked toward it. Moving quickly but cautiously, keeping one eye on the action.

The cordon of soldiers advanced and the Arabs retreated, but not smoothly. Scuffles broke out as authority confronted resistance—shoving matches punctuated by hate-filled screams, grunts of pain, the dull, insulting abrasion of metal against flesh.

Marciano lifted a megaphone to his lips and barked an order.

The rear row of the cordon fired its rifles in the air and a shudder coursed through the mob.

For a moment it seemed as if the Arabs were ready to disperse. Then some of them began shrieking PLO slogans and sitting down on the asphalt. Those who'd begun to retreat backed into them, stumbling and falling; they were lifted by front-line soldiers and pushed back. The sitters were quickly removed, picked up by the scruff and shoved over to MPs who propelled them toward the vans. More resistance, more arrests, a bedlam of bodies, boiling and spitting.

Within seconds the Arabs had been forced back several meters. All at once, several large rocks arced from the center of the mob and rained down upon the cordon. One landed near Daniel and he ran for cover, crouching behind a nearby jeep.

He saw soldiers raise their arms protectively, a blossom of blood spring from the cheek of one unlucky private.

Marciano bellowed into the megaphone.

The soldiers fired several volleys, this time over the heads of the crowd. The Arabs panicked and ran backward; a few stragglers were trampled in the process.

More slogans, more stones.

A soldier crumpled.

Megaphone orders. Stones. Soldiers with rifles fired rubber bullets directly into the mob. Several Arabs clutched arms and legs in agony and fell, writhing.

The mob was a thing of the past, now, the Arabs fanning out toward Hebron, each man for himself. Tripping over one another in a hasty sprint for safety.

Suddenly a long-haired, bearded man of about twenty materialized out of the human swirl, dashing wild-eyed toward the troops, a long knife in one hand, a jagged hunk of concrete in the other.

He raised the knife, threw himself at the soldiers, who closed ranks and fired. Lead bullets.

The long-haired man's body seemed to take off in flight, floating and gyrating, billowing smoke puffs, spouting ragged black holes. Then the holes filled with red and overflowed. Blood spurted out of him. Just as abruptly as he'd appeared, he collapsed, expelling his life-juices into the dirt.

Some of the dispersing Arabs had turned to watch him die. They stopped, frozen, mouths shaped into paralyzed ellipses.

The cordon advanced, walking around the dead man, pushing the remaining Arabs back. Moving forward inexorably until every rioter was in custody or fleeing.

The road was devoid of movement now, decorated with blood, prostrate forms, and spent cartridges.

Ambulance attendants rushed forward with stretchers, picking up wounded soldiers and Arabs, leaving for last the dead knife-wielder.

"Let him rot!" shouted a Gvura man. Other settlers took up the cry and turned it into a chant. They began moving forward. Colonel Marciano spoke into the megaphone; the rear row of the cordon reversed itself and faced the Gvura people.

"Go ahead," screamed one woman. "Shoot Jews! Damned Nazis!"

The soldiers remained impassive. Granite eyes in baby faces.

Daniel walked up to Marciano. The colonel was surrounded by subordinates but acknowledged him with a nod as he delivered order after order in a calm, even voice.

Marciano was a huge man—two meters tall—with an egg-shaped body that seemed to balance precariously on long, stilt-like legs. His head was egg-shaped, too—bald, brown, deeply seamed, with a large, fleshy nose and a chin that could have used some reinforcement. Soft-spoken without his megaphone, he was a career man, a hero of the '67 Sinai assault and Yom Kippur, in charge of Judean security for the past two years. An organized thinker and reader of philosophy and history who seemed to take it all in stride.

When the subordinates had left to carry out his orders, he gripped Daniel's hand and said, "It's over."

"The call I received said it had to do with my case."

"Could be. One second."

Two soldiers were carrying the dead Arab to the side of the road, holding him low to the ground so that his buttocks dragged in the dirt. Marciano picked up his megaphone, said, "Lift him," sharply. Startled, the soldiers complied.

Before the loudspeaker had been lowered, an army lieutenant came over and said, "What about them, Barukh?" Pointing to the Gvura people, who were still shouting and cursing.

"Inform Shimshon in Hebron that movement north of the city limits is restricted for twenty-four hours," said Marciano. "Maintain a line of troops one hundred meters to the south, and see to it that no one without legitimate business crosses it for the rest of the day. Once the line's established, leave them alone to blow it off."

The lieutenant wiped his brow and left.

"Come on," said Marciano. He loped to the back of the truck, climbed in, and Daniel followed. The two of them sat on the hot corrugated-steel floor of the truck bed. Marciano lit a cigarette and dragged deeply, then pulled a canteen off his belt, took a swig, and passed it to Daniel. The water inside was cool and sweet.

Marciano stretched out his long legs.

"This is what happened," he said. "About two hours ago, one of the Gvuranik women was standing out in front of the settlement, waiting for a lift to Jerusalem—a pregnant one. She had an appointment at Shaarei Zedek Hospital. One of Kagan's deputies—American named Arnon—was on transport duty, supposed to be coming back with a carful of schoolbooks, then making a return trip to pick up a Torah and take her to her appointment. He was late. She waited by herself for a while, knitting booties.

"Suddenly this car drives up." Marciano pointed to the mud-colored Fiat. "Three Arabs get out, two with butcher knives. The other's packing a pistol—one of those cheap Czech jobs, as likely to blow up in your hand as fire. They start moving on the pregnant one. She's terrified, can't move. They're saying something about blood sacrifices and sin offerings, revenge for dead virgins. She starts to scream. They clamp a hand over her mouth, start pulling her into the car.

"Meanwhile Arnon pulls up, sees what's happening, and runs over to help. He's got a pistol, runs toward them waving it but is afraid of hitting the woman. The Arab with the gun starts shooting—misses three times even at close range but finally gets Arnon in the belly.

"Arnon's down. The pregnant woman manages to break free, starts running and screaming at the top of her lungs. The Arabs go after her. Mrs. Kagan happens to be taking a walk near the outskirts of the settlement, hears the gunshots and the screams and rushes over. *She's* packing an Uzi, pulls it into firing position. The Arab with the gun shoots at her, misses, then starts to run away. Mrs. Kagan goes after all three of them, opens up on the car, kills two of them right away, wounds the third. By now, Gvuraniks are streaming out. They pull the wounded Arab out of the car and beat him to death."

Marciano paused for a drag on his cigarette. "Pretty picture, eh, Dani? Wait, there's more. Seems the three Arabs were only part of the gang. There are four others waiting in a flat in Hebron—knives, shroud, looks like they had a revenge party in mind. When the Fiat doesn't show up, these guys drive up the road to investigate, see Gvura people standing over the dead bodies of their comrades, and pull out *their* Czechis. The Gvuraniks spot them, go after them—lots of shooting, no one hit. The Arabs step on the gas, speed back to Hebron telling everyone that the Jews are on a rampage, murdering Palestinian heroes. To make matters worse, some professor from Bir Zeit—asshole punk named El Said—is visiting an uncle, hears the news, and steps out in the middle of the *souq* with an impromptu speech that whips up a mob. The rest you saw."

Marciano smoked some more, took another swallow from the canteen. A chorus of ambulance sirens rose shrilly and diminished, backed by racing engines, the still-lusty epithets of the Gvura people.

"In terms of your case," said the colonel, "we found a newspaper article in the Fiat—you know the one I mean."

"I haven't read the paper today," said Daniel.

"In that case I'll get it for you." Marciano got on his knees, stuck his head out of the truck, and called an MP over.

"Get the bag labeled Number Nine out of the evidence case."

The MP trotted off.

"Where's Kagan?" asked Daniel.

"With his wife. Shooting those Arabs seemed to shake her up. She collapsed shortly afterward—they took her to Hadassah for observation."

Daniel remembered the woman's quiet grace, hoped she was all right.

"What's the casualty situation?" he asked.

"The three dead ones from the Fiat. The pregnant one received only a few scratches, but it wouldn't surprise me if she loses her baby. Arnon's belly wound looked serious, lots of blood loss—when they carried him off he was unconscious. You just saw the one with the knife—no doubt he'll be a hero by this evening. Stupid bastard didn't leave us much choice. Six of my boys received flesh creases. Bunch of Arabs with rubber bullet injuries. We took another ten in custody, including El Said and the four gangsters in the second car—we're taking them to Ramle. You can have a go at them by evening, though I doubt you'll learn anything—just another action-reaction."

The MP came back with a paper bag. Marciano took it, pulled out a folded newspaper and gave it to Daniel.

This morning's *Al Quds.* A front-page headline that read: NEW EVIDENCE IN BUTCHER MURDERS POINTS TO ZIONIST MURDER PLOT. An

Arabic translation of a wire service story by Mark Wilbur, augmented by florid inserts authored by the local editor.

"It ran in our papers too," said Marciano. "Without the extra bullshit."

"I've been out in the field since sunrise," said Daniel, immediately regretting the apologetic sound of it. *The field*. Walking the desert near the murder cave, his beeper signal weakened by the surrounding hills. Walking in circles, like some Judean hermit. Hoping to find . . . what? New evidence? Cosmic insight? Cut off from reality, until he returned to his car, got the riot call from Shmeltzer.

He read the article, grew progressively angrier with each sentence.

Mark Wilbur claimed to have received a message from someone—an *anonymous* someone, who the reporter strongly implied was the Butcher himself. A blank piece of paper upon which had been pasted two paragraphs excised from a Hebrew-language Bible, the precise translation and references supplied by "biblical scholars."

The first, according to Wilbur, was "the traditional Old Testament justification for the Judaizing of Palestine":

> AND BECAUSE HE LOVED THY FATHERS, AND CHOSE THEIR SEED AFTER THEM, AND BROUGHT THEE OUT WITH HIS PRESENCE, WITH HIS GREAT POWER, OUT OF EGYPT; TO DRIVE OUT NATIONS FROM BEFORE THEE GREATER AND MIGHTIER THAN THOU, TO BRING THEE IN, TO GIVE THEE THEIR LAND FOR AN INHERITANCE, AS IT IS THIS DAY. (DEUTERONOMY 4:37–38)

The second was termed "a collection of Mosaic sacrificial rituals taken from the Book of Leviticus":

> AND IF HE BRING A LAMB AS HIS OFFERING FOR A SIN-OFFERING, HE SHALL BRING IT A FEMALE WITHOUT BLEMISH. (4:32)
>
> BUT THE INWARDS AND THE LEGS SHALL HE WASH WITH WATER. (1:13)
>
> WHATSOEVER SHALL TOUCH THE FLESH THEREOF SHALL BE HOLY; AND WHEN THERE IS SPRINKLED OF THE BLOOD THEREOF UPON ANY GARMENT, THOU SHALT WASH THAT WHEREON IT WAS SPRINKLED IN A HOLY PLACE. (6:20)

Shall he wash with water, thought Daniel. Except for those close to the investigation, no one knew about the washing of the bodies. Barring a leak, that meant the paragraphs might very well be the real thing. Material evidence that Wilbur had failed to turn over.

He tightened his jaw, read on:

". . . cannot dismiss the possibility of religious-ethnic motivations behind the Butcher slayings. Both victims were young Arab women, and though police have refused to discuss the details of the case, rumors of sacrificial mutilation have persisted since the discovery, almost a month ago, of the first victim, Fatma Rashmawi, 15."

The article went on that way for several more paragraphs, discussing the conflicts between "right-wing religious settlers on the West Bank and the indigenous Palestinian population," noting that "although prayer has replaced animal sacrifice in Jewish worship, frequent references to sacrificial ritual remain an important part of the liturgy," quoting choice phrases from Moshe Kagan's most inflammatory speeches, stressing the Gvura leader's use of the Bible to justify "coercive territorial expansion." Citing the growing anger among many Israelis toward "what are perceived as random terrorist acts on the part of disenfranchised Palestinians."

Reminding everyone of the tradition of revenge in the Middle East.

Coming as close as possible to blaming the Gvuraniks, or someone like them, for the murders, without actually spelling it out.

But doing it subtly—managing to come across as objective and truth-seeking. Wreaking more damage with nuance and implication than by direct accusation.

"Wonderful thing, freedom of the press." Marciano smiled.

Daniel put the newspaper back in the bag, said, "I'll keep this. What else do you have?"

"All the weapons, tagged and ready for fingerprinting. We've tried to keep the car clean, too, but Gvura people were all over it. The Hebron revenge flat's sealed and guarded. When can your people get to it?"

"Right away. Can you patch me to French Hill?"

"Easy enough," said Marciano, crushing out his cigarette.

The two of them climbed out of the truck bed and back up

into the cab. The colonel punched a few buttons, handed Daniel the radio, said good-bye and good luck, and stepped out. Daniel watched him stride onto the asphalt, stooping to examine a bloodstain, conferring with an underling, gazing neutrally at the Gvura people, who were beginning to return to their homes.

The pace of activity had slowed. Only the heat remained constant. A flock of ravens rose from the vineyard, flying overhead in formation, then reversing itself and settling in the fig trees. Big, lazy-looking birds, their well-fed bodies sheathed by blue-black wings as glossy as an oil slick. Perched with uncharacteristic silence on the gray, knobby branches.

Suspicious creature, the raven. Noah had sent one out to seek dry land; it had come back before completing the journey. Convinced, according to the rabbis, that Noah had designs upon its mate.

Daniel stared at the birds for a moment, then got on the radio.

51

Wilbur never heard them coming. He was celebrating the Butcher-letter story—the biggest pickup ever—rounding off the afternoon at Fink's with a belly full of steak and chips washed down with shots of Wild Turkey and Heineken chasers. The place was empty—all the others were scrambling to write up the Gvura riot thing. Far as he was concerned, that was the same old stuff, be stale by sunrise. He was enjoying the solitude, easing down his fifth chaser and fading into a nice summer high, when he felt his elbows in the vise-grip, saw the gray sleeve hook around his neck and flash the badge in his face.

"What the—" He tried to turn around. A big, warm hand clamped around him and held his head still, exerting pressure behind the ears and keeping him staring straight ahead. Another hand took hold of his belt and pushed forward, preventing him from backing off the barstool.

He looked for the bartender, someone to witness what was going on. Gone.

"Police. Come with us," said a dry voice.

"Now wait one sec—" He was lifted off the stool, all booze-limp, marched out the door to a waiting car with its motor idling.

As they dragged him, he tried to clear his head, zero in on details.

The car: white Ford Escort four-door. No chance to look at the plates. The driver was shielding his face with a newspaper.

The rear door opened. He was eased in, next to a young guy. Good-looking. Tan. Bearded. Skintight red polo shirt, tight designer jeans. Angry face.

"Seat belt," said Dry Voice, and he got in, too, sandwiching Wilbur and slamming the door shut. Wilbur examined him: an older one, limp gray suit, glasses, pale face, beak-nosed and thin-lipped. Semitic version of the guy in "American Gothic." Something about him made Wilbur's stomach queasy.

He fought to suppress his fear, telling himself: No problem, this is a democracy. No Tontons Macoute/Savak types here, unless . . . they weren't policemen. All he'd seen of the badge was a flash of metal—cops in a democracy weren't supposed to behave like this.

Nasty thoughts flashed through his mind. Israeli mafia. Or some crazy Arab group—even though neither of the two in the back looked like Arabs. Maybe Gvura crazies getting back at him for the riot.

A fourth man came around from the rear of the car and got in front, next to the driver. Bushy black hair, big and broad—had to be the one who'd grabbed his neck. Black polo shirt. Huge, hunched shoulders—weight lifter's shoulders. The seat creaked when he moved.

"What the hell is going on?"

"Seat belt," repeated Dry Voice, and when Wilbur hesitated, both he and Handsome reached over and fastened the belt themselves, yanking it tight over his midriff.

The driver put the Escort in gear. Kinky-haired, modified Afro with a yarmulke bobby-pinned to the crown. Crocheted black yarmulke with red roses around the border. Band of dark skin showing above a white shirt collar—a black Jew?

Kinky backed out HaHistadrut Street, onto King George,

drove north, shot the amber light at the Yafo intersection and continued on Straus, weaving in and out of traffic like some joyrider.

Straight out of a second-rate foreign film, thought Wilbur. French or Italian. Only this was real and he was scared shitless.

The Escort hurtled along at breakneck speed until coming to a red light at Malkhei Yisrael, at which point Kinky hooked into an alley so narrow its stone walls threatened to scrape the sides of the car. Kinky maintained his pace, dodging potholes and rubbish.

Wilbur's fingernails dug into his knees. His tailbone was taking a beating, though most of the impact was absorbed by the bodies of Handsome and Dry Voice, compressing him shoulder to shoulder. They stared straight ahead, paying no attention to him, as if he were too insignificant to deal with. Smelling of cologne and sweat. Dry Voice kept one hand in his jacket.

Very subtle.

The alley hairpinned. Kinky kept speeding.

Wilbur stared at the floor in order to keep from heaving.

They emerged on Yehesqel, turned left on Shmuel Hanavi, and Wilbur thought: They *are* police. Taking me to National Headquarters on French Hill.

Outrageous.

He permitted himself to get angry, began selecting the precise wording of his official protest.

Then the Escort bypassed the police compound and continued north and he felt the fear rise again in his gut, stronger, mingling with booze-tinged nausea.

"I demand to—" Croaking. Sounding like a wimp.

"Quiet," said Dry Voice, meaning it.

Kinky kept up the speed. They zipped through the northern suburbs, passed Ramot Eshkol, and the city stopped looking citylike.

Goddamned desert. Empty stretches that preceded the Ramot. Then the northern heights themselves.

Ramot A.

Ramot B.

Wilbur forced himself to keep concentrating on the details, keeping his mind on the story that would come out of all this. The story he was going to shove down these bastards' throats: Reporter abducted; State Department protests. International scandal. Exclusive story by Mark A. Wilbur. TV interviews, talk shows. Dinner at the White House. No problem selling *this* screenplay . . . Who'd be right to play him? Redford? Too flat . . .

On the story, *off* reality.

The four men in the car didn't talk. They *really* didn't seem concerned with him.

That scared him.

Details:

Apartment tracts knocked up quickly for new immigrants—clusters of no-frills rectangles, cinder block faced with limestone, sitting on dry beds devoid of landscaping. Depressing. Like the housing projects back in New York, but these had a ghost-town quality to them, separated from one another by acres of sand.

Laundry on lines.

A vest-pocket park shaded by pines and olives. Kerchiefed women pushing strollers. Hassid types walking with their hands clasped behind their backs. A small shopping center.

A handful of people. Too far away to notice what was happening.

Or care.

The Escort kept barreling along, traveling so fast the chassis was rattling.

Ramot Pollin.

Fewer people, then none. Things were starting to look downright desolate.

Half-finished foundations. Scaffolding. The skeletal underpinnings of buildings. A prefab gas station on a concrete pad, the windows opaque with dust and still X-taped, four oblong trenches where the pumps were going to be.

But no workers, no signs of construction activity. Some goddamned strike, no doubt.

Trenches. Tractor treads. Craters occupied by dormant bulldozers and cranes, the dirt pushed up around the rims in soft brown pyramids.

Unfinished roads bleeding off into dust.

Quiet. Silent. Too damned silent.

A roller-coaster hump in the road, then a sharp dip, another construction site at the bottom, this one stillborn, completely deserted: a single story of cinder block, the rest wood frame. Off in the distance, Wilbur could see tents. Bedouins—where the *hell* were they taking him?

Kinky answered that question by driving off the road, down a muddy ditch, and onto the site. He circled the cinder-block wall until coming to a six-foot opening at the rear and driving through it.

Another car was parked inside, half-hidden by shadows. Red BMW, grayed by dust.

Kinky turned off the engine.

Wilbur looked around: dark, damp place, probably the future subterranean garage. Roofed with sheets of plywood and black plastic tarp. Garbage all over the dirt floor: nail-studded wood scraps, plasterboard fragments, shreds of insulation, bent metal rods, probably a healthy dose of asbestos particles floating in the air.

During orientation, Grabowsky had amused him with stories of how the Israeli mafia buried their victims in the foundations of buildings under construction. Religious Hassid types who were *kohens*—some special kind of priest—afraid of going into the buildings because Jewish law prohibited them from being near dead bodies.

No longer amusing.

No, couldn't be. Kinky wore a yarmulke. Nice Jewish boy, no mafia.

Then he remembered some of the stuff that guys with yarmulkes had pulled off in the diamond district.

Oh, shit.

"Okay," said Dry Voice. He opened the door. Wilbur saw the gun bulge under his suit jacket. Wool suit—asshole wasn't even sweating.

All of them except Kinky got out of the car. Dry Voice took Wilbur's elbow and led him a few feet past the front bumper.

Handsome and Iron Pumper folded their arms across their chests, stood there staring at him. Iron Pumper turned full face. Wilbur saw he was an *Oriental*—goddamned Oriental giant with cold slit eyes. This *had* to be a dream. Too much booze—he'd wake up any moment with a four-plus hangover.

A door slammed. Kinky was out of the car now, holding an attaché case in one hand, the paper he'd used to shield his face in the other.

Wilbur looked at the paper. This morning's international Trib, his Butcher-letter story on page two.

Dry Voice held on to his elbow. Handsome and Slant-Eye

had backed away into the shadows, but he could still sense their presence.

Kinky came closer. Small guy—not black, more like a mixed-blood, the kind you saw all over Brazil. But with weird golden eyes that shone in the dimness like those of a cat. The hand holding the paper was a mess—stiff-looking, covered with shiny pink scars. Real contrast to the rest of him, which was all brown and smooth and seamless. Baby face. But the eyes were old.

"Hello, Mr. Wilbur." Soft voice, barely an accent.

"Who are you?" *Who the fuck are you!*

"Daniel Sharavi. I understand you've been asking about me."

Goddamned geezer at the archives. They all stuck together.

"In the course of my work—"

"That's what we want to talk to you about," said Sharavi. "Your work." He waved the *Herald Tribune.*

Wilbur felt the anger return. More than anger—rage—at what the bastards had put him through.

"This stinks," he said. "Kidnapping me like some—"

"Shut your fucking mouth," said Dry Voice, tightening the hold on his elbow. Heavier accent than Sharavi, but no mistaking the words or the tone.

Sharavi glanced at Dry Voice, smiled apologetically, as if excusing an errant brother. So this was going to be one of those good-cop–bad-cop routines . . .

"Have a seat," said Sharavi, motioning to a plywood board suspended on cinder blocks.

"I'll stand."

Dry Voice led him to the board and sat him down. Hard. "Stay."

Wilbur stared up at him. Asshole looked like an *accountant.* IRS auditor delivering bad news.

Wilbur kept eye contact. "These are Gestapo tactics," he said.

Dry Voice knelt in front of him, gave a very ugly smile. "You're an expert on Gestapo?"

When Wilbur didn't answer, the asshole stood, kicked the dirt, and said, "Shmuck."

Sharavi said something to him in Hebrew and the guy moved back, folded his arms over his chest like the others.

Sharavi lifted a cinder block, brought it close to Wilbur, and sat on it, facing him.

"Your article today was very interesting," he said.

"Get to the point."

"You used a biblical scholar to locate the precise references of the passages."

Wilbur said nothing.

"May I ask which scholar?"

"My sources are confidential. Your government assures the right—"

Sharavi smiled.

"Mutti Abramowitz isn't much of a scholar. In fact, his father told me his grades in Bible Studies have always been very poor."

Little guy put his hands on his knees and leaned forward, as if expecting an answer.

"What's your point?" said Wilbur.

Sharavi ignored the question, opened his attaché case, and rummaged in it. Head concealed by the lid, he asked, "Where were you three Thursdays ago?"

"Now, how am I supposed to remember that?"

"The day before Juliet Haddad's body was found."

"I don't know where I was, probably following some . . . Whoa, wait a minute. I don't have to do this." Wilbur stood. "I want a lawyer."

"Why do you think you need one?" Sharavi asked, mildly.

"Because you people are trampling on my rights. My strong advice to you is quit right now and minimize the damage, because I'm going to raise a stink the likes of which—"

"Sit down, Mr. Wilbur," said Sharavi.

Dry Voice took a step forward, hand in jacket. "Sit, shmuck."

Wilbur sat, head swimming with booze and bad vibes.

"What were you doing three Thursdays ago?" Sharavi repeated.

"I have no idea. I'd just gotten back from Greece, but you guys probably know that, don't you?"

"Tell me everything you know about the murders of Fatma Rashmawi and Juliet Haddad."

"My articles speak for themselves."

Dry Voice said, "Your articles are shit."

"Tell me about the wounds on Juliet Haddad's body," said Sharavi, almost whispering.

"How the hell would I know anything about that?"

Sharavi unfolded the *Herald Tribune,* searched for a place with his finger, found it, and read out loud: "'. . . rumors of sacrificial mutilation have persisted.' Where did you hear those rumors, Mr. Wilbur?"

Wilbur didn't reply. Sharavi turned to the others and asked, "Have you heard such rumors?"

Three head shakes.

"We haven't heard any such rumors, Mr. Wilbur. Where did *you* hear them?"

"My sources are confidential."

"Your sources are shit," said Dry Voice. "You're a liar. You make them up."

"Inspector Shmeltzer lacks tact," said Sharavi, smiling, "but I can't argue strongly with him, Mr. Wilbur." Little bastard held out his hands palms up, all sweetness and light. The palm of the messy hand was puckered with scar tissue.

"Mutti Abramowitz as a biblical scholar," he said, shaking his head. "A clown like Samir El Said as a sociological scholar. Rumors of 'sacrificial mutilations.' You have a vivid imagination, Mr. Wilbur."

"Lying shmuck," said Dry Voice.

"Listen," said Wilbur, "this good-cop–bad-cop stuff isn't going to work. I've watched the same movies you have."

"You like movies, don't you?" Sharavi reached in the briefcase, took out some papers, and handed them to Wilbur.

The notes and title page for his screenplay. Not the original, but photocopies.

"You have no right—"

"Very interesting reading," said Sharavi. "You seem to have many ideas about the Butcher."

"That's fiction—"

Sharavi smiled. "Many ideas," he repeated. "It was you who named him the Butcher, wasn't it? So in one sense you invented him."

"What else did you steal from my office?"

"Tell me everything you know about the murders of Fatma Rashmawi and Juliet Haddad."

"I already told you—everything I know is in my stories."

"Your stories are shit," said Dry Voice—Shmeltzer.

"This is outrageous," said Wilbur.

"Murder is always outrageous," said Sharavi.

"Breaking into my office, stealing my personal—"

"Just like Watergate," suggested Sharavi.

"Wilburgate," said Shmeltzer. "Shitheadgate." He said something in Hebrew. Handsome and Slant-Eye laughed.

Sharavi shook his head. The others quieted.

"A good imagination," he said, returning his attention to Wilbur. "You hear rumors that the police haven't heard, receive letters from someone you claim is the Butcher—"

"I claimed nothing of the sort, I simply—"

"You implied it strongly. Just as you implied that the Gvura people were responsible—"

"I analyze facts," said Wilbur. "Do my research and come up with feasible hypotheses—"

"Feasible hypotheses?"

"You got it, chief."

"You seem to know more about the Butcher than anyone. His motives, his 'sacrificial mutilations,' what goes on inside his head. He must appreciate your understanding, think of you as a friend, because he sends you a letter—a letter without postage. A letter without any fingerprints or serum traces except the ones that match those removed from your liquor bottle and typewriter. Your fingerprints. Your serum type."

"That envelope was stuck in my mail."

"Yes, that's what Mutti says. However, the mail lay in the box there for an hour before he collected it and brought it to you."

"Meaning what?"

"Meaning perhaps you placed it there yourself."

"That's absurd."

"No," said Sharavi. "That's a *feasible hypothesis*. Mutti Abramowitz as a biblical scholar is *absurd*."

"Why would I do something like that?" asked Wilbur, knowing the question was stupid, the answer obvious. "I report the news," he said. Talking to the walls. "I don't create it."

Sharavi was silent, as if digesting that.

"This morning," he said, finally, "five men died, a woman will probably lose her baby, another man, a good portion of his intestines. Several others were injured. All because of 'news' that you invented."

"Blame the messenger," said Wilbur. "I've heard it before."

"I'm sure you have. *My* research reveals you have a history of inventing the news. Mardi Gras ritual murders that turn out to be suicides, exposés that end up exposing nothing."

Wilbur fought to stay cool. "We have nothing to talk about."

"But that's old mischief," said Sharavi. "My primary concern is how far your current inventing went. Could you have been hungry enough for a juicy crime story to supply the crime?"

Wilbur shot out of his chair.

"What the hell are you saying!"

Sharavi closed his attaché case, placed it on his lap, and smiled.

"Learning by doing, Mr. Wilbur. It ensures realism."

"This conversation is over." Wilbur's heart was pounding, his hands shaking. He forced a cool tone: "Nothing more without my lawyer."

Sharavi waited a long time before speaking. Let the silence sink in.

"Where were you three Thursdays ago, Mr. Wilbur?"

"I don't *know*—but I was in *Greece* when the first one was killed! Across the goddamned Mediterranean!"

"Sit down," said Shmeltzer.

"Bullshit," said Wilbur. "Pure and total bullshit harassment."

Sharavi waved Shmeltzer away and said, "Remain on your feet if you like." The gold eyes remained steady. "Tell me, Mr. Wilbur, what sharp-bladed instruments do you own besides the Sabatier cutlery in your kitchen and the Swiss Army knife in your desk?"

"Absurd," said Wilbur. His damned heart wouldn't quiet.

"Do you rent another flat besides the one on Rehov Alharizi?"

"I want a lawyer."

"You've quoted Samir El Said, extensively. What's the nature of your relationship with him?"

Wilbur didn't answer.

"Talk, shmuck," said Dry Voice.

"I have nothing to say. This whole thing is a crock."

"Are you engaged in a homosexual relationship with Professor El Said?"

That took Wilbur by surprise. He tried to maintain a poker face but, from Sharavi's smile, knew he'd been unsuccessful.

"I thought not," said the little bastard. "You *are* a little old for him."

"I'm not homosexual," said Wilbur, thinking: Why the hell am I defending myself?

"You like women?"

"Do *you*?"

"I don't like cutting them up."

"Oh, Christ."

"Shmuck's religious," said Dry Voice.

"I have nothing to say," said Wilbur.

"Look," said Sharavi, "we have plenty of time. When it gets dark, we'll use flashlights to chase away the rats."

"Suit yourself," said Wilbur.

But the stonewall didn't work.

Sharavi proceeded to question him for another hour and a half about the murders. Times, places, where he bought his linens, what kind of soap he used, how many kilometers a day he drove. Were his eyes healthy, what drugs he took, did he shower or take baths. What were his views on personal hygiene. Seeming irrelevancies. Picayune details that he'd never thought about. Asking the same questions over and over, but changing the phrasing ever so slightly. Then coming out of left field with something that sounded totally irrelevant and ended up being somehow tied in with something else.

Trying to confuse him.

Treating him like a goddamned murderer.

He was determined to resist, give the little bastard nothing. But eventually he found himself relenting—worn down by the smiles and the repetition, Sharavi's unflappable manner, the way he ignored Wilbur's outbursts, refused to take umbrage at Wilbur's insults.

By the time the reporter realized he was losing, he'd already lost, answering questions with numbed docility. His feet tired from standing, but refusing to sit for fear of underscoring his submission.

As the interrogation wore on, he rationalized it away by telling himself the little bastard was giving in too. Acting nicer.

Treating him like an adviser, not a suspect.

Believing him.

After ninety minutes, Sharavi stopped the questions, chatted with him about trivia. Wilbur felt himself loosen with relief. Sat down, finally, and crossed his legs.

Twenty minutes later, the chatting ceased. The basement cavity had grown darker, colder. Nightfall.

Sharavi said something to Slant-Eye, who came over and offered Wilbur a cigarette. He refused. Finally, Sharavi clicked the attaché case shut, smiled, and said, "That's it."

"Great," said Wilbur. "Drop me back at Beit Agron?"

"Oh, no," said Sharavi, as if the request had taken him by surprise.

Slant-Eye put a hand on Wilbur's shoulder. Handsome walked over, put handcuffs on him.

"This is Subinspector Lee," said Sharavi, looking at the Oriental. "And this is Detective Cohen. They'll be taking you back to Jerusalem. To the Russian Compound, where you'll be booked for obstructing a criminal investigation and withholding evidence."

A flood of words rose in Wilbur's gullet. He lacked the will to expel them and they stagnated.

Sharavi dusted off his trousers.

"Good afternoon, Mark. If there's anything else you wish to tell me, I'll be happy to listen."

When the BMW had driven off, Daniel asked Shmeltzer, "What do you think?"

"Only thing I got from his eyes is alcoholism—you should have seen the bottles in his flat. As far as the grin goes, we didn't give him much chance to smile, did we, Dani? Nothing we've turned up in the flat or the office implicates him, and the Greek thing checks out as an alibi for Fatma's murder—though if he's got pals, that's meaningless. What did Ben David tell you about the letter?"

"That the Bible quotes could mean a real fanatic or someone wanting to sound like one. One thing's for certain: Whoever wrote it is no true scholar—the passages from Leviticus are out of sequence and out of context. The one about washing the legs refers to a male animal. It smells deceptive—someone trying to distract us."

"Someone trying to pin it on the *Jews,*" said Shmeltzer. "Exactly this Wilbur shmuck's style." He spat into the dirt. "Ben David have anything to say about the printing used for the address?"

"The block letters were written very slowly and deliberately by someone familiar with writing English. Along with the fact that English was used for the address instead of Hebrew, that could support our foreigner angle, except that the Bible quotes were in Hebrew. But Meir Steinfeld came by just before I picked you guys up, told me about the prints and the serum and shed some light on the Hebrew. The text matched that of a gift edition Hebrew-English Bible—common tourist item, printed locally. Mass-market—no use checking bookstores. He showed me a copy, Nahum. The text is printed correspondingly. Anyone could read the English, then cut out the matching Hebrew verse. Addressing the envelope would be a different matter."

"Some fucking anti-Semite," said Shmeltzer. "Fucking blood libel."

"The alternative, of course, is that whoever sent the letter knows Hebrew *and* English and used both languages to play games with us, show off how clever he is. That kind of posturing is consistent with serial killers."

"If the letter-writer's the killer."

"If," agreed Daniel. "It could be pure mischief. But there's the washing reference."

"Press leak," said Shmeltzer.

"If it was, someone in the press would have used it. Even Wilbur made no mention of it specifically, just talked in general terms about sacrifices. And Ben David thought it looked promising from a handwriting perspective, said the slowness and the pressure of the writing indicated calculation and suppressed anger—lots of anger. The tearing of the paper shows that the anger is threatening to break through the suppression."

"Meaning?"

"If the writer's our killer, we're probably in for another murder. Maybe soon—today is Thursday."

"Not if Wilbur's our guy and we keep him locked up," said Shmeltzer.

"Not necessarily. You're the one who likes the group theory."

"I like this guy, Dani. Wouldn't mind cooling his ass at the compound for a while, see what a little tenderizing does to his memory for detail. At the very least we can tie him up for a while on the obstruction thing, fucking bastard."

"You enjoyed the interrogation, didn't you, Nahum?"

"Labor of love."

The two of them got in the Escort. Daniel revved up the engine, drove out of the basement and across the rocky surface of the site. Gravel spattered the underside of the car. Only a semicircle of sun was visible over the horizon. The darkness had turned the partially framed building into something ephemeral. Atrophied.

"Speaking of obstruction," said Shmeltzer, "Drori, the anesthesiologist, is eliminated. Night of both murders he was on duty at the hospital, working emergency surgeries. Thing that pisses me off is that the Thursday night that Fatma was killed, Krieger—the one who informed on him—was there too. They did an operation together. Krieger was trying to harass the guy."

"Personal thing, as we suspected," said Daniel.

Shmeltzer gave a disgusted look. "I tailed Drori to find out where he goes on those middle-of-the-night drives when Krieger's on duty. Straight to Krieger's flat to fuck Krieger's wife. Same old jealousy shit—bastard was trying to use us as his henchmen. If we weren't so busy, I'd pull him in, teach him a lesson."

"Anything on the desert hikes?"

"University and the Nature Conservancy still checking—the usual bureaucratic bullshit."

Daniel steered the Escort onto the road and headed south. They rode for a while without speaking, past the upper Ramot, and down toward A and B. Just ahead of them, an Egged bus had pulled up to the curb. Dozens of dark-garbed yeshiva boys alighted; their mothers, waiting at the bus stop, greeted them with soft bosoms, kisses, and snacks. The bus swung out sharply, moving nonchalantly into the path of the Escort, and Daniel had to weave sharply to avoid hitting it.

"Idiot," muttered Shmeltzer. His glasses had been knocked loose and he straightened them. A hundred meters later he said, "Busting a journalist, *Herr* Pakad. Going to bring down big buckets of political shit."

"I'll wear a hat," said Daniel. He pressed his foot to the floor and sped back toward the city and its secrets.

52

Wonderful, wonderful, wonderful, thought the Grinning Man, masturbating. Then, thinking: I sound like Lawrence fucking Welk, and starting to giggle.

But it *was* wonderful. Sand-niggers and kikes chewing each other up. Ripping and squeaking like the little hook-nosed rodents they were.

And he, the trainer.

Project *Untermensch*.

He flashed a mind picture of opposing rat hordes, charging at each other on little rat feet. Pouring out of sewer pipes, up out of putrid storm drains, bubbling to the surface of sinkholes.

Little brown sand-nigger rats with little rag heads and black whiskers. Little pink-and-gray kike rats with yarmulkes and chin-beards. Yammering and shrieking and snapping, biting off snouts and lips and leaving gaping holes like the pictures in Dieter Schwann's big green book.

Chomp. There goes a tail.

Chomp. There goes an ear.

Chewing each other up until there was nothing left but little bone piles and little moist rat stains that you could clean up really good.

And blessed silence—space for a white man to walk.

No more bad-machine noises.

Plenty of elbow room.

Chomp.

What a terrific feeling, to set something into motion and watch it work out just the way you planned.

Real power.

Real science.

Power. The thought of it made him come sooner than he'd planned. He was lost in the orgasm for a few brain-shattering moments, rocking back and forth on the bed, stroking and squeezing himself with one hand, caressing the half-healed swastika wounds on his thighs with the other.

Mind control.

The kind he'd wielded over Doctor, though the fucker had been only one rat and now he had lots of them scampering on command.

But an important rat, a mind-fucker par excellence.

The Michelangelo of mind pictures.

No. Dali. *There* was a mind-fucker—limpo clocks, quails cooked in their own shit. And they said he was a kike. Lies!

Power over Doctor. He'd been careful not to overdo the extortion thing—dear old dad was a greedy pig, didn't give a shit about him. Push him too far and no telling what he'd do.

The important thing was to keep a good sense of balance. Hit the fucker for favors that were really important. Squeeze him hard and fast, no mercy, then disappear. The rest of the time, let him go about his life deluding himself that he was a free man.

The squeeze: cash. Lots of it—more than anyone else his age had, but nothing that would break Doctor—fucker kept *cracking chests* and raking it in, all those apartment buildings he owned, blue-chip stocks and certificates of deposit.

Money junkie, like all of them.

How do you teach a Jewish baby to swim?

Throw a penny in the pool. The rest takes care of itself.

The little bit he squeezed added up surprisingly quickly. Some of it went into a savings account, some in a safe deposit box, along with the bonds.

Tax-free municipals and high-yield corporates—he clipped coupons every month, saved the principal, pocketed the interest. Doctor told his attorney the time had come to pass some of his holdings along to his beloved son in order to get around the inheritance tax.

Estate planning. Gee, what a neat dad.

Cash and bonds and growth stocks that he could sell whenever he wanted. Doctor introduced him to his broker, told the slimy button-down asshole he wanted his beloved son to learn the financial ropes at a young age, be able to make his own decisions.

Superdad.

And the cars—the Jag totally cool but always in the shop. Perfect once in a great while for cruising in high style, feeling like King Shit, the Emperor of Real Science. The Plymouth ugly but dependable, plenty of trunk space for toys and whatever.

Doctor gave him three gas credit cards. The maintenance bills and insurance premiums were always paid right on time.

He had the house to himself—Doctor had moved out, lived in a condo near the hospital. *She* was grokked-out all the time now, sleeping and pissing in her bed, brain circuits totally fried.

Doctor, terrific husband that he was, hired private-duty nurses to take care of her. Different ones each week, fat nigger broads and swishy faggots—they just sat there doing crossword puzzles and smoking, changed the sheets, stole jewelry and food.

The maids were gone; in their place, a retardo nigger who came in once a week to dust and clear away the dishes.

The house had started to smell old and stale. Like death. Only his room was clean. And the library.

He cleaned those himself.

Cleanliness next to godliness.

Nice quiet house—he was Lord of the Manor.

He made a stab at junior college, taking Mickey Mouse courses and attending just often enough to pass. Kept his job at the hospital for fun, working three afternoons a week delivering mail—richest fucking mailboy in the city.

He read journals and books in the hospital library, learned a lot. Snuck into the pathology lab, opened body drawers and fondled the cadavers, rubbed himself against cold flesh, ogled welcome holes and jars of organs. Coded new mind pictures.

Nighttime was the right time.

Cruising Nasty Boulevard, ogling the geeks, freaks, junkies, slime-os, and whores. Using the Jag for show, the Plymouth for serious business. He craved new identities, sought out the theatrical supply shops on Nasty and bought disguises: hats, glasses and sunglasses, false mustaches, beards and wigs, to make himself look different. *Be* different. Practiced talking different voices, using different mannerisms.

He could be anyone!

In the beginning he just cruised and ogled. Passed the motel where he'd caught Doctor and the candy-striper, saw only soft cars, a different slant at the desk.

He stopped, closed his eyes, and wondered what was going on inside. How many whores were fucking how many geeks, the things they were doing, a treasure trove of mind pictures.

Whores, the ultimate females.

He decided to relate to them, cruised by them for weeks, catching smiles, but not ready to make contact, then finally doing it, heart pounding the same way it had when he sat on the stairs.

He picked one at random, from a hot-pants hen party leaning against a lamppost. Spoke his lines like a robot and didn't even bother to notice what she looked like until she'd gotten in and he'd driven a couple of blocks.

Total downer: fat nigger bitch, Ubangi lips and white eye shadow. Sagging tits, stretch marks—she had to be forty.

They pulled off on a side street in the Plymouth, agreed to a blow-job in the front seat.

He finished fast; the bitch coughed and spat him out into a handkerchief as if he were garbage. Wholly unsatisfactory, but a start.

The next few times were the same, but still he liked it, collecting pictures for the memory file. Lying in bed hours later, imagining himself later opening up the whores, exploring their welcome holes, cleaning them and feeling totally cool and in charge.

Then he met Nightwing.

She worked by herself, on a quiet corner several blocks east of the hot-pants hens. Good bone structure despite the red-black lipstick, chalk-white Vampira makeup, and mile-long false eyelashes. Meaty thighs bulging out of a black silk microskirt. All in black.

A little older than he, early twenties probably. Short and stacked, long dark hair, big dark eyes, a terrific face.

A Sarah face!

That was the main thing! The resemblance totally freaked him out—so much that the first time he saw her he sped up and drove by without doing a thing. Drove for a mile until he'd gotten hold of himself, then circled back on the boulevard, hanging a U and cruising slowly toward her street corner.

In the Jag, top down, tweed jacket, deerstalker cap, bristly mustache. Identity: British sophisticate.

She was talking to this fat spic, haggling. The spic shook his head and walked away. She flipped him the bird.

He slowed down, took a good look at her, at the Sarah face.

She saw the car first, shiny bumpers, sloping headlights,

hard-on front end. Smelled money, looked up at him and licked her lips.

Sharp little white teeth. Cat teeth.

Hey, cutie, wanna party?

Strange accent. Wop? Spic?

Still freaked, he passed her by again, looked in the rearview mirror and saw her flip him off.

Next night he was in the Plymouth, different hat, no fake hair. No recognition.

Hey, cutie.

He leaned over and pushed the door open: Hop right in, babe. Saying it movie-stud cool, but so nervous a tickle would have made him pee his pants.

She came to the curb, leaned in, tits hanging out of a black vinyl halter.

Well, hello there. Looking him over.

Hi, babe.

More once-over, the false lashes opening and closing like moth wings. Then backing off, the you're-not-no-cop-are-you game.

Charming smile: Do I look like a cop, babe?

No one looks *like a cop, cutie.*

Hold the smile, flash the cash: If I wanted to talk all night, I'd have joined a rap group.

She hesitated, looked around, scratched a fishnet knee.

He edged the Plymouth forward an inch.

Hold on, cutie.

Now *she's* smiling, all cat teeth, evil-Sarah. Watching her, he got totally turned on. His hard-on like a ton of galvanized pipe.

She got in, closed the door, and stretched. Catlike. Named a price.

Fine, babe. So casual.

She studied him again. Stretched.

Go three blocks and hang a right, cutie.

What's there?

A nice comfy spot for partying.

Two minutes later, the old front-seat head-in-lap cliché, but different: He'd expected to shoot off right away, but the Sarah-resemblance created mind pictures that kept him going for a while. He made her work, pushed down on her head, wrapped her hair around his fingers, then gave it to her.

All *right!*

And this one didn't spit: *Yum*. With a smile.

Lying through her teeth, but he loved it nonetheless.

Loved *her*.

Because it was true love, he paid her more than they'd agreed on, looked for her the next night and the next, not knowing her name, not knowing who to ask for—Sarah who swallows? Went home hungry, cruised, stole a stray dog and feasted on science and the memories until the third night, when he spotted her on a different corner, even farther east.

Still in black, still beautiful.

No recognition, until she got close.

Well, hello, cutie.

Weird accent, but definitely not spic.

After she did him, he asked what her name was.

Nightwing.

What kind of name is that?

My street name, cutie.

What's your real name?

The street is *real, cutie. You ask too many questions. Talk's a waste of time.* Cat smile. *Well, well, would you* loo-ook *at that . . . Hey, Youngblood—how about seconds? You're so cute, I'll give you a discount.*

I'll pay you regular.

Well, aren't you sweet—ooh, so impatient. Go ahead, push my head, pull my hair—a little harder, even, if it gets my cutie off.

They dated regularly, at least once a week, sometimes twice. Driving farther and farther away from Nasty, up into the hills that overlooked the boulevard. Parking on cul-de-sacs and tree-blackened side streets, always blow-jobs—neither of them wanted anything messy.

Casual dates, no holding-hands-in-the-movie-theater bullshit. He liked the honesty, the fact that neither of them felt a need for conversation and other lies.

But learning a little about her anyway—she liked to talk when she reapplied her lipstick.

She was from out of town, had worked Nasty for six months, first with a pimp but going it alone now. The pimp, some evil nigger named BoJo, had accused her of holding out cash and cut her up. She showed him the scar under one tit, bumpy pink zipper. He licked it.

Being an independent meant she had to cover her ass at all times, stay away from the pimp-slaves, restrict herself to quiet corners. Which was getting tougher to do—the pimps were spreading out, pushing her east, away from the Nasty Strip hot spots. But the hills were okay. Everything was okay:

I got no problems, cutie. I got no problem making ends meet—if you dig what I'm saying, cutie pie.

She'd volunteer a little info, but wouldn't answer questions, not even about the accent, which he still couldn't place—gypsy?

The secrecy didn't bother him. In fact, he liked it.

None of that *peace-love-confiding-and-relating* scam.

He paid; she sucked. He started keeping an ice chest in the trunk of the Plymouth, brought beer, Pepsi, and orange soda along. She washed her mouth out afterward, licked his nipples through his shirt with a cold tongue. Most of the time it got him going for seconds.

He was becoming an expert, could go longer and longer now, volunteered to pay her for her time instead of by the act. She squealed with delight, told him he was a total sweetie. Went down on him with fake enthusiasm so real it made his head spin, gagging and whispering that she'd do anything for him, just name it.

Just do what you're doing, babe.

He gave himself a street name, too: Dr. Terrific.

Mind picture: DT LOVES N carved into the cerebral cortex.

C'mon, cutie. You're too young to be a doctor.

You'd be surprised.

But you got money like a doctor, don't you?

Want to earn some more?

Right on.

Later:

If you're a doctor, you probably got all sorts of far-out drugs, right?

Drugs are bad for you.

You're putting me on now, right?

Mysterious smile.

After their twentieth date, she snorted heroin and offered him some. He said no, watched her get all drowsy and mellow, played with her body while she lay there half-grokked.

True love.

* * *

At nineteen, he could tell from the way people ogled him that he was good-looking. Was certain that he looked older—maybe twenty-four or -five. At nineteen and a half, life got cleaner: *She* died, just stopped breathing in bed and lay there in her own filth for two hours before one of the hired nurses came up from the kitchen and noticed.

The house was *totally* his now. It hadn't taken much to "convince" Doctor to let him keep living in it.

Nineteen and a half, and totally on top of the world: his own pad, endless bucks, and head-in-lap true love.

He cleaned out the Ice Palace, had the carpets ripped up, gave everything away. Told the retardo nigger to spray it with disinfectant, open all the windows. Decided it would stay empty forever.

He woke up one morning feeling terrific and filled with a sense of purpose. He'd been waiting for the right time to start the investigation, knew this was it, and started looking in the Yellow Pages under Private Detectives.

He wanted a one-man agency; the big firms were all fat on big-business bucks, not likely to take him seriously.

He found half a dozen possibles, all in low-rent areas, phoned them, listened to their voices, and made an appointment with the one who sounded the hungriest.

Slimeball named J. Walter Fields, bad address not far from the Nasty Strip.

He made an appointment for late in the afternoon.

The office was on the fourth floor of a decaying walkup, winos dozing near the front entrance, half the suites unoccupied, shit-colored cracked linoleum, bare light bulbs and empty sockets, the hallways stinking of piss.

Fields's place was a glass-doored single room with the men's john on one side, an answering service company on the other.

RELIABLE INVESTIGATORS.

J. W. FIELDS, PRES.

Inside was pure Late Show cliché: old-clothes smell, grimy walls, portable fan on a chair, metal desk and file cabinets. A flyspecked window offered a view of inert neon signs and the tar-paper roof of the walkup across the alley.

Fields was a short, fat bag of slime in his late fifties. Wet, hungry eyes, bad suit, and receding gums. He kept his feet up on the desk and popped licorice drops in his mouth while raising one eyebrow and staring at his visitor. Making a big show of being bored.

"Yeah?"

"We have an appointment." Speaking in a deep voice.

Fields glanced down at a big old-fashioned metal desk calendar resting on a rust-specked metal base. "You're Dr. Terrif, huh?" Pronouncing it *tariff*.

"That's right."

"The fuck you trying to pull, kid? Get outa here. Don't waste my time."

"Pressed for time, are you?"

"Watch your mouth, kid." A grubby thumb pointed to the door. "The fuck out."

Boyish shrug. "Oka-ay." Pulling out a thick roll of bills, putting it back, and turning to go.

Slimeball let him get to the door, then spoke up. Straining to keep the hunger out of his voice.

"Whoa, what's on your mind, kid?"

"Doctor."

"Sure, sure. You're a doctor, I'm Mr. Universe."

Scornful look at the slimeball: "We have nothing to talk about." Saying it with class, swinging the door open and walking out.

He'd gone ten paces down the hall before hearing Fields's cheap-shoe shuffle.

"C'mon . . . Doc. Don't be *sensitive*."

He ignored the whining, kept on walking.

"Let's *talk*, Doc." Fields was trotting to catch up. "C'mon, Dr. Terrif."

Stopping, swiveling, staring at the pathetic slime.

"Your manners stink, Fields."

"Listen . . . I didn't—"

"Apologize." Power.

Fields hesitated, looked sick, as if standing on a diving board suspended over a cesspool.

Tick-tock, licking his lips. You could see the dollar signs bounce like slot-machine fruit in the fucker's eyes.

Split-second later, he sucked in his breath and dived in: "You got to understand . . . Doc. My business, you get all types, all kinds of scams. Just trying to cover my butt. . . . You got a young face, good genes, lucky guy, Doc. . . . Okay, I'm sorry. How say we start over?"

Back in the rathole of an office, Fields picked up a gray mug that had once been white and offered to fix him instant coffee.

I'd rather drink snake-jizz, fucker. "Let's get down to business, Fields."

"Sure, sure, at your service. Doc."

He told the slime what he wanted. Fields listened hard, trying to imitate an intelligent life form. Popping licorice and saying "Uh huh" and "Uh huh, Doc."

"Think you can handle it?"

"Sure, sure, Doc, no problem. This guy Schwann, you into him for bucks or vicey versey?"

"That's none of your concern." Saying it automatically, in a totally cool way. The deep voice making him sound just like a rich guy, totally in charge—which he was, when you got down to it. Built to rule.

"Okay, no problem, Doc. Only sometimes it helps to know about the *motivation,* if you know what I'm sayin'."

"Just do what I pay you for and don't worry about motivation."

"Sure, sure."

"When can you have the information?"

"Hard to tell, Doc. Depends on lots of things. You ain't givin' me much to work with."

"Here's your advance. Plus." Standing and peeling off bills, a hundred more than the slime had asked for. Doing it offhand, in a totally cool manner.

"I got expenses, Doc."

Another hundred passed into the slime's paw. "Have the information in three weeks and there's an extra two hundred in it for you."

Fields nodding energetically, just about coming in his cheap-suit trousers. "Okay, sure, Doc, three weeks, you're top priority. Where can I reach you?"

"I'll reach *you.* Sit down. I'll see myself out."

"Yeah, sure, pleasure doing business with you."

After leaving the office, he closed the door, stood to the side for a moment, and heard the slime say "Fucking rich kid."

* * *

Nightwing started using heroin in front of him on a regular basis. Snorting the first few times, then skin-popping.

I don't mainline, cutie. That's how you really get fucked up.

But ten dates later, she was shooting it into a vein behind her leg.

I can handle it.

He'd read plenty of medical books on addiction, knew she was full of shit, biochemically hooked, but didn't say anything. When she nodded off, he used the time to explore her body. She knew what he was doing, smiled and made little cat sounds while he poked and probed and nibbled and tasted.

One night, while parked on a side street in the hills, Nightwing sprawled across the front seat of the Plymouth, he heard racing engines, saw red lights—pair of cop cars speeding by, on their way to check out something in one of the hill houses. Break-in? Silent burglar alarm? If so, the cops would be back, cruising the hills, looking for suspects. He thought of the heroin in Nightwing's black vinyl purse and began to freak out.

A bust for dope—the perfect life blown to bits!

He put the Plymouth in neutral, coasted downhill with his lights off. Nightwing stayed fast asleep, rolling with the motion of the car, snoring like a little sow. At that moment he saw her as filth, hated her, wanted to open her up, dive in, clean her. Then love thoughts took over and replaced the scientific ones.

He coasted all the way to Nasty, turned the engine and headlights on, merged with the traffic, and tried to calm down. But he stayed freaked at the thought of being busted for dope, had read about prison in psychiatry books, and knew what happened to fresh young white meat.

Deprivation-induced homosexuality: Locked in a cell with psycho niggers who'd ream his ass. His hold over Doctor loosened, the fucker'd be in charge of the lawyers, be able to keep him there as long as he wanted. Maybe even hire some nigger to slice him with a homemade shiv.

He pulled off the boulevard, drove six blocks, parked, and reached over for Nightwing's purse. The strap was under her ass. He tugged. She stirred but didn't wake.

Quickly, frantically, he rummaged through gum wrappers and tissues, plastic wallet, comb, makeup, breath-mint roll, foil rubber packets, and all the other crap she kept in there, before finding the little glassine envelope. Tossing it out of the car, then driving another half mile before feeling safe.

He pulled over again, under a street light, cut the engine. The purse was in his lap. Nightwing was still sleeping.

As he calmed down, curiosity overpowered his fear. He opened the purse, removed the plastic wallet.

Inside was a driver's license, picture of Nightwing without Vampira makeup, just a pretty, dark girl, Sarah-twin.

Lilah Shehadeh. Five two, hundred and fourteen. Birth date that made her twenty-three. Address in Niggertown, probably from her days with BoJo.

Shehadeh. What the hell kind of name was that?

When she awoke, he told her about ditching her dope. She sat up sharply, started to get all pissed.

Oh, shit! That was China fucking White!

What was it worth?

Hundred bucks.

Bullshit, babe.

Fifty—and that's no bullshit. China White's heavy duty—

Here's sixty. Buy yourself some more. But don't carry it when you're with me.

She snapped up the money. *Fun guy,* you *are.*

Flames of rage seared him from throat to asshole. The bad-machine noise grew deafening.

He gave her a long, heavy stare, totally scornful, just like the one he'd used to whip Fields into shape.

This is our last date, babe.

Panic under the mile-long lashes: *Aw, c'mon, cutie.*

It's not fun for me either, babe.

She reached out, ran her long black fingernails over his forearm. He felt nothing—being cool was easy.

Aw, c'mon, Dr. Cutes. I was just kidding. You're real fun, the best. Grab. *The biggest.*

He removed her fingers, shook his head sadly.

Time for both of us to move on, babe.

Aw, c'mon, we been having so much fun. Don't let a little—

She was whining. The bad-machines echoed in his head, making him feel hollow. Useless.

His hand was around her neck in a flash. Thin neck, soft neck, nice and fragile under his grip. He pushed her back against the door of the car. Saw the terror in her eyes and felt his hard-on grow gargantuan.

A little pressure on the carotid, cut off the blood flow to the brain for a split second, then release, let her breathe. Let her know what he could do if he wanted. That she was a bug over a flame. Dangling in the grip of a pair of tweezers.

Let her know who controlled the tweezers.

Listen carefully, babe. Okay?

She tried to talk. Fear had frozen her vocal cords.

I'm perfectly happy to date you—you're terrific. But we've got to come to an understanding. Okay? Nod if you agree.

Nod.

The beauty of this relationship is that we give each other what we need. Right?

Nod.

Which means both of us have to stay happy.

Nod.

I don't care if you want to kill yourself with heroin. But I don't want you putting me in danger. That's fair, isn't it?

Nod.

So no dope when you're with me, please. A beer's okay, one or two at the most. If you ask my permission and I give it. No surprises. I respect your rights and you respect mine. Okay?

Nod.

Still friends?

Nod, nod, nod.

He let go of her. Her eyes stayed big with fear—he could see the respect in them.

Here, babe. He gave her an extra fifty. This is for goodwill, let you know I only want the best for you.

She tried to take the money. Her hands were shaking. He tucked it between her tits. Pointed at his crotch and said, I'm ready to go again.

After they finished, he asked her:

What kind of name is Shehadeh?

Arabic.

You're an Arab.

Fuck, no, I'm an American.

But your family's Arab?

I don't want to talk about them. Defiantly. Then looking at him in panic, wondering if she'd pissed him off again.

He smiled inside. Thought: The relationship's climbed to a new level. Still casual dating and true love, but now the roles were set. Both of them knew their parts.

He held her face in his hands, felt her tremble. Kissed her on the lips, no tongue, just friendly. Gentle—letting her know everything was okay. He was merciful.

They'd have a long, happy life together.

He met with Fields three weeks after giving the slime the assignment. Grubby little fucker was surprisingly thorough, had a thick file labeled SCHWANN, D. clutched in his grubby little hands.

"How you doin', Doc?"

"Here's your money. What do you have?"

Fields stuffed the money in his shirt pocket. "Good news and bad news time, Doc. The good news is I found out all about him. The bad news is the sonofabitch is dead."

Saying it with a twinkle in his eye that signed his own death certificate.

"Dead?"

"As a doorknob." Slimeball shrugged. "Sometimes in these bad-debt cases you can sue the estate in probate court, try to collect, but this Schwann was a foreigner—goddamned Kraut. His body was shipped back to Krautland. Try to collect from over there, you're gonna need an international lawyer."

Dead. Daddy dead. His roots completely severed. He sat there, numb, flooded with pain.

Fields mistook the numbness for disappointment over the debt, tried to comfort him with "Tough luck, eh, Doc? Anyway, guy like you, being a doctor and all that, should be able to write it off, pay less taxes this year. Could be worse, eh?"

Babbling. Making things worse for himself.

The slime was staring at him. He shook himself out of the numbness.

"Give me the file."

"I got a report for you, Doc. All summed up and everything."

"I want the file."

"Eh, usually I keep the file. You want a copy, I got Xeroxing charges, extra expenses."

"Would twenty dollars take care of it?"

"Uh, yeah—thirty would be more like it. Doc."

Fields took the three tens and held out the folder.

"All yours, Doc."

"Thanks." He stood up, took the folder with one hand, picked up the old-fashioned desk calendar with the other, and slammed the fucker across the face with the rusty metal base.

Fields went down without a sound, slumping on the desk. A red stain spread from under his face and saturated the blotter.

He wrapped his hands in tissues, lifted the slime, and inspected him. The front of Fields's face was flattened and bloody, the nose a soft smear. Still a weak wrist pulse.

He put him facedown on the desk, slammed him on the back of the head with the calendar base, kept slamming him, enjoying it. Making him pay for Schwann, for the twinkle in his slimy eyes.

No pulse—how could there be? The medulla oblongata had been turned to shit.

Looked out the window: only neon, and pigeons on the roof. He drew the shade, locked the door, searched for any mention of his or Schwann's names in any other file or in the calendar, then wiped his hands and everything he'd touched clean with a handkerchief—the important thing was to clean up properly.

A little blood had spattered on his shirt. He buttoned his jacket; that took care of that.

Picking up the Schwann file, he left the fucker lying there leaking, stepped out into the hallway, and walked away casually. Feeling like a king, the emperor of everything.

Dr. T.

Those good feelings grew as he drove home on Nasty. Looking at the geeks and pimps and junkies and bikers, all thinking they were bad, so bad. Thinking: How many of you losers have gone all the way? Remembering what Fields's face had looked like after being slammed. The weak pulse. Then nothing.

One giant step for Dr. Terrific.

Back home, he put the Schwann file on his bed, stripped naked, masturbated twice, and took a cold bath that made him angry and hungry for bloody mind pictures. After toweling himself dry, he jerked off some more, came weakly but nicely, and, still naked, went in and got the file.

Noble Schwann, dead.

Cut off at the roots.

The bad-machines started grinding.

He should have taken his time with Fields, really punished him. Brought the slime's body back here, for exploration, real science.

Except the guy's body would have had to be putrid, a real stinker. So no loss.

Anyway, no use crying over spilt milk . . . spilt blood, ha ha.

He grinned, took the file into the stale, empty space that had once been the Ice Palace, sat on the bare wooden floor, and began to read.

53

Fourteen minutes before Thursday night surrendered to Friday morning, Brother Roselli exited the Saint Saviour's monastery and began walking east on St. Francis Street.

Elias Daoud, swaddled in a musty Franciscan habit and concealed in the shadows of the Casa Nova Hospice, was not impressed. The farthest Roselli had ever gone was down the Via Dolorosa, tracing Christ's walk in reverse, to the doors of the Monastery of the Flagellation. Hesitating at the shrine, as if contemplating entry, then turning back. And that was a long-distance hike—usually Roselli walked no farther than the market street that bisected the Old City longitudinally, separating the Jewish Quarter from the Christian Quarter. And the moment he got there, he jerked his head back nervously and turned around.

Hardly worth the effort of following him.

Strange bird, thought Daoud. He'd come to resent the monk, deeply, for the numbing boredom he'd brought into his life. Sitting, hour after hour, night after night, as inert as the cobblestones beneath his feet, wearing the coarse, unwashed robes or some beggar's rags. So stagnant he feared his brain would soon weaken from disuse.

Feeling the resentment grow as he thought about it, then plagued by guilt at harboring anger toward a man of God.

But a *strange* man of God. Why did he stop and go like some wind-up toy? Setting out purposefully, only to reverse himself as if manipulated by some unseen puppeteer?

Conflict, he and Sharavi had agreed. *The man is in conflict over something.* The Yemenite had told him to keep watching.

He'd begun, eventually, to resent Sharavi too. Keeping him away from the action, stuck on this dummy assignment.

But let's be truthful: It wasn't the boredom that bothered him. A week wasn't that long—he was patient by nature, had always enjoyed the solitude of undercover, the shifting of identities.

It was being excluded.

He'd done his job well, identifying the Rashmawi girl. But no matter—now that things had gotten political, he was unwanted baggage. No way would they trust him with anything of substance.

The others—even young Cohen, little more than a rookie, with no judgment and no brains—banded together as a team. Where the action was.

While Elias Daoud sat and watched a strange monk walk two hundred meters and turn back.

He knew what was in store for him when this assignment ended: Off the Butcher case, back to Kishle, maybe even back in uniform, handling tourists' purse-snatches and petty squabbles. Maybe another undercover some day, if it wasn't political.

Working for the Jews, everything was political.

Not a single Arab he knew would regret seeing the Jews disappear. Nationalistic talk had grown fashionable even among the Christians. He himself couldn't muster much passion for politics. He had no use, personally, for the Jews, supposed an all-Arab state would be better. But, then again, without Jews to complain about, Christians and Muslims would surely turn on one another; it was the way things had been for centuries. And given that state of affairs, everyone knew who'd win—look at Lebanon.

So it was probably best to have Jews around. Not in charge, to be sure. But a few, as a distraction.

He stepped out on St. Francis Street and looked east. Roselli's outline was visible a hundred meters up, just past Es Sayyida Road; the monk's sandal-shuffle could be heard clear up the street. Daoud wore sandals, too, but his were crepe-soled. Police issue. The discrepancy concealed by the floor-length robes.

Roselli kept walking, approaching the market intersection.

Daoud stayed out of sight, flush with the buildings, prepared to duck into a doorway when the monk reversed himself.

Roselli passed the Abyssinian monastery, stopped, turned right onto Souq El Attarin, and disappeared.

It took a moment for the fact to register. Caught by surprise, Daoud ran to catch up, his boredom suddenly replaced by anxiety.

Thinking: What if I lose him?

To the east, the *souq* was ribbed with dozens of narrow roads and arched alleyways leading to the Jewish Quarter. Tiny courtyards and ancient clay-domed homes restored by the Jews, orphanages and one-room schools and synagogues. If someone wanted to lose himself at night, no section of the city was more suitable.

Just his luck, he lamented, sprinting silently in the darkness. All those stagnant nights followed by split-second failure.

A Thursday night, too. If Roselli was the Butcher, he might very well be prepared to strike.

Constricted with tension, Daoud sped toward the *souq*, thinking: Back in uniform for sure. Please, God, don't let me lose him.

He turned on El Attarin, entered the *souq*, caught his breath, pressed himself against a cold stone wall, and looked around.

Prayers answered: Roselli's outline, clearly visible in the moonlight streaming between the arches. Walking quickly and deliberately down stone steps, through the deserted market street.

Daoud followed. The *souq* was deserted and shuttered. Rancid-sweet-produce smells still clung to the night air, seasoned intermittently by other fragrances: freshly tanned leather, spices, peanuts, coffee.

Roselli kept going to the end of the *souq*, to where Attarin merged with Habad Street.

Pure Jewish territory now. What business could the monk have here? Unless he was planning to head west, into the Armenian Quarter. But a Franciscan would have little more to do with the Pointed Hats than he would with the Jews.

Daoud maintained his distance, ducking and weaving and maintaining a keen eye on Roselli, who kept bearing south. Past the Cardo colonnade, up through the top plaza of the Jewish Quarter, the fancy shops that Jews had built there. Across the large parking lot, now empty.

Two border guards stood watch on the walls, turned at the sound of Roselli's sandals and stared at him, then at Daoud following moments later. A moment of analysis; then, just as quickly, the guards turned away.

Two brown-robes, nothing unusual.

Roselli passed under the arch that, during the day, served as an outdoor office for the Armenian moneylenders, showing no interest in either the Cathedral of Saint James or the Armenian Orthodox monastery. Daoud followed him toward the Zion Gate, mentally reviewing the Roman Catholic sites that graced that area: the Church of Saint Peter of the Cock-Crowing? Or perhaps the monk was headed outside the Old City walls, to the Crypt of Mary's Sleep—the Franciscans were entrusted with the tomb of Jesus' mother. . . .

But neither shrine proved to be Roselli's destination.

Just inside the Zion Gate was a cluster of Jewish schools—yeshivas. Newly built structures constructed on the sites of the old yeshivas Hussein had reduced to rubble in '48, Arab homes built by the Jordanians confiscated in '67 to make way for the rebuilding of the schools.

The typical Jerusalem seesaw.

Noisy places, yeshivas—the Jews liked to chant their studies for the world to hear. Black-coated longbeards and kids with skimpy whiskers hunched behind wooden lecterns, poring over their Old Testaments and their Talmuds. Reciting and debating without letup—even at this hour there was activity: brightly lit windows checkering the darkness; Daoud could hear a low sing-song drone of voices as he walked past.

Heretics, for sure, but one thing you had to give them: They had great powers of concentration.

Roselli walked past the larger yeshivas, approached a small one set back from the road and nearly obscured by its neighbors.

Ohavei Torah Talmudic Academy—domed building with a plain facade. Meager dirt yard in the front; to one side a big pine tree, the boughs casting spidery shadows over four parked cars.

The monk ducked behind the tree. Daoud closed the distance between them, saw that beyond the tree was a high stone wall separating the yeshiva from a three-story building with sheer stone walls. Nowhere to go. What was the monk up to?

A moment later, the monk emerged from the tree, a monk no longer.

The robes gone, just a shirt and pants.

One of those Jewish skullcaps on his head!

Daoud watched in astonishment as this new, Jewish-looking Roselli walked to the front door of Ohavei Torah Talmudic Academy and knocked.

A kid of about sixteen opened the door. He looked at Roselli with clear recognition. The two of them exchanged words, shook hands; the kid nodded and disappeared, leaving Roselli standing in the doorway, hands in his pockets.

Daoud was suddenly afraid: What was this, some Jewish plot, some cult? Had the Bible-quote letter sent to the American journalist been truthful? All the talk of Jewish blood sacrifices more than the idle rumors he'd taken them for?

Just what he needed: *Arab detective unearths Jewish murder plot.*

They'd be as likely to accept that as elect Arafat Prime Minister.

Behead-the-messenger time—what likelier scapegoat than Elias Daoud. Even success would bring failure.

It is my destiny, he thought, to remain humble. *Kismet*—if a Muslim blasphemy could be permitted, dear Lord.

But what was there to do other than perform his duties? Slipping between two parked cars and crouching, he continued his surveillance of the yeshiva.

Roselli was still standing there, looking like a red-bearded Jew with his skullcap. Daoud itched to approach him, confront him. Wondered what he'd do if the monk entered the building.

And what else was going on inside there, besides chanting? A helpless Arab girl chained in some dungeon? Another innocent victim, prepared for ritual slaughter?

Despite the warmth of the night, he shuddered, felt under his robes for the reassuring weight of his Beretta. And waited.

Another man came to the door. Rabbi-type. Tall, fortyish, long dark beard. In shirtsleeves and trousers, those strange white fringes hanging over his waistband.

He shook Roselli's hand too.

Congratulating him?

For what?

Roselli and the rabbi left the yeshiva and began walking straight toward the parked cars, straight toward Daoud.

He ducked lower. They passed him, turned right, and walked, side by side, southward through the Zion Gate and out to Mount Zion—Al Sion, the portion of Al Quds traditionally allocated to the Jews. They named their movement after it, glorified it by calling it a mountain, but it was no more, really, than a dusty mound.

He got up and trailed them, watched them pass the Tourist Agency office and David's Tomb, climb down the dirt drive that led to the Hativat Yerushalayim highway.

The road was deserted. Roselli and the rabbi crossed and climbed over the stone ridge that bordered the highway.

And disappeared.

Down into the dark hillside, Daoud knew. The rocky slope that overlooked the Valley of Hinnom. To the left was Silwan; only a few lights were burning in the village.

Daoud crossed the highway.

Where had they gone? What awaited them on the hillside, another murder cave?

He stepped over the ridge, careful to tread silently in the dry brush. And saw them immediately. Sitting just a few meters away, under the feathery umbrella of a windswept acacia.

Sitting and talking. He could hear the hum of their voices but was unable to make out their words.

Carefully, he stepped closer, trod on a dry twig, saw them raise their heads, heard the rabbi say, in English: "Just a mouse."

Holding his breath, he took another step forward, then another. Toward another tree, a stunted pine. Getting just close enough to discern their speech. Slowly, he sat, leaned against the trunk of the pine, pulled the Beretta out from under his habit, and rested it in his lap.

"Well, Joseph," the rabbi was saying, "I've refused you three times, so I suppose I must listen to you now."

"Thank you, Rabbi Buchwald."

"No need to thank me, it's my duty. However, it's also my duty to remind you what an enormous step you're taking. The consequences."

"I'm aware of that, Rabbi."

"Are you?"

"Yes. I can't tell you how many times I've set out to see you, froze in my tracks and turned back. For the last two months I've done nothing but think about this, meditating and praying. I know it's what I want to do—what I have to do."

"The life changes you'll impose upon yourself will be agonizing, Joseph. For all practical purposes your past will be erased. You'll be an orphan."

"I know that."

"Your mother—are you willing to consider her as dead?"

Pause.

"Yes."

"You're sure of that?"

"Even if I weren't, Rabbi, she's sure to cut me off. The end result will be the same."

"What of Father Bernardo? You've spoken of him fondly. Can you cut *him* off just like that?"

"I'm not saying it will be easy, but yes."

"You'll most certainly be excommunicated."

Another pause.

"That's not relevant. Anymore."

Daoud heard the rabbi sigh. The two men sat in silence for several moments, Roselli motionless, Buchwald swaying slightly, the tips of his woolly beard highlighted by starglow.

"Joseph," he said finally, "I have little to offer you. My job is bringing lapsed Jews back into the fold—*that's* what I'm set up for, not conversion. At best there'll be room and board for you—very basic room and board, a cell."

"I'm used to that, Rabbi."

Buchwald chuckled. "Yes, I'm sure you are. But in addition to the isolation, there'll be hostility. And I won't be there to cushion you, even if I wanted to—which I don't. In fact, my explicit order will be that you stay away from the others."

Roselli didn't respond.

The rabbi coughed. "Even if my attitude were different, you'd be an outcast. No one will trust you."

"That's understandable," said Roselli. "Given the realities of history."

"Then there's the matter of your fallen status, Joseph. As a monk, you've acquired prestige, the image of a learned man. Among us, your learning will be worthless—worse than nothing. You'll start out at the lowest level. Kindergarten children will have things to teach you."

"None of that is important, Rabbi. I know what I have to do. I felt it the moment I set foot on holy ground, feel more strongly about it than ever before. The core is Jewish. All the rest is extraneous."

Buchwald snorted. "Pretty talk—the core, faith, all that intellectual stuff. Now throw it all out—*forget* about it. You want to be a Jew. Concentrate on what you *do*. Action talks, Joseph. The rest is . . ." The rabbi threw up his hands.

"Tell me what to do and I'll do it."

"Just like that, eh? Simon says."

Roselli was silent.

"All right, all right," said Rabbi Buchwald. "You want to be a Jew, I'll give you a chance. But your sincerity will be tested at every step." More chuckling. "Compared to what I have in store for you, the monastery will seem like a vacation."

"I'm ready."

"Or think you are." The rabbi stood. Roselli did likewise.

"One more thing," said the monk.

"What is it?"

"I've been questioned about the Butcher murders. The first girl who was killed lived at Saint Saviour's for a while. I'm the one who found her wandering, tired and hungry, near the monastery and persuaded Father Bernardo to take her in. A police inspector interrogated me about it, then came around after the second murder to talk again. I can't be sure, but he may consider me a suspect."

"Why would that be, Joseph?"

"I honestly don't know. I get nervous talking to the police—I guess it comes from the old protest march days. I was arrested a couple of times. The police were nastier than they had to be. I don't like them; it probably shows."

"Confession is for Catholics," said Buchwald. "Why are you telling me about this?"

"I didn't want you, or the yeshiva, to be embarrassed if they come looking for me again."

"Have you done anything that would embarrass us?"

"God forbid," said Roselli, voice cracking. "Taking her in is the extent of my involvement."

"Then don't worry about it," said the rabbi. "Come, it's late. I have things to do yet."

He began walking. Roselli followed. They passed meters from Daoud's tree. He held his breath until they neared the highway, then got up and followed.

"When will you be moving in?" asked Buchwald.

"I thought Monday—that would give me enough time to tie up loose ends."

"Tie all you want. Just let me know in time to prepare my boys for our new student."

"I will, Rabbi."

They climbed to the edge of the highway, stepped over the ridge, and waited as a solitary delivery truck roared by.

Daoud, crouching nearby, could see their lips moving, but the truck blocked out any sound. They crossed the highway and began the gentle climb up Mount Zion.

Daoud followed at a safe pace, straining his ears.

"I've had nightmares about Fatma—the first victim," Roselli was saying. "Wondering if there's something I could have done to save her."

Rabbi Buchwald put his hand on the monk's shoulder and patted it. "You have excellent capacity for suffering, Yosef Roselli. We may make a Jew of you yet."

Daoud trailed them to the door of the yeshiva, where Roselli thanked the rabbi and headed back north, alone. A quick-change under the big tree preceded his reemergence as a monk.

Hypocrite, thought Daoud, fingering his own habit. He was angry at all the foolish talk of cores and faith, the idea of someone tossing away the Christ like yesterday's papers. He vowed to stay on Roselli's rear for as long as it took, hoping to unearth other secrets, additional trapdoors in the monk's screwed-up head.

When Roselli reached the Jewish Quarter parking lot, he stopped, climbed the stairs to the top of the city wall, and strolled along the battlement until coming to a stop under a crenel. The pair of border guards stood nearby. Two Druze, he could see, with big mustaches, binoculars, and rifles.

The guards looked Roselli over and approached him. He nodded at them, smiled; the three of them chatted. Then the Druze walked away and resumed their patrol. When the monk was alone, he hoisted himself up into the crenel, folding himself inside the notch, knees drawn up close to his body, chin resting in his hands.

He stayed that way, cradled in stone, staring out at the darkness, silent and motionless until daybreak. Unmindful of Daoud, hidden behind the Border Patrolmen's van, watching Roselli tirelessly while breathing in the stinking vapors from a leaky petrol tank.

54

Friday morning, no new body. Daniel had spent much of the night talking to Mark Wilbur and directing surveillance of Scopus and other forested areas. He left the interrogation at four A.M., convinced the reporter was intellectually dishonest but no murderer, went home for three hours of sleep, and was back at Headquarters by eight.

As he walked down the corridor to his office, he observed someone in the vicinity of his door. The man turned and began walking toward him and he saw that it was Laufer.

The deputy commander strode quickly, looked purposeful and grim. Swinging his arms as if marching in a military parade.

Dress-down time: the fallout from Wilbur's arrest.

They'd locked the reporter in a solitary holding cell, using the mischief he'd provoked at Beit Gvura to invoke the security clause and withhold counsel. Slowed the paperwork by having Avi Cohen handle it—for all Daniel knew the poor kid was still breaking his teeth on the forms. But by now, someone was bound to have found out; the wire service attorneys were probably pouring on the threats, the brass catching them and passing them down the line.

Laufer was three meters away. Daniel looked him in the eye, readied himself for the assault.

To his surprise, the D.C. merely said "Good morning, Sharavi," and walked on.

When he got to the office, he saw the reason why.

A man was sitting opposite his desk, slumped low in the chair, chin on knuckles, dozing. A half-consumed cigar lay smoldering in the ashtray, letting off wisps of strong, bitter smoke.

The man's chest heaved; his face rolled. A familiar, ruddy face above a corpulent, short-limbed body that filled the chair, ample thighs stuffed into trousers like sausages in casing, spilling over the seat. The cleft chin capped by a tiny white goatee.

Daniel knew the man was seventy-five but he looked ten years younger—good skin tone and an incongruously boyish thatch of yellow-gray hair. The collar points of an open-necked white shirt spread over the lapels of a rumpled gunmetal-gray sport coat, revealing a semicircle of hairless pink flesh.

The tightly packed trousers were dove-gray and in need of pressing; the shoes below them, inexpensive ripple-soled walkers. A maroon silk handkerchief flourished from the breast pocket of the sport coat—a dandyish touch at odds with the rest of the ensemble. Another incongruity, but the man was known for surprises.

Daniel closed the door. The corpulent man continued to sleep—a familiar pose. Newspaper photographers delighted in catching him napping at official functions—slumping, dead to the world, next to some stiff-backed visiting dignitary.

Narcolepsy, his detractors suggested; the man was brain-damaged, not fit for his job. Others suggested it was an affectation. Part of the stylized image he'd wrought for himself over twenty years.

Daniel edged past the pudgy gray knees, went behind his desk, and sat down.

As Shmeltzer had promised, a file labeled TOUR DATA was right there in front of him. He picked it up. The sleeping man opened pale-gray eyes, grunted, and stared at him.

Daniel put the tour file aside. "Good morning, Mr. Mayor."

"Good morning, Pakad Sharavi. We've met—the Concert Hall dedication. You had a mustache then."

"Yes." Three years ago—Daniel barely remembered it. He had served on the security detail, hadn't exchanged a word with the man.

Having done away with pleasantries, the mayor sat up and frowned.

"I've been waiting for you for an hour," he said, totally alert. Before Daniel could reply, he went on: "These murders, all this nonsense about butchers and sacrifices and revenge, it's creating problems for me. Already the tourist figures have dropped. What are you doing about it?"

Daniel began summarizing the investigation.

"I know all that," the mayor interrupted. "I meant what's *new*."

"Nothing."

The mayor picked up the now-cold cigar, lit it, and inhaled.

"An honest man—Diogenes would be happy. Meanwhile, the city is threatening to boil over. The last thing we need is a tourist slump on top of the recession. That note, with the Bible passages—any validity to it?"

"Possibly."

"No evasions, please. Are we dealing with a Jew? One of the black-coats?"

"There's no evidence of any particular group at work."

"What about Kagan's bunch?"

"No evidence. Personally, I doubt it."

"Why's that?"

"We've checked them out thoroughly."

"Avigdor Laufer thinks they're a suspicious lot."

"Avigdor Laufer thinks lots of things."

The mayor laughed. "Yes, he is a jackass." The laughter died abruptly, making it seem false.

"The note," said Daniel, "may be someone trying to blame it on religious Jews."

"Is that a professional opinion, or just your *kipah* speaking?"

"The Bible quotes were out of sequence, out of context. There was a manufactured quality to the note."

"Fine, fine," said the mayor with seeming uninterest. "Point is, what are we doing about it?"

"Our procedures are sound. The only choice is to continue."

The mayor narrowed his eyes. "No excuses, eh?"

Daniel shook his head.

"How long before progress?"

"I can't promise you anything. Serial killers are notoriously hard to catch."

"Serial killers," said the mayor, as if hearing the term for the first time. Then he muttered something that sounded like "killer ants."

"Pardon me?"

"This Wilbur, when are you releasing him?"

"He has yet to be arraigned on the obstruction charge. The paperwork is in progress."

"You're not actually expecting to take him to trial?"

"He's being treated like any other—"

"Come now, Pakad, we're not two Kurdis in some fertilizer factory, so stop shoveling shit."

"He withheld material evidence."

"Is he a murderer?"

"It's possible."

"Probable?"

"No."

"Then let him go. I don't need extra headaches on top of your . . . serial butcher."

"He may prove useful—"

"In what way?"

"If the killer contacts him again—"

"He won't be contacted in prison, Pakad."

"He can be released pending trial and kept under surveillance."

"And if he chooses to leave the country?"

"That can be prevented."

"You want to hold him hostage to use him? What is this—Beirut?"

"We have sufficient—"

"Let him go," said the mayor. Suddenly his tone was waspish, his face hard as granite. He leaned forward and jabbed his cigar. Like a bayonet. A coin of ash fell on Daniel's desk.

"With all due respect—"

"If you respect me, stop arguing and let the idiot go. I've talked to his boss in New York, chairman of the corporation that owns the wire service. They know his conduct was unprofessional, promise to keep his arrest under wraps, transfer him somewhere he can't do any damage—not immediately, within a month or two. The appearance of capitulation must be avoided. But the deal's only good if we release him immediately."

"In the meantime he writes."

"He writes, but his articles—all articles concerning the Butcher case—will be reviewed by the security censor."

"No one—not the locals or the foreigners—takes the censor seriously," said Daniel. "They know we pride ourselves on being more democractic than the Americans. Everything gets through."

"His won't. One month, then the bastard's gone," said the mayor. "We've tolerated worse." Another layer of ash dropped. "Come on, Pakad, I need your pledge of cooperation, immediately. Wilbur's boss—this chairman—is visiting Jerusalem next month. Prides himself on being some kind of amateur archaeologist. I'm meeting him at the airport with the official bread and salt, have arranged a tour of the Allbright Institute, the Rockefeller, some of the local digs. I'd appreciate it, Pakad, if everything goes smoothly."

"Please pass the ashtray," said Daniel. He took it from the mayor's padded hand, brushed the fallen ash into it, and wiped the desk with a tissue.

"One hand washes the other, Pakad. All the little ants are happy. To you it probably smacks of immorality; to a realist, it's mama's milk."

"I'll need permission from the prosecutor's office to dismiss the charges," said Daniel. "But I suppose that's been taken care of."

"Such a detective." The mayor smiled. He waved the cigar like a baton. "Stop looking so offended. That kind of self-righteousness is reserved for soldiers and pilgrims. And all soldiers and pilgrims ever did for this city was leave it in ruins."

"Sender Malkovsky," said Daniel. "What kind of hand-washing led to that?"

The mayor was unruffled. "One needs to take the long view, Pakad Sharavi. This city is a collection of little anthills, different color ants, little ant armies, each one thinking God or Allah or Jesus ordered it to devour the others. Think of it: all that potential for bloodshed. And for two thousand years that's what we've had. Now we've got another chance, and the only way to keep things from spilling over is to maintain a balance. Pluralism. Every ant an emperor in his little hole. A balance your Butcher is threatening to upset."

"Malkovsky is no ant. He rapes children."

The mayor inhaled his cigar, brushed away the comment and the smoke. "From that perspective, Malkovsky can be viewed as a mistake. But in the larger scheme of things, it was no mistake at all. Let me tell you something, Pakad: The big conflict in Jerusalem isn't going to be between Arab and Jew. *We'll* be in charge for a long time. *They'll* continue to *kvetch*, but it's all for show. Down deep they enjoy everything we give them: the schools, the medical care. The Jordanians never did it for them; they know they never would. Arafat's a paper hero, a member of the Husseini clan—the Arabs remember how the Husseinis confiscated their land and sold it cheap. So they'll adapt, we'll adapt—a status quo that will never be kissy-kissy, but we'll get by.

"The *big* problem is going to be between Jew and Jew—the black-coats and everyone else. They're fanatics, don't recognize the state, want to tear down everything we've fought for, turn it into another Iran run by Jewish ayatollahs. Think of it: no cinema, no cafés, no museums or concert halls, fanatics telling us to hang *mezuzah*s on every door and *daven* three times a day or be flogged in Zion Square. And they're breeding heavily—nine, ten kids a family. Thousands of them emigrating from ghettos in America in order to build ghettos here. They huddle in their yeshivas all day, live off the dole—not one of them does a day of army service. Thousands of enemies of the state and future enemies—and dangerous because they're repressed—sexually, emotionally. You know how violent they can get, the bus burnings we had every Saturday night in Mea She'arim. Even the soccer field we built them didn't drain off all the aggression."

The mayor relit his cigar.

"Violent," he repeated. "Which is why the religious implications of the note didn't sound all that implausible to me—those blackies are capable of doing violence to anyone who offends them. However, you inform me there's no evidence of any particular group at work."

"Malkovsky," Daniel reminded him.

The mayor's expression said the whole issue was trivial.

"Malkovsky's *rebbe*—the Prostnitzer—is a potential asset, someone definitely to be reckoned with. He's a cousin of the Satmar *rebbe,* broke off from the Satmar three years ago because of some dispute about the line of succession. That, of course, is no big deal—they're always fighting with each other. But as part of establishing his own identity, the Prostnitzer adopted a pro-state stance. Think of it: your basic ultrafanatic type—black hat, side curls, fur hats, leggings—and he's coming out saying righteous Jews should support the state."

"Agudah's been doing that for years."

"Agudah's of no importance. All they want to do is build kosher hotels and get rich. This Prostnitzer is a man with stature. *Charisma.* When he tells his Hassidim the '67 victory is a sign from *Messiah,* it carries weight."

"I never heard him say that," said Daniel.

"He's said it in private, to me. He's waiting for the right time to go public. The Malkovsky thing has pushed the date up a bit, but he's made a commitment, requested only a few favors in return. *Small* favors, which I'm more than happy to grant him because the stakes are high. Exposing one of his followers as a pervert would only be destructive. Think of it: an inroad to the fanatics, a first wedge driven into their intransigent ranks. They're followers by nature. Conformists. One begins; others follow suit; pretty soon you've introduced ambiguity into their belief system—creative tension. Lack of absolutes weakens fanaticism. The battle lines become obscured, strengthening the vitality of our *pluralism*."

"Ants crawling from hole to hole?" asked Daniel.

The mayor looked at his watch and stood.

"It's late. I've spent too much time on theoreticals. I expect Mark Wilbur to be released immediately, with no further harassment. You're obviously an intelligent fellow. If you wish to discuss ant holes further, feel free to call me at the office or at home—both numbers are listed. We'll set up an evening, break out the schnapps, open a few philosophy books. But not yet. After you clear up this Butcher nonsense."

Alone, Daniel read the tour file. The university had provided lists of participants in nine field studies in the general vicinity of the murder cave, three expeditions a year for the past three years. Exploration had been going on since '67, but older lists hadn't turned up. ("D: You should see their files, what a mess," Shmeltzer had noted. *"Professors.")*

The most recent trip had taken place last summer, a surface dig one and a half kilometers north of the cave, sponsored by the Department of Archaeology. The others were a pair of water-retention surveys conducted by Geology. Participants were faculty members, students, and visiting scholars. Only the names of the professors were listed, the same half-dozen over and over. Two were out of the country; Shmeltzer had interviewed the other four, three of them women, coming up with no leads and an incomplete list of student names gleaned from cluttered academic memories. The students were all Israelis, with the exception of one Nigerian who'd returned to Africa six months before the first murder. They had yet to be questioned.

None of the private tour companies visited that part of the desert, which wasn't surprising—nothing flashy down there. When the tourists asked for desert, they were shown the camel market in Beersheva, Masada, Ein Gedi, the Dead Sea mud spas.

The Nature Conservancy had taken a single group of hikers into the area six months ago, a lecture tour on annual desert flora. The guide was a woman named Nurit Blau, now married to a member of Kibbutz Sa'ad. Shmeltzer had called her; she had a new baby, sounded fatigued, remembered nothing about the tour other than that a freak rain shower had ended it prematurely. No, none of the participants was memorable. Some of them might have been foreigners, she really didn't remember—how could one be expected to remember that far back?

A check at the Conservancy office turned up no names; reservation lists weren't kept past the day of the hike. The lists were incomplete, anyway. Most hikers never bothered to reserve, simply showed up at a designated location the morning of the hike, paid cash, and tagged along.

Sum total: skimpy. Besides, lists didn't prove anything; anyone could take a walk in the desert. Still, procedure was procedure. It wasn't as if they were deluged with leads. He'd have Cohen and the Chinaman interview the students, try to obtain the names of the missing ones, check them out too.

At eight twenty-five he went down the hall, made a couple of turns, and ended up at the unlabeled locked door of Amos Harel's office. He knocked, waited several moments for it to open, and found himself staring into the undercover man's gray eyes.

Harel held a smoldering Gauloise in one hand, a felt-tip pen in the other. He wore a T-shirt and jeans. The full white beard he'd worn on his last assignment was gone, revealing a pale, lean face, the jawline marred by shaving nicks.

"Morning, Dani."

"Morning."

Harel didn't invite him in, simply stood there waiting for him to speak. Though ten years Daniel's senior and a rav pakad, he never pulled rank, just concentrated on the job. The toughest of the tough guys, though to look at him you'd never know it—the narrow shoulders, the bent back that housed three splinters of shrapnel, courtesy Anwar Sadat. He had an emotional barometer that never seemed to register and a bloodhound's nose for subtle irregularities and suspicious parcels.

"Morning, Amos. Is your man still watching Wilbur's mailbox?"

"He checked in two hours ago—nothing happening."

"Wilbur's out of jail—string-pulling from way up. You may

get a request to end the surveillance. Do me a favor and take your time about pulling out."

"String-pulling." Harel frowned. "How much time do you need?"

"A day or so, maybe a day and a half until I get one of my own men ready for it. Shouldn't be any problem for you to conceal the delay."

"No," said the Latam chief. "No problem at all."

Thanking him would have been superfluous; Daniel turned on his heel and walked away. Back in his own office, he phoned Shmeltzer at the Russian Compound jail, wanting to know the status of Mossad's search for Red Amira Nasser. The older detective wasn't at the lockup, and he considered contacting Mossad himself. But those guys were touchy about improvisation. Better to stick to the official liaison routine.

"Connect me with Subinspector Lee," he told the jail desk officer.

A minute later the Chinaman came on and Daniel told him about his morning visitor.

"Snoozy himself, huh? What's he like?"

"Charming. He sees the world in insect terms. Anyway, Yossi, if you have any more questions for Wilbur, ask them now. He'll be walking soon."

"He already walked. Two tight-assed guys just slow-waltzed him out. Can I help Avi finish the papers? Kid's sweating buckets."

"Sure. Get anything more from Wilbur?"

"Not a thing. We fed him, gave him coffee. The guy broke down—not much substance to him at all. But all he gave us was bullshit. The last hour or so he did nothing but talk about his childhood. Seems he had a mean daddy, big-shot lawyer, wanted him to be a lawyer, too, never thought much of scribblers." The Chinaman yawned into the phone.

"Where's Nahum?"

"After he'd called Wilbur *shmuck* for the hundredth time, he stomped out—said something about interviewing students."

"Names from the university desert tour list. Try to reach him and help him with those interviews. Tell him, also, that I want an update on the Amira Nasser search. Take Cohen with you to speed things up but let him off by two. He's replacing Latam on the mailbox watch. Tell him to go to Hamashbir, buy some new clothes—nothing fancy, something a kibbutznik would wear. Also, he has to shave off his beard, get a short haircut and nonprescription eyeglasses."

"Mistreatment of the troops," laughed the Chinaman. "I'll catch his tears in a bottle, save it as evidence for the Review Board. Listen, Aviva called—she's got a morning off. Okay with you if I go home and get some breakfast?"

Daniel thought about it. The student hikers could wait. "Get in touch with Nahum, first. Then all of you go have breakfast."

"Last-meal time for Cohen," said the Chinaman, still chuckling.

At eight-forty, Daniel called his own wife.

"I love you," he said. "Sorry I had to rush out. Guess who was waiting for me in my office?"

"The Prime Minister?"

"More powerful."

"You're serious."

"Very."

"Who, Daniel?"

"The mayor."

"In your office?"

"I opened the door, there he was, dozing away."

"I always thought that sleep stuff was for the benefit of the media."

"This morning it was for my benefit."

"What did he want?"

"To have the American reporter released and check me out in the process."

"I'm sure he was favorably impressed."

"He'd be more impressed if I could solve the murders, which he sees as a civic nuisance."

Laura said nothing for a moment, then: "Pressure."

"Nothing unexpected."

"Listen, before I forget, Gene called about fifteen minutes ago, said he tried phoning you at the office but had trouble getting through."

"Is he at the Laromme?"

"I think so. You know they're due to leave this Sunday for Rome."

"Already?"

"It's been four weeks, honey."

Daniel sighed.

"There'll be other opportunities," said Laura. "Luanne's already talking about coming back next year. Anyway, they're coming over for Shabbat dinner, tonight. Will you be able to make it home by three?"

"Sure."

"Good. There's wine and pastries to pick up at Lieberman's. The other woman in your life's got a new dress she wants you to approve before she wears it."

"Tell her I love her. Tell all of them."

He phoned Gene at the Laromme.

The black man picked up on the first ring, said, "I was hoping that was you. Been having a devil of a time getting through your switchboard. What is it, security?"

"Bad lines, more likely. What's new?"

"McGuire phoned me with the computer data. I think I've got something juicy for you. Got a pen and paper?"

"Now I do. Go ahead."

"They've got five hundred and eighty-seven unsolveds that fit into possible serial patterns. Two hundred and ninety-seven involve some use of knives. Out of those, the machine spat out ninety-one cases with wound patterns similar to yours over the last fifteen years—the data bank goes back longer than I thought, but stuff from the last five years is relatively sketchy."

"Ninety-one," said Daniel, visualizing heaps of mutilated corpses.

"Not that many, considering your wounds were darn-near generic," said Gene. "But most of them differ from yours in terms of mixed *modus:* knife and gun, knife and strangulation. And victim demographics: males, kids, old ladies, couples. In my opinion, that doesn't eliminate them—some of these monsters get pretty indiscriminate about who they kill and how they do it. But there's no use tackling something that huge. Thing to do is start breaking it down into subsets."

"Young females," said Daniel.

"Exactly. Fifty-eight in the seventeen- to twenty-seven-year-old range. By playing statistical games with it, the FBI broke that down into seven groupings that appear to be the work of the same killer or killers, though there's overlap. The cutoffs aren't perfectly clean. But when you plug in dark complexion, multiple blades, and drug OD, it narrows way down and starts to get *real* interesting: seven cases, none of them strangled, which in itself is unusual. One additional case that matches everything, except no mention is made of multiple blades. The first is an L.A. case: girl found cut up fourteen years ago, March 1971, in a *cave*—how do you like *that*?"

"There are caves in Los Angeles?" asked Daniel, gripping the edge of his desk.

"Plenty of them in the surrounding mountain areas. This particular one was in Griffith Park—big place just north of Hollywood, thousands of acres. There's a zoo and a planetarium there, but mostly it's wilderness."

"Was she killed in the cave?"

"FBI says yes."

"What was the physical layout of the cave?"

"They don't have that kind of detail programmed yet. Hold on a second—there's something else I want you to hear: Victim's name was Lilah Shehadeh; she's listed as a twenty-three-year-old female Caucasian, black hair, brown eyes. But Shehadeh's an Arab name, isn't it?"

"Yes," said Daniel, feeling the excitement grow within him. "Go on."

"Multiple stab wounds from several different weapons, death from exsanguination—poor gal bled to death. Heroin overdose to the point of general anesthesia, severed jugular, decimation of the genitals, no trace evidence other than residue of Ivory soap—sounds like she was washed."

"At the cave?"

"Printout didn't say that either. There are streams in Griffith Park—in March they could still be full from the rains. Let me see what else I've got . . . Shehadeh was an addict and prostitute. I racked my brains to see if I could remember her case but I couldn't. I was working Southwest Division back then, clear across town. To be honest, a single hooker-cutting wouldn't get much notice. I just got off the phone with a buddy in Hollywood Division, asked him to dig up the file, call me back and dictate the details."

"Thank you, Lieutenant Brooker."

"Onward: Number two occurred over two years later, July of '73, in New Orleans. Another prostitute, named Angelique Breau, drugged out—this time with Demerol—and cut identically to Shehadeh. Traces of soap and shampoo: Dial and Prell—he's not strict about his brands. The body was killed somewhere else, but found in a crypt in the St. Louis cemetery—which is kind of cavelike, wouldn't you say? And she and Shehadeh fit your genital destruction-removal sequence—Shehadeh's vaginal vault was cut up; Breau's ovaries were removed. She's listed as a female Cauc, black and brown, nineteen years old, but New Orleans is famous for race-mixing. If you put *Caucasian* on your driver's license application, no one's going to argue with you. Name like Breau she could be lily-white Parisian, swamp-rat Cajun, Creole mulatto, or any mixture thereof."

"Dark. Mediterranean-looking," said Daniel.

"Good chance of it."

"She could have been an Arab, too, Gene. Some of them—Moroccans, Algerians—have French names."

"Hmm. Maybe. But the next two are definitely *not* Arab, so it appears the killer's going after a certain look, not nationality."

Dark women, thought Daniel. The streets of any Levantine, Mediterranean, or Latin American city were teeming with them. Yet the killer—if it was the same killer—had come to Jerusalem.

It had to be more than a look that he was after. . . .

"The third one took place April of '75, twenty-one months after Breau," said Gene. "Northeast Arizona, desert area outside of Phoenix. Victim's name: Shawnee Scoggins, female Native American—Indian. Eighteen years, black and brown. Ovaries *and* kidneys removed. Murdered somewhere else, but the body was found off the highway near one of the Indian reservations. Reservation police handled the case. Girl had a history of delinquency, drug problems. Fresh needle marks in her arm, heroin OD, no fiber traces, no mention of soap. But this is the one that doesn't list multiple weapons either, so we could be talking about a failure on the part of the locals to report all the facts, poor investigatory procedure, or a slipshod autopsy. Everything else fits. I'd suggest you include her."

"All right."

"After Scoggins there's a thirty-two-month lapse until December of '77. Back in California again, but up north near San Francisco. *This* one I remember: nude dancer named Maria Mendoza, twenty-one, black and brown, history of prostitution and narcotics convictions. What was left of her was discovered near a *cave* up in Mount Tamalpais."

"Not *in* the cave?"

"I asked McGuire about that. Printout said *near*—didn't say how near. Hard to understand why they put some data in, leave other stuff out."

"Was she killed up there?"

"No. Somewhere else, site unidentified. This one was very messy, Danny. *All* the internal organs were removed—she was literally skin and bones. San Francisco police had been dealing with a bunch of unsolved homicides attributed to some crazy who wrote letters to the papers calling himself Zodiac. The last suspected Zodiac killing was in October of '75, farther east, in Sacramento. San Francisco thought he'd come back to haunt them. Reason I remember the case is that one of the primary Zodiac suspects moved down to L.A. shortly after Mendoza's body was found, and we were alerted. We watched him—it came to nothing."

"What was his name?"

"Karl Witik. Weirdo biology student. White guy but rented a house in Watts, had squirrels and mice running wild inside the place. But don't worry—he's not your man. He blew his brains out in early '78. Two more possible Zodiacs went down in '79 and '81, so he probably wasn't San Francisco's man either."

"Eight," said Daniel, looking at his notes. "Four more."

"Four more," said Gene. "And they keep getting nastier. Mendoza's the last intact body on the list. The rest are all dismemberments: August 1978 in Miami, Florida; July 1980, Sun Valley, Idaho; March '82, Crater Lake, Oregon; January '84, Hana, Hawaii. Young, dark women, no fiber or prints, soap traces, heroin residue in the tissue, bone rills indicating multiple knives, body parts tossed in wooded or desert areas. Three of the victims have never been identified, including one whose head was never recovered. The one from Crater Lake was ID'd as Sherry Blumenthal, seventeen-year-old runaway from Seattle. Same old song: drug history, prostitution busts. 'Remains found in state of advanced decomposition on the north bank of the lake.' "

Gene paused. "Sounds like your guy, doesn't it?"

"The *modus* is identical," said Daniel. His sweaty hands made wet marks on the desk. "A traveling killer."

"Beast of the highway," said Gene. "The more we coordinate our interstate records, the more we keep turning up. Looks like this one traveled far."

Daniel scanned his notes again. "Two murders took place in California. Perhaps that's his home base."

"Same state, but L.A. and San Francisco are four hundred miles apart," said Gene. "Maybe he just likes the weather."

Daniel examined the list of murder sites again. "All these places have good weather, don't they?"

"Hmm, let me see: Oregon, Louisiana—you get your rain and chill there, but yes, generally they're mild."

"Places to visit on holiday?"

"I suppose so. Why?"

"The time lapse between the murders averages almost two years," said Daniel. "Perhaps the killer lives normally for a while, goes out on holiday to murder."

"Let me take a look at the dates," said Gene. He grew silent for several moments, then: "No, I don't think so. January in Hawaii is the off-season, cloudy and rainy. New Orleans and Miami are hot and sticky in July—folks fly down there in the *winter*. Anyway, there are plenty of guys who don't need a vacation to travel: drifters, truckers—anyone with a job that puts him on the road. And don't depend too much on the time lapse. He may have killed plenty of others in between—FBI estimates six undiscovered victims for every one in the file."

Five hundred eighty-seven by six. "Over three thousand undiscovered murders," said Daniel. "How can that be?"

"Runaways, throwaways, orphans, missing persons who remain missing. Big country, big mess—it's not like over here, Danny."

Daniel put the numbers out of his head, returned to his notes. "The first murder was fourteen years ago, which tells us something about his age. The youngest he could have been at the time would be, what—fourteen?"

"I've heard of sex murders committed by kids," said Gene, "but they're usually a lot more impulsive-looking. Sloppy. From the care taken on these—cleaning up the evidence, using dope to knock them out—my guess is they were committed by an adult. Eighteen, nineteen at the youngest, probably early twenties."

"Okay, let's be cautious and say sixteen," said Daniel. "That would make him at least thirty today, most likely older."

"If Shehadeh was his first."

"If she wasn't, he could be much older. But not much younger."

"I can buy that," said Gene.

"Thirties or older"—Daniel thought out loud—"an American, or one who travels to America frequently." Thinking to himself: If he's not an American, all those trips to the U.S. will show up on his passport.

"Hundred to one, he's American," said Gene. "He knew the terrain, knew where to kill, where to dump. Some of those dump spots are out of the way. Americans are suspicious of foreigners. If one was lurking around, you'd expect it to surface in at least some of the investigations. Unless," he added, "you've got Interpol suggesting otherwise."

"No, I'm still waiting for Interpol. A question, Gene: In America, he's a traveling killer, goes from city to city. Here, he stays in Jerusalem. Why didn't he murder one girl in Jerusalem, another in Tel Aviv, move on to Haifa?"

"Maybe Jerusalem's got some special meaning for him. Defiling the holiness or something."

"Maybe," said Daniel. But his mind was racing:

Defiling the holiness of three faiths. Defiling women. Dark women. Arabs. A Mexican stripper. An Indian girl. Maybe a Louisiana mixed-blood. Maybe a Jew—the Blumenthal girl from Oregon could be Jewish.

Every identified victim a member of a racial or ethnic minority.

But here, only Arabs. The *main* ethnic minority.

A racist killer?

A Jewish killer? Kaganism justified by the Bible and carried to bloody extreme?

Or blood *libel,* as Shmeltzer insisted. Someone blaming it on the Jews?

Whoever had sent that note to Wilbur had defiled the Bible, too. Cutting the text out and pasting it up like some ransom note. What observant Jew would do that, when the sentences could just as easily be copied?

Unless you didn't know Hebrew.

Addressing the envelope in English block letters.

He didn't know Hebrew. A foreigner.

An outsider.

Fomenting hatred, setting Jew against Arab? Semite against Semite?

A *genuine* anti-Semite.

A racist American maniac. Amira Nasser's story about the

crazy-eyed foreigner was sounding better and better: crazy eyes, strange smile . . . Dammit, where were the Mossad hotshots when you needed them?

" . . . still only general, we need specifics," Gene was saying. "Best thing is to take a look at the original police files, or at least get the important details over the phone. I can help you with San Francisco and New Orleans. The rest I've got no personal contacts with but they may cooperate, one American cop to another."

"You've done more than enough, my friend. I'll call them myself. Do you have the addresses and phone numbers?"

Gene dictated them, then said, "It's no problem my calling them, Danny. It'll go faster, believe me."

"You've only got four days left in Jerusalem, Gene. I don't want to take up the remainder of your holiday."

The line went silent.

"Listen," said Gene, "if you need me, I can postpone leaving."

"Gene, Rome is a beautiful—"

"Danny, Rome is more churches. Bigger ones. Shrines and murals. Murals on ceilings always give me a stiff neck."

Daniel laughed.

"However," said the black man, "I think there're still a few holy places around here that Lu hasn't seen. Just this morning she was complaining about missing a lecture series on ancient pottery whosits or something. So there's a chance I can persuade her to modify our itinerary if you need me. Have to know soon, though, or we run into problems with changing the tickets."

"I need you, Gene."

"Nice to hear. You can tell me again at dinner tonight. Meantime, let me get going on those calls. Bye."

Daniel put the phone down, thought more about the traveling killer.

America to Israel.

Europe in between?

He phoned Friedman in Bonn, knowing it was barely morning in Germany and not caring if the Interpol man got yanked out of sweet dreams.

The same detached secretary's voice came on the line. Reciting a recorded message.

He slammed the phone down, studied his notes, let his mind run with the facts, expand them. Kept returning to one thought:

A racist killer.

Calculating. Careful.

Manipulative.

He remembered the phrase that had come to him while reading the books and monographs on psychopathic killers:

Street-corner Mengeles.

He thought, again, of the disgusting paperbacks in Ben David's office. *The Black Book of Fascist Horror.*

Read the chapter on "Murder for Profit," the psychologist had said. *The surgical experiments.*

I found myself thinking about them in Nazi terms . . .

You see, you don't need me. Your unconscious is guiding you in the right direction.

His unconscious. It had been languishing, sick with frustration, withering from disuse. But the data on the FBI list—the link—had breathed new life into it. Now, an image of the killer had been sculpted in his mind—a soft sculpture, to be sure, a wax outline, gross features melting in the glare of uncertainty. But an image nonetheless.

He was certain he was right.

The killer was no Jew, no Arab.

An American with strange eyes, a diseased mind, and a racist scheme. *A beast of the highway stalking the herd.*

Americans, thousands of them living and visiting here, but the only ones under surveillance were Roselli and Wilbur. Not very promising: The reporter was unethical, but no killer; the monk's big secret was that he wanted to be a Jew.

Which made him intriguing, but no suspect.

Unless he had more than one big secret.

From what Daoud had overheard, the monk knew he was under suspicion. Was the move to the yeshiva a means of covering something up?

Daniel had instructed Daoud to stay on Roselli. The Arab's "Yes, Pakad" had been reflexive but strained. Poor guy was probably cross-eyed with boredom by now. If nothing came up soon, Daniel resolved to put his talents to better use. Any further observation of Roselli could be carried out by one of Harel's Latam boys, wrapped in robes and *kaffiyah.*

He thought about Roselli again. From monk to yeshiva student.

A spiritual quest? Or just another impulsive shift for an unbalanced mind?

Another crazy American. With crazy eyes?

Thousands of Americans walking the streets of Jerusalem—find the one with the crazy eyes. Like sifting granules of gold for a single speck of dross.

Big mess, but small country. An outsider couldn't submerge himself indefinitely.

He took pen in hand, outlined his plan.

Airline cross-checks, page-by-page reviews of tens of thousands of uncomputerized passport records—the tedium the Chinaman had dreaded out loud but which was the surest way to fine-carve the sculpture. Canvasses of hotels, *pensiones,* hostels, dormitories, housing agents and automobile rental firms, travel and tour companies, kibbutzim and *moshavim* that took on foreign volunteers.

The evil bastard couldn't hide deep enough. He'd root him out, put an end to the defilement.

For the first time in a long time he felt lightened with hope. The mastery of the hunter.

His thoughts were interrupted by a knock on the door.

"Yes?"

The door opened a crack and a uniform stuck his head in. Young, gawky, with a peach-fuzz face, he had to be barely out of the training course. He blinked rapidly, bobbed his head, looking everywhere but at Daniel.

"Pakad Sharavi?"

"Yes? Come in."

The patrolman's body remained in the corridor; only his head bobbed around inside the office, jumpy and vigilant, like a chicken watching out for the *shohet*'s knife.

"What is it?"

The uniform bit his lip and chewed air. When he finally got the words moving, they tumbled out in a rush:

"Pakad, a dead body, they said to call you, you'd know all about it. In Talpiyot, along the industrial stretch. Not far from the lot where we tow the parking violators."

Book Three

55

Dr. Levi's promptness was commendable. Within hours of the removal of the body to Abu Kabir, the necropsy findings were phoned to Daniel.

But the pathologist might just as well have taken his time. The wounds on number three were identical to Fatma's and Juliet's, save for one bit of information that Daniel had anticipated: The killer had removed Shahin Barakat's ovaries and her kidneys.

Just as he'd done, ten years ago, to his third American victim. The Indian girl, Shawnee Scoggins.

Shahin's body had been found, dumped like garbage in a stand of eucalyptus, reeking of encroaching decay and menthol. Only meters from the police tow yard.

Thumbing his nose at us.

Shahin. Another pretty face preserved intact above the gaping neck wound. Nineteen years old, black hair lustrous, thick, and wavy. Dainty pierced ears, the earrings missing.

But, unlike the others, married. The husband had been hanging around the Kishle substation for days, dogging the uniforms, begging them to find his wife.

"Ex-wife." Patrolman Mustafa Habiba had been quick to clarify, the moment Daniel entered the substation, telling his side of the story, then rushing off to fetch the Pakad an unrequested cup of Turkish coffee and a piece of baklava wrapped in wax paper. The Arab policeman was a leftover from the days of Jordanian occupation, unschooled, nearing sixty, and waiting for his pension from the Jews. Allowed to remain on the force because of his familiarity with the back alleys and their denizens, the desire by the brass to maintain the illusion of continuity.

"He kicks her out, gives her three times *talaq*, then changes his mind and wants us to be the marriage counselors. How were we to know, Pakad?"

Habiba needed a shave. His grizzled face twitched with fear; his uniform needed ironing. Daniel had brought him back to Headquarters and he looked out of place in the sterile emptiness of the interrogation room. An antiquity.

Forty years of pocketing petty baksheesh and dishing out bureaucratic indifference, thought Daniel, and now he's terrified that indifference is going to be twisted into something cruel.

"There was no way to know," Habiba repeated, whining.

"No, there wasn't," said Daniel. The man's anxiety was starting to wear on him.

"What difference would it have made had we looked for her?" insisted Habiba. "When this Butcher wants someone, he gets her."

There was awe in the old policeman's voice when he spoke of the killer. Awe undercoated with contempt for his own police force.

He thinks of the bastard as superhuman, some kind of demon—a Jewish demon. The helplessness—the homage to evil—angered Daniel and he had to restrain himself from dressing the old policeman down.

"Marriage counselors," muttered Habiba. "We're too busy for that kind of nonsense."

Anger overtook restraint.

"Of course you are," said Daniel. "Feel free to return to Kishle. Don't let a murder investigation keep you from your pressing business."

Habiba flushed. "I didn't mean, Pakad—"

"Forget it, Officer Habiba. Go back to Kishle. Don't worry, your retirement's intact."

Habiba started to say something, thought better of it, and left the room.

Daniel looked at his watch. Six P.M. Goodbye, family; goodbye, Shabbat. The husband was in another room, being comforted by relatives under the watchful eye of the Chinaman and Shmeltzer. Daniel had tried to get something out of him but the poor guy was too distraught, frozen silent, near catatonic, only the hands moving—scratching his face bloody. The imperviousness to pain chilled Daniel's heart.

Maybe Daoud could do better. He was due over from the Old City any minute. No mistaking the joy in his voice at being reeled in—jubilation at being regarded as someone with special talents. And relief at being pulled off the Roselli surveillance. The timing couldn't have been better—last night's watch had now provided the monk with an ironclad alibi.

Daniel tried to imagine Roselli as a yeshiva student, wondered how long the monk would stay faithful to his latest mistress. The spartan lodgings and seventeen-hour days Buchwald demanded from his students might not prove too different from the rigors of monkhood. But Daniel suspected that Roselli was one of those philosophic grasshoppers, leaping from creed to creed. A searcher destined never to find what he was looking for, because you had to fill your own void. No rabbi or priest or mullah could do it for you.

Not that the searchers would ever stop searching. Or flocking to Jerusalem. The city was a psychic magnet, drawing in the Rosellis of the world and those who promised them salvation. At that first meeting at The Star, Shmeltzer had bemoaned the influx of fanatics and nut cases as if it were a new phenomenon, but the attraction was as old as Jerusalem itself. Pilgrims and self-flagellators, crucifiers and false messiahs, visionaries, dervishes, charlatans, and the willfully blind. Determined to squeeze blood out of every rock, hallucinate sacred flames licking from every arid clump of mesquite.

Searchers, some of them undoubtedly mad, others teetering on the brink of madness. Yet, despite them, the city endured wave after wave of destruction and rebirth. Or maybe *because* of them.

Mad but *benign,* seeking internal order.

Unlike the slashing, plundering, mocking monster *he* was after.

Beast of the highway.

Disorder, internal collapse—hell on earth—was what this one craved.

Daniel resolved to burn him.

He sat behind a one-way mirror and watched Daoud conduct the interview. Hardly a sophisticated concealment, but if Abdin Barakat noticed it, he gave no sign.

The Arab detective had all the right moves—authority, compassion, patience, appeals to a husband's desire to find his wife's murderer and avenge her death. But to no avail in the beginning: Barakat blocked him out as completely as he had Daniel.

If grief was proportional to devotion, no man had ever possessed greater love for a woman than Abdin Barakat for Shahin. His grief was silent but all the stronger for it, as eloquent an opera of woe as Daniel had ever heard.

He looks dead himself, Daniel thought. Sunken-cheeked, stiff, lifeless features, lusterless eyes half-hidden in the darkness of cavernous sockets. The coarse complexion bleached pale as gauze bandage.

A young man mummified by suffering.

Eight years older than Shahin, but that still made him young. Tall, sparely built, with short, poorly cut hair, the cracked fingernails and grease-stained clothes of a working man.

An ironworker in one of the stalls in the Old City. Repairer of pots and pans, family business—the father was the boss. And the landlord. For four married years, home had been two rooms tacked on illegally to the top story of the Barakat family dwelling in the Muslim Quarter. A cooking space and a tiny bedroom for Abdin and Shahin—their names rhymed; it implied a certain harmony—because without children, what need was there for more?

The childlessness was at the root of the divorce, Daniel was sure. Four barren years would have stretched the tolerance of Abdin's family. The Muslims had no use for a woman who didn't bear, made it exquisitely easy for a man to dispose of her: *Talaq,* verbal denouncement unencumbered by justification, set the divorce process in motion. Three denouncements, and the break was final.

On the other side of the mirror, Barakat began weeping, despite himself; the breakdown was beginning. Daoud handed him a tissue. He clutched it, wept harder, tried to force back the tears but failed. Burying his face in his hands, he moved it back and forth, as if shaking his head no.

Daoud pulled out another tissue and tried again.

Patience paid off. Eventually, after two hours of listening and tissue-offering and gentle prodding, Daoud got Barakat talking—softly but rapidly, in near-hysterical spurts.

A fragile victory, and the Arab detective knew it. He put his body language into the interrogation, bringing his face so close to Barakat's that they could have kissed, placing his hands on the husband's shoulders and exerting subtle pressure, his knees touching Barakat's knees. Shutting out the room, the universe, so that only questioner and answerer existed in empty white space.

"When's the last time you saw her, Mr. Barakat?"

Barakat stared at the floor.

"Try to remember. It's important, Mr. Barakat."

"M-Monday."

"This past Monday?"

"Yes."

"You're certain of that?"

"Yes."

"Not Sunday or Tuesday?"

"No, Monday was the day—" Barakat burst into tears, buried his face in his hands again.

Daoud looked past the heaving shoulders, through the mirror at Daniel, raised his eyebrows, and tapped the table silently. Glancing at the tape recorder on the table, he waited until Barakat's sobs diminished to sniffles before continuing.

"Monday was the day *what*, Mr. Barakat?"

"It was . . . complete."

"What was complete?"

No answer.

"The third *talaq*?" prompted Daoud.

Barakat's reply was barely audible: "Yes."

"The divorce was final on Monday?"

Jerky nods, tears, more tissues.

"Was Shahin scheduled to leave your house on Monday?"

"Yes."

"Where was she planning to go?"

Barakat uncovered his face. "I don't know."

"Where does her family live?"

"There is no family, only a mother in Nablus."

"What about the father?"

"Dead."

"When did he die?"

"Many years ago. Before the . . ." Tears flowed down the sunken cheeks, wetting the lacerations and causing them to glisten.

"Before you were married?"

"Yes."

"What about brothers or sisters?"

"No brothers or sisters."

"An only child? Not a single male in the family?" Daoud's tone was laden with disbelief.

"Yes, a great shame." Barakat sat up straighter. "The mother was a poor bearer, useless organs, always with the female sicknesses. My father said . . ."

Barakat stopped mid-sentence, turned away from the detective's eyes. One hand picked absently at the scratches on his face.

"What did your father say?"

"That . . ." Barakat shook his head, looked like a dog that had been kicked too often.

"Tell me, Abdin."

A long moment passed.

"Surely the words of one's father are nothing to be ashamed of," said Daoud.

Barakat trembled. "My father said . . . he said that Shahin's mother's loins were cursed, she'd been possessed by a spirit—a *djinn*. He said Shahin carried the curse too. The dowry had been obtained deceitfully."

"A *djinn*."

"Yes, one of my old aunts is a *kodia*—she confirmed it."

"Did this aunt ever try to chase out the *djinn*? Did she beat the tin barrel?"

"No, no, it was too late. She said the possession was too strong, agreed with my father that sending Shahin away was the honorable thing to do—as a daughter, she, too, was afflicted. The fruit of a rotten tree."

"Of course," said Daoud. "That makes sense."

"We were never told of the *djinn* before the wedding," said Barakat. "We were cheated, my father says. Victimized."

"Your father is a wise businessman," said Daoud. "He knows the proper value of a commodity."

Daniel heard sarcasm in the remark, wondered if Barakat would pick it up too. But the young man only nodded. Pleased that someone understood.

"My father wanted to go to the *waqf*," he said. "To demand judgment and reclaim the dowry from the mother. But he knew it was useless. The crone no longer owns anything—she's too far gone."

"Far gone?"

"Up here." Barakat tapped his forehead. "The *djinn* has affected her up here as well as in her loins." He scowled, sat up higher, square-shouldered and confident, the guilt-ridden slump suddenly vanished. Reaching out, he took a drink from the water glass that, till then, had gone untouched.

Watching the change come over him, Daniel thought: Plastering over the rot and mildew of sorrow with a layer of indignation. Temporary patchwork.

"The mother is mad?" asked Daoud.

"Completely. She drools, stumbles, is unable to clean herself. She occupies a cell in some asylum!"

"Where is this asylum?"

"I don't know. Some foul place on the outskirts of Nablus."

"Shahin never visited her?"

"No, I forbade it. The contagion—one defect was bad enough. The entire line is cursed. The dowry was obtained deceitfully!"

Daoud nodded in agreement, offered Barakat more water. When the young man had finished drinking, Daoud resumed his questioning, searching for a link to Shahin's whereabouts after her expulsion, inquiring about friends or acquaintances who might have taken her in.

"No, there were no friends," said Barakat. "Shahin shuttered herself in the house all day, refused to have anything to do with other women."

"Why was that?"

"Their children bothered her."

"She didn't like children?"

"At first she did. Then she changed."

"In what way?"

"They reminded her of her defect. It sharpened her tongue. Even the children of my brothers made her angry. She said they were ill-trained—a plague of insects, crawling all over her."

An angry, isolated woman, thought Daniel, no friends, no family. Stripped of the security of marriage, she'd have been as helpless as Fatma, as rootless as Juliet.

Picking off the weak ones.

But where had the herd grazed?

"Let's go back to Monday," said Daoud. "The last time you saw her, what time was it?"

"I don't know."

"Approximately."

"In the morning."

"Early in the morning?"

Barakat tapped his tooth with a fingernail and thought. "I left for work at eight. She was still there . . ." The sentence died in his throat. All at once he was crying again, convulsively.

"She was still there *what,* Abdin?"

"Oh, oh, Allah help me! I didn't know. Had I known, I never . . ."

"What was she doing when you left for work?" Daoud pressed softly but insistently.

Barakat kept crying. Daoud took hold of his shoulders, shook him gently.

"Come, come."

Barakat quieted.

"Now, tell me what she was doing the last time you saw her, Abdin."

Barakat muttered something unintelligible.

Daoud leaned closer. "What's that?"

"She was . . . Oh, merciful Allah! She was cleaning up!"

"Cleaning what up?"

Sobs.

"Cleaning what up, Abdin?"

"The kitchen. My dishes. My breakfast dishes."

After that, Barakat became withdrawn again, more mannequin than man. Answering Daoud's questions but perfunctorily, employing grunts, shrugs, nods, and shakes of the head whenever they could substitute for words, muttered monosyllables when speech was necessary. Pulling the information out of him was a frustrating process, but Daoud never flagged, taking the husband over the same territory time and time again, returning eventually to the issue that had driven a wedge between him and Shahin.

"Did she ever take steps to correct her defect?" Phrasing it so that all the responsibility rested on the woman's shoulders.

Nod.

"What kind of steps?"

"Prayer."

"She prayed, herself?"

Nod.

"Where?"

"Al Aqsa."

"Did others pray for her as well?"

Nod.

"Who?"

"My father petitioned the *waqf*. They appointed righteous old men."

"To pray for Shahin?"

Nod. "And . . ."

"And what?"

Barakat started to cry again.

"What is it, Abdin?"

"I—prayed for her too. I recited every *surah* in the Quran in one long night. I chanted the *zikr* until I fainted. Allah shut his ears to me. I am unworthy."

"It was a strong *djinn,*" said Daoud. Playing his part well, thought Daniel. He knew what Christians thought of Muslim spirits.

Barakat hung his head.

Daoud looked at his watch. "More water, Abdin? Or something to eat?"

Shake of the head.

"Did Shahin ever consult a doctor?"

Nod.

"Which doctor?"

"A herbalist."

"When?"

"A year ago."

"Not more recently?"

Shake of the head.

"What's the herbalist's name?"

"Professor Mehdi."

"The Professor Mehdi on Ibn Sina Street?"

Nod.

Daoud frowned, as did Daniel, behind the glass. Mehdi was a quack and illegal abortionist who'd been busted several times for fraud and released when the magistrates took seriously his lawyer's claims of ethnic harassment.

"What did Professor Mehdi advise?"

Shrug.

"You don't know?"

Shake of the head.

"She never told you?"

Barakat started to throw up his hands, got midway to his shoulders, and let them drop. "He took my money—it didn't work. What was the use?"

"Did she see a medical doctor?"

Nod.

"After she saw Professor Mehdi or before?"

"After."

"When?"

"Last month, then later."

"When later?"

"Before she . . ." Barakat chewed his lip.

"Before she left?"

Nod.

"When before she left?"

"Sunday."

"She saw this doctor the day before she left?"

Nod.

"Was she going for treatment?"

Barakat shrugged.

"What was the purpose of her appointment?"

Tension, then a shrug.

Daoud tensed also, looked ready to throttle Barakat. Tapping the table with his fingertips, he sat back, forcing a reassuring smile onto his face.

"She saw this doctor the day before she left, but you don't know for what."

Nod.

"What was the doctor's name?"

"Don't know."

"Didn't you pay his bill?"

Shake of the head.

"Who paid the doctor, Abdin?"

"No one."

"The doctor saw Shahin for free?"

Nod.

"As a favor?"

Shake of the head.

"Why, then?"

"A U.N. doctor—she had a refugee card. They saw her for free."

Daoud edged his chair closer to Barakat's.

"Where is this U.N. doctor's office?"

"Not an office. A hospital."

"*Which* hospital, Abdin?"

There was an edge in the detective's voice and Barakat heard it clearly. He pressed himself against his chair, shrinking back from Daoud. Wearing an injured look that said *I'm doing the best I can.*

"Which hospital?" Daoud said loudly. Getting to his feet and standing over Barakat, abandoning any pretense of patience.

"The big pink one," said Barakat, hastily. "The big pink one atop Scopus."

56

Patients began arriving at the Amelia Catherine at nine-thirty, the first ones a ragtag bunch of men who'd made the walk from the city below. Zia Hajab could have started processing them right then, but he made them wait, milling around the arched entry to the compound, while he sat in his chair sipping sweet iced tea and wiping his forehead.

This kind of heat, no one was going to rush him.

The waiting men felt the heat, too, shuffling to avoid baking, grimacing and fingering their worry beads. Most of them bore obvious stigmata of disease or disability: bandaged and splinted limbs, sutured wounds, eye infections, skin eruptions. A few looked healthy to Hajab, probably malingerers out for pills they could resell—with what they were paying, pure profit.

One of the men lifted his robe and urinated against the wall. A couple of others began grumbling. The watchman ignored them, took a deep breath and another sip of the cool liquid.

What they were paying, they could wait.

Only ten o'clock and already the heat was reaching deep inside Hajab, igniting his bowels. He fanned himself with a newspaper, peered into the tea glass. There was a lump of ice floating on top. He tilted the glass so that the ice rested against his teeth. Enjoyed the sensation of chill, then nibbled a piece loose and let it rest upon his tongue for a while.

He turned at the sound of a diesel engine. A UNRWA panel truck—the one from Nablus—pulled up in front of the hospital and stopped. The driver got out and loosened the tailgate, disgorging twenty or thirty men who limped down and joined the grumblers from the city. The groups merged into one restless crowd; the grumbling grew louder.

Hajab picked his clipboard off the ground, got up, and stood before them. A sorry-looking bunch.

"When may we enter, sir?" asked a toothless old man.

Hajab silenced him with a look.

"Why the wait?" piped up another. Younger, with an impudent face and runny, crusted eyes. "We've come all the way from Nablus. We need to see the doctor."

Hajab held out his palm and inspected the clipboard. Seventy patients scheduled for Saturday Men's Clinic, not counting those who walked in without appointments, or tried to be seen with expired refugee cards or no cards at all. A busy Saturday made worse by the heat, but not as bad as Thursdays, when the women came—droves of them, three times as many as the men. Women were weak-spirited, crying *Disaster!* at the smallest infirmity. Screeching and chattering like magpies until by the end of the day, Hajab's head was ready to burst.

"Come on, let us in," said the one with the bad eyes. "We have our rights."

"Patience," said Hajab, pretending to peruse the clipboard. He'd watched Mr. Baldwin, knew a proper administrator had to show who was in charge.

A man leaning on a cane sat down on the ground. Another patient looked at him and said, *"Sehhetak bel donya"*—"without health, nothing really matters"—to a chorus of nods.

"Bad enough to be sick," said Runny Eyes, "without being demeaned by pencil pushers."

A murmur of assent rose from the crowd. Runny Eyes scratched his rear and started to say something else.

"All right," said Hajab, hitching up his trousers and pulling out his pen. "Have your cards ready."

Just as he finished admitting the first bunch, a second truck—the one from Hebron—struggled up the road from the southeast. The engine on this one had an unhealthy stutter—the gears sounded worn, probably plenty else in need of repair. He would have loved to have a go at it, show what he could do with a wrench and a screwdriver, but those days were gone. *Al maktoub.*

The Hebron truck was having trouble getting over the peak of Scopus. As it lurched and bucked, a white Subaru two-door came cruising by from the opposite direction—from the campus of the Jews' university. The Subaru stopped, rolled several meters, and came to a halt directly across the road from the Amelia Catherine. Probably a gawker, thought Hajab, noticing the rental plates and the yellow Hertz sticker on the rear window.

The door of the Subaru opened and a big guy in a dark suit got out and started walking toward the Amelia Catherine. The sun bounced off his chest and reflected something shiny. Cameras—definitely a gawker—two of them, hanging from long straps. From where Hajab sat they looked expensive—big black-and-chrome jobs with those oversized lenses that stuck out like noses.

The gawker stopped in the middle of the road, oblivious to the approaching truck despite all the noise it was making. He uncovered the lens of one of the cameras, raised the machine to his eyes, and started shooting pictures of the hospital.

Hajab frowned. That kind of thing just wouldn't do. Not without some sort of payment. His commission.

He pushed himself out of his chair, wiped his mouth, and took a step forward, stopped at the sight of the Hebron truck coming over the peak and headed straight for the guy with the cameras, who just kept clicking away—what was he, deaf?

The driver of the truck saw him late, slammed on the brakes, which squealed like scared goats—another job for an expert mechanic—then leaned on his horn. The guy with the cameras looked up, waved hello like some kind of mental defective, and stumbled out of the way. The driver honked again, just for emphasis. The guy with the camera bowed and trotted across the road. Headed right for Hajab's chair.

As he got close, Hajab saw he was a Japanese. Very big and broad for one of them, but Japanese just the same, with the goofy tourist look they all had: ill-fitting suit, wide smile, thick-lensed eyeglasses, the hair all slicked down with grease. The cameras hanging on him like body parts—Japanese babies were probably born with cameras attached to them.

They were the best, the Japanese. Rich, every one of them, and gullible—easy to convince that the commission was mandatory. Hajab had posed for a group of them last month, gotten five dollars from each one, money he still had in a coffee can under his bed in Ramallah. His own bed.

"No pictures," he said sternly, in English.

The Japanese smiled and bowed, pointed his camera at the rose garden beyond the arch, snapped a picture, then swung the lens directly in line with the front door.

"No, no, you can't take pictures here," said the watchman, stepping between the Japanese and the door and wagging his finger in the big yellow face. The Japanese smiled wider, uncomprehending. Hajab searched his memory for English words, retrieved one Mr. Baldwin had taught him: "Forbidden!"

The Japanese made an O with his mouth, nodded his head several times, and bowed. Refocusing his camera—a Nikon; both of them were Nikons—on Hajab. The Nikon clicked and whirred.

Hajab started to say something, was distracted for a moment by the rattle of the Hebron truck's tailgate chains, the slamming of the gate on the asphalt. The Japanese ignored the noise, kept shooting Hajab's portrait.

"No, no." Hajab shook his head.

The Japanese stared at him. Put the first camera down and picked up the second. Behind him the Hebron truck drove away.

"No," Hajab repeated. "Forbidden."

The Japanese smiled, bowed, started pressing the second camera's shutter.

Idiot. Maybe "no" meant *yes* in his language—though the ones last month had understood. Maybe this one was just being obstinate.

Too big to intimidate, Hajab decided. The best he could do was disrupt the photographs, follow up with a little pantomime using his wallet.

He told the idiot: "U.N. say, must pay for pictures," put his hand in his back pocket, was prevented from proceeding by the swarm of Hebron patients hobbling their way to the entry.

Aggressive bunch, they pushed up against him, tried to get past him without showing their cards. Typical Hebron animals. Whenever they were around, it meant trouble.

"Wait," said Hajab, holding out his palm.

The Hebron patients pressed forward anyway, surrounding the big Japanese and beginning to stare at him with a mixture of curiosity and distrust as he kept taking pictures.

"Cards," announced Hajab, spreading his arms to prevent any of them from getting through. "You must show cards! The doctors won't see you without them."

"He saw me last month," said a man. "Said the card wasn't necessary."

"Well, it's necessary now." Hajab turned to the Japanese and grabbed hold of his arm, which felt huge under the suit sleeve: "Stop that, you. No pictures."

"Let the man take his pictures," said a man with a bandaged jaw and swollen lips, the words coming out slurred. He grinned at the Japanese, said in Arabic: "Take my picture, yellow brother."

The Hebron ruffians laughed.

"And mine."

"Mine, too, I want to be a movie star!"

The Japanese reacted to the shouts and smiles by snapping his shutter.

Hajab tugged at the Japanese man's arm, which was hard as a block of limestone and just as difficult to budge. "No, no! Forbidden, forbidden!"

"Why can't he take his pictures?" a patient demanded.

"U.N. rules."

"Always rules! Stupid rules!"

"Forget the rules! Let us in—we're sick!"

Several patients pushed forward. One of them managed to get around Hajab. The watchman said, "Stop, you!" and the sneak halted. Stooped-over little fellow with sallow skin and a worried face. He pointed to his throat and his belly.

"Card?" said Hajab.

"I lost it," said the man, talking with effort in a low croak, still holding his belly.

"The doctor won't see you without it."

The man moaned in pain.

"Let him in!" shouted someone. "He vomited in the truck, stunk it up."

"Let me in—I have to vomit too," said another voice from the crowd.

"Me, too. I have loose bowels as well."

Laughter, followed by more crudities.

The Japanese seemed to think the merriment was directed at him; he responded to each jest and rude remark with a click of his shutter.

A circus, thought Hajab, all because of this camera-laden monkey. As he reached up to pull down the Nikon, several rowdies made for the door.

"Stop your pictures!" he said. "Forbidden!" The Japanese smiled, kept clicking away.

More patients were pushing through now. Heading for the front door, not a single one of them bothering to show his card.

Click, click.

"Forbidden!"

The Japanese stopped, lowered his camera and let it rest against his broad chest.

Probably out of film, thought Hajab. No way would he be permitted to reload on hospital property.

But instead of reaching into his pocket for film, the Japanese smiled at Hajab and held out his hand for a shake.

Hajab took it briefly, withdrew his hand, and held it palm up. "Twenty dollars, American. U.N. rules."

The Japanese smiled again, bowed, and walked away.

"Twenty dollars," laughed a patient as he walked by.

"Twenty dollars for what, a kiss?" said another.

Hajab thought of going after them, stepped aside instead. The Japanese stood in the middle of the road again, pulled a third camera, a smaller one, out of his jacket pocket and took more of his damned pictures, then finally got in his Subaru and drove off.

Nearly all the Hebron patients had gotten to the door. Only a few stragglers remained, limping or walking the stingy, halting steps of the truly disabled.

Hajab headed back to the shade of his chair. Hot day like this, it didn't pay to expend precious energy. He settled his haunches on the thin plastic seat and wiped his brow. If things got crazy inside, that wasn't his problem.

He sat back, stretched his legs, and took a long sip of tea. Unfolding the paper, he turned to the classified section, became engrossed in the used car ads. Forgetting his surroundings, forgetting the Japanese, the jokers and malingerers. Not paying the stragglers one bit of attention, and certainly not noticing two of them who hadn't arrived on the truck with the others. Who'd emerged, instead, during the height of the commotion created by the Japanese, from a thicket of pines growing just outside the chain-link border at the rear of the hospital compound.

They wore long, heavy robes, these two, and dangling burnooses that concealed their faces. And though they hadn't been required to use them, in their pockets were refugee cards closely resembling the ones issued by UNRWA. Reasonable facsimiles, printed up just hours before.

Inside the hospital, things were indeed crazy. The air-conditioning system had broken down, turning the building into a steam bath. Two volunteer doctors hadn't shown up, appointments were already running an hour behind schedule, and the patient load was heavy, injured and sick men spilling out of the waiting room and into the main hallway, where they stood, squatted, sat, and leaned against the plaster walls.

The stagnant air was fouled by unwashed bodies and infection. Nahum Shmeltzer staked out a place against the north wall and watched the comings and goings of doctors, nurses, and patients, with a jaundiced eye.

The little false mustache was ridiculous, perched above his lip like a piece of lint. He hadn't shaved or showered and felt as unclean as the rest of them. To top it off, the robes Latam had provided him were abrasive as horsehair, heavy as lead. He was sweating like a sick man, starting to feel really feverish—how was that for method acting?

The only bright spot was the smile the costume had elicited from Eva. He'd picked her up at Hadassah, taken her home, tried to get her to eat, then held her for four hours before falling asleep, knowing she'd be up all night, waiting by the phone. The old man was close to death; she kept wanting to return to the hospital, afraid of missing the moment he slipped away.

Still, when Shmeltzer had gotten up at five and put on the Arab get-up, the corners of her mouth had turned up—only for a moment, but every little bit helped. . . . Shit, he was uncomfortable.

Daoud didn't seem to mind any of it, he noticed. The Arab stood across the hall, blending in with the others, cool as rain. Making occasional eye contact with Shmeltzer, but mostly just fading into the background. Backing up against the door of the Records Room and waiting for Shmeltzer's signal before making unobtrusive movements with his hands.

Movements you wouldn't notice if you weren't looking for them. The hands busy at the lock but the face blank as a new note pad.

Maybe Arabs weren't bothered by this kind of thing, thought Shmeltzer. If they could be trusted, they'd make great undercover men.

Arabs. Here he was, surrounded by them. Except for prison camp duty in '48, he'd never been with so many of them at one time.

If they knew who he was, they'd probably tear him apart. The Beretta would pick off a few, but not enough. Not that they'd ever find out. He'd looked in the mirror after putting on the outfit, surprised himself with what a good Arab he made. Ahmed Ibn Shmeltzer . . .

Someone lit a cigarette. A couple of others followed suit. A guy next to him nudged him and asked if he had a smoke. All that despite the fact that the American nurse, Cassidy, had come out twice and announced *No Smoking* in loud, lousy Arabic.

The Arabs ignored her; a woman talking, she might just as well have been a donkey braying.

"Smoke?" repeated the guy, nudging again.

"Don't have any," Shmeltzer said in Arabic.

The Cassidy girl was out in the hall again, calling out a name. A beggar on crutches grunted and bumped his way toward her.

Shmeltzer looked at the nurse as she escorted the cripple to an examining room. Plain as black bread, no breasts, no hips, the type of dry cunt always exploited by greasy sheikhs like Al Biyadi.

A few minutes later, the sheikh himself stepped out of another examining room, all pressed and immaculate in his long doctor's coat. He glanced at the mob of patients with disdain, shot his cuffs, and exposed a flash of gold watch.

A white swan among mud ducks, thought Shmeltzer, and he knows it. He followed Al Biyadi's path across the hall and into the Records Room. Daoud had moved away from the door, sat down, and was feigning sleep.

Al Biyadi used a key to open the door. Arrogant young snot—what the hell was he doing working here instead of renting a suite of offices in Ramallah or on a good street in East Jerusalem? Why lower himself to stitching up paupers when he could be raking in big money attending to landowners' families or rich tourists at the Intercontinental Hotel?

The initial research had shown him to be a playboy with expensive tastes. Hardly the type to go in for do-gooding. Unless there was an ulterior motive.

Like access to victims.

Dani's theory was that the Butcher was a psycho with something extra—a racist out to cause trouble between Jews and Arabs. Shmeltzer wasn't sure he bought that, but if it was true, it only strengthened his own theory: Al Biyadi was a closet radical and best bet for the Butcher. He'd said as much at the emergency staff meeting last night. No one had agreed or disagreed.

But he fit, the snot, including the fact that he'd lived in America.

Ten years ago, Nahum, Dani had objected. Their typical debate.

How do you know?

Our passport records confirmed it during the initial research.

Ten years. Four years too late to match two of the murders from the FBI computer.

But Shmeltzer wasn't ready to let go of the bastard that easily. Before settling in Detroit, Michigan, for college, Al Biyadi had lived in Amman, attending a high-priced boarding school, the same one Hussein's kids went to. Rich kid like that, he could have easily gone back and forth between Jordan and America as a tourist, using a Jordanian passport. Any trips taking place before his return to Israel wouldn't show up in their files.

American Immigration would have records of them, though. Dani had agreed to get in touch with them, though if past history was any indicator, getting the information would take weeks, maybe months.

Meanwhile, as far as Nahum Shmeltzer was concerned, the book was still open on Dr. Hassan Al Biyadi. Wide open.

Anyway, there was no reason to be wedded to the American murders. Maybe the similarity was just a coincidence—a strong one, granted, what with the caves and the heroin. But maybe certain types of sex maniacs operated in patterns, some common psychological thread that made them carve up women in similar ways, dump them in caves. Dani's black friend had said the match was too close for coincidence. An American detective would know plenty about that, but even he was theorizing. There was no hard evidence. . . .

Al Biyadi came out of the Records Room bearing several charts, locked it, stepped over Daoud, and pursed his lips in distaste.

Prissy, thought Shmeltzer. Maybe a latent homosexual—the head-doctor had said serial killers often were.

Look at the woman he chose: The Cassidy girl had no meat on her—not much of a woman at all, especially for a hotshot rich kid like Al Biyadi.

A strange pairing. Maybe the two of them were in it together. Closet radicals intent on fomenting violent revolution—a killing team. He'd always liked the idea of more than one murderer. Multiple kill spots, a partner to help carry stuff to and from the cave, serve as lookout, do a nice thorough washing of the bodies—nursie serving doctor.

And a *female* partner, to make it easier to snag victims. A woman would trust another woman, especially a do-gooder in a white uniform. Believe her when she said *Relax. This little shot is to make you feel better.*

Trust . . . Maybe Cassidy had done the first two American ones by herself—a female sex maniac. Why not? Then, four years later, Al Biyadi comes to America, meets her at Harper Hospital, the two of them find they have a common interest and start a killing club.

It sounded far-fetched, but you never knew. Anyway, enough speculating. It was giving him a headache. What was needed was good old-fashioned evidence.

The old Swiss nurse, Catherine Hauser, walked out into the center of the corridor and called out a name. Her voice was too soft amid the white noise of small talk, and no one heard her.

"Quiet," ordered Al Biyadi, just about to enter an examining room. "Quiet immediately."

The men in the hall obeyed.

Al Biyadi glowered at them, nodded like a little prince granting favors. "You may read that name again, Nurse Hauser."

The old one repeated it. A patient said, "Me," and got up to follow her. Al Biyadi pushed the door open and disappeared inside.

Shmeltzer leaned his elbows against the wall and waited. The man next to him had managed to get a cigarette from someone else and was blowing thick plumes of smoke that swirled in the hot air and took a long time to die. Across the hall Daoud was talking to a guy with a patch over his eye. Ahmed Ibn Dayan . . .

The two other doctors—the older Arab, Darousha, and the Canadian, Carter, came out of a room with an Arab between them. The Arab had one foot in a cast and was stumbling along as they propped him up, his arms on their shoulders.

How sweet.

Do-gooders. As suspects, Shmeltzer thought they were weak. True, a Canadian was almost like an American. Carter would certainly have had easy access to a big open border. But if the American murders cleared anyone, it was him: The initial research placed him in South America during four of the killings. A hitch in the Peace Corps in Ecuador during his last year in medical school, a return trip years later, as a doctor. Real do-gooder, the soft, hippie type, but probably an anti-Semite down deep—anyone who worked for UNRWA had to be. But his references from the Peace Corps were all glowing: devoted physician, saved lives, prevented outbreaks of cholera, helped build villages, dam streams, blah blah blah. To believe it, Dr. Richard Carter pissed champagne.

Darousha also shaped up as one hell of a *tzadik*: reputation for kindness, no political interests, got along with Jewish doctors—took courses at Hadassah and received high marks. So clean he'd never even had a traffic ticket. Everyone said he really liked making people feel better, was especially good with children.

Only mark against him was the fact that he was queer—and a real Romeo. Shin Bet had just firmed up some rumors connecting him with a series of male lovers, including a married Jewish doctor three years ago. The latest boyfriend was the moronic watchman out in front. What a pair they'd make—two pudgy guys bouncing around in bed.

But being homosexual meant nothing in terms of this case, decided Shmeltzer. According to the head-docs, the magic word was *latent*. The theory was that the violence came about because the killer was repressing his homosexual impulses, trying to overcompensate by being supermasculine and taking control of women by destroying them.

If Darousha was *already* overtly queer, didn't it mean he'd *stopped* repressing? Had nothing to hide, nothing to be upset about? Unless he thought no one knew about him . . .

All bullshit, anyway, the psychology stuff. Including the bullshit profiles Dani's black friend had quoted from the FBI: Men who cut up women were usually sadistic psychopaths. Which was like saying you could make something smaller by reducing it in size. Nice guy, the black—no doubt he had more experience than any of them, and Nahum Shmeltzer was the last person to refuse help from outsiders. But only if they had something solid. Like evidence.

Which was what they were after this morning, stuck here in the midst of all this stink and pestilence. He looked over at Daoud, hoped the chance came soon. Goddamned robes itched like crazy.

At one in the afternoon the doctors took a lunch break. Free coffee and pastries were offered to the patients, who went after the food like starving animals, rushing out to the front courtyard of the hospital where folding tables had been set up.

Moving damned fast, noticed Shmeltzer, for guys on crutches and canes. He signaled for Daoud to make *his* move.

Shielded by the commotion, the Arab detective sidled up to the Records Room door again, worked the pick out from inside his sleeve, and played with the lock.

Slow, thought Shmeltzer, keeping one eye on the hallway. One minute more, he'd have a try at it himself.

Finally the lock yielded. Daoud turned and looked at Shmeltzer, who looked up and down the corridor.

Coast was clear, but the hallway was emptying, their cover was dissipating.

Go, Shmeltzer signaled.

Daoud opened the door, slipped inside, and closed it after him.

The corridor grew silent. Shmeltzer waited for the Arab to do his work, standing watch five meters to the east of the door. Then footsteps sounded from around the corner. A man appeared, a Westerner, walking quickly and purposefully.

Baldwin, the administrator—now *there* was an American. Real uncooperative bastard, according to Dani. And the shmuck had been out of America only for the last two murders in the FBI file, which were dismemberments anyway, no ID on the victims—far from clear that they belonged with the first ones.

A pencil-pushing bastard. Shmeltzer would have liked to see him as the killer. No doctor, but he'd hung around hospitals long enough to learn about drugs, surgical procedures.

Look at him, wearing a Great White Father safari suit and shiny black boots with hard leather heels that played a clackety drumbeat on the tile floor. Gestapo boots.

Shmuck was walking fast but his eyes were buried in a magazine—*Time*. A large ring of keys dangled from one hand as he approached.

Heading straight for the Records Room, realized Shmeltzer. Hell of a disaster if Daoud stepped out right now and came face to face with the bastard.

Shmeltzer backed up so that he stood in front of the door. Heard rustling inside and knocked a signal to the Arab, who locked the door and stopped moving.

Baldwin came closer, looked up from his magazine and saw him.

"Yes?" he said. "Can I help you?" Heavily accented Arabic.

Shmeltzer leaned against the door, clutched his chest, and moaned.

"What's the matter?" said Baldwin, looking down on him.

"Hurts," said Shmeltzer in a whisper, trying to look and sound feeble.

"What's that?"

"Hurts."

"What hurts?"

"Chest." A louder moan. Shmeltzer fluttered his eyelids, made as if his knees were giving way.

Baldwin grabbed his elbow, dropping his *Time* magazine in the process. Shmeltzer went semi-limp, let the bastard support his weight, smiling to himself and thinking: Probably the first real work he's done in years.

The American grunted, fumbled with his key ring until he'd attached it to his belt, freed his other hand to prop up Shmeltzer's steadily sagging body.

"Have you seen the doctor yet?"

Shmeltzer gave a miserable look and shook his head. "Waiting. Waiting all day . . . oh!" Letting out a wheezing breath.

Baldwin's pale eyebrows rose in alarm.

"Your heart? Is it your heart?"

"Oh! Ohhh!"

"Do you have a heart problem, sir?"

"Oh! Hurts!"

"All right. Listen," said Baldwin. "I'm going to lower you down. Just wait here and I'll go get one of the doctors."

He let Shmeltzer slide to the floor, propped him against the wall, and jogged off back toward the east wing. The moment he rounded the corner, Shmeltzer got to his feet, rapped on the Records Room door, and said, "Get the hell out!"

The door opened, Daoud emerged, eyes alive with excitement. Success.

"This way," said Shmeltzer, pointing west.

The two of them ran.

As they put space between them and the Records Room, Shmeltzer asked, "Get anything?"

"Everything. Under my robes."

"Mazel tov."

Daoud looked at the older man quizzically, kept running. They passed the examining rooms and the X-ray lab. The hallway terminated at a high wall of windowless plaster marked only by a bulletin board.

"Wait," said Shmeltzer. He stopped, scanned the board, pulled off a clinic schedule, and stashed it in his pocket before resuming his run.

A right turn took them into a smaller corridor lined by a series of paneled wood doors. Recalling the Mandate-era blueprints they'd examined last night, Shmeltzer identified their former function: servants' quarters, storage rooms. The Brits had pampered themselves during their reign: The entire west wing had been devoted to keeping them well clothed and well fed—quarters for an army of butlers, maids, cooks, laundry room, linen closets, silver storage, auxiliary kitchen, auxiliary wine cellar.

Now those rooms had been turned into flats for the do-gooders, doctors' and nurses' names typed on cards affixed to each door. Al Biyadi's room was next to Cassidy's, Shmeltzer noticed. He took in the names on the other cards too. Committing all of it to memory—automatically—as he continued to run.

Behind them, from behind the corner, came the sound

of distant voices—echoing voices full of worry, then surprise.

The voices grew louder. As did the footsteps. Hard Gestapo heels.

At the end of the smaller corridor were French doors that yielded to the turn of a brass handle. Shmeltzer and Daoud ran out onto a stone landing guarded on both sides by reclining statuary lions, leaped down half a dozen steps, and found themselves facing the rear grounds of the hospital—neglected estate grounds, once elaborately landscaped, now just an expanse of red dirt bordered by the ragged remains of privet hedges and walled by tall old pines. Empty flower beds and patches of rusty earth interrupted by seemingly random copses of younger trees. To the far west of the grounds was an enclosed pen for animals; all else was open space.

But the entire property was enclosed by three meters of chain link.

Trapped.

"Where now?" said Daoud, running in place.

Shmeltzer stopped, felt his knees aching, his heart pumping furiously. Thinking: Funny if I got a real heart attack.

He surveyed the grounds, looked back at the hospital. Much of the rear of the huge pink building's ground floor consisted of glass panels—more French doors leading out to a canopied sun porch. A solarium back in Mandate days—goddamned Brits sunning themselves while their empire rotted out from under them. Now the dining room.

The sun porch was unoccupied, but if anyone was inside the dining room looking out, he and the Arab would be easy to spot. A real mess.

Still, what was the alternative?

"Keep going," he said, pointing to the north end of the property.

What had once been a rolling lawn was now dirt coated with stones and pine needles. They ran for the shelter of a copse of pines, ran through several meters of shade before exiting the trees and finding themselves on steeply sloping barren ground leading directly to the northern perimeter of the property—a cliff edge. A hinged rectangle had been cut out of the chain link, framing blue sky. A door to the heavens.

Hell of a view, thought Shmeltzer, taking in the distant

cream-and-purple contours of the desert, the terraced hills of Judea, still coated with greenery.

Sapphire sky above; big dry blanket below. Hills for folds. Caves for moth holes.

Caves.

He looked back through the trees, saw two figures on the sun porch, one of them in khaki, the other in white. They stood there for a while, went back inside.

Who the hell cared about one sick old Arab?

Daoud had opened the chain-link door. Was gazing out at the wilderness.

"What's it look like over the side?" Shmeltzer asked him.

The Arab dropped to the ground, crawled to the edge, and peered down.

"Small drop, easy," he said, surprised. "Looks like a hiking trail."

They lowered themselves over the side, Daoud first, Shmeltzer following. Landed on flat, soft earth, a wide terrace—three meters by two. The first of several oversized steps notched into the hillside.

"Like stairs," said Daoud.

Shmeltzer nodded. Below the steps was a thick, coarse growth of water-spurning shrubbery. Ugly stuff, green-gray spikes and coils, some of it browning in the heat.

He noticed a split in the brush, a parting like the Red Sea. The two detectives climbed down the steps and entered it, edging through a narrow pathway, barely one person wide. Beneath their feet, flat surface rounded to a concave ditch; they sank suddenly and had to use their arms for balance. But soon they grew used to the concavity, were walking steadily and rapidly down the side of the hill. Bent at the waist to avoid being snagged by the thorny branches overhead.

Shmeltzer slowed and looked up at the branches. An arch of greenery—the classic Jerusalem arch, this one fashioned by nature. Opaque as a roof except for frayed spots where the sun shone through, letting in shards of light that cast brilliant white geometric patterns upon the hard-packed earth.

A tunnel, he thought. Leading straight down to the desert, but from the air or below you'd see only brush, a serpentine line of gray-green. Probably fashioned years ago by the Brits, or maybe the Jordanians after them or the Turks before them. An escape route.

"How you doing?" he asked Daoud. "Still got the stuff?"

The Arab patted his middle. "Still got it."

"Okay, let's follow this. See where it leads."

57

After a while, Nightwing got more open about herself, lying in his arms in the backseat of the Plymouth after she did him, and talking about her childhood—growing up fat and pimply and unpopular, terrorized by an asshole father who crawled into her bed every night and raped her. The next morning he'd always feel guilty and take it out on her by slapping her around and calling her a whore. The rest of the family going along with it, treating her like scum.

Once he saw tears in her eyes, which nauseated him; hearing about her personal shit made him sick. But he didn't stop her from spilling it out, sat back and pretended he was listening, sympathetic. Meanwhile he was filling his mind with pictures: real science experiments on whimpering mutts, touching the stiffs in the path lab, memory slides of what he'd done to Fields, how the slimeball's head had looked all bashed to trash. Thinking: It's easy to be a shrink.

One night they were driving on Nasty, headed for a parking spot, and she said, "That's him—that's BoJo!"

He slowed the car to get a good look at the pimp, saw a short, skinny nigger in a purple suit with red fake-fur lapels and a red hat with fake leopardskin band and peacock feathers. Little slime was standing on a corner talking to two fat blond whores, his arms around them, showing lots of gold tooth.

Nightwing slumped low on the seat and prodded his arm. "Speed up. I don't want him to see me!"

He slowed the Plymouth, smiled. "What, you're scared of a little shit like that?"

"He may be little, but he's bad."

"Yeah, right."

"*Believe* it, Doctor T. C'mon, let's get out of here!"

"Yeah, right."

After that, he started watching the nigger.

BoJo was a creature of habit, showed up on the boulevard Wednesdays, Fridays, and Sundays, always around eleven P.M. Always driving from the south side of town in a five-year-old lacquer-flake purple Pontiac Grand Prix with gangster whitewall tires wrapped around chrome reversed mag wheels, silver sparkle vinyl top, etched opera windows, fake ermine tuck-and-roll interior with purple piping, "BJ" monogrammed in gold on the doors, and blackened windows with stickers on them warning that the entire shitty mess was protected by a supersensitive motion-detector alarm system.

The pimpmobile was always left in the same no-parking zone on the south side of Nasty. Cops never checked; Grand Prix never got ticketed. When BoJo got out of the car, he always stretched, then lit an extra-large gold-tipped purple Sherman's with a gold lighter shaped like a Playboy rabbit, before setting the alarm with a little handpiece. Repeated the same song-and dance-on his way back to the car.

The little shit's evenings were just as predictable: a westward stroll on Nasty, collecting from his whores until midnight, then the rest of the night spent drinking at a puke-stinking pimp bar called Ivan's Pistol Dawn on Wednesdays and Fridays. Ogling the dancers at a strip joint called the Lube Job on Sundays.

Dr. Terrific followed him. No one noticed the clean-cut guy in the windbreaker, T-shirt, freshly laundered jeans, and blue tennies. Just another soldier on leave, looking for action.

Soldier of destiny.

Once in a while BoJo left with one of the Lube Job strippers or a whore. Once in a while another nigger, a big, light-skinned, muscle-bound type, hung around him playing bodyguard. But usually he did his thing alone, swaggering along the boulevard as if he owned it. Probably feeling confident because of the nickle-plated pistol he carried—big .45-caliber cowboy job with a white fake-pearl handle. Sometimes he took it out of the glove compartment and waved it around like some kind of toy before sticking it back in his waistband.

Fucker certainly *seemed* confident, dancing and prancing, laughing all the time, his mouth a fucking gold mine. He wore tight, satin-seamed pants that made his legs look even skinnier than they were, custom-made ticky-tacky wide-shouldered jackets, and patent-leather shoes with high stacked heels. Even with the heels he was short. Black dwarfshit.

Easy to spot.

He watched the scuzz for weeks, was there one warm Friday night, waiting, when BoJo returned from his prowl/party at three-thirteen A.M. Had been waiting in the shit-stinking alley for four hours, standing next to a shit-stinking dumpster, but not the least bit tired. Letting the garbage smells pass right through him, floating above it like some angel, his mind pure and free of thoughts.

Seeing only Fields's face, then BoJo's, then the two of them merging into a white/nigger slime mask.

Pow. His hands itched.

BoJo turned off Nasty and onto the side street, snapping his fingers and staggering—probably stoned out of his gourd from too much juice or weed or whatever. He paused a block away from the Pontiac, the way he always did, hitched up his pants, and lit his Sherman's. The flame from the rabbit lighter illuminated his monkey face for one brief, ugly moment.

Soon as the flame died, Dr. Terrific came running silently out of the alley, all superhero clean-cut and full of destiny.

Sliding a crowbar out from under the windbreaker, he jogged over to the Grand Prix on bouncy tennie feet, raised the crowbar over his head, and brought it down as hard as he could, pulverizing the windshield. The sound of shattering glass still sweet in his ears, he zipped around to the passenger side, squatted low on the sidewalk.

The supersensitive motion-detector alarm started screaming.

BoJo had been dragging on his cigarette. It took a second for the pimp to realize what was happening. Another second before he started screaming too.

In harmony with the alarm.

Soul music.

Fucker pulled out his gun, ran/staggered to the Grand Prix as fast as those faggy high heels could take him. Tripping and cursing, finally getting there and staring open-mouthed at the rape of the windshield. Meanwhile, the alarm was still screaming out its mechanical painsong.

BoJo jumped up and down, swung the .45 in an arc, and looked from side to side, spitting and cursing, saying "Come here, mothah*fuckahs,* goddam fuckin' mothah*fuckahs*!"

The alarm continued pouring its little electronic heart out.

Meanwhile, *he* was staying still as a dead man, crouching with the crowbar in his hand. Ready. Stupid nigger never saw him, never thought of checking the passenger side of the car. Just kept jumping and spitting and cursing, leaning over to finger what was left of the windshield, staring at whole chunks of safety glass that had come loose, hundreds of bubbles of glass all over the fake-ermine tuck-and-roll dashboard, stuck in the high-pile fake-ermine bucket seats.

Repeating "Mothah*fuckah,* fuckin' mothah*fuckah*" like some spear-chucker chant, stomping his little high-heeled foot, waving the gun around, then finally putting it away, taking the handset out of his pocket and turning off the alarm.

The screaming died; the silence seemed even louder.

Dr. T. held his breath.

"Shit," said BoJo, removing his hat and rubbing a balding head. "Oh, fuck, mothahfuckin' *shee*-it."

Nigger opened the driver's door with a gold-plated key, brushed glass from the seat and the dashboard, listened to the sad-song tinkle as it fell to the curb, said "*Shee*-it" again, then got out to reexamine the windshield, as if it had all been a bad dream, next time he looked everything would be okay.

It wasn't.

"Mercy fuck. *Shee*-it."

Famous last words, because when the fucker straightened up, he was staring into a clean-cut superhero face, hearing:

"Hi, I'm Doctor Terrific. What seems to be the problem?"

"Say wha—" Feeling, without really comprehending, the stunning pain as the crowbar smashed him square across his nose, pulverizing his face, driving bone slivers into whatever poor excuse for cerebral tissue he carried in that ugly black monkey skull.

So easy, just like Fields.

So easy, it made him hard.

Blackberry jelly, he thought, as he hit the nigger slime again and again, stepping back and wiping himself with tissues each time, so that the blood wouldn't spatter his clothes. Wiping the crowbar clean, and leaving it next to the body. Using the tissues to extract the .45 from the slime's waistband and laying the gun on top of the pimp's crotch.

"Umgawa, umgawa. Suck this, coonshit."

Then heading back to the alley, where he retrieved his Polaroid camera, returned to the heap of wet blacktrash, and snapped a flash picture before sauntering off, soooo casual.

He stopped under a streetlight three blocks away, found a few tiny blood freckles on his shoes and T-shirt. The shoes he wiped. The shirt was quickly concealed by zipping up the windbreaker. Then he walked on. Two blocks farther was the Plymouth, nice and comfy. He got in it, drove a mile to another alley with dumpsters. Opened the trunk of the car and wet some rags with alcohol and water from plastic hospital bottles he'd stored there. Pulled the camera apart with his hands, enjoying the cracking sound and imagining it was the nigger's body he was breaking. Wiping each piece, then throwing them into three separate dumpsters.

Riding on and tossing the tissues in four separate sewer drains, tearing off the corner of the one with the most blood and eating it.

He rewarded himself by getting a beer out of the ice chest in the trunk. Drinking it slowly, so casual.

Twenty minutes later he was back on the boulevard, foot-cruising among the geeks and creeps and night-crawling slimeballs, knowing they were *his*, knowing he could have any of them any time he wanted.

He found a twenty-four-hour fast-food stand—greasy, run-down joint with a pockmarked slant behind the counter. After staring the slant into giving him the key to the men's room, he washed up, examined his face, touched himself, not quite believing he was real.

Then he went back to the counter, ordered a double cheeseburger and vanilla shake from the slant, sat on a cracked plastic stool, eating. Really enjoying his dinner.

The only other customers were a pair of stinking biker faggot types in black leather, stuffing their faces with teriyaki dogs and onion rings. They noticed him, nudged each other, tried to stare him down, tried to give him the evil eye.

His grin changed their minds.

He thought Nightwing would be impressed by the snapshot

of all that dead black jelly, overcome with *My Hero!* gratitude. Instead she gave him a weird look like he was dirty. It made him feel bad for a moment, kind of nauseous and scared, like when he'd been a kid sitting tight-sphinctered on step number six, terrified of being caught.

He stared back at her stare, heard the bad-machine noise get louder, and thought: Stupid ungrateful cunt. Hot rage-pain clawed at the roof of his mouth; he felt the cold rolled steel of the crowbar in his hands. Cooled it with a chest-ballooning deep breath and mind-pictures of the nigger as he'd gone down. Patent shoes black with nightblood.

Be casual. Patient.

But he knew she was hopeless. The romance was over.

He tore the picture in little pieces, ate them, and grinned. Stretched and yawned. "I did it for you. Now you're safe, babe."

"Yeah." Forced smile. "G-great. Thanks—you're terrific!"

"My *pleasure,* babe." A command.

A minute later: "Do me again, babe."

She hesitated, saw the look on his face, then said, "Yeah, sure, *my* pleasure, gratis," and lowered her head.

After that their relationship changed. They continued to date, she took his money, did what he wanted, but held back. Emotionally. He could tell.

No more boyfriend/girlfriend, this was heavy duty love/respect, like a kid for a parent.

Which was okay. He was sick of hearing her sob stories, mean old daddy, all the johns who couldn't get it up, dribbled on her legs, the ones who liked to hurt her.

Fuck that noise. Power was better than closeness any day of the week. Far as he was concerned, they could have continued that way for a while.

But she fucked it up. What happened was her fault, when you got right down to it. The thoughtlessness, dirtying his heritage.

Dirtying Schwann.

He'd say one thing for Fields: The shitbag had been thorough. Checking foreign phone books, employment and immigration records, physicians' directories, licensing board rosters, motor vehicle registrations. Medical journal obituaries.

Being a private eye was clearly more busywork than brainwork, all that TV stuff pure bullshit.

He learned something: Lots of information was just lying around for the taking, if you knew where to look for it.

One downer: The best information Fields had gotten hold of came right out of Schwann's hospital personnel file—Doctor's hospital, the same hospital he'd been working in for two years! In the Pathology Department, of all places—he'd delivered mail there at least a thousand times, was still doing it, had fondled a stiff there just last week.

All those sacred facts right under his nose and he'd paid a dumb slime to find them!

Overlooking it made him tremble, want to cut himself. He cooled himself down with a beer and a stroke, told himself it was okay to make mistakes as long as you learned.

He'd learned. From a dead man, a fucking scumbag.

It paid to keep an open mind.

Visually, Fields's report was a mess, just what you'd expect from a lowlife slob: cheap paper, ink smudges, bent corners, the text typed on a cheap machine with chipped letters, and marred by typographical errors and slipping margins. In those margins, Fields had scrawled little handprinted comments—the slime had obviously planned on squeezing more money out of him by coming across superhelpful. Writing in an oily buddy-buddy tone that made him wish he could bring the fucker back to life in order to smash him to trash again.

Despite all that, the file was sacred, a bible.

Bless you, Daddy.

He set aside bible time every day, sitting naked on the floor of the ice palace, touching himself. Sometimes he worshipped more than once, memorizing the text, every word was sacred. Staring at the hospital ID photo for hours until the image of Schwann's face was burned into his brain.

His face.

The same face. Clean-cut and handsome.

Handsome, because Schwann had wanted to pass the superhero legacy on to him, had squeezed those face-chromosomes into *her* filthy womb.

Dominating her inferior tissue with Schwann supersperm. The line of command from father to son, a sparkling clone chain.

Looking at his face, anyone knowing Schwann would have to know. Doctor had been a stupid kike fuck not to have caught it.

No one else had ever mentioned it because they were kike-dupes. Doctor had paid them off.

He intensified his bible studies, started reading the file after every meal. The New New Testament. Book of Dieter, Chapter One, Verse One.

In the beginning, Dieter Schwann was born.

Only child—like him!—of Hermann Schwann and Hilde Lobauer Schwann.

Date of the blessed event: April 20, 1926.

The sacred place: Garmisch-Partenkirchen, Germany.

("Fancy ski resort for the rich, Doc," Fields had scrawled. "Family probably had money, may still have some. You could try to attach some of their bank accounts but overseas stuff is hard to pull off without an internt'l attorney—be happy to get you a referral.")

Grandma Hilde: Fields had little to say about her. ("Nothing traceable. Died 1962, haven't been able to find out who inherited her estate. A foreign trace might obtain you more.") But *he* was certain she was beautiful. Clean and cool. And blond.

Grandpa Hermann: a doctor, of course. An *important* one —*two* doctorates, M.D. *and* Ph.D. Professor of Surgery, University of Berlin.

Herr Doktor Professor Hermann Schwann, M.D., Ph.D. ("Died, 1952. A Nazi. I checked the Periodicals Index and his name turned up in a 1949 *Life* magazine article on the Nuremberg trials. Seems he ran experiments at Dachau, was convicted of war crimes and imprisoned after the war. Died in jail. Tough luck for the bastard, eh, Doc?")

Tough luck for slime-o Fields, eh?

Chapter Two, Verse One: Dieter Grows to Manhood.

Supercloner had been a doctor too. A brilliant one—you could tell by reading between the lines of the bible/report:

"M.D., 1949, University of Berlin"—which made him a doctor at 23! "Residency and fellowship in surgical pathology, '49–'51"—they didn't give that to just anyone! "Immigrated to the U.S. on a student visa in '51 for a post-doctoral fellowship in micro-anatomy research. Finished up in '53, and went to New York as a staff pathologist at Columbia Presbyterian Hospital."

Reading between the lines revealed a dual mission to the emigration:

A. Put the finishing touches on a brilliant medical education.

B. Shoot superhero sperm into a womb-receptacle until it cloned to perfection.

Fuck the womb—the seed lives on!

Dr. Terrific, alias Dieter Schwann, Junior—no, *the second.* No, Roman numerals: II. II. II.

Dr. Dieter Schwann, II.

Herr Doktor Professor Dieter Schwann, II: Famous—*world-renowned* physician, surgical pathologist, micro-anatomist, life giver and taker, cleanser of dirt and scum, mind-picture artist, and man-about-town.

Dieter Schwann had died for the sins of the world, but his seed lived on.

Lived.

A noble story, but the end of the report couched it in lies. The Apocrypha. By trying to conceal the truth, Fields had justified his death a million times over.

It had happened too fast. The slime had deserved a lesson. Real science.

No more Mr. Nice Guy.

Still, he didn't tear out the lies, not wanting to alter any part of the bible. Forced himself to read, in order to strengthen his will, harden his heart.

"Schwann left Columbia in '59. They wouldn't say why—his file was closed. (I picked up a hint of something smelly in the ethics department, which makes sense when you follow what happened to the guy.) After that, the State Board has him working in a storefront medical clinic in Harlem—that's a bad black neighborhood—from '60 through '63. The first dope arrest is in '63. He got probation, lost his license, appealed, and lost. No employment record after '63. Second arrest, '64, possession of heroin and conspiracy to sell. A year at Rikers Island—that's a New York City jail—released on probation after six months. Arrested again in '65, sent to the state prison at Attica for seven years. Died of a heroin overdose in prison in '69."

In the margin: "Like father, like son, eh?"

He read the scrawled note for the millionth time, became inflamed with rage. Rubbed his cock until the skin was raw and pinpointed with blood. Clawed at his thighs, tore the skin, pushed through the bad-machine noise, which was as loud as thunder, strong as a tidal wave.

"No records of burial service," wrote Fields. "Probably a potter's field situation (pretty low for a doctor, eh?). No bank accounts or credit cards, no permanent address since '63." In the margin: "I wouldn't count on getting your dough, Doc. This guy may have made a good living at one time but he pissed it all away on dope. Top of that, it's been a couple of years. The foreign angle seems our best bet. What do you think, Doc?"

He thought—he thought—hethoughthethought.

NOTHING!!!

One summer, two tourist girls from the Midwest got raped and stabbed to death near Nasty and the politicians got all hot and bothered about the crime situation. The cops responded like good little robots, enforcing a ten P.M. curfew, raiding bars and skin joints, busting heads, hauling geeks and creeps off to jail for spitting on the sidewalk.

A threat to his relationship with Nightwing, but no problem for Dr. T.—he was ready to break it off with the ungrateful cunt anyway. Had been figuring out the best way to do it. The best plan.

She was a shallow person, had stopped acting scared but the emotional distance was still there. But *she* wanted *him,* said:

"Listen, Doc, no reason for you to boogie away. I found another place. A safe one."

He thought for a while.

"Sure, babe."

There was a big park in the hills north of the boulevard, huge place with a zoo and an observatory and a dozen gates. She told him to drive there, directed him to an obscure gate on the east side, almost completely hidden by giant eucalyptus—a swinging metal frame crossed by wood beams that the park rangers never bothered to lock. She got out of the car, pushed it open, got back in, and they drove through.

The park was oil-black at night. Nightwing pointed left, to a winding road that circled one of the mountains that formed the core of the park. He drove slowly and carefully, with his headlights off, aware of sheer drops on both sides, the city lights that got smaller as they climbed.

They cruised nearly to the top of the mountain, came to a flat turnoff before she said, "Right here. Park under those trees and turn off the engine." When he hesitated: "Come on, don't be a party pooper."

He parked. She got out. "Come on. There's something I want to show you."

He got out carefully. Walked down a twisting dirt path, through walls of trees.

Spooky. But not scared. His body was hard and strong from hours of self-torture and weight lifting, his eyes cat-sharp in the darkness—he *was* part cat, now. Snowball's contribution to his Aryan *ubermensch* superconsciousness.

Ubermensch. Kultur. Das Reich. He sang the sacred words to himself as he followed Nightwing's ass-wiggle. *Arbeit macht frei.*

So many things you could learn in the library.

The librarian at the junior college was an older woman with big tits, not bad-looking, but not his type.

Excuse me . . .

Smile. Yes, what can I do for you?

Uh, I'm doing a term paper on racist literature for Soc. 101. What kind of reference material do you have?

Let's see. The general references would be in the card catalogue—you could try bigotry, racism . . . prejudice, possibly ethnicity. How far back do you want to go?

Twentieth century.

Hmm. We also have a special collection of Nazi and neo-Nazi literature just donated a few months ago.

Oh? (I know, bitch. A truckload of stuff donated by the wimps at the Coalition Against Racism. Long-haired kikes and spics and niggers wanting to expose the student body to the evils of prejudice, raise the fucking student *consciousness.* Fucking candlelight ceremony with some hook-nosed rabbi mouthing off about the peace-love-brotherhood scam. Campus paper covered it big—he'd cut out the article, put it in his research file.)

Is that something you'd be interested in looking at? Smiling. The tits jiggling as she talked.

I guess so.

She kept him waiting, went into the back room and came back pushing a trolley of file cases.

Here you go. It can't be checked out. You'll have to read it right here.

Thanks. You've been a great help.

Smile. That's what we're here for.

He wheeled the trolley to a table against the wall, away from everyone else, opened the cases, and found a treasure trove.

Mein Kampf, in English. Gerald L.K. Smith. George Lincoln Rockwell. *The Thunderbolt. The Klansman.* And classic stuff: *Protocols of the Elders of Zion. Der Stürmer* with those terrific cartoons.

Truth-tellers.

Their words gripped him, set off something inside of him that he knew was right and real.

He wanted to eat all of it, chew up and swallow every book and pamphlet, infuse it directly into his genetic code.

But not the liars' books.

Whiny, whimpering shit written by kikes and kikesymps about the SS, the death camps, Josef Mengele, M.D., Ph.D. Photos of twin victims, piles of bodies, supposed to repulse.

But they turned him on.

Among the lies, a find: a book on the Nuremberg trials written by some kike lawyer who'd been there. A list at the back, naming the defendants. Noble *Herr Doktor* Grandpa occupying a place of honor in the *S* column. His sweet name shining like a beacon.

A fuzzy group picture of defendants at the docket.

The same face!

Hermann to Dieter to Dieter II.

The seed lives!

He returned to the library, again and again, got the trolley and wheeled it to a quiet corner—such a studious boy. Lived with the treasure for weeks while he copied sacred sentences into spiral notebooks, preserving the words, burning the truth into his mind.

The kikes were behind the drug trade, world communism, diseases of the genitals. War and crime. Out to turn the world hook-nosed and filthy.

Gerald L.K. Smith said so. So did George Lincoln Rockwell, Robert Shelton. They proved it with facts, exposed Holocaust lies, the kike-banker conspiracy.

The Führer, persecuted. Grandpa Hermann, framed, dead in a prison cell.

Daddy Dieter dead in a prison cell!

Crucified by nigger-pimp-pushers and the kike drug bankers who bankrolled all of it.

Heil Daddy! He felt like crying. . . .

Thin fingers on his arm brought him back to the park, the night air. They'd reached the end of the pathway. Nightwing stroked his hair.

"Come on, Dr. T., it's cool, no patrols. Nothing to get freaked about!"

He looked at her, through her.

Stupid cunt had her mesh blouse unbuttoned, revealing her tits, hands on her hips, trying to look sexy. The moonlight hit her face, turned her into a skeleton, then back to a girl, then back to a skeleton again.

Shifting layers.

The beauty beneath the surface.

"C'mon, cutie." Pointing to a cave. Taking his hand and leading him into it.

Dark, mildew-smelling place. She took a penlight from her purse, switched it on, revealing grooved rock walls, sloping rock ceilings. A June bug, momentarily paralyzed by the light, came to its senses and scampered for cover. Other insects wiggled in the corners of the cave—spiders and whatever. Ignoring them, Nightwing crawled to the far end, showing him her ass under her microskirt, the line of black panties splitting the cheeks. There was a filthy-looking army blanket wedged near the wall. She lifted it, dragged out a cheap vinyl suitcase and opened it.

Watching her practiced movements, seeing the suitcase, he knew she'd been there before, thousands of times, with thousands of other men. Had shared the secret place with them, but not him.

Stupid, unfeeling cunt! After all he'd done for her, she hadn't trusted him enough to show him her little hidey-hole. Not until thousands of others had come up here first, filling her with their lies and their scuzzy jizz.

The last straw. Be casual.

"What's in the case, babe?"

"To-oys." Licking her lips.

"Let's see them."

"Only if you promise to be a good *bo-oy."*

"Sure, babe."

"Prom-ise?"

"Promise."

The "toys" were predictable: novelty-shop S&M props, the stuff seen in the ads at the back of fuck books—whips, chains, spiked boots, an oversized black dildo studded with bumps, a leather domination helmet with straps and buckles all over it.

Yawn.

She put on the boots, lifted her leg to give him a beaver shot while she did it.

Double yawn.

Took off the mesh blouse, put on a leather bra with holes cut out for the nipples.

Borrring.

Then she pulled out the hat. Black silk Nazi officer's hat with a shiny black brim, the SS death's-head insignia above the center of the crown. Under the grinning skull, the double lightning bolts that stood for:

Schwann-Schwann.

"Where'd you get that? Babe?"

"*Some*-where." Leaning close and running a long-nailed finger down the side of his arm, thinking she was turning him on when all she was doing was shoving hot needles into his flesh.

Putting on the hat. Raising her arm in salute.

"Heil, Nightwing! Da dum, da dum." Putrid smile. Bad German accent: "Vont me to poot it on ven I do you, little Adolf? I giff grreat hat!"

Keep cool. Stay in control. "Sure, babe."

"Hey, feel *that*! You *like* this Nazi shit, don't you? *Thought* so." Salute. "Heil blow-jobs!"

Touching him, unzipping him.

"Look at me, Fraulein Adolfa Titler, ready to suck you all the way to the Fourth Reich. God, you're hard. You *really love* this, don't you? I found your *thing*!"

He could have done her the same way he'd done Fields and the nigger, but that was wrong. She deserved better.

Gluing his jaws together, fighting back the noise, acid tears, he said: "Sure do, babe."

She gave a death-eating smile, went down.

They went to the cave three more times after that. The third time, he put sheets, soap, a bunch of water bottles, and the knives in the trunk of the car. The dope was in her purse. He knew from her leg tracks that she'd developed a heavy Jones. Wasn't surprised to find out she was carrying blatantly, disobeying him. Because that was the way a junkie functioned. As addicted to sneakery as the needle.

When he pulled her works out of her purse, she was scared shitless. Relieved—grateful—when he didn't get angry.

Downright orgasmic when he said, "No sweat. I've been too uptight about your getting off, babe. You want to fix, go ahead."

"You're sure?" Already breathing hard.

"Sure, babe."

Before he finished talking, she'd jumped on the works, was panting, fixing, smiling, nodding off.

He waited. When she was totally out of it, he walked back to the car.

The morning after his last date with Nightwing, he woke up with a new sense of purpose, knowing he was ready for bigger and better things. After he'd touched himself to the accompaniment of new real science pictures, he went to work at the hospital, delivered the mail to the Surgery Department, and cornered Doctor in his office.

"What do you want?"

"Been a long time, stud. Cash-in time. I want to go to med school."

Kikefuck was blown away.

"That's crazy! You haven't even finished two years of junior college!"

Shrug.

"Have you taken any science courses?"

"Some."

"Are your grades any better?"

"I'm doing fine."

"Sure you are—oh, great. Terrific. Straight D's and you want to be a doctor."

"I'm *going* to be a doctor."

Fucker slammed his hand on the desk. His eyes were popping out of his ugly purple face. Mad because an Aryan warrior was breaking into the kike medico conspiracy.

"Now you listen—"

"I want an M.D. You're going to fix it for me."

"Jesus Christ! How the hell do you expect me to pull something like that off!"

"Your problem." Stare-down, melting the fucker by being totally cool.

He walked away with a spring in his step, ready for a bright new future.

58

Saturday, seven forty-three P.M. Daniel had just finished praying *ma'ariv* and *havdalah,* bidding farewell to a Sabbath that, for all practical purposes, had never existed. Talking to God with all the devotion of a nonbeliever, his mind on the case, chewing on the new information as if it were fine filet steak.

He put away his *siddur* and had started to assemble his notes for the staff meeting when the operator phoned and said a Mr. Vangidder was on the line.

Unfamiliar name. Foreign. "Did he say what it was about?"

"No."

Probably some foreign reporter. Despite Headquarters' blackout on Butcher information, journalists were being their usual persistent selves. "Take his number and tell him I'll call him back."

He hung up, made it to the door when the phone rang again. He considered ignoring it, let it ring, finally answered.

"Pakad?" said the same operator. "It's about this Vangidder. He says he's a policeman calling from the Netherlands, says you'll definitely want to speak to him. It has to be now—he's leaving tonight for a one-week holiday."

Dutch police? Had the Interpol man finally done his job?

"Put him on."

"Okay."

He waited anxiously through a series of electronic bleeps, hoping he hadn't lost the call. In light of what Shmeltzer and Daoud had found at the Amelia Catherine, information from Europe could narrow the investigation.

The bleeps were followed by a serenade of static, a low, mechanical rumble, then a high-pitched, cheerful voice, speaking in flawless English.

"Chief Inspector Sharavi? This is Joop Van Gelder of the Amsterdam police."

"Hello . . . is it Chief Inspector?"

"Commissaris," said Van Gelder. "It's similar to a chief inspector."

It was, Daniel knew, a rank above chief inspector. Joop Van Gelder was unassuming. Instinctively, from thousands of miles away, he liked the man.

"Hello, Commissaris. Thank you for calling and sorry for the delay in putting you through."

"My fault, really," said Van Gelder, still cheerful. "I neglected to identify myself as a police officer, was under the impression that your Interpol man had passed my name along."

Thank you, Friedman.

"No, I'm sorry, Commissaris, he didn't."

"No matter. We've got more important things to chat about, yes? This morning, your man passed along some homicide data that so clearly matched an unsolved murder in our city that I knew I had to get in touch with you. I'm off-duty, packing for a holiday to England. Mrs. Van Gelder won't tolerate any further postponements, but I did manage to find the file on the case and wished to pass the information along to you before I left."

Daniel thanked him again, really meaning it. "When did your murder take place, Commissaris?"

"Fifteen months ago."

Fifteen months ago. Friedman had been right about the Interpol computer.

"Ugly affair," Van Gelder was saying. "Clearly a sex killing. We never cleared it up. Our consulting psychiatrist thought it had all the characteristics of the first in a series of psychopathic killings. We weren't certain—we don't often get that kind of thing."

"Neither do we." Or didn't.

"The Germans do," said Van Gelder. "And the Americans. One wonders why, yes? In any event, when no second murder occurred, we weighed two alternatives: that the psychiatrist had been mistaken—it does occur, yes?" He laughed. "Or that the murderer was someone passing through Amsterdam and had departed to do his killing elsewhere."

"Traveling psychopath," said Daniel, and told him about the FBI data.

"Horrifying," said Van Gelder. "I began an inquiry into the FBI files myself. However, the Americans were less than helpful.

They put up bureaucratic barriers and when a second murder didn't occur, given our work load . . ." The Dutchman's voice trailed off, guiltily.

Knowing it would be rude to brush off the lack of thoroughness, Daniel said nothing.

"We can check suitcases for bombs," said Van Gelder, "but this kind of terrorist is harder to spot, yes?"

"Yes," said Daniel. "A person can buy knives anywhere. Even if he uses the same ones over and over, there are ways to transport them that can be legitimately explained."

"A doctor."

"It's one of our hypotheses."

"It was one of ours too, Chief Inspector. And for a while I thought it would help solve the case. Our records check revealed no matching homicides in the rest of the Interpol countries, but an almost identical crime did take place in September of 1972 in Sumbok—it's a tiny island in the southern region of the Indonesian complex that used to be a Dutch colony. We still consult to the local police in many of the colonies—they send their records to us biannually. One of my clerks was sifting through the biannual reports and came across the case—an unsolved mutilation homicide of a sixteen-year-old girl.

"At first we thought there might be a tribal link—our Amsterdam victim was an Indonesian—half-Indonesian, really. Prostitute by the name of Anjanette Gaikeena. It seemed possible that her murder might have been related to some primitive rite or revenge plot—an old family score to settle. But her family turned out to have no connection whatsoever to Sumbok. The mother is from Northern Borneo; the father is Dutch—met the mother while serving in the army and brought the family back to Amsterdam eighteen years ago.

"When I read about a sex murder there, I was puzzled, Chief Inspector. Sumbok really is an insignificant little bar of sand and jungle—a few rubber plantations, some cassava plots, no tourist trade at all. Then I remembered that a medical school once existed there: The Grand Medical Facility of St. Ignatius. No connection to the Catholic Church—the 'saint' was used for its official sound. It was a fourth-rate place at best. Unaccredited, the barest of facilities, but charging very high tuition—a moneymaking scheme, really, run by unscrupulous American businessmen. There was a dispute about taxes; the Indonesian government closed it down in 1979. But back in '72 it was functioning, with over four hundred students—mostly foreigners who'd been denied acceptance anywhere else. I managed to obtain a '72 faculty list and student roster, ran a check with our passport files during the time of the Gaikeena murder, but unfortunately found no match."

While Van Gelder talked, Daniel had pulled out the list of American homicides from the FBI data bank. Shehadeh: March '71. Breau: July '73. The Sumbok homicide fell neatly in between.

"Do you have that roster handy, Commissaris?"

"Right here."

"I'd like to read some names for you, see if any of them appear on it."

"Certainly."

None did.

"Too easy," said Van Gelder. "It never is, yes?"

"Yes. I'd like to see the roster anyway."

"I'll cable it to you, today."

"Thank you. Tell me more about your homicide, Commissaris."

Van Gelder described the Amsterdam killing: Anjanette Gaikeena's savaged body had been found in a fish-cleaning shed near one of the docks on the northeast side of town.

"It's a rough part of the city," said the *commissaris*. "Just above our famous red light district—have you been to Amsterdam, Chief Inspector?"

"Just once, last year, on stopover. What I saw was beautiful, but I had no real chance to tour. However, I did see the district." No chance to do anything but wait out a two-day sentence of house-imprisonment in an apartment suite, babysitting half a dozen Olympic rowers and football players. Listening to the athletes' nervously rowdy jokes with half an ear, one hand wedded to his Uzi. The athletes had grown irritable and difficult to manage, had finally been allowed a single excursion. Unanimous choice: the famous whores of Amsterdam.

"Everyone sees the district," said Van Gelder, somewhat sadly. "However, the part of the dock where Gaikeena was found isn't one of our toursist spots. At night it's deserted, except for prowlers, drunken sailors, and other undesirables. The shed was left unlocked—nothing to steal but herring bones and a warped old table. She was on the table, laid out on white sheets. The wounds match your first one precisely. Our pathologist said she'd been anesthetized with heroin, at least three knives were used, sharp as a surgeon's scalpel, but not necessarily a surgeon's scalpel. What impressed him was how clean she'd been washed—not a trace of fiber evidence, no semen, nothing for serum typing. A local soap had been used on the body and the hair, the brand most commonly provided by many hotels, but millions of bars are sold each year here—that's not much of a lead. We tried to trace the purchaser of the sheets, with no success."

"Was she killed on the spot?"

"Unclear. However, she was definitely washed and drained there. The shed contained a large trough for gutting and washing fish, large enough to hold a woman of Gaikeena's size. It ran out to sea, but there was a bend in the pipe before it reached the sluice gate. Traces of human blood were found mixed in with the fish waste."

Thorough procedure, thought Daniel. But useless.

Van Gelder was thinking the same thing. "We reviewed our list of known sex offenders and knife-wielders, put every one of them through hours of interrogation, talked to the girl's habitual customers, interviewed every prostitute and procurer in the district to see if they remembered who she went off with that night. There was no shortage of leads, but all were false. Given what we know now about this traveler, it was a waste of time, yes?" The Dutchman's voice lost its cheer and took on a sudden intensity. "But now you may have him, my friend. We'll work together."

"Those names I read you," said Daniel. "It would be nice if any of them turn up on your passport records."

"All of them are serious suspects?" asked the Dutchman.

"As serious as we've got." Daniel knew Van Gelder wanted more, a ranking of the names in terms of seriousness; he regretted not being able to provide it. "Anything you can find out about any of them would be tremendously helpful."

"Should a passport check prove positive, we'll be glad to pursue it with the hotels, the airlines, tour bus operators, canal boat drivers, local merchants. If any of those people were in Amsterdam during Gaikeena's murder, we'll provide you with the most precise records of their whereabouts and activities that we can muster. I'll be in England for a week on holiday. While I'm gone, the man to talk to is Pieter Bij Duurstede." Van Gelder spelled it, said, "He's a chief inspector, a very conscientious fellow. He'll contact you immediately if something turns up."

Van Gelder gave Daniel Bij Duurstede's direct-dial phone number, then said, "Meanwhile, I'll be watching the changing of the guard at Buckingham Palace."

Daniel laughed. "Thank you, Commissaris. You've been tremendously helpful."

"Doing my job," said Van Gelder. He paused. "You know, we Dutch pride ourselves on our tolerance. Unfortunately, that tolerance is sometimes mistaken for passivity." Another pause. "Let's catch this madman, my friend. Show him we have no tolerance for his brand of evil."

59

Everyone was on time, even Avi, looking like a schoolboy with his short haircut and clean-shaven face; the skin where the beard had been, a sleek bluish-white.

Daniel turned to the summary of the medical charts and began:

"All three of them were patients at the Amelia Catherine. Nahum and Elias obtained the files this morning and I've abstracted the contents. Both Fatma and Shahin were seen at the Woman's General Health Clinic, which is held three out of four Thursdays a month. The second Thursday each month is devoted to specialty clinics for women—gynecology and obstetrics; eye diseases; ear, nose, and throat; skin; and neurology. Juliet attended Neurology Clinic to get a refill of her epilepsy medicine.

"Fatma first: The Thursday before she left the monastery, she was seen, treated for a vaginal rash and pubic lice. The American nurse, Peggy Cassidy, seems to have done most of the actual examining and treating. According to her notes, Fatma came in claiming she was a virgin, had no idea where she could have picked up the lice, or the rash—which turned out to be a yeast infection, something called *Candida albicans*. During the health screening interview, however, she quickly broke down, admitted she'd been having intercourse with her boyfriend, had brought shame upon her family, and had been kicked out of her home. Cassidy described her as 'suffering from an agitated depression, fearful, isolated, and lacking in psychosocial support.' In addition to the guilt about losing her virginity and fear of her family, Fatma was convinced she'd given the lice to Abdelatif and was terrified he'd find out and leave her—though we know from Maksoud, the brother-in-law, that the reverse was probably true. Abdelatif consorted with prostitutes, had infected Maksoud's entire family with lice more than once.

"Cassidy dispensed ointment—neomycin sulfate—for the infection and had Fatma take a delousing bath. Her dress was laundered in the hospital washing machine. Cassidy also tried to counsel her psychologically, but wrote that 'the language barrier and the patient's defensiveness prevented the development of a therapeutic bond.' A recheck appointment was scheduled for the following week; Cassidy expressed doubts Fatma would show up. But she did, right on time, at nine-thirty in the morning—consistent with Anwar Rashmawi's account of observing his sister and Abdelatif leave the New Gate Thursday morning and go different ways. Abdelatif walked to the east side bus station and bought a ticket for Hebron. Now we know where Fatma went.

"Cassidy's notes for the second appointment indicate the infection had cleared up, Fatma was free of lice, but emotionally she was worse—'profoundly depressed.' Counseling was tried again, with no more success. Fatma was told to return in two weeks, for the next General Health Clinic. Cassidy raised the possibility of a psychiatric consultation. Her notes for both visits were co-signed and concurred with by Dr. Hassan Al Biyadi."

The detectives were stone-faced. No one spoke or moved.

"Now, Juliet," said Daniel. "She was seen the following Thursday at Neurological Clinic, though the distinctions between the clinics may be in name only. She, too, was seen first by Peggy Cassidy, who noticed the needle marks on her arms and legs, inquired about drug use, and received a denial. Cassidy didn't believe her, wrote: 'Patient presents us with symptoms of addiction, as well as mental dullness, perhaps even retardation; possible aphasia due to narcotics abuse, chronic grand mal seizure disorder, or a combination of both.' The fact that Juliet was a new arrival from Lebanon, lacked family connections and psychosocial support was also recorded."

"Another perfect victim," said the Chinaman.

Daniel nodded. "Cassidy termed Juliet 'high-risk for noncompliance,' also suggested she be given only a small amount of medication to ensure that she returned for an electroencephalogram and intelligence testing. Al Biyadi examined her, dispensed a week's worth of phenobarbitol and Dilantin, and co-signed Cassidy's notes. That evening Juliet was murdered."

Shmeltzer grunted and shook his head. He'd allowed his beard to grow for several days, looked haggard and old.

"Our new one, Shahin Barakat," continued Daniel. "She was seen three times within the last six weeks at the General Health Clinic, the first time by Cassidy and Dr. Carter; the other two by Cassidy and Dr. Al Biyadi. She came in requesting a general checkup, which Cassidy performed and Carter co-signed. Other than an outer-ear infection treated with antibiotics, she was found in good health, though Cassidy noted that she looked depressed. Cassidy also wrote that she 'related well.' "

"Translate: gullible," said Shmeltzer.

"The second visit was a recheck on the ear, which was fine. However, Cassidy noted that she looked even more depressed—sounds familiar, doesn't it?—and when she was asked about it, began talking about her infertility problems, how being barren had shamed her in the eyes of her husband and his family, how her husband had once loved her but now he hated her. He'd already denounced her once. She was certain he'd complete the *talaq* and kick her out. To quote Cassidy, she 'probed for family support and psychosocial resources. Patient reports no siblings, father deceased, a living mother whom she describes as "very sick." When asked about the nature of the maternal "sickness," patient responds with visible tension and ambiguous evasions, suggesting some sort of psychiatric problem or other stigmatizing condition.'

"Cassidy suggested Shahin undergo a pelvic exam as the first stage of diagnosing the cause of her infertility. Shahin asked if any female doctors were available. When informed none were, asked Cassidy to do the exam herself. Cassidy told her she wasn't qualified for that. Shahin refused to be examined, saying no man other than her husband was allowed to touch her intimately. She also insisted upon an Arab doctor. Cassidy told her the nearest female Arab physician working for UNRWA was a general practitioner who volunteered once a month at a mobile clinic set up in the Deir El Balah camp in Gaza—she'd be happy to arrange a referral. Shahin refused, saying Gaza was too far to travel. At that point, Cassidy gave up, writing: 'Patient is still firmly in the denial stage regarding her infertility and the status of her marriage. As the marital stress increases she may be more amenable to diagnostic evaluation.'

"Shahin's final visit was two days ago. At that time, she was described by Cassidy as 'profoundly depressed.' Her husband *had* completed the *talaq*, she had nowhere to go, nothing to eat. A weight check showed she'd lost three kilos during the month since the second visit. She explained to Cassidy that she'd lost her appetite, hadn't eaten or slept since being banished, had camped under one of the old trees near the Garden of Gethsemane, didn't care if she lived or died. Cassidy found her blood pressure to be very low, got her some food and a bath, and tried to offer 'supportive counseling.' Shahin expressed fears that she was going insane, admitted that her own mother was mentally ill and her husband had always told her she'd inherit it. Cassidy suggested temporary bed rest in one of the hospital wards, with eventual placement at a women's shelter. Shahin refused, though she did accept more food. Then, according to Cassidy, she walked out of the hospital against medical advice. Al Biyadi never saw her but he co-signed Cassidy's notes and concurred with them."

Daniel looked up from the summary.

"Three rootless women, two of them scared and depressed and abandoned, the other a mentally deficient drug addict on the run, with no family ties. As Yossi said, perfect victims, except that the killer hadn't counted on Abdin Barakat's enduring love for Shahin. If Elias hadn't gotten him to open up, we'd still be wondering about the common thread."

Daoud acknowledged the compliment with the stingiest of nods.

"Cassidy and Al Biyadi saw all three of them," said Daniel. "Carter saw one of them. Both doctors' contacts appear to have been minimal—a quick look and out the door. Given the patient load at the clinics, it's possible Fatma's and Juliet's names wouldn't have meant anything to them. But Peggy Cassidy spent time with them. She'd be likely to remember, so at best she withheld material knowledge. At worst—"

"*At worst* is more like it," said Shmeltzer. "Motive, opportunity, means. She and Lover Boy, together."

"What's the motive?" asked the Chinaman.

"What Dani's been saying: The two of them are PLO symps, want to pit us against the Arabs, cook up a revenge bloodbath."

Daniel noticed Daoud smile at the use of the word *us*, then lose the smile, quickly. He, too, was unshaven, fatigued. Sitting next to the older man. Scruffy comrades-in-arms.

"A perfect setup," Shmeltzer said. "Hundreds of patients coming in and out of that place, the women one day, the men the next. Cassidy screens them, selects the vulnerable ones. As a woman, it's easy to get them to trust her. To *relate*. She reassures them the needle is going to make them feel better, calm them down. Then Lover Boy enters and . . ." Shmeltzer drew a finger across his throat.

Stalking the herd, thought Daniel. Picking off the weak ones.

"Three kill spots," continued Shmeltzer. "The cave and each of their rooms." He turned to Daoud. "Show them the plans."

Daoud unfurled the Mandate-era blueprint of the Amelia Catherine's ground floor and spread it across the center of the conference table. Everyone leaned forward. Daoud pointed to several rooms on the west wing freshly relabeled in red.

"These were formerly servants' rooms," he said. "Now they're staff quarters. Nahum memorized the door plates."

"*He* did, also," said Shmeltzer. Frowning at Daoud: "False modesty's no virtue."

"Al Biyadi's room is right here at the end, closest to the back door," said Daoud. "Cassidy's is here, right next to his."

"No big surprise if there's a connecting door between them," said Shmeltzer. "Two sinks, two bathtubs, plenty of space to butcher and wash at leisure. Easy access to dope, knives, sheets, towels, soap, the hospital washing machine. A few steps to the rear door of the hospital and a quick walk in the darkness down to that tunnel we found."

"How far is the end of the tunnel from the murder cave?" asked Daniel.

"Good couple kilometers," said Shmeltzer, "but if you went down at night, you could easily escape notice. One of them carries the body; the other, the equipment. All that brush offers a straight, camouflaged track from the hospital to the desert. An aerial view would show one strip of green among many—we could probably get some photos from the air force to prove it."

"If they've got two rooms, why the cave?" asked the Chinaman.

"Who the hell knows? They're crazy," said Shmeltzer. "Political, but two crazy assholes—a marriage made in hell."

Daniel studied the blueprint, then rolled it up and put it next to his notes. "Any chance you were noticed going over the side?"

"Doubtful," said Shmeltzer. "They didn't look for me seriously. Baldwin probably saw it as one crazy old Arab who'd limped off somewhere to die—*high risk for noncompliance.* They're probably used to it."

Daoud nodded in agreement.

"What about the missing files?" asked Daniel.

"Sure, if someone was looking for them," said Shmeltzer. "But why would they?"

"Why would Cassidy and Al Biyadi do something as obvious as killing their own patients?" asked Daniel. "And why would they leave records? Why not destroy the charts?"

"Arrogance," said Shmeltzer. "Typical U.N. arrogance. They've been violating their charter every day since '48, getting away with shit for so long, they think they're invulnerable. On top of that, Cassidy and Al Biyadi are both arrogant as *individuals*—she's a cold bitch; he prances as if he owns the place, treats the patients as if they're subhuman."

"Sounds like any doctor," said the Chinaman.

Daniel recalled his first and only encounter with Al Biyadi, the young physician's nervous hostility. He remembered the frosty reception Baldwin had given him, how the Amelia Catherine people had made him feel like a foreigner on his own native soil.

The big pink building had been the logical place to begin. The killer had done his initial dirty work close to home, studying Yaakov Schlesinger's disciplined schedule, knowing when it was safe to cross the road and dump Fatma's body. Then dumping Juliet and Shahin across town to divert attention from Scopus.

Now the investigation had come full circle.

Two deaths later.

His mind started to fill with maddening hindsights. Again. Should-haves and could-haves that gnawed at him like tapeworms.

"Anyone at the hospital could have been watching for vulnerable patients," he said. "Not just Al Biyadi and Cassidy. Anyone could have gained access to those charts—look how easily you got hold of them. And let's remember Red Amira Nasser's weird-eyed American. No way could Biyadi be mistaken for a Westerner. In light of what we know, Amira's story may be irrelevant, but it would still be nice to get a detailed description from her. Is Mossad still claiming they can't find her in Jordan, Nahum?"

"Not a trace," said Shmeltzer. "It could be the truth, or just more of their cloak-and-dagger bullshit. Either way, I think her story *is* irrelevant, one of Little Hook's fantasies. We found no record of her being treated at the Amelia Catherine. She doesn't fit the mold. And if you want a weird-looking American, why not Cassidy? Maybe she dressed up like a man—she's a mannish type, anyway. Maybe *that's* what impressed Nasser as being weird."

"Maybe," said the Chinaman, "she had one of those sex-change operations." He chuckled. "Maybe she had balls sewn on 'cause she wanted to be another Golda."

Weak smiles all around.

"With clinics every Thursday, why the time lag?" said Avi. "Two murders a week apart, then nothing until last Friday."

"If Amira Nasser's story is true," said Daniel, "he made a play for her exactly a week after Juliet's murder. A break in *modus*, but Ben David says psychopaths sometimes do that—it's evidence of a breakdown in their impulse control. Maybe his failure to snare her gave him pause for a couple of weeks, made him careful."

"The Amira story is fantasy," said Shmeltzer. "More likely that the right victim didn't show up during the next couple of clinics. Not stupid or vulnerable enough."

"Good point, Nahum. But we've got eight matching American homicides that aren't fantasies. When Al Biyadi was being denied a visa, his history was looked into pretty carefully, and according to our records, he was in Amman until 1975, no American trips. That encompasses the first killing in Los Angeles and the second one in New Orleans. I've taken seriously your suggestion that he could have traveled back and forth between Jordan and America prior to '75, as a tourist. I asked the Americans to check their records, in case we missed something the first time. But that means getting their State Department involved and whenever that happens it means paperwork and long delays. In order to shortcut the process I've asked Lieutenant Brooker to use his American connections to help me trace the Amelia Catherine staff's American activities—see what else we can learn about Al Biyadi and Cassidy and the others.

"In terms of the others, the Canadian, Carter, examined Shahin the first time. He's fair-haired, would have had free entry to America. Everything we know about him comes from the Peace Corps report. Let's take a closer look at him. Then there's the administrator, Baldwin, who *is* an American. He runs the hospital, has easy access to every file, keys to every room. I also got the impression that he and his Lebanese secretary, Ma'ila Khoury, have a thing going—maybe he has a love/hate relationship with Arab women.

"Dr. Darousha and Hajab seem clean," he continued. "According to Shin Bet, neither has been out of the country since '67. Hajab's never even been issued a passport. But we'll look at them again, anyway. Same for the old nurse, Hauser, whom I can't imagine harming anyone. The volunteers will be more of a problem. Shin Bet's passed along a list of about two dozen foreign doctors, nurses, and technicians who volunteer at the Amelia Catherine on an occasional basis. They're generally affiliated with one of the church groups as well as UNRWA, spend most of their time in the camps. Shin Bet had an old list they'd gotten hold of, didn't want to burgle the U.N. at this particular time, and obtained this list from a plant in one of the Gaza camps. Just a compilation of names, doesn't give any idea which volunteers, if any, were present at the Amelia Catherine the days our victims were examined."

The Chinaman lit a cigarette, offered the pack around. Avi and Daoud accepted. The room went thick with smoke.

"One more piece of information," said Daniel. "Just before coming here, I received a call from Holland that strengthens the foreigner angle."

He recounted his conversation with Van Gelder, said, "None of the permanent Amelia Catherine staff people or volunteers show up on the Indonesian medical school list. It's possible one of them attended St. Ignatius under a false name—or under a *real* name which was changed later. The school had a bad reputation; it was eventually closed down. A doctor who managed to transfer to an accredited institution might very well have wanted to disassociate himself from Sumbok. Thinking along those lines also brought me back to Baldwin—a professional medical administrator. Sometimes people who fail to become doctors establish careers working *with* doctors."

"Boss over the doctors," said Shmeltzer.

"Exactly. He could have begun medical studies at Sumbok, been unable to transfer to a legitimate school, and gone into pencil pushing. The same logic could apply to one of the volunteer technicians. In any event, the Dutch murder could come in handy—the Gaikeena girl was killed fifteen months ago. Van Gelder is certain no other similar European homicides have been discovered by Interpol, though I'm still trying to confirm that. If the killer went from Amsterdam straight to Israel, he'd probably be using his current name on his passport. Amsterdam's working on their passport records—I expect a call, soon. I've also requested the original American homicide files, which may contain some helpful details, and the Sumbok medical school list. We'll be trying to trace where the St. Ignatius students went—graduates and dropouts—if any of them filed for name changes. Gene Brooker will take the Americans; I'll look at everyone else. If we can place anyone in Amsterdam during the time of the Gaikeena murder, and here during our killings, we'll move on them."

"And if not?" said the Chinaman.

"If none of our traces is fruitful, we'll have to start looking at all post-Gaikeena travelers from Amsterdam as well as those arriving on any other flight or cruise that stops over in Amsterdam—which includes a good portion of the New York flights. Big numbers."

"Bigger than that," said Shmeltzer, "if the killer went from Amsterdam to Paris, London, Zurich, Istanbul, Athens, Rome, et cetera, *and* didn't kill anyone in those places. Just spent enough time to get hold of a false passport before getting on the plane to Ben Gurion. There goes our match."

"It's possible," Daniel admitted.

"Are we planning to check every person who's entered the country since Gaikeena, Dani? Meanwhile, in five days another bunch of potential victims will be herded into that hospital. Why don't we go the hell in there, have a look at those staff rooms, try for some physical evidence?"

"Because the brass says absolutely no. They're furious about our lifting the Amelia Catherine files without informing them first. Trying to get in there legally is also out of the question—no way will the U.N. capitulate without putting up a fuss. The brass is viewing this case primarily in political terms. During the last week, the United States covertly killed seven Arab-sponsored attempts to condemn us in the Security Council because of the murders. There've been three more revenge attempts on Jewish women since the Beit Gvura riot. One came dangerously close to tragedy. I didn't know about any of them until Laufer told me. Did any of you?"

Shakes of heads.

"That shows you how serious they are about keeping this quiet. The early ID on Shahin allowed us to keep the story of her murder completely out of the papers. Two Arab dailies found out anyway, through the Old City rumor mill, and tried to sneak through back-page items on her. They had their presses shut down for seventy-two hours. But we can't control UNRWA. A confrontation with them will shove the entire case back in the limelight. As will a bungled covert—I know that won't happen, Nahum, but the guys with the wood-paneled offices don't share my level of confidence. In neither case are they willing to risk a special session of the Security Council based on three medical charts."

"That's not just Laufer trying to stick it to us?" said Avi.

"No. Since the mayor's visit, Laufer's been relatively quiet, though he's starting to lean on me again. He's under plenty of pressure to have the case solved, wouldn't mind some action. The clear message from on top is we need to give them more evidence before they can authorize a move."

"Shmucks," said Shmeltzer. He made circular motions with his hands. "We have to give them evidence before they'll allow us to look for evidence—what the hell do they want us to do?"

"Keep a watch on the hospital, on everyone who works there, log who goes in and who goes out."

"Surveillance. Very creative," said Shmeltzer. "While we sit on our asses, the wolves inspect the lambs."

"As you said, we've got five days until the next clinic," said Daniel. "If nothing further turns up by then, a pair of female Latam officers will infiltrate the clinic, prevent any outright abduction. In the meantime, let's talk about the surveillance."

Shmeltzer shrugged. "Talk."

"Latam has been authorized to give us ten officers—eight men and the two women. Given the size of Amos Harel's staff, that's generous, and they're all good people—Shimshon Katz, Itzik Nash, guys of that caliber. I briefed them this afternoon. They'll be keeping a general watch on the hospital premises, check out the volunteers, be at our disposal for backup. It's still a thin spread, but better than nothing. Avi, I want you to stick with Mark Wilbur, keep an especially close eye on his mailbox. This killer is power-mad, craves the attention all those stories brought him. He'll be watching the papers for something about Shahin. When nothing turns up, he may get angry, do something dramatic to get Wilbur's attention. It's crucial you don't get made, so change your appearance frequently—*kipot,* hats, eyeglasses, dirty clothes. Litter-skewer and dustbin one day; felafel wagon, the next."

"Litter-skewer—there goes your love life, kid," said the Chinaman, holding his nose and slapping Avi on the back.

The young detective rubbed his naked jaw and feigned misery. "Worth catching the bastard just so I can grow it back."

"The rest of you, these are your assignments."

Back in his office, Daniel checked his desk for the Amsterdam wire, found nothing, and asked the message operator about a call from Bij Duurstede.

"Nothing, Pakad. We have your message to call you immediately."

He depressed the button, released it, and phoned Gene at the Laromme.

The black man picked up on the fourth ring, said, "Nothing interesting, so far. I reached all the medical and the nursing schools, Baldwin's college in San Antonio, Texas. Far as I can tell, everyone seems to have gone to school where they said they did—this is only verification of graduation I'm talking about. All the clerks promised to check their complete records. I'll get back to them by the end of their working day, see if they keep their word. They think I'm calling from L.A. Just in case they bother to check, I phoned my desk sergeant, told him to certify me kosher. But they could end up talking to someone else, so fingers crossed. What about those directories of medical specialists I mentioned—does your library have them?"

"No, only a list of Israeli doctors."

"Too bad. Okay, I can call one of my buddies, have him do a little legwork for me. Anything new from your end?"

Daniel told him about the call from Amsterdam.

"Hmm, interesting," said Gene. "A world traveler."

"The wounds on the Amsterdam victim matched our first one. Yet ours duplicates the American pattern. To me it seems like he used Amsterdam as a dry run, Gene. Preparing for something big, here."

"Something personal," said Gene. "Fits with the anti-Semite thing." Silence. "Maybe that island med-school roster will speed things along."

"Yes. I'd better go now, see if the wire's arrived. Thanks for everything, Gene. When I hear more I'll let you know. When are you moving?"

"Right now. I was just out the door. You sure this is necessary?"

"I'm sure. Your phone bill's already enormous. If you won't let me compensate you, at least use my phone."

"Who compensates *you*?"

"I'll put in a requisition form; eventually they'll reimburse me. Explaining you would be harder."

"All right, but I already gave my hotel room as the mailing address to half the departments I spoke to. Someone's going to have to be checking all the time to see if something comes in."

"I'll do the checking—you do the phoning. Laura's expecting you. She's cleared the desk in her studio. There'll be sandwiches and—"

"Drinks in the refrigerator. I know. Lu and I were over for Shabbat lunch. Shoshi made the stuff herself, showed me how she wrapped it all in plastic. They're all planning on going out for ice cream tonight. Call soon—you might still catch them."

"Thank you for the tip. Shalom."

"Shalom," said Gene. "And *Shavua tov*." The traditional post-Shabbat wish for a good week.

"Where'd you learn that?"

"Your kids have been educating me."

Daniel laughed, fought back the loneliness. Said, "*Shavua tov*." Wishful thinking.

Talking to Gene made him want to call home. Laura answered the phone with tension in her voice.

He said, "*Shavua tov*. Sorry I haven't called sooner—"

"Daniel, the dog's gone."

"What?"

"Dayan's *gone*, run away. He didn't get out this afternoon, so Shoshi took him for a walk in the park. She met a girlfriend, started talking, and let go of the leash. When she turned around, he'd disappeared. The two of them looked all over for him. She didn't want to come home, is locked in her room at this moment, hysterical."

"Let me speak to her."

"Hold on."

He waited for a moment. Laura came back on, said, "She's too upset or ashamed to talk to anyone right now, Daniel."

"How long ago did it happen?"

"Right after Shabbat."

Over an hour ago. No one had called him.

"He's never done this before," said Laura. "He's always been such a coward, clinging to your pants leg."

No pants leg to cling to for a while, thought Daniel.

"How are the boys?"

"Uncharacteristically quiet. Mikey even tried to kiss Shoshi, so you can imagine what it's been like."

"He'll come back, Laura."

"That's what I think too. I left the lobby door unlocked in case he does. We were planning to go out for ice cream, but I don't want the poor little guy trotting up and finding us gone."

"Gene will be over soon. As soon as he arrives, go out—it will be good for all of you. In the meantime, I'd check with the Berkowitzes on the second floor—Dayan likes their cat. And Lieberman's grocery—Shoshi takes him by there regularly. Lieberman gives him chicken scraps."

"The Berkowitzes haven't seen him and he wasn't hanging around near the grocery. I just got off the phone with Lieberman—he's home, not opening until tomorrow at ten. I asked him to check for Dayan when he comes in. How'm I doing, Detective?"

"*Aleph*-plus. I miss you."

"I miss you too. Anything new?"

"Some progress, actually. Far from solved, but the net is tightening, bit by bit."

She knew better than to ask for details, said, "You'll get him. It's just a matter of time." Then: "Will you be home tonight?"

"I'm planning on it. I'm waiting for a wire from overseas, will head home as soon as I get it. Where will you be going for ice cream? I can pick up Gene—maybe we can catch you."

Laura laughed. "What are the chances of that?"

"Just in case," said Daniel.

"Just in case, I thought Café Max. The boys took long naps—

they might be able to handle the late hour. If not, we'll eat on the run, maybe drop in on your dad." Laura's voice broke. "I feel so bad about that little dog. I never wanted him in the first place, but now he's become a part of us. I know it's not important compared to what you're dealing with but—"

"It *is* important. When I get out of here, I'll drive around and look for him, okay? Was he wearing his tag?"

"Of course."

"Then, one way or another, we'll find him. Don't worry."

"I'm sure you're right. Why would he go and do this, Daniel?"

"Hormones. He's probably feeling romantic. Probably found himself a girlfriend—a Great Dane."

Laura laughed again, this time softly. "Put it that way, and I don't feel so sorry for him."

"Me, neither," said Daniel. "I feel jealous."

60

Gone, all three charts.

Predictable. Boring.

Borrring.

He thought about it and stretched his grin until it threatened to split his face, visualized his face dividing in two and reconstituting. Mytosis—wouldn't that be something? Two superior Aryan Schwann-hemi-faces rolling over Kikeland like nuclear mace balls, churning up the soup, steamrolling the scum . . .

Three charts, big deal. They probably thought they had a fucking bible, but they were limited thinkers, predictable. Let it lull them into a false sense of superiority.

Meanwhile, he'd be creative. The key was to be creative.

Stick to the plan, but allow for improvisation. Float above the scum-sump, trading identity for triumph.

Clean up afterward.

No doubt they were watching.

No doubt they thought they had it all figured out.

Like Fields had, so long ago. Grand Prix BoJo, all the real science girls.

All his little pets, now purified, part of him.

Nightwing.

Pet names, private identities. Remembering them made him hard.

Gauguin Girl, washing clothes by the river when he found her. *Hi!*

Voodoo Queen, talking gris-gris and mojo and other spooky jive in the light of a wet, yellow Louisiana moon. Taking him to the cemetery, trying to come on evil. But fading without struggle, just like all the others.

Pocahontas. Trading it all for powdered trinkets.

Jugs. Twinkie. Stoner. Kikette. Still, white shells lying emptied, explored. All those welcome holes the ultimate memory picture. All the others. So many others. Pet names, limp limbs, last looks before fading to final bliss.

Last looks full of trust.

And here: *Little Lost Girl. Beirut Bimbo. The Barreness.*

These sand-nigger females the most trusting of all; they respected a man, looked up to a man of position—a man of science.

Yes, Doctor.

Do with me what you will, Doctor.

He'd come to Kikeland with just a general blueprint for Project *Untermensch.* Discovering that cave on the nature hike had put it all in place—an inspiration jolt straight to the brain, straight to the cock.

Nightwing II. *Meant to be.*

Executive command to Dieter II, directly from the Führergod.

His own nature hike with Little Lost Girl.

Wet cavework, then spread out.

Spread them all out, wiping his ass all over Kike City.

He started to stroke himself, one hand resting on the dog collar, fondling the dog tag with the kike letters stamped into it—what did it say? Kikemutt?

Knowing it wouldn't take long, the safari almost over.

Rest in peace. Pieces. Clean-up time.

Surprise, surprise!

Bow wow wow.

61

At ten P.M., Amsterdam called. Van Gelder's man was a slow talker, deep-voiced. No policeman-to-policeman chit-chat: This one was all business.

"Am I speaking to Chief Inspector Daniel Sharavi?"

"You are."

"This is Pieter Bij Duurstede, Amsterdam police. Have you received the St. Ignatius medical school list?"

"Not yet, Chief Inspector."

"We wired it to you some time ago. Let me verify."

Bij Duurstede put him on hold, came back moments later.

"Yes, I've verified that it was wired and received. Twenty minutes ago."

"I'll verify on my end."

"Let me give you something else first. You requested a cross-reference of eight names with our passport list at the time of the Anjanette Gaikeena homicide. Five out of the eight turned up. I'll read them to you, in alphabetical order: Al Biyadi, H. M.; Baldwin, S. T.; Carter, R. J.; Cassidy, M. P.; Hauser, C."

Daniel copied the names in his notebook, just to keep his hands busy.

"They arrived from London five days before the Gaikeena homicide," said Bij Duurstede. "All of them traveled on the same flight—Pan American Airlines, number one twenty, first-class passage. They were in London on a one-day stopover, arrived there on Pan American flight two, from New York, first-class passage. In London they stayed at the Hilton. In Amsterdam, at the Hôtel de l'Europe. They were here a total of six days, attended a three-day United Nations conference on refugees held at The Hague. After the conference, they did some sight-seeing—canal rides, Volendam and Marken, Edam, the Anne Frank house. The tours were arranged by an agency here—I have the records."

The Anne Frank house. A street-corner Mengele would have enjoyed that.

"Over a hundred delegates attended the conference," added Bij Duurstede. "It's held every year."

"How close is the De l'Europe to where Gaikeena was found?"

"Close enough. In between is the red light district."

The narrow, cobbled streets of the district came into focus again. Bass-heavy rock music blaring from nearby bars, the night air clammy, the waters of the canals black and still. The athletes, bug-eyed at the brazenness of the place: milk-fed blondes and sloe-eyed Orientals selling themselves as easily as chocolate bars. Some working the streets, others posed, half-naked, in blue-lit window tableaux, inert as statuary.

Passive. Made to order for a fiend with control on his mind.

He visualized a late-night stroll, a solitary stroll after cocktails and small talk at a hotel lounge—the De l'Europe? A respectable-looking killer, wearing a long coat with deep pockets for the knives. Checking out the herd, eyeing the long-lashed come-hithers, then selection: a flash of thigh, the exchange of guilders. Extra money for something different—something a little kinky. Intentions camouflaged by shyness. Maybe even an embarrassed smile:

Could we—uh—go down by the docks?

What for, honey? I've got a nice warm bed.

The docks, please. I'll pay for it.

Got a thing for water, handsome?

Uh—yeah.

Plenty of water right around here.

I like the docks. Will this be enough?

Oh, sure, honey. Anjanette loves the docks too. The tides, going back and forth . . .

"Gaikeena was killed the day after the convention," said Bij Duurstede. "Your five left the next morning for Rome, along with twenty-three other U.N. people. Alitalia flight three seventy-one, first class. The U.N. always travels first class."

Daniel picked up the list of Amelia Catherine's volunteer staff, compiled by Shin Bet.

"I have some other names, Chief Inspector. I'd appreciate your checking if any of them attended the convention as well."

"Read them to me," said Bij Duurstede. "I have the convention roster right in front of me."

Soon Daniel had added five more names to those of the permanent Amelia Catherine staff: three doctors, two nurses. A Finn, a Swede, an Englishman, two Americans. Same arrival, same hotel, same departure.

"Any idea why they went to Rome?" he asked.

"I don't know," said Bij Duurstede. "Maybe an audience with the Pope?"

He placed a call to Passport Control at Ben Gurion Airport, pinpointed the arrival of ten U.N. staffers from Rome on a Lufthansa flight one week after the Gaikeena murder. Two more calls, to Scotland Yard and Rome police, confirmed that neither had experienced similar murders during the New York to Tel Aviv time frame. By the time he hung up, it was ten-thirty—forty-eight hours since he'd bathed; the last thing he'd eaten was a water biscuit at eight in the morning.

His head itched. He scratched it, looked at his open notebook, frustrated.

After the Amelia Catherine covert and Van Gelder's call, he'd felt the case starting to resolve. *The net tightening*. He'd put faith in the second Amsterdam call—too much faith—hoping for a magical intersection of geographical axes: a single name singing out its guilt. Instead the net had loosened, accommodating a larger catch.

He had ten suspects to consider. Individually or in pairs, triplets—cabals. Maybe Shmeltzer *had* something, with his group-conspiracy theory.

All of the above. None of the above.

Ten suspects. His men and Amos Harel's undercover backups would be stretched to capacity. The chance of getting something before next Thursday's women's clinic seemed slimmer than ever.

The Sumbok wire. Bij Duurstede had sent it, but *he* hadn't received it. He left his office to check with Communications and, midway down the corridor, met a female officer carrying the printout.

Taking it from her, he read it in the hall, running his finger down the names of St. Ignatius students, and getting even more frustrated when he saw the size of it.

Four hundred thirty-two students, fifteen faculty, twenty "ancillary" staff. Not a single match to his ten.

Four hundred sixty-eight surnames followed by first initials. None of them identified in terms of nationality. About half the names sounded Anglo-Saxon—that could mean British, Australian, New Zealanders, and South Africans as well as Americans. And, for that matter, Argentinians—some of them had names like Eduardo Smith. And some of the Italian, French, German, and Spanish names could have belonged to Americans too.

Useless.

He scanned the list for Arabic names. Three definites: Abdallah. Ibn Azah. Malki. A few possibles that could also have been Pakistani, Iranian, Malaysian, or North African: Shah, Terrif, Zorah.

Another waste of time.

He returned to his office, suddenly exhausted, forced himself to call Gabi Weinroth, the Latam man stationed atop the law building at the Scopus Hebrew U. campus with an infrared telescope focused on the Amelia Catherine.

"Scholar," answered Weinroth, in code.

"Sharavi," said Daniel, eschewing the name game. "Anything new?"

"Nothing."

The fifth "nothing" of the day. He reiterated his home number to the undercover man, hung up, and left for the place that matched it.

He drove around Talbieh and the neighboring German Colony, looking for Dayan, seeing only the luminescent eyes of stray cats, part of nocturnal Jerusalem for centuries.

After three go-rounds, he gave up, went home, opened the door to his flat expecting family sounds, was greeted by silence.

He entered, closed the door, heard a throat clear in the studio.

Gene was in there, using Laura's drawing table for a desk, surrounded by stacks of paper. The stretched canvases and palettes and paint boxes had been shoved to one side of the room. Everything looked different.

"Hello, there," said the black man, removing his reading glasses and getting up. "The Arizona and Oregon files came this morning. I didn't call you because there's nothing new in them—the local investigations didn't get very far. Your boys are sleeping over at your dad's. The ladies are catching a late movie. I just got a call from the night manager at the Laromme, very dependable fellow. Another package arrived for me. I'm going to run down and pick it up."

"I'll go get it."

"No way," said Gene, looking him over. "Take some time to clean up. I'll be right back—don't argue."

Daniel acquiesced, went into his bedroom, and stripped naked. When the front door closed, he gave an involuntary start, realized his nerves were frayed raw.

His eyes felt gritty; his stomach sat like an empty gourd in its abdominal basket. But he felt no desire for food. Coffee, maybe.

He put on a robe and went into the kitchen, brewed some Nescafé double-strength, then padded to the bathroom and took a shower, almost falling asleep under the spray. After dressing in fresh clothes, he returned to the kitchen, poured himself a cup, and sat down to drink it. Bitter, but warming. After two sips, he put his head down on the table, awoke in the midst of a confusing dream—bobbing in a rowboat, but no water, only sand, a dry dock . . .

"Hello, sweetie."

Laura's face smiling down at him. Her hand on his shoulder.

"What time is it?"

"Eleven-twenty."

Out for half an hour.

"Gene found you this way. He didn't have the heart to wake you up."

Daniel got up, stretched. His joints ached. Laura reached out, touched his unshaven face, then put her arms around his waist.

"Skinny," she said. "And you can't afford it."

"I didn't find the dog," he said, hugging her tightly.

"Hush. Hold me."

They embraced silently for a while.

"What movie did you see?" he asked.

"Witness."

"Good?"

"A police story. Do you really want to hear about it?"

He smiled. "No."

Finally they pulled apart and kissed. Laura tasted of peanuts. Cinema peanuts. Daniel reminded himself of the reason for the movie distraction, asked, "Where's Shoshi?"

"In her room."

"I'd better go talk to her."

"Go ahead."

He walked through the living room, down the hall toward the rear bedroom, and passed by the studio. Gene sat hunched over the table/desk, eating and working. With a pen in one hand and a sandwich in the other, he looked like a student cramming for exams. Luanne reclined, shoeless, on the couch, reading a book.

Shoshi's door was closed. He knocked on it softly, got no response, and knocked louder.

The door opened. He looked into green eyes marred by swollen lids.

"Hello, *motek*."

"Hello, Abba."

"May I come in?"

She nodded, opened the door. The room was tiny, barely room to walk, plastered with rock-star posters and photos cut out of tabloids. Above the bed was a bracket shelf crammed with rag dolls and stuffed animals. The desk was piled high with schoolbooks and mementos—art projects, a cowrie shell from Eilat, his red paratrooper's beret and '67 medals, a Hanukah menorah fashioned from empty rifle shells.

Incredible clutter, but neat. She'd always been a neat child—even as a toddler she'd tried to clean up her crumbs.

He sat on the bed. Shoshi leaned against a chair, looked down at the floor. Her curls seemed limp; her shoulders drooped.

"How was the movie?"

"Fine."

"Eema said it was a police story."

"Uh huh." She picked at a cuticle. Daniel restrained the impulse to tell her to stop.

"I know about the dog, *motek*. It wasn't your fault—"

"Yes, it was."

"Shoshi—"

She wheeled on him, beautiful little face suffused with rage. "He was my responsibility—you always said that! I was stupid, blabbing to Dorit—"

He got up and reached out to hold her. She twisted away. One of her bony knuckles grazed his rib.

She punched her thighs. "Stupid, stupid, stupid!"

"Come on," he said, and pulled her to him. She resisted for a moment, then went limp. Another rag doll.

"Oh, Abba!" she sobbed. "Everything's coming apart!"

"No, it's not. Everything will be fine."

She didn't answer, just continued to cry, drenching the front of his clean shirt.

"Everything will be fine," he repeated. As much for his benefit as hers.

62

Sunday noon, and all was quiet at the Amelia Catherine, medical activities suspended in honor of Christian Sabbath.

Up the road, at the Scopus campus, everything was business as usual, and Daniel made his way unnoticed through throngs of students and professors, up the serpentine walkway, and through the front door of the Law Building. He traversed the lobby, took the stairs to the top of the building, walked to an unmarked door at the end of the hall, and gave a coded knock. The door opened a crack. Suspicious eyes looked him over; then the crack widened sufficiently to admit him. Gabi Weinroth, in shorts and T-shirt, nodded hello and returned to his position across the room, sitting at the window. Daniel followed him.

Next to the Latam man's chair was a metal table bearing a police radio, a pair of walkie-talkies, a logbook, three crushed, empty cola cans, a carton of Marlboros, an ashtray overflowing with butts, and greasy wax paper wrapped around a half-eaten steak pita. Under the table were three black hard-shell equipment cases. A high-resolution, wide-angle telescope equipped with infrared enhancement was set up almost flush with the glass, angled eastward so that it focused on the entire Amelia Catherine compound.

Weinroth lit a cigarette, sat back, and hooked a thumb at the telescope. Daniel bent to look through it, saw stone, wrought iron, chain link, pine trees.

He pulled away from the scope, said, "Anyone leave besides the watchman?"

The Latam man picked up the logbook, opened it, and found his place.

"The older doctor—Darousha—left fifty-three minutes ago, driving a white Renault with U.N. plates. He headed north—Border Patrol picked him up on the road to Ramallah. Our man Comfortes confirmed his arrival back home. The watchman showed up a few minutes later. Both of them went into Darousha's house and closed the shutters—probably planning a midday tryst. These U.N. types don't work too hard, do they?"

"Anything else?"

"A couple of brief in-and-outs," said Weinroth. "More romance: Al Biyadi and Cassidy jogged for half an hour—eleven-eleven to eleven forty-three. Down the Mount of Olives Road and back up again past the hospital and all the way to the east campus gate. I was tilted almost straight down—lost them for a bit, but picked them up again as they headed back for the Amelia Catherine. Short run, about five and a half kilometers, then back inside. Haven't seen them since. She's a better runner than he is, good strong calves, barely breathing, but she holds herself back—probably doesn't want to break his balls. The administrator, Baldwin, took a stroll with the Arab secretary, more Romeo and Juliet stuff. If you would have let us plant some audio surveillance, I might have picked up some sweet talk."

Daniel smiled at the Latam man, who smiled back pleasantly and blew smoke rings at the ceiling. Weinroth had pressed him on the microphones—hi-tech types loved to use their toys. Codes and toys. But Daniel had judged the risk too high: If the killer/killers caught on to the surveillance, there'd be a pullback, stalemate. The madness had to end.

"Want me to videotape any of it?" asked Weinroth between puffs. "I can easily interface the recorder with the scope."

"Sure. Anything else? Any sign of Carter or Hauser?"

Weinroth shook his head, simulated snoring.

"Pleasant dreams," Daniel told him. By the time he reached the door, the Latam man was up and fiddling with the latches on one of the equipment cases.

* * *

Sunday, eight P.M., and the old man was dead, Shmeltzer was sure of it. He could tell by the nurse's tone of voice over the phone, the failure resonating from every word, the angry way she'd refused to let him talk with Eva, insisted Mrs. Schlesinger was in no condition to speak with anyone.

Telling him without telling him.

"She'll speak with me," he'd insisted.

"Are you family?"

"Yes, I'm her brother." Not really that much of a lie, considering what he and Eva had established between them.

When the goddamned nurse said nothing, he repeated: "Her brother—she'll want to speak with me."

"She's in no condition to speak with anyone. I'll tell her you called, Adon Schnitzer."

"Shmeltzer." Idiot.

Click.

He'd wanted to call the bitch back, scream: *Don't you know me? I'm the shmuck always with her, every free moment I've got. The one waiting out in the hall while she kisses a cold cheek, wipes a cold brow.*

But the nurse was just another pencil pusher, wouldn't give a damn. Rules!

He hung up the phone and cursed the injustice of it all. Since the first time they'd met, he'd stuck with Eva like paste on paper, absorbing her pain like some kind of human poultice. Holding, patting, drinking it in. So much crying on his shoulders, his bones felt permanently wet.

Faithful Nahum, playing big strong man. Rehearsing for the inevitable.

And now, now that it had finally happened, he was cut off. They were cut off from each other. Prisoners. She, chained to the goddamned deathbed. He, shackled to his assignment.

Keep an eye on the fucking sheikh and his fucking dog-faced girlfriend. Down from the hospital in his big green fucking Mercedes, a shopping trip at the best stores in East Jerusalem. Then watch them enjoy a late supper at their fucking sidewalk table at Chez Ali Baba.

Stuffing their bellies along with all the other rich Arabs and tourists, ordering the waiters around as if they were a couple of monarchs.

Two tables away, the Latam couple got to eat too. Charcoal-broiled kebab and shishlik, baked lamb and stuffed lamb, platters of salads, pitchers of iced tea. A flower corsage for the lady . . .

Meanwhile, Faithful Shmuck Nahum dresses as a beggar, wears false sores, and sits on the sidewalk just out of sniffing range from the restaurant. Sniffing garbage fumes from the restaurant's refuse bins, absorbing curses in Arabic, an occasional kick in the shins, a rare donation—but even the few goddamned coins he'd earned by looking pathetic would be returned to the department, cost him a half hour of paperwork logging the money.

Any other case, he'd say fuck it, time to retire. Run to Eva.

Not this one. These bastards were going to pay. For everything.

He turned his attention back to the restaurant.

Al Biyadi snapped his fingers at the waiter, barked an order when the man approached. When the waiter left, he looked at his watch. Big gold watch, same one as at the hospital—even from here Shmeltzer could see the gold. Bastard had been checking the time a lot during the last half hour. Something up?

The Latam couple ate on, didn't seem to notice, but that was their job, noticing without being noticed. Both were young, blond, good-looking, wearing high-priced imported clothes. Looking like a rich honeymoon couple absorbed in each other.

Would he and Eva ever have a honeymoon?

Would she have anything to do with him after being abandoned at the Crucial Moment? Or maybe he was sunk anyway—abandonment had nothing to do with it. She'd suffered with an old guy through terminal illness. Now that he was dead she'd be ready to put her life together—last thing she'd want was *another* old guy.

She was a fine-looking woman; those breasts were magnets designed to pull men in. Younger men, virile.

No need for bony wet shoulders.

The waiter brought some sort of iced drink to Al Biyadi's table. Big, oversized brandy snifter filled with something green and frothy. Pistachio milk, probably.

Al Biyadi lifted the snifter, Cassidy hooked her arm around his, they laughed, drank, nuzzled like high school kids. Drank again and kissed.

He could have killed them both, right then and there.

* * *

At eleven P.M., Gabi Weinroth completed his shift at the top of the Law Building and was replaced by a short, gray-haired undercover man named Shimshon Katz. Katz had just been pulled off a three-month foot surveillance of the Mahane Yehuda market and sported a full Hassid's beard. Twelve weeks of playing rabbi and looking for suspicious parcels—he felt pleased that nothing had turned up but was drained by the boredom.

"This isn't likely to be any better," Weinroth assured him, gathering up his cigarettes and pointing at the telescope. "Mostly blank space, and if you see anything sexy, you broadcast it on the security band—the other guys take it from there."

Katz picked up a stack of photographs from the table and shuffled through it. "I'm supposed to commit all of these to memory?"

"These eight are the main ones," said Weinroth, taking the stack and pulling out the permanent Amelia Catherine staff members. He placed them faceup on the table. "The rest are volunteers. I haven't seen one of them come near the place yet."

Katz studied the seven, lingering on a candid of Walid Darousha, whom the camera had caught scowling.

"Nasty-looking character," he said.

"He's in Ramallah with his boyfriend, and according to Major Crimes, he's low priority. So don't play psychoanalyst—just look and log."

"Up yours," said Katz jovially. "Which ones are *high* priority?"

Weinroth jabbed the photos. "These, for what it's worth."

Katz stared at the pictures, drew a line across his forehead. "Etched permanently on my mind."

"For what *that's* worth," said Weinroth. "I'm off." He took two steps, turned, and leered. "You want me to look in on your wife and comfort her?"

"Sure, why not? Yours has already been taken care of."

Avi sat low in the unmarked car, strained his eyes, and watched the front door of Wilbur's apartment building on Rehov Alharizi. The moon was a low white crescent, the dark street blinded further by the hovering bulk of the tall buildings that rose from the east. The Chief Rabbinate, the Jewish Agency, Solel Boneh Builders, the Kings Hotel. Important buildings—official buildings.

As a child he'd spent plenty of summer days in official

buildings, harbored dim memories of official visits perceived from a waist-high perspective: shiny belt buckles, rippling paunches, jokes he didn't understand. His father convulsing with laughter, his big hand tightening with amusement, threatening to crush Avi's small one . . .

Forget that crap and concentrate.

The hum of an automobile engine, but no headlight flash, no movement up and down the block.

Nothing suspicious in the mailbox or at Wilbur's office at Beit Agron—the latter he could personally verify because he'd delivered the office mail himself, covered the entire press building. No one but the janitor had approached Wilbur's suite all day. At six the reporter left, in shirtsleeves, with no briefcase, and walked toward Fink's for his usual soak. By eight he hadn't returned, and, following the plan, Avi was relieved by one of two Latam men who'd been watching the reporter's flat. He drove to Alharizi and parked half a block down from Wilbur's building, a nicely kept, two-story fourplex. Then he waited.

And waited. For all he knew, the bastard wasn't even coming home tonight, had picked up some chick and was sacking out at her place.

The street was deserted, which meant none of his daytime identities—street cleaner, postman, sausage vendor, yeshiva boy—were of any use; the costume changes lay tangled and unused in the trunk of the unmarked car.

And what an unmarked! His own wheels were out of the question—the red BMW stood out like a fresh bloodstain. In its place Latam had dredged up a terminally ill Volkswagen, oppressive little box, the gears protesting every nudge of the shift lever, stuffing coming out of the seats in rubbery tufts, the interior smelling of spoiled food, leaking petrol, and stale cigarette smoke.

Not that *he* could smoke—the glow would give him away. So he sat doing nothing, his only company a plastic two-liter Coke bottle to piss in. Each time he was through with it he emptied it in the gutter.

Sitting for almost four hours, his ass had fallen asleep; he had to pinch himself to get the feeling back.

Nash, the Latam guy at the back of the building, had the better deal: run a dry mop up and down the hallway, then stake out the alley. Fresh air, at least. Exercise.

Every half hour the two of them checked in with each other. The last check had been ten minutes ago.

Aleph, here.

Bet, here. Grunt.

Not a very social guy, Nash, but he supposed most undercover types weren't picked for their conversational skills. The opposite, even: They were to be seen and not heard.

He checked his watch. Eleven-forty. Reached for the Coke bottle.

Midnight, Talbieh, the Sharavi household was silent, the women and children all asleep.

Rather than return to the hotel alone, Luanne had chosen to stay for the night, sleeping in the master bedroom, on Daniel's side of the bed. She and Laura came into the studio, nightgowned and cold-creamed—the borrowed gown half a foot too short on Luanne—and gave their husbands quick kisses before trundling off together. Daniel heard little-girl giggles, conspiratorial whispers through the thin bedroom door before they fell asleep.

A pajama party. Good for them. He was glad they were coping by keeping occupied, had never seen Laura so busy: museum outings, shopping trips to the boutiques on Dizengoff Circle and the Jaffa flea-market stalls, lectures, late movies—now that was a change. She'd never been much of a cinema buff, rarely stayed up past ten.

Changes.

And why not? No reason for her to give up her life because the case had turned him into a phantom. Still, a small, selfish part of him wanted her to be more dependent. Need him more.

He finished chewing one of Shoshi's chicken sandwiches—dry, but an architectual masterpiece, so lovingly prepared: the bread trimmed, the pickles quartered and individually wrapped. He'd felt guilty biting into it.

He wiped his mouth.

"Whoa," said Gene. "Whoa, look at this."

Daniel got up and walked to the black man's side. Next to three sandwich wrappers and the Sumbok roster was the newly arrived homicide file on Lilah "Nightwing" Shehadeh, spread out on the table/desk, opened to one of the back pages. The file was thick, stretching the limits of the metal fasteners that bound it to the manila folder, and anchored to the desk top by Gene's large thumb.

"What do you have?" Daniel leaned over, saw a page of photocopied murder photos on one side, a poorly typed report on the other. The quality of the photocopy was poor, the pictures dark and blurred, some of the printed text swirling and bleeding out to white.

Gene tapped the report. "Hollywood Division never figured it for a serial because there was no follow-up murder. Their working assumption was that it was a phony sex-killing aimed at covering up a power struggle between Shehadeh's pimp and a competitor. The pimp, guy named Bowmont Alvin Johnson, was murdered a few months before Shehadeh; bunch of other fancy boys were interviewed—all had supposed alibis. Shehadeh and Johnson had split up before he was killed, but the same detectives handled both cases and they remembered finding a purse at his apartment that his other girls identified as once belonging to Shehadeh. The purse was stored in the evidence room; after she turned up dead, they took a closer look at the contents. No trick book—she probably took that with her when she left—but the next-best thing: some scraps of paper with names that they figured to be either her dope suppliers or customers. Twenty names. Eight were never identified. One of them was a *D. Terrif.* There were also several *D.T.*'s. Now the punch line. Look at this."

He lowered his index finger to a spot at the center of the Sumbok page.

Terrif, D. D.

Daniel remembered the name. One of the three he'd thought might be Arabic.

His hands were trembling. He put one on Gene's shoulder, said, "Finally."

"Bingo." Gene smiled. "That's American for 'we done good.' "

A Latam detective named Avram Comfortes sat in the soft mulch beneath the orange trees that surrounded Walid Darousha's large, graceful Ramallah villa, inhaling citrus fragrance, shooing away mice and the night moths that alighted upon the trees and sucked nectar from the flowers.

At fifteen minutes past midnight, the metal shutters to Darousha's bedroom window cranked open. They'd been sealed shut for an hour, since Darousha and the watchman had finished a late supper, the doctor cooking, the watchman eating.

An hour. Comfortes had a good idea what had been going on inside, was glad he didn't have to look at it.

The window was small, square, laced with grillwork—the old-fashioned kind, ornate enough for a mosque. Framed inside was a clear view of the doctor's bedroom. A large room, painted blue, the ceiling white.

Comfortes lifted his binoculars and saw a sepia-tone family portrait on the far wall, next to an old map of pre-'48 Palestine—they never gave up. Under the map was a high, wide bed covered with a white chenille spread.

Darousha and Zia Hajab sat under the spread, side by side, naked to the waist, propped up by wildly colored embroidered pillows. Just sitting there, not talking, until Hajab finally said something and Darousha got up. The doctor was wearing baggy boxer shorts. His body was soft, white, and hairy, generous love handles flowing over the waistband of the underpants, breasts as soft as a woman's, quivering when he moved.

He left the bedroom. Alone, Hajab fingered the covers, wiped his eyes, stared straight in Comfortes's direction.

Seeing, the undercover man knew, only darkness.

What did guys like that think about?

Darousha came back with two iced drinks on a tray. Tall glasses filled with something clear and golden, next to a couple of red paper napkins. He served Hajab, leaned over and kissed the watchman on the cheek. Hajab didn't seem to notice, was already gulping.

Darousha said something. Hajab shook his head, emptied the glass, wiped his mouth with the back of his hand. Darousha handed him a napkin, took the empty glass and gave him the second one, went back to his side of the bed and just sat there, watching Hajab drink. Looking happy to serve.

Funny, thought Comfortes, he would have expected the opposite, the doctor in charge. Then again, they were deviates. You couldn't expect them to be predictable.

Which made them well worth watching.

He picked up his logbook, made a notation. Writing in the dark, without benefit of seeing the letters. But he knew it would be legible. Plenty of practice.

* * *

At twelve-thirty, from his perch atop the Law Building, Shimshon Katz saw movement through his telescope. Human movement, originating at the rear of the Amelia Catherine, then hooking around to the front of the hospital and continuing southeast on the Mount of Olives Road.

A man. Swinging his arms and walking in a long, loose stride. The relaxed stride of someone without a care in the world.

The man stopped, turned. Katz saw him quarter-face, enough to match him with his photo. He resumed walking and Katz followed him through the scope, using one hand to switch on the videotape interface. Hearing the whir of the camera as it began to do its job.

Probably nothing, just a walk before bedtime. The administrator, Baldwin, had done one of those twenty minutes ago, along with his cute little Lebanese girlfriend: a stroll along the ridge, stopping for a couple of minutes to look out at the desert, then back inside. Lights out.

But this nightwalker kept going, toward the city. Katz watched the silhouette grow smaller, turned up the magnification on the scope, and nudged it gently in order to keep the departing figure in his sights.

He continued following and filming until the road dipped and the figure dropped from view. Then he got on the police radio, punched in the digital code for the security band, and called Southeast Team Sector.

"Scholar, here. Progress."

"Relic speaking. Specify."

"Curly, on foot down the Mount of Olives Road, coming your way."

"Clothing and physicals."

"Dark sport coat, dark pants, dark shirt, dark shoes. No outstanding physicals."

"Curly, no vehicle, all dark. That it, Scholar?"

"That's it."

"Shalom."

"Shalom."

The communication was monitored by Border Patrol units stationed in the desert above Mount Scopus and near the Ras el Amud mosque, where the Jericho Road shifted suddenly to the east. The man who'd answered the call was a Latam man, code-named Relic, stationed near the entry to the Rockefeller Museum at the intersection of that same road and Sultan Suleiman, the first link in the human chain that made up Southeast Team Sector. The second and third links were undercover detectives positioned on Rehov Habad at the center of the Old City, and the Zurich garden at the foot of Mount Zion.

The fourth was Elias Daoud, waiting nervously at the Kishle substation for word that a suspect was headed due west of the city walls.

The radio call came in at Daniel's flat when he was on the phone to the American Medical Association offices in Washington, D.C., trying to find out if a Dr. D. Terrif was or had ever been a member of that organization. The secretary had put him on hold while she consulted with her superior; he handed the phone to Gene and listened closely to what Katz was saying.

Wondering, along with the rest of them, if Dr. Richard Carter had anything else in mind tonight, other than a casual stroll.

63

A miracle, thought Avi, watching Wilbur stumble toward his front door, carrying something in a paper bag. Amount of liquor the *shikur* had inside of him, it was a miracle he hadn't ended up in some gutter.

One forty-three in the morning—late-ending party or an all-nighter cut short?

Through his binoculars he saw the reporter fumble with his keys, finally manage to find the right one, scratch around the front-door lock.

Put a little hair around it. Though from the looks of this jerk, even that wouldn't help.

Wilbur finally got the key in and entered the fourplex. Avi radioed the Latamnik in back to let him know the subject was home.

"Aleph here."

No answer.

Maybe the reporter had walked through the building straight to the back alley—to throw up or get something from his car—and the undercover man couldn't give himself away by answering. If that was the case, any transmission would be a betrayal.

He'd wait a while before trying again, watch for some sign that Wilbur was up in his room.

For ten minutes he sat impatiently in the Volkswagen; then the lights went on in the reporter's second-story window.

"Aleph here."

The second radio call went unanswered, as did a third, five minutes later.

Finally, Avi got out of the car, jogged the half block to Wilbur's building on brand new Nikes, and tried the radio again.

Nothing.

Maybe Nash had seen something, followed Wilbur into the building, and he should hold back.

Still, Sharavi's clear instructions had been to stay in regular contact.

Follow orders, Cohen. Stay out of trouble.

He was in front of the fourplex, enveloped by darkness. The light in the reporter's flat was still on, a dim amber square behind blackout shades.

Avi looked up and down the street, pulled out his flashlight, and insinuated himself in the narrow space between Wilbur's building and its southern neighbor. He walked over wet grass, heard a crunch of broken glass, stopped, listened, and inched forward until he'd slipped completely around the building and was standing in the alley.

The back door stood partially open. The section of corridor it revealed was black as the night. Wilbur's leased AlfaSud was parked in the small dirt lot along with three other cars. Avi made a mental note to record their license plates, continued slowly toward the door.

He smelled something foul. *Shit*. Really ripe shit, had to be close by—he wondered if he'd gotten any on the Nikes or his pants. Wouldn't that be wonderful!

He took a step closer; the shit smell was really strong now. He had visions of it coating the bottom of his cuffs, clicked on the low beam of the flashlight, ran it over his trousers, then onto the ground in front of him.

Dirt, a bottle cap, something odd: shoes.

But vertical, pointing up at the sky. A pair of running shoes attached to white ankles—someone else's trouser legs. A belt. A shirt. Splayed arms.

A face.

In a split second he made sense of it: the body of the Latamnik, some sort of cord drawn tight around the poor guy's neck, the eyes open and bulging, the tongue distended and sticking out from between thickened lips.

A froth of saliva.

The smell.

Suddenly his homicide course came to mind, the English-language textbook that had made him sweat. Suddenly he understood the shit smell: death by strangulation, the reflexive opening of the bowels . . .

He turned off the flashlight at once, reached frantically under his shirt for his Beretta; before he could get it out, felt stunning, electric pain at the base of his skull, a cruel flash of insight.

Then nothing.

Bitter-mouthed and queasy, Wilbur dragged himself out of the shower, made a halfhearted attempt at drying himself off, and struggled into his robe.

What a night—crap topping off crap.

They'd gotten to him, the Chosen People had.

CP: 1. MW: 0.

No more Butcher stories, not a single sentence since Sharavi and his storm troopers had put him through their Gestapo . . .

Jesus, his head hurt, he felt feverish, sick as a dog. Stupid broad and her cheap brandy—thank God he'd had the presence of mind to pick up the bottle of Wild Turkey.

Thank God he hadn't wasted it on her. The bottle was waiting, still sealed, on his nightstand.

Ice cubes in the freezer; he'd filled the tray this morning—or was it yesterday morning? No matter. Important thing was, there was *ice.* And *Turkey.* Pop the seal—*deflower* the seal—and get some good stuff in his system.

A single, solitary cheerful thought at the end of a very crappy day.

Several crappy days.

Wiring his stories and watching for pickups, but not a single goddamned line in print. Good stories, too: human-interest follow-up on the Rashmawis, most of it made up but *poignant—goddamned* poignant. He knew poignant when he saw it. Another one with a Tel Aviv U. shrink armchair-analyzing the Butcher. And an interview with a disgruntled former Gvura creep exposing how Kagan cadged funds out of rich, respectable American Jews, silk-stocking types who insisted their names be kept secret. The piece he'd written had busted the secret wide open, listing names along with dollar amounts. He'd tacked on a tasty little summary tying the whole thing in with a Larger Social Issue: the conflict between the old Zionist idealism and the new militaristic . . .

Big fucking deal. Not a word of it picked up.

Nada. They'd erased his identity—for all practical purposes, murdered him.

At first he'd thought it was a delay, maybe an oversupply of stories holding up his. But after four days he knew it was something else, grabbed the phone and called New York. Making noise about state censorship, expecting outrage, backup, some Freedom of the Press good fellowship, *we're behind you, Mark, old buddy, will get right on it, yessir.*

Instead: hemming and hawing, the kind of talking without saying anything politicians did when they wanted to avoid a cutting question.

New York was part of it.

He'd been laid out on the altar for sacrifice.

Just like the Butcher victims: the unsung victim—how long before they buried him?

Nebraska. Or Cleveland. Some dead-end desk job purgatory. Meanwhile all he could do was bide his time, work on his screenplay, send letters to L.A. agents—if that panned out, fuck 'em, he'd be eating duck pizza at Spago . . .

Until then, though, a cycle of wretched, empty days. A good romp would have eased the pain.

Romp and Turkey.

Thank God he hadn't wasted the good stuff on her, the phony.

Australian reporter, shoulders on her like a defensive lineman. But a nice face—no Olivia Newton-John, but good clean features, nice blond hair, good skin. All those buttermilk freckles on her neck and chest—he'd been curious as hell to know how far down they went.

Way she came on at Fink's, he was sure he'd find out. He'd bought the Wild Turkey from the bartender—double retail plus tip, on his expense account. He sat down at her table. Five minutes later, her hand was on his knee.

Wink and a whistle, my place or your place?

Her place.

Dinky single, just a couple of blocks from his, almost no furniture—she'd just arrived from kangaroo land. But the requisite party toys: stereo, soft-rock cassette collection. A futon mattress on the floor, candles. Bottles.

Lots of bottles: cheap brandy, ten varieties, every fruit you could think of. A cheap-brandy freak.

They'd tossed back shot after shot, sharing a jam jar. Then her little secret: little chocolate-colored hashish crumbs inserted into a Dunhill filter tip—an interesting buzz, the hash softening the edges of the bad booze.

Mind candy, she'd whispered, tonguing his ear.

Soft lights, soft rock on the tape deck.

A tongue duel, then lying back. Ready to dive into their own personal Down Under. Nice, right?

Wrong.

He let the towel fall to the floor, felt the cold tile under his soles, shivered, and swayed unsteadily. Vision blurred, nausea climbed up to his throat.

God, he felt like heaving his guts out—how much of that swill had he ingested?

He leaned over the sink, closed his eyes and was hit by an attack of the dry heaves that left him weak and short of breath, needing to hold on to the sink for support.

Pure swill—he didn't want to think about what it was doing to his intestinal tract. And had the hash been anything other than hash? He recalled a night in Rio, Mardi Gras craziness. Weed laced with some kind of hallucinogen, he'd walked on rubber sidewalks for three days.

But *she'd* put away an entire bottle by herself, not even blinking.

Australians—they were bottomless pits when it came to booze and dope. Descended from criminals, probably something in the genes . . .

He felt his heart pounding. Irregularly. Brushed aside heart-attack terror, closed the commode and sat down on the lid, having trouble getting a good deep breath. Trying not to think of tonight's disaster, but the more he tried, the more the memories forced themselves into his muddy consciousness.

The two of them lying side by side on the futon, his hand on her thigh—hefty, freckled thigh. Tossing back swill and smoking hash and tossing back more swill, his hand in her blouse, she, letting him, smiling goofy-eyed and saying *cheers* and burping and putting it away as if it were Perrier.

Everything going well, goddamned salvation after all those shitty days. Then she suddenly gets the talkies—all she wants to do is jabber.

Off goes the blouse—big girl, big freckled tits to make a centerfold jealous, just like he'd imagined. Big brown nipples; she let him suck on them, play with her—we're heading home, Marko—but she kept right on *talking*.

Dope-talk. Fast and furious, with an undercurrent of hysteria that made him nervous, as if one wrong move and she'd be sobbing uncontrollably, screaming rape or something.

Crazy-talk. Sliding from one topic to the next without benefit of logical association.

Her ex-husband. Exotic birds. Her parents' taste in furniture. High school drinking parties. A cactus collection she'd had in kindergarten. Homesickness. An abortion in college. Her brother, the sheep shearer.

Then lots of weird stuff about sheep: shearing sheep. Dipping sheep. Watching sheep fuck. Castrating sheep—not exactly the lexicon from which erotic alphabet soup sprang . . . What the hell was he talking about? Her craziness was catching.

His head felt ready to split open. After several attempts he finally got to his feet, lurched into the bedroom, and made for the Turkey bottle. The ice could wait.

The light was off. Funny, he thought he'd left it on.

The mind gone, memory cells blasted to hell—he was sure she'd put something in the hash. Or the rotgut.

The darkness better anyway. His eyelids felt crammed with gravel, the darkness more soothing, just a little soft glow from the foyer highlighting outlines . . .

He went for the Turkey on the nightstand, groped air.

It wasn't there.

Oh, shit, he'd put it somewhere else and forgotten about it. He was really blasted, had really done it this time. The stupid broad had poisoned him with her blackberry-peach-pear rotgut. Jerked him around and poisoned him.

And how he'd been jerked. She'd let him do anything, everything, allowing him into her pants, passive as a coma victim. Letting him spread her big freckled legs, accommodating him as he slipped it in like a finger in a greased glove. So accommodating he wondered if she felt it—was she used to something bigger? He moved to *make* her feel it, stroked her, used every trick he knew, but all she did was lie there staring at the ceiling and *talking,* as if he were doing it to someone else, she wasn't even a part of it, was in some talktalk twilight zone.

Putting up no resistance, but jabbering until he lost his hard-on, pulled out, stood up.

Jabbering, spread-eagled, even as he put his clothes on, grabbed the unopened Turkey bottle. He could still hear her jabbering as he closed the door to her apartment. . . .

He stumbled around the room, feeling for the Turkey.

Where the hell was the goddamned bottle?

Mind, gone; memory, gone. He stomped around the room, checking the floor, the bed, his dresser, the closet, feeling the panic starting to rise—

"Looking for this?" said someone.

His heart shot up into his chest, collided with the roof of his mouth. Unexpelled breath stagnated painfully in his chest.

Outline in the doorway, backlit by the foyer bulb. Some guy, hat, long coat. The light glinting off eyeglasses. The fuzz of a beard.

The guy came closer. Smiling. Grinning.

"What the hell—"

"Hi, I'm Dr. Terrific. What seems to be the problem?"

He could see teeth. A grin.

Too weird.

Oh, shit, Dr. Terrific: D.T. The D.T.'s.

A Delirium Tremens Demon. You always heard about it hitting some other guy, never thought it would happen to you. He remembered the warning of the Brazilian doctor with the soft, wet hands: *Your liver, Mr. Wilbur. Easy on the daiquiris.*

Off the sauce, he promised himself, first thing tomorrow morning. Three squares a day, more B vitamins . . .

"Looking for this, Mark?" repeated the D.T. Demon, extending the Turkey bottle.

Definitely hallucinating.

Poisoned hash. Laced with something—LSD . . . The demon in the hat grinned wider. Looking awfully goddamned real for a hallucination . . .

Wilbur sat down on the edge of the bed, closed his eyes, rubbed them, opened them again, hoping to find himself alone.

He didn't.

"What the hell—"

The demon/man shook his head. "Talk respectfully, Mark."

Using his name, as if he knew him intimately, were *part* of him. Like one of those cartoons he'd watched as a kid. *This is your conscience speaking, Mark.*

He waved it away. "Up yours."

The demon reached into its coat, pulled out something long and shiny. Even in the dimness, Wilbur knew right away what it was.

Knife. Biggest goddamned knife he'd ever seen—blade had to be close to a foot long, maybe longer. Gleaming metal blade, pearl handle.

"Respectfully, Mark."

Wilbur stared at the knife glinting light. Cold and clean and cruel and real . . . Could this be real? Oh, God—

"I've missed your stories about me, Mark. I feel as if you've abandoned me."

And then he knew.

"Listen," he forced out, "I wanted to. *They* wouldn't let me."

The man kept grinning, listening.

A hundred shrink interviews reeled through his head: *Buy time,* goddammit. Establish a bond. Empathy.

"Censorship—you know what it's like," he said. Forcing a smile—oh, Jesus, how it hurt to smile. That knife . . . "I did several stories—you want to see them, I can show them to you—out in my desk in the living room." Slurring his words, sounding like a drunk. *Be clearer!*

"In the living room," he repeated. Front room, make a lunge for the door . . .

"Another thing, Mark," said the grinning bastard, as if he hadn't heard a word. "You called me a butcher. That implies sloppiness. Crudeness. I'm a professional. A real scientist. I always clean up afterward."

No, no, no, make this go away—got to get out of this room, this goddamned room, make a run for it . . .

"I'm sorry, I didn't mean—"

"Despite that, I've really missed those stories, Mark. We had a relationship. You had no permission to end it without consulting me."

The man in the hat and long coat came closer. What a weird face, something wrong with it—off kilter, he couldn't place it. . . . Hell with that—don't waste time wondering about stupid things.

Buy time.

"I know what you mean. I'd feel the same way if I were you. But the system stinks, it really does." Now *he* was jabbering. Going on about New York, the Chosen People, how both of them were victims of Zionist censorship. The grinning man just standing there, bottle in one hand, knife in the other. Listening.

"We can work together, Doctor. Tell your story, the way you want it told, a big book, no one will ever know who you are, I'll protect you, once we're out of this stinking country no more censorship, I can promise you that. Hollywood's crazy for the idea. . . ."

The grinning man didn't seem to be listening anymore. Distracted. Wilbur moved his aching eyes down from the off-kilter face to the asshole's hands: the Turkey bottle in one hand, the knife in the other. He decided to go for broke, wondered which one to grab.

The knife.

He readied himself. A long moment of silence. His heart was racing. He couldn't breathe, was suffocating on his own fear . . . Stop that! No negative thinking—buy time.

Distract the asshole again.

"So," he said, "tell me a little about yourself."

The grinning man came closer. Wilbur saw his eyes and knew it was useless. Over.

He tried to scream. Nothing came out. Struggled to get up off the bed and fell backward, helpless.

Paralyzed with fear. He'd heard that animals about to be ripped to shreds by predators slipped into protective paralysis. The mind shut off. Anesthesia—oh, Lord, he hoped so. Make me an animal, numb me, take away these thoughts, the waiting . . .

The bearded face hovered over him, grinning.

Wilbur choked out a feeble squeak, covered his face so as not to see the knife, scrambled to fill his mind with thoughts, images, memories, anything that could compete with the pain of waiting.

God, how he hated knives. So unfair—he was an okay guy.

The hand with the knife never moved.

The one with the bottle did.

64

The Ali Baba closed at midnight, but Al Biyadi slipped the waiter some dollars and he and Cassidy were allowed to sip another pistachio milk as the lights went out around them.

Quite a few dollars, thought Shmeltzer, as he watched the waiter bring them a plate of cookies topped off by a sonata of bows and scrapes.

Cassidy took a cookie and nibbled on it. She seemed bored, no expression in the sexless face. Al Biyadi drank, consulted his watch. Just another couple out on a date, but Shmeltzer's instincts told him something was up—the shmuck had looked at the watch fourteen times during the last hour.

The more he studied them, the more mismatched they seemed—the sheikh in his tailored dark suit and shiny shoes, Cassidy trying to feminize herself with that upswept hairdo, the dangling earrings and lacy dress, but ending up far short of success. Touching the sheikh's arm from time to time but getting only half-smiles or less.

Shmuck was definitely nervous, his mind somewhere else.

A young dark-haired woman dressed in white work clothes and equipped with a mop and pail emerged from the back of the restaurant, knelt, and began cleaning off the sidewalk. Al Biyadi and Cassidy ignored her, kept playing out their little scene.

Waiting? For what?

The Latam couple had paid their check and left the restaurant ten minutes ago, conferring briefly with Shmeltzer before walking off hand in hand, north on Salah E-Din. To the casual observer a goyische twosome, headed for fun in a suite at the American Colony Hotel.

Al Biyadi looked at his watch again. Almost a nervous tic. Cassidy put the cookie down, placed her hands in her lap.

The scrubwoman dragged her mop closer to their table, making soapy circles, then right up next to them.

She knelt, kept her hands moving, her narrow white back to Shmeltzer. He half-expected Al Biyadi to say something nasty to her—guy was class-conscious.

But instead he looked down at her, seemed to be listening to her. Tensing up. Nodding. Cassidy making a grand show of looking off in the distance.

The scrubwoman dragged her pail elsewhere, scrubbed for a few seconds, then disappeared back into the restaurant. Half the sidewalk was still dirty. Al Biyadi slapped down more bills, pinned them under the candle glass, got up, and brushed off his trousers.

Cassidy stood too, took his arm. Squeezed it—through his binoculars, Shmeltzer could see her fingers tightening like claws around the dark fabric.

Al Biyadi peeled them off, gave her a tiny shake of the head, as if to say *not now*.

Cassidy dropped her hands to her sides. Tapped her foot.

The two of them stood on the sidewalk.

Moments later, Shmeltzer heard sounds from the back door of the restaurant. The door opened, freeing a beam of ocher light and kitchen clatter. He pressed himself into a dark corner and watched as the scrubwoman, now dressed in a dark dress, walked out and fluffed her hair. Short girl—petite. Pretty profile.

She began heading north on Salah E-Din, duplicating the Latam couple's route.

Shmeltzer could see she was a bit flatfooted, could hear her shuffle. When her footsteps had died, he moved forward, looked at her, then back at the Ali Baba.

The restaurant's front lights had been turned off. The waiter was folding up tablecloths, extinguishing candles, collapsing tables.

Al Biyadi and Cassidy began walking north, too, following the scrubwoman.

They passed within two meters of him, keeping up a good pace, not talking. Shmeltzer radioed the Latam couple. The woman answered.

"Wife, here."

"They just left, followed a short woman in a dark dress, shoulder-length dark hair, early twenties. All three of them coming your way on Salah E-Din. Where are you?"

"Just past Az-Zahara, near the Joulani Travel Agency."

"Stay there. I'll take up the rear."

He put the radio under his beggar's robes, back in the pocket of his windbreaker, cursed the heat and all those layers of clothes, and followed a block behind.

Goddamned caravan.

Sheikh and girlfriend kept walking fast. A few stragglers were still out on the streets—lowlife, porters and kitchen help from the Arab hotels going off-shift—but he found it easy to keep an eye on his quarry: Look for a female head bobbing next to a male. You didn't see many men and women walking together in East Jerusalem.

They passed Az-Zahara Street, walked right by the Joulani Agency where the Latam couple was waiting, invisibly, and the American School for Oriental Research, and continued toward the Anglican Cathedral of Saint George and its four-steepled Gothic tower.

Just above the cathedral they reunited with the scrubwoman, exchanged words that Shmeltzer couldn't hear, and made their way—a strange threesome—east, then south, down Ibn Haldoun. The street was narrow and short, dead-ending at Ibn Batuta and the front facade of the Ritz Hotel.

But they stopped short of the dead end, walked through a wrought-iron gate into the courtyard of an elegant old walled Arab house, and disappeared.

Shmeltzer waited across the street for the Latam couple to arrive, saw them enter the mouth of Ibn Haldoun and trotted up the street to greet them. The three of them retreated twenty yards up Ibn Haldoun, away from the glare of street lamps.

"All three of them in there?" asked the man.

Shmeltzer nodded. "They entered just a minute ago. Do you know anything about the building?"

"Not on any list I've seen," said the woman. "Nice, for a street scrubber."

"She resembles the first three Butcher victims," said Shmeltzer. "Small, dark, not bad-looking. We've been thinking they plucked their pigeons right out of the hospital, but maybe not. Maybe they make contact during medical visits, arrange to meet them later—money for sex." He paused, looked back at the house.

Two stories, fancy, carved stone trim. "Be nice to know who owns the palace."

"I'll call in, put in for a Ministry of Housing ID," said the woman, removing her radio from her purse.

"No time for that," said Shmeltzer. "They could be doping her up right now, laying her out for surgery. Call French Hill, tell them the situation and that we're going in. And ask for backup—have an ambulance ready."

He looked at the man. "Come on."

They sprinted to the house, opened the gates, which were fuzzy with rust, entered the courtyard, Berettas drawn. A front-door back-door approach was called for but access to the rear of the house was blocked on both sides by Italian cypress growing together in dense green walls. Returning their attention to the front, they took in details: a single door, at the center; grated windows, most of them shuttered. Two front balconies, the courtyard planted nicely with flower beds. Maybe a subdivision into flats—most of the big houses in Jerusalem had been partitioned—but with only one door there was no way to know for certain.

Shmeltzer waved his gun toward the door. The Latam man followed him.

Locked. The Latam guy took out picks. This one was fast; he had it open in two minutes. He looked at Shmeltzer, waiting for the signal to push the door open.

Shmeltzer knew what he was thinking. A place this fancy could have an alarm; if it were the kill spot, maybe even a booby trap.

Too old to be doing this, he thought. And to save an Arab, yet. But what could you do—the job was the job.

He gave the door a push, walked into the house, the Latam man at his heels. No ringing bells, no flurry of movement. And no shrapnel tearing through his chest. Good. Saved for another day of blessed existence.

A square entry hall, round Persian rug, two more doors at the end. Shmeltzer and the Latam man pressed themselves against opposite walls, took one door each, jiggled the handles.

The Latam guy's was open. Inside it was a spiral staircase, uncarpeted stone.

Shmeltzer walked up it, found the landing at the top boarded up, the air dust-laden and smelling of musty neglect. He tried the boards. Nailed tight, no loose ones. No one had come up here tonight.

Back down to the ground floor, signal to the Latam guy to try the second door. Locked. Two locks, one on top of the other. The first one yielded quickly to the pick; the second was stubborn.

The minutes ticked away, Shmeltzer imagined drops of blood falling in synchrony with each one. His hands were sweat-slick, the Beretta cold and slippery. He waited as the Latam man *potchked* with the lock, thought of the scrubwoman, naked on some table, head down, dripping into a rug. . . .

Too damned old for this shit.

The Latam guy worked patiently, twisting, turning, losing the tumblers, finally finding them.

The door swung open silently.

They stepped into a big dark front room, gleaming stone floors, heavy drapes blocking rear windows, swinging Dutch doors leading to a corridor on the right. A low-wattage bulb in a wall sconce cast a faint orange glow over heavy, expensive-looking furniture—old British-style furniture, stiff settees and bowlegged tables. Lace doilies. More tables, inlaid Arab-style, an oversized inlaid backgammon set, a potbellied glass-doored breakfront full of silver, dishes, bric-a-brac. A guitar resting on a sofa. Ivory carvings. Lots of rugs.

Rich. But again, the senile, old-clothes smell of neglect. Set up like props on a theater stage, but not lived in. Not for a long time.

The front room opened to a big old-fashioned kitchen on the left. The Latam man peeked his head into it, came back signaling *nothing*.

The Dutch doors, then. The only choice.

Damned things squeaked. He held them open for the Latam man. The two of them stepped onto an Oriental runner. Doors, four of them. Bedrooms. A hyphen of light under one on the left. Muted sounds.

They approached the door, held their breath, listened. Conversation, Al Biyadi's voice rising in excitement. Talking Arabic, a female replying, the words unclear.

Shmeltzer and the Latamnik looked at each other. Shmeltzer motioned him to go ahead. The guy was younger—his legs could take the punishment.

The Latam man kicked in the door and the two of them jumped in, pointing their Berettas, screaming: "Police! Drop down! Drop! Drop down! Police!"

No murder scene, no blood.

Just Al Biyadi and two women standing open-mouthed with

astonishment in a bright, empty room full of wooden crates. Most of the boxes were covered by canvas tarpaulins; a few were bare. Shmeltzer saw the words FARM MACHINERY stenciled on the wood in Hebrew and Arabic.

A crowbar lay on the floor, which was littered with packing straw. A crate in the center of the room had been pried open.

Filled to the brim with rifles, big, heavy Russian rifles. Shmeltzer hadn't seen so many at one time since they'd taken the weapons off the Egyptians in '67.

Al Biyadi was holding one of the rifles, looking like a child caught with his hand in the biscuit bin. The women had dropped to the floor, but the shmuck remained standing.

"Drop it!" Shmeltzer screamed, and pointed the Beretta at his snotty, sheikh face.

The doctor hesitated, looked down at the rifle and up again at Shmeltzer.

"Put it down, you fucking little rat!"

"Oh, God," said Peggy Cassidy from the floor.

Al Biyadi dropped the rifle, a second short of dying.

"On the ground, on your belly!" ordered Shmeltzer. Al Biyadi complied.

Shmeltzer kept his gun trained on Al Biyadi's spine, advanced carefully, and kicked the rifle out of the bastard's reach. He was to find out, moments later, that the weapon had been unloaded.

65

So pretty, thought the Grinning Man, eyeing the young cop's body laid out naked on the table.

Every muscle outlined in relief, like fine sculpture, the skin firm and smooth, the facial features perfectly formed.

Adonis. No hook-nose.

Hard to believe this one was kikeshit. He'd searched the dumbfuck's pockets, hoping to find a non-kike ID, something indicating he was an Aryan who'd somehow been duped into working for the kikes.

But there was no wallet, no papers. Just a Star of David on a thin gold chain stuffed into one of the pockets.

Hiding the kikeness. The dumbfuck was kikeshit.

It was wrong, an insult.

The dumbfuck was a genetic fluke, sneak thief of Aryan genes.

But *pretty*. The last time he'd seen anything male that looked this good was years ago, back in stinkhole Sumbok. Fourteen-year-old Gauguin Boy brought in dead to the Gross Anatomy Lab—sold for small change by his family, ninety pounds of medical research material.

Ninety pounds of prime protoplasm: coppery skin, smoky long-lashed eyes, glossy black hair. Little slant had died from acute bacterial meningitis; once he'd sawed open the skull and exposed the cerebral cortex, the damage was obvious, all that yellow-green mucus clogging the meninges.

But, despite the brain-rot, the body remained beautiful, firm, smooth as a girl's. Smooth as Sarah. Hard to believe he was a hundred percent slant—hard to believe he was *male*.

But rotten to the core, even in death:

The little slant bastard had ruined his plans!

It reaffirmed his code:

Males were to be finished fast: the kill-blow to the face or a tracheal-rupture death-choke. The power-jolt, that final look of surprise before the lights went out.

Now you know who's in charge.

Bye-bye.

Females were to be savored. Saved. For real science.

But this one on the table was pretty. Near-female.

Female enough?

His first impulse after cold-cocking the dumbfuck had been to finish him off as he lay there, one good boot-stomp to the face, leaving him behind the reporter's building along with the other kikeshit.

Then he looked at the face, the body, saw something that made him shake.

So pretty.

He got hard.

Disturbing thoughts, as painful as bee stings, darted around in his head:

Pretty as a faggot?

Girl or boy?

He swatted away the thoughts, concentrated on the dumbfuck lying inert, under his control.

Dumbfuck was a faggot.

The SS had known what to do with faggots.

Grandpa Hermann had known what to do with faggots.

Real science. The prospect of adventure: *That's* what had made him hard.

He took a deep breath, held it; the bee-sting thoughts flew away. Quickly, he went through the pockets of the faggot's designer jeans, found car keys, confiscated them along with the gun the faggot had dropped, then gave the faggot a nighty-night shot of H to keep him quiet. Then, out front to the street, trying car doors until he found the lock that matched the keys.

Taking risks but enjoying the endocrine-rush. His Mideast safari almost over, why not squeeze out every bit of pleasure before moving on to the next project?

He found the car soon enough: beat-up VW bug—faggot had left it unlocked. He drove it back to the alley, dumped the faggot's unconscious body in the trunk. Found costume changes, identity changes—dumbfuck thought *he* knew how to play that game! Then a five-minute drive to the German *Haus*, the VW stashed in the garage next to his Mercedes. Another five minutes and Faggot Adonis was stretched out and tied up on the dining room table.

Kike Adonis. Too pretty—very wrong. An affront to the Schwann-code, it was up to him to avenge it.

Improvise.

And why not? Improvisation was fine if you did it with style. After all, his final act would be a *grand* improvisation, the ultimate fuel-jolt that really got Project *Untermensch* off the ground.

Surprise, surprise. Let the games begin.

The dumbfuck stirred on the table, made a clicking sound from deep in his throat.

He reached over, checked the faggot's pulse and respiration, made sure he wasn't about to vomit and choke on it.

All systems functioning normally.

Dumbfuck was quiet again. Pretty.

Yes, *definitely* pretty enough for a real science excursion.

Exploring the faggot cavity—Grandpa Hermann would approve.

Expand the boundaries: males, females, dogs, cats, rats, reptiles, *Arachnida, Coelenterata*—all soft tissue and pain receptors. The differences were minor when you got right down to it. Arbitrary. When you opened a body, looked into the welcome hole, the visceral mural, you realized the sameness. Everyone was the same.

In terms of meat.

Not mind.

A fine Aryan Schwann-mind was in a different cognitive sphere from *untermensch* hollow-head brainscum.

And this young, naked one on his table was ikey-kikey faggot kikeshit, wasn't he?

Pretty.

But *male.*

More bee stings:

He'd explored a male before. It had ruined his plans.

Since then he'd been disciplined. The males finished lightning-fast, the females for exploration.

But he'd come a long way since then. Learned how to be careful, how to clean up perfectly.

Sting.

Swat.

Fuck it! He was in charge; no need to be hemmed in any longer by what Gauguin Boy had done to him.

Just the *opposite:* He needed to *break free* of constraints. Liberate himself. Dieter Schwann and Grandpa Hermann would want that, would be proud of his creativity.

Suddenly he knew why the young cop had been delivered to him: The dumbfuck was there to *save* him, to be savored by him. Dessert after the final act. A bouquet of roses tossed onstage after a bravura performance.

Roses from Dieter, a message: Free thyself.

His decision was clear.

Keep the dumbfuck tied up nice and snuggly-wuggly; pump him with enough H to keep him calm; then, after the final curtain had fallen, come back, wake him up, give him some more H—no, *curare,* just like the dog. Motor paralysis accompanied by total mental awareness!

Lying frozen as ice, corpse-helpless, but hearing and seeing and smelling. *Knowing!*

Exactly what was going on.

Exactly what was being done *to* him.

The terror all in the eyes.

Bow wow wow.

A superb plan. He finalized it in his head, started preparing a batch of new needles, thinking:

This will free me forever from Sumbok memories.

But as he thought about it, Sumbok memories bore through his mind, making high-pitched bad-machine noises, like termites crunching through masonry.

He touched himself, stroked himself, trying to get past the noise. Dropped a glass syringe on the floor and barely heard it shatter as he grappled with images. Doctor's smug, puffy face:

Well, I finally found a place for you. Not much of a med school, but a med school. Cost me a fortune to convince them to take you. If you manage somehow to get through four years and pass the foreign graduate exam, you might be able to find an internship somewhere.

Fucking smugsmile. Translate: You'll never do it, stupid.

Showed how much *he* knew, the lame fuck. For all practical purposes, he was already a doctor; all that was left was to make it legal by matching his Dr. Terrific hands-on experience with boring books, paper formalities. Then, claim his birthright:

Dieter Schwann, II., M.D., Ph.D., Aryan conqueror of the welcome hole. Mengele-magician-artisan, painting the visceral mural.

The seed preserved!

He'd filled out the application forms with a sense of joy and purpose, readied himself for the adventure, masturbating to happy graduation pictures: himself ten feet tall, in black satin doctor's robes collared with velvet, a satin mortarboard tilted with just the right cockiness. Collecting certificates of honor, delivering the valedictory, then dedicating the Dieter Schwann, M.D., Chair in Surgical Pathology and Visceral Exploration at the University of Berlin.

Bravo.

Living off those pictures for two butt-numbing days of air travel to Djakarta, only to feel the joy die inside of him as the rattling shuttle prop landed on that putrid, humid shithole of an island.

A lumpy brown patch. Water all around, like some cartoon. Sand and mud and droopy trees.

Where are we?

The pilot, a rotten-toothed half-breed, had turned off the

engine, opened the door, and tossed his luggage out onto the landing strip.

Welcome to Sumbok, Doc.

Reality: mosquitoes and swamps and grass huts and pock-marked Gauguin-scum hobbling around in loincloths and T-shirts. Pigs and goats and ducks living in the huts, mounds of shit everywhere. On the south side of the island, a muck-filled stagnant bay, jellyfish and sea slugs and other disgusting things washing up on the beach, putrefying, sliming the sand. The rest of it jungle: snakes, nightmare bugs as big as rats, rats as big as dogs, hairy things that gibbered and shrieked in the night.

The so-called *school:* a bunch of rusting Quonset huts, cement-floored wooden cabins for dormitories, the bunks hooded with mosquito netting. One big, crumbling stucco building for classrooms. In the basement, the Gross Anatomy Lab.

A hand-painted tin sign over the front door: *The Grand Medical Facility of St. Ignatius.*

Big joke, ha ha.

Except that he was *living* it.

The so-called *students:* a bunch of losers. Morons, dopers, chronic complainers, perverts of sullied ethnic origin. The *faculty:* slant creeps with M.D.'s from dubious places. Delivering their lectures in pidgin accents no normal person could understand, taking delight in insulting the students, insisting on being addressed as Professor. He felt like hate-beaming into their slant-eyes, smiling:

Heavy starch in the shirts, One Hung Low.

Total scam, no one gave a shit. Most of the students gave up and went home after a few months, forfeiting two years' tuition paid in advance. The others got the energy leeched out of them and turned into bums—pissing away days sunning themselves on the beach, nights given over to smoking dope, jerking off under the mosquito netting, wandering the island trying to seduce twelve-year-old Gauguin-girls.

Depraved. He knew if he let himself be sucked into their apathy, he'd be sidetracked from the Schwann mission. Wondered how to insulate himself, decided an identity change was in order—identity changes always cleansed the mind, renewed the spirit.

And he knew which identity to assume, the only one that would enable him to float above it all.

He went and talked to the dean. Slantiest slant of all, nasty little shit with greasy Dracula hair, oily yellow skin, pig eyes, pencil-line mustache, potbelly as if he'd swallowed a melon. But with a fancy Dutch name: Professor Anton Bromet Van der Veering, M.D., D.Sc.

Pretentious little scrotebag.

Sitting behind a big, messy desk, surrounded by books he never read. Smoking a meerschaum pipe carved in the shape of a naked woman.

Slant took a long time to light the pipe, made him stand there for a while before acknowledging his presence. He filled the time by visualizing smashing the scrote's face, meerschaum chips atop the bloody yellow pulp like confectioners' sugar on a lemon tart. . . .

Yes, what is it?

I want to change my name, Dean.

What? What are you talking about?

I want to change my name.

Surely this is a legal matter, to be taken up with—

Legal matters don't concern me, Dean. This is a personal issue.

Talking low and serious, one doctor to another, the way he'd seen Doctor confer with his associates while discussing a case.

Scrote was confused. Dense. *I really don't see what—*

From now on I want to be known as Dieter Terrif.

Spelling it.

Confusion in the pig eyes: *This your real name? Terrif?*

In a manner of speaking.

I don't—

It's my real name.

Then why did you enroll as—

A long story, Dean.

Charming smile: And for our purposes, irrelevant. The important thing is from now on I want to be known as Dieter Terrif. When I graduate, the diploma will say Dieter Terrif, M.D., Ph.D.

A slip. The scrote caught it, pounced on it:

We don't grant Ph.D.'s, Mister—

I realize that. I'm planning on continuing my studies past the M.D. Surgical pathology, histological research.

Scrote was definitely confused. That was the problem with dealing with inferior types.

Really, now, this is highly irregular.

Scrote fondled the breasts of the meerschaum lady, pig eyes widening as he watched the money land on his desk.

One, two, three, four, five hundred-dollar bills, fanned out like a green poker hand.

Will this help regularize it?

A greedy hand reaching out. Then, hesitation. More greed.

Five hundred more landed on the desk.

What do you say, Dean?

Well, I suppose . . .

Little shit held a grudge against him after that, looked at him strangely every time they passed each other.

No matter. His new identity cleansed him. Six months of medical studies went by fast, despite tropical storms and heavy rains that brought more mosquitoes to the island; a plague of hairy spiders, spiny lizards, and other creepy-crawlies making their way into the dormitories, scuttling across night sheets, melding bad dreams with reality.

His fellow students woke up screaming. More morons started dropping out, talking about pharmacy school, chiropractic.

None of that second-rate bullshit for him.

He floated above it, cracking the books. Filling his head with doctor-words, taking special pleasure in Gross Lab, spending extra time there. Alone in the basement.

He had little use for food or sleep, was preparing himself for his rightful role as prizewinning pathologist on the staff of Columbia Presbyterian Hospital.

Then came the day they wheeled Gauguin Boy into the lab, brain-ravaged, but the body so beautiful.

The cadaver got assigned to another student. He bribed the moron, exchanged a disgusting, shriveled old man, plus cash, for the boy.

Came back late at night to study. And cut. Lit the lamp over his dissecting table, left the rest of the room dark. Opened the black leather case, took out a dancer and made a real science Y incision. Cracked the sternum, pinned back the skin flaps.

And saw the internal beauty.

He wanted to dive in, swim among the colors, unite with the cells, the structure, the primal soup of life.

Be as one.

And why not?

Moving automatically, without thinking, he was stripping off his clothes, his nakedness delicious and holy. The lab, hot and humid and reeking of formaldehyde and rot, crickets chirping inside and out. But he wasn't afraid, wasn't sweating, so cool with purpose, floating above it all.

Then descending. On top of the boy, the hole a window to beauty, welcoming him.

Merge.

Coolflesh.

A moment of indescribable ecstasy, then betrayal:

Pidgin curses. The lights sharp and blinding.

Professor Anton Bromet Van der Veering, M.D., D.Sc., standing in the doorway, pipe in hand, the naked-lady meerschaum resembling a tiny female victim struggling in his slimy yellow fingers.

Staring, the piggy-slant eyes so bugged out they'd become round.

Fucker expelled him that night, gave him three days to leave the island. Remained resolute, beyond the lure of more money.

The first time in St. Ignatius history. Hot death-shame took hold of him and made him tremble as he packed. He considered letting a dancer jitterbug along his own wrists, ending it all, then realized it was an honor to be expelled.

He was lucky: set free from a *shitpile,* separated from stink. Too clean and noble for this place. It was all part of a plan—of Schwann's plan.

Dieter-Daddy had better things in mind for him. Cleaner things.

He put aside failure-thoughts and gave himself a bon voyage party. Gauguin Girl down by the river, washing clothes. Exchange of smiles. *Hi, I'm Dr. Terrific.* The sweet bliss of real science, in the creamy green silence of the jungle.

He used her bucket and river water to wash her. Left her lying under an enormous mango tree—more bloody fruit to match the soft, festering ones that had fallen to the ground.

Bye-bye, stinkhole.

A stopover in Amsterdam, sluts in windows—he would have loved to play real science with them, but no time.

Back home, he went to see Doctor in his office at the hospital. Kikefuck said nothing, shot him I-told-you-so taunt-beams with his silence.

You'll find me another school. A real one.

Oh, sure, just like that.

Bet on it. Knowing he had the fucker's balls in his pocket.

But a week later the fucker was history. Keeled over in the operating room, dropped dead right on top of a patient.

First-class joke: Famous heart surgeon dies of heart attack. Raking in big bucks bypassing other people's arteries; meanwhile, his own were sludging up.

Funny, but not funny. In death, the fucker got in his last licks: left him out of the will. Everything signed over to Sarah.

As if she needed it, out of Harvard, Mass General, a psychiatrist with a brand-new Boston practice. And married to that fat little hook-nosed kikeshit, also a shrink; on top of everything else, his family was filthy rich. The two of them raking it in, with their Beacon Hill town house, summer home "on the Cape," Mercedes, good clothes, theater tickets.

He and Sarah barely noticed each other at the funeral. He stared at her tits, but kept to himself, talked to no one. She interpreted it as heavy-duty grief, wrote him a letter stinking of phony sympathy, signing over the deed to the pink *Haus* to him.

Throw a bone to stupid little brother.

One day he'd kill her for it.

Deprived of his ball-hold on Doctor, he took time to reassess his situation: He owned his cars. The portfolio was doing nicely—couple of hundred thou. The savings account had forty-two thou—money he'd saved up over the years from his hospital job, pill profits. His clothes, his costumes. The books in the library. The big green book. The Schwann bible. The dancers in their velvet leather crib.

He sold the pink house cheap and fast, took in another four hundred thousand. After taxes and commission, two hundred thirty thou was left.

He put it all in the bank. Boxed the books, stashed them in the Plymouth, drove around looking for a place to live, and found an apartment near Nasty: two bedrooms, two baths, clean and cheap. Twenty bucks a month extra for two parking spaces.

He spent two days scrubbing the place from floorboard to ceiling, set up bedroom number two as a lab. Went back to the hospital and got his mail-delivery job back, stole more pills than ever, and sold them for higher profit margins. Added to his fortune, spent his free time in the library.

His vacation time was set aside for travel. Medical conventions, pleasure trips, using interesting identities, becoming new people.

Travel was *fun*. Trapping and hunting.

Now, he'd really expanded his vistas, was an international hunter.

Back in Europe: nightwork in Amsterdam. After all those years, he'd gotten back there, found a slant window-slut, took her down to the docks, and initiated her into the world of real science.

Bought H from a diamond-eared nigger on Kalverstraat near the Dam Square, packed it without worry—U.N. luggage got V.I.P. treatment. Besides, who would think of bringing the stuff *into* the Middle East?

Then on to Kikeland.

A German *Haus* in Kikeland.

So real, so right.

While drawing up his safari plan in New York, he'd known he wanted a second place, his own place, away from the others. There was an all-night newsstand on Broadway, near Times Square. He went to it one Friday night and bought *The Jerusalem Post,* U.S. edition. Took it home and checked the classifieds under *Dwellings, Jerusalem—Rentals* and read magic words:

VILLA, GERMAN COLONY, 3 RMS, AMENITIES, FURN, 1 YR. MIN.

A phone number in New York.

The German Colony. He looked it up at the main branch of the New York Public Library, in the *Encyclopedia Judaica.* Old southern Jerusalem neighborhood named after the German Templar sect that had lived there from the 1870's until the Führer's Holy War, when they were kicked out by the British for distributing Nazi literature.

Aryans in Kikeland, brothers in spirit! So real, so right!

The kikefuck who'd run the ad was a professor named Gordon, on sabbatical at City University of New York. More than happy to rent him the place, especially after he offered a year's rent up front in cash, plus damage deposit.

Phony name, Manhattan post office box as an address.

Everything conducted over the telephone.

Cash in the mail, keys mailed to the box three days later.

A month later he was walking through the place, knowing it was rightfully his.

Old, dark, tile-roofed *Haus,* shadowed by big trees, hidden from the road. A main entrance in front and another through the back. A closed double garage. And a bonus he learned about months later: just south of Liberty Bell Park, hop, skip, and jump to the tower where the nigger-kike Sharavi lived.

A clear view of the tower.

Him and his dog and his nigger friends and his kikey-ikey family.

Had to be fate, everything coming together.

He'd made himself comfy in his German *Haus.* Would have given anything to see the look on Gordon's hook-nosed face when he returned next year and found out what had been done to his little kikenest, the trade he'd made for the fucking *damage deposit.*

But Doctor Terrific would be long gone, by then. On to new adventures.

The faggot-cop on the table stirred again, pretty eyelashes fluttering, lips parting as if for a kiss.

He filled a syringe with H, then decided to hold off.

Let him wake up, see the swastikas on the walls, the heads and pelts and messages from Dieter. Then put him back under.

Faggot opened his eyes wide. Then his mouth, which was quickly filled with a wadded-up cloth.

Taking in the room, gulping and thrusting and straining against the ropes.

"Hi, I'm Dr. Terrific. What seems to be the problem?"

66

Monday, two A.M. The cries and pleadings of Margaret Pauline Cassidy still filled Daniel's ears as he left the interrogation room.

A Mossad guard man handed him the message slip: Rav Pakad Harel needed to speak to him immediately. He left the subground interrogation suite, took the stairs up to the third floor, and wondered what the Latam chief had come up with. As he climbed, his thoughts returned to Cassidy.

Pathetic young woman. She'd entered the session spitting defiance, still believing Al Biyadi intended to marry her, that their relationship had something to do with love.

Shmeltzer had torn into her, stripped away those fantasies in no time at all.

It opened her up fast. The tape recorder was gorging itself on names, dates, and numbers by the time the brass stormed in: Laufer, *his* boss, high-ranking tight-lipped boys from Mossad and Shin Bet. Taking over. The case was now national security, Shmeltzer and Daniel allowed to stay but relegated to observer status.

Priorities were clear, Laufer's attitude an excellent barometer. Since the Amelia Catherine covert, the deputy commander had abandoned his hands-off stance, insisted upon receiving daily progress reports, copies of the medical charts, the Sumbok list, the logs of the surveillance from the law building. But this morning he had no time for any of it, showed not the slightest curiosity about the case.

Fine, fine, Sharavi. Rushing past Daniel in order to question the terrorists.

Daniel watched, too, sitting behind one-way glass, as a Mossad investigator walked the soil Shmeltzer had plowed.

Three interrogations proceeded simultaneously. A marathon.

Al Biyadi in one room; next door his cousin, the phony charwoman. Both of them toughing it out, silent as dust.

But Cassidy had spilled to Nahum. He'd ignored her insults, the anti-Semitic slurs, kept picking and tearing at her resistance until he made her see that she'd been used and demeaned.

When the insight hit her, she did an immediate about-face, turning her wrath upon Al Biyadi, vomiting out her shame and hurt, talking so fast they'd had to slow her down, tell her to speak so that the recorder picked up more than mush.

And talk she did: How Hassan had seduced her, strung her along with promises of matrimony, a big house back in America, back in Huntington Beach, California. Children, cars, the good life.

Just one more assignment before settling down to eternal domestic bliss. A dozen *one more*'s; a score.

She'd started by composing and distributing PLO literature for him in Detroit, typing and proofreading the English versions, delivering boxfuls at out-of-the-way night drops. Meeting men in cafes, smiling Arab men. In retrospect she realized they'd had no respect for her, had been mocking her. At the time she'd thought them mysterious, charming.

Running errands. Picking up parcels at Detroit Metropolitan Airport. Making coded phone calls and taking down incomprehensible messages. Side trips up to Canada, delivering packages to a row house in Montreal, returning with other packages to Michigan. Serving coffee and donuts to Hassan's friends as they met in the basement of a Black Muslim mosque. All of it in her spare time—going off shift at Harper Hospital and heading straight for her unpaid second job. But reimbursed by love, freeing her lover to complete his medical studies. The lack of romance sometimes painful. But telling herself that he was a patriot with more important things on his mind than movies and dinner dates. A patriot in jeopardy—the Zionists were watching him; he needed to maintain an apolitical stance.

He made love to her infrequently, told her she was a warrior-heroine, the kind of woman he wanted as mother of his children.

They signed up for the U.N. job together, planned to carry their activism to Palestine. Here, too, he doctored while she did the dirty work.

She composed twenty different propaganda pamphlets, found a printer in Nablus who could make them up in English, French, and Arabic. Made contact with the PLO operatives who came to the Amelia Catherine disguised as patients, growing close to one of them—Hassan's cousin, Samra. A pretty, dark girl, also trained as a nurse but working full-time for the liberation of Palestine. Hassan introduced them to each other in one of the examining rooms; an easy bond of friendship followed soon. The two women became confidantes, tutor and student.

Samra coached, Peggy performed well.

In February she was promoted to more important functions: serving as a conduit between Hassan and arms smugglers in Jordan, making payoffs, overseeing early morning transfers of the wooden crates to the big house on Ibn Haldoun.

Samra lived in a flat in Sheikh Jarrah, but the house was hers, deeded to her family—a rich family, like Hassan's. Her father had been a judge in East Jerusalem before escaping to Amman in '67.

Good friend, Cousin Samra.

In reality she was no cousin at all, but a wife. The one and only Mrs. Hassan Al Biyadi. A Jordanian marriage certificate found in her purse proved it, complete with signature by her father the judge.

Shmeltzer had waved the dogeared piece of paper in Cassidy's face, told her she was a gullible idiot, a stupid, stupid girl who deserved to be deceived.

She screamed denial. The old detective slapped her out of her hysteria and continued to attack her verbally, savagely, to the point where Daniel thought of intervening. But he didn't and finally the denial gave way to a new grasp on reality. Peggy Cassidy sat in her chair, shaking, gulping water, bubbling at the mouth, unable to spill her guts fast enough.

Yes, she'd known the first two Butcher victims were Amelia Catherine patients—Hassan's patients. Had wanted to tell someone—Mr. Baldwin, at least. But Hassan forbade it, said their cover was more important, they couldn't afford police probing around the hospital.

She began weeping: "Those poor women!" Hassan hadn't cared, didn't care about anyone! He was a pig—the Arabs were all pigs. Filthy, sexist pigs, she hoped they all rotted in hell, hoped the Jews killed every single one of them.

One extreme to the other.

An unstable girl. Daniel wondered how she'd cope with prison.

Amos Harel was waiting outside his office, pacing and smoking. Unlike him to show nervousness; something was wrong.

Gauloise butts littered the floor. The door was closed. As Daniel came closer, he saw the look on the Latam chief's face and a flame ignited in his belly.

"One of my men is dead," said Harel hoarsely. "Itzik Nash, strangled in the alley behind the reporter's building. Your man, Cohen, is missing—no trace of the car we gave him. We found his radio near Itzik's body. They were supposed to maintain regular contact—Cohen was probably checking up on Itzik when he got hit. The reporter's also dead, bludgeoned to pulp up in his flat, swastikas painted in blood all over his bedroom walls—his own blood, according to Forensics. They're still there swabbing and dusting. The Canadian, Carter, is the only suspect who was out last night. No one knows where the fuck he is."

Daniel knew Itzik Nash—they'd attended Police School together. A roly-poly guy with a ready arsenal of lewd jokes. Daniel visualized him wearing the thick-tongued idiot's yawn of the strangulation victim. Thought of Avi in the Butcher's hands and found himself trembling.

"God. What the hell happened!"

Harel took hold of the doorknob, twisted savagely, and shoved the door open. Inside his office sat a Latamnik—the man who'd broadcast as Relic. He was staring at the floor. Harel's throat-clearing raised his face, and Daniel saw that his eyes were lifeless, filmed over. He looked withered, a husk of himself. The code name strangely apt.

"Get the hell out here and tell him what happened," ordered Harel.

"He faked us out," said the Latamnik, coming to the doorway.

Harel put his face close to his man's, sprayed Relic with spittle as he talked: "No *vidduy*, just facts."

Relic licked his lips, nodded, recited: "Carter took the predictable path, Ben Adayah to Sultan Suleiman, walked right by me. I picked up his trail the moment he passed the Rockefeller, followed him up Nablus Road and into the Pilgrim's Vision Hotel. Place was empty, just the night clerk. Carter registered, went up the stairs. I leaned on the clerk; he told me the room number—three-oh-two—and that Carter had ordered a whore. I asked if Carter had ever stayed there before—did he have any particular whore in mind? The clerk said no to both. There was only one roundheels working this late—she was up in one of the other rooms, would be free in fifteen minutes. He was planning to send her up then. I warned him not to let on anything was up, took a house key, and waited in the room behind the desk. When the whore showed up and picked up the key, I followed her to three-oh-two, let her go in, waited maybe fifteen seconds, then went in myself."

The Latamnik shook his head, still unbelieving. "She was all alone, Pakad, sitting on the bed reading a comic book. Not a trace of Carter. The window was bolted, dusty—it hadn't been opened recently. I looked everywhere for him, tried other rooms, the communal lavatory. Nothing. He must have slipped out the back way—there's a rear stairway leading out to Pikud Hamerkaz."

"Didn't you call for backup?" demanded Daniel. His hands were clenched at his sides, his abdomen searing. His body so tense the muscles threatened to burst through the skin.

"Sure, sure. I know the layout of the hotel—we watched it

last winter on a dope surveillance. I radioed for help first chance I had—while waiting for the whore to show up, maybe three minutes after Carter arrived. The closest guy was one of ours, Vestreich on Habad Street, but if he left, it meant no coverage for the Old City. So your Arab, Daoud, came over from Kishle, maybe five, six minutes later, and stationed himself out back."

"Could Carter have known you were following him?"

"No way. I stayed twenty meters behind, always in the shadows. God wouldn't have spotted me."

"Could anyone have warned Carter about you?"

Relic pressed himself against the corridor wall, as if trying to shrink. "No way. I had my eye on the clerk at all times; no one else around. I wanted to have him phone Carter's room to confirm the bastard was up there, but the Palace is a shithole, half a star, no phone service to the rooms, no way to send a message. I tell you, Daoud was out back in five minutes—he didn't see him leave."

"Plus the three minutes before you called makes eight," said Daniel. "Plenty of time."

"Four wouldn't have been enough—bastard never went up to the room in the first place! Never made it to the third floor, at all. He probably climbed one flight, walked through to the back stairs, and slipped out before Daoud arrived. He used the goddamned hotel as a tunnel."

"Where's Daoud now?"

"Looking for Cohen," said Relic. "If Carter had gone south, back on Sultan Suleiman, Daoud would have run right into him, so he must have headed north, up Pikud Hamerkaz, maybe west to Mea She'arim or straight up to Sheikh Jarrah. We alerted Northwest and Northeast Sectors—no one's seen a damn thing."

The Latamnik turned to his boss. "Fucking bastard faked us out, Amos. We were told he was probably unaware of the surveillance, but that's bullshit. The way he acted, he had to suspect something was up—he paid cash, didn't register in his own name—"

"Terrif," muttered Daniel. "He registered as D. Terrif."

"Yes," said Relic, feebly, as if another surprise would tax his heart. "How'd you know?"

Daniel ignored him, dashed away.

He ran down the four flights to subground, insisted, over the protests of the Mossad guard, that Deputy Commander Laufer be pulled out of the interrogation.

Laufer came out flushed and indignant, ready to do battle. Before he could open his mouth, Daniel said, "Be quiet and listen. Harel's Itzik Nash is dead. Avi Cohen may be dead too." As he related the details of the surveillance disaster, Laufer deflated like a punctured tire.

"Shit. Cohen. Was the kid ready for something like this?"

Stupid bastard, thought Daniel. Even now, he's looking to pin blame. "Carter's out there somewhere," he said, ignoring the question. "Cohen's car is nowhere in sight, which could mean it's garaged. It supports our suspicion of a second place—a second kill spot, away from the hospital. I want authorization to go into the Amelia Catherine, go through Carter's room and see if we can come up with an address. And a release of the bastard's picture to the press in time to make tomorrow's editions."

Laufer shifted his weight from one foot to another. "I don't know."

Daniel restrained himself from grabbing the idiot's collar. "What's the problem!"

"The timing's bad, Sharavi."

Daniel curled the fingers of his bad hand, raised the ravaged flesh in front of the deputy commander's face. "I've got a maniac on the loose, a new hire in danger of being slaughtered—what does it take!"

Laufer stepped back, looking sad, almost sympathetic. "Wait," he said, and went back into the interrogation room. Daniel waited while the minutes flowed slowly as honey, drowning in inertia, chafing to be *doing* something. Despite the frigid air-conditioning, the sweat was pouring out of him in cold rivulets; he caught a whiff of his body odor. Acrid. Toxic with rage.

The D.C. came back shaking his head.

"Not yet. Mossad wants no attention drawn to the hospital —no tip-offs—until all the members of Al Biyadi's terrorist cell are in custody. Most are local assholes—they're being round-up right now. But the big boss—the one directing Al Biyadi—left for Paris through Damascus, last week. We're waiting for confirmation that our French operatives have him."

"What about *my* operative, damn you! What about Cohen laid out on some table for dissection!"

The D.C. ignored the insubordination, talked softly and rhythmically, with the exaggerated patience reserved for mental defectives and hostage-takers. "We're not talking about a long delay, Sharavi. A few hours until the local busts are accomplished. The Paris data could arrive any minute—a day at the longest."

"A day!" Daniel spat on the floor, pointed toward the closed door of the interrogation room. "Let me go in there and talk to them. Let me show them pictures of what this monster does."

"Pictures won't impress them, Sharavi. They have a nice scrapbook of their own: the Japs mowing down pilgrims at Ben Gurion, the Ma'alot school bus, Qiryat Shemona, Nahariya. That house was a fucking arsenal—pistols, Kalashnikovs, fragmentation grenades, a fucking *rocket launcher*! They had plans to shoot up the Western Wall during Shabbat *shaharit* services—preferably during a big tourist Bar Mitzvah. Schematics of the best places to place bombs at the Rabinovitz Playground, the Tiferet Shlomo Orphans' Home, the zoo, Liberty Bell Park—think of the pictures that would create, Sharavi. Hundreds of dead kids! Cassidy says there are two other arms storehouses—in Beit Jalla and Gaza. Cleaning up a mess of that magnitude is more important than one maniac." He stopped, hesitated. "More important, even, than one detective, who's probably dead already."

Daniel turned to go.

Laufer grabbed his arm.

"You're not being fucked over totally. As of this moment, finding Carter is top departmental priority—*as a covert.* The hospital is being watched—asshole shows his face, he's in custody before his heart takes another beat. You want men, you've got them, the entire goddamned Latam, the Border Patrol, airplanes, whatever. Every cruise car will have a picture of Carter—"

"Six cars," said Daniel. "One's in the shop."

"Not just Jerusalem," said Laufer. "Every city. You're worried five cars can't cover our streets—take my goddamned Volvo. I'll put my goddamned driver out on patrol, okay? You want an address on Carter? Check housing records, utility bills, the goddamned phone bills—every clerk and computer in the goddamned city is at your disposal. The slightest whiff of bullshit, call me immediately. The moment the cell's been busted, the hospital's open territory."

"I want access to U.N. records."

"You'll have to wait on that," said Laufer. "One of Al Biyadi's terrorist chums is a secretary at U.N. headquarters on the Hill of Evil Counsel. No surprise, eh?"

Laufer's fingers were moist on his arm. Daniel pried them loose.

"I've got work to do."

"Don't fuck up," said Laufer. "This is serious."

"See me smiling?" Daniel turned and began walking away.

"You and Shmeltzer will get credit for the armory bust," Laufer called after him. "Service medals."

"Terrific," said Daniel, over his shoulder. "I'll give them to Cohen's mother."

He reached the Chinaman by radio at three o'clock, Daoud five minutes later. Both had been cruising the city for signs of Avi or the Volkswagen. He called them in, convened a meeting with his three remaining detectives and Amos Harel.

"Goddamned kid," said the Chinaman. "God damn him. Probably pulled some John Wayne stunt before he got hit."

"Everything indicates he was playing by the rules," said Daniel. But Laufer's question had come back to haunt him: The kid was less than dependable. *Had* he been ready?

"Whatever," said the Chinaman. "What now, pictures of the bastard in all the papers?"

"No." He informed them of the Mossad restriction, felt the anger in the room harden into something dark and menacing.

Daoud expelled breath, closed his eyes and rubbed his temples, as if in great pain. Shmeltzer got up and circled the room like an old jackal. Harel took out a Gauloise and crushed it, unlit, between his fingers.

"Goddamned cloak-and-dagger mothercunts!" exploded the Chinaman. "I tell you—"

"No time for that, Yossi," Daniel cut him off. "Let's get organized, make sure he doesn't get away this time. Amos is giving us every man we need—he'll be coordinating lookouts along the Jerusalem to Tel Aviv Road and up the coastal road, train stations, bus stations, Ben Gurion, every harbor including the freighter docks at Eilat. When I'm through, he'll give you the details.

"The army's on alert in the territories—Marciano's in charge in Judea; Yinon in Samaria, Barbash in Gaza. The Border Patrol's conducting individual searches at the Allenby Bridge and Metulla, tightening things up along all perimeters and within the Old City. They're also staking out forested areas and are stationed near the murder cave. Telescopic surveillance of the Amelia Catherine has been expanded to another infrared from the desert aimed at the rear of the compound."

He unfolded several sheets of paper. "These are the home numbers of records clerks and their bosses at the phone company, the Licensing Office, the Ministry of Construction and Housing, the Ministry of Energy, all the banks. We'll divide them up, start waking people, try and find the home away from home. Look for Carters and Terrifs—include all spelling variations. Now that we know who he is, he won't be able to get far."

But to himself he thought: Why should catching a madman be easier than finding my own dog.

He worked until six, setting up and monitoring the search for Richard Carter, before allowing himself a cup of coffee which his dry throat and aching stomach rejected. At six-ten he went back to his office and pulled out the notes he'd taken during his first and only meeting with Carter. Read them for the twentieth time and watched Carter's face materialize before his mind's eye.

An unremarkable face, no monster, no devil. In the end it was always like that. Eichmanns, Landrus, Kurtens, and Barbies. Disappointingly human, depressingly mundane.

Amira Nasser had supposedly talked about mad eyes, empty eyes. A killer's grin. All he remembered about Carter's eyes were that they were narrow and gray. Gray eyes behind old-fashioned round eyeglasses. A full ginger beard. The shambling, careless carriage of a backpacker.

Former hippie. A dreamer.

Some dreamer: a nightmare machine.

He forced coffee down his throat and recalled something else—incongruous chuckling in response to his questions.

Something amusing, Dr. Carter?

Big fingers running through the beard. A smile—if there had been something evil about the smile, it had eluded him.

Not really. Just that this sounds like one of those cop shows back home—where were you on the night and all that.

The bastard had seemed so casual, so relaxed.

Daniel punished himself with self-scrutiny. Had he been careless, missed something? A psychopathic glint in the gray eyes?

Some near-microscopic evidence of evil that he, as a detective, was expected to pick up on?

He replayed the mental movie of the interview. Reviewed his notes again. Questions, answers, the smiles.

Where were you on the night and all that.

And where are you tonight, Richard Carter, you murderous scum?

67

At seven A.M. Shmeltzer brought him a list of names gleaned from phone books, utility bills, and housing files. Two Carters in Jerusalem, five in Tel Aviv, including a senior officer at the American Embassy. One in Haifa, three more scattered throughout the Galilee. No Richards. Three Trifs, four Trifuses, none of them Richards or initial D's. No Tarrifs or Terrifs. All old listings. He dispatched men to check out the local ones anyway, had the other divisions do the same with the people in their bailiwicks.

At seven-twenty he called home. Laura answered. He heard the boys hollering in the background, music from the radio.

"Good morning, Detective."

"Hello, Laura."

"That bad?"

"Yes."

"Want to talk about it?"

"No."

Pause. "Okay."

He felt impatient with her, intolerant of any problem short of life and death. Still, she was his lover, his best friend, deserved better than to be dismissed like a subordinate. He tried to soften his voice, said, "I'm sorry. I really can't get into it."

"I understand," she said. Automatically.

"I don't know when I'll be home."

"Don't worry. Do what you have to do. I'll be busy all morning with straightening up and finishing the painting for Lu and Gene. After school, Lu and I are taking the boys to the zoo, then to dinner. Shoshi didn't want to go. She's sleeping over at Dorit Shamgar's house—the number's on the refrigerator."

Daniel thought of Mikey and Benny frolicking at the zoo, remembered what Laufer had said about the schematics found in the house on Ibn Haldoun. Horrific bomb-blast visions filled his head. He chased them away—a steady diet of those kinds of thoughts could drive a man crazy.

"Why didn't she want to go to the zoo?" he asked.

"It's for babies; she and Dorit have more important things to do—she wants to be on her own, Daniel. Part of establishing her identity."

"It's not because she's still upset over the dog?"

"Maybe a little of that too. But she'll work it through— Here's Gene. He worked most of the night, refuses to go home and get some rest."

"Okay, put him on. Bye."

"Bye."

"Danny," said Gene. "I've been following up this Terrif thing and—"

"Terrif's a name used by Richard Carter," said Daniel. He filled Gene in on the night's events. Talking to a fellow policeman after excluding his wife.

Gene listened, said, "What a mess. Terrible about your man." Silence. "Carter, huh? Sonofagun. Everything I've got on him spells clean. The records from McGill check out—the med school transcripts clerk said the guy was an honor student there, did very good research on tropical diseases. The Peace Corps said he continued that research with them, saved plenty of lives. With the exception of a bust for marijuana when he was in high school, no one has a bad word to say about him."

"I do," said Daniel. "The records are probably falsified. It would be the least of his sins."

"True. I've got more info for you. Got a minute?"

"Sure."

"I started thinking about the American murder sites—your point about nice weather, vacation spots. Vacation cities are also popular with organizations when it comes to locating their conventions—as in *medical* conventions. I've managed to get through to the chambers of commerce in New Orleans and Miami, convinced them to go through their '73 and '78 convention records, respectively, and found one common thread: The Society for Surgical Pathology held conventions in both. It's a relatively small group of hotshot doctors, but the conventions are attended by lots of people—scientists, technicians, students. I called their headquarters in Washington, D.C. The '73 roster had been tossed out, but they still had the one from August '78. Sure enough, a D. Terrif attended the Miami convention, registered as a student. The convention began two days prior to the murder and ended five days after. My info on Richard Carter is that he was still a student in '78—got his M.D. in '79. But he was doing his first Peace Corps bit in Ecuador that summer."

"How do we know he didn't leave Ecuador and fly to Miami for a week? Used the Terrif name to conceal his identity, then returned to doing good deeds as Carter."

"Dr. Carter, Mr. Terrif. Split personality?"

"Or just a clever psychopath."

"Yeah, it would fit with something else I came up with. After we found that D. Terrif reference in the Shehadeh file, I called one of my buddies at Parker Center, asked him to check all the files for someone by that name. He came up empty, even in the social security files. No such person ever received a card—which is just about every adult who pays taxes in America. Now, Carter's a Canadian, so it wouldn't apply to him, but my buddy said something interesting: that Terrif didn't even look like a bona fide name, that the first thing he thought of was that it was an abbreviation for Terrific."

Daniel thought about it. The kind of linguistic nuance that he'd fail to catch, working in a foreign language.

"D. Terrific," said Gene. "Maybe the D stands for some other name or maybe it stands for Doctor."

"Doctor Terrific."

"Like a superhero. Scum takes on an alter ego when he goes out to kill."

"Yes," said Daniel. "It feels right."

"Doesn't seem immediately helpful," said Gene, "but when you get him to trial, it could be." He started to yawn, stifled it.

"Absolutely," said Daniel. "Thanks for doing all of this, Gene. Now please go back to the hotel and get some sleep."

"Soon. First I want to look into Canadian Terrifs, then see if I can find an old Ecuador-to-Miami plane reservation made out to any Carters or Terrifs. A very long shot, because it was seven years ago, but you never know what pays off. Where you going to be?"

"In and out," said Daniel. "I'll check in with you at the end of the day, if not before."

"Okay. Good luck. And be sure to call me when you catch the scum."

68

Monday, five P.M. One of the local members of Al Biyadi's terrorist cell continued to avoid capture, no word from Paris, and Mossad was still stalling.

Richard Carter had been spotted sixteen times throughout the state of Israel, as far north as Quneitra, as far south as Eilat. Sixteen fair-haired, ginger-bearded men were pulled off the streets for questioning, all eventually released: five Israelis, four Americans, two Britons, two Germans, a Swede, a Dane, and one unfortunate Canadian tourist detained for five hours by Tel Aviv detectives and left behind by his tour group as they boarded an excursion flight to Greece.

Two Volkswagens matching the one Avi Cohen had driven were located and impounded, one on Kibbutz Lavi, the other in Safed. Both owners were interviewed intensively. The Safed car belonged to an artist of wide reputation and mediocre talent who protested loudly that he was being harassed because of left-wing political views. Verification of ownership and registration of both vehicles was obtained.

At six, Daniel and Amos Harel reviewed the written logs of the Amelia Catherine surveillance:

Six-thirteen A.M.: A blue Renault panel truck from the Al Aswadeh Produce Company in East Jerusalem drove around to the rear of the hospital. The chain-link gate was locked. One man got out, walked to the front. Sorrel Baldwin's secretary, Ma'ila Khoury, came out, spoke to him, went back inside. Minutes later,

Khoury unlocked the gate and signed for the groceries. Delivery completed, the truck departed six twenty-eight A.M. License plate number recorded and verified as registered to Al Aswadeh.

Seven-ten A.M.: Zia Hajab arrived at the East Jerusalem bus station on the Ramallah-to-Jerusalem bus. He bought a cold drink from a street vendor, walked from the station to the hospital. By eight A.M. he was sitting at his post.

Nine-twenty A.M.: Dr. Walid Darousha returned from Ramallah in his Peugeot, parked in back, entered the hospital.

Ten-fifteen A.M.: Ma'ila Khoury left the hospital in Sorrel Baldwin's black Lancia Beta and drove to Hamashbir Letzarkhan on King George Street. Spent two hours in the department store, purchasing panty hose, a negligee, and a foam-rubber pillow. Paid for the merchandise with Sorrel Baldwin's U.N. Visa card. Serial number recorded and verified. Ate lunch at Café Max and returned to the hospital at one forty-three P.M.

Eleven A.M.: Fourteen male patients lined up at the entrance to the hospital. Zia Hajab kept them waiting for twenty-two minutes, then let them in. All were gone and accounted for by two forty-five P.M.

Three-eleven P.M.: A Mercedes truck with green cab and metal van painted with the name, address, and phone number of the Bright and Clean Laundry Service of Bethlehem drove around to the back of the hospital. Ten sacks removed, six delivered, along with numerous folded tablecloths and sheets. Some of the sacks were judged large enough to hold a human body. Enlarged photographs of the delivery men revealed all of them to be Arabs, none bearded, none bearing the slightest resemblance to Carter. The truck departed three twenty-four P.M. License plates recorded and verified as registered to Bright and Clean.

Four forty-two P.M.: A new Mercedes glass-top bus brought a group of Christian tourists from the Intercontinental Hotel on the Mount of Olives to the Amelia Catherine. Twenty-three tourists. Nine men, excluding the driver and the guide. No male tourists under the age of sixty. The driver and guide were both Arabs, not tall, dark-haired; one was bearded. Their heights estimated at a meter seven, each. Zia Hajab was given money by the guide, the tourists permitted to enter the courtyard of the hospital, take pictures. The bus departed at four fifty-seven. License plate recorded and verified to Mount of Olives Tour Company, East Jerusalem.

Five forty-eight: A white Mercedes-Benz diesel sedan with United Nations plates drove around to the back of the hospital. A man wearing a *kaffiyah* and Arab robes removed several cardboard boxes labeled RECORDS in Arabic and delivered them to the hospital. Two of the boxes were judged possibly large enough to conceal a human body if the body was bent to the point of contortion. The man was estimated to be approximately the same height as Richard Carter. Several photographs were taken and enlarged. Headdress and position of subject prevented a full-face photo. A partial profile shot revealed a hairless chin and small dark mustache, no spectacles, no resemblance to a computer-enhanced portrait of Richard Carter minus his beard. License plate recorded and verified to U.N. Headquarters at Government House.

"It doesn't say he left," said Daniel.

"He arrived fifteen minutes ago, Dani," said Harel, pointing to the time. "You got this hot off the press. If he spends the night, you'll be the first to know."

At six-fifteen, Daniel drove home for a shower and change of clothes, parked the Escort near the entrance to his building. A faint breeze blew, causing the jacaranda trees to shudder.

He walked to the pebbled-glass exterior door and found it locked. Had the dog returned?

As he fitted his key in the lock, he heard shouts, turned, and saw a rotund figure half a block away, trotting toward him and waving. A white apron flapping in the breeze.

Lieberman, the grocer. Probably a pickup Laura had forgotten.

He waved back, waited. The grocer arrived moments later, breathing hard, wiping his forehead.

"Good evening, Mr. Lieberman."

"Pakad," huffed the grocer, "this . . . is probably nothing, but . . . I wanted to tell you . . . anyway."

"Easy, Mr. Lieberman."

The grocer took a deep breath, patted his chest.

"Football days . . . long gone." He smiled.

Daniel smiled back. He waited until the grocer's breathing had slowed, then said, "What's on your mind, Mr. Lieberman?"

"Probably nothing. I just wanted to keep you in touch—you know how much I see, sitting behind the counter: the human parade. I figure it's my duty to let you know."

"Absolutely, Mr. Lieberman."

"Anyway, about an hour ago, your daughter went off with a guy. Big blackie, said he'd found her dog."

"My American guest is black," said Daniel. Thinking: Good for Gene. The ultimate detective.

"No, no. I've met Mr. Brooker. Not a *shvartze*—a blackie, a fanatic—long black coat, black hat, big beard."

"A Hassid? Shoshi went off with a Hassid?"

"That's what I'm telling you. She'd just come by the grocery. She and her friend were baking cookies, they ran out of chocolate, and Shoshi came by to get some. After I rang her up, she left, had gone maybe five meters and this blackie steps out of a parked car and starts to talk to her. I figured maybe he was one of her teachers or some friend of the—"

"What kind of car?"

"White Mercedes diesel, made a lot of noise—"

Daniel's heart stopped. "Did you see the plates?"

"No, sorry, I—"

"Go on. What happened?"

"This blackie said something about finding the dog. It was injured—he'd take her to it. Shoshi thought about it for a moment. Then she got into the Mercedes and the two of them drove off. A few minutes later I started wondering about it—the guy was religious, but she hadn't seemed to know him. I called your wife—no one answered. I thought maybe I should—"

A voice inside Daniel screamed no, no, no! He gripped Lieberman's soft shoulders. "Tell me what this Hassid looked like."

"Big, like I told you. About your age, maybe older, maybe younger. Full red beard, glasses. Big grin, like a politician. Let me see, what else—"

Daniel's grip tightened. "Which way did they go?"

The grocer winced. "That way." Pointing north. "She's okay, isn't she?"

Daniel let go of him and raced toward the Escort.

69

No! Please God. Pleasegod, pleasegod.

I should haves, I could haves. Prayers shrieked through a deafening nightmare storm. His right leg pushed the gas pedal to the floorboard; his hands were welded to the steering wheel.

Not my baby, my first baby, my little mongrel.

Precious, precious. No, not her. Anyone else.

Unreal. But too real.

Nightmares, the nightmare machine.

Silence it!

Tears flowed from his eyes like blood from a mortal wound. He forced himself to stop crying, keep his head clear.

Keep speeding, stretch the minutes.

Please, God.

A red light came on at the King David intersection; the boulevard was congested with traffic. Opposing traffic beginning to move, turning directly in his path.

He leaned on the horn. No one moved. Steered the Escort onto the sidewalk, swerving to avoid hitting terrified pedestrians. Waddling tourists in peacock clothes. A mother and a baby carriage.

Out of the way.

Got to save *my* baby!

Whistles and screams, a fury of horns. Hitting the rim of the central island, then over the curb and on it.

Scraping the underside of the Escort, ripping metal, hubcaps springing loose.

More screams. *Maniac! Asshole!*

Off the island, skidding, swinging left, dodging cursing motorists. Filthy-mouthed taxi drivers.

Fuck you—not your baby on the altar.

A shouting, gesticulating traffic officer near the King David Hotel tried to block his passage.

Move or die, idiot.

Not your baby.

The idiot moved at the last moment.

Please God, please God.

Speed.

Making deals with the Almighty:

I'll be a better person. Better husband daddy Jew human being.

Let her be—

More traffic, endless ribbons of it, a plague of metal locusts.

Can't slow down.

Weaving through it, around it, up sidewalks, off, knocking trash baskets into the streets.

Brake squeals. More curses.

Careening, wrestling with a wild animal steering wheel.

Fighting for control.

No time to put on the magnetic flasher.

No time to phone for backup—he wouldn't do it even if there were.

Another fuck-up: Sorry, Pakad, we lost him.

Not with my baby.

Oh, God, no.

He emptied his mind, chilled it, shut out time, space, everything. Even God.

The city a glacial wasteland. Speeding through layers of dirty ice, the Escort a power-sled.

Smooth. No risks.

Onto Shlomo Hamelekh, downhill full-speed ahead.

More red lights to defy, swooshing by, oblivious to cause and effect.

Only my baby.

Coming for you, *motek*.

A steep drop. Up through the air and down so hard the impact sent electric currents through his spine.

Good pain, welcome pain.

Alive. Let her be alive. Abba's coming, *motek*, sweet little mongrel.

Willing the Escort to be an airplane, a jet fighter, flying north, retracing the early morning ride of a month ago.

Fatma's body in the white sheet.

Shoshana.

Prettiness. Innocence.

Pretty faces, bodies juxtaposed, blood sisters— No, back to the glacier!

Uphill. The Escort struggled. Go faster, fucking damn fucking car, go faster or I'll rip you apart—

Rip *him* apart.

Fueling himself with boiling blood. Weapons assessment: only the 9 mm. The Uzi back at Headquarters.

He had his hands.

One good one.

Speeding past Zahal Square, more close calls, hateful shouts from the ignorant. If they knew the truth, they'd cheer him on.

Onto Sultan Suleiman through a scatter of frightened faces.

The Old City. Not beautiful anymore. A bloody city. Conquest upon conquest, graveyard upon graveyard.

Jeremiah lamenting.

Mothers eating babies as the Romans besieged the walls.

Blood running down limestone. Altars.

Christian Crusaders wading knee-deep in blood, slaughtering the innocent—

Not my innocent.

Shoshi.

Fatma. Shoshi.

Fatmashoshi.

Torturing himself with policeman's knowledge that cracked the glacier:

His *motek*, Number Four—no!

Amsterdam, a dry run.

The Israeli butchery replicating the American butchery.

American Number Four.

Gene's voice: *This one was very messy, Danny . . . all the internal organs*— No!

Abba's coming, angel.

Motek, motek, hold on, hold on. Make yourself live. Force it.

Literally skin and bones—

No!

Should have been there, should have been a better daddy.

Promise to be better.

God allowed back: making deals.

An old Arab man wheeled a barrowful of melons across the street. Daniel sped by. A bus coming from the opposite direction kept him from swerving far enough, and his rear bumper nicked the front end of the barrow.

Rearview mirror story: Melons rolling down Sultan Suleiman. Old man lying flat, then rising, shaking his fists.

Fuck your melons.

My fruit is precious.

Let her be alive.

Ben Adayah empty, a clear climb: God responding.

A single tour bus bumping its way down the Mount of Olives Road.

Dodging to avoid him.

Idiots pointing, chattering.

Fly by them, fly!

Onto Scopus.

Bloody eye of a bloody city.

Abba's coming!

The fucking slaughterhouse of a hospital, rosy pink, the pink of diluted blood.

He aimed the Escort at the entrance, screeched to a halt, blocking it. Took hold of the Beretta, checked the clip, and jumped out.

The Arab watchman, Hajab, on his feet. Shaking a fist.

"Halt! You cannot park there!"

Ignore the idiot. Running through the courtyard.

Hajab stepping in front of him, trying to block his way.

Idiot face flushed with indignation. Idiot mouth opening: "Halt! You are blocking the entrance! Trespassing on United Nations property!"

Charging the idiot.

Idiot arms spread to halt him.

"I am warning you, when Mr. Baldwin returns you'll be in big—"

Swinging the Beretta and hitting the idiot square in the face. Hearing bones crunch, the rustle and thud of collapse.

Running, flying, through the courtyard, trampling flowers. Gagging on sickly-sweet roses.

Funeral flowers.

No funeral today—coming, *motek*!

Through the door, mentally unfolding the Mandate-era blueprints.

West wing: servants' quarters. Staff quarters. Tagged doors.

The slaughterhouse, empty.

He ran, gun in hand.

Someone heard him, peeked a head out.

The old nurse Hauser, dressed in starched white, a white cap. Touching her hand to her lips in fear.

She shouted something. Ma'ila Khoury, the Lebanese secretary, stepped out into the corridor on awkward high heels. Saw his face and ran back into her office, slammed the door and locked it.

He transformed himself into a bullet. Shot round the corner.

Names on doors. Baldwin. DaroushaHajab. Blah blah blah. Carter.

Carter.

Nazi scum.

He turned the doorknob, expecting to find it closed, ready to aim the Beretta and blast the lock.

Open.

Carter in bed, blue pajamas. Under a top sheet.

Ghost-pale, propped on pillows, his mouth a dark hole in the beard, an elongated O.

No Shoshi! Too late—oh, no, oh, God!

He pointed the gun at Carter. Screamed:

"Where is she!"

Carter's eyes opened wide. Yellow corneas around gray eyes. "Oh, shit."

Daniel came closer.

Carter covered his face with his arm.

Daniel took in the room as he ran to the bedside.

A real mess. Pig of a Nazi. Dirty clothes and papers everywhere. The nightstand crowded with pill vials, tubes. A plate of half-eaten food. A stethoscope.

The room reeked of medicine and flatulence and vomit.

Sickness-stench.

He forced Carter's arm down. Ripped off the Nazi's eyeglasses and flung them across the room.

Shattering glass.

Carter blinking. Shaking. "Oh, God."

Nazis prayed too.

He put his knee on Carter's chest, pressed down. Nazi gasped.

Transferring his gun to his bad hand, he used the good one to grab Carter's neck. Big neck, but soft.

He squeezed.

"Where is she, damn you? Where is she! Damn you, tell me!"

Nazi gurgled. Made an unhealthy-sounding squeaking noise from deep inside of him.

He let go. Carter coughed, gulped air.

"Where is she?"

"Wh-who?"

Slapping the monster hard. Handprints materializing like Polaroid images on the pale Nazi flesh.

Choking the monster again.

Carter's eyes rolled backward.

Daniel let go. "Where is she?"

Carter shook his head, tried to scream, produced more squeaks.

"Tell me or I'll blow your fucking head off!"

"Wh—"

"My daughter!"

"I don't kn—"

Slap.

Tears, gasps.

"Where is she!"

"I swear . . ." gasp-gulp . . . "I don't kn-know wh-what . . ." gasp . . . "you're talking about."

"My daughter! A beautiful girl! Green eyes!"

Carter shook his head frantically, began sobbing, coughing, retching.

"Cohen," said Daniel. "Nash. Fatma. Juliet. Shahin. All the others, you filth!"

Raising his hand.

Carter cried out, cowered, tried to slide under the covers.

Daniel grabbed his hair, pulled up hard. The Nazi's scalp hot, the hair greasy with sweat.

"Last chance before I blow your filthy head off."

An acid smell filled the room, a wet stain spread on the sheet near Carter's groin.

"Oh Guh-God," croaked Carter. "I sw-swear it, please buh-believe me. Oh, shit—I do-don't know what you're ta-talking about."

Hand around the throat again.

"Tell me, you—"

A voice at his back, female, indignant: "What are you doing? Get off him, you!"

Hands pulling on his shirt. He shook them loose, kept his

knee on Carter, put the gun against the monster's temple, and swiveled.

The movement knocked Catherine Hauser loose. The old nurse stumbled backward. She fell, legs spread, revealing tallowy thighs encased in white stockings. Sensible shoes.

She pushed herself up, brushed off her uniform. Her face was mottled. Her hands shook.

"Out of here," said Daniel. "Police business."

The old woman stood her ground. "What do you want with poor Richard?"

"He's a killer. He has my daughter."

Hauser stared at him as if he were mad.

"Nonsense! He's killed no one. He's a sick man!"

"Out of here right now," Daniel barked.

"Gastroenteritis," said Hauser. "Poor man's been sick in bed for the last four days."

Daniel turned and looked at Carter. The Canadian made no effort to move. His breath was rapid, shallow.

Identities.

Stage actor. Manipulator.

"Not that sick," growled Daniel. "Early this morning he took a walk into the city and killed three men, then abducted my daughter."

"Ridiculous!" snapped Hauser. "What time this morning?"

"He left around midnight, stayed away all day, returned just before six."

"Absolute nonsense! Richard was in this room from eight until now—throwing up, diarrhea. I've been here myself, caring for him. I cleaned out the emesis basin at twelve-thirty, gave him sponge baths around two and four, and have been checking on him since then, every hour on the hour. I took his temperature twenty minutes ago. He's got a fever—feel his forehead. Dehydrated. He's taking antibiotics, can barely walk."

Daniel removed the gun from Carter's brow, touched the Canadian's face with the top of his hand.

Burning.

Carter shook with sobs.

Hauser looked at him, raised her voice to Daniel.

"The poor man can't walk two steps, let alone hike into the city. Now I'm warning you, Inspector Whatever-your-name-is:

The U.N. authorities have been called. If you don't stop brutalizing him, you'll be in serious trouble."

Daniel stared at her, then at Carter, who was whimpering and breathing hard. His neck was red and raw, already starting to swell. He coughed, gurgled.

Daniel stepped away from the bed. Hauser moved between him and Carter.

"I'm sorry about your daughter, but you've tormented an innocent man."

A hard-faced old woman.

He stared at her, knew she was telling the truth.

Carter was vomiting onto the sheets. Hauser brought a metal basin, held it under his chin, wiped him with a washcloth.

Sick as a dog. Four days in bed.

Not Carter on the nightwalk.

Shifting identities.

A manipulative psychopath.

Carter rocked and shook violently. Spit up clear mucus and groaned.

Not acting.

"Please *leave,* Inspector," said Hauser.

Not Carter. Then who?

Oh, God, who?

Then he thought of the watchman's warning: *When Mr. Baldwin returns you'll be in big—*

When Mr. Baldwin returns from *where?*

According to the surveillance log, the administrator hadn't left the Amelia Catherine since Sunday morning.

Shifting identities.

Exchanging identities.

Dr. Terrific.

Runs the place. Boss over the doctors.

Takes on an alter ego when he goes out to kill.

Carter on nightwalk—but not Carter.

False Hassid.

False Arab driving a white Mercedes diesel. Carrying cardboard boxes labeled RECORDS. No beard.

Judged possibly large enough to conceal a human body if the body was bent to the point of contortion.

Or small.

A child's body.

He granted Hauser her wish. Ran for the door labeled BALDWIN, S. T.

Locked.

He aimed the Beretta, shattered the lock, stepped in, ready to kill.

A large room, tile-floored and whitewashed, twice the size of Carter's.

Blueprint recall: storage pantry.

Big, cast-iron bed. The covers drawn and tucked military tight. Neat and clean, everything in its place.

A Hassid's clothes folded neatly on the bed. False red beard, eyeglasses.

Something shiny and green.

A butterfly pin, silver filigree with malachite eyes.

Not a sign of the monster.

No Shoshi.

He followed the Beretta into the bathroom.

No one.

Luggage in the corner: three suitcases, packed tight and fastened.

A messy one, Danny.

Swallowing his fear, he opened them.

Only clothes in the two bigger ones, neatly folded. He scooped his hands under the garments, tossed them out, opened the smallest.

Toiletries, a shaving kit. False mustaches, wigs, more beards, bottle of hair dye, tubes of theatrical makeup.

In the shaving kit was a one-way ticket on a Greek-registered ship to Cyprus, leaving tomorrow from Eilat Harbor.

He faked us out, Pakad.

He searched the closet: empty.

Looked for attic passages, trapdoors.

Nothing.

Where? The cave? Border Patrol staked out down there—he would have been notified.

He sank to his knees, looked under the cast-iron bed. Silly ritual, like checking for ghosts.

Saw brass hinges, a rise in the tile. Wood.

Trapdoor in the floor.

Blueprint recall: the auxiliary wine cellar.

Moving the bed.

The door a solid hardwood rectangle stretching from the center of the room to one wall. The doorknob had been removed, the hole plugged with wood.

Pry marks around the edges. A crowbar or something like it.

He looked for the tool. Nothing—bastard had taken it down with him.

He struggled to pry it open, lost his hold several times, mashing his nails and tearing skin from his fingers. Finally he managed to pull up hard enough. Opened the door, then stepped back.

Darkness below.

He slipped into it.

Abba's coming!

70

He descended silently, frantically, on narrow stone stairs. A score of them, pitched steeply.

The darkness absolute, dizzying. Touching moist stone walls for support and orientation.

Please, God.

The passageway twisted, shifting direction, then more stairs, a dank chill rising from unseen depths.

He sped down blindly.

A deep cellar. Good—perhaps the sound of the gunshot hadn't penetrated.

Another twist. More steps.

Then the bottom, gripping the Beretta, extending his bad hand. Metal. He explored, fumbling with damaged fingers, holding his breath. A low metal door, rounded at the top. Sheet metal—he could feel the seams, the bolts. Took hold of a handle, turned, and pushed.

Opening. Silence. No monster.

But he was assailed by icy white light.

Momentarily sightless, he stepped back reflexively, shielding his eyes and blinking. His pupils constricted painfully. When they were partially adjusted, he took a step forward, saw that he was in a small, cavelike room, empty save for a troughlike double sink and two floor drains encrusted with something unhealthy-looking.

The floors, walls, and ceilings were rough-hewn stone, the entire space scooped out of bedrock. Age-blackened rock streaked with greenish-blue mold and overlaid with a warped wooden exoskeleton—widely spaced pine laths laid cross-hatched over the walls; knotted overhead beams from which hung panels of fluorescent tubes on chains.

Dozens of fluorescent tubes—half a hundred, emitting an eye-searing flood of light.

He heard laughter, turned toward it.

At the end of the room, beyond the light, was another door—old, flimsy, wooden, banded with rusty iron. He ran to it, nudged it open, stepped into another room, somewhat larger than the first, the light brighter, tinted an odd silvery lavender.

Cold air, chemically bitter. Another trough, more drains.

At the center was a long steel-topped table on stout metal legs that had been bolted to the floor.

Daniel stood at its foot, looking down on soft whiteness, white buds—the soles of two small feet. Two fragile calves, a hairless pubis, spindle ribs, concave belly, flat chest.

His baby's naked body, the dusky skin blanched by the light.

She lay motionless in a nest of white sheeting, a pinpoint of red in the crook of one limp arm.

Her neck and shoulders had been propped up on several rolled pillows, thrusting the head back, chin upward, mouth open. Her lily-stem throat forced into the most vulnerable of convexities.

The sacrificial arch.

He yearned to rush to her, cover her, was stopped by the knife that caressed her trachea. Long-bladed, double-edged, pearl handled.

White on white.

So still. Oh, God, no—but no blood other than the needle mark, the body sculpture-perfect, not a wound. Her chest rose and fell in a shallow, narcotized cadence.

The gift of time . . .

Behind her, a mass of white. White hands—big hands, thick-fingered. One gripping the handle of the knife. The other submerged in her curls, entangled. Stroking, caressing.

Ugly laughter.

Baldwin, standing at the head of the table—looming, naked, Shoshi's head shielding his chest, her life contingent upon the turn of a wrist.

Leering, confident.

The tabletop bisected him at the navel. What was visible of his upper torso was massive, armored with muscle, slathered with something oily.

The fluorescence had bleached him an unearthly lavender-gray. Despite the cold, he was sweating, his thin hair plastered in strands, like wet twine, across the bare gray crown.

His body was shaved girl-smooth and prickly with goose bumps, the flesh glowing moist, shiny, slick as some nocturnal burrowing grub.

He stood slightly right of table-center, left leg exposed. Swastika-shaped scars covered his thigh—malignant purple brands. A fresh swastika wound had been incised just above the knee, the surrounding skin rosy with smeared blood.

Staring at Daniel, the eyes cold, flat, twin peepholes into hell.

Laid out before him was a sparkling array of surgical instruments—knives, needles, scissors, clamps—on a precisely folded napkin of white linen. Next to the napkin was a hypodermic syringe half-filled with something milky.

Shoshi dead-still.

Abba's here.

A carotid pulse bounced bravely under the knife blade. Daniel aimed the Beretta.

Baldwin pulled Shoshi's head higher, so that her curls bearded his chin. He laughed again, unalarmed.

"Hi, I'm Dr. Terrific. What seems to be the problem?"

All at once the knife began sawing across Shoshi's neck. Daniel stopped breathing, started to scream, pounce—but no blood.

Laughter.

A game. The grin widening. More sawing.

"Like my fleshfiddle, kikefuck?"

The pearl handle of the knife caught the light and tossed it back in Daniel's face.

White on white.

On white.

A white swastika painted crudely on the dark stone floor. Painted words, familiar English block letters:

HEIL SCHWANN!! THE SCHWANN SEED LIVES!!!

Baldwin's face constricted with ecstasy. Drunk on the game, not noticing as Daniel shifted to the right. Took a step. Another.

"Don't move, kikefuck."

The warning uttered around that sickening grin. A harsh voice. Mechanical. No trace of the cowboy drawl.

Deep, yet topped by a strident tentativeness—echoes.

The echoing screams of abandoned, victimized women. Daniel swore he could hear them, wanted to cover his ears.

Baldwin's mouth spread the grin wider.

The fingers of his left hand fanned down over Shoshi's face, spatulate tips fondling her cheekbones, her lips, as the right one held the knife in place. Baldwin moved it back and forth in a horror-tease.

A giggle: "Never had one this tender."

Daniel moved another centimeter to the right.

"Drop the bang-bang or I'll whittle on her." Grin. Long white teeth. Purple tongue. Lavender lips.

Daniel lowered the Beretta slowly, watched Baldwin's eyes follow the weapon down—poor concentration. He pushed forward with his toes. Another quarter-step, and another. On the right side of the table now. Closer.

"I said drop it, nigger-kike. All the way." Baldwin pressed the flat side of the knife blade against Shoshi's neck, obscuring the pulse. He stretched luxuriantly, gorging himself on power. But shifting to the right, simultaneously, in unconscious defense.

It exposed his crotch. His penis was semi-erect, a starched-white cylinder hovering tentatively above the branded thigh.

He removed his left hand from Shoshi's body, lowered it to himself, began stroking himself. Leering.

"*Two* weapons." Giggle. "Real science."

Daniel lowered the gun until it was level with the organ. Took another step forward.

Baldwin laughed, quickened his stroke. Kept sawing the knife in counterpoint.

"Silly millimeter, bye-bye kikette."

The voice rising in pitch, the erection hardening, tilted upward.

Power was everything with this one. Control, the key.

Daniel played along with it. Said, "Please."

"Please," laughed Baldwin. He masturbated a while longer, stopped, and ran his nail along the upper cutting edge of the knife. The lower edge still resting on Shoshi's windpipe.

"This is a Liston amputator, kikescum. It knows how to fast-dance, cuts through bone like butter." Grin. Giggle. The knife lifted, then descended.

"Please. Don't hurt her."

"Blink the wrong way and we'll be playing football with her fucking head."

"Please. I *beg* you."

Baldwin's eyebrows arched. He licked his lips.

"You really mean that, you insignificant piece of roach shit, don't you?"

"Yes." Forward.

"Yes, *Doctor*."

"Yes, Doctor." Begging, putting on a servile face and keeping Baldwin's eyes off his legs. Moving close enough to Shoshi's leg to grab her ankle, pull her away. But the knife was still kissing her flesh. A muscle twitch could sever her jugular.

"Yes, please, Herr Doktor Professor!"

"Yes, please, Herr Doktor Professor."

Baldwin smiled, sighed. Then his face creased abruptly into a livid hate-mask.

"THEN DROP THE BANG-BANG, FUCKHEAD!"

Daniel lowered the Beretta further. Begging for mercy as he did it. Scanning the room and taking in the layout.

No more doors. This was the end point.

"Please, Doctor, don't hurt her. Take me instead."

Idiocy, but it amused the bastard, purchased time.

Shiny things hanging from a nail embedded in a lath. Gold hoop earrings. Three pairs.

In the corner, an ice cooler. Next to it a crowbar. Too far.

Wall racks holding two large flashlights, more sheets, pillows. Stacks of folded clothing: Dresses, undergarments. A white dress striped with blue, torn, a strip missing.

Next to the clothing, jars filled with clear liquid and labeled with gummed stickers. Soft, pinkish things floating within.

Two he recognized as kidneys.

Others, unfamiliar. Roundish, clearly visceral.

"DROP IT, SHITBRAIN, OR I CUT HER!"

Bellowing, but subtle aftertones of panic.

Cowardice.

A passive monster, picking off the weak. Even after he had them in his clutches, putting them to sleep before doing his dirty work—terrified of resistance. Cutting himself superficially, but Daniel knew he'd chance nothing that endangered him.

He lowered the gun all the way. Baldwin was distracted, again, by its descent.

Daniel moved closer to the head of the table, looked at Baldwin, then past him, at a stuffed animal perched on the rack below the jars. Then he saw the black patch over the eye, realized it was Dayan. Stiff as a toy. Dead. No—paralyzed, the big brown eyes moving back and forth, *following* him. Begging for rescue.

"ON THE FLOOR OR FOOTBALL!" screamed Baldwin, sounding like a child having a tantrum.

Daniel said, "Yes, Doctor," and flipped the Beretta across the room, to the left. It hit the side of the sink-trough, clattered to the ground.

During the instant that Baldwin's eyes followed its trajectory, his knife hand lifted.

A millimeter of air between blade and throat.

Daniel lunged for Baldwin's wrist with both of his hands, pushing the knife up and away from Shoshi. Lowering his head, he drove it hard into Baldwin's oily abdomen, pushing the monster back.

Monster was heavy, a twenty-kilo advantage. Rock-hard. Thick wrists. A head taller. Two good hands.

Daniel injected the full force of his rage into the attack. Baldwin stumbled backward, against the wall racks. The laths vibrated. A jar tilted, fell, shattered. Something wet and glossy skidded across the floor.

Earrings tinkling.

Baldwin opened his mouth, roared, charged, swinging the knife.

Daniel backed away from the death-arcs. Baldwin stabbed air several times in succession. The inertia threw him off-balance.

Big and strong, but no trained fighter.

Daniel used the moment to head-butt Baldwin again, drove his fists into the monster's belly and groin, kicking at naked shins, reaching upward, grabbing a wrist, struggling to gain possession of the knife.

Baldwin fought free. Stab, miss. Stepped on broken glass, cried out.

Daniel stomped on the wounded foot, went for the knife with his good hand, tried to claw Baldwin's chest with his bad one. The fingernails made contact with oily flesh, slid off ineffectually.

He looked for the gun. Too far. Kicked at Baldwin's knee. Punishing, but not damaging. Got both hands around Baldwin's hand, felt the smooth pearl of the knife handle.

Go for the fingers, stuffed with nerve endings.

He tried to bend back Baldwin's index finger, but Baldwin held fast. Daniel's leverage was poor, his hand slipped, came perilously close to the knife blade. Before he could regain his hold on the handle, Baldwin yanked upward, gear-shifting the knife, up and down, back and forth, stabbing, wrenching, controlling it, as Daniel held on and pivoted to avoid being slashed.

The pinkie of Daniel's bad hand grazed the blade. The nail split open, then the soft flesh under it. Electric pain. A warm bath of blood.

He kept his good hand on the handle, gouging at Baldwin's fingers.

Baldwin saw the blood. Laughed, was renewed.

He lowered his teeth to Daniel's shoulder, sank them in.

Daniel twisted away, torn, on fire. A deep wound, more blood—his shirt began soaking up scarlet dye. No problem, he had plenty to spare, wouldn't stop until he was drained.

But escaping from Baldwin's bite had caused him to lose his grip on the knife.

Baldwin raised the giant blade.

Daniel held out his bad hand, palm-first.

The knife came down.

Went through him.

Enough nerves left to register pain.

Old pain, memory pain.

Back on the hillside. Back in The Butcher's Theater.

Baldwin twisted the knife, both hands on the handle, the big blade eating muscle, severing tendons, threatening to separate the metacarpal bones, split the hand clear up to the finger webs.

The monster growling. Gnashing his teeth. The eyes empty, obscene.

Intent on destroying him.

Baldwin drew himself up to his full height, bearing down on the knife. Pushing, churning, forcing Daniel down.

Tremendous pressure, crushing, relentless. Daniel felt his knees bend, buckle. He sank, skewered.

Baldwin's grin was wider than ever. Triumphant. He pressed down, panting, sweating, the oil mixing with the sweat, running down his body in viscous streams.

Daniel looked up at him, saw the swastika brands.

The crowbar—too far away.

Baldwin laughing, shouting, churning the knife.

Daniel pushed up with all his strength; the knife blade continued devouring his hand, extended its scarlet dominion.

He bit back screams, locked onto Baldwin's eyes, held the monster fast, refused to succumb.

Baldwin laughed, swallowed air.

"You . . . first . . . her . . . for . . . dessert."

Daniel felt the blood leave him, the strength leeching out of his muscles, and knew he couldn't hold out much longer.

He pushed up again, harder, made his arm a rigid, jointless length of steel. Held his own, then let go suddenly, ceasing all resistance, falling backward in a paratrooper's roll, the impaled hand slamming to the ground, the knife pursuing it, but purposelessly, fueled by gravity, not intent.

The tension-release caught Baldwin off guard. He stumbled, held on to the knife, and went down after it, bending awkwardly at the waist to maintain his grip on the weapon.

Daniel kicked up at his knee, again.

This time hearing something snap.

Baldwin howled as if betrayed, clutched his leg, collapsed. Falling full force on top of Daniel, one hand bent under him, the other still clutching the knife.

Baldwin closed his eyes, pulled up on the blade, trying to free the Liston, go for a kill-zone.

But the knife was lodged between bones, refused to spread them. All he could do was saw it back and forth, open more blood vessels. Knowing time was on his side. The nigger-kike's pain had to be terrible—he was puny, inferior, bred for defeat.

But the little fuck was holding on, fighting back!

Hard blows stung his Aryan nose, cheeks, chin, mouth. His lower lip burst open. He tasted his own blood, swallowed it—hero-sweet but it made him gag.

The blows kept coming like razor-rain and his own pain got worse, as if the nigger-kike was taking everything he'd absorbed and spitting it back at him.

He forced a D.T. grin, looked down, searching for signs of fadeout.

Kikefuck was smiling back at him!

The scum—this *fucking untermensch scum*—didn't *care* about pain, didn't *care* about the Liston dancing on him, eating him alive.

He marshaled all his strength, pulled up on the knife. Scumshit used his hand as a weapon, pushed back, stuck to it.

Suddenly brown fingers were imbedded in his cheek and raking downward. Shreds of flesh peeling down like tree bark.

Oh, no!

Blood—*his* blood—splashing in his face, his eyes, everything red.

He sobbed with frustration, said farewell to the Liston and let go of it. Used one hand to block the endless blows, tried to clamp the other around the niggerfuck's throat.

Daniel felt big wet fingers scrambling over his larynx.

He rolled free. Punched Baldwin's nose, mouth, chin. Aiming for the cheek-gouges. Erase that grin, forever.

Keep smiling. It scared the coward.

Baldwin regained the stranglehold.

Getting a grip on the larynx. Squeezing, crushing. Trying to rip it out of Daniel's throat.

Daniel felt the breath leave his chest in a sad hiss. The perimeters of his visual field turned gray, then black. The blackness spread inward, blotting out the light. His head filled with hollow noises. Death rattles. His lungs filled quickly with wet sand.

He kept striking out, tearing at the monster's face. The big fingers kept choking him.

The knife still piercing in his hand, lodged tight, hurting so intensely.

Two loci of pain.

Baldwin cursed, spat, throttled him. The blackness was almost complete. Acid flames raged in his chest, licked upward, scorching his palate, advancing toward his brain.

So hot, yet cold.

Fading . . .

The monster, stronger than he. Intent on destruction.

Her for dessert.

No!

He reached inward, beyond himself, beyond sensation, mined a last filament of strength, embraced the pain, went past it. Arching his body, blind, breathless, he bucked, groped, found one of Baldwin's fingers. Took hold of it, bent it backward, breaking it in a single, swift movement.

A popping sound, then a distant cry. The grip around his neck loosened. A drink of air.

Two more fingers grasped together. Bent, broken. Another.

Baldwin's hand flapped loose. He screamed, flailed aimlessly.

Daniel pushed him hard, threw himself upon the big oily body, dived after it as it went down.

Baldwin was bawling like a baby, eyes closed, flat on his back, clutching his hand, unprotected.

Daniel pulled the knife out of his hand. Baldwin thrashed wildly, one of his feet caught Daniel in the solar plexus, knocking the wind out of him.

Daniel gagged, gasped for breath. The knife fell loose, clattering on stone.

Hearing it, Baldwin opened his eyes, sat up, reached for the weapon with his unbroken fingers.

Daniel threw himself upon Baldwin, avoided gnashing teeth, clawing fingers. Baldwin snarled, head-butted, tried to bite Daniel's nose. Daniel pushed back reflexively, felt something soft. Familiar. Yielding.

His fingers had discovered Baldwin's left eye. He closed them around the orb, pried, ripped it loose.

Baldwin shrieked, reached for his face, touched the empty eyehole, shrieked again, and sank his teeth into Daniel's shoulder. Finding the wound, chewing it, enlarging it.

Daniel felt his flesh give way—he was being consumed.

Nearly blacked out from the pain, he forced thoughts of Shoshi into his mind, struggled for consciousness, plumbed Butcher's Theater memories, and went for the other eye.

Realizing what was happening, Baldwin twisted maniacally out of reach. But Daniel was pure intent now, his hand a hungry land crab, stalking its prey, undistractable. It found what it was looking for, seized it, tore it loose.

His world immutably blackened, Baldwin whipped and

pitched, weeping blood from empty sockets. But his teeth remained embedded in Daniel, crushing, gnawing, the force of the bite intensified by agony.

Daniel punched at Baldwin's scarlet-washed face. His fists grazed bone, skin, gristle. Finally he managed to get the heel of his good hand under Baldwin's chin and give a sudden, sharp push. Baldwin's jaws relaxed involuntarily. Daniel pulled himself free.

Baldwin struggled to his knees, a moaning, swooning ghost. His face a bleached-white death mask, the holes below his brow yawning, black and bottomless.

He screamed and swung his arms wildly, seeking context in the void.

Daniel retrieved the knife, clutched it in his good hand. Stepped in fresh blood, slipped, and staggered backward.

Baldwin heard the sound of the fall. He got to his feet, staggering and groping for support.

And found it. Broken fingers embraced the cold metal rim of the surgical table, then advanced with a mind of their own.

A hellish smile spread across Baldwin's face, corroding its way through pain and blindness.

His unbroken hand, huge, blood-slick, lowered itself onto Shoshi's face, turned claw-like.

Now it was Daniel's turn to scream. He charged forward and up, shoving his torn shoulder into Baldwin's rock-hard torso and pushing him away from the table.

Baldwin flailed, took a drunken step backward, and embraced him, ripping his nails into Daniel's back. Blood-pinkened teeth chattered and lowered, searching for a familiar target.

Daniel struggled to break loose, felt Baldwin's grip tighten around him. Despite what had been done to him, strength remained in the monster. Daniel's hand was gripped around the handle of the knife, but the blade was pressed between them, flat against their torsos. Useless and inert.

Baldwin seemed impervious to the coldness of surgical steel against bare chest. He raised his hand, buried it in Daniel's hair, and yanked hard. Daniel felt his scalp separate from his skull.

Baldwin yanked again.

Daniel twisted the knife free, found the spot he was looking for just under Baldwin's rib cage.

Baldwin snaked his fingers through Daniel's hair, over Daniel's forehead, onto Daniel's eyes.

He scrabbled, placed thumb and forefinger around the eyeball, and cried out triumphantly just as Daniel shoved upward with the knife. The blade entered silently, completed its journey quickly, passing through diaphragm and lung, coming to rest in Baldwin's heart.

Baldwin pulled back, convulsed, opened his mouth in surprise, and expelled a wave of blood. Clutching Daniel in one final spasm, he died in the detective's arms.

71

More whiteness, everyone in white.

They were protecting him, entertaining him. Insinuating their comfort between him and his thoughts. Standing around the bed, kind strangers. Smiling, nodding, telling him how well he was doing, everything sewed up fine. Pretending not to notice the bandages, bags of blood, bottles of glucose, tubes running in and out of him.

Gurgling when they talked. Usually he had no idea what they were saying, but he tried to look as if he were paying attention so as not to hurt their feelings.

They'd given him something to silence the pain. It worked but encased him in wet cement, turned the air liquid, made staying alert an effort, like treading water wearing sandbags.

He tried to tell them he was okay, moved his lips. The people in white nodded and smiled. Gurgled.

He treaded water a while longer, gave up, sank to the bottom.

The second day, his head cleared slightly, but he remained weak and the pain returned, stronger than ever. He was disconnected from his tubes, allowed to sip liquids, given pain pills that he concealed under his tongue and discarded when the nurse left.

Laura sat by his bedside, knowing what he did and didn't

need. When he drifted off to sleep, she read or crocheted. When he awoke, she was there, holding his good hand, wiping his forehead, tilting a water glass to his lips before he asked for it.

One time, toward evening, he woke up and found her sketching. He cleared his throat and she flipped the sketch pad around, showed him what she was working on.

Still life. Bowl of fruit and wine bottle.

He heard himself laughing. Sank back in pain, then slept and dreamed of the day they'd met—a hot, dry morning, the first September of a unified Jerusalem. Just before Rosh Hashanah, the birth of a new year that promised nothing.

He was a patrolman, still in uniform, nursing a soda at Café Max. Winding down after a rotten day in the Katamonim: the bad hand aching from tension, a bellyful of verbal abuse from *pooshtakim,* and the torment of wondering if he'd made the right decision. Had Gavrieli used him as a pawn?

Across the café sat a group of art students from Bezalel. Young men and women, long-haired, nonconformist types with laughing mouths and graceful hands. Their laughter grated on him. They took up three tables, drank iced coffee, gobbled cheese toast and cream pastries, and filled the tiny restaurant with cigarette smoke and gossip.

One of the girls caught his eye. Slender, long wavy blond hair, blue-eyed, exceedingly pretty. She looked too young to be studying at the institute.

She smiled at him and he realized he'd been staring. Embarrassed, he turned away and finished his soda. Calling for the check, he reached into his pocket for his wallet, fingered it clumsily, and dropped it. As he bent to pick it up, he caught another glimpse of the art students. The blond girl.

She seemed to have separated from the others. Had moved her chair so that she faced him, and was drawing in a pad. Looking right at him, smiling, and sketching.

Doing his portrait! The nerve, the intrusion!

He glared at her. She smiled, continued to sketch.

Bubbles of pent-up anger burst inside of him. He turned his back on her. Slapped down a few bills and stood to leave.

As he exited the café, he felt a hand on his elbow.

"Is something the matter?"

She was looking up at him—short girl. Had followed him out. She wore an embroidered black smock over faded jeans and sandals. Red bandanna around her neck—playing artist.

"Is something wrong?" she repeated. American-accented Hebrew. Terrific, another spoiled one, spending daddy's money on fantasies. Wanting a fling with a uniform?

"Nothing," he said in English.

The force of the word startled her and she took a step backward. Suddenly, Daniel felt boorish, at a loss for words.

"Oh," she said, looking at his bandaged hand. "Okay. It's just that you were staring at me, and then you got angry. I was just wondering if something was wrong."

"Nothing," he repeated, forcing himself to soften his tone. "I saw you drawing my portrait and was surprised, that's all."

The girl raised her eyebrows. Broke out laughing. Bit her finger to stop. Continued giggling.

Spoiled baby, thought Daniel, angry once more. He turned to walk away.

"No. Wait," said the girl, tugging on his sleeve. "Here." She opened her sketch pad, flipped it around so he could see it.

Still life. Bowl of fruit and wineglass.

"Pretty bad, huh?"

"No, no." *Idiot, Sharavi.* "It's very nice."

"No, it's not. It's dreadful. It's a cliché, kind of a joke—an art school joke."

"No, no, you're a very good artist. I'm sorry, I thought—"

"No harm done." The girl closed the sketch pad and smiled at him.

Such a wonderful smile. Daniel found himself hiding his scarred hand behind his back.

Awkward silence. The girl broke it.

"Would you *like* your portrait done?"

"No, I don't, I have to—"

"You have a terrific face," said the girl. "Really. Great contours." She raised a hand to touch his cheek, pulled it back. "Please? I could use the practice."

"I really don't—"

She took his arm, led him up King George. Minutes later he was sitting on green grass, under a pine tree in Independence Park, the girl squatting across from him, cross-legged and intent, sketching and shading.

She finished the portrait. Tore the paper out of the pad and handed it to him with lovely, smudged fingers.

At this point in the dream, reality receded and things got strange.

The paper grew in his hand, doubling, trebling, expanding to the size of a bed sheet. Then larger, a banner, covering the sky. Becoming the sky.

Miles of whiteness.

Four faces rendered in charcoal.

A thoughtful Daniel, looking better than life.

Three laughing, round-faced infants.

This doesn't make sense, he told himself. But it was *nice.* He didn't fight it.

The portrait took on color, depth, achieved photographic realism. A sky-sized mural.

Four giant faces—his own face, smiling now. Beaming down from the heavens.

"Who?" he asked, staring at the infants. They seemed to be smiling at him, following him with their eyes.

"Our children," said the girl. "One day we'll make beautiful babies together. You'll be the best father in the world."

"How?" asked Daniel, knowing her, but not knowing her, still dream-baffled. "How will I know what to do?"

The blond girl smiled, leaned over, and kissed him lightly on the lips. "When the time comes, you'll know."

Daniel thought about that. It sounded right. He accepted it.

At eight-thirty, Gene and Luanne arrived with flowers and chocolates. Gene chatted with him, slipped him a cigar, and told him he expected a speedy recovery. Luanne said he looked great. She bent and kissed his forehead. She smelled good, minty and clean. When they left, Laura went with them.

The next afternoon was spent tolerating a visit from Laufer and other members of the brass. Faking drowsiness in the middle of the D.C.'s little speech.

Laura returned at dinnertime with the children and his father, bringing shwarma and steak pitas, cold beer and soda. He hugged and kissed all of them, stroked Mikey's and Benny's buttery cheeks, let them play with the wheelchair and fiddle with the television. Watched Shoshi stare out the window, not knowing what to say.

His father stayed late, taking out a Tehillim and singing

psalms to him in a sweet, soothing voice, using ancient *nigunim* from Yemen that synchronized with his heartbeat.

When he woke up, it was nine forty-five. The room was dim; his father was gone. Only the psalmbook remained, closed on his nightstand. He picked it up, managed to open it one-handed, chanted the old tunes softly.

Shmeltzer burst into the room minutes later. A heavyset nurse followed on his heels, protesting that visiting hours were long over; this patient had already had too many visitors.

"Off my back, *yenta*," said the old detective. "I've put up with your rules long enough. This is official police business. Tell her, Dani."

"Official police business." Daniel smiled. "It's all right."

The nurse placed her hands on her hips, adjusted her cap, said, "It may be all right with you, but you don't make the rules, Pakad. I'm calling the attending doctor."

"Go, call him," said Shmeltzer. "While you're at it, take a tumble with him in the linen closet."

The nurse advanced on him, fumed, retreated. Shmeltzer dragged a chair to the bed and sat down.

"Bastard's real name was Julian Heymon," he said. "American, from Los Angeles, rich parents, both dead. A loser from day one, kicked out of Sumbok—why, we don't know, but a place like that, it had to be serious. He couldn't get into any other medical school and tramped around the U.S., living off inheritance and attending medical conventions using false identities. Our busting him helped the FBI close fourteen murders. There are at least five other possibles. Don't hold your breath waiting for thanks.

"The real Sorrel Baldwin was a medical administrator from Texas, bright young guy on his way up—earned a master's degree at the American University and stayed on to work at their hospital when Beirut was still Zurich East. He stayed a year, returned to the U.S. in '74, took a position running a fancy pathology lab in Houston that catered to heart surgeons—Heymon's father was a heart surgeon, a Yid—do you believe that! So there may have been some weird connection there. In the shit we found in the German Colony house, there are multiple references to another father, some guy named Schwann. We're still trying to sort that out, along with boxes of the preserved animal corpses and Nazi shit that he scrawled on the walls. He filled a couple of notebooks, too, labeled them EXPERIMENTAL DATA: REAL SCIENCE, but it was mostly incoherent crap—psycho ravings, torture experiments. From what I can tell, you were right about the racial angle. We found the phrase *Project Untermensch* several times—something about using the murders to set us against the Arabs, them against us, until we wiped each other out. Finishing off—"

Shmeltzer stopped. Cleared his throat, looked out the window. "Anyway, that's the long and short of—"

"Finishing off Shoshi was his final ploy," said Daniel. "He planned to mutilate her, leave a note next to the body attributing it to an Arab revenge group."

Shmeltzer nodded. "According to his notes, his next destination was somewhere in Africa—South Africa or Zimbabwe. Pit whites against blacks. Far as I'm concerned, it was all bullshit. Shmuck enjoyed killing, plain and simple. Tried to gussy it up with political motivation. Whatever you did to him was too good."

Daniel closed his eyes. "What happened to the real Baldwin?"

"That's one to feel sorry for," said Shmeltzer. "Poor devil was on top of the world until he attended a medical finance convention in New York, back in '75. Had dinner with some other administrators, went out for a stroll, and was never heard from again."

"Ten years ago," said Daniel, remembering what Gene had said about America: Big country, big mess. Missing persons who stayed missing.

"Heymon was patient, I'll say that for him," said Shmeltzer. "He held on to Baldwin's papers—for four years used them only to get duplicates, transcripts. We found other false IDs in the German Colony house, so the bastard had his pick. In '79 he got a job, as Sorrel Baldwin—an administrator in an abortion clinic in Long Beach, California. Four years later, he hooked up with the U.N.—Baldwin's résumé was first-rate, not that they're that picky. He pushed U.N. paper in New York for a while—probably enjoyed working for Waldheim, eh?—studied Arabic, then applied for the Amelia Catherine job and got it. The rest is history."

"What about Khoury, the girlfriend?"

"She claims to be as shocked as anyone. We've got nothing that proves otherwise. She says she knew Baldwin—Heymon—was a weird one. Never tried to get her in bed, happy just to hold hands and gaze at the stars, but she never suspected, blah blah

blah. We'll keep an eye on her anyway. Maybe I'll assign Cohen to it—she's a looker, comes on strong."

"How's *he* doing?"

Shmeltzer shrugged. "According to him, perfect—big John Wayne thing, for the moment. When you get down to it, he didn't go through that much. Your finishing off Heymon gave his heroin dose time to wear off. Cohen woke up all by himself, saw the animal heads, and probably thought he'd died and gone to hell. But he denies it, says it was funny—some joke, eh? He wriggled to a phone, put a pencil in his teeth, and dialed 100. By the time Daoud and the Chinaman got there, he was out of his ropes, bragging how simple it had been. He'll get credit for the German Colony bust, a promotion, like all of us. You're the only one who got bruised—tough luck, eh?"

"Me and Richard Carter," said Daniel.

"Yeah, tough luck for him too," said Shmeltzer. "Guy's at Hadassah, but he'll live. The watchman, Hajab, got a split mouth. The teeth you knocked out were false—let the fucking U.N. buy him a new bridge. Needless to say, the bastards from the Hill of Evil Council tried to raise a stink, bring you up on charges, but the brass and the mayor stood up for you. Something about tearing down the fucking hospital for national security purposes."

Daniel coughed. Shmeltzer poured him a glass of water, held the glass to his lips.

"Two other tidbits, Adon Pakad. Amira Nasser, the redheaded whore, supposed to be in Amman all this time? Rumor has it that she was on Shin Bet's payroll, free-lancing for dollars, on top of her street work, in order to pick up on bomb talk. When she encountered Heymon, started talking about it, Shin Bet pulled her off, sent her to a safe house in the Negev."

Daniel sat up, was hit with a wave of pain. "Nice guys. They couldn't have let us talk to her, given us the ID?"

"Bad timing, low priority," said Shmeltzer. "Rumor has it that she didn't get a good look anyway."

"Rumor has it, eh? Your friend been getting talkative?"

Shmeltzer shrugged again, adjusted his glasses. "My famous fatal charms. She thinks I'm still available, wants to get on my good side."

"What's the second tidbit?"

"More wonderful timing. Remember that pregnant kibbutznik I talked to—Nurit Blau, used to be a tour guide for the Nature

Conservancy, had total amnesia? She saw Baldwin's picture in the papers, this morning. Called me up and said, oh, yeah, that guy, he was on one of my tours, snooping around. Anyway, I can be of help, blah blah blah—idiot, probably give birth to a cabbage."

Daniel laughed.

The door opened. The heavy nurse stormed in, a young doctor at her side.

"Him," she said, pointing at Shmeltzer.

"Finished so soon?" Shmeltzer said to the doctor. "Tsk, tsk, not good at all, got to work on your staying power."

The doctor was perplexed. "Adon," he began.

"Good night, Pakad." Shmeltzer saluted, and left.

72

A candle burned on the nightstand.

At least another two kilos gained, estimated Daoud, as he watched Mona get into bed. She'd unbraided her hair and combed it out to a black, glistening sheet that hung past her waist. And what a waist! Her softness concealed by a tent of soft cotton nightgown, but the curves coming through—all that comforting roundness.

She got in beside him, causing the bed coils to creak, laid her head on his chest, and sighed. Fragrant of cologne and the sweets he'd bought her: sugar-coated almonds, Swiss chocolate filled with fruit paste, honeyed figs.

"Was the dinner acceptable?" she asked timidly.

"Yes."

"Is there anything else you'd like to eat or drink?"

"No."

She lay there, breathing heavily. Waiting, the way a woman should, for him to make the first move.

The closet-sized bedroom was silent; an open window revealed a starry Bethlehem sky. All six children and Grandma finally put to bed. The rugs beaten, the kitchen washed down and aired.

Time to rest, but even after the heavy meal and sweet tea, he was unable to unwind. All those hours spent in the shadows, waiting, watching, and now it was over. Like that.

Thank God, no more murders. But still, a letdown.

He'd done his job well, there were promises of promotion, but when the end had come, he'd been sitting and watching and waiting.

Much talk of all of them being heroes, but the Yemenite was the true hero, had met the killer face to face, washed his hands in the devil's blood.

He'd visited Sharavi in the hospital, brought him a cake Mona had baked, moist and rich, spiced with anise, stuffed with raisins and figs.

The Yemenite had eaten with him. Commended his performance, repeated the promises of promotion.

Still, he wondered what lay ahead.

Walking the line. Serving at the pleasure of strangers.

Cases like the Butcher came up once in a century. What further use would they have for him, waiting and watching? Betraying his Arab brethren? Making more enemies, like the one in Gaza?

Mona's dimpled hand caressed his chin. She purred like a well-fed cat, eager, ready to take him in, make another baby.

He rolled over, looked at her. Saw the pretty face, cushioned, like a piece of gift glass.

She closed her eyes, pursed her lips.

He kissed her, propped himself up, hiked up his nightshirt, and prepared to climb atop the mountain.

Mona parted her thighs and extended her hands toward him.

Then the phone rang in the sitting room.

"Oh, Elias," she murmured.

"One moment," he said, climbed out of bed, and went in to answer it.

He picked up the receiver. The ringing had wakened the baby. Covering one ear to blot out its cries, he placed the other against the phone.

"Daoud? Chinaman here."

"Good evening."

"I'm at French Hill. Got an assignment for you, interrogation."

"Yes," said Daoud, smoothing his shirt down, suddenly alert. "Tell me."

"You know all those confessors that have been crawling out of the woodwork since the Butcher thing closed? Finally we've got one that looks promising—for the Gray Man. Old plumber in gray work clothes, marched into Kishle a few hours ago, carrying a knife and crying that he did it. They would have kicked him out as a fake, but someone was smart enough to notice that the knife matched the pathologist's description. We hustled it over to Abu Kabir—blade fits right into the wound mold. Guy's an Arab, so we thought you'd be the one to handle it. Okay?"

"Okay."

"When can you be here?"

The baby had gone back to sleep. Daoud heard a sound from the bedroom, turned and saw Mona, filling the width of the doorway. A plaintive look on her face, like a kid begging for goodies but not expecting any.

Daoud calculated mentally.

Mona clasped her hands across her pendulous belly. The nightgown rippled. Her earrings shone brightly in the candlelight.

"Ninety minutes, maybe less," said Daoud. Then he hung up and pulled off his nightshirt.

73

The best disco in Tel Aviv: huge, tropical motif, silk ferns and papier-mâché palms, green-and-black velvet walls and aluminum-rainbow ceiling, strobe lights, a high-tech German sound system that could make your ears bleed.

The best drinks too. Russian vodka, Irish whisky, American bourbon, French wine. Freshly squeezed orange and grapefruit juice for mixers. And food: barbecued lamb ribs at the bar. Fried eggplant, steak on bamboo skewers, shwarma, shrimp, Chinese chicken salad.

American rock, all back-beat and screaming guitars.

The best-looking girls, going crazy to the music, making love to every note. Scores of them, each one a perfect doll, as if some horny Frankenstein had invented a Piece of Ass Machine and turned it on full-force tonight. Firm breasts and jiggling tushes, hair tosses and glossy white smiles turned multicolor by strobe flashes.

Hip-thrusting, wiggling, as if the dance were sex itself.

Avi sat smoking at a corner table near the bar, by himself. Wondering if it had been wrong to come.

A slim brunette at the bar had been making eyes at him for five minutes, crossing and uncrossing silver lamé legs, sucking on a straw, and letting one high-heeled slipper dangle from her toes.

But a hungry look on her face that made him feel uneasy.

He ignored her, ate a shrimp without tasting it.

Another guy came over and asked her to dance. The two of them walked off together.

Twenty-dollar cover charge, plus drinks, plus food. He had thought this would be the way to wipe his head clean, but was it?

The noise and drinks and laughter seemed only to make everything worse. Emphasizing the difference between good clean turn-ons and what had happened to him. Like putting what had happened into a picture frame and hanging it on the wall for everyone to see.

It was crazy, but he couldn't help feeling branded, couldn't shake the thought that everyone knew about him, knew exactly what the fucking pervert had done to him.

Those eyes. Bound and gagged, he'd looked up into them, seen the grin, known the meaning of evil.

I'm saving you, pretty one. Thank me for it. . . .

Another girl sat down at the bar. Strawberry blonde, tall and fair, not his usual type. But nice. She spoke to the bartender, lit a cigarette while he prepared her something lime-green and foamy in a brandy snifter, a piece of pineapple stuck on the rim.

She smoked, drummed her fingers on the bar top, bobbed in time to the music, then started looking around. Her eyes fell upon Avi. She checked him out, head to toe. Smiled and sipped and smoked and batted her lashes.

Nice lashes. Nice smile. But he wasn't ready for it.

Didn't know when he'd ever be.

Frame it and hang it on the fucking wall.

Everyone knew. Though the secret sat like a stone in his chest.

Last night he'd awakened, smothered by the stone, cold and damp and relentless. Struggling against dream bonds, unable to breathe . . .

Pretty one.

The strawberry blonde swiveled on her stool in order to give him a full front view. Lush figure, all curves. Red brocade shorty jacket over black leotard. Low cut. Healthy chest, lots of cleavage. Long, shiny hair that she played with, knowing it was gorgeous. Maybe the color was natural—he wasn't close enough to tell for sure.

Very nice.

A flash of green strobe light turned her into something reptilian. It lasted for only a second but Avi turned away involuntarily. When he looked again she was bathed in warm colors, nice again.

He smoked.

She smoked.

Big-shot Lover Boy.

Everyone had nice words for him—Sharavi, the Arab, even old Shmeltzer.

Far as they knew, he'd slept through it all, dosed up on heroin.

Didn't know the maniac had let him come out of it, didn't know what the fucking shit had done with him.

To him.

Making *him* the woman. Calling him *pretty one,* cursing in German as he played out his filthy . . .

The agony, the shame. After the fucking shit left, he bloodied his hands freeing himself, dressed himself before they had a chance to find out the truth.

The next day, he'd driven all the way to Haifa, found a doctor up on the Carmel, and using a false name, told a lame story about bleeding hemorrhoids which the doctor hadn't even pretended to believe. Cash up front had stifled any questions. Ointments, salves, the blood test results back yesterday.

Everything normal, Mr. Siegel.

Normal.

The secret intact. He returned to Headquarters a hero.

If any of them ever found out, they'd never look at him the same.

He wanted desperately to put the memories out of his mind,

but they kept returning—in dreams and daydreams, filling empty moments, dominating his thoughts.

Filth. He wanted to remove his brain, dip it in acid.

The strawberry blonde had gotten up, was walking toward him.

Leaning low. Giving him a tease-glimpse of nipple before tugging up her top.

Really a gorgeous one.

She posed, smiled, tapped a foot, and made her chest shake.

He felt a warm stirring in his jeans. But vague, removed, as if it were happening to someone else's body.

He said nothing, did nothing.

She looked confused. "Hey. Do you want to dance?"

Avi looked up at her, trying to collect his thoughts.

"Hey," said the girl, smiling again, but hurt. "I didn't know it was a life-or-death decision."

She turned to leave.

Avi stood, took hold of her.

"It's not," he said, twirling her around and putting on a smile of his own, the one the South African girl had called devilish, the one they all went for.

Keeping the smile plastered on his face, he squired her onto the dance floor.

74

On the fourth day, Daniel went home and slept until evening. When he awoke, Shoshi was in the room, sitting in a chair by the window, big-eyed, silent, picking at her cuticles.

Far away . . .

He remembered Ben David's visit, yesterday. The disquieting feeling of waiting for a comparative stranger to tell him about his own child.

I won't tell you she's perfect. She's shaken up—traumatized. Expect some sleep problems, maybe nightmares, appetite loss, fearfulness, clinginess. It's normal, will take time to work through.

What about addiction?

No chance. Don't worry about that. In fact, the heroin turned out to be a blessing. She was spared the gory details. All she remembers is his grabbing her suddenly, holding her down for the injection, then waking up in the ambulance.

Hearing the psychologist talk about the abduction had made him want to cringe. He'd suppressed it, thought he'd done a good job of hiding his feelings. But Ben David's look was penetrating. Appraising.

What, Eli?

Actually, what worries her the most is you—that you'll never be the same, that it was all her fault, you'll never forgive her.

There's nothing to forgive, Eli.

Of course not. I've told her that. It would help if she heard it from you.

"*Motek?*"

"Yes, Abba?"

"Come here, on the bed."

"I don't want to hurt you."

"You won't. I'm a tough guy. Come on."

She got up from the chair, settled near his right shoulder.

"How's the dog, Shosh?"

"Good. The first night he cried until morning. I put him in my bed. But last night he slept well. This morning he ate everything I gave him."

"And how about you—how are you sleeping?"

"Fine."

"No bad dreams?"

"No."

"And what did you eat for breakfast?"

"Nothing."

"Why not?"

"I wasn't hungry."

"Dieting?"

A tiny smile formed on her lips. She covered her mouth with her hand. When she removed it, the smile had vanished.

"No."

"What then, Yom Kippur? Have I been here so long that I've lost track of time?"

"Oh, Abba."

"Not Yom Kippur. Let me see—a boy. You want to look skinny for a boy."

"Abba!"

"Don't worry about what the boys think, what anyone thinks. You're beautiful just the way you are. Perfect." He lifted her hand to his lips, touched the palm to his unshaven cheek. Feeling the warmth, capillaries brimming with lifeblood. Exulting in it.

"Smooth or scratchy?" Old game.

"Scratchy. Abba—"

"Perfect," he repeated. Pause. "Except, of course, for the way you treat your brothers."

The smile again, but sad. Fingers twisting her hair, then touching the wings of the silver butterfly.

"Have you done your homework today?"

"There is no homework. School's out in two days. The teachers let us have parties. And they're wild animals."

"Your teachers are wild animals?"

"Mikey and Benny!"

"Oh. What species?"

She stiffened, pulled her hand away. "Abba, you're being silly, treating me like a baby and trying to avoid the subject."

"And what subject is that?"

"That I was stupid to go with a stranger—all those times you and Eema told me about strangers, and I went. I thought he was a rabbi—"

"You cared about Dayan—"

"It was stupid! Retarded! And because of it I hurt you, hurt you badly—your shoulder, your hand. It was all my fault!"

She tore at her hair, her little face crumpled. Daniel pulled her down to him, tucked her head under his neck, felt her fragile body convulse with sobs.

"I won't lie to you, Shosh, it was a mistake. But even mistakes turn out well—because of you, an evil man was caught before he could hurt anyone else. All part of God's plan."

Silence. "You killed him, didn't you, Abba?"

"Yes."

She sat up, stared out the window for a long time. Daniel followed her gaze, over the domes and spires of the Old City. The sun was setting, casting rosy shadows across the wilderness of Judea. Rose dappled with soft blue. He wished he had an artist's memory. . . .

"I'm glad you killed him. But it was still stupid and now your hand is ruined."

"It's injured, not ruined. It'll get better. I'll be fine."

"No!" Shoshi shook her head furiously. "In the hospital—I heard a doctor talking in the hospital. He said it was ruined—you'd be lucky to get any use out of it."

She began to cry again. Daniel clasped her to him, started crying too.

He held her, tried to absorb her grief. Waited until she'd calmed and took her chin in his hand, stared into her huge wet eyes. Smoothed back her hair, kissed tear-streaked cheeks, and forgot the pain.

"I'm not ruined, Shosheleh. I'm very, very whole. Please believe that. Abba doesn't lie to you, does he?"

A shake of the head.

"Then believe me, please, sweetie. I'm whole, complete. No man could be more complete. Do you believe me?"

Nod.

He cradled her in his arms, remembering baby days, changing diapers, spoon-feeding mush, the first clumsy steps, inevitable pratfalls. The privilege of watching it—watching all of them.

The room grew dark. Daniel said, "Get me my *siddur, motek*. It's time to pray *ma'ariv*."

While she fetched the prayerbook, he recited a silent *modeh ani*—thanking the Almighty for restoring his soul. A morning prayer, twelve hours too late.

But it felt like morning.